"It's come to this, hasn't it?" Lagganvor said.

"I fear so," Adrana said.

Lagganvor popped out his eye and bounced it off his palm in slowly increasing parabolas, smiling like a street huckster until the eye's apex took it level with Darkly's face and it stopped, suspended with an iron stillness. Lagganvor stood back and the eye began to pulse with a soft pink glow. The glow intensified, the pulse quickening, the orb drifting nearer to Darkly, concentrating its cycling light on his own two eyes. Darkly made a small clicking sound in the back of his throat. Lagganvor's eye clearly had some powerful paralysing influence on him: he could not blink, avert his vision, or twist his face away.

The clicking continued and a tremble spread down from his neck, his limbs quivering against their restraints. The chair creaked on its pedestal.

"Enough," Adrana whispered.

"Oh, just when we were starting to have fun."

"Enough!"

Lagganvor lifted a finger and the eye backed off, the light dimming very slightly.

"That can get worse, Mr. Darkly," Lagganvor said. "Very much worse."

Darkly was drooling. Adrana dabbed it away with the edge of his collar.

"Give us the Clacker's number, or better still his address. Once we've verified that the information's accurate, we'll return to set you free. Better still, persuade him to come here directly. That will end our involvement the soonest."

"I don't . . ." Darkly cleared his throat with a hacking wet cough, and Adrana dabbed at his mouth again. "I don't need to persuade him to come to me."

"I think for your sake you do," Lagganvor said, flicking a curtain of hair down over his enucleated eye-socket.

"You misunderstand me," Darkly answered. "There's no need to call or summon the Clacker. He's already here."

Praise for Alastair Reynolds

"This wonderfully complicated, fascinating space opera carries on the adventures of teen sisters Adrana and Arafura Ness, who find themselves over their heads in deep space intrigue.... [A] marvelous mix of character study and space adventure."
    —*Publishers Weekly* (starred review) on *Shadow Captain*

"*Shadow Captain* does what a great sequel should do: it builds upon, rather than replicates, the earlier work while escalating the drama and upping the stakes.... The worlds'-shattering conclusion has us very much looking forward to our next voyage with the Ness sisters."   —*B&N Sci-Fi & Fantasy Blog*

"Comparisons to Dune abound.... At a time when large-scale SF is flourishing, *Absolution Gap* is as good as it gets, and should solidify Alastair Reynolds's reputation as one of the best hard SF writers in the field."   —*SF Site*

"A book of great fascination, rich description, and memorable action."   —*Locus* on *Absolution Gap*

"Reynolds writes a lean and muscular prose where the intense action scenes are leavened with the kind of bright, shining, mind-boggling science talk that characterizes the best of post-modern space opera."   —*Science-Fiction Weekly* on *Absolution Gap*

"Alastair Reynolds continues his rise to the top of... SF.... Revelation, Redemption, Absolution... Reynolds provides them all."
    —*Guardian* on *Absolution Gap*

"Fulfills all the staggering promise of [Reynolds's] earlier books, and then some.... A landmark in hard SF space opera."
    —*Publishers Weekly* (starred review) on *Absolution Gap*

"A leading light of the New Space Opera movement in science fiction."   —*Los Angeles Review of Books*

"A fascinating hybrid of space opera, police procedural, and character study."   —*Publishers Weekly* on *The Prefect*

"One of the giants of the new British space opera."   —*io9*

"It's grand, involving, and full of light and wonder. *Poseidon's Wake* is one of the best sci-fi novels of the year."   —*SciFiNow*

"Reynolds blends AIs, mysterious aliens, intelligent elephants, and philosophical ruminations on our place in the universe in a well-paced, complex story replete with intrigue, invention, and an optimism uncommon in contemporary SF."
                              —*Guardian* on *Poseidon's Wake*

"Few SF writers merge rousing adventure with advanced futuristic technology as skillfully as Alastair Reynolds."
                              —*Toronto Star* on *On the Steel Breeze*

"Reynolds is a master of the slow buildup leading to apocalyptic action, and *On the Steel Breeze* is no exception."
                              —National Space Society

"His writing mixes spartan style, provocative ideas, and flashes of dark humor....Reynolds excels at weaving different threads together."   —*Los Angeles Review of Books* on *Slow Bullets*

"Alastair Reynolds is a name to watch....Shades of Banks and Gibson with gigatons of originality."
                              —*Guardian* on *Revelation Space*

"If you like hard SF...with fast-paced action and hard-boiled characters...you're in for a great ride."
                              —*SF Site* on *Redemption Ark*

BONE SILENCE

By Alastair Reynolds

The Inhibitor Trilogy

Revelation Space
Redemption Ark
Absolution Gap

Chasm City
Century Rain
Pushing Ice
House of Suns

The Prefect Dreyfus Emergencies

Aurora Rising (previously published as *The Prefect*)
Elysium Fire

The Revenger Series

Revenger
Shadow Captain
Bone Silence

Short Story Collections

Diamond Dogs, Turquoise Days
Galactic North

BONE SILENCE

The third book of Revenger

ALASTAIR
REYNOLDS

www.orbitbooks.net

Copyright © 2020 by Dendrocopos Ltd
Excerpt from *Revelation Space* copyright © 2000 by Alastair Reynolds

Cover design by Blacksheep & Lauren Panepinto
Cover images © Depositphotos
Cover copyright © 2020 by Hachette Book Group, Inc.
Author photograph by Barbara Bella

Orbit
Hachette Book Group
1290 Avenue of the Americas
New York, NY 10104
www.orbitbooks.net

First U.S. Print Edition: April 2020
Originally published in Great Britain by Gollancz and in ebook in the U.S. by Orbit in February 2020

Orbit is an imprint of Hachette Book Group.
The Orbit name and logo are trademarks of Little, Brown Book Group Limited.

The publisher is not responsible for websites (or their content) that are not owned by the publisher.

The Hachette Speakers Bureau provides a wide range of authors for speaking events. To find out more, go to www.hachettespeakersbureau.com or call (866) 376-6591.

Library of Congress Control Number: 2019957612

ISBNs: 978-0-316-46275-4 (trade paperback), 978-0-316-46273-0 (ebook)

Printed in the United States of America

LSC-C

10 9 8 7 6 5 4 3 2 1

This one's also for my mum

1

It had begun as a distant glimmering dot; now it was unmistakably a world.

At the front of the rocket launch, from her control position behind the forward windows, Fura Ness tried to fly exactly like any other prospective visitor. Too confident in her approach, and she would draw attention to herself. Too cautious, and she would look as if she had something to hide.

Which—of course—she did.

The sweep was bouncing range-location pings against the outer shell of Mulgracen. A dial showed their closing speed, now down to just six thousand spans per second.

"That will do nicely," Lagganvor said, as he leant over her shoulder to study the instrument board.

Fura took her time answering. She flipped a switch or two, worked a lever, tapped her nail against a sticky gauge.

"This ain't my first approach, Lag."

Lagganvor's reflection smiled back from the burnished metal of the console.

"Nor mine."

Fura applied a little more counterthrust, dropping them to five thousand five hundred spans per second. They were threading through the orbits of other ships gathered around Mulgracen that ranged from little runabouts like their own to fully-rigged sailing vessels, albeit all close-hauled so near to the gravity well of a swallower.

"All this way for a pile of bones," Prozor said, in a familiar complaining tone.

"Bones we happen to need," Fura answered.

Prozor rubbed the dent in her head where a metal plate had been put in. "*You* need 'em, girlie. The rest of us is quite satisfied never goin' near those horse-faced horrors."

"I share your reservations," Lagganvor said, directing a confiding smile at Prozor. "But I also appreciate the need for up-to-date intelligence. Without a viable skull, we're operating blind."

"And this intelligence," Prozor said. "It wouldn't have anything to do with gov'm'nt men turnin' over every rock in the Congregation to look for us, would it? Gov'm'nt coves with ships and guns and undercover agents and plenty of intelligence of their own?"

Lagganvor scratched at his chin. "It might."

"Then why in all the worlds is we...goin' anywhere near a world?"

"We've been over this," Adrana Ness said, turning to face Prozor from the seat immediately behind her sister's control position. "It's all very well keeping to the margins, picking off other ships for essential supplies—that's served us well enough since The Miser. But it's not sustainable. We've only adopted piracy as a temporary measure, not a business for life."

Prozor nodded at the forward windows, where Mulgracen was now large enough for surface details to be visible. "And offerin' our necks on the choppin' board by voluntarily going to a world—that's meant to be an improvement?"

"It has to be done," Fura said, sighing hard. "None of the skulls we've found on other ships were worth a spit by the time we got our hands on them. So we've no choice but to shop. But I ain't taking silly risks. Mulgracen's a long way out and there's no likelihood that anyone will be expecting us. It won't be like Wheel Strizzardy..."

"The risk was supposed to be contained there as well," Prozor said.

"It was," Fura answered through gritted teeth. "Just not contained enough."

*

Mulgracen was a laceworld, orbiting the Old Sun in the Thirty-Fourth Processional. It was neither entirely hollow, like a shellworld, nor entirely solid, like a sphereworld. It was, instead, a sort of sugary confection, made up of many thin and brittle layers, each nested delicately within each other and inter-penetrated by voids, shafts and vaults through which a ship could move nearly as freely as in open space. The outer surface—from which the launch was bouncing its range-finding pulses—was only loosely spherical. There were gaps in it, some of which were whole leagues across. Between these absences were irregular plates of uninterrupted surface, some of them joined by thick necks of connecting material and some by only the narrowest, most perilous-looking of isthmuses. Nowhere was this surface layer more than a tenth of a league thick, and in places it was considerably thinner. Little domed communities, never more than a quarter of a league across, spangled against the firmer-looking bits of surface. Now and then a tiny train moved between them; a luminous worm hurrying through a glassed-over tube.

With their speed reduced to just five hundred spans per second, Fura dropped the launch down through one of the larger gaps. The thickness of the surface plate swept up past them, and then they were into what was technically the interior of Mulgracen. There was little sense of confinement. In many directions it was still possible to see stars, as well as a dozen or so nearer worlds and the purple-ruby glimmer of the greater Congregation. Beneath them, about a league below, was a smaller broken surface, ornamented with domes and the fine, glistening threads of railway lines. There were domes and lines above them as well, for there were communities attached to the underside of the outer shell, as well as to its outer surface. Only the thinnest of connecting structures bridged the two layers, and it seemed quite impossible that these feeble-looking columns and walls could support anything, let alone many square leagues of habitable ground.

But they did, and they had, and they would. Mulgracen was already millions of years old, and it been claimed and lost and re-claimed many times during the long cycles of civilisational collapse and rebirth that made up the recorded history of the Congregation.

Fura dropped their speed further still. Traffic was thick all the way into Mulgracen. Rocket launches were coming and going in all directions, with little regard for any sort of organised flow. Cargo scows and rocket tugs growled by on their slow, ponderous business. For every ship about the size of their own launch, though, there must have been ten or twenty smaller craft that were only used for shuttling within and around the world, and these seemed even more cavalier about navigational etiquette. They were nosey about it, too, swerving close to the launch and only breaking off at the last second. The anti-collision alarm was going off so frequently that in the end Fura cuffed it into silence.

They went down another level. Only now was it getting hard to see any clear part of space, and the communities at these depths had to rely on artificial lights at all times of day. There were more of them, packed more closely together, and in places the towns had merged so thoroughly that they were now merely the districts of city-sized settlements, easily the rival of anything on the Ness sisters' homeworld. The domed-over buildings were huge, multi-storied affairs, and their windows so numerous that they seemed to emanate a soothing golden glow of comfort and prosperity. Carved animals reared up from roof-lines, picked out by spotlights; neon advertisements flickered on the buildings' sides, traffic lights threw red and green hues across pavements and intersections. People were still too small to see except as moving dots—even the trams and buses were like tiny gaming pieces—but it was not hard to imagine being down there, dressed for the season and strolling along lovely marbled boulevards lined with grand shop windows and no shortage of enticing places to dine and dance.

Fura looked at her sister, wondering if Adrana felt any pangs of homesickness at this spectacle of bustling civilisation.

"I'd forgotten—" Adrana began.

"—how pretty things could be," Fura finished darkly, and her sister met her eyes and gave the merest nod of mutual understanding. "How nice decent society looks, from the outside. How pleasant and inviting. How ready to accommodate our every wish. How devious and deceitful! It's a trap, sister, and we ain't falling for it."

"I didn't say I was about to."

Fura slowed them again. They descended through the gap between two domes, then continued on down through the thickness of another layer, until they emerged beneath its underside. There was one more layer below, totally enveloped in a single glowing mass of buildings. That was the closest settlement to the swallower, which was somewhere deep inside that final sphere. They didn't need to go quite that deep, though, which pleased Fura as it meant a little less expenditure of fuel.

"There," Lagganvor said, jabbing a finger at the windows. "The landing wheel."

Fura had been forewarned about the arrangements, but that did not make her any less apprehensive as she brought them in for the final approach. The landing structure was a very odd sort of amenity. It was like a carnival wheel, jutting down from a slot in the ceiling, so that only the lower two thirds of it was visible, turning sedately. There were platforms on the rim of this wheel, each large enough to hold a ship, and some cogs or counterweights kept them level even as the wheel rotated, lifting the ships up into the slot and the hidden part of their rotational cycle.

A third of the platforms were empty. Fura selected one and brought them in belly-first, toggling down the launch's undercarriage and cutting the jets at the last moment. She'd chosen the rising part of the wheel, and it did not take long for its rotation to take them into the slot and up to the apex, where ships moved through an enclosed reception area on their smoothly rising and descending platforms. Fura and her crew were not yet ready to leave the ship, and they were already descending by the time they had completed their suit preparations and gathered in the main lock.

"Names and back-stories?" Fura asked.

"Drilled into us so hard I might be in danger of forgettin' my actual name," Prozor answered. "Come to mention it…what is my actual name?"

"Doesn't matter, so long as you don't slip up," Fura said.

Prozor knelt to squeeze some oil into a knee-joint.

"Anyone would think you wasn't overly sympathetic, girlie."

"I'm not." Fura knuckled the chin-piece of her brass-coloured helmet. "I'm sympathetic to my neck, and to keeping it attached to something. And that means sticking to our roles."

"I think we are tolerably prepared," Lagganvor said. "Now, may we discuss the division of chores? I think I would be most effective, and speedy, if I were permitted to operate independently. Obviously I can't help with the procurement of a new set of bones, but the other items on our shopping list…"

"The sisters can take care of the shivery stuff," Prozor said. "You can stick tight by me, Lag, seeing as you know the terrain."

"I have been here once, dear Proz; that hardly makes me qualified to write a tourist brochure."

They made a last-minute inspection of each other's suits. By then the platform was just coming back round to the apex. Fura opened the lock and they tramped down the access ramp with their luggage, onto the platform's gridded metal surface. At the edge they waited for the platform to come into line with the fixed surface of the reception chamber, and then stepped briskly from one to the other. It was a nimble operation, but no crew who had just come in from a string of bauble expeditions would be fazed by such a test. From there it was a short walk into a reception lock, after which it was possible to remove their helmets.

They found themselves at the back of a shuffling line of crews being questioned by immigration clerks and revenue men. The room was full of low murmuring, bored questioning, the occasional stamp of a document. Once or twice a clerk stuffed some papers into a pneumatic tube that took them further up the administrative hierarchy.

The line moved sluggishly. Fura and the others put down their luggage and nudged it along with their boots as another crew joined the line behind them, and then another.

It was brazen, just being here. They had avoided any contact with civilisation for months. Nor was Mulgracen some outlaw world, where a blind eye might be turned. It was prosperous, long-established, well-connected: unusually so, given its orbit within the Frost Margins. It did a lot of trade, and that was the crux of Fura's gamble: she had been relieved, not disheartened, when she saw how many other ships were coming and going, and it pleased her now to be at the back of a grumbling, slow-moving queue.

From behind them a gruff voice raised a complaint as one of the clerks abandoned their desk and left a "closed" sign, forcing two lines to converge into one.

"You did well," Fura whispered to Adrana.

Adrana dipped her nose, looking at Fura over the bridge of her spectacles. "High praise."

"For once I wasn't the one making the choices. It's good for you to show a little…initiative…now and then."

"Don't think too highly of me. All I did was pick a world we could reach that wasn't too far in and had a halfway decent selection of bone shops." She glanced back at the crew behind them, who were grumbling about the closed desk. "Any other benefits are…incidental."

"Incidental or otherwise, they'll serve us nicely." Fura dropped her voice. "I'd say 'well done, sister,' but perhaps it's about time we slipped into character."

"Whatever you say, Captain."

The line moved in fits and starts, and after about thirty

minutes it was their turn to be questioned. Fura put their papers onto the table and stood with a hand on her hip, affecting a look of mild but compliant impatience. She was still wearing her vacuum suit, and for once she had a full sleeve and glove over her artificial hand, instead of the pressure-tight cuff she normally wore.

"Captain...Tessily...Marance," said the clerk, a heavy-jowled man with a persistent low cough. "Captain Tessily Marance. Tessily Marance."

"Don't wear it out," Fura said.

He held one of her papers, squinting as he compared the photograph with her face.

"In from the Empty, are you?"

"No law against it."

He licked his fingertips, turning pages quickly.

"Where was your ship registered?"

"Indragol."

"Describe it."

"It's about four hundred spans long, with rooms inside and lots of sails and rigging."

He looked at her with a stone-faced absence of humour.

"The world, not the ship."

"Why, are you planning a holiday? All right, Indragol. It's a cesspit down in the Twenty-Eighth. Tubeworld. Besides the *Grey Lady*, the only other good thing to come out of it was my father..."

"His name?"

"Darjan. Darjan Marance."

He shifted his gaze onto Adrana. "Who is she?"

"She can speak for herself," Fura said.

Adrana looked down her nose at him. "Tragen Imbery."

"Occupation?"

"Sympathetic." Adrana leaned in and added, in a near-whisper: "That's a Bone Reader, you know."

He held up a different page. "Take off your spectacles."

Adrana complied, staring at him with a fierce, level gaze. He continued holding up the page, frowning slightly, and beckoned one of his colleagues over. The first clerk handed the papers to the second, murmuring something in regard to Adrana. The second clerk sat down and began going through their papers with a heightened attentiveness, taking out a pocket magnifier and consulting a reference document, presumably looking for tiny flaws in their forged credentials. Meanwhile, the first clerk began asking Prozor and Lagganvor questions.

Off to one side of the desk, a small flickerbox was showing successive grainy images of the faces of various felons and persons of interest.

Fura started to sweat. She had thought that being combative and surly might help her case, because it was the last thing anyone would expect if the actual Ness sisters were trying to sneak their way through immigration. Now she was starting to wonder if she had taken the wrong tack.

The second clerk leaned into the first and cupped a hand to his mouth. The first clerk scratched at a roll of jowl and reached for an empty pneumatic tube canister. He was beginning to curl some of Fura's papers up, preparing to stuff them into the tube.

"Did you say Darjan Marance?" asked the gruff voice from behind them.

Fura turned around with an imperious lack of haste. "What if I did, cove?"

"Darjan Marance took two hundred leagues of triple-filament yardage from us, down in Graubund. An' he never came back with payment." The speaker—a tall, scar-cheeked, rough-voiced woman with a stiff brush of green hair—shook her head in mocking disbelief. "I never believed this day would come. Been keeping eyes and ears out for Marance's crew these last ten years in case we crossed paths, but I never thought you'd be so stupid as to use your own name, right in front of me." She pushed forward, interposing herself between Prozor and Lagganvor, and pointed at the clerks. "She's a thief. I don't care if it was her father stole that yardage, she inherits the crime—she and her whole scummy crew." She waggled her finger. "You don't go letting 'em into Mulgracen. They'll be out and away before I see them again. You get 'em locked up *now*, and I'll fill out any papers you need me to, laying out what she owes us."

Lagganvor raised his hands, smiling hard. "My dear... Captain? Perhaps we might come to an... amicable settlement? If there has been some... entirely innocent confusion? I'm not reliably acquainted with the current rate for triple-filament yardage, but I should think six hundred bars might be not unfair recompense, for any grievous... misunderstanding?"

The green-haired woman gave a derisive snort. "Six hundred bars, cove? Is that some sort of joke? Have you any idea what six hundred bars'll get you, nowadays?"

Lagganvor grinned desperately. "Presumably... not *quite* enough to settle this matter?"

"Arrest them, all of them," the green-haired captain said. "I'll do whatever it takes. It's not about the money, it's the principle. I don't mind if I have to take two hours or six setting down our side of the story..."

Behind her, her crew began to groan. Clearly they had other plans for the day.

The first clerk looked from the green-haired captain to Adrana, then back to Fura. He leaned over and confided something to his colleague. The second clerk shook his head ruefully, pinched at the corners of his eyes, then pushed himself up from the desk. The jowly clerk still had the semi-bundled papers, nearly ready to go into the canister. He hesitated for a second, then flattened them out again, before reaching for his stamping tool and punching his way through each of their sets of personal documents. "You're lucky, Captain Marance," he said, eyeing Fura. "Normally we take a very dim view of such allegations."

Fura looked at the clock above the clerk's position. It was only twenty minutes off noon, and more than likely that was the end of the clerk's shift. Perhaps his colleague's, as well. The last thing either of them wanted was to activate a process that involved additional checks, more paperwork, superiors, interview rooms and so on, all on the doubtful say-so of a crew whose past might be equally blemished.

"She's got the wrong Marance," Fura said, but with a touch more politeness than before. "I'm...grateful not to be delayed, all the same."

"Spend your quoins while you can," the clerk said, handing back their papers.

*

"That was a good try, earlier on," Adrana said to Lagganvor, as they ascended to street level. They were alone in a cramped elevator car, squeezed in with their luggage around their legs, while Fura and Prozor took the next car along.

"A good try?"

"About it making sense to go off on your own."

Lagganvor's living eye gleamed with vain amusement. The other—the duller, glassier eye—stared through her with a supercilious indifference.

"I was only thinking of making the best use of our time."

She placed a hand on his shoulder, almost affectionately, and allowed her fingers to wander to his collar. They were not wearing vacuum suits now. They had taken them off, leaving them at an office on the same level as the immigration department, and changed into the ordinary clothes they had brought for their time in Mulgracen. Adrana's knuckles brushed against the stubbled side of his cheek and Lagganvor smiled, but not without a certain wariness. Then she pushed her hand behind his neck, seized a thick clump of his shoulder-length hair, and twisted it hard.

"Bringing you here was a risk," she said, as Lagganvor squirmed and grimaced. "But less of a risk than leaving you on the ship, where you could easily signal your masters."

"Signalling my masters," he said through gritted teeth, "is a thing I do for your benefit, not my own. While they know I am alive and monitoring you, they are content and not attempting a long-range kill."

"That logic works while we're out in space," Adrana said, still clutching his hair, and still twisting it. "But now we're on a world, I thought you might start having other ideas. Like calling in the reinforcements to take us alive, while we're preoccupied with shopping."

"I wouldn't dream of it."

"Be sure you don't. We'll be sticking together like glue, Lag. Just you and me. And if you so much as raise an eyebrow in the wrong direction, never mind anything to do with that eye of yours, I'll tell Fura exactly what you are."

"That…might not go down very well for either of us."

"She'll understand why I had to shelter you."

"I'm glad you have such faith in your sister's continued capacity for reasonableness," Lagganvor said, reaching up to dislodge her hand. "Me, I might need a little more persuading." He sighed and looked her hard in the eyes. "You can trust me not to go against my word. I signalled them twenty days ago, feeding them an erroneous position and heading; they won't be expecting another update until we're long clear of Mulgracen. They have no knowledge of your whereabouts here, nor your plans beyond it." He caught his reflection in the elevator's side and began to fuss with his fringe. "Incidentally…what *are* those plans?"

"I think it would be for the best," Adrana said, "if those plans stayed between Fura and I. Just for now. Oh, and *Brysca*?"

He blinked, discomfited by the use of his real name.

"Yes?"

"You're quite right; I wouldn't take a chance with Fura. It'd be far less trouble to kill you myself."

*

They met at the top of the elevator shafts, at the five-fold intersection of Virmiry Square, which was itself near the centre of Strenzager City, one of the larger conurbations at this level of Mulgracen. Fura craned her neck back, taking her first proper breath since she left *Revenger*. A city's flavours filled her lungs. Brake dust, pavement dirt, animal grease, monkey sweat, hot oil, electric fumes, kitchen smells, sewerage stink, the vinegar-tang of a drunk stumbling out of a nearby bar, the steam of an all-night laundry. It was a sort of poison, taken in extremis, but after months in space breathing nothing that had not been reprocessed through the vegetable membranes of lightvine, nothing that did not taste subtly, pervasively green and slightly stale, it was as fine and thrilling to her senses as a perfumery or chocolatier. She had missed the smell of cities. She had missed the smell of worlds, of life.

She had better not start getting used to it.

"One drink," she declared, "then we split up. Adrana and I will cover different bone shops, since it's far too risky to be seen together while being open about our talents. We'll stay in touch by squawk and meet when we've got something to discuss. But I *do* need a drink, and—"

"Something's happening," Adrana said, nodding beyond the nearby bar.

A group of people were gathering at the corner of one of the intersections where the five main boulevards met Virmiry Square. They were pressing together, almost like a throng of theatre-goers waiting for the doors to open. Above them rose a grand edifice with complicated ornamental stonework and numerous floors. It might have been a huge department store, or perhaps the head offices of an insurance firm. At the back of the gathering a small child was hopping up and down to get a better look at whatever was going on.

Adrana stepped between trams and joined the rear of the gathering, Fura, Lagganvor and Prozor close behind. Adrana was craning to look up at something. There was a slow-rising scream, like some kind of siren starting up.

Fura looked up as well, tipping back the brim of her hat. She could see all the way up past the tops of the buildings, beyond the neon signs and the scissoring search-lights, out through the fine-fretted glass of the pressure dome over this part of the

4 • Alastair Reynolds

city, up and up through a league of vacuum, criss-crossed by
the fast-moving motes of ships, all the way to the next interior
layer of Mulgracen, where a pattern of inverted cities—whose
buildings hung like pendants—lay strung across that broken
surface like an imaginary constellation, made up of smeared
and twinkling stars of every hue.

The scream—which was coming from a throat, not a machine—had its origin only twenty or so stories up. There was an
open window, a tall sash-window that faced out onto a prepos-
terously narrow balcony, and a tiny pale form was trembling as
it gripped the lower pane and stared down to the pavement and
the gathering crowd, of which the Ness sisters were now on the
periphery, clotting around whatever it was that had last come
through that window.

A hand settled on Fura's shoulder. Something cold and sharp
touched the skin of her neck.

"One good turn could be said to deserve another. Wouldn't
you agree, Captain Marance?"

Fura turned around slowly with the cold point still pressing
against her skin.

Adrana, Prozor and Lagganvor were standing back with
expressions of abashed helplessness. They had been caught off-
guard. Lagganvor was the only one of them who had a weapon,
but to reveal it—even without the actual use of violence—
would have drawn exactly the sort of attention they were trying
to avoid.

"You never knew my father," Fura said.

The woman—the green-haired captain—gave a half laugh.
"I'm not sure you did, either." She was out of her suit now, her
hands ungloved. She scraped a black nail down one of her own
scarred cheeks, leathery and wrinkled as an old book's spine,
cocking her head thoughtfully, but with some small amusement
at Fura's expense. "Was any part of that true?"

Fura thought for a second. "In fairness, Indragol is a cess-pit."

"On that, at least, we can agree."

Fura nodded back to the crowd, which had swollen by a third

since their arrival. The people were so engrossed that a tense stand-off between two newly-arrived crews went totally unnoticed. Up above, the screaming person was still screaming. It seemed quite impossible that a single pair of lungs could produce such a continuous, harrowing exclamation.

"Do you know what that's all about?"

"A squelcher," the green-haired captain said. "It's the new thing— an employment initiative. All the rage across the Congregation. Or have you not been paying attention to the news?"

"As I said, in from the Emptyside."

The point moved away a little. "Then I'll bring you up to date, a little. About six months ago, every quoin, everywhere in the Congregation—in every pocket, every purse, every safe and vault, every bank, every investment house, every chamber of commerce—*every single quoin* underwent a randomised resetting of its intrinsic value."

"I heard something along those lines."

"Would've been hard not to. It's the single biggest financial upset to hit the Congregation since the start of the present Occupation. Makes every other slump or crash seem like a pleasant dream. The banks are calling it the Readjustment. Makes it seem distant, abstract—not something that affects real people, real lives." The woman's tone became wistful. "But then, I suppose they had to call it *something*."

"I suppose they did."

"The thing is—the curious thing..." The woman shook her head. "Well, it's silly. But there's a rumour doing the rounds that two sisters had something to do with it."

"Two sisters?"

"Two prim-and-proper little madams from Mazarile who ran away, got a ship—a very fast, dark ship—and poked their noses into something they oughtn't have. Something that made *this* happen."

"I wouldn't know about that," Fura said.

"No," the woman said, appraising her. "I don't suppose you would."

There was a silence. Fura reached up and very gently deflected the tip of the blade.

"If you knew about these sisters, would you turn 'em in?"

"That'd depend. There's many that would. That Readjustment has hit people hard, and not just those who could stand to lose a little money. It might be months since it happened, but the banks are still going through their accounts, telling their clients what they now have in their savings. It'd be bad enough if it was just a case of the quoins changing value; then it would just be a simple accounting exercise. But the truth is, no one's sure what a single bar means now. Is a ten-bar quoin worth more now than a ten-bar quoin six months ago? Or less?" She nodded out over the heads of the gathering. "You can be sure *that* fellow got some unwanted news."

"People lose fortunes all the time," Fura said.

"Well, that's true. Harsh, but undeniably true. And the fact is—even though the banks have put up a small fortune for the Ness sisters—not everyone thinks too fondly of those institutions to begin with. You know how it is when you desperately need a loan to keep your ship operating, and the institutions don't oblige."

Fura nodded tentatively. "I can't say my family was treated too well by 'em."

"May I...intercede?" Lagganvor asked gently. Very slowly he opened his coat, and with equal caution he dipped into an inner pocket and drew out a plump purse, jangling with quoins.

"What're you proposing, cove?"

"A gesture for your kindness in digging us out of that hole at the immigration desk."

"Someone had to. Your captain's mouth certainly wasn't doing you any favours."

Lagganvor bounced the purse on his palm, then offered it to the other captain. "That figure I mentioned earlier, relating to the non-payment of the yardage? There's about the same in here, maybe a little more. Does that suffice, as a token of our gratitude?"

She snatched the purse from him, stuffing it into a pocket of her own without once glancing at the contents.

"Let's say it does."

"Then we're square," Fura said, dry-mouthed.

The woman's blade retracted with a snap. It had vanished back into a tiny bird-like brooch, far smaller than the blade it contained, which she pinned back onto her collar.

"We're square. But two things before we part. The first is that not every crew feels as ambivalent about that reward as we do, so the Ness sisters would do well to watch their backs. The second thing... there's a message you might pass on to them, if your paths ever cross."

Fura nodded earnestly. "And...what would that message be?"

"Tell them they'd better be damn sure they know what they're doing."

*

The white-whiskered man in the bone shop looked up from his bench, peering at Adrana over a pair of complicated spectacles set with many interchangeable lenses. She was taking her time, moving around his shelves, picking up and examining his wares. It was tourist tat for the most part: nothing that was of any practical use to a genuine Bone Reader. There were fist-sized skulls made out of bits of old rat, cat and dog, sutured together until they looked passably alien, and then stuffed with a few glinting threads of something that might, in a cooperative light, just about fool someone into thinking it was active twinkly. There were fragments of larger skulls that had, possibly, been alien at some point, but were now useless except as ballast.

"I see you have an eye for the good pieces, my dear," the man said, as Adrana examined one of the larger faked-up skulls.

"I have an eye for a con," Adrana answered levelly, before placing the skull back on its shelf. "To your credit, Mr....." She picked up one of the neat little tags attached to one of the skulls, moving her lips as she read it: *Darkly's Bone Emporium, 62 Boskle Lane,*

Virmiry West, Strenzager City, Pellis Level, Mulgracen. "Mr. Darkly…that *is* you, Mr. Darkly? To your credit—your very minor credit—there's nothing here's actually labelled as being authentic; you are merely content to let the unwary make the assumption for themselves. Do you get many takers?"

Mr. Darkly set down his tools. There was a skull on the bench before him, positioned on a padded cradle, and it was three times as large as any of the counterfeit pieces. If it was fake, it could only have come from a camel or a carthorse. If it was real—real and alien and ancient—then it was at the smaller end of the typical range of specimens. But she had seen smaller, in other emporia.

"There's no harm in servicing a demand for souvenirs. If tourists want a little skull to take back Sunwards with them, something to put over a fireplace and remind them of a nice holiday in Mulgracen, why should I deny them that harmless little pleasure?"

"It's tricked-up junk," Adrana said, studying him through her own glasses. "Worthless scraps. I wonder where you get the bones from. Do you have a little deal going with the local veterinarian? Do you set traps in the back alleys, then boil the animals down?"

Darkly pulled his complicated spectacles off his large, red-veined nose and set them down on a half-folded newspaper next to the skull. He brushed crumbs from his bib. "Ask yourself a different question: the tourists will have their souvenirs, and they'll pay for them. Deep pockets, even now—anyone who can *afford* to get here isn't down to their last quoin. Would you rather they were sold a harmless replica, a perfectly nice and harmless trinket, or that a real, functioning skull went out of circulation, ending up locked away where no crew could ever benefit from it?"

Adrana sniffed, disliking his logic even as she was persuaded by it.

"I suppose that would depend on whether you actually have any real skulls to offer me."

"I might," Darkly said, with a faintly salacious half-smile. He was a scrawny, liver-spotted man of advanced age, with two eruptions of white hair either side of a perfectly bald pate, the two flanking tufts lovingly combed into up-sweeping swan's wings, their effect carefully augmented by nimbus-like growths of hair sprouting from his ears. "The question is, my dear, would you recognise them if I did? You don't have the look of a sympathetic—"

"There's a look to us?" Adrana asked with sharp surprise.

"I would've said you're past the age…or near the limit." He stopped himself, shaking his head once. "But you know your bones, it seems. There are…other wares in the back room. Some that I think may be a bit more attractive to you."

"Excellent, Mr. Darkly. I should like to test one or two samples."

A tram rumbled past the shop, and the smaller bones rattled on their glass shelves.

"You are welcome to test any of our wares. I should warn you that we have a swallower near us, as well as all the disturbances of the city, so you mustn't judge the skulls too harshly. They'll all work much more reliably in open space. But…I imagine you knew that."

Adrana reached into her jacket and took out a small pouch. "I brought my own neural crown. I trust that won't be a problem? It eliminates a number of variables."

"You do what you must, my dear."

Darkly was moving to the door to flip the "open" sign while he was engaged with Adrana in the back room when another customer came in, the bell over the door tinkling. It was a black-haired man, tall, broad-shouldered, and dressed very finely. He looked around the shelves and cabinets, hands in his pockets, swivelling on his heels, grinning like a boy who had found the secret door to a sweet shop.

"Are these all real?"

Darkly nodded gravely. "They are indeed real bones, sir."

The man flicked back his dark fringe. He had slightly mis-matched eyes: one livelier and gleaming more than the other. "And these skulls…they're old?"

"The atoms in them, sir, are as old as the stars."

"And…aliens used these?"

"These bones have seen a great deal of employment, sir." Darkly turned the sign around and shut the door from inside, leaving the key in the lock. "May I…direct your attention to that shelf to your left? The topmost selection? Some of our finer wares. They are not for everyone, but I see you are a man of taste and discernment…please, take your time, while I attend to another customer. We shan't be too long."

Adrana left Lagganvor front of shop while she went through a beaded curtain, along an unpromising corridor and into the rear of the premises. Although she kept her wits about her there was nothing too sinister about this arrangement. Most bone shops did their business in squalid, windowless back rooms, with customers who rightly disdained the trinkets in the window display. This was where the serious, profitable stuff was kept, and if her manner had been a little brusque, it had earned her the right to be treated with respect.

"This way, please," Darkly said, opening a heavy metal door that led into a low-ceilinged room with many dusty cabinets, teetering piles of cardboard boxes and great wads of packing paper on the floor. He closed the door behind her, and all remaining sounds of the city were abruptly silenced. The room was acoustically sealed, and probably electrically isolated as well: not up to the level of insulation around a ship's bone room, but as good as one could reasonably hope for on a world.

It was half testing chamber, half storeroom. A partly finished meal sat mouldering on a tray. A bucket of something unspeakable stood in one corner. In the middle of the space was an inclined chair with a padded head support, and next to it was a trolley stacked high with metal boxes. The boxes were electrical devices, connected together by cables and with glowing dials and screens on them. The ensemble gave off a faint, anticipatory hum. Somewhere else in the room some old plumbing gurgled to itself.

"We don't need to run an aptitude test on you, do we?"

"You can if you wish," Adrana said, settling herself into the chair. "Or we could get on and test some bones." She took her neural crown out of its pouch and began to unfold the delicate, skeletal device.

Darkly slurped down whatever was left in a mug, then wheeled over another trolley. Instead of metal boxes, this one had a flat platform on top. He took down one of the larger cardboard boxes, only just managing it on his own, and set it on the trolley. He folded back the box's flaps, partially exposing a medium-sized skull with a very strong mottled brown colouration. It had been extensively repaired, with zip-like suture marks and many metal staples driven into the weaker parts. One eye-socket was intact, the other partially collapsed, and the front part of the upper mandible was missing completely. Input sockets in various stages of corrosion knobbed the skull like metal warts. A damp, soil-like odour drifted out of the box. It was an ugly specimen, to be sure: not the sort of thing to tempt a magpie-eyed tourist into opening their purse. But almost certainly *real*, Adrana thought, unless she had greatly underestimated her own gullibility. Whether it would oblige, whether it would mesh with her talent, was a different question.

"Would you suggest an input point?" she asked, drawing out the contact line from her neural crown, now settled down over her freshly-trimmed hair.

"Try that one there, on the cranial mid-line. I'll dim the room and…give you some privacy. Try a few inputs. You'll know before long if there's anything to be had. Are you quite comfortable?"

Adrana wriggled in the chair. "Well enough."

"Good. I shan't rush you—that other customer may have need of my attention—but there are two or three more I think you might try, if you don't take to the first."

"I'll try as many as I'm able before making a decision," Adrana said, not adding that any really promising skulls would need to be tested by Fura as well, before any money changed hands:

there was no point acquiring a skull that only suited one of them. She watched as Darkly turned off the main lights, leaving only dim red secondary illumination as he shut her into the testing room. She did not hear a lock being turned, but the heavy metal door was the only way in or out, so there was no chance of her stealing a skull, nor of making her escape if she damaged the wares. She had no intention of doing either thing: her identity might be subject to concealment, but she was here on honest business, and she believed she could afford any skull on sale.

This one was viable, at least. The twinkly glimmered out of its sockets, like a play of faint, reflected carnival lights. That *might* be faked, but these emporia tended to draw a sharp line between the dubious goods front of house, and the real items in the back. Fleecing a few tourists was all right, but making enemies of crews was very bad for the long-term viability of a business.

She collected herself, took a few deep breaths, decided that her mind was as clear as it was going to get, and plugged in on the mid-line socket.

There was nothing.

It was as comprehensively, resoundingly dead as an unplugged telephone. She tried the next socket along and there was something, just possibly, at the absolute limit of her detection faculty. Though it might have been a carrier signal, or some stray noise coming through the circuits. She unplugged and tried again, in a site bored into the thin bone behind the damaged eyehole. There it was, a shade stronger than before. A faint, faint hint of a conversation going on, some interchange between two distant ships, somewhere out in the vast spaces of the Congregation and the Empty that surrounded it, but it was as if she had her ear pressed to a thick dividing wall between two houses, able to sense the presence of dialogue without once detecting a coherent word or phrase. It could have been in any language around the Old Sun. It might, ultimately, have been all in her imagination. But she was not too discouraged: if a skull worked at all this close to a swallower, it stood a good chance of working much better in the bone room of a ship. Adrana unplugged. There were still plenty of sockets she had yet to try, but she had an intuition about these things and felt it was worth testing a couple more skulls before she spent too much time on one candidate. She began to leave the chair; she could open a few boxes herself until the proprietor returned. He had not exactly forbidden it.

Darkly returned. Lagganvor was with him.

"Turn on the lights," Lagganvor said.

Darkly did as he was instructed. He had little choice in that particular matter: Lagganvor was pinning his arm back firmly, while using his other hand to hold a small, sharp tool against the man's neck.

"Oh, must we," Adrana said, sighing as she took off the neural crown. It had been a calculation, having Lagganvor remain front of shop while she went back, but on this evidence she had been right to chance it. "He seemed almost helpful."

"I'm sure he was," Lagganvor said, grunting as he restrained the man. "So helpful that as soon as he was front of shop he was onto his telephone. There was a newspaper on his bench, next to that skull he was digging into. Turned to a snappy if sensationalist little column-filler about the on-going search for the Ness sisters, and with two admittedly not very clear images of said sisters."

Adrana extricated herself from the chair and dipped her neural crown back into its padded pouch. "Did he make his telephone call, Lag?"

"Mercifully not."

"That's lucky for us. I should have cut straight to the chase, I suppose, but it seemed rude not to show a little interest in his wares."

"Very rude," Lagganvor agreed. "Would you like to squawk our friends?"

"Not just yet: I think we've got the matter agreeably in hand, for now. Put Mr. Darkly in the chair, if you wouldn't mind. There must be some string or rope in here somewhere."

"String will suffice," Lagganvor said, shoving Darkly into the chair she had just vacated.

"Don't hurt me," the whiskered man pleaded.

"I'm not going to," Adrana said. "At least, not while you cooperate, which you can start doing right away."

"Take a skull. Take any skull. Take *two* skulls."

"I'll be honest, Mr. Darkly: this was never really about the bones. My sister's out shopping, and she can take care of that bit of procurement well enough on her own."

His jaw wobbled. "I was hoping...I was hoping you'd deny it. I only thought you *might* be one of the sisters."

"And now that I've admitted it, now you've seen my face... you know there's no hope for you?" She shook her head at him, pityingly. "I don't know what they printed about us in that rag, but I doubt even a tenth of it's true. You help me, and no harm'll come to you."

"She means it," Lagganvor added, rummaging through boxes while Darkly stayed in the chair.

Adrana took off her glasses, polishing them against her sleeve. "I have a minor confession...I didn't just stumble into *Darkly's Bone Emporium, 62 Boskle Lane*. I was after a well-connected man that might have useful connections, and my...information...suggested you were a very, very promising candidate. About three years ago—closer to four now, I suppose—Bosa Sennen sent a man to speak to you."

Darkly swallowed hard.

"Did she?"

"Oh, don't pretend you've forgotten. His name was...well, it's complicated and confusing enough for me, so I won't trouble you with that. But you'd remember him well enough. A very persuasive fellow, and if you saw him next to my companion here, in a dark alley, you might mistake one for the other."

Darkly looked stricken and perplexed.

"The point," Adrana continued cheerfully, "is that this man was sent to ask you about another individual, a gentleman called the Clacker. Now it seems—and I admit I can't be too sure about this—but it *seems* Bosa's man never quite got as far as meeting the Clacker; that there was some snag or interruption that prevented him from making the desired rendezvous. And what I'd like from you—no, strike that—what I'm going to *get* from you, is an introduction to this gentleman."

"I've never met the Clacker."

Lagganvor was busy securing Darkly to the chair with some string he'd found. He glanced up from his work. "But you know of him?"

"No...not until she mentioned the name."

"Mm." Lagganvor made a regretful grimace. "That's not what our research tells us, Mr. Darkly. The Clacker is one of your favoured bone brokers. An intermediary between you and the other aliens...a black-market go-between. And you must have his telephone number."

"You've got the wrong man. I don't know this...Clacker. I don't deal with aliens. Clackers, Crawlies...they've got their business, I've got mine."

"It's come to this, hasn't it?" Lagganvor said.

"I fear so," Adrana said.

Lagganvor popped out his eye and bounced it off his palm in slowly increasing parabolas, smiling like a street huckster until the eye's apex took it level with Darkly's face and it stopped, suspended with an iron stillness. Lagganvor stood back and the eye began to pulse with a soft pink glow. The glow intensified, the pulse quickening, the orb drifting nearer to Darkly, concentrating its cycling light on his own two eyes. Darkly made a small clicking sound in the back of his throat. Lagganvor's eye clearly had some powerful paralysing influence on him: he could not blink, avert his vision, or twist his face away.

The clicking continued and a tremble spread down from his neck, his limbs quivering against their restraints. The chair creaked on its pedestal.

"Enough," Adrana whispered.

"Oh, just when we were starting to have fun."

"Enough!"

Lagganvor lifted a finger and the eye backed off, the light dimming very slightly.

"That can get worse, Mr. Darkly," Lagganvor said. "Very much worse."

Darkly was drooling. Adrana dabbed it away with the edge of his collar.

"Give us the Clacker's number, or better still his address. Once we've verified that the information's accurate, we'll return to set you free. Better still, persuade him to come here directly. That will end our involvement the soonest."

"I don't..." Darkly cleared his throat with a hacking wet cough, and Adrana dabbed at his mouth again. "I don't need to persuade him to come to me."

"I think for your sake you do," Lagganvor said, flicking a curtain of hair down over his enucleated eye-socket.

"You misunderstand me," Darkly answered. "There's no need to call or summon the Clacker. He's already here."

2

A few blocks away, a stop or two down the Green and Purple Peripheral Interurban Lines, yet still within the Virmiry West district of Strenzager City, the younger Ness sister was also doing back-room business.

"I'm startin' to think," Prozor was saying, as they ascended a flight of stairs, "that this was never about bones to begin with."

"It was always about bones," Fura retorted sternly, glancing back over her shoulder. "We've need of a skull, and that need ain't evaporated. But I reckon we can depend on Adrana to sort us out a skull that meets our requirements. When she's found one, which won't take her long, I'll examine the relevant item and decided for myself whether it's a suitable purchase. But there ain't any sense in the both of us doing donkey-work. I have..."

"Loftier concerns?"

"Not the exact phrase I'd have chosen, but...not far off the mark, either."

At the top of the stairs was a short corridor, floored in red carpet worn through to a beige stripe down the middle. At the end of the corridor was a sturdy wooden door, flanked by a pair of potted plants. Fura pulled her metal fist out of her pocket, raised it in readiness to knock, and then looked into Prozor's eyes for some confirmatory sign, some reassurance that she was on safe ground.

"Whatever's behind that door, girlie, it's between you and your conscience. You've been spooked ever since that green-haired captain had your mark, ain't you? Rarely seen you so twitchy. No wonder you couldn't get a peep out of any of those bones, the state you've been in."

"I don't like being recognised."

"Nor me. I know you were applyin' some reverse psychology at that immigration desk, playin' difficult, 'cause that's exactly how Fura Ness wouldn't behave, if she was tryin' to sneak her way into a world...but next time, if there is a next time, maybe try a bit of forward psychology as well. Never know, girlie—it might help." Prozor pushed her sharp features into half a smile. "I wouldn't worry about that captain—I think she meant what she said: that there's some against us and some for us, and she wanted to let the Ness sisters know that they can count on some support...unless you really make a mess of things."

"That's meant to help?"

"All I've got, girlie."

Fura rapped on the door, her gloved hand sounding like a series of hammer blows. She dipped her fist back into her pocket and stood back. There was nothing to be gained in knocking again; their arrival could not fail to have been noticed.

"It wasn't just the captain," she said quietly.

"The thought of that cove, splattered all over the pavement?"

"You could put it a *touch* more delicately."

Prozor touched the dent in her head where the metal plate had been put in. "They knocked the delicacy out of me when they screwed this into my noggin. Not that there was much to be knocked out even then."

"You astonish me."

"I know you're thinkin' what happened to that cove had some-thin' to do with what you did to all those quoins..."

Fura touched a finger to her lip. "Proz..."

"It ain't a secret between us, girlie, and if anyone's thinkin' of listenin' in, it's 'cause they already know who and what you is, and most of what you done. You shouldn't dwell on that cove, though. I ain't here to be your conscience, or your voice of reason, but I am here to let you know that not everythin' that happens—or will happen—has to be your fault."

"They must've lost something in the crash, Readjustment, whatever they want to call it."

"And maybe their troubles were brewin' long before the Ness sisters went off to space. The point is, girlie, you weren't to know what'd happen when you brought those quoins together. True, you might've given it a little more consideration before you started pokin' your nose into somebody else's onions, but it wasn't you made things the way they are. There was somethin' rotten goin' on long before you drew a breath."

"Just tell me I haven't made it worse," Fura said.

"Sometimes things have to get worse before they get better. And that ain't always bad."

A latch sounded and the door opened. A strange, dead-eyed girl stood on the other side, with a continuation of the corridor beyond her. She was nearly as tall as Fura, thin to the point of cadaverousness, with a slumping, lop-sided posture that made it seem as if she were hanging by invisible puppet strings. She had ribbons in her hair and was dressed in the sort of pretty, pink-and-blue striped dress a girl might wear for her tenth birthday party, yet Fura felt certain that she was at least sixteen, and perhaps older still. Her mouth was a toothless slash, smeared around with black lipstick.

"Who?" she asked, in a rasp of a voice.

"Captain Tessily Marance," Fura said.

"Hirtshal," Prozor added.

The girl had a notebook. She flipped its pages and dragged a black-nailed finger down a column.

"The Pharmacist will see you."

They followed her. She had ballet shoes on and moved on tiptoes, hardly in contact with the floor. The carpet in the corridor beyond the door had been replaced more recently and there were photographs and paintings on the wood-panelled walls. At the end was a door constructed mostly of pebbled glass, through which penetrated a trembling green light. The girl opened the door and beckoned them into the room beyond, which was as cool and damp as a crypt.

It was an aquarium, or rather a room filled with many individual aquarium tanks. They covered the walls and quite a lot of the floor. Each tank was lit from within, and each was full of countless luminous fish of many sizes and varieties. They moved in restless shoals, swimming around coral formations and diving in and out of miniature caves and fabulous sunken cities made of jewelled stone.

Fura gawped for a few seconds, half saddened and half delighted. She had forgotten how much she used to enjoy the aquarium house at the Zoological Gardens in Hadramaw. Just being in this room, with its smells and noises—the dampness, the low illumination, the quiet gurgle of pumps—made her think of ice-creams and souvenirs and fine days away from indoor chores.

"Captain Marance and her associate for you," said the girl.

"Very good, Pasidy—wait a moment, will you? Excuse me, Captain—my little darlings must be attended to."

The speaker—the Pharmacist—had his back to them. He was propping himself up on a stick while he sprinkled feed into the open top of the one of the central tanks. Behind him was an old-fashioned wheelchair made mostly of wood and wicker. The fish—little blue darts with fiery slashes down their sides—pushed their mouths up to the surface as the Pharmacist shook loose the last few granules from his bag. "Please come over, Captain Marance—I am very eager to make your acquaintance."

Fura and Prozor walked up to the man. He settled the lid back on the tank very carefully, then eased back down into the waiting wheelchair. The girl—Pasidy—lingered slump-shouldered and sullen at the door for a few moments, biting at a strand of hair.

"Thank you for agreeing to see me at such short notice," Fura said.

"I should congratulate you on your industry in finding me as easily as you did. For reasons that I need not dwell on, I maintain a deliberately low profile." The man flicked a patterned blanket across his knees. He was very nearly as cadaverous as the girl, with stick-thin wrists jutting out of the sleeves of a white surgical smock, buttoned at the sides and over one shoulder. A tide of damp green licked around his rolled-up cuffs where he had immersed them in the water. He had a permanent grin, one that was so fixed that its effect was maniacal rather than reassuring. His eyes were heavy-lidded and copiously bagged, drooping away from either side of a long, steep-sloping nose. His ash-coloured hair was combed sharply from one side of his scalp to the other, forming an asymmetric wave that dipped down over half his face. Fura could not begin to estimate his age: he was either a young man gone to precociously early seed, or a geriatric who had smuggled a few faint traces of youth into advancing years. "You have the necessary list?"

Fura passed a piece of twice-folded paper to the Pharmacist. He took it in his fingers, pressed it against his nose, smelled it carefully, then opened it out and read down the column of items Eddralder had prepared for her.

"You have a physician in your service, I see. Would it not have been quicker and easier for him to come to me directly?"

"He prefers to stay on the ship. Anyway, he said there wasn't much here that would be difficult to find."

He ticked his finger down the list, mouthing softly. "Tranzerome, ten standard measures at the usual dilution. Twenty ampules of Theramol. Six units of oral Axanox..." He lifted his eyes to her. "A dangerous game, bauble-hunting?"

"I never said I was in that line of work."

"Whatever other work is there, for an honest captain? These are the medical supplies of a crew expecting injury, above and beyond the common ailments of space travel."

Fura shrugged. "There are risks."

"Can you supply the girlie with what she needs, is the question," Prozor said.

"Yes…yes." He looked at her with a faint flash of irritation. "For the most part."

"For the most part?" Fura asked.

"The bulk of this is straightforward enough…you'll be paying black market prices, you understand, but I guarantee the product and you won't have the trouble of going through any official channels. For a reasonable surcharge, I'll supply enough export documentation to grease any wheels on your departure."

"We can pay," Fura said.

"The only difficulty is…your man has requested twenty vials of Mephrozine?"

"If it's on the list then we need it."

"Mephrozine is *very* difficult to come by. Very difficult, and very expensive. I can't supply twenty vials, not at short notice. Ten is the best I can do, and I guarantee you won't have any more success elsewhere in Mulgracen."

Prozor jammed her hands on her hips, giving him her best sceptical look. "Got the market sewn up, have you?"

"Let's just say that the little Mephrozine that circulates through Mulgracen tends to pass through my hands. Might I…" He was looking sharply at Fura.

"What?" she asked.

"Mephrozine has several uses…but one of the principal ones is to counter the advance of *acute progressive parasitic lightvine syndrome*, or the glowy." He frowned, studying her with a deeper interest. "You have it, don't you? The skin patterning may be concealed, to a degree, but less so the presence of it in your eyes, and I see the glints. The spores reach the eyes via the optic nerve; so it is already in your brain, beginning to affect your cognitive processes."

There was no denying it, so Fura stiffened her jaw and shrugged. "Do you have the Mephrozine or not?"

"Ten vials."

"I'll take them all."

The Pharmacist examined the list again. "Six thousand bars will cover this. Six-thousand-three-hundred for the goods and the export papers. For that, I'll throw in a box as well—it'll save you stuffing your pockets."

Fura looked at Prozor, who dug into her coat for the bag of quoins she was carrying. Six-thousand-three-hundred bars was extortionate, but she wanted the medicines now and without too many other questions asked. Prozor sorted through the bag, squinting at the bar patterns on the quoins until she had something close to the desired figure. When she was done, she handed over twelve of the medallion-sized objects.

"We're twenty short, but you ain't going to quibble about that, are you?"

"I don't suppose I am." The Pharmacist took the quoins and sifted through them with a quick and attentive eye. He held a quoin up to the wavering green light, peering into the interlocking pattern of bars on its face—criss-crossing threads suspended over an impression of depth much greater than the thickness of the quoin. "Pasidy—take this list and fill out a travelling box. Captain Marance may have all ten of our remaining vials of Mephrozine. Her need is not in doubt."

The girl took the paper and left through a back door between two rows of tanks. "She won't be long," said the Pharmacist. "Pasidy is *very* efficient, bless her." He stuffed the quoins into his tunic pocket, wheeled his chair along a pace or two, then pushed himself back up so he could feed the fish in the next tank along. "These must be trying times for someone in your line of work. The Readjustment has caused all sorts of difficulties. When credit can't flow, neither can commerce. Local economies like Mulgracen can just about function, but things are much worse between the worlds. Luxury goods continue to move, but the less glamorous items, where the margins were always...*marginal*—things like foodstuffs, medicines, or the chemicals need to make them—they're hardly moving at all."

"Bad times for honest captains and their crews," Fura

said. "Bad for legitimate wholesalers. Not quite so bad for black-marketeers."

He leaned further over the tank, sprinkling the food. "One must make hay while the Old Sun shines, Captain. Would you rather I wasn't in business?" He strained, leaning further, and some quoins tipped out of his tunic pocket and into the water.

Fura watched with only faint interest as they submerged, descending edge-down.

"You're careless with your money," she said.

"No harm shall come to them, and Pasidy can fish them out later. She has the reach for it."

Fura folded her arms and angled a heel against the floor, willing Pasidy back with the medicines. Idly she watched the quoins sink, descending with their faces pointed back out of the tank's side. The last of them was coming into its final alignment; it ceased its axial rotation as neatly as if it had come into contact with an end-stop. Then it continued descending, until—along with the others—it sank its rim into the silt at the bottom of the tank.

Fura's curiosity prickled like an itch behind her forehead. "Is there something magnetic in the frame of that tank?"

"Why do you ask?"

"No reason," she answered, realising that he had seen nothing unusual in the way the quoins descended; nothing in their curious alignment.

The door opened again and the girl entered with a heavy wooden box swinging against her hip. The Pharmacist had settled back in his wheelchair, shaking the last few crumbs of fish food from his fingers. He pointed at Fura, and Pasidy gave her the box, leaning forward at the waist like a crudely-jointed puppet, then jerking back up as the tension was released. Her arms waggled by her side and her head lolled as if her neck was broken.

"You may examine the goods," the Pharmacist said.

The box was the sort of portable chest that hinged open down the middle, with four layers of separate drawered compartments, each of which was stuffed with drugs. On top was a sheath of plausible-looking paperwork. Fura took out a set of vials, holding them up to the ceiling and squinting at their labels.

"They're either real or they're not," she said, directing her words at Prozor. "Either way, only Eddralder's going to be able to tell."

"Is the Meph in there?"

Fura nodded. She had already identified the black wallet containing the Mephrozine doses. "It'd better be genuine," she to the Pharmacist. "We'll find out if it isn't, and Mulgracen's not exactly off the beaten track. You wouldn't be a hard man to find a second time."

"Which is why I'd never countenance selling anything I didn't have confidence in. You may depend on the articles. Use them cautiously, of course…some of them are *very* potent. Especially the Mephrozine."

Fura returned the items to the chest and latched it closed. "Pity you couldn't sell me more of it."

"Hopefully that will tide you over—if you haven't left it *too* late, of course." His grin unwavering, he regarded her with tissue-thin sympathy. "I do hope you haven't."

3

The four of them met again on the tram back to the docking wheel. Lagganvor had called through to Prozor on the portable squawk, saying that he and Adrana were on their way back to the launch, that their shopping had gone well, and that it might not be a terrible idea if Fura and Prozor were to join them. He said no more than that, and kept to their false names, but Fura could not help but pick up on an undercurrent of urgency.

Fura and Prozor came aboard via the rear door. It was a squeeze, standing room only, but they pressed their way through the other passengers until they were within muttering distance of Adrana and Lagganvor. Fura had sworn she would limit contact with her sister while they were in Mulgracen, but they had got on at different stops and would only be sharing the tram for a short distance. In the squeeze of all the other passengers, she thought they would be safe. Everyone was too close to everyone else anyway, and many of the passengers were already arguing or complaining to themselves. Fura had not exactly endeared herself to anyone, coming aboard with the hefty, square-edged medical chest, but she was far from the only passenger with luggage. "I paid my ticket, cove," she said in reply to one muttered complaint. "Ain't no law says I can't bring my belongings with me."

Adrana was not making herself much more popular. She had

a huge and unfamiliar item of luggage at her feet: a rectangular case with metalled edges. Fura noticed it with a measure of relief, thinking that a container of that size could only be used for one purpose.

Over the hubbub she mouthed: "I hope it's a good specimen. You must've had a great deal of confidence in it, to buy it without my say-so."

"I have a great deal of confidence in it," Adrana replied, while Lagganvor observed their exchange with a look of quiet if strained amusement. "But it isn't the item you think." She dipped the direction of her gaze down to the box Fura had brought aboard. "Yours, on the other hand...I presume you had equal confidence in that? It's an odd sort of container; smaller than I was expecting. I do hope you spent wisely."

"I spent very wisely indeed," Fura said.

"She ain't got the thing you're thinkin' she has," Prozor said to Adrana. "And if I'm not too mistaken, you ain't, either."

Adrana lowered her nose, looking down at Fura over the tops of her spectacles. There was something scolding and older-sisterly in her expression. "We had one objective. One reason alone for coming to Mulgracen."

"We did," Fura agreed. "Which I was counting on your fulfilling."

"And I was counting on you. You are...the more adept one." Adrana winced, as if this one admission had cost her physical pain. "I thought I could depend on you."

Fura kept her voice level, but there was an edge to it. "I thought I could depend on *you*."

"Voices, down," Lagganvor said, in a friendly but emphatic tone, smiling doggedly. Their tense exchange had begun to draw glances, with travellers lowering their newspapers or breaking off from their own arguments to watch this far more interesting interaction. "Might I ask, dear Captain Marance, about the contents of that very handsomely made chest?"

"Medicines."

Lagganvor turned to Adrana, shrugging good-humouredly. "You cannot deny that we needed medicine, dear Tragen.

Perhaps not as urgently as we might have needed another item, but it's not a frivolous purchase."

"And your box?" Fura asked. "Something nice in that as well? I'll give you this—whatever it is, it looks big and heavy."

"Pals," Prozor said, in a sudden and urgent manner.

The tram had stopped and two dark-hooded figures had boarded via the same rear door Fura and Prozor had used. Fura understood why Prozor had clocked them immediately: there was something instantly wrong about these newcomers; something alarming in the casual manner in which they were shouldering their way forward, utterly unconcerned about the other passengers.

"We have to get out," Adrana said, squeezing her way to the forward part of the tram. The "stop" light above the front windows was already illuminated, but Adrana rang the bell twice more, yanking her own box along despite the ankles of the increasingly irate passengers who were standing between her and the door.

"Would you like me to stop them?" Lagganvor asked mildly, beginning to lift up his fringe.

"No!" Fura said.

The two figures were halfway down the tram now. They had ash-grey coats on, with oil-cloth extensions over the shoulders and their hoods drooping low so their faces lay mostly in shadow. Fura caught a pale flash of a pocked and stubbled jaw from one; a half-crescent gleam of yellowing teeth from the other. Someone took exception to being barged aside and delivered a swipe with their umbrella. The stubble-jawed one seized the umbrella without glancing aside, then tossed it through the open ventilator above one of the side windows. Another man had his broadsheet raised too highly, and too far into the aisle: the yellow-toothed man ripped a fist through it and tossed it to the floor, grinding it into a greasy mess under his heels. Both men continued their advance, and the tram was carrying on, crossing junctions but showing no signs of approaching its next stop.

Adrana was ahead; Fura and Prozor had now slipped past Lagganvor. He was still regarding the men, holding his ground and fingering the skin around his eye.

"Don't do this, Lag," Fura said. "You'll make more trouble than we need."

"I rather think the trouble has already arrived."

"Who are they?"

"Men who would rather we didn't leave with Adrana's box."

"It *was* paid for, wasn't it?"

"Payment," said Lagganvor, with a faint sidelong smirk, "is not *entirely* the issue here."

"What the chaff is in it?"

The tram slowed hard as its brakes went on. Passengers jostled into each other, and for a moment the stubbled man looked on the point of tripping. He reached up to support himself on the back of one of the seats, then used his free hand to dig into his ash-grey coat. Fura had just enough time to glimpse something small and bone-white between his fingers, like a skeleton key or some elaborate toothpick.

The tram had braked at some lights, but it was not a scheduled stop and when Adrana tried to push open the door the driver barked something at her and raised a warning finger from his enclosed control booth. Adrana turned around and pressed her face to the window separating her from the driver, shouting something. Ahead, the lights changed to green, though the driver waited for some pedestrians to clear the crossing in front of the tram before ringing his bell. Prozor squeezed in next to Adrana and started shouting through the glass. Lagganvor pressed himself against the side of the tram and let the stubbled man approach his level.

Fura glanced around and realised that this unwanted attention was nothing to do with their being the Ness sisters, at least not directly. The men had never given her a glance, and if they hadn't recognised her, then their apparent interest in Adrana might be solely connected to the item in her possession.

She breathed in, collected herself.

"Do nothing," she mouthed to Lagganvor.

The tram started moving again, nosing its way across a busy intersection, and following close behind another tram on the same line. The stubbled man passed Lagganvor, never giving him a second glance. His companion, behind him, mouthed something into a grilled box tucked under his collar.

Fura waited for her moment. The stubbled man was nearly level with her, and the space before her had opened up a bit. Trusting that its contents were snugly secured, she swung the medicine chest as hard and high as her surroundings permitted, and with the entire force of her being.

She caught the stubbled man on the chin and dislodged his hood, which slipped back away from his face to reveal...

She would never forget what it revealed.

The man was not a man. The upper two thirds of his face, from the point where his nose might have begun, was a jumble of insect parts stitched together like the pieces of a rag doll. Instead of skin he had plates of glossy integument; instead of a nose he had a proboscis from which projected a cluster of twitching sensory feelers; his eyes were huge and faceted, and there were two mis-matched sets of them, jammed into the jigsaw of his face with no thought for symmetry. His eyes' facets glittered with shades of ultramarine and lapis lazuli.

She saw all this in an instant. She was still following through with the swing of the medicine chest, and it knocked away the man's glove, as well as the white thing he had been holding. His hand was...not quite a hand, she saw, but a sort of whiskered pincer.

Lagganvor saw his chance and grabbed for the white thing before it hit the floor. He appraised it for a bare instant, then drove the sharper end of it into the creature's neck. The would-be attacker twitched and slumped as screams and startled cries spread down the length of the tram. Some brave soul flicked down the hood of the other pursuer, and the head that was revealed was no less grotesque than the first.

"Muddleheads," Lagganvor said with an odd finality, as if that utterance resolved every question she might have had.

Fura gathered her breath. The second one was still advancing. He was put together differently from the first, as if assembled from a different box of scraps, yet with the same disregard for form and harmony.

What were these creatures?

Ahead, Adrana was using her own hefty box as a bludgeon, swinging it repeatedly against the forward doors. The driver was yelling at her, and Prozor was yelling at the driver. They were so engrossed in this exchange that the business with the muddlehead had gone entirely unnoticed. Lagganvor still had the white thing between his fingers, and seemed to be evaluating its usefulness to him, versus the proven efficacy of his eye. The muddlehead on the ground was twitching, and perhaps regaining strength. Fura pressed her boot heel onto the creature's chest, pressing down through the ash-grey coat and whatever layers of clothing were underneath. Something gave way with a sudden soggy collapse, like a piece of rotten floorboard, and a horrible moaning gasp came out of the twitching muddlehead.

The tram stopped with a lurch. The driver's fist came down on a pneumatic control and the front doors wheezed open. Adrana almost fell out, the box tumbling ahead of her. Prozor was next, then Fura, her boot heel nastily sticky under her, and then Lagganvor. Decamping from the tram, he raised a hand to the driver, a sort of apologetic half-wave. A commotion was still going on inside, as the second muddlehead progressed toward the front door. Alarmed passengers were already spilling out at the rear.

Lagganvor helped Adrana regain her footing, then grabbed the larger box. They were in the middle of an intersection. Fura still had the medicine chest, clutched so hard to herself that it hurt her ribs. Prozor pointed away from the tram and the immediate focus of the commotion; Lagganvor nodded and they all moved as one. The streets were still busy and it was surprising how quickly they lost themselves in the anonymity of the crowd. Fura looked back over the heads of street-goers.

She could still see the tram, and it was still stopped, but no one would have given it a second glance now.

Prozor's intuition had taken them down a secondary street: a little less busy than the main thoroughfare that the tram had been on, but not so quiet that four newcomers stood out. It was lined with neon-lit saloons and dining parlours that were a step below from those on the main drag; just a little seedier and more run-down looking. Above the narrow channel formed by the opposed rows of buildings was the fretwork of the dome, and far above that the lights of the next layer. They seemed as distant as the fixed stars, and Fura began to wonder whether she would ever see the space beyond this world.

"They were going to kill us," she said, realising that she was out of breath. "Weren't they?"

"Our welfare was certainly not uppermost in what passed for their minds," Lagganvor said. "They had one objective, and that was the recovery of the box now in our possession."

"What…in the worlds…were they?"

"Muddleheads," he said. Then, because some clarification was evidently in order: "Sometimes called motleys. Temporary agents, operating for the benefit of aliens. They knit them together out of body parts—monkey or alien; anything that will do, anything that can be made to shuffle around for a few hours—and give them just enough volition and free-will to accomplish a job. Is that not right, Proz?"

"Heard of 'em, Lag, but never got myself into such deep water that I had to discover they was real."

"Well, they are real—*very* real. I confess I had some dealings with muddleheads during my time in Wheel Strizzardy. It was never agreeable. I had rather hoped not to run into the likes of them again…" Lagganvor tensed and slowed.

"What?" Fura asked.

"That's what," Prozor said.

Two more muddleheads—for that was surely what they were—had stepped out into the street ahead of them. Like the first two, they were garbed in heavy coats and face-concealing hoods. Fura might have passed a hundred such men in the course of the evening and not given them a second glance, but now she was attuned to their nature and she thought she would recognise a muddlehead anywhere.

There was no traffic coming up and down this secondary street, and as if by decree, all the other pedestrians and by-standers had melted back into shops and shadowed alleys. It was just the four of them, standing in line, facing the two muddleheads. One of the pair was muttering something into his collar, just like the one on the tram.

"Let us by," Adrana said. "Let us by, and there'll be no trouble."

The other muddlehead pushed back his hood a fraction. A wash of yellow neon caught the angle of his jaw, which was too sharp and pale to be anything but raw bone. A buzzing electrical voice came from him, while his mouth stayed completely still.

"Give us the box. We only want the box. Then you may leave."

Adrana shook her head. "No. He's mine now."

Fura looked at her sister. There were many things she would have liked to ask Adrana, starting with the question of who "he" was, and what "he" had to do with the box she was carrying.

"He has committed wrong acts," the buzzing voice said. "He has betrayed confidences and risked the integrity of respectable institutions. These crimes of his are not your concern. If you shelter him, they become your concern. Then you become our concern."

"Who?" Fura hissed.

"A Clacker," Lagganvor said quietly. "*The Clacker*. Apparently."

"A Clacker?" She gasped out her fury. "Why in the worlds are we troubling ourselves over a filthy alien? They want him, they can have him."

"No," Adrana said. "He's with us. I gave him our protection."

"I wasn't consulted."

Adrana gave a tiny shrug. "I wasn't consulted about whatever's in that medicine chest. The alien's our responsibility now. He's made enemies of his own kind, and others. Do you know what that makes him to us?"

"A nuisance."

"No, it makes him useful to us. He knows things. Things that you'd like to know as well. That's why he's running, why they want him dead, and why he's coming back with us. That's why this *isn't* a negotiation."

"Give us the box," the muddlehead stated again. "Then you may leave."

"How much does the cove know, exactly?" Prozor asked.

"Enough," Adrana said.

Lagganvor reached up to his eye, making it seem like a thoughtless mannerism, a nervous reaction. "It's not like we had a chance to become intimately acquainted, Proz. As soon as we met the gentleman, it became imperative to move him. Now we must get him as far and as quickly away from Mulgracen as we may." With one quick twitch of his fingers he had the eye out, and had tossed it in the direction of the muddleheads. A whip-crack sounded and the entire street flashed pink-white. Fura reeled: half blinded, half deafened. The muddleheads were black paper silhouettes; one stooping, one reaching into the folds of his coat. A pure white beam lanced out, slicing an arc toward them. Lagganvor shouted and Fura started running. His eye flashed again. One of the muddleheads fell into two pieces, littering the road like garbage. The other was still coming after them.

Adrana stumbled her way into a narrow alley between two of the saloons. Lagganvor and Prozor followed her. Fura collected her breath and came up behind them. Adrana propped the box against the side-wall of the alley, while Lagganvor pressed himself against the corner. The alley was dark, and the street they had just escaped was still being lit by the pink-white flashes of his eye and the purer white of the muddlehead's weapon. It was as if they were in the darkened stalls of a theatre, watching some inscrutable performance up on the stage.

It was impossible to tell what was happening.

"They got him," Adrana said.

Fura looked down. "What?"

"His box is damaged. They got a shot at him."

Grey smoke was seeping from a corner of Adrana's box, where it had been caught by the energy beam. From somewhere inside it came ruby sparks and a powerful acrid gas.

"Well, he's useless to us now," Fura said. "Whatever we got mixed up in here, it doesn't have to continue."

"I said the box is damaged, not that he's dead," Adrana countered. Even in the alley's gloom, her scolding look was obvious. "He comes with us. He knows about quoins, sister. He knows what we've started and what it means. That's enough for you, isn't it?"

Prozor laid a hand on Fura's shoulder. "If she's done a deal with him, he has to come with us."

"We've got papers for the medicines," Fura said, grinding her teeth. "How are we supposed to take an alien with us when he's already got half of Mulgracen trying to find him?"

The pink-white flashing was at last abating. Lagganvor stiffened and raised a hand, and the sphere of his eye whisked around the corner and into his palm. He rolled it in his fingers as if it were either very hot or very cold.

"I suggest," he said, "that we do not delay our departure. There will be others, I'm sure."

A muddlehead staggered into view. His gait was lop-sided and foot-dragging. He stepped over the bisected remains of his colleague, one half of which was still twitching, still attempting some parody of animation. Lagganvor stepped back, the eye still in his palm.

"Do something," Fura said.

He looked back, flashed a guarded smile.

"I have."

The muddlehead came apart, collapsing like a tower of laundry that had been piled too high. His scissored edges sparkled with pink embers. Lagganvor waited a moment, then walked over to what had been the head and upper torso of the muddlehead.

"You ought to have let us leave," he said, with a surprising reasonableness as if, despite all that had passed between them, he bore the muddlehead no ill-will. "Then we wouldn't have had to go through with this."

"Is it dead?" Fura asked, joining him.

"Deader."

She inspected the head where the hood had fallen away. It was assembled from a different selection of monkey and alien parts, with the eyes resembling clusters of chimneys rather than faceted orbs. There were grasping, feeler-like things jutting from gaps in the cheekbones, and a glassy, green-filled transparency over what ought to have been the brain-case.

"Would they have killed us, Lag?" she asked.

"Most certainly. Not because they have any interest in our exploits—I do not think they even realised who we are—but because we stood between them and their quarry. They wanted the Clacker very badly."

Fura went back into the alley, where Adrana had the box horizontally against the ground and its lidded side hinged up. She laughed: a hollow, disappointed laugh.

The box was empty.

"Whatever that trouble was about, sister, someone obviously saw you coming. If there was an alien in the box when you saw it, they must have—"

"He's still here."

Adrana beckoned her sister closer, indicating she should kneel next to her and extend a hand into the apparent emptiness of the box. Fura did, as much to please her sister as to satisfy any curiosity of her own, and felt a cold tingle slither up her metal fingers.

She withdrew the hand, unsettled, but at a loss to explain the cause of her disquiet.

Lagganvor was standing over her. "Effector-displacement systems. Either Clacker-indigenous or fifth or sixth Occupation Occultist technology."

"I don't—" Fura began.

"The alien is still in there," Adrana said. "But he's concealed, along with his life-support apparatus. There's a field, to make him invisible, and a device that moves the atoms of your hand somewhere else, temporarily, so that you feel as if you're reaching into an empty space."

Fura pushed her hand back into the box, detected that cold, then pulled it out, flexing her fingers and warming them in the palm of her other hand. "It's like Ghostie technology."

"Perhaps not unrelated," Lagganvor said.

"Feels just as wrong."

"But very *right* if it helps us spirit this fellow away, which it will." The box flickered, and just for an instant there had been *something* in it; a box-within-the-box, a sort of mechanical container with windows, and something pressed into that, something folded and alien and breathing. "We should not delay," he added. "The damage done to the box is affecting the effector-displacement systems. If they fail, there'll be no hiding the fact that there's a Clacker in our luggage."

Fura rubbed her metal fingers. The cold had bitten them thoroughly. "What would've happened...what would've happened if I'd had my hand in there when it failed?"

"Nothing advisable," Lagganvor said.

*

Two hours later they were in the launch, slipping free of Mulgracen. To Fura's relief and surprise they had not been detained on their way out: the papers in the medicine chest had satisfied the customs officers, and the curiously empty box in which the alien resided had drawn only a few quizzical looks. No one had even bothered reaching into the seemingly-empty space. The effector-displacement mechanism had kept working precisely as long as was needed, and the Clacker's presence had not been disclosed. They had gone through without a second question, and even their suits had still been where they left them in storage.

"I thought there might be a block on anyone leaving," Fura said, as Adrana worked the launch's controls and navigated them through the congestion of local traffic, threading between runabouts and taxis out into the clear space where their main ship floated. "After all that bother we got into..."

"Those muddleheads were not acting in any sort of official capacity," Lagganvor said, absently picking dirt from his fingernails. "The forces behind them depend on anonymity for free movement, and they won't get that by blabbing to customs officials and asking for some innocent crew to be detained at their pleasure. There'll be something about a disturbance in the morning papers, but I very much doubt that the customs men had any idea of the trouble that happened tonight. I was entirely confident we'd sail through."

"So why were you sweating like the rest of us?" Fura asked.

"That, dear Captain, was a necessary part of the act. Any halfway honest crew would be sweating a bit on the way out." He paused and dug into a pocket of the inner layer of his vacuum suit. "I smuggled this about my person, just in case we *were* questioned. It always helps if you give them something to find, so they can go home feeling terribly clever." He took out a small stoppered bottle, unscrewed it, sniffed at the aroma, took a sip, gasped theatrically, then passed it to Prozor. They were under gravity from the thrust of the launch's rocket, so it was entirely possible to sip from a bottle, and she did, generously, before wiping the top with her sleeve and returning it to Lagganvor.

"Very tasty, Lag."

"You are more than welcome, dear Proz."

"But you *was* sweatin', all the same."

Lagganvor put on a pained expression. "Of course I had *some* concerns for the welfare of our new companion. Especially after the poor fellow was shot. But the damage seems to be confined to the outer box, not his principle hibernation casket." He patted the sturdy container, which was wedged into the space next to his feet. "He will be quite safe in here, and he won't eat into our supplies on the ship. The casket supplies all that he needs."

"I thought you said he'd be useful to us," Fura said.

Adrana twisted around from the console. "He will."

"Not much use if he's dozin'. What if I want to get some answers out of him, like you said?"

"All in good time," Lagganvor said. He rubbed his hand along the edge of the box. It had metal edges, inlaid with black. "We communicated with him very briefly—just enough to establish the terms of our cooperation. He needed to get away from Mulgracen, and we had the means. But that casket of his has a fixed minimum sleep interval. Now that he's gone into it at the deepest setting, he won't be roused for at least two or three months, perhaps longer."

"We'll see," Fura said.

"He's our guest," Adrana said. "Not our prisoner, not our pet, not our plaything to be interrogated."

"Who is he, anyway?"

"A fugitive, renegade, whistle-blower, whatever you wish to call it. Bosa Sennen was seeking him because of the information he holds, and if he was of interest to her, then I think it safe to say that he is of interest to us." Adrana's look was pointed. "Do you disagree, sister?"

"Depends what he knows. Depends what he wants."

"Passage," Lagganvor said grandly. "Free passage to Trevenza Reach, where he has allies. And he has promised us that in delivering him to Trevenza Reach, we will find answers to some of the questions that have troubled us."

"Some?"

"And perhaps answers to one or two you haven't even thought of."

Fura moved the fingers of her metal hand. They still carried some memory of the chill she had picked up from the Clacker's box. "How long ago was this all planned?"

"It wasn't 'planned,'" Adrana said. "I had a lead from Bosa's journals, which you could just as easily have found for yourself. I meant to find us a skull—that was always the intention—but I saw no harm in asking about the Clacker while I was about it."

"We visited a bone merchant called Darkly," Lagganvor said. "It seemed likely he'd know of the Clacker's whereabouts, since the Clacker was part of his supply chain. Adrana only wanted to be put in touch. What we didn't realise was that Darkly was already sheltering him. He'd got the Clacker in the same room where he lets his customers test the bones, since the shielding stopped the Clacker's enemies locating him with their trackers."

"He could've stayed there."

"No, he could not. The muddleheads were getting nearer, and it was only a matter of time. Darkly woke the Clacker up temporarily and explained the situation. He agreed to throw in his lot with us, accepting a heightened risk of capture if there was a way off Mulgracen."

"So we've inherited a trackable alien that some other people want dead." Fura dropped her eyes to the metal-edged box. "As far as I'm concerned, there's only one question. Front lock, or belly door. Which do you think?"

"We've given our word to look after him," Prozor said.

"Queer how I don't remember being consulted about that."

"And I don't remember being consulted about the purchase of those expensive medicines," Adrana said. "They had better be worth it."

"Take it up with Eddralder—he gave me the shopping list."

"And the rest of it," Prozor said.

"The rest of what?" Adrana asked.

"You may as well come clean about the special medicines," Prozor said to Fura. "Then both of you'll have clear consciences, won't you?"

Fura growled, angry at her friend, and yet angrier still with herself, for she knew that Prozor was right, and she had no moral advantage over her sister. "I purchased some Mephrozine. Eddralder said it was the only thing that stood a chance of arresting my glowy."

Adrana nodded slowly. "How much did you get?"

"About half what I was hoping for. And it's no miracle cure; Eddralder never promised me that. But it's better than nothing, and if it stops it getting as far as it did with Glimmery, or slows it..."

"You should have told me," Adrana said.

"Because you'd have argued me out of it?"

"Because I would have agreed and told you to use every quoin in our possession, if it would make a difference."

The two sisters were silent for a few moments. Lagganvor offered Prozor another sip from his bottle, the two of them watching with the nervous air of spectators in a bare-knuckle boxing den.

"I s'pose I ought to have told you."

"And I ought to have mentioned the Clacker. But I didn't want to build up your expectations until I was sure we had him."

Fura felt some easing within her. There had been differences between them these last few months, and there were days when she was certain Adrana was hiding secrets, uncomfortable secrets, so she much preferred it when they were of one mind, and such times had come to feel finite and precious to her, like the last dwindling days of some long holiday.

"I think we can agree that a skull would still come in handy."

"No dissent from me. The Revenue ships haven't had any easy time finding us while we could be anywhere in or around the Congregation. But Lag says they're concentrating their efforts within a month or so's sail of Trevenza."

Fura regarded Lagganvor. "Had your ear close to the ground, have you?"

"While the opportunity was there. I'm not saying we go back on our word to the Clacker. Quite the contrary: we should deliver him with the utmost urgency. But those ships will be out there, and on high alert for us."

"We'll dodge 'em," Fura said. "Done it before, we can keep doing it. Of course, a skull would still be very nice to have. Very nice indeed."

"Pity the poor crew you have to steal it from," Lagganvor said.

4

In the control room of *Revenger*, ninety days out from Mulgracen, the only sound was the dependable ticking of an antique
stopwatch. Fura had started the timepiece when the first coil-
gun went off, and now she was counting the seconds until the
sail-shot began to arrive at its target. Based on Paladin's ranging
estimates, the relative speeds of the two craft, and the muzzle
velocity of the sail-shot, she expected to see impact signs after
thirty-two seconds.

"Twenty-five," Fura said. "Keep 'em peeled, Lag."

"Nothing yet," came Lagganvor's hollow-sounding voice, drifting down via speaking-tube. He was inside the sighting room: a
pressurised observation bubble pushed out from the hull on a
hydraulic ram.

"Thirty," Fura said.

"Nothing."

"Thirty-two."

"Still nothing."

Fura paused before replying, the stopwatch's ticking filling
the room like an amplified heartbeat.

"Verify your aim."

"Nothing wrong with my aim," Lagganvor answered. "Wait a
moment. I think I see...yes. Sail-flash." Now his tone shifted

from mild affront to one of clinical reportage. "Multiple speckles, spatial spread, increasing."

Fura snapped the button on the stopwatch, freezing the ticking and recording the delay between the first salvo and the first instance of sail-flash.

"She's slipped a little further from us," Adrana said, twisting Fura's stopwatch around to see the face for herself.

"Tryin' to run," Prozor said, with a no-good-will-come-of-it shake of her head. "Poor saps. Better off bowin' to the inevitable."

"They are," Fura said, with a predatory delight. "They just don't know it yet." Then, raising her voice: "Paladin, recompute and prepare for a second volley."

Paladin's mechanical mind might have been ensconced in the captain's quarters, but he had eyes and ears and mouthpieces throughout the ship.

"Do you wish to gauge the damage done by the first?" he asked in his deep, tutorly voice, one that the sisters had known throughout childhood and adolescence. "It may already be sufficient, judging by Mister Lagganvor's report."

"No," Fura said. "We'll offer 'em a little bit more encouragement, just so they don't get any silly ideas."

"As you wish, Captain."

Lagganvor spoke from the speaking grille. "Sail-flash is heavy and widely distributed."

"Good," Fura said. "Dish 'em another helping."

Paladin let off the coil-guns for a second time, the middle of the three volleys that were possible without breech-reloading.

Clang, clang, clang.

Fura initialised the stopwatch and restarted it with a firm depression of her metal thumb.

Tick, tick, tick...

Sail-flash meant that their sail-shot was ripping into the other ship's rigging and sails, disrupting them badly. Square leagues of sail were being torn away or shredded, free to flap and twist beyond the captain's discretion, and therefore maximising the chances of casting sunlight in an adverse direction.

Thirty seconds passed, then five more, and Lagganvor reported a second wave of sail-flash superimposing itself on the tail-end of the first.

"Multiple heavy flashes, maybe some hull incidence..."

No one doubted his observations. With his artificial eye, Lagganvor had the keenest acuity of any of the breathing crew.

"Hold the third wave," Fura said, stopping the timer and holding up her flesh fist by way of emphasis.

She had not intended to score direct hits against the hull, but it was a known risk given the uncertain ranging, and she would not compound matters by sending more sail-shot.

"Open squawk, short-range only," Fura continued. "Be ready for return fire. Lag, you can come back in; tell Merrix she's up next."

"Squawk is open and ready," Paladin answered.

Fura pocketed the stopwatch and snatched one of the squawk handsets from its wall-mounting. "Do you want to do the honours, dear heart? Has to be said you've got a sweeter way with it than me."

Adrana took the handset from her sister, raising it to her lips, the coiled line stretching out from the wall.

"Unidentified craft: this is Captain Ness. We've crippled you and are about to board. If you abide by our conditions, there'll be no need for any trouble. We'll take what we want, but no more, and we'll leave you alive and capable of making port. Our physician will be with us, and if you have injured parties he'll see to your needs. All of that, though, is contingent upon your total cooperation. Our guns stay on you the whole while. If we see so much as one warm coiller, you'll be destroyed outright. There'll be no clemency, no mercy, no taking-of-prisoners, no kindly treatment for your wounded." She breathed in, fingers caressing the switch on the squawk handset. "This is my last word on the matter. Prepare to submit, or prepare to die: the choice is yours."

She closed the transmission.

"How was that?"

"Commendably done. If you weren't my own blood, I think I might be a little afraid of you as well." Fura returned to the speaker grille and selected a different channel. "Surt, Tindouf. Ready the launch."

*

Fura brought the launch to a crawl when it was a league from the other ship. With another control she brought up the flood-lamps, brushing fingers of light across the rigging, sails and hull of the injured craft.

"Oh dear," she said, with a false sympathy. "What have we done to 'em."

It was a spectacle of chaos, a dark, visceral conundrum of knots and tangles, and the phantom-like forms of limp or collapsed shrouds and gallants, some parts of them still moving. There was a time when the damage would have been inscrutable to her, but now she gauged the success of her action with a keen and confident eye. A few parts of the sail-shot had struck the hull—there were bright, clean wounds to prove it, where paint or cladding had been ripped back to bare alloy—but so far as she could gauge there had been no puncturing. The innermost elements of sail and rigging had not been badly touched; it looked worse than it was because the outermost areas had been drawn back in under the tension of sail-control gear, once they had lost the counter-balance of photon pressure to hold the torque-lines and stay-preventers under load.

Fura reached into a pouch on her left hip and took out a little purse-like affair made of cushioned material. With the tips of her metal fingers she extracted a rough-edged rectangle of smoky glass, then slipped it into her other hand, where she was not yet wearing a gauntlet.

Raising the stone to her eyes, she squeezed very gently. The lookstone responded, becoming dark instead of smoky, and she pivoted her gaze very slowly, stars oozing across that letterbox of darkness until the other ship came into view. She squeezed a little more and the ship's outer cladding melted away, disclosing a ghostly, wobbly impression of its interior compartments and mechanisms.

"Anything?" Prozor asked in a whisper.

"Five, maybe six individuals." Fura was concentrating intently, trying to make out the dense knots of bone and muscle that were the ship's crew. "Four of 'em cooped up in one place, which I think might be the galley, and another two back near the stern, very close together."

"Do you see coil-guns, anything like that?" Lagganvor asked, holding his helmet in his hands.

"Maybe a small piece or two, aft and stern, but no broadside batteries." She passed the lookstone to Prozor, who—like Lagganvor—was pressing in behind her pilot's position. "See if you can spot any hideaways. I don't want to go into the ship thinking there's just six of 'em, and have another dozen spring out of hatches. That box the Clacker came in has got me worried about things that might be hidden away."

"Effector-displacer systems are very rare," Lagganvor said, in a low confiding tone. "And valuable. Any crew that was lucky enough to have such a thing wouldn't need to be scrabbling around in this neck."

"We are," she said.

"But we have ulterior motives."

"Let's hope *they* don't."

"I'm only seein' six so far," Prozor said, making a curious spectacle of herself as she held the lookstone up to her own face, for there now seemed to be a rectangular tunnel stretching all the way through her, out beyond the launch and into open space.

Fura opened the short-range squawk back to *Revenger* and reported on their findings so far, informing her sister that she did not believe the crew capable of putting up any significant resistance.

Cautiously, she edged the launch deeper into the carnage, closer and closer to the hard form of the hull. Loose rigging scratched along the smooth lines of their hull, making a dry rustling sound. A fragment of sail snagged on one of the fins, then a corner of it fluttered against the flame of the exhaust and the entire scrap vanished in a soundless white deflagration.

"Do you see a name?" Lagganvor asked.

"Not yet."

Prozor handed back the lookstone. "I still ain't seen more than six. I also ain't seen much in their holds, either."

"If they have a skull, I'm happy." Fura slipped the lookstone back into her purse, and the purse back into her pouch. "Doctor Eddralder: are you ready?"

"Tolerably so," Doctor Eddralder said. The tall physician with the tombstone face was making a final inspection of his medical chest: the same one that Fura had brought him from Mulgracen, although now stocked only with the drugs and instruments that were likely to be useful in the immediate aftermath of a boarding operation.

"I see something," Lagganvor said, jabbing a finger at the windows as the launch came around to the other ship's mouth-like prow. "Red letters, nearly faded away." He tapped a finger against his temple, sending an acoustic signal to his eye. "The *Merry Mare*, I think. Is this a ship known to anyone?"

"Not me," Prozor said.

"They'll be just like we were," Fura said. "Just some happy, hapless saps out of their depth. If they ain't from Mazarile, they'll be from somewhere just as dirt-poor and hopeless, betting everything on one big score." She set her jaw. "Well, I'm sorry to bring their dreams crashing down."

"I just saw a face flash against one of those large windows," Doctor Eddralder said.

"Good," Fura said. "Always nicer to have a welcome. I expect they're putting the tea on for us already."

*

They docked. The two craft made a solid, resonant contact, and a moment later Fura activated the capture latches so that the launch could not be shaken loose.

She unbuckled and worked her way back from the console position. There was a lightweight hatch in the treaded walkway that ran between the launch's two rows of seats. Fura flipped it up, exposing a heavier door beneath, with a spoked locking wheel set into its face. She bent down to spin this wheel, which in turn unlatched the inner pressure door of the belly lock. She lowered herself down into this cramped space, then set about loosening a second wheel set into the outer pressure door. Lagganvor and Prozor leaned in above her, directing crossbows over her shoulders as she worked. It was a two-handed job and Fura could not bring a weapon to bear until she was done with it.

"Brace yourselves," Lagganvor said, his voice emerging through his visor, but also communicated to the others via suit-to-suit squawk, so that it had a double-edge to it, one muffled, the other buzzy and sharp.

With the boarding party all suited, it would not have mattered if the door led to vacuum, but when Fura had opened the outer door—with the inner one still open—there was no drop of pressure.

Facing them was another door, but painted brown this time. It belonged to the *Merry Mare*.

"The sooner some clever cove comes up with a substitute for breathin'," Prozor was saying, "the happier I'll be. Spent half my life going in and out of ships."

"And the other half complaining about it," Fura said, twisting around to take Prozor's crossbow and using the haft to hammer firmly against the brown door, before passing it back again. There were a few seconds of silence, then a faint metallic scuffling from beyond the door. Fura reached beneath her chest-pack and closed her artificial hand around the hilt of a long-bladed Ghostie knife. She detached the knife, and brought it into her line of sight. Though she ought to have been able to see it plainly, the Ghostie weapon resisted her attention, weaselling out of focus unless she averted her gaze.

The brown door began to hinge open in their direction. Fura eased back to allow it room to swing, ready with the blade should she need to hack or stab.

Prozor and Lagganvor covered her with the crossbows.

A round, helmetless face bobbed out of darkness, like a pale balloon unmoored from its string.

"I know you're going to kill us," the man said, defiant and cocksure in the same breath. "But if you've one shred of decency left in you, Bosa Sennen, you'll make it quick."

They faced each other across the threshold of the lock, Fura behind her visor with its grillework and surrounding ornamentation of spikes and bone-parts, the man's head protruding from a tall, wide neck-ring marked with badges and emblems of service.

"I ain't Bosa Sennen, cove."

"We heard your threats," the man said, fighting—or so it now seemed to Fura—to keep a tremble out of his voice. He had a freckled face, eyes set wide beneath a prominent, sweating brow, a dusting of red hair on the scalp. His gaze slipped to the Ghostie knife then just as easily slipped off it. "I heard what you said you'd do to us."

"That was just a little bit of…patter. A bit of persuasion to get you agreeing to our terms and conditions," Fura said.

"We know what you've done. What you've always done. We'll keep to your terms and still you'll slice us up. That's what you do." He spat at her, and his spit formed a drunken cobweb across the grille of her visor.

"Kill me. Torture me. Whatever you will. But show the others some mercy, if you still know the word."

Slowly and deliberately, Fura pulled back the Ghostie blade and fixed it back under her chest-pack. It clacked into place by means of a magnetic latch.

"What's your name?"

"Cap'n Werranwell, as you must already know." His face wobbled beyond the glistening strands covering her visor. He set his jaw, trying—it was obvious to Fura—to look and sound more assured than he felt. "Werranwell, of the expeditionary-privateer *Merry Mare*."

She reached out her metal hand, as if they might shake on terms there and then.

"Much obliged to make your acquaintance. That's a fine ship you have…had, I mean. I'm Captain Ness, as was already explained."

He spat at her again. This time it formed a slimy membrane between her fingers.

"Ness, Sennen, whatever you choose to call yourself. To hell with you and your crew."

She shook her hand, trying to dislodge the spit. "We're getting off on the wrong footing here, Werrie. Why'd you not shoot us while you had the chance, by the way? You had chasing pieces. They'd have been worth a go, wouldn't they?"

He sighed, rubbed at his forehead. "Lasling would have had me risk a positioning sweep, and maybe a volley or two. But it wouldn't have been guaranteed to stop you, and all we'd have done is give you a juicier target to aim for. We're a bauble-skipper, not a plunderer—just an honest ship trying to make an honest living. Still, I wish I'd listened to Lasling…"

"Well, you're right—it wouldn't have helped. But it's not all doom and gloom, Werrie." She put her finger under his chin. "Be sweet with us, don't try anything silly, and we'll be out of your hair in two shakes. Then you can be back about your business…"

He managed a mordant laugh.

"Business? My ship is finished. Or did you not notice that, as you were destroying our sails and rigging and throwing a few shots at the hull for good measure?"

"Necessary damage," Fura said.

Prozor and Lagganvor jabbed the crossbows past her shoulders for emphasis. Captain Werranwell retreated back to clear the lock and allow Fura to pass through onto the *Merry Mare*. She remained alert and ready for action as she did so, trusting nothing, especially not the captain's apparent capitulation.

It was no ruse, though. She was convinced of as much as she

drifted into the *Merry Mare*'s galley and took in the collective mood of the gathered crew, assembled in the chaos left after the engagement. Game pieces, cooking utensils and cutlery drifted free, knocked loose from magnetic tables and latches. A chair had shattered into wooden splinters. Blobs of water had become quivery, mirror-like forms, drifting around like strange alien pets. Lightvine, ripped free from the walls, formed loose, writhing tendrils of glowing colour.

There were three besides Werranwell: two men and a woman. The four figures she had seen through the lookstone. They were beaten, dejected, thoroughly surrendered to their fates. They all wore suits or parts of suits, but none of them had helmets and only one, the woman, had got as far as fitting her gloves on. There were no weapons or defensive items to be seen, not even a little dagger or energy pistol.

"Don't think we wouldn't have put up a fight if we thought it would get us anywhere," the woman said in a low, measured voice shot through with bitter acceptance. "A trip or two ago, we'd have given you something to remember us by. But we've been short-handed since we lost Ives and Mauncer at His Foulness, back in ninety-nine. Then we traded our last good piercing piece for a better skull, thinking intelligence would serve us better than armament, in the long run."

"And did it?" Fura asked, with what almost sounded like genuine curiosity.

The woman affected a pitying, sarcastic look. "Oh, it's worked out handsomely, wouldn't you say?"

"You were at His Foulness?" Prozor asked, following Fura into the galley and sweeping her crossbow into the room's cluttered corners with a quick, confident manner, as if it was something she hardly needed to think about.

"Does that mean something?" Fura asked.

"It means they're either lyin', or they deserve our respect."

"Is this the lot of you?" Lagganvor asked, looking around. Clever, Fura thought: testing the captain's veracity, rather than reveal that they already knew about the other pair.

"This is my crew," said Werranwell, lifting his chin. "Save Meggery, who was injured in your action, and Ruther who's with her. They're in the sick-bay."

"What's up with Meggery?" Fura asked.

"What's it matter?" asked the woman, raking a hand over her dark red hair, which she wore combed to the right of her head, the left side completely shorn, and the hair braided into an elaborately stranded tail that was long enough to reach the small of her back. She was exceedingly skinny, sharp-cheekboned, small-chinned, with a jangle of earrings on the shaved side of her head. "We'll all be going Meggery's way soon enough."

"Let me clarify something," Fura said. "I mean what I said—what we promised you on the squawk."

Werranwell cut across her. "You sounded different when you were laying out your terms."

"Does it matter how I sounded?" Fura turned to call back in the direction of the lock. "Doctor Eddralder! Shift your sticks! Got some employment for you here." She refocused on the crew before her. "What are your names, besides your captain here?"

"Why d'you care?" asked the woman, fingering the tip of her hair-braid. Some lingering pride apparently caused her to collect herself, glance at her colleagues, and say: "I'm Cossel: Assessor/Opener on the *Mare*, and a damned fine one when I had the chance."

"Vouga," said the compact-looking man to her left, who was completely bald, with curiously small ears, two deep grooves between his long-curved nose and his small, nearly feminine mouth, and what appeared to be a permanent doubtful set to his lips, like a doll that had been given a fixed expression for life. "Wrestler, circus strongman and general enforcer." He frowned at himself. "No, wait: Integrator. That's what I meant to say: Integrator."

"I'm Lasling," said the larger man to Cossel's right, who was very broad across the shoulders and very narrow at the hips, so that he formed an inverted triangle, accentuated by the fact that his legs ended at the knees, with his suit trousers sewn into closed-off stumps like the bottoms of lungstuff canisters. He had a wide, flattened face, with a nose that had obviously been broken and mashed to one side, then allowed to heal in that position. When he spoke, his mouth showed an assortment of teeth that were missing, broken, capped in metal or replaced entirely. His face was a canvas for bumps and blemishes, his ears blobby extrusions of malformed cartilage, his lips swollen and nicked with numerous scars. "Master of Sail," he stated, before glancing down at his legs. "I was an Opener, until life decided I needed a change of career."

Fura nodded at him as if they were old acquaintances. "You'd be the cove who was trying to talk your captain into a positioning sweep?"

Lasling shrugged, as if the point was of vanishing consequence. "Maybe it was me. What would you've done?"

"Exactly what you were advocating."

Doctor Eddralder was coming into the galley, unbending himself like a cleverly hinged walking cane. His visor was a sheet of curved glass, lacking any armoured grilles or frets, so his long, faintly equine face was easily visible. His large eyes, pale as hard-boiled eggs, searched the scene, looking for signs of injury or distress.

"You said I might be of assistance, Captain?"

"Yes, back in their sick-bay—someone called Meggery, with another crew member in attendance." Then, to the four who were gathered in the galley: "Captain Werranwell, we'll keep you busy for a little while, so will you deputise one of these to take Doctor Eddralder to your sick-bay and help him as needed?"

"Oh, are we going to play a game of sides?" asked Vouga, with a faint frowning interest.

Fura sighed hard and reached up for her visor. "I wanted to rattle you a bit, and I meant some of what I said, but I'm also going to leave you all alive and able to get back home." She hinged open the visor, allowing her glowy-charged skin to shine out into the galley. "I'm Fura Ness. Not Bosa Sennen, nor any other name you might be expecting. I took her ship, as you might have heard, but I didn't take her methods, or her temper."

Cossel scratched at the shorn side of her skull.

"Well, that's me reassured."

Fura looked the woman hard in the face. "You're the Assessor, you said?"

"What of it?"

"You can help me and Lagganvor take our pick of your treasure, such as it is. Vouga or Lasling, would one of you accompany Doctor Eddralder to the sick-bay?"

"I'll help if there are treats in it," Vouga said.

"That leaves Lasling," Fura said, ignoring Vouga. "It's handy that you're the Master of Sail."

The broad, stump-legged man asked: "Why?"

"With Prozor's help you can itemise the damage done to your rigging, and what you need from us to put it right."

"Well, isn't that generous," Lasling said. "It's like being stabbed in a back-alley, then having the same cove tell you they can help with the bleeding."

Doctor Eddralder braced his arm against a wall-rib and turned to address Lasling. "Difficult as it may be to believe— and I understand your misgivings—these people will keep their word. They did my daughter and I a very considerable kindness, and I remain in their debt. Are your injuries recent?"

Lasling seemed to debate with himself before giving his answer.

"Enough to keep me awake some nights."

"Then I will attend to you, once I've seen to the other party. Mister Vouga—would you be so kind as to show me the way?"

"Kind? I'll bend over backwards. There's nothing pleases me more than helping pirates pick our own ship to cat-scraps…"

Vouga glanced back at his captain, who—after a moment's deliberation—gave a single short nod.

"Your physician is either a sincere man," Werranwell said to Fura, "or a very persuasive liar."

*

While the boarding operation was in progress, Adrana sat in the captain's quarters, trying to distract herself from the dangers at hand. She had journals and private letters to look through; she had the Clacker's box to observe—just in case it did anything, which was highly unlikely—she had Merrix in the sighting room if she wished for conversation, and of course Strambli, Surt and Tindouf were elsewhere in the ship, and so never far away. Paladin was immediately at hand, his head—all that remained of him—fixed to the desk like a large glass ornament.

"You seem agitated, Miss Adrana," he remarked, as she turned another page in one of the old, mostly cryptic journals that she and her sister had inherited from Bosa Sennen. "May I allay your concerns, to some degree? We have chased down other ships, without injury or loss to ourselves. With each instance, we are getting better at it—colder and more efficient, you might say. With each—"

"There is a game they play in some of the worlds, Paladin," she interrupted, although not unkindly. "They take a particular sort of pistol, with a revolving chamber, and load only one shot into it. Then they spin the chamber and place the pistol against their heads, by way of a wager. They shoot, and spin, and shoot again. For a little while their luck holds: the pin falling on an empty chamber. Would you say that they are getting better at it, if that keeps happening?"

"I am not sure that the analogy is *entirely* merited."

"I am not sure that it is entirely *not* merited, Paladin," she countered. "We tested our luck in Mulgracen; there is nothing to say we are not testing our luck here."

"And yet, you are in agreement with your sister that having a skull is vital."

"It would help us."

"Well, then."

"And yet we have done quite well without one so far. Lagganvor's right: we would benefit from improved intelligence. But the advantages of a skull have to be weighed against the risks in acquiring one."

"I might venture to say that the time for weighing one against the other has now passed."

"You never used to be so sarcastic."

"Your father would never have tolerated me if I had been. Nor, for that matter, would you."

It was true. Fura had been devoted to Paladin, as fond of him as she might have been of an uncle or kindly older brother. Adrana had been…less enamoured. She had viewed Paladin as fundamentally stupid and failing: a blindly loyal instrument of her father, extending his kind but over-protective and controlling regime into their bedroom and playroom.

To a degree, she had not been wrong. But she had underestimated what Paladin had once been, and what he could be again. It had taken Fura to bring him back to himself, by unlocking memory banks and decision-action circuits that had long been frozen. He had been a soldier once; now he was a soldier once more.

He had also been damaged so badly that his old body, with its arms and wheels, had been abandoned for scrap when Fura made her escape from Mazarile, on her way to rescue Adrana.

What remained of him was a transparent three-quarter sphere full of chattering relays and flickering lights, with fine sutures in the glass where the pieces had been fixed back together, and shards and chips that were from elsewhere, stained different colours, but carefully cut to replace the missing parts of him, mostly by the nimble-fingered Surt, who had taken a personal interest in his welfare. The base of the globe was attached to a collar, and the collar in turn was fixed to the desk, providing a means for circuits to come and go between Paladin and the rest of the ship. If he had a body now, then perhaps it was the ship as a whole, with its sails and rigging, its coil-guns and ion-fluke, its sweeper and squawk.

Perhaps, for Paladin, it was not so very bad a trade.

"I worry, that's all," Adrana said, casting a glance at the Clacker's box. That was the real source of their troubles, if she was going to be honest: all else was incidental.

And she was the real cause of the Clacker.

Adrana had hoped that finding him would be a simple matter, and that once in her presence he would gladly (or perhaps with a little persuasion) answer the questions that preoccupied her. Or if not answer them directly, at least direct her toward possible sources of those answers.

But the Clacker, instead, had become a liability. He might be able to help them, but that cooperation was now contingent on his being delivered to Trevenza Reach. And in the thirteen weeks that had passed since Mulgracen, as they sailed around the edge of the Congregation, they were venturing nearer and nearer to the volume of space where they were likely to run into the squadron of ships assigned to hunt them down. And since their chances of slipping around or through that squadron would be greatly improved by the interception of intelligence on its movements and intentions, they had to have a skull. And since they had to have a skull...

Paladin used to read them a picture story. It was a sort of moral parable about a chain of consequences, each leading to something worse. It began with a horse not being shod properly, for want of a nail. It ended with the collapse of an entire interplanetary empire.

Paladin had been very good at stories. Adrana remembered all of them very well. The more of their stories he read, the more he fed their rules and conventions into his circuits, and the better he was at making up new stories. He could even draw pictures to go with them, projecting them onto the walls of their room.

And for want of a skull, a ship was taken. And for want of caution...

"Miss Adrana?"

"Yes," she answered, jolted back to the room.

"I think there may be another ship nearby. It would appear that we have just been swept."

5

"I almost feel bad about it," Fura said, as they passed one empty compartment after the next. Empty except for the usual junk and clutter of any ship in service: scraps of sail and line, bits of vacuum suit, odd-shaped scabs of hull material that had been cut away during repairs and deemed too precious to discard. "Adding to your tally of bad luck, I mean. The worst of it is I can see how you deserved better than what you got."

"You feel you know us, do you?" Werranwell asked.

"I know a crew that's got the short end of the stick," Fura said. "Mainly 'cause I've been on one. My first ship was under Rackamore, and he did all right for himself—kept his accounts clean and was generally popular. Then I signed on with Trusko, and that was a different story altogether."

"I don't know him," Werranwell said.

"Oh, I knew him," said Cossel, who—along with Lagganvor— was accompanying the two captains. "It was all over the squawks for a week or two; even made the papers and flickers. He'd been borrowing from the banks to keep his operation going, and if there's one thing the lending institutions *really* don't like, it's someone defaulting on their credit by having the bad grace to die."

"The poor fellow can hardly be blamed for being killed by Bosa Sennen," said a smirking Lagganvor, who was carrying a crossbow in case of trouble, but generally keeping it aimed discreetly away from Cossel and her captain. Setting aside this admitted awkwardness, the party of four could easily have been mistaken for a group of acquaintances visiting a museum or gallery, peering into each exhibit with a steadily draining forbearance. Not friends, exactly, but colleagues or distant relatives, thrown together and forced to rub along for an hour or two.

"Not that anyone's credit really matters a damn anymore," Cossel said.

"Were you hit bad?" Lagganvor asked, the object of his enquiry needing no clarification.

"I daresay others were hit worse," Werranwell said. "But yes, it was very bad. We had done quite well in ninety-six and seven, running a string of successful raids—Wedza's Eye, the Cuckoo, Black's Talon among them." He directed a sharp eye at Fura. "Check the chambers of commerce if you doubt me—I can tell you exactly where and when we did business. We were successful, and I make no apology for it." A rueful tone entered his voice. "Too successful, perhaps. Our treasure was exactly what the market was looking for, and we converted our assets into quoins very readily. Then we banked quite a lot of those quoins, and I gather that most of the institutions are guaranteeing those deposits, up to certain thresholds. But I have always been cautious where the banks are concerned, and so we salted half our earnings in private deposits, where there are no such guarantees. After the Readjustment..."

"Such an innocent-sounding thing," Cossel said, interrupting her captain without a thought.

"What do you expect?" Lagganvor asked. "It was the banks that caused that trouble; it's only fitting they be the ones to put a name to it."

They paused at another compartment, small as a kitchen larder. It was bare except for a person-sized sack with a cinch around the neck. Werrenwell reached into the compartment and dragged it out.

It jangled as it drifted.

"The banks have made no statement as to the cause of the Readjustment," Werranwell said. "And for once—despite my better instincts—I am inclined to believe that they do not really understand its origins. Sometimes these financial upsets help the banks, you see—or at least help the aliens, which may amount to the same thing. But the Readjustment was nothing like the slumps and crashes we have all come to know. I don't think it benefited the banks at all. That is why they are so very angry about the whole thing—for once, it exposes their weakness."

"I wouldn't believe everything I hear about quoins," Fura said. She took the bag from Werranwell, loosened the cinch, and peered inside. There were about a hundred quoins inside, she judged, respectable enough even if the denominations were low. But she doubted very much that it would be any sort of fortune, never mind the sort of money that was needed to furnish a ship and its crew. "This your only stash?" she asked.

"Regrettably," Werranwell said, and if it was a lie it was very persuasive one. "Take it. I'd sooner not be reminded of our poor decisions."

She tossed the bag to Lagganvor. "Leave three quarters in the bag by denomination, near as you're able. We'll let 'em keep the rest."

Lagganvor rummaged one-handed through the contents of the bag, cradling the crossbow in the other. He'd had plenty of practice at this sort of thing, Fura reflected. He had been in the service of Bosa Sennen, once, and although she had turned against him—not without provocation, it had to be said—he had not forgotten the common arts of piracy, of which efficient accounting was a principal one.

"We must be a disappointment," Cossel said.

"We're not finished with your holds just yet, cove," Fura said. "We can also use fuel, lungstuff, yardage, tar, bread, butter, almost anything you care to mention." A buzz sounded in her helmet. She reached up, turning on the squawk. "Dear heart, how are we faring?"

Adrana's voice came through, but faintly, and not just because they were inside another ship, and subject to the screening influence of its own hull. She must have had the squawk strength turned down nearly as far as it would go.

"We're in trouble."

Fura smiled. "When are we ever not, dear?"

"Paladin picked up a sweep, then a second at a higher energy and tighter focus. The first feels like a general search sweep; the second more like a targeting action."

Fura took the news as stoically as she could, not wanting to give anything away to Werranwell's crew.

"May we speculate on...distances?"

"No—Paladin can't say. Merrix hasn't seen anything, so they're unlikely to be too close to us. But something's out there, and it's just taken an interest in us. It's the wreck they're picking up, of course, but since we happen to be sitting practically on top of that wreck...I want you back here. Paladin is monitoring a rising weather trend, and Tindouf and Surt will be standing-by to receive the launch."

"We shan't be too long now. It's not exactly rich pickings, I'm afraid." She shot an aggrieved, apologetic look at Cossel and Werranwell. "Lag's just rummaging through our winnings as I speak. Doctor Eddralder's with an injured cove, and Prozor's sorting out the materials they'll need to fix their rigging."

"Understood, but get back as quickly as you can."

"That is exactly my intention. We'll speak soon, fondest."

Fura ended the transmission. She smiled at Lagganvor, who was just finishing off with the bag of quoins, and beckoned him nearer, so she could whisper.

"We have to leave."

"An excellent proposition, all told." He passed about twenty loose quoins to Werranwell, who scooped them close to his chest and then sent them drifting, back into the compartment. They clattered and jangled against the compartment walls, then came to a gradual halt. Fura watched them guardedly, reminded of the quoins in the Pharmacist's aquarium.

There was no mistaking it, now she had seen it: their faces were falling into a common alignment, like spectators at the racetrack watching a single dog.

"There's nothing else," Cossel said.

"And I'd love to believe you," Fura said, "but that's exactly what I'd say if there was something you didn't want us to know about. Like a pretty alien skull, just waiting on a new owner. Show me to your bone room."

*

"What if they don't come back?" Strambli asked.

"They will."

"But what if they don't? What if something keeps 'em there, and whoever sent those pulses comes near enough to get a shot at us? Do we just sit here, or do we move?"

"They will come back."

"But what if..."

Adrana raised a warning hand. "Strambli, please. This isn't helping."

She was at the control room, next to the Glass Armillary. It was a complex, lacy assemblage of nested rings, representing the Congregation and some tiny fraction of the worlds that constituted that little cradle of civilisation. *Revenger* had dipped into its outer layers to visit Mulgracen, but now they were back out in the relative sanctuary of the Empty, where the only worlds were bare rocks or uninhabited baubles, and where the distances between the ships could usually be measured in millions, rather than thousands, of leagues. Trevenza Reach—their intended destination—was still seventeen million leagues and two months distant. It was the one exception to the usual rule: a world that was both fully inhabited, and yet travelling through the Empty. That was because its orbit was uncommonly elliptical, so that it only spent a portion of its time inside the Congregation.

"I don't mean to be jumpy, Adrana. It's just since we brought that scaly cove onboard..."

"You mean the Clacker. You mean our passenger, to whom we have an obligation."

"He ain't said a word to us!"

"He said a word to me, before we left Mulgracen. We entered into an arrangement. Now we are discharging that arrangement. We will convey him to Trevenza Reach, and we will evade our hunters, as we have done before." She looked at the other woman searchingly. "You mustn't lose faith, Strambli. We have the fastest, darkest ship anywhere in the Congregation, and our guns are without equal. We *shall* prevail."

"I know it, Adrana. I just don't feel it." She let out her sigh. "Something's changed in me since Wheel Strizzardy, and not just because of that Ghostie splinter they had to dig out of my leg. I ain't sure I'm suited to this new life of ours." Hastily she added: "It's not that I'm a coward..."

"No one would ever say that of you."

"But stalking ships like this, taking their prizes, leaving their crews all shivered-up..."

"It's a temporary occupation, that's all. Think of a good person who lost their home and had a choice between starving and freezing on the street, or picking the odd pocket. As long as they do it kindly and understand that what they're doing isn't a vocation..." Adrana moved one of the adjustable stalks on the Glass Armillary, taking account of a revised estimate of their exact position. "This is not our new life, Stramb. It's just something we have to get through. Once we have delivered the alien, and gained the answers to some of the questions we seek—"

"You seek."

"I seek, then. But once that is done, all this will seem like a mere footnote. We'll find a way to slip back into normal life, normal society. Those of us who wish to remain in ships may do so, but any who don't will be free to do whatever they choose."

Strambli rubbed at the area of her leg where Eddralder had cut out the Ghostie shard. Fura had seen her do it before, and she supposed it was some itch or tingle that flared up whenever Wheel Strizzardy came up. Strambli had nearly died there, after all.

"You do always make it seem as if everything's going to be all right forever," Strambli said.

"I think it shall," Adrana answered. "I hope it shall be, for all our sakes."

Strambli lifted her eyes to the Glass Armillary. "Mister Lag said we wouldn't run into that squadron, not if we were careful, and definitely not this far from Trevenza."

"I am inclined to agree with his assessment. There are other ships operating out here, and they don't all have to be engaged on some hunt for us. I think we shall find that those two sweeps were not meant for us personally. All the same...I should also be very glad to see that launch on its way back to us."

*

"That swab again, if you'd be so kind," Eddralder said, lifting his gaze to acknowledge Fura's arrival, then immediately returning to the object of his attention.

He was bent over a female patient who was stretched onto a surgical couch and fixed there by grubby straps. A very young man was keeping a close observation on both, floating next to the couch with his legs tucked under him. Eddralder had his medical chest opened, and the young man was holding some of the necessary items, passing them to Eddralder upon request.

"The skull is loaded," Fura declared, "and Lagganvor's completed his inventory of the holds. We've all that we wish to take, and I'd like to be underway very shortly, before the weather worsens..." Or before another sweep comes in, she thought to herself.

The lad passed Eddralder the swab.

"Take a look at what you've done," he said, gesturing at the woman being treated.

"Easy, lad," cautioned Werranwell, who was just behind Fura. She nodded. "You'd be Ruther, would you?"

"Never mind me," the boy said hotly. "It's Meggery you should be bothered about."

Meggery had her face turned away from Fura and a burn-like wound covering her shoulder and neck. From what Fura could judge of her, Meggery was a small, muscular woman with a large head and a great cloud of curly black hair floating above it. She had as many scars as she did tattoos; so many that it was no simple matter telling which was which. On her right side, opposite the new injury and masking some old serpentine wound, a seahorse curled around her shoulder and collar bone. Chains of stars pocked her wrists and forearms. Lacy blue cobwebs patterned her hands. She was missing the smallest finger on her left arm, snipped off cleanly at the knuckle and long healed-over.

"I took your ship, Ruther," Fura answered imperiously. "That's what happens in piracy. It ain't nice when it's done to you, but lots of things in life ain't nice. Besides, there was no hull penetration. I didn't put a shot through you. Unless she was outside, I don't see how she could've come to any harm."

"Meggery is our Master of Ions. When you started hacking us up, Captain Werranwell asked her to give us all possible thrust from the ion-emitter, in the sure knowledge that we were about to lose our sails." Ruther nodded at his captain. "It was the right thing, too."

Fura shrugged. "And?"

"Meggery was down in the ion room when one of your shots hit our hull, and the recoil sent her right into the rectifier vanes. That's an electrical burn, and a bad one."

"Then I'm sorry to add one more scar to her collection."

"It's more than a scar," Ruther retorted, spittle bursting between his teeth. "It knocked her right out, and your doctor reckons there could be neurological impairment as well as tissue damage."

Fura ignored the boy and directed her question at Eddralder. "Have you patched her up?"

"The electrical burn should heal," Doctor Eddralder said, without looking up from his work. "If it doesn't, a graft will be possible."

"You have no idea what you've done," Ruther said.

"I've spared her, is what I've done. And the rest of you, while I was at it. Just because I'm keeping to my word doesn't mean things couldn't have gone very differently."

"Your word," Ruther said, disgustedly. He was sixteen or seventeen, slight of build, with a sharp chin beneath a heart-shaped face. His eyebrows were arched, his eyes a surprising deep blue. The only aspect of his appearance which ran counter to the overall impression of youth was a stripe of pure white hair, running from his forehead all the way to his crown and beyond. "What does their word mean to someone like you?"

"Push me and you'll find out," Fura said, beginning to run out of patience with the boy. Then, to Eddralder: "Will she be all right?"

"Probably. But I'd like to keep her under close observation. If she takes a bad turn, I might be required to go in."

"Go in?" queried Werranwell, drifting close to the patient, and bracing himself by his fingers.

Eddralder looked at the captain.

"Cranial surgery. But it would need to be done on *Revenger*. None of the facilities here are suitable. The swab again, please, Ruther."

Fura seethed, but by great force of will she managed to bottle most of it in. Though it felt like a hot red tide lapping against the lower part of her eyelids, ready to gush out.

"This critical period, Doctor Eddralder. What are we looking at, exactly? Hours, days, weeks?"

Eddralder deliberated before offering his answer.

"Two days of close observation will be sufficient, but if there is a downturn I would need to operate very quickly. There wouldn't be time to convey Meggery back to *Revenger*, not unless you brought it closer."

Werranwell met her eyes. "Your doctor is indeed a man of his word, Captain Ness. But it looks as if you'll be taking back one more trophy than you planned."

*

The great sails were traced in chalkboard scratches of purple and indigo, framing acres of perfect black. The ordinary sails—those they had stitched into the rigging to disguise her nature—had been hauled in before they began stalking the *Merry Mare*, so all that remained were vast square leagues of catchcloth.

In the central focus of the sails, a red mouth gulped wide.

Fura spun the launch around, backing into the docking bay with tiny, expert puffs of the steering jets, so that when it finally touched its berthing cradle the impact was as tender as a pleasure boat kissing against its quay. Doctor Eddralder thanked her for taking such pains not to disturb Meggery, but in truth she was thinking mainly of the skull, and how sad it would be if she smashed it now.

Surt and Tindouf were still in their vacuum suits to help secure the launch, with Adrana and Strambli waiting on the other side of the lock as soon as the doors were opened.

"I took the decision to unfurl the main sheets as soon as Paladin confirmed you were on the way back," Adrana said. "We can set a course as soon as you wish, but for the moment I thought it better to be moving somewhere."

"You can furl them back again," Fura said. "We ain't going anywhere."

any of you, he'll be your physician as much as ours."

"Equal terms, then?" Vouga asked, lifting an eyebrow.

Fura crimped her lips. "We'd need to draw up those articles."

"Well, we could start now," the Integrator said, with a hard and avaricious gleam in his eye. "The loot in your hold. What you took from us, and what you've taken from others. We want an equal share of that now."

"What we took from you," Fura said, "wouldn't fill a doll's thimble." But she gave an effortless shrug. "Of course you'd be equal partners. I wouldn't countenance any alternative. If our hulls are lashed close, we can come and go like neighbours."

Cossel gave a little shudder.

"Never did get on with my neighbours."

"Your sister has joint captaincy?" Werranwell wheezed out.

"She does, sir."

"And you rate her capabilities as well as you do your own?"

The others started to glance among themselves, evidently doubtful of where Werranwell was headed with this line of questioning.

"I do," Fura said, nodding emphatically. "She's as tenacious and determined as me, and she's taken to this new life very well. We've got our different ways of doing things, neither of us would deny, but I've looked up to Adrana for as long as I remember."

"It must be difficult, sharing the responsibilities of one ship."

"We make do. I won't say we don't squabble over this and that, but…well, we love each other, and we want the same things for our crew, and now that includes all of us."

"I am about to die," Werranwell said.

"There's still time to summon Eddralder, and he'd be able to give you a second opinion…"

"A third, or a fourth, wouldn't make any difference. Meggery? Tell her the arrangement we discussed, while she was on her way over."

"This ship is short-handed," Meggery said. "Has been since we lost Ives and Mauncer. Now we're about to be short of a captain."

"Meggery doesn't want the position," Werranwell said. "Nor

does Lasling, or Cossel, or Vouga. Ruther's too young. They're all much too wedded to their specialisations, in any case, and I can hardly blame them for that." He forced a look of fond recollection, perhaps the last of a lifetime. "I was like that, when I had to take over from Haligan, the captain who preceded me. They had to tear me away from the sails."

"Why did you agree?" Fura asked.

"Because there wasn't a more willing candidate. It strikes me, though, that your own ship is presently over-burdened with captains." He interrupted himself, gathering his strength to go on. "The Ness sisters are strong and capable, or they wouldn't have made it this far. One of you will make an excellent replacement for me."

Fura shook her head, denying the idea before it had time to take root. "Your crew won't accept us."

"They will, if I ask them to. I have a choice, Captain Ness: either I anoint a replacement, or risk friction and suspicion tearing my crew apart—and perhaps yours with it. So, I declare that one of the Ness sisters will take my ship, and the loyalty of her crew."

Fura turned to Meggery. "You accept this?"

"It's the captain's wish," she answered. "And if he wishes it, we abide by it. You might not have my affection, or gratitude. But you'll have my word, and that goes for every cove on this ship."

"I... don't know what to say."

"So you accept the delegation?" Werranwell asked. The sucking sound from his chest was more horrible now, slower, and somehow more cavernous, as if issuing from some deeper, darker part of him, far beyond the reach of surgery.

"I do. One of us will take command," Fura said.

"Good... good," Werranwell answered. "That is... most comforting to me, Captain Ness. There is just one pre-condition, call it a down-payment, which Meggery made me insist upon..."

*

Condensation dimpled the inside of Fura's faceplate. It was like the pebbled panes that had been set into the tall, narrow walls on either side of the main door of their house in Mazarile, through which tradespeople became jigsaw puzzles of broken colour and form. Prozor too had become a jigsaw of herself, the pieces not quite knitted together. She bundled Fura out of the lock, into the main compartment of the rocket, and then helped her wrestle off the sweat-and-condensation-drenched helmet. Fura took a deep inhalation of what passed for fresh lungstuff.

"If you're back, that has to be mean something," Adrana said.

"We were expecting you to stay silent, but not for quite as long as this," Lagganvor said.

"I left them my squawk," Fura said, between ragged inhalations. "We'll fix 'em up with something better, but it'll do for communications in the short term. Just until...we figure out how to bring our two ships in close."

"Then...they are amenable?" Adrana asked. "Despite everything, they've agreed to our arrangement?"

"They took some...time to come around to the sense of it." She sucked in more lungstuff, fighting to get her breathing back onto some sort of seemly tempo. "Werranwell died. He was alive when I got there, dead by the time I left."

Lagganvor raised an eyebrow.

"Negotiations went that badly?"

"He'd been injured in the attack, beyond anything we could do to help him. He was...not against my proposition. They've agreed to be lashed to us and accepted our help with their repairs. As soon as we can, we'll draw up common articles." Fura grimaced against a sudden sharp pain. "That way we can pass ourselves off...pass as two innocent ships...just happen to be sailing in from the Empty."

Adrana swapped a look with Prozor.

"To what end?"

"I'll think of one." Fura was still breathing rapidly, clenching her jaw against the pain—which was both worse than she had anticipated, and yet just distant enough to be tolerable, provided she had words to spit out. "Strambli's my main worry. How she fares will determine any action I...we...decide upon."

"What's wrong with your arm?" Adrana asked.

Fura had her artificial arm tight against her chest, clenching its fist so tight that she risked plunging her metal nails right through her alloy palm and out the other side.

"Show us, girlie," Prozor said, taking her arm as gently as she could and persuading it away from her chest. But the fist was still balled, and no monkey strength was ever going to be sufficient to uncoil those fingers. Prozor touched the closed fist, sending a spasm of fresh agony right into Fura, and came away with something damp and snot-coloured on her own fingers, which she sniffed cautiously. "She's bleedin'...something."

Doctor Eddralder pushed to the front of the little knot of gathering. "What happened?"

"Open it up for him," Prozor said, placing one hand on Fura's shoulder, the other at her elbow. "Goin' to have to do it sooner or later, so might as well get it over with."

Fura knew this to be true, but the only thing holding the pain at any sort of bearable level had been the pressing of that arm against her chest, and the balling of her fist. Still, she had to do it. She bit down hard, grunted, forced open her fingers. It took all her will to bend them straight. The pain bludgeoned her instantly, her grunt becoming an anguished exclamation. The oily seepage, which had contaminated Prozor's hand, began to gush and bubble freely. It was some liquid component of the hand that she had never suspected was there.

"Oh, Fura," Adrana said.

Lagganvor rushed for a cloth and pressed it against the source of the seepage.

"Hold it open," he commanded.

"What did they do to you?" Eddralder asked.

She forced herself to look. She had lost a finger from her hand. The smallest digit had been wrenched out and away, leaving a ragged socket where it ought to have plugged into her knuckle. That was where the seepage was coming from, spurting out in rhythmic pulses as if driven by her own heartbeat.

The agony rose and fell on that same cycle.

To her surprise she found that she could bear it, for the moment.

"They didn't...*do*...anything," Fura said. "Nothing I didn't agree to, at any rate. There was just...a little account-settling."

"They took this off you...how?" Adrana asked, taking over from Lagganvor with the cloth, which was already sodden with the green ichor. "Looks to me like they did it with a pair of shears."

Fura tried to force her breathing into something like a normal rhythm. "Didn't care how they took it off. Only that they did it and got it over. Didn't think it would hurt. Not this much. Never really felt a part of me...until now."

"You agreed to this?" Lagganvor asked, shaking his head as if she had just dismantled his last certainty.

"A small price to pay," she said, deciding that the only thing now was to grin her way through the pain, and laugh a little at what she had allowed to be done. "I got you a ship, sister," she said to Adrana. "I'm giving you the *Merry Mare*, and her crew!"

"Meggery was missing the same digit, on the same hand," Eddralder said, before Adrana had a chance to react to this development.

"She was," Fura said, still grinning.

"Then this was at her demand, I take it? She insisted you lose the finger?"

"She said...I'd cost her something. Something that couldn't be replaced. So it was only fair I gave something back, something that meant a lot to me."

Eddralder shook his head. "You had nothing to do with the loss of her finger. That was very clearly an old injury, totally unconnected with our action."

"It wasn't the finger she was cross about," Fura said. "It was what was on the skin before it got burned. What had to be cut away. A little tattoo. Two tiny birds on a vine."

"I fail to see how the one loss may be measured against the other," Eddralder said.

"Mauncer did it for her."

"Mauncer being...?"

"One of the coves they'd already lost, before we found 'em," Prozor said, sparing Fura the need to elaborate. "Lasling told me some of it, when me and him was sortin' out what sail materials they needed. Mauncer and the other cove, Ives, was the ones who got stuck inside the bauble when Lasling lost his pins. Seems Mauncer was the one who got the rest of 'em inked up, when it suited him." She looked down at her own hands and palms, scarred and age-spotted as they were, but otherwise unblemished, then shook her head, more in wonderment than denial, at the fact of the universe once again managing to surprise her with its wicked and playful cruelty. "Can't say I've ever been one for the ink."

*

The sisters had not been long back aboard *Revenger*, discussing plans for the cooperation, when Merrix summoned them to the Kindness Room.

As always, Adrana steeled herself before going inside. She had left too much of herself behind in here: too much of her innocence, too much of the girl she had once been. Doctor Eddralder's many salves and unguents gave off their own odours but somewhere beneath it all was a stench that could never be erased, a chemical memory suffused with pain and terror and all the many colours of madness.

Fura sensed her hesitation. She closed a kind hand—her good hand—around Adrana's forearm.

"We have to be strong for each other. Let's see how bad the news is."

"Don't let him take it off," Strambli said, raising her eyes as soon as she realised she had new visitors. "It ain't time for that. I've been feeling better these last few days, I know I have..."

"Merrix," Eddralder said. "Would you be so kind as to remove the dressing, as gently as you can?"

Adrana moved to the side of the bed-bound Strambli. She was strapped down, just as Meggery had been. The restraints were there for her own welfare, done up no tighter than was necessary to prevent her drifting free and hurting herself, but the sight still pushed a hard stone into Adrana's throat.

"The Doctor won't do anything unless it's your life's that's at stake, Stramb," Adrana said. "And you know how much you mean to us."

"What happened to you, Captain Arafura?"

Strambli had enough wits remaining to notice the recent injury. Fura smiled quickly, making light of it. "Nothing that Surt can't fix in jiffy, Stramb. Just a little finger, too—can't say I ever had much use for it until now, and I'm not sure I'll miss it."

"I'll miss my leg, if he has to saw it off. Tell him he doesn't have to saw it off, won't you?"

"We're a long way from that," Adrana said soothingly. "It's just an infection, something we treated once and can treat again. Isn't that so, Doctor?"

She ought to have deduced from his demeanour that matters were not that straightforward.

"The wound is…changing," Merrix said, carefully peeling the dressing away from the affected area. It was sticky with antiseptic salve, and the process of removal was clearly uncomfortable for Strambli. It had to be done, Adrana supposed, but she had a horrible sense that she was abetting Strambli's distress.

"It doesn't look as red as before," Fura said, lifting a puzzled eyebrow in Eddralder's direction. "That's good news, isn't it? Your potions are working. Just keep treating her, and…" But she slowed, seeing what was already evident to Adrana's eye.

"It's…turning," Eddralder said, with a fearful reverence, as if to speak of the matter at all was to encourage it. "Some cellular transformation is taking place, not far beneath the skin."

"What does he mean?" Strambli asked, with a rising anxiety.

"I noticed there was a pearliness to the affected area," Merrix said quietly. "The redness was in retreat, and in its place the skin…

the tissue…had a colourless quality. I thought it was some necrosis, but Father…"

"It's not a medical process," Eddralder said.

"What is it?" Fura asked.

"Take a closer look. Since Merrix made her initial observation, the transformation has extended itself. I cannot say if it is pushing deeper, or extending outward more vigorously, but it is definitely more developed."

Fura and Adrana almost knocked their heads together as they peered at the wound. Each gave the same intake of breath, the same shudder of disquiet. The surface pearliness which Merrix had mentioned was now a window of smoky transparency, as if a thumb-sized portion of Strambli's skin had turned to smeared glass. Beneath that vile little window—hemmed by a moat of pink inflammation, not nearly as angry as it had been—was an impression of colourless crystal depths, as if they were looking down into an icy crevasse.

"Have you seen anything…" Fura began. "No, what a ridiculous question. If you'd seen something like this, you wouldn't have that terrified look about you."

"I am very sorry," Eddralder said, and it was hard to say whether his apology was meant for the Ness sisters, or the patient in the bed.

"I told you it made me stab me," Strambli said. "Been saying so since I had the accident. 'Cept it wasn't no accident, was it? It was that blade jabbing a bit of itself into me. I know what you're thinking and none of you wants to say it."

"We oughtn't to jump to conclusions," Adrana said, swallowing hard.

"You don't have to," Strambli said, with a ghoulish delight in her own predicament. "We know what's going on. It's turning me. It's making me into Ghostie gubbins."

10

The lull in the solar weather continued. Over the next thirty-six hours, the launch sped back and forth between *Revenger* and the *Merry Mare* with the tireless industry of a shuttle in a weaving loom. It would dock, unload supplies, transfer personnel, then make the return journey and restock. Such was the efficiency of this process that the launch's exhaust gases barely had time to dissipate before it was nosing back through them.

Gradually the two parties got to know each other better. Lasling's legs gave him no trouble moving outside the ship, and he was needed to get the ruined rigging into some sort of condition that would enable the *Mare* to be hauled close to *Revenger*. Watching his arduous, careful progress, Tindouf was quick to propose helping him. Fura was sceptical, but they rapidly formed an efficient, good-natured partnership, and within a day of their first joint shift the wreck of the *Merry Mare* was deemed sufficiently stable to be dragged without risk of further damage. This was accomplished in two stages: first with the rocket launch serving as a tug, coupled to the wreck by six lines of triple-filament yardage; and then by *Revenger's* own sail-control winches, slowly hauling in the same lines.

Fura and Adrana watched proceedings with acute unease, well aware how suddenly and badly things could turn. There was always tension on yardage when a ship was under sail, but that strain acted in familiar ways, along force-vectors that were well understood. It was never a happy moment when a line or winch gave way, but when it went wrong the ensuing damage usually played out in a predictable pattern. Accordingly, crews who valued life and limb knew where it was inadvisable to be and, just as crucially, where to scurry to at the first intimations of disaster.

Such hard-won experience counted for little now. The winches and yard-lines were being put to unintended usages, and if they failed they would do so in unpredictable fashion. Even being inside the ship was not much guarantee. If a line broke, and whiplashed back at *Revenger*, it could cut through glass and hull with impunity. If a well-anchored winch sheared off, it might take a generous part of the ship with it, plunging her compartments into sudden vacuum.

Yet in the six hours that it took to complete the final union of the two ships, six hours in which catastrophe was only ever a single act of malice or inattention away, no accident occurred. No further damage was inflicted on either ship, and no additional toll upon the workers save exhaustion and a fresh catalogue of scrapes and bruises.

When the hull of the *Merry Mare* was finally secured to *Revenger* by a prodigious web of lines and chains, tensioned against the slightest movement, Surt and Vouga fashioned a connecting passage between the two pressurised compartments, so that the repair teams might come and go without the encumberment of full vacuum gear. There was just as much that had to be fixed within the *Merry Mare* as without, and the passage would permit the interior chores to be completed as quickly as possible, freeing up hands to work to restore a full spread of sail. The *Merry Mare* would not be able to extend her own acreage until she was flying freely, or else her lines and sails would tangle with *Revenger*'s, but there was much that needed to be done to the navigation and control gear before that desired eventuality, and yet more to consume the masters of their varied professions.

When the two weary crews mingled in the two galleys, close enough that they could almost sing or shout from one table to the next, Fura dispelled any fears she might have held about any immediate insurrection from the other party. Lasling, Meggery, Ruther, Cossel and Vouga were far too exhausted to put up any sort of fight, and her own crew were scarcely in better condition. Better fed, perhaps, and not as sickly to begin with, but the business of joining the ships had enacted a deep and wearying toll on them all. She was glad, very glad indeed, that the marriage—however temporary or inharmonious it might prove—was now complete.

"We heard that one of your number was sick," Lasling said, facing her across the galley table in *Revenger*. "Nothing contagious, I suppose?"

"If it was, do you think we'd be so quick to fraternise?" Fura asked.

Merrix, who was also sitting at the table, said: "It isn't anything that's catching, sir, and if it were we'd have made sure you knew about it. You've met my father already—Doctor Eddralder. He's doing all that he can for Strambli."

"He did well by Meggery, and seemed to want to help me, within his means."

"He will, sir."

"Lasling." He extended a bruised, swollen-knuckled hand in Merrix's direction. "Zancer Lasling, although Lasling will serve you fine. Your father told me you'd both been done a kindness by the Ness sisters, and he considered himself in their debt."

"He does, sir—both of us do." Merrix looked at Fura, who was the only Ness sister present, Adrana being entertained aboard the *Merry Mare*. "We were in trouble on Wheel Strizzardy, and they helped us escape the place."

"I heard there was all kinds of trouble at Wheel Strizzardy," said Cossel, the only other present. "Even then, I can't imagine how bad it must have been for *this* life to seem any sort of improvement."

"Then you should consider yourself very fortunate," Merrix said, staring down at her cutlery.

Lasling, who seemed to take it upon himself to act as informal peacemaker, tore off a chunk of bread and sniffed it tentatively. "Not quite at its best, I suspect, but a distinct improvement on the green crumbs we've been making do with. And this ale is... almost tolerable." He lifted his tankard, with its hinged lid, before taking a sip through the drinking hole. "Our association may not have begun in the most conventional manner, but this hospitality is appreciated. I fear the reciprocal arrangements on the other ship may fall a little short."

"You... ain't at fault for that," Fura said, smiling decorously. "You had a run of misfortune such as might befall any honest crew. We were the penultimate part of that misfortune, but I hope, in some small way, also the beginning of the turning of your luck."

"I'm struggling to see how that might work," Cossel said.

"We're fully equal partners now," Fura said, reaching across and laying her metal hand on the woman's fingers before she had a chance to draw them away.

Cossel flinched, but kept her nerve.

"Then you won't mind sharing some of that bread and ale between the two ships. And anything else that doesn't have maggots swimming in it."

"Our own reserves ain't as generous as they might seem—" Fura started, for when she had talked about sharing she had been thinking more of tar and lungstuff and yardage, not the edible provisions.

"But if we're equal partners, we will share what we have," Merrix said, cutting across her. "Won't we, Captain? Or else we aren't really equal at all, no matter what we say."

Fura nodded emphatically, furious with the girl for interrupting but making every effort to look placid. "Of course, Merrix— that goes without saying."

"And Father will want them to have equal access to any medicines that they need. Medicines and his services, in all respects."

"Without question. Although Strambli is his priority…"

"She is—but since neither of us knows what's to be done with her, it's mostly a question of keeping her comfortable and monitoring the progression of her…condition. That won't take up all his time, and he said he'd do more for Mister Lasling… Lasling, sir, I mean."

"I'm not an urgent case," Lasling said, yet there was a stiffness in his smile as of someone grinning through pain, and Fura supposed that even in weightlessness such arduous work would cause old wounds to complain. "As for your friend… is the condition as serious as you just made it sound, Merrix?"

"If I may answer for her," Fura said, "it's only the lingering complication of an earlier treatment." But she took on a grave, downcast look. "Still, it forces our hand. We were committed, in a very general sense, for Trevenza Reach. Now our arrival there is a matter of life and death."

"We are not in a fit position to sail anywhere," Lasling said.

"Not now, and not for the three or four weeks it'll take to get you shipshape," Fura said. "But as we've discussed, there's nothing to prevent *Revenger* from sailing quite tolerably, even with the dead weight of…" She smiled hastily, reminding herself that the mortal remains of Captain Werranwell still reposed on the *Merry Mare*, and that her crew might be sensitive to that fact. "I mean that it ain't any inconvenience to us, to have your hull lashed to ours, and to keep about our repairs even as we sail. Tindouf and Paladin already have a plausible crossing for us, allowing for the vagaries of solar weather, taking just seven or eight weeks. But we'll be within sweeper range of Trevenza Reach long before we arrive."

"What is the significance of that?" Lasling asked.

"Before they see us," Fura said, "our ships'll need to be far apart, and moving on plausibly different courses, so that there's no hint of an association between us."

"Wait," Cossel said, squinting and frowning as intently as if she had a splinter in her eye. "Wait. Why are *both* ships required to go to Trevenza Reach? Only one of 'em will have a sick party aboard."

"It suits our purposes equally, Cossel. We've got our pal Strambli to think of, as well as another passenger, and you've been done a great injustice by that squadron. At Trevenza Reach you may seek restitution."

Lasling shifted on his stumps. "You said civilisation wasn't safe for us."

"Then it's as well that Trevenza Reach doesn't quite count as civilised." Fura picked up a quoin that was serving as a paperweight, holding down a napkin. She tapped it against the table as she made her argument. "They came off badly after the crash of '99, and even worse after the Readjustment. Banks treated 'em shabbily. There wasn't much love for the financial institutions before all that, and there'll be even less now. Better, Trevenza's always been welcoming to privateer crews, preferring to do business with them rather than the bank-rolled combines. They won't have any truck with that squadron, and they'll be very sorry to hear about your woes. You'll get a sympathetic hearing, is all I'm saying, better than anywhere else in the Congregation, and once you've got your story out, the other worlds'll have no choice but to take notice."

"After which, it's happy-ever-after," Cossel said.

"I ain't saying there won't be a few kinks along the way," Fura said. "But we'll cross them as they come. The chief thing is to agree that our interests are all served in Trevenza Reach." She let go of the quoin, allowing it to float just above her palm, and watched as some faint, invisible torque began to turn its face to the Old Sun. Then she closed her fist around it again and smiled at the gathering. "May we agree on that much?"

"Tell us about this other passenger," Lasling said.

*

One by one, the crew of the *Merry Mare* were brought into the Clacker's presence. Adrana would have gladly introduced them all at once, but Fura would not agree to any more than one visitor in their cabin at a time, at least not until loyalties were firmly established, and that was going to take more than a few hours.

"He came with us from Mulgracen," Adrana said, resting a hand on the outer casing of his box. "He was stuck on that world, needing urgent passage away from it, having made enemies—very serious enemies, of his own kind and others—and they were closing in on him. He was being sheltered by a man called Darkly, who used to buy bones from the Clacker."

It was Ruther's turn for the introduction. The boy knelt close to the box, and Adrana let him examine its shell, including the area where it had been damaged by the muddleheads. "How did he end up making enemies, Captain Ness? I thought those aliens stuck together like glue."

She had been asked permutations of this question by them all. "There wasn't time to speak to him in any depth before he went into the box for the last time. But it probably has something to do with the way our world works. I mean all the worlds; everything that makes up the Congregation, and everything we know of it. Something to do with quoins, very likely, but that'll only be part of it."

"Then you should wake him and ask him."

Adrana smiled to herself at the boy's naivety. By all objective measures he was only a few years younger than her, and it was entirely possible that he'd already had a longer career in space. But she felt a gulf of experience between them, colder and less readily traversable than the leagues between the worlds. She had already seen more and known more and questioned more than this guileless child ever would. She had always wondered how it would feel when she eventually slipped across the boundary between adolescence and adulthood, feeling as if it ought to be some definite threshold, a crossing between one pole of experience and another, accompanied by the sudden reversal of compass needles. But it had happened and she had been unaware of it, until Ruther provided her with this point of reference, a gauge to measure her own progress.

"We would have woken him, if it were that easy," she said, not wanting to be too hard on the boy, for she knew how affected he had been by the death of his beloved captain. "But he's gone into an automatic hibernation interval, and we can't speed up the clock or risk opening his box ahead of time."

"How long will it be?"

"From this point on, there's no telling. He's been with us for three months, nearly to the day, and from what we understand that was the minimum sleep interval. But how much longer he spends in there will depend on factors totally beyond our control—if he comes out of it at all."

Ruther looked disappointed, as if he had been presented with lavishly-wrapped gift and then told he would never get to open it.

"So your passenger could spend forever in that box?"

"No—I don't think it will come to that. When we get to Trevenza Reach, there'll be friends of his waiting. They'll know how to bring him out safely."

"But it would be them speaking to him, not you."

"I admit…there are questions I would like to ask of him myself."

"I saw one of their ships," Ruther said brightly. "It was around Hazzardy, I think. Captain Werranwell made us all come to the window and watch as it came in. It looked like…well, I almost can't say. Not like this ship, or any other ship of ours. Vouga said it was like a piece of frozen smoke; Cossel said it was more like a shard of dirty ice, with lights in; I thought it looked more like an old grey tooth. It didn't have any sails, though. They don't need sails to go where they go."

"Sails are all well and good for the distances of the Congregation," Adrana said, in a patient, tutorly manner. "But they're no use at all for the spaces beyond—the Empty, and the vast gulf between the stars. Once, we probably had the means to cross those distances, and you can bet we didn't do it at a few thousand leagues per hour. A few million leagues per hour, perhaps, if even that was fast enough. The aliens that come to do business with us must have something much better."

"We should ask them for it," Ruther declared, as if no one in history had ever entertained such a thought.

Adrana almost felt bad about pricking his enthusiasm. "I do not think they would be in any sort of rush to let us have it. There is a *system* here, Ruther—one that suits everyone involved. We monkeys get to live around the Old Sun and have quite a tolerably nice life, if only for a short time. Occasionally, the aliens help us—with medicine, or even certain types of technology, though they maintain a careful control of it. They, in turn, find us quite useful. We have the means to extract quoins from baubles, something that the aliens are unable or unwilling to do for themselves. They run our banks for us, and that is one less thing we have to do for ourselves, which *might* be considered a kindness. But there is something in it for them, as well. The quoins flow from the baubles into the banks' reserves, and from that point on what happens to them is anyone's guess. They have a value to the aliens beyond our own use as a form of currency, and we are the means of production. That is the system, and the aliens will do nothing that risks harming it, not so long as there is a viable civilisation around the Old Sun. Eventually all of this will end—this brief, glorious Occupation of ours—and the aliens are either the cause of that termination, or are in some way powerless to prevent it. I am not sure which I prefer. It is comforting to think of them as having greater powers than us, isn't it?" Ruther nodded meekly at this question, and she continued. "But perhaps those powers aren't as superior as we might wish. Just because they have strange ships, and can come and go as they please, does not mean they have the means to save us from ourselves."

"This Occupation will be different," Ruther said. "I'm sure of it. The others...well, they weren't us. They did things the wrong way. Got greedy, or made mistakes." With the firmness of youth, he added: "We shan't."

"We'll be the exception, where twelve civilisations before us all failed? Including the Epoch of the Bauble-Makers, the Council of Clouds, the Glass Queens, the Incarnadine Multitudinous, the High Instrumentality? Each of which was comfortably in advance of our own culture? You think *we* will do better, Ruther?"

"I think we must try," he said, doubtfully.

"Then there are already cracks in your certainty. As there must be." Adrana patted the Clacker's box again. "There is an answer in here, or a partial one. He knew about the quoins; their true purpose. And more, I think. That is why his enemies were so intent on silencing him. That is why he matters to us, and why I will not break our promise to deliver him to Trevenza."

"They'll arrest you there," Ruther said. "You do realise that, don't you? And the rest of us will do well if we merely avoid being arrested as your accomplices."

"Would you rather we never went near a world again?"

"No," he admitted, averting his face, as if to admit such a thing were a kind of shame.

"We won't be arrested. Or, at least, we shall take great pains to prevent it. We have false identities, and they've not worked too badly on two previous worlds. And this time we shall have two ships, and our former crews dispersed between them. There'll be nothing to help the authorities make the connection to *Revenger*."

"You seem so sure."

"I am not," Adrana confessed. "But we have no other path before us. It is not an easy one, but walk it we must."

She kept her hand on the Clacker's case, thinking how the alien's fate was now braided with her own, and by extension the whole of her crew. She wished it to survive, so that it might furnish her with answers. But to help the alien survive, she needed to put them all in harm's way by chancing another encounter with a world. A pledge was a pledge, though. If she surrendered every fine part of herself to her new career, her word would be the last thing she gave away.

The box jolted lightly under her palm, and deep inside it something made a low clicking sound, like a clock gear moving from one ratcheted position to the next.

She jerked her hand away.

"What is it?" Ruther asked.

"I don't know," Adrana said, for she owed the boy the truth if nothing else.

*

Over the next few days Adrana and Fura were rarely out of the presence of the Clacker's box, and if neither of them was present in the captains' quarters, then Paladin was under strict orders to maintain the closest possible surveillance.

That something had happened was beyond dispute, for if either of the Ness sisters pressed their heads to the box's side, they now heard a distant, continuous whirring. Very occasionally they chanced to open the outer casing, and when they did that the inner box—the true hibernation device—was mostly invisible and intangible, except in the flickering instants when the concealment machinery faltered. The sisters theorised that the box was having to divert some of its energies into sustaining that illusion of absence, and that it might be better to allow it to use all of its powers to facilitate whatever process was now in force, be it the repair of damage, or the slow awakening of the occupant.

They did not know, and intervention seemed no wiser now than it had a day earlier. So they waited, and waited, and gradually realised that whatever was happening, no haste seemed to be involved.

"Now that we're together," Fura said, during one of their joint vigils, "we may as well discuss the thing we haven't been discussing. We can't pretend that there isn't a set of bones in the bone room."

"Were we pretending?"

"You know what I mean. Ever since that...contact...we've avoided any talk of going near the skull again."

"For good reason."

"We weren't prepared for him," Fura said. "We'd be prepared the second time."

"That…boy…would also be prepared. He nearly had the better of us; we'd be fools to give him a second chance. What if some part of our intention slipped between the skulls, and alerted him to our chosen destination?"

"We can hold it back."

"No," Adrana answered. "We'd think we could, but we don't know how deep his capabilities run. We both sensed it: he's at least our equal, and perhaps better than us, and that scares me. I know we went to a lot of trouble to get that skull, and by some reckoning that action cost Captain Werranwell his life. But that doesn't mean we have to use it, just because it's there. Part of me says we'd be better off smashing it to chips, just to remove the temptation. Or at the very least welding the bone room shut, until we're sure that that boy isn't going to be a problem."

"You're right to be concerned about his learning our plans," Fura said. "Our destination's one thing. But a captain also knows her ship's instantaneous position and vector. Imagine if he could pluck those numbers straight from our heads, just because we were skullbound!"

"I am not sure what you're driving at. You seem to be agreeing with me that there is too much hazard in using that skull, and yet I have never known you change your position so readily."

"We're forgetting about the boy," Fura said. "The other boy, I mean: Ruther."

"What of him?"

"He can read the skull. It's the one he's used to. If we put Ruther into the bone room, there's much less chance of the other boy learning anything useful."

"Other than our destination, which Ruther already knows."

"But he doesn't know our detailed plan, and there's no reason he ever has to know it. We can insulate him from anything that'd be useful to the squadron. No navigational figures; no knowledge of the disposition of our sails or armaments. Nothing he could inadvertently pass to the enemy."

"His knowing about Trevenza Reach might already undo us. If that squadron managed to cut ahead of us, blockade our approach…" Adrana shook her head. "It is still far too great a risk, sister. We'd never be sure that Ruther couldn't give something away…and besides, I didn't care for the feeling of his mind trying to worm into my own. We might not be stronger than the boy, but I think we may agree that we are stronger than Ruther. It would be reckless of us to expose him to something he doesn't have the defences to resist."

"Ruther's useless to us, then," Fura said, with a deliberate coldness. "Just another mouth to feed. The only question is which lock we throw him out of."

"He may be helpful to us in a thousand ways that don't depend on the bone room."

"His knowledge of that skull could still be an asset, even if he doesn't take the crown," Fura conceded. "If—when—we chance another contact, Ruther might be able to help with the input settings. That other boy can't be monitoring his own skull around the clock, so if we can get in and out quickly…"

"It's still too risky."

"But it'd be foolish to disregard Ruther's knowledge completely—or put ourselves in a position where it can never be exploited."

"Again, I am not sure where you are driving."

"I'm only saying that Ruther should remain with the skull that he knows the best. If this harmonious little union doesn't fray at the edges between now and the separation of our ships, there'll need to be an inter-mingling of the crews anyway. That way there will be no chance of any lingering enmities resurfacing once we are apart."

"You mean for Ruther to remain on *Revenger*."

"Anything else would be foolishness, dear heart." Fura smiled. "But I know you see that as plainly as I do."

11

By common consent between the various expert parties—
Tindouf, Lasling, Surt, Vouga—and factoring in the not-
entirely-disinterested opinions of Lagganvor and the Ness
sisters, a plan of works was agreed upon. It would require slightly
more than three weeks to execute, and ought to be comfortably
achievable in four, even allowing for the occasional mishap. At
the end of that interval, the ships would be cut loose and take
their independent courses. Both would sail for Trevenza Reach,
but by somewhat indirect means, to cover all trace of their
former association.

There was much to be concerned about after the separation,
but Fura dared not count on anything until the first few days
were behind them, and she vowed she would not begin to relax
until they were into their second week of work.

It was tense, to begin with. The crews were starting to know
each other, but not quite well enough to know their limits. An
ill-chosen remark here, a jest-too-far there, might prove a sharp
provocation. It would not take much, Fura knew, to turn their
fragile truce into brawling disharmony, and not much beyond
that to rip the crews apart for good. They were never more vulnerable than at the present time. Fura therefore instructed her
own subordinates to show exceptional forbearance; to come
to her before responding in kind, and at all times to consider

the injustices wrought upon Werranwell's crew, and their own footnote in that sorry saga.

And yet, to her rising astonishment, as the days turned into that first week, and first week became a second, the flashpoint never came. The crews melded. There were hints of actual friendship. Lasling and Tindouf seemed to like each other without complication or impediment, and Tindouf celebrated this unlikely partnership by fashioning Lasling a new pipe, which he presented with all due ceremony.

Vouga and Surt circled each other like wrestlers, probing their areas of knowledge and ignorance. Fura would catch them in the galley at odd hours, peering at each other over tight-clasped drinks, cross-examining each other in terse, interrogatory bursts, giving the bare minimum away yet slowly, inexorably, establishing the basis for a mutual respect, whether they desired it or not. It turned out that while they had areas of shared expertise, agreed upon grudgingly, each was also good at some area in which the other was lacking. They would have made a good team, for any captain who could afford to keep two Integrators on the payroll.

Cossel, meanwhile, was a source of fascination to both the Ness sisters, for she had survived something in the region of thirty bauble expeditions without loss of life or limb, and in the course of her career she had visited ten or so of the most notorious baubles, including His Foulness, but also The Night Clock, The Shadow Castle, The Labyrinthine, The Milk Churn, The Flytrap and The Croupier. She had not always left these baubles with treasure—Cossel had never got rich under any of her captains—but she had got out with her life, and that was no small accomplishment. Fura and Adrana were more than content to hear Cossel reminisce about these expeditions, and if some gentle persuasion was initially needed to loosen Cossel's tongue—it turned out that she had a healthy enthusiasm for alcohol—once started, there was little stopping her. Like many Assessors, her knowledge had been gained through experience and word-of-mouth rather than book-learning, but it was no less deep or comprehensive for that. Fura tested her once or twice, throwing in a comment that contained an error about some historical subdivision of an Occupation, and Cossel never failed to pick up on the slip. She would have made an excellent asset for any crew, but for that awful, lingering suspicion that she was in some way a magnet for bad luck. For while it took uncommon skill to survive thirty consecutive expeditions, it was rather odd not to have stumbled on even a minor fortune during that span of employment. Fura was not superstitious, though, and she apportioned no blame to Cossel in this matter. Perhaps her captains had been over-cautious, their Openers not the quickest, their auguries and maps never the most up to date.

So, as these alliances and bonds of respect hardened into something barely distinguishable from companionship, so the weeks passed, and the work progressed. Fura was mildly amazed that there had not been more trouble, until she considered the other crew's evident depth of loyalty to Werranwell. They had liked him so much that they were ready to submit to his last order without rancour, for to turn against one or other of the Ness sisters was to disobey their beloved former captain, and that was unconscionable.

"I reckon he was a good man," Fura said, while Adrana prepared her next injection of Mephrozine. "A good man, with a good crew, and a good ship. And it was his very *bad* misfortune to run into us. I'd almost prefer that we'd taken a rotten crew, under a hated captain. Perhaps they'd have switched their loyalties just as easily."

"You forget," Adrana said, jabbing the needle in, and surprised at how little sympathy she felt when Fura flinched. "They haven't switched their loyalties at all. They've merely accepted his choice of successor. They're not dishonouring his memory—quite the contrary. It was wise of him, too. He tried to devise the best way to keep his people alive. I think he loved them and felt that he owed them much more than what they'd received."

Adrana injected the Mephrozine and withdrew the needle.

Fura swabbed the sore spot where it had gone in. "I wonder what to do with him. I've had Lagganvor ask around, very delicately, and it appears that none of the older ones were acquainted with his funeral plans."

"Did Lagganvor speak to Ruther?"

"I don't know. Why would Ruther be any wiser, when the others weren't?"

"Because he was Werranwell's boney, and therefore the one that the captain was most likely to confide his secrets to." Adrana set about packing away the syringe and vials. "Are you still fixed on the idea of one dose every two days?"

"Ain't see any reason to change my mind."

"That was the fifty-sixth injection. Less than half your supply remains."

"There's still an excellent margin of safety."

"But a diminishing one."

"What would you have me do, sister? The current dose may be the minimum effective measure to hold the glowy at bay. If I stretch out the intervals further, the glowy'll pounce." She gave an involuntary shudder, remembering a muscled man in a bath of milk, the glowy shining out of him like the pages of an illuminated manuscript. Flashing back to his madness and the torment when the glowy's late-stage fits had their fierce hold on him. "I won't become *him*. Perish the worlds, but that will not be *my* fate."

"I think there was already plenty wrong with Glimmery before the glowy got into him." Adrana sealed the wallet with her usual care. "I can't push you, I know. It has to be your choice."

"Just as it was my choice to survive on lightvine so I could come back and rescue you." Fura touched her face, which was already starting to tingle as the Mephrozine took effect. "This isn't just a mark of something that happened to me on the *Monetta*. This is a mark of you being alive."

"I haven't forgotten. Nor am I ever likely to."

*

Fura was visiting Eddralder and Merrix in the Kindness Room, where Strambli remained in their care. The two ships had been joined for eighteen days, and only a few hours earlier Adrana had given her the fifty-eighth dose of Mephrozine, nearly exhausting the sixth vial. For the first time in weeks, her sister had completed the procedure without the slightest suggestion of increasing the intervals between injections. Fura felt less as if she had won an argument, than that she had adhered with stubborn tenacity to an indefensible position, and therefore triumphed by default. A nagging part of her still wondered if Adrana was correct to have her concerns.

"The work is going well, Doctor," she said to Eddralder, "and the *Merry Mare* nearly repaired well enough to sail on her own."

Eddralder dipped his head like the jib of a steam-crane.

"I am grateful for the information."

"Very shortly, decisions will be taken concerning who goes with which ship. I thought we would do well to consider Strambli's situation, while we have the option."

Eddralder lifted an eye to his patient, who had been sleeping since Fura's arrival. "If you are looking for reassurances, I may have to disappoint you. The....complaint...is not in retreat. It advances a little some days, and pauses others, but there is no indication that any of my treatments are capable of arresting it."

"And her chances once we get to Trevenza Reach?"

Merrix looked up silently.

Her father answered: "Not excellent."

"But are they better than what can be offered on this ship?"

"That would depend on your definition of 'better.' Radical surgery is always a possibility. She does not wish to lose the limb, but there may come a point where all other interventions have failed."

"Such a procedure would be better off done in Trevenza Reach?"

"There might be marginal benefits. On the other hand, this room is very well outfitted. Better still, there need be no secrecy between the parties involved."

"Could you…do it?"

Eddralder regarded Merrix. Some wordless exchange passed between father and daughter.

"Yes. Between us, we could do what had to be done."

Fura nodded gravely.

"I'm grateful for your candour, Doctor."

"I presume it has some bearing on the coming decisions?"

"One ship may arrive ahead of the other. At the moment I'm minded to send the *Merry Mare* by the swiftest route, partly because she'll never have our speed and nimbleness, and she's less well-armed so needs an advantageous course, and partly because there's much less chance of that ship being connected to the Ness sisters and *Revenger*. She should make port in three or four weeks, following our separation. Once at Trevenza, Adrana may lay the ground for our arrival, which I shouldn't imagine will be too many days afterward."

"Lay the ground in what sense?"

"Contacting such allies as we may find and procuring those supplies that are necessary for both ships."

"You are starting to become concerned about the Mephrozine."

"No, I am entirely unconcerned. But it will do no harm if Adrana finds some more while we are still sailing. Having her do the procurement will make very good sense. One look at me and they may start inflating the price, seeing how obviously I depend on the drug. Adrana isn't so affected, and so may strike a fairer price."

He glanced at the patient to verify that she was still unconscious. "And the bearing of all this on Strambli?"

"By your own admission, there's no reason for her to leave *Revenger*. She won't be greatly assisted by an early arrival at Trevenza, and of the two ships, ours is by far the best equipped for her care."

"I concur."

"I'm very glad of it, doctor. You'll remain with Strambli, and of course Merrix must remain with you. Might I…" An awkwardness forced a pause upon her. "You mentioned Mephrozine."

Eddralder looked at her with a distant curiosity.

"I did."

"I know it has other uses, besides treating the glowy. There couldn't be any benefit to Strambli, could there?"

Merrix looked up again, but her father was the one who answered. "There is very little in the literature to suggest that Mephrozine is an effective agent against the glowy. Besides... you have definite need of that drug, and it *is* proving satisfactory in your case. It would be foolish to squander what little supplies remain on a wing and a prayer."

Fura felt some small but definite weight lift off her. "I...am relieved. Not for Strambli—I'm still concerned about her—but at the thought that I might be able to do something and wasn't. You understand, don't you?"

"It is an entirely reasonable sentiment."

Fura was glad of the doctor's words and wished to believe his assurance. For a few moments she did, wholeheartedly. Until something in Merrix's face gave her cause to doubt.

*

On the twentieth day, Paladin detected a sudden change in the condition of the Clacker, and alerted the Ness sisters to make all haste to the captains' quarters. Fura came down from the sighting room, Lagganvor taking over from her, and Adrana arrived from the *Merry Mare*, where she had been helping Vouga update their charts and almanacks, as well as gaining some familiarity with the layout and temperament of her own new command.

When they arrived, they found that the outer box was still sealed and cross-buckled to the side-wall of the cabin, but it was shaking visibly, and some dark green bubbling seepage issued from the part that had been shot through by the muddleheads. The box was making a continuous but off-tempo knocking sound, quite unlike the soft, distant whirring that had been coming out of it these past weeks.

"What's that stuff?" Fura asked, recklessly dipping her fingers into the green seepage, and then just as recklessly sniffing it.

"I think we should open the outer box again," Adrana said. "It doesn't matter if we overload the effector-displacement device; for all we know he could be drowning in that stuff and unable to fight his way out."

"We could kill him by opening it."

"We could kill him by *not* opening it. We can't be sure, but since I brought him aboard the responsibility ought to be mine and my instinct is that we need to open that box. Help me with these buckles. We'll lay it down on the floor."

Gingerly, they removed the restraints and lowered the box against the surface that they agreed to call the floor, even in the near-weightless conditions under which *Revenger* now operated. The two sisters knelt close by the box, watching as the green bubbles continued to emerge. They formed a sticky, clotting froth.

"We should call Eddralder down," Fura said.

"Alien medicine is as foreign to him as it is to us. We mustn't hesitate."

She reached forward and sprung open the catches on the outer container. The lid hinged wide. Inside was a very curious spectacle. The green seepage was defining the boundaries of the inner container, yet the container itself was still invisible for at least four seconds out of five. In the moments when it showed itself—in intervals that were longer than any they had witnessed before—it became clear that the damage was not confined solely to the outer casing. The inner box, which was of entirely alien fabrication and embellishment, was cracked and buckled in places. The green seepage was oozing out of it in prodigious, breath-like surges. The box—or the volume of space it occupied—was jolting around like loose luggage on a bumpy tram.

"I thought the muddleheads only got the outer part," Fura said.

"We were mistaken. Or we were right, and something else has gone wrong with it."

"It's spending more and more time visible. It reminds me of the surface of a bauble, showing through a field just before it collapses."

"Perhaps there's some relation between the two technologies, however distant. Or they both depend on a similar science. What was the height of sophistication to the bauble-makers of the Fourth Occupation may be bread and butter to a Clacker. Do not do that!"

Fura had jabbed her hand into the space occupied by the box, in the diminishing intervals between its fits of visibility. She jerked back her metal fingers and pressed them to her lips.

"Brrrr."

"The box wants to do something," Adrana said. "That's why it's rattling around in there like an old washing machine. Perhaps it wants to open, and it can't, not when it's wedged into the outer part."

"Then we've got to take it out. But only when it's visible. If our hands slip into the space it's occupying, and then it comes back… what did Lagganvor say would happen?"

"Never mind Lagganvor. We must do this." Adrana looked at her sister with a firm authority. "We'll have one chance, so there must be no hesitation. I'll take this side, you the other. We pull as hard as we can, for half a second, and if the box doesn't come free immediately, we let go. We can't risk our hands being trapped. You have one fewer to spare as it is."

The box flickered out again, was absent for a second or two, then came back. Adrana sprung her hands onto its cold, slippery edge—greasy with that green lather—and pulled with all the force and determination she had. So did Fura. They had not needed to signal each other; they had not needed to exchange a word. There was a moment of stubbornness and then the box popped out as easily as a rotten tooth—tumbling at them just as the sisters fell back on their haunches.

Fura laughed. So did Adrana. They had done it, and as perfectly as they could have wished, and both still had a nearly full tally of digits. The box had come to rest before them, and after a few flickering transitions it became fully visible.

The sisters drew a collective breath. They sensed that something was about to happen.

So it did. The box gave a short exhalation, a snort of trapped gas—which was sweet-smelling, rather than foul—and sprung wide open, disclosing its occupant, which was shivering and shaking like a newborn.

The Clacker was tucked into a foetal ball and covered over in a slime of that same green material that had been forcing its way out of the box. Gluey wires and cables lay suspended in this quivering matrix, pale as worms.

"What do we do?" Fura asked.

"Help him," Adrana said. She leaned forward and scooped the Clacker out of the box, the wires and cables falling away as she did so, and leaving only faint impressions of where they had been in contact with the alien. It felt more like a warm doll than a truly living form: a heavy, bulky doll that had been played with recently. The limbs moved under the pressure of her embrace, and she had the impression of some faint general stirring through the alien's body, even as it kept its face pressed to its chest or belly. As if it were surfacing through peculiar alien dreams, back to whatever passed for consciousness in its breed.

"Is all in hand?" Paladin asked.

"I think it's too soon to say," Adrana answered. "But I am equally sure that there's nothing you or I or anyone else on this ship can do that will make any difference."

Fura swivelled around to face his globe. "Have you met Clackers, Paladin?"

"If I ever had that pleasure, it is long since lost in the regrettable degradation of my memories. Of course, I do know something of the species. Their immediate needs are not too far from your own. They breathe a similar mix of gases, tolerate a similar range of temperatures, and may sustain themselves with our food and water—not indefinitely, but most certainly for several months, before deficiencies of certain elements and compounds cause them a range of complaints."

"You are very well informed," Adrana said.

"On the contrary, I am quite grievously ill-informed about almost everything. But I am particular about the little islands of knowledge I still contain."

The Clacker was showing signs of further resuscitation. Adrana held it completely, but it was an awkward embrace, and would not have been possible on a world such as Mazarile. The Clacker was dense for its size, indicative of thick, heavy bones, which she supposed had something to do with its place of origin. Now the short yet muscular arms and legs were beginning to fidget, as if—distantly—it sensed both that it was awake, and also in a kind of restraint.

"Set him down," Fura said softly. "I think he wants to wake but isn't quite aware of his surroundings."

Adrana set it down before her, allowing the faint force of their sail-generated acceleration to nudge it to the floor. The Clacker had two legs and four arms, the former appendages terminating in two toes, and the latter in two fingers and a thumb. The topmost pair of arms were attached to its body by shoulders at more or less the conventional location, with the lower pair, which were slightly smaller and more delicate, sprouting from just below the armpits of the upper set.

It sat on its haunches, with its legs curled in front of it. It was clothed, if that was the word, in a single thin garment that was made of an open weave, enclosing all parts of it except the head, with its great resonant casque. The garment was a dark silver colour. Pale green skin, mottled in places, showed through the weave. If the garment was there to protect the Clacker while in hibernation, or otherwise preserve its dignity, it was also open enough to allow the wires and fronds to find their way into flesh.

The fidgeting had abated, but now the remarkable head, which made up nearly half the Clacker's bulk, began to tilt up. The casque had a sort of crescent-shape to it, with a continuous convex curve running from front to back, the bulge of its resonant chamber below that, and then—less distinctly, because it merged with the face and neck—the concave undersurface. The crescent's front horn tapered down to meet the tip of a long, wide, lizard-like mouth, and the rear horn protruded backwards, curving down at the same time, and thus was it rumoured that a Clacker was the only living creature that could scratch the small of its back with its own head. The casque was a similar pale green to the rest of it, but had a lovely deep lustre to it, as of some fine varnished stone, and there were hints of blue and turquoise in the mottling. But it was also riven by large holes, with sharp ragged edges, which did not look like any natural part of the creature's physiology.

The Clacker was drowsily opening its eyes. There were two of them, one on either side of its head, tucked under the bulge of the casque's resonant cavity, and each situated just above the rearmost part of the mouth, and emplaced in a deep fortification of wrinkles. The eyes were mostly white with small dark pupils, and much better at looking sideways than peering directly ahead.

A wet, slurry-like sound came out of the Clacker. After a few seconds of this, it switched to the most disgusting liquid snorting.

"What's it trying to say?" Fura asked.

"I don't know. That first sound is how it builds up a picture of its surroundings, or how it tries to. The casque is a resonant structure, and very well evolved for sense-gathering. But it's obviously broken, and it can't make speech sounds properly, either."

"Was it like this on Mulgracen?"

"No. Lagganvor and I were able to speak to it quite easily. Whatever's happened must have come about when we met the muddleheads."

The Clacker's eyes were open but gummed over with yellow-green slime. It reached up with its upper forelimbs and, with some delicacy, scuffed them clean. Perhaps only then becoming aware of its situation, it gave a very creditable impression of a startled blink.

"Can you understand me?" Fura asked, in a loud and strident

manner, as if she were addressing a dim-witted child. "You're on my ship now. You arranged passage with us from Mulgracen. We're on our way to Trevenza Reach."

The Clacker looked at the Ness sisters, fixing them with first one eye and then the other, twisting its whole body as it did so, as if it doubted the evidence of either eye without corroboration from the other. Then it made more of that wet, snorting, slurry-like sound: a horrible hawking emanation. The snorting intensified in speed, although there was no sense to be made of it.

"We can't understand you," Adrana said, frustratedly. "You remember me, don't you? We met you in Darkly's emporium, but there was an attack on the way to port…"

The Clacker gave up on its sounds and made a quick repeated gesture with its lower two hands. One hand made a palm shape, the other swiped across it.

"I might venture," Paladin said, "that the individual is in want of pen and paper."

Fura dashed to her desk and found what was required. She brought the items to the Clacker, and pressed them against its upper pair of hands. The Clacker examined the materials by touch, looking down and waggling its head, then began to write. The Ness sisters watched with a degree of amazement as the words appeared, in a slanting, sinuous, long-tailed script of such exacting neatness, precision and elegance that it would have served as an example to be copied, laboriously and without error, during one of their more tedious parlour lessons.

It said:

My Dear Captains,

I am grateful for your assistance.

I trust that you will expedite my delivery to my friends with all urgency.

All the answers you seek—and more—may be found in Trevenza Reach.

But only with my assistance, and survival.

On that matter, I must regretfully inform you that I am in very imminent danger of dying.

There may be less time than all of us would wish for.
Tazaknakak

*

"He never wanted to go back to any world," Ruther said, raking fingers through the white shock of his hair. "Not because he didn't love the worlds—he did, with all his heart—but because there wasn't one of them he liked more than the rest, and he said he'd come to like the view of them from outside. He said it was the prettiest spectacle anywhere in the Congregation, or out of it, and that was what he'd like his eyes fixed on, between now and the Old Sun's passing. He said we should find him a spare bit of plate from the hull, lash him to it in a suit we didn't mind not having, and fix a scrap of sail to the other side of the plate by a league or two of yardage, just enough to keep him facing the worlds, but not so much that he got blown away out into the Empty at the first solar gust." Ruther swallowed, looking for all the world as if he was betraying some trusted confidence. "He said he didn't think it would be too much trouble for us, once he was gone, but if it turned out that it *was* too much trouble..."

"It won't be," Fura said, with a firm but kindly assertiveness. "Not too much at all, if you're certain that was his wish."

"I am," Ruther said, dropping his eyes.

"If he told you this," Adrana said, "then he did so for a reason. Not because he meant you to keep it to yourself, but because he could trust you to disclose it when the time was right. You served him well, Ruther—and you serve him well now. We shall make the arrangements."

"I think it might be fitting..." Ruther began.

"If the plate came from the *Merry Mare*?" Fura nodded, guessing his meaning. "I'd insist on it. She was a good ship—she *will* be a good ship. And we'll find that yardage and enough sail to keep him steered to the Old Sun. He'll warm his face for a few more Occupations, I think."

Fura's sentiments were sincere, in a fashion, but at the back of her mind was her determination to preserve the present cordiality, and do all in her power to ensure its prolongation. Even if it cost her a little in materials to do right by the dead captain, she would abide by his request; indeed, she considered herself to have done well out of it, for he could very easily have demanded something more expensive and troublesome to arrange.

So a suit was assembled for him, made up out of constituent parts that were damaged or unreliable, while still presenting a not-undignified whole, and a piece of hull plating about two spans by four was easily provided out of the repairs done to the *Merry Mare.* Werranwell was put into the suit and strapped to the plate. Yardage and ordinary sail-cloth was bundled into a package and, with both crews in solemn attendance, the whole was ejected into space with a slight spin to ensure the deployment and tensioning of the sail. Within an hour the ensemble had stabilised, with the sail catching flux and Werranwell serving as a counterpoint at the Sunward end of the rigging. Within another hour, watched by all, he had drifted far enough from the linked ships to be on the cusp of invisibility. He would bob around the Old Sun now, his orbit unpredictable, its average diameter gradually increasing in size, yet so slowly that it might be many centuries before he fell beyond the common haunts of ships, and at any point some kindly captain might find his corpse and nudge it back toward the light and life of the Congregation, understanding that though this man might not have wished burial on any world, nor had he forsaken them.

12

Tindouf's axe came down in a clean arc. There was a jerk as it separated the last line, a moment of strange hiatus, and then the two ships fell slowly away from each other.

A muted cheer sounded over the short-range squawk, reverberating through helmets and compartments.

There was no haste to scramble back inside either ship. The *Merry Mare* still had to run out its full spread of sail, and *Revenger* had hauled in much of its acreage for this most perilous stage of separation. Neither ship was accelerating, and the distance between their hulls was increasing at an extremely leisurely rate. It would be hours before they were too far apart for their crews to cross between them in tethered suits, and several days before it became inconvenient to use the launch. Yet, as the suited parties drifted this way and that, tidying up loose lines and securing tools and material, there was a sense that what had been done could not be revoked, and the sooner this separation was consummated by the formalities of an assigned captaincy, so much the better.

"You decreed that I should take the *Merry Mare*," Adrana said. "Did you ever give any consideration to the alternative?"

"I did, for all of three seconds." Fura paused, tap-tap-tapping the nib of a pen against a blotting pad. "Face it, dear heart: they'd never take me to their hearts as readily as you. I was the one who came aboard with a knife, looking like I meant to use it."

"Meanwhile, you get sole command of this ship—and sole access to Paladin."

Fura looked pained. "I'm *gifting* you a ship, sister—you can hardly claim to be getting the raw end of the deal." She sniffed. "A perfectly fine ship, too—in much better condition than when we found it. Of course, if you don't like the idea of having a ship of your own..."

"I like it very well—just not the mechanics by which I arrived at my command."

"What's done is done."

"Yes—and if only all our difficulties could be brushed aside so easily." Adrana stiffened, as if bracing herself for some onerous duty. "I will take the ship—I could hardly not, given how tenaciously you mean to hold onto this one. But there are conditions."

"Naturally."

"I must complete the faster crossing and arrive ahead of *Revenger*. It's as little as three weeks to Trevenza, if the weather's kind, and we run into no trouble. You may only be a week behind us, but there can be no delay where Tazaknakak is concerned. Therefore he must come with me." She turned her gaze to the makeshift crib they had made for him, in which the alien was now—judging by the irregular, wet, snoring-like noises coming out of him—in some state of slumber. "He can't be helped by Eddralder, unlike Strambli, but there's a real chance his friends may be able to do something, if we reach them soon enough. Besides, he has been my responsibility from the outset, and he remains my responsibility now. I won't abandon him to an uncertain fate on *Revenger*."

"And yet you would abandon Strambli?"

"I didn't say that at all. We both know that her chances have very little to do with what ship she's on, or how quickly she's brought to Trevenza. Though she has a marginal advantage in being close to Eddralder, should an operation be needed."

"That seems...agreeable," Fura said.

"Good. I rather expected you to dissent, which makes me wonder what it is you want from me."

Fura jammed the pen into its inkwell and opened one of her many journals, flattening it wide with magnetic paper-weights. "Nothing very much. I was merely thinking of the detailed rostering of our two ships, and who'd be of most benefit at your side. For a while we may be able to send signals to each other by optical telegraph, but that will become difficult at long-range and in any case should be reserved for emergency communications only. Obviously using the squawk is completely out of the question. There'll inevitably come a point when we can't communicate, even by telegraph, and each of us will be totally alone, except for the wise counsel of those at our sides. That's why I would like you to take Prozor. She's wily, versed in many skills, and I think quite generally liked by Werranwell's party. In return I should take the boy, Ruther."

"Why Ruther?"

"Because, dear heart, you have no skull and I do."

"We discussed this. You may have Ruther, but only for the purposes of guidance concerning the use of that skull. He mustn't use it at all, and I would advise *you* against using it except in emergency. But I won't have Prozor."

This drew a sharp, quizzical look from Fura. "You've taken against her?"

"Far from it. I like her very much. I think you like her too, but find her an uncomfortable and constraining influence on your actions: a conscience you would sooner banish to another ship."

Fura twitched. "You do not know me half as well as you imagine, sister."

"I know you a third as well, and that is sufficient. Prozor remains with you; I will take Lagganvor."

"He was my prize, not yours."

"You found him, admired him as you would a shiny new hat-pin, and then grew bored of him. Once his intelligence led you to The Miser, you had no further need of his services."

"A little harsh," Fura conceded. "But not a million leagues from the truth." She elevated her palm, as if she were bestowing some rare pardon. "You may have him."

There was no farewell kiss, no embrace. But Adrana reached for her sister's hand and for a moment they looked into each other's eyes with a giddy mutual astonishment at the journey that had brought them to this point: this parting, each about to take sole command of a fully-rigged sunjammer.

"I look forward to our reunion," Adrana said.

"As do I," Fura answered. "My last visit to Trevenza Reach ended on something of a sour note. I don't intend to let history repeat itself."

*

Adrana was going through the books and journals, packing any that she thought she might need—and that Fura might plausibly do without—into a sturdy leather satchel. Captain Werranwell's library was not nearly so well-furnished as that on *Revenger*, and there would soon come a point where it would be impractical to signal for information concerning matters of navigation or shipmastery.

She sneezed as she ruffled the pages of a scuffed but otherwise serviceable copy of *The Book of Worlds*, turning to the entry for Trevenza Reach:

A spindleworld of some modest renown. Its celebrity is in no small part due the peculiarity of its orbit, being highly eccentric in comparison to the common population of habitable bodies constituting the Congregation. Because it may at any given time lie inside the Thirty-Fifth Processional, or some prodigious distance beyond it, the prospective traveller is well advised to consult reliable almanackal tables before committing to what may be a lengthy and costly crossing. The word of crews is not to be depended upon.

Some ten leagues from end to end, and very agreeably disposed with regard to the provision of gravity, Trevenza Reach has, at the most recent census, a population of one and two tenths of a million…

"You was intending to say goodbye, girlie, wasn't you? Or was it your plan to scuttle off to your new ship and hope I didn't notice? I got word that I wasn't your preferred candidate."

Adrana snapped shut the book. Its pages exhaled a snort of dust and she slipped it into her satchel.

"I would like to have you on that ship very much, Proz."

"Then why's it come to me that I'm stayin' aboard this hulk, and Mister Lag's taking my natural seat on the other?"

Adrana buckled the satchel. She had enough books for now.

"You would be an asset to either crew, Proz. If I had expressed a firm preference for your company, and Fura had relented, you would be badgering her with exactly the same questions. The fact is there is only one of you, and whichever ship you are not aboard will be handicapped."

"Well, if you mean to flatter me…"

"I do not—you are much too wise and sure of yourself to be swayed by flummery. I merely state the facts. You are as beneficial to a ship as a well-tuned sweeper or a fine chasing coiller. But one of us must have you, and one must manage without. The choice is made." She gave a small unconcerned shrug. "It might as easily have been decided by rolling dice."

"And this dice-rolling—did that apply equally to Mister Lag?"

Adrana stiffened. "You are natural counterparts," she said carefully. "If one ship lacks Prozor, there may be some compensation in Lagganvor."

"Fura says you pleaded to be able to take Lag, over me."

"That is not…" Adrana had started harshly, so she silenced herself and recommenced in a more conciliatory tone. "That is *not* the case. I promise you as a friend. We horse-traded. If anything, I was the one who made the sacrifice. You know how forceful Fura can be, when she has her mind set on an outcome."

"I know how forceful both of you can be," Prozor said.

"I assure you there is no malice in my accepting of Lagganvor instead of you. Besides, this arrangement—this division of crews—is only a convenience until we make Trevenza. After that the cards may be reshuffled. I do not even think of this sole captaincy as a permanent state of affairs."

"So you not wantin' me, that's nothing to do with you wantin' him more?"

Adrana sighed. "How well do we know each other? I would take one of you over a hundred of him."

"Which begs the question, girlie…why do you want him with you? I might be a bit addled in the noggin these last few months, but I don't think it's 'cause you're sweet on the cove." She narrowed her eyes. "You ain't sweet on the cove, are you?"

Adrana smiled thinly. "No…decidedly not."

"But you do want him around. Well, he's useful, I'll grant that. But there's more to it, ain't there?"

"I assure you there is no more to it."

"Thing is, I ain't so green as not to have noticed a few things. You keep a very close eye on Mister Lag. You always have done, nearly from the day he came aboard."

"He was a former associate of Bosa Sennen. It behoved us all to keep our eyes on him."

"But yours especially. In Mulgracen, you went off shoppin' with Mister Lag, not your natural kin."

"Perhaps it suited Fura and I to have a few hours apart. Do not make more of this than is needed, Proz."

"You've got more than a few hours of separation comin' up, that's for sure. But you still want Mister Lag where you can watch him. Well, I shan't poke any more where I'm not wanted."

"Thank you," Adrana said tersely.

"But I will say this: if there's reason enough to think he ain't to be entirely trusted, you should've confided in old Proz. I'd have been fair with you…understandin' even. And if I found myself forced into holding a secret from my captain…one of my captains, I should say—well, it wouldn't have been the first time." Prozor reached down into her collar and tugged on a leather drawstring. She came out with a little pill-shaped box, sheathed in dark blue velvet. "Been keepin' this about me long enough; might as well pass it on to someone likely to benefit. He gives you any trouble, you might think of givin' this a squeeze. It won't kill him, but it might put the cove at a disadvantage, you get my drift."

Adrana felt stricken by her lies to Prozor. It was all the worse for the fact that Prozor had nearly guessed the truth—perhaps, indeed, had guessed it completely—and still Adrana denied her the truthful admission she was owed. It was all she could bear not to confess her position there and then.

But she could not. No matter how well she trusted Prozor, a secret shared was a secret imperilled.

"I don't need any gifts, Proz. We aren't saying farewell. We're just going off on different ships for a few weeks."

"But you'll take it anyway." Prozor opened Adrana's palm and pressed the box into it. "It ain't much, just a Firebright. But they're rare nowadays and I always thought it'd be a shame if it didn't go to a deserving cause."

"I am not deserving," Adrana said quietly, and if there was to be an admission, that was the extent of it.

Perhaps it was sufficient.

"You take it nonetheless, girlie." Prozor closed Adrana's fingers around the box. "And we *are* sayin' farewell. It don't mean goodbye for the rest of eternity. Just—travel well. And I want you to travel well."

Adrana re-opened her satchel and placed the box inside, nestled next to *The Book of Worlds*.

"Travel well, Prozor. I shall see you in Trevenza Reach."

*

Within a day of the separation, both ships had gathered their final crews into their hulls. The launch was the last thing to make the crossing, transferring a few final supplies from *Revenger* to the *Merry Mare* before scuttling back to its mother vessel. Just before the point of last contact, Doctor Eddralder had proposed that his daughter should transfer to the other ship, but Fura had denied it without equivocation. Eddralder said that it would be useful to have someone with a tiny bit of medical knowledge on both ships, and while there was a force to that argument, Merrix was a pair of hands that Fura could not afford to lose. Besides, as Adrana recognised, Eddralder's principle motivation was to make sure that his daughter was on the ship that he felt had the best chance of making it to port without molestation, and in his view that ship was not *Revenger*.

And so, with their rosters settled, and their captains formalised in name, the two ships were at last far enough apart for each to run out a full spread of sail without risk of entanglement. It was a stern test for any crew at any time, but doubly so in a ship that had been lately repaired, and whose particular new foibles were not yet documented.

Lasling was Adrana's new Master of Sail, and he had every incentive to ensure that the work went without complication, and so it proved. Lasling called for a pause at various intervals, pressing his eye to strain-gauges and torque-dials, and twice he went outside to make inspections and adjustments that could not be completed except in vacuum, and he conferred with Meggery at urgent moments, for a Master of Ions could make or break the process with an elegant or clumsy cooperation. Once he signalled Tindouf, and the two men conversed in the strange and specialised argot of their similar professions, for Tindouf was far from ignorant about the problems Lasling now faced.

But despite these hiatuses there was no serious hitch at any stage in the process, and the running out and tensioning of ordinary sail, rather than catchcloth, now seemed to Adrana to be a rather unremarkable and drab business. Over the coming days— weeks, even—there would be a gradual process of adjustment and finessing of the arrangements, requiring many hours of vacuum operations, but that was part of the ordinary business of any ship and crew, and in any case had the added benefit of keeping the hands from going too mad with confinement.

While all this was going on, the crew of *Revenger* had their own sails to attend to, and since she must soon pass muster as a friendly privateer, rather than a creature of ambush and shadow, *Revenger* was obliged to swap a measure of her catchcloth for the same ordinary sails as bedecked the *Merry Mare*. They had done this before, on the approach to Wheel Strizzardy, The Miser and Mulgracen, but in recent months they had been running mostly on catchcloth alone, except when navigation demanded otherwise, and now that black perfection had to be marred by the intrusion of square leagues of mirror-bright sail, easily detectable across great distances, and greatly susceptible to sail-flash.

There was no alternative. As soon as both ships fell into the threshold of Trevenza Reach's sweeper range, which could happen sooner than anticipated, they had to look entirely unthreatening. They might also need to pass inspection at closer range, which was why *Revenger*'s crew, once they were done with the sails, soon had to start papering over her gun-ports with tar-stiffened sheets and paint. Again, it was work they had done before, and which to a degree had been only partially undone by the recent engagements.

Soon the ships were a thousand leagues apart, and not long after that, as the solar wind bore on their sails, ten thousand. It was a greater distance than the average mind could easily comprehend, yet only a scratch compared to the fifty million leagues which separated one side of the Congregation from the other.

And even that was nothing—less than nothing—compared to the immensity of cold emptiness in which the Congregation floated, bright and tiny as a single mote of dust, lit for an instant as it drifted through a vast, unthinking solitude of darkness and silence.

*

With the gentlest of touches, she attempted to rouse the alien in its crib. The Clacker had been making disagreeable liquid noises while it slept—if that was indeed an accurate term for its condition—and although she wished to have him in her cabin at all times, she had been obliged to press stoppers into her ears if she wished to get any thinking done.

"Tazaknakak. Please wake."

Vouga floated behind her, watching with his arms folded. "You didn't think you'd be better off leaving him on Mulgracen?"

"Even with this snoring," Adrana said, "I am not sorry to have him with us. But it would be so much easier if he wasn't troubled by this injury."

"So much easier for you, not having to put up with that gurgling racket?"

"For the both of us, Vouga—although I won't deny that there's a degree of self-interest. I'm starting to hear that snorting in my dreams. Do you really think you can help him?"

"He'll need to be the judge of that. I've got enough on my conscience without adding the death of an alien."

"We shall endeavour to ensure it doesn't come to that. But he is ill, and I think this intervention may help him, in a small way." She shook the alien more vigorously, until his eyes opened to narrow squints. Tazaknakak rolled out from the balled form he adopted when sleeping, unpeeling his six limbs and stretching the upper two pairs. He gave off a sweet, slightly stale smell, like the crumb-flecked bottom of a cake box. "Tazaknakak, please awaken. This man has something that may make you feel better."

She passed the alien a writing block and pen. He fumbled for both and wrote:

I do not think this is the same ship.

"It isn't," she answered. "I've taken control of another vessel, the *Merry Mare*, and this man Vouga is one of her crew."

Our arrangement is annulled?

"No: my pledge to you still stands. *Revenger* is shadowing us, and somewhere behind both our ships is a hostile squadron. Arafura and I agreed that the best way to get you to Trevenza Reach was for you to come aboard this ship and make the fastest possible crossing. We've already been sailing on separate courses for four days—you were unconscious the whole while, or I would have informed you of our plans."

Please do not wake me again. I will go back to sleep very shortly and conserve my energies as best I can. If I am not dead when we reach Trevenza, return me to the preservation box. It is very badly damaged, but the effector-displacer device may function long enough to smuggle me onto that world. Once there you must make contact with my friends—if they do not make contact with you first.

"Tazaknakak, I wouldn't have woken you without good reason. I know that what's happened to your casque is very bad. You can't form a sense-picture and you can't make monkey speech sounds."

His pen moved again.

You wake me to remind me of the awfulness of my predicament?

"Vouga, show him."

Vouga came forward tentatively. He knelt next to Adrana, by the Clacker's crib and opened his apron, spilling out an assortment of tools and materials. "I've got a clever resin, your alien-ness. It's rare stuff, and ordinarily we'd save it for emergencies…but I suppose if anything counted as one, it's you."

A resin?

"Tell him, Vouga."

"It's called quickglass. If you get a crack in your visor, you mix some up and spoon it on. It flows into the crack and forms a seal. It's cleverer than that, though. It knows what it has to do. If there's a curve to the visor, it'll form the same curve. And once it's cured, which only takes a few minutes, it goes the same colour and transparency as the old stuff. The match is so good you'll never see where the old stuff ends and the quickglass begins."

The alien looked up at her. Although its eyes were small, and only a secondary faculty, she thought she saw in them a desperate hopefulness; a yearning tempered only by the terrible fear that what was being offered might be a hoax or a phantom.

"Vouga was thinking this resin might be able to seal up your casque," Adrana said. "We don't have too much in our stores—it's Ninth Occupation technology, so very precious—but he's measured the quantities, and he thinks there's enough to put right the damage. If the quickglass works with living tissue as well as it does inert matter, it ought to form a repair with the same resonant properties. You would be able to sense and speak again."

But there is a risk.

"Yes...yes there is. Perhaps you know better than me, Tazaknakak, but I do not think this has ever been attempted with a living organism. Let alone a Clacker."

You desire my consent.

"More than that," Adrana said. "This is a delicate matter, Tazaknakak, but it needs to be said. When we meet your friends, as I hope we shall, it would be best for all concerned if you're still alive. But if that isn't the case...well, then I should be very glad indeed to have a letter from you, in a hand that couldn't possibly be forged, indemnifying us against any responsibility for your death."

The alien nodded slowly. He scribbled out his answer.

You are right. That is indeed a delicate matter.

"What of it, Tazaknakak?"

Tell your man to prepare his resin. By the time he is ready you shall have your letter of indemnity.

*

The slip of paper had been double-folded, like a lover's note, then pushed into the seam between the door to the captains' quarters and the pressure bulkhead into which it was set. For a second when she saw it, Fura thought it was some small pale moth that had somehow travelled with them from the worlds, entirely undetected until this moment, haplessly batting itself against the door.

She pinched it out with forensic delicacy, carried it to her desk, opened it, allowed it to rest before her, washed over in Paladin's pink-red light. Even opened out, it was a small rectangle of paper, seemingly torn from the corner of a journal, and there was only one line of writing on it. The words were neatly done, and she recognised the hand from Merrix's turns in the sighting room.

The message said:

My father did not tell you the truth.

That was all.

It was enough.

She unlocked her desk drawer and took out the wallet with its vials and little glass syringe. She had completed sixty-five doses, all but sixty-three of which had been injected into her by Adrana. The last two, since the ships had parted, she had done herself—clumsily and hesitantly, but with eventual success. She could have gone to Eddralder, or even Prozor, but now that Adrana was away she saw no reason not to strive for independence.

She was halfway through the seventh vial; only three completely full vials remained. Thirty-five doses; less than half of what she had already used, but sufficient for seventy more days if she held to her present regime. The *Merry Mare* would be at Trevenza in three weeks; *Revenger* would arrive in four, depending on weather and course corrections. That would still leave her with about a month's supply in hand.

A month was a long time, she told herself. A very great many things could be achieved in a month.

"I'm going to see Eddralder, Paladin," she said. "Call me if anything arises, from your own instruments or the sighting room."

She pressed Merrix's note into her journal and left the captains' quarters. She went through the galley, along the yellow-green of corridors lit by lightvine, past coil-gun batteries and sail-control gear and down into the Kindness Room.

She had braced herself before entry, anticipating a sickly smell—she remembered well the stench of Strambli's initial wound when it had begun to turn—but there was none of that now, only the lingering chemical background of potions and disinfectant products.

Strambli was strapped loosely to the bed, under light sheets, with Merrix taking her temperature as they arrived. Her eyes were open, her face turning toward Fura as she came into the room. But there was no alteration in her expression, which remained blankly absent of feeling or interest.

"There's been no change," Eddralder said, lifting his eyes from a medical almanack, before slipping a bookmark into the pages. "I would have informed you if there was anything to report."

"Strambli?" Fura asked.

The face locked onto her with a fraction more attentiveness, but the eyes seemed to be focused beyond Fura, fixated on something distant and curious. "When is Captain Trusko coming to see me?" Strambli asked, mouthing the words in a half-whisper. "They said he'd come."

"Captain Trusko won't be coming," Fura answered. "He's been dead a long time, Strambli. Don't you remember?"

"They said he'd come."

"He died. I'm your captain now. Captain Fura Ness. Do you know which ship you're on?"

Strambli showed puzzlement, then the mask of her face produced a sudden and disconcerting smile. "I know which ship! The *Nightjammer*! *Dame Scarlet*! Bosa Sennen took us and made us her crew!"

"No...not that ship. It was once, but it's not now."

"I see the glowy in you, Captain!" She lifted an arm, pointing at Fura, that same grin splitting her features. "I see you! You've got it good and shiny, ain't you! There's *glimmery* in your eyes!"

In a low voice, Eddralder said: "She is lucid now and then, but these intervals of confusion are becoming more common than the lucidity. At other times, she is unconscious. I would not call it sleep, exactly. And when she is lucid, she complains terribly of the cold."

"It's a fever, then—a sign that her body's fighting the infection."

"There is no fever," Merrix answered. "No heightened temperature. No indication of any infectious response."

"Something's wrong with her."

"Of that," Eddralder said, "we may be in no doubt. But whatever was happening to her wound early on, when she stole from my supplies, was a phase that's passed. Her body's stopped resisting. It's as if it accepts the inevitable—that the transformation will continue, relentlessly."

"May I see?"

Eddralder elevated the sheet so that Strambli's leg was exposed. Fura controlled her reaction, although it took some considerable force of will to do it. If there was even the slightest chance that Strambli was taking any of this in, she did not want her to be unduly distressed. But perhaps her silence, and her strained composure, would have been all the indication Strambli needed to realise all was not well.

The last time she had seen the wound—however one wished to define it—there had been a translucence to Strambli's skin, and a hint of colourless crystal depths beneath. Now that point of transformation had extended itself to encompass almost the entire extent of her lower leg. From her toes to her knee, the skin had turned waxy and colourless, and a large area around the original wound had gained that familiar translucence, so that equally pale and glassy structures were becoming visible beneath it. At the extremities, there were still hints of uncorrupted tissue, which looked curiously unaffected, lacking any visible indication of necrosis.

"How is blood reaching those areas?"

"It isn't," Eddralder said. "At least, it can't be, judging by what we can see of the transformed regions. Yet by some means, there is preservation of life, and nervous function, until the translucence penetrates, and transforms. Which it is doing, quite relentlessly."

Fura eyed Strambli again.

"You have to remove it. She was right. It's turning her into... something else."

"Ghostie gubbins," Merrix said quietly.

"I'm going Ghostie!" Strambli said, delightedly. "That's my fate! I'd like pretty glimmery eyes like yours, but it's Ghostie gubbins for me! There's glass in my bones now! There's glass swimmin' into my noggin! Shoaly fishy glass! Soon you won't see me!"

"She's gone insane."

Eddralder did not contradict her.

"If she does, and fully, it may be a mercy. But there is still enough of her left to understand her predicament."

"Could Mephrozine help her?"

The tiniest flicker of surprise showed itself in Eddralder's face. "I answered that question already."

"You said there wasn't much in the literature to suggest it would be helpful. Which leads me to think there must be something, or you'd have made a flat-out denial."

"I told her," Merrix said. "I found the chapter you'd been reading, and I saw that it said there was a possibility of using Mephrozine in cases of Ghostie progression."

"You should never have done that," Eddralder said.

Merrix turned to him with a calm defiance.

"It was the truth."

"Is she right, Doctor?" Fura asked. "Can it do something for Strambli? And don't blame Merrix: if there's even a chance of this helping, she was right to let me know."

"There is hardly any chance at all. That is why I did not bring it to your attention. Besides... even if I were to put my faith in those old accounts..."

"What?" Fura asked sharply.

"You do not have enough Mephrozine to spare."

"Doesn't that depend on how much she needs? I could begin rationing you some of my supply from this point on."

"That isn't how it works. The dose would need to be given to her in one go, not parcelled out over weeks."

"Tell her," Merrix said.

"There is no account of a successful intervention with anything less than ten units. And that is an outlier. Of the few remaining anecdotes... those to which I would ascribe any reliability... a twenty-unit dose seems to be the effective minimum."

"I have thirty-five remaining, Doctor." She swallowed hard. "So I would only have fifteen units remaining. That might see me

Eddralder pre-empted Fura's question with a short shake of his head. She hardly needed his answer, anyway. It only took a glance at Strambli's form to tell her that there had been no improvement, dramatic or otherwise.

"Is it possible that it still needs time?" Fura asked.

"It has been eight days," Merrix answered, pausing to mop Strambli's brow. "Those old accounts never agreed on much, but they all said that if the Mephrozine was to have any useful effect, it would be obvious within a few hours."

"I am afraid your charity may have been wasted," Eddralder said.

"The Mephrozine's still inside her?"

"Broken down into useless metabolic products, beyond any hope of recovery. I suppose you are angry, that this sacrifice was for nothing?"

"I'm angry," Fura said, and privately wondered how plainly that emotional state now showed in her face. "But not with you, Eddralder. You never promised me success. I *am* angry that the universe has done this thing to Strambli, and we're powerless to stop it." She flexed her fists. Her fingers, flesh and metal, were tingling. Her cheekbones prickled as if they had the first touches of frostbite. She had just taken an injection of her own, after a four-day interval. The Mephrozine had hit her harder than ever, and the consequent stirring of the glowy was taking longer than usual to fade. If indeed it was fading at all.

"I see it in your eyes, more visibly than of late," Eddralder informed her.

"I'm aware. I'm also…composed." This was true, to a degree, but it was the composure of some fractured, crumbling wall damming back an immense, testing pressure. "It was worth trying, no matter the cost. It would be worth trying again, if we had enough Mephrozine to spare."

"By my estimation you are down to twelve units."

She nodded meekly. "And I'm all for hopeless gestures, but I doubt very much that another twelve would be any good for Strambli, when twenty failed?"

"I wouldn't permit it under any circumstances. It was a kindness, Captain Ness, and worth attempting. But now we must resign ourselves to the inevitable. I must attempt to cut it out of her."

Strambli murmured: "Ghostie shoaly fishies! I'm half-past Ghostie! It's gubbins-time for me!"

Strambli was delirious but otherwise unconscious—had been so the whole while, and whenever Prozor had been to visit—and Fura counted this as the one small mercy of the whole affair. It allowed them to speak plainly. "You will take the leg, if you must?"

"Worse things have happened. If I had the confidence that would be an end to it, I would do so now. But you have seen the unusual paleness of her eyes."

"Then what good will only cutting out a part of it do?"

"That is where I will begin. If we can excise the root of the infection, she may have the reserves to fight the rest of it on her own."

"You don't know."

"I see no other option than to try. If you are willing, Merrix and I will proceed after the conclusion of the next watch. That will give us time to rest and prepare for what I presume will be a difficult procedure."

"You have my permission." Fura shifted her gaze to the other patient in the Kindness Room. "What of Ruther? If you've even a speck of good news, Doctor, I'd very much welcome it."

"Then I shall strive to give you good news. He isn't worsening, which is something. He has been in a condition of deep unconsciousness since the incident, but these last few watches he seems to be surfacing...gradually. He has been muttering to himself. There is...coherence to his words, even if he seems troubled. That at least tells us that there can't be profound neurological damage."

"Troubled?" Fura asked.

"The boy seems tormented by bad dreams. Merrix has been party to more of them than me. I think she understands some of it, even with his half-severed tongue. Tell her, Merrix."

"There's a cave, or a cell," Merrix said. "A sort of dungeon. He's in it, I think, and there's something trying to get inside with him, something coming out of the floor. He screams, then slips back into silence. He's calm for hours, then it starts again."

"You do not need that happening while you're busy with an operation," Fura said.

"I admit it would be a distraction we might well do without," Eddralder said. "I also admit that, besides monitoring him, there is little more that we are able to do for the boy. I think he will wake, in time. But it cannot be rushed."

"Have Tindouf bring him down to my cabin," Fura said. "If there's any screaming to be done, I should be the one to put up with it."

"Fishy Ghosties swimmin' in me half-noggin! I'm gubbinsy-gubbinsy!"

*

Adrana decanted a measure of Trennigarian brandy into a small, weightless glass, the sort with a fine hinged lid and a drinking teat, and lifted it to Lasling as he came into her quarters.

"I've just taken a navigational bearing," she said. "We're sailing as true and fast as any honest ship ever did, and no small part of that must be due to your hard work with the sails and rigging. You are done with the vacuum work now, I trust?"

Lasling was still wearing most of his suit, including two improvised peg-like extensions he had strapped onto his stumps. "Truth to tell, Cap'n, it was all but done three or four shifts ago. But there was always something that could be made a little sweeter."

"And Lagganvor?" she asked, trying not to make it as if she cared too much about the answer. "He came in at the same time as you?"

"The gentleman said he wanted to admire the stars and

Congregation for a few minutes, so I left him to it. But I daresay he'll be in directly."

"I daresay he shall as well, Lasling." She bid him sit opposite her and pressed the glass into his fingers, which were raw at the tips from all the recent work. "Thank you for working so industriously. Every hour that we shave from our crossing is helpful to us, and helpful to my sister as well."

Lasling dipped his eyes to the Clacker's crib, where Tazak-nakak was dozing silently, recuperating after Vouga's repair work. "I hope your passenger is worth the trouble. There are some that'd say it's worth more than their lives to get mixed up with alien affairs. Is he on the mend?"

She injected a deliberate note of caution into her answer.

"To the degree that any of us can say, Lasling, it would appear so. But only Tazaknakak will be able to tell us, when at last he comes around. I am confident though. That quickglass was an excellent suggestion. If the resonant chamber is intact, Tazak-nakak will be able to form a sound-picture and use our own language without difficulty. They speak very well: it comes much more readily to them than to a Crawly."

"And the ones who did that to him in the first place, putting all those holes through him? They have something to do with Incer Stallis and his squadron?"

"Let us just say that neither has our best interests at heart." She nodded encouragingly. "But he has fortitude, and so must you, to have come through your own injury."

He shrugged off her concern. "Once we limped into dock at Ishimvar, I was all right."

"And the pain you still suffer?"

"A reminder that I got out of that bauble, when Mauncer and Ives didn't." He collected himself for a moment. "I can still hear their screams, on the other side of that door. They had no injuries, but they knew they were never getting out of that tomb. I bet they'd have killed to have one more day, even with a little pain. Anyway, pain's too big a word. Mostly it's just an ache, or some soreness."

"Which was keeping you from sleeping."

"When you've been in this life for a few years, there are a lot of things to keep you up all night. Most of us carry a few scars on the outside, but it's the ones inside that give the most trouble."

"That I can believe. It's no easy life, even when we don't have pirates or squadrons to contend with. What was it brought you to the baubles, if I may ask?"

A half-smile creased his lips. "A weakness."

"Go on."

"I liked to gamble. From a very early age, I had to be betting on things. It didn't matter what, or how poor the odds. Street tricks with cups and buttons. Cards and dice. Dogs, if we'd had 'em on my world, which mostly we didn't. But anything else that ran, or hopped, or scrapped, that was fair game. Eventually I took up brawling myself, offering wagers to anyone who felt they could take me on, and I spilled blood—nearly all my own—in every bar and fighting den from the Ramer Docks to the Furnax Gate. Bought stowage on ships when I could afford it, and sneaked and lied my way aboard when I couldn't. Saw a hundred worlds and slowly learned some of the ways of sunjamming. But I couldn't stop gambling, and day by day I was losing everything. I'd stolen from or cheated all my friends, and burned every kindness ever offered to me. I was a wreck: a slave to the grog, bones set by back-room physicians who were usually at least as fond of the bottle as I was, my teeth like tombstones—those that were left—and me starting to see phantoms in daylight, and worse when I was sleeping. My last real fight was somewhere down near the Conjugates. So hazy now that I can't even tell you when and where." He paused, and some rueful self-deprecation had him shaking his head, disgusted and amazed in the same moment. "But I do remember the cove I took on. Him I'll never forget, because he took me to the edge of death and then spared my life. Saved it, you could say. There was nothing to him, just a skinny runt who looked as if he'd snap if you breathed on him too hard. But he could fight like no one I ever met before or since. His name was Paley, and he was an Assessor on a ship called *Midnight's Mistress*. Not that I knew that when he peeled me off the ground, rinsed the blood off my face, and slapped me around the cheeks until I wasn't quite seeing double. He rummaged in my pockets for his prize money, and when he came out with scraps and tokens, I think he was more inclined to pity than disgust. He sat me down on a step near the den and forced a jug of cold coffee into my throat. Then he asked me what I thought I was doing with my life."

"And what did you tell him?"

"That I had this thing in me I couldn't satisfy. Paley nodded at that, and said he wasn't unfamiliar with the condition. Then he surprised me: he said I had to accept that I wasn't going to change. The only question was what I did with that urge. Keep at it the way I was going, Paley explained, and soon I'd have no teeth, no bones that hadn't been reset, and every chance of meeting another runt like himself who wasn't quite so inclined to hold back. I laughed, but he wasn't laughing."

"He could have killed you?"

"Easily. But he didn't, and as we were talking—me still spitting out bits of tooth between gulps of that coffee—Paley asked me what I knew about baubles. He'd spotted that I'd been on ships by then, picked up on the tattoos and piercings that showed I wasn't local to that world—wherever it was we were—and he figured I might have just enough wits left to sign onto a bauble-cracker. Going into a bauble, he said, was the only thing in life worth gambling on. The only stake worth dying for—and the only thing that was ever going to satisfy that urge in me, because nothing in the worlds compares to the chance and mystery of bauble-cracking."

"Did he mention the part about sometimes getting stuck inside them for the rest of eternity?"

"Oh yes. If he'd pulled his punches when he was laying me out on the ground, he didn't hold back now. Told me a dozen horror stories there and then, of things that had happened to his pals. But he knew it wouldn't deter me, only make me want it more. He was laying out the rules of the greatest game in the Congregation, and he knew I wouldn't be able to turn back."

"Paley must have seen something in you."

"In all the worlds I don't know what it could have been. But he did, I suppose, and through him I got a berth on the *Midnight's Mistress*. That was my first time on a real privateer, rather than some cosy merchanter or passenger scow, and it was as if I'd never been into space at all. Hard months, while they knocked some shape into me. Nearly a year of proving myself before I was allowed into a bauble, and then only on the condition I stuck to Paley like his own shadow. But it was enough. From the moment we went in, I knew I'd found my vocation. All I needed to do was become good enough at it to get useful."

"And did you?"

"In the end. Decided I liked the idea of Opening, more than Assessing, so that's where I applied myself—learning every last thing I could squeeze into my head about doors and locks and traps and all the secret wizardry of the monkeys who came before us. The *Mistress* had a fine Opener of her own in Chenzel, but she came down with Gribble's Palsy, which is a condition of the nervous system, causes the hands to shake. It's a common side-effect of bauble-cracking, if you live long enough, and not normally a problem in an Assessor."

Adrana fished into the collar of her blouse and drew out the blue velvet box Prozor had given her before their separation.

"I'm sure some of that Assessor's lore is still in your head. Tell me what you make of this."

"Is this a test?"

"Not at all. This was a gift, and supposedly of some rarity, but I confess I don't quite know what it is. The box opens by that catch on the side."

Lasling's fingers were no longer made for fine work, but he persuaded the catch open and peered into the little box. With even more care, he dug his thumb and forefinger inside and pinched out a small, glass-like thing with a stellate shape.

"It's a light-imp," he said, frowning slightly. "But unless you've never opened the box, you'd have seen that for yourself. It is of some rarity, I suppose. Light-imps are always in short supply, becoming scarcer, and there isn't a crew that holds them in anything other than favourable regard." He offered a smile. "Well, it's a nice enough gift."

"I was told it was something else—something called a Firebright."

Lasling seemed on the verge of saying something, then caught himself. He turned the light-imp over in his fingers, then placed it carefully back into the box. "It's a pretty piece. And a light-imp does have value. I...wouldn't turn my nose up at such a thing."

"I'm not." Hiding her disappointment as well as she could, Adrana slipped the box and its contents back into her blouse. "It was well-meant, and that is the main thing. Your fingers are steady enough, I notice. I presume you took over Chenzel's position?"

"Eight or nine baubles in, I was ready. Chenzel didn't resent it—she understood that she couldn't carry on. Gave me all her books and gubbins, and I worked hard to fill her boots. Which I did, and not too shabbily. Gradually I got a name for myself, and when the *Mistress* went insolvent—no fault of any of us—I was able to sign on under Werranwell."

"Did Paley come with you?"

"No. He died in a bauble called the Yellow Jester. Went back for a chest of Atomist treasure when we should have been well on our way to the surface. Our auguries were a little off and the field started thickening up sooner than predicted. He never made it out."

"Poor Paley."

"I owed him everything. But I learned a lesson that day, which was that sooner or later the baubles always win. It might be the greatest game, but it's rigged from the start. The...trick...is knowing when to quit."

Adrana could not prevent her eyes darting to Lasling's legs. "Life made that choice for you."

"It did, and if it wasn't for the friends we lost that day, I'd have no complaints."

"But your...compulsion. First you gambled and brawled, and then the baubles gave you an outlet for that urge. When you knew you could never go back into a bauble...?"

"You would think the compulsion ought to have returned?" He met her eyes and shook his head. "On that part, at least, dear old Paley was wrong. I could change and I did. When they pulled me out of His Foulness, I left more than just my legs behind. That...compulsion...had gone completely, and it hasn't troubled me since." He drew a hand across his lips, then set down the glass. "Hardly touched a drink since, either, although it'd have been rude to turn down your kindness. I have been... contented...to be what I am. A Master of Sail might not have the glamour of an Opener or an Assessor, but a fair crew splits its earnings equally and I have come to enjoy my profession."

"I am very glad to have you as my Master of Sail, Lasling. I'm only sorry that it could not have happened under happier circumstances." She hesitated, feeling that something more needed to be said. "I may hope that I have your confidence?"

He shrugged, as if the question were beneath consideration.

"Werranwell appointed one of you captain and that's all I need to know. I'll help you as you wish, and shut up otherwise. I am sure you will prove yourself very capable. Your friend, Lagganvor, seems a dependable ally?"

"He has the necessary experience," she answered, with the merest trace of terseness.

"I should hope he does." It was Lagganvor speaking; he was leaning in a very indolent way against the doorframe, tugging off a pair of vacuum gloves. His fringe was low across his eyes, like a half-drawn visor.

"Did you enjoy your view?"

"Most certainly."

"We all get a bit homesick at times," the other man observed.

She extended her hand, palm upraised. "Join us. I was just congratulating Lasling on his work. With the wind at our backs we might even cut a day off our arrival in Trevenza."

Lagganvor dragged up another chair and lowered himself into it with great delicacy. There was scarcely any need for either man to be seated, given the feebleness of the *Merry Mare*'s acceleration, but it suited Adrana to host her guests as if they were in a Mazarile drawing-room, resting their knees after a long afternoon at the races.

"I spoke to Cossel on the way down," Lagganvor said. "The sweeper is clear, and there's not been a squeak on the optical telegraph since that news about Incer Stallis. We shall soon be at the limit of practical signalling, in any case."

"Sail-flash?"

"Not a glimmer there, either. If that squadron is aft of *Revenger*, they are sailing with excellent discipline."

"So long as *Revenger* stays dark, they won't find her," Adrana replied.

"She will be running out a spread of ordinary sails ahead of port," Lagganvor reminded her.

"But not until it is imperative. I know my sister. She will take no silly chances." Adrana poured another measure and passed it to Lagganvor. "Show Lasling your eye, Lag."

"My eye?"

"He hasn't seen it, and I think he would find it interesting. There needn't be any secrets between us now, need there?"

He took a sip of the drink, gasped admiringly, and held the little glass up the light. Then he set it down, pushed back his fringe, and popped his eye out onto the table.

"A remote," he said, as Lasling's gaze veered between the empty socket and the perfectly veined and coloured object that had only just been occupying it. "Bosa Sennen gave it to me, to aid in her spy craft. It has...certain capabilities."

"It can see through things?"

"Not as well as lookstone. But it can travel independently of me, scouting ahead. It can kill, if it has to."

"Make it move," Adrana said.

"I'd rather not."

"Lasling will think there is nothing there except a glass eye."

"Lasling is fine," Lasling said, with a genial dismissiveness. "I believe whatever I am told."

Lagganvor reached out a hand and suspended it over the eye. He raised the hand, and the eye levitated from the table as if suspended by an invisible thread. "What our good captain doesn't quite appreciate," he said, through mildly gritted teeth, "is that none of this happens without effort. The control binding is very demanding. It leaves me...drained. Which is why I prefer not to use the eye unless there is an urgent need." He stiffened his hand, angled the palm until it was upright, and sent the eye speeding away. It travelled to the Clacker's crib, spun around and returned.

Lagganvor caught it between his fingers.

"Satisfied?"

"Thank you for the demonstration," Adrana said, smiling emphatically.

Lagganvor fixed the eye back into place, his look guarded, as well she expected it to be. He ruffled his fringe back into place, then took another hard sip from his glass. "With luck, Lasling, that'll be the last time you ever see my eye anywhere other than in this socket."

"I should not be too sorry if that were the case, Mister Lag." Lasling smiled awkwardly, as might anyone who had sensed the fringes of some tense business without having the least idea of its true shape and extent.

There came a stirring from the crib. Tazaknakak pushed away his blankets using his upper arms to paw around the repair work that had been done to his casque. He probed himself, cautious around the margins between his normal tissue and Vouga's quickglass. His eyes opened: sleepy and small as those of a pale, docile whale Adrana had once seen in the Mazarile public aquarium. Then he began to make a sound like a child's rattle, amplifying and intensifying in speed, until the individual clacks of the rattle blended into each other, and some longer, slower pattern emerged.

"A moment alone with my guest, if you would be so kind," Adrana told her two visitors. "I don't want him to be overwhelmed with sudden company."

15

She lifted the Clacker from his crib and helped him into the seat which Lagganvor had been using, with a cushion stuffed under him to bring his face to her eye-level.

"You have not died on us, Tazaknakak. I take that to be an encouraging sign. Has the resin been successful?"

"It would seem so...I...congratulate your man on his... perspic...ik...ik...ik...acity."

She had to strain to understand him, but that was not atypical of Clackers, at least those few of which she had experience. The sounds he generated in his casque were a marvel of subtlety and fluidity, but they had never been intended to emulate the output of a monkey's larynx. The wonder was not that discoursing with Tazaknakak demanded concentration, but that it was possible at all.

"We spoke a little in Mulgracen, if you remember, but your voice sounds different to me now. Vouga has done well, I think, but there are bound to be changes in the resonant cavities. It must be like learning to speak all over again. As well as that, you are out of the habit."

"I will soon adjust. But even if I could not speak...ik...ik... a word of your tongue again, I am beginning to see the world anew. You cannot know what it is to lose the gift of sound-sight, Captain Ness. There is no analogous handicap among your kind."

"I am certain you know us well enough to be sure, Tazak-nakak. Is it really coming back to you?"

"Yes. I am forming a sound-picture of you even as I speak. It is...imperfect. The crudity of resolution would disgrace a newly-hatched. But it is vastly better than no sound-picture at all."

Beneath the rapid rattling and clacking that enabled him to generate speech sounds was a constant ululation at a much higher pitch. It was nearly at the limit of her hearing and she presumed most of what was being generated was in fact beyond any possibility of detection.

"If we have been able to help you in any way, I am glad of it." She coughed lightly. "I am sure there will be much more that your friends are able to do for you, beyond our poor attempts at medicine."

"You have done your best, Captain, and no more can be expected of you."

"If you have any immediate needs, don't hesitate to bring them to my attention. Do you have much idea of the time that's passed since you gave your letter of indemnity?"

"I confess I have none."

"We operated on you only a day or two after our ships took their separate courses. We've been sailing like that for two weeks now. You were...recuperating...for most of that time. We felt it best to let nature take its course."

"How much sailing lies ahead of us?"

"No more than a week."

"These ships of yours are so intolerably slow. I wonder how you put up with it."

"We do things at our own speed, Tazaknakak, and for the most part it suits us very well. There are twenty thousand settled worlds in the Congregation, and none is more than a year's sailing from another. Most are mere weeks; even days for the more favourable crossings. We do not desire to be faster. Being faster just means being bored and disappointed by things sooner than otherwise. We desire to be safe, and prosperous, and free of worry for our future."

"You cannot miss what you have never known."

"I know your ships are faster than ours, but that doesn't make them better. Do you have need of men such as Lasling or Tindouf on your clever Clacker ships? I doubt it very much. I imagine those ships need about as much love and consideration as a lightbulb. They do what is asked of them, when it is asked of them, and they are forgotten about when they are not needed. This ship..." She stroked the edge of her table. "This ship may be slow, but it runs on sweat and patience and the sort of wisdom it takes half a life to acquire."

"It is good to be content with one's situation."

She was starting to get the first faint, dawn-like intimations of a headache. She had heard about that somewhere. It was something to do with being in close proximity to a Clacker: the constant ultrasonic influence of their auditory sense-gathering. "Concerning our situation..." she began.

"You wish to bring up the real purpose of this conversation."

She sighed, disappointed in herself for being so transparent. "It would be remiss of me not to discuss it, given that every second brings us closer to Trevenza Reach. Are you confident that your friends will be waiting for you?"

He knitted both sets of hands together, managing to convey an impression of intolerable smug self-satisfaction.

"Perfectly so."

"I wish I had your confidence. Those muddleheads on Mulgracen nearly stopped you leaving. Nearly killed you, if I'm not mistaken."

"They were the blunt instruments of fools. There would have been no difficulty with them if I had left on my own schedule. Alas, matters were disrupted by your arrival, and your insistence that I leave according to your timetable, not mine."

She bridled, and did well to keep her composure. "It's such a shame you had no other choice of ship, Tazaknakak—and such a shame that we had no other choice of passenger. But our obligations will soon be discharged—won't they?"

"You will deliver me safely."

"And you will answer my questions."

"Not before our arrival. What guarantee would I have that you wouldn't let me die as soon as I have served my usefulness to you?"

"One: I'm not a monster. Two: I'd rather hand you over to your friends breathing. But it might not hurt if you demonstrated a little goodwill."

"How so?"

"My questions are complex and inter-twined. It won't take one answer to satisfy them, as well you know. So why not show you are sincere by giving me something now, instead of when we reach Trevenza?"

"It is true," said Tazaknakak, "that it will take more than one point of light to illuminate the vast landscape of your ignorance."

"Then we'll begin with one answer. I'll ask you two questions. You can decide for yourself which you respond to. The other will wait until we arrive."

"And the price for this...premature disclosure?"

"Our continued good relations, Tazaknakak. Which I'm sure neither of us would wish to jeopardise. Here are the questions. I should like to understand why quoins have begun to demonstrate an affinity for the Old Sun. My sister noticed it first. This is a new behaviour, something that was never seen before the Readjustment, and it must be telling us something profound about their true nature. But I cannot see it for myself. That is the first question."

"And the second?" he asked hopefully, as if it might be more to his taste.

"A curious riddle that has been puzzling me since our encounter with the muddleheads in Mulgracen. Lagganvor told me that they are temporary agents, stitched together from bits of monkey and bits of alien. They are...animated, infected with a purpose, and enough wits to serve that end. But I cannot see how they are possible."

"You live in a world in which the inexplicable is commonplace, Captain Ness. Skulls. Bauble fields. Ghostie relics.

Effector-displacer devices. You understand none of these things, yet you do not seem troubled by that lack of comprehension. Why perturb yourself about one more trifling thing?"

"Because I am not sure that it is trifling. Where my sister and I grew up was a place called Neural Alley. I am sure there are similar places on a thousand worlds."

"Doubtless. Concerning the quoins—"

"Let me finish. There were shops in Neural Alley where vendors sold novelty animals. We saw them in cages or tanks in the shop windows. They were marvellous to us, and a little terrifying. They had been manipulated by genetic means, using technologies and methods that the vendors barely understood, but which were repeatable. They could take one trait from one creature and splice it onto another. By that means, the vendors created frogs that glowed like night-lights, birds that had the lustrous wings of dragonflies, snakes that had multitudes of legs, and so on. Chimeric organisms, they were called. They could not propagate, but they were alive, and could only exist because of the innate similarity of their biological grammar. Deep, deep in the past, they shared common ancestors. This was how fragments of forgotten genetic language could be reawoken or copied between species. Because it was not truly alien."

"Your observations are most creditable. If I may address your former question, relating to the deep nature of quoins—"

"If the means by which the muddleheads are made are not so different to the means used by those vendors, then it must be… it can *only* be… are you listening, Tazaknakak?"

"This is… not a desirable line of enquiry, Captain."

"I did not imagine it would be. I shall tell you where it has been leading me, though. I think we are not so different from each other as is generally assumed. If the muddleheads are made up from bits of monkey, and bits of alien… then what we think of as monkey and alien cannot be as far apart as is commonly believed. There must be a similarity, an underlying biological connection…"

"There is not," Tazaknakak said.

"A flat assertion does not constitute an answer to my question."

"We each know our histories, Captain. Yours is a tale of Occupations stretching back ten million years or more. A broken, disjointed tale, with an uncertain prologue. You do not even remember how long ago you decided to dismantle your eight old worlds. Our history is not like yours. It is unbroken, and immense. A tapestry reaching back billions of years, without a single thread out of place. You might ask the same of our colleagues the Crawlies, or the Hardshells, or any of the alien cultures who have offered their assistance. You would receive a similarly humbling lesson in differing perspectives."

"And a similar evasiveness, Tazaknakak?" She sighed and shrugged, certain she had got as far as she was likely to. "All right—the quoins. They're drawn to the Old Sun. This can't have escaped your attention. What does it signify?"

"It signifies—"

A buzz sounded from her desk. Adrana regarded her guest, thought for a moment of having him leave, or of taking her call in the control room, then leaned forward and pressed the intercom button.

"Captain's quarters. What is it?"

A voice scratched out of the grille, as muffled and reedy as someone blowing down an organ-tube.

"This is Meggery, calling down from the sighting room. I see something, Captain Ness. It's faint, but I think it's another telegraph coming in from *Revenger*. I'm transcribing it as I speak."

*

Eddralder's daughter was just outside the Kindness Room, peeling off a pair of surgical gloves in a slow and disconsolate manner, while the only noises coming from inside the room were the methodical chinks of instruments and medicines being put away.

"Is she still alive?" Fura asked.

Merrix rubbed a clean knuckle against a red-rimmed eye. "I

don't know. In a fashion, I suppose. But she won't know that you're here. I don't think she knows anything at all now."

"I'd like to see her."

"Father did all that he could." A sudden pleading look took over her. "You understand that, don't you?"

"I was under no illusions, Merrix. I don't doubt for an instant that you both did everything that was possible, given our situation. But I still want to see Strambli."

"Go in, then. But you won't like it."

She went past Merrix, pushing through the curtain they had put over the doorway, then squeezing around the bulky machines that had been assembled for the operation. They were all dormant now, their leathery bellows no longer huffing and puffing, their chugging blood pumps stilled, their green-gridded oscilloscope screens turned dark. Eddralder was holding a huge glass syringe up to his eye, checking it for cleanliness before placing it into a precisely formed slot in a velvet-lined medical box. Strambli was still on the operating bed, her body obscured by a gauzy curtain pulled around her on a rail.

Fura appraised the indistinct form. There was a sheet over her legs and torso, and that made it difficult to be sure, but there was no obvious sign that Eddralder had got very far in cutting out the Ghostie infection.

Eddralder continued with his packing-away.

"What happened?"

"I failed her."

"We all failed her," Fura said.

"No, the fault is with me. I was too hesitant, too fearful, too hopeful that those old accounts might be relied upon. I wasted your Mephrozine, when I should have operated as soon as she came to me."

"None of us knew how this was going to progress."

Merrix had come in behind Fura. "Show her, Father," she said, in a low but commanding tone.

Eddralder whisked back the curtain between them and Strambli, and lifted aside the sheets.

Fura stared, not at first believing the evidence of her own senses. It crossed her mind, fleetingly, that the doctor and his daughter must have conspired to arrange a sort of prank, a dark joke at her expense. The absurdity of this premise was almost easier to accept than the reality before her.

The Ghostie transformation had enveloped the whole of the affected leg, turning the limb colourless and semi-translucent. It looked wasted and near-skeletal. Faint structures, shadows of veins and bones, arteries and tendons, were embedded in that translucence like wisps of frozen smoke. They shivered into blurry indistinction the more Fura pressed her concentration upon them. It was as if they were furtive, always holding themselves at a distance somewhere other than the point at which her eyes were focused.

This was bad—there was clearly no hope whatsoever of salvaging the limb—but equally distressing was the fact that the Ghostie transformation had begun to encroach its way down the other leg. The upper thigh had the onset of grey pearliness that would eventually become translucence, while the leg below the knee looked almost healthy.

"This ain't possible," Fura said.

"Yet it is happening," Eddralder said. He paused, glanced at Merrix. "I've measured the blood temperature in the unaffected part of the leg. It's colder than it should be. I think between her heart and the leg, her blood…goes somewhere. It goes somewhere else, along with her bones and nerves, and then comes back to us. It's how these disconnected parts of her remain alive."

Fura felt cold as well. "What do you mean by 'somewhere else'?"

"He doesn't know," Merrix interjected. "No one could."

"The transformation must depend upon a continuously living host," Eddralder said. "It needs that substrate. So as it encroaches, it does something to the living flesh. Displaces it, cell by cell, structure by structure, into some realm we can't sense. Some cold place, yet not so cold that the blood freezes. That way there is a preservation of life...of consciousness...almost until the end."

"Until the end of what?"

Merrix elevated the sheet so that Strambli's entire torso was visible. A pearly tide had lapped nearly halfway up her chest. Her hips had the same translucence as her legs. In that translucence floated a grey impression of pelvic structures, like an anatomical photograph that had not been properly developed.

"At the first touch of my knife, the process accelerated. I tried to cut it out, to reach the margins of the transformation. There was no hope. It raced ahead, faster than we could act. We could see the spread of it with our own eyes."

"It's slowed down again now," Merrix said. "But only because it must know it's won. It must have used up a lot of energy in that burst of transformation, and now it needs to recuperate."

"Even so, it won't be long now," Eddralder said. "Will you signal the *Merry Mare*, to let them know that we've failed?"

"If I had something definite to tell them. But what would I say? Doctor Eddralder operated, and now she's more Ghostie than not? If she were dead, it would be so much simpler for all of us." Fura moved to Strambli's head. Her eyes were glassier than before, and now the skin around them had begun to be drained of colour and opacity. "Is it in her mind?" she asked, softly.

"It will have consolidated its hold. Clearly it infiltrates the nervous system before it reaches the external tissue. If it is any consolation, I doubt that Strambli has any awareness of her condition."

"I don't want her to suffer."

"Nor do we."

"If there's the least part of her still in there, still capable of feeling, I want her to be spared any distress."

"I cannot make that judgement," Eddralder said.

"Then I'll make it for you. You have drugs. I know what some of them are capable of. End this." Fura made to push herself away from Strambli's side, her eyes beginning to sting. "I'm so sorry we couldn't do more," she said, speaking directly to the unconscious form. "You deserved better."

*

Adrana took a direct transcription of the message sequence Meggery was sending down from the sighting room. There were inevitably some errors and drop-outs in the sequence, for Meggery was using her own eyes at the limit of reliable signalling distance, but since the message repeated itself twice, there was no difficulty in creating a clean version.

While Lagganvor and Cossel looked on, Adrana spread out this message transcription—which was still in raw code—and began to work laboriously through it with one of the standard cipher books weighted open beside her.

"'Strambli...worsening,'" she said, pausing deliberately between each word. "'Eddralder forced to operate.'" She stroked a finger up and down the densely printed columns of the cipher book, frowning as she lost her place. "'Missing...gas... mixtures...for...an...an...'"

"Anaesthesia," Lagganvor said quietly, before gesturing at the code. "May I?"

She regarded him for a second.

"Please do."

He read, as quickly and confidently as if the dots and dashes were his native tongue. "'Merrix believes tables in your infirmary: consult the red book on second shelf: ninth edition *General Pharmacopium*. Send figures in sixth appendix by way of return, telegraph only, with all haste.'"

"Silly of him to leave that book in the wrong ship," Cossel said.

"These things happen," Adrana answered. "We must oblige, in any case."

"Squawk'd be the quickest," Cossel said.

"And the quickest way of exposing our position to Incer Stallis and inviting a ranging shot. We might accept the risk to ourselves, but we also have our passenger to consider."

"And how is our friend?" Lagganvor asked. "Suitably loquacious?"

"He gives me a headache just being near him," Adrana said. "There is only so much of that I shall be able to tolerate. But I think he has a lot more to tell us, and I intend to get some of it out of him before we dock. I worry about him disappearing as soon as we arrive."

Lagganvor nodded. "That *would* be a tad on the unfortunate side. Still, he's better off with you than Fura."

"Why so?"

"If your sister had the first inkling he wasn't being as forthcoming as she'd like, she'd have Surt whip up a set of thumb-screws. Or whatever would suffice."

"I am not Fura."

"Speaking of your sister," Cossel said, turning around the transcription Adrana had made from Meggery's report. "This has to be from her, doesn't it? There's no way it could have come from one of Incer Stallis's ships, just happening to lie along the right line o'sight?"

"We would be foolish to rule it out," Adrana said. "But I do not see how Stallis can possibly know about Strambli's condition, or Eddralder's intention to operate, or the presumed existence of that book." She flicked the briefest of glances at Lagganvor. "We can verify the fact of the book very easily. If it turns out to be real, then the request must be authentic."

Lagganvor rubbed at his chin.

"I don't like it, Adrana. It smacks of something to me—some ruse that we can't quite see. But as you so correctly state—the proof will be in the mere existence of that book."

Cossel went off to the infirmary and was back very promptly, with a fat red volume in her hands. She set it down next to the daybook and the crib-sheet. Adrana stared at it for a few moments, then leafed through to the section on gas mixtures for anaesthetic medicine.

She easily found the table of values that Eddralder had requested.

"He needs only these sets of numbers," she said, dragging a nail down the main columns of the table. "We should be able to transmit them fairly quickly. Eddralder will know immediately what to do with them." She tore a sheet off the daybook and copied the relevant figures down, omitting any supplemental information that she felt Eddralder could manage without. When she was done, she passed the sheet and the pen to Cossel.

"Can you formulate this for me, then come to the main lock? As soon as we are suited, Lagganvor and I will go out with the telegraphic box."

Cossel bit on the end of the pen for a moment, then began to mark down the code sequence.

*

The outer door opened and they left the ship, stomping out onto the curve of the hull. All the normal lights had been dimmed—they had never been bright to begin with—and so their suits were illuminated by only two diffuse sources: the purple and ruby shimmer of the Congregation on one side, with the Old Sun's dusky radiance at the heart of that enchanting lantern show, and on the other side the fainter and paler starlight of all the suns beyond their own agreeable little pocket of civilisation: all the fixed stars which were near enough to see as individual glints, even though they might yet be hundreds or thousands of light years distant, and far beyond them, like a vast, faceless audience against which these closer objects were merely a troupe of scattered actors, the nearly numberless stars of the Swirly. The near stars wore faint tinted masks: reds and golds. The more distant ones were blue or pearly, if indeed Adrana apprehended any colour at all.

"Did Cossel give you the out-going code?" Lagganvor asked.

"A little late to ask me now, but yes, she did. I asked her to keep it brief."

"Very sensible. But you realise it'll be much harder for them to pick up our message, no matter how well we send it?"

"Meggery only made a few mistakes. Here. You can read the code back to me, while I do the sending."

Lagganvor closed his glove around the paper. "Luck was on Meggery's side—as well as dark skies, and a very accurate alignment from the other ship, no doubt assisted by Paladin. We can't count on such fortune. They'll be seeing us against the backdrop of the Congregation, which will make our signal harder to discriminate."

"He needs those gas mixtures, Lag. They wouldn't have asked if they didn't think there was a hope of reading our reply."

Never taking more than one magnetic sole off the hull at a time, they worked their way around the curve of the ship until the Congregation lay at their backs and the star-mottled darkness of the Empty was before them.

The gyro-compass was built into the top of the telegraphic box, with a ring of lamps to indicate the alignment of the whole device relative to the desired direction. If she had the box properly aimed, only a central green lamp would activate; otherwise red lamps in sectors of the ring would flicker on in accordance with her pointing error. It was only as accurate as the initial gyro-lock, and that was perfectly good so long as the two ships maintained a fixed posture. That was seldom the case in celestial navigation, though, and most certainly not the case now. It was the best anyone could do, though, without harnessing a robot mind to run the changing calculations.

Adrana stood with the box before her, held by its double handles. The red lamps guided her onto the approximate alignment, and she adjusted it very carefully until the green lamp glowed unwaveringly. Fortunately, it took only minimal effort to hold the box, and there were additional gyroscopes inside it to aid with the pointing stability.

"You have it, I believe," Lagganvor said.

There were paddle-like control levers set into the handles. Adrana used one to open the flaps at the front of the box, exposing the delicate optics. She pressed another which propelled a light-imp out of a cartridge, positioning it within cradle at the focal point. At the same time, a spring-loaded mechanism drove a ram down onto the light-imp, crushing it, and thereby activating its stored luminosity. Light-imps were transient light sources, but they were much brighter than any neon tube or incandescent bulb, and ideally suited to short intervals of telegraphic transmission.

Through gill-like slits in the side of the box, directed back at the operator, a wavering glow signified that the imp was giving off its stored flux.

"I'm ready," Adrana said. "Give me the message."

Lagganvor looked down at the code sequence and began to speak.

"Open, shut, open, shut, open, shut. Long open. Long shut. Open, shut, open, shut. Long shut. Open. Long shut. Long open, shut, open, shut, long open..."

Adrana's thumbs worked the iris controls as he continued relating the code. She felt the mechanism working, a faint but definite *twitch* with each activation. The aiming lamp was holding green, but that was no guarantee that she was pointed in exactly the right direction, or that there was anyone at the other end picking up her signal.

"...open, shut, long open, shut, open, shut, open, long shut, open, shut, open, shut, open, shut." He paused. "That's all there is. Do you think you sent it cleanly?"

"If there was a mistake, I didn't make it."

"We should re-transmit, all the same."

"Two more times, while the gyro-lock is still valid."

They re-sent it twice more.

When they were done, Lagganvor swept an arm at the nearest line of rigging, where a pale indigo emanation traced the filament's edge. "I see some ghost-light forming. The weather must be on the turn."

"We've done what needed to be done," Adrana answered.

She closed the main flaps, lowering the box so that it pointed at the hull. The light-imp was still giving off its flux, but by the evidence of the glow spilling from the gills it was beginning to flicker and die.

*

There was no good aspect to Strambli's passing, except that it had been facilitated quickly. It was an odd blessing to count on, Fura supposed, that it had still been within Eddralder's power to end a life so efficiently, and at her order. All the same she was as glad as she could be that his medicines had retained their potency, even if they were put to the most harrowing of ends.

Merrix and Eddralder had been present as the injection served its purpose, and Ruther was still mumbling and turning in his sleep in her quarters, so the only two other members to pay their respects were Surt and Tindouf, and they could not hide their discomfort at the strange and distressing condition of their late colleague.

"I never saw such a thing, or ever want to again," Surt said, after she had given Strambli's form the shortest, most flinching of glances. "And I'll never go within a million leagues of anything Ghostie, if I know my own right mind."

"Few of us would argue with that sentiment," Fura said.

"What's we to do with her?" Tindouf said, consternation and puzzlement making a creased map of his brow. "It don't seems right to take her back to a world like that, not the way she is."

"You both knew her better than I did," Fura said. "Did she leave any instructions, the way Captain Werranwell did?"

"She weren't plannin' on dyings quite so early," Tindouf said, scratching at the corner of his eye. "Oh, Stram. Why'd you have to be so careless around the Ghostie gubbinses?"

"She said it weren't carelessness," Surt remarked. "She said that knife had a mind of its own, when it jerked in her hand. As if it meant to put a bit of itself into her. I know we didn't credit her at the time, but now I'm minded to think diff'rently."

"Does you think the Ghostie gubbins wanted to make more of itselfs?" Tindouf asked.

"I don't know, Tinnie. I don't think I want to know."

"Whatever was happening to her, we stopped it," Fura said, with rather more confidence than she felt. "Doctor Eddralder said the Ghostie transformation couldn't keep happening if she wasn't alive. The drugs he put into her were enough to kill a horse several times over. She went peacefully, and she went fast, and now it's done."

"But you still don't know what to do with her," Surt said.

Fura nodded meekly. "We can't just leave her somewhere without a thought to what she's become. She's Ghostie gubbins now, part of her, and we owe it to other crews not to have 'em stumble on her unawares and do themselves harm. Casting her into space, the way with we did with the captain, ought to be safe enough for a century or two...or we could find some out-of-the-way bauble, one that won't pop back open for a long time, and stash her there. Her remains, I mean. I think we have to burn the parts of her that'll burn."

Surt looked stricken. "On a ship?"

"We can discuss the practicalities later. I'm just saying that we have responsibilities to meet—to our friend as well as other crews. Of course, if she had left instructions, even just something she'd mentioned in passing..." Fura trailed off, willing either of them to come up with something, even if it was a white lie conjured up on the spur. "Well, rack your memories," she said, on a despondent falling note.

"If we leave Strambli somewheres," Tindouf mused, "then I'd be very glad if we left the rest of the Ghostie gubbinses with her. Some good dids come of it, but not much, and I'd be happier in my bunk knowing they weren't shiverin' up the ship."

"We'll cross that line," Fura said, "when we're sure we don't have any further need for sharp cutting things."

16

Adrana waited for Lagganvor, turning the gargoyle head in her hands, watching with devout concentration as its eyes and tongue lolled in and out. How old might it be, she wondered. Younger than skulls, she supposed, for its purpose depended on them, but that hardly narrowed matters down. How nice it would have been, she thought, to have Fura with her now, so that they might marvel over the strange thing and offer their individual theories as to its provenance and function. Until it was denied her, she had not realised how pleasant it was to have a sister to talk to in such idle moments; how fine a thing it was to have Fura's imagination as counterpoint to her own. How splendid it had been, for all their differences and adversities, to be adventuring together, rather than alone.

"You've finally found out what that ugly thing is for?" Lagganvor asked as he came in. "If so, please be so kind as to put me out of my ignorance."

"I do know its purpose, yes." She poured another measure of the spirit she had offered him during their last conversation. "You may as well finish it off, since it was so evidently to your taste. Will you sit down?"

He took his seat. He had removed the outer parts of his vacuum suit, but was still wearing the padded under-garments with their numerous tubes and wires somewhat resembling an inverted anatomy of arteries and intestines. Patches of sweat darkened the fabric, some it baked-in through long use and some of it new.

"The drink is..." He elevated the glass to his nose, sniffed. "Thrispan brandy? I meant to ask."

"Close. Trennigarian"

"Close indeed. I'm surprised you didn't share a drop of it with me while we were on *Revenger*."

"I couldn't have. The stuff was under lock-and-key: Werranwell's private stash. For a man of austere tastes, it seems he wasn't above a treat or two—and I don't think sharing it with anyone was uppermost in his thoughts."

"We mustn't judge the poor fellow too severely. I doubt there are any captains in all the Congregation who don't have at least one thing they'd prefer to keep from their crew—even if it's just a bottle of Trennigarian brandy." He searched the room, frowning slightly. "I realised something was missing, but I couldn't put my finger on it. Where is the Clacker?"

"I had Vouga take him to the sick-bay."

"Nothing wrong, I take it?"

"No—but we want to make sure that there aren't any complications arising from the fusion of the quickglass and his living tissue. Vouga is making a very careful examination of the margins, something we hardly dared risk when Tazaknakak was asleep. He'll be a little while. That's fine, though. It allows us to speak candidly."

Adrana had prepared a measure of Trennigarian brandy for herself. She drank from it with her right hand, keeping her left below the table. "To go back to Werranwell: do you think your brother was also the sort to keep secrets?"

"My brother had his private concerns. They were secrets of a sort. But I don't think he intentionally withheld them from his crew."

"He withheld you."

Lagganvor shrugged. "He had his reasons. If I might have the time again, I would not treat him the way I did." He creased his lips. "He'd suffered enough as it was, clearly. But I couldn't act as if I'd never warned him. I told him repeatedly that he was flirting with disaster."

She nodded, thinking of the partial account she'd heard from Prozor.

"By taking Illyria with him on those voyages."

"I understood his attachment to the girl. She was the living embodiment of her mother, in many ways—a constant reminder to him. Heartache, as well as solace."

"What happened to her mother?"

"One of the plagues."

Adrana nodded slowly. "Then I feel for Illyria, if I didn't already. That's how Fura and I lost our mother—how we ended up being raised by our father alone, on Mazarile."

"Then the consequences would have been familiar to you. The father's attachment increased. Pol's daughter became more precious to him than ever before."

"Then why in the worlds did he risk taking her on bauble-hops?"

"He didn't, to begin with. He went off, while I remained home as Illyria's guardian. I was a little younger than Pol, and not as settled in my mind that a career cracking baubles was the life for me. That's not to say that I didn't want to see the worlds, but I thought there might be other ways to do that." He glanced at the little glass, which was still pinched between his fingers, as if some flavour in the Trennigarian brandy had only just revealed itself to him. "I set my sights on joining the mercantile intelligence services, in the end. Pol had already gone off to make his fortune, but there were years of study ahead of me, and no reason at all that Illyria couldn't remain in my care. He saw her often enough, and I always made sure to draw a line between my role and his. She always understood who her father was, and she admired his occupation. Admired it too much, I should say. She argued to join on one of his jaunts. Pol was against it, initially. But she persuaded him, and nothing I could say made any difference." He made a fluttering gesture with his free hand. "Off they went. There was no misadventure, that time. They came back a few months later, and she remained with me while he was off on his next trip. But she'd got the taste for it by then."

"She insisted on becoming a permanent fixture on his ship."

"Pol caved in to her. He gave her quarters of her own and arranged for her continuing education. I...expressed my disapproval. It was to no avail whatsoever. I..." He set down the cup, eyeing it with a faint but developing suspicion. "I feel a little fuzzy around the edges."

"That would be the sedative I put into the brandy."

He absorbed this news with a surprising pragmatism. "I see. And the reason for this...sedative?"

"So you don't make any sudden, rash movements. I have a weapon aimed at you beneath the desk."

He nodded. "I did wonder about the other hand."

"But not enough to think that I might actually intend to kill you." Now that the matter was in the open, she raised her arm and settled it on the table. She held a dainty, jade-coloured energy pistol. "I found this in Werranwell's belongings as well. It's a fanblade, I believe; a very specific weapon from the Eighth Occupation. Have you heard of such a thing?"

"I may well have."

"I'll jog your memory just in case. Another name for it is 'gut-spiller.' It emits a beam of particles with a short half-life, moving very rapidly from side to side in a twenty-degree arc." She gave it an admiring pout. "It's pretty, isn't it? I think it may be one half of a duelling set."

"I'm thinking it's rather a shame I don't have the other half," Lagganvor said.

*

The boy had been muttering in his sleep again, fragments of sentences and words turned to near-mush by the damaged condition of his tongue. She held her pen above her journal, listening as he slurred out something about a dungeon and a candle; something else about a wooden door in the floor, and something that was under that door. Ruther became increasingly agitated: whimpered words of fear and distress becoming moans of wordless terror, and then a shriek so loud and sudden that it jolted him quite awake. Wide-eyed and shivering, still in the slackening coils of that night-terror, he looked around at the cabin in which he found himself.

Fura got up from her desk and went over to him with a tankard of water.

"Drink this."

Ruther pressed his lips to the tankard and sipped tentatively, then with gathering strength.

"I'zh very..." He paused, looked at her with wide and surprised eyes, then dabbed a finger into his mouth, probing the tip of his tongue. "Wha'sh...what'sh happened to me?"

"Nothing that won't heal, according to Eddralder. You nearly bit your own tongue off while you were skullbound with Incer Stallis. Do you remember any of that?"

Ruther looked doubtful, and for a second or two seemed to have no recollection whatsoever of the episode that had tipped him into unconsciousness. Then his face began to tighten, just as if he had registered the first faint sting of an injury and knew that a greater pain was on its way.

"I couldzhn't shto...couldzhn't *shtop* him."

"It wasn't your fault. He was nearly too strong for me and Adrana, and I was silly enough to think we'd catch him off-guard if you used the skull instead of me. But he was much too clever for that."

"Why...why am I here?"

"You were making too much racket to stay in the Kindness Room. Bad nightmares. You were just having one now."

Ruther touched his cheekbones and jaw, examining the outline of his face as if it might have taken on some other aspect while he was asleep. He ran a hand through the white blaze of his hair, ruffling it as one might ruffle the fur of a dog.

"He wazh...I felt him come into my head." He took some more of the water she had offered him. "I could feel him, like I'd become a puppet, or some hollow thing made of wood. Just a marshk…a mask, with some eye-holzh…"

She nodded, believing him, yet puzzled as to how his memories of the contact with Stallis related to the nightmare of the dungeon. She turned this puzzle over in her head, came to no agreeable solution, and not for the first time had cause to regret the absence of her sister, who could always have been depended upon for some useful insight or shrewd observation. Had she been too hasty to gift Adrana a ship of her own, when some other arrangement might have prevailed? It was one thing to be annoyed by her sister's interjections and quibbles when she was nearby, quite another to be aware of the widening gulf between them, and how much she would now have given for Adrana's counsel.

"You don't have to speak for now," she said, trying to find a kinder manner than her earlier brusqueness. "Let your tongue heal. Eddralder sewed it back together, but he said it'd be swollen for a few more days. You served me well, in any case, and I won't ask you to go back into the bone room; not until I know Stallis won't be on the other end."

"My head feelzh…" Ruther frowned as he sought the word he needed. "Sh…tained."

"There was something in you that left a bad trace of itself. I felt the same thing, when I had a dose of him. But you're strong, Ruther."

Her praise drew a bashful smile from the boy. She doubted that he was more than two years younger than herself, but for all that he had lately seen some action, she still felt as if a lifetime's worth of experience separated them: a gulf of horror and loss and sharp learning that could never be undone.

"You think…too highly of me."

"We made an error, but so did Stallis. He showed too much of himself. When he took you over I got a far stronger sense of his personality than I ever did before. And it made me want to…" She looked around the immediate environs of the cabin for some hapless bug, some innocent creature she could mash to a squirming smear under her metal thumb, but for once there was nothing. "I want to seek restitution," she said. "And I'll have it."

Ruther nodded in a way that made it clear that her words left in him no doubt at all.

"How long wazh... how long was I out for, Captain?"

"All in all, about twelve days. Eddralder kept a very close eye on you, and made sure you didn't waste away while you were under. We've been sailing independently of the *Merry Mare* for sixteen days. We still have about two weeks ahead of us, in case you have any fears about missing the excitement."

"Two weeks izhn't... isn't so bad. Is the sh...shquadron... anywhere near?"

"It's possible. But we don't know where they are, exactly, and they obviously don't know our own position very well. If they did, they'd have been peppering us almost continuously with sail-shot."

"He felt near, Captain. I can't say how or why, jusht that he did. Izh... isn't there any way we can tell?"

"I wish there was, Ruther. Sometimes it's worth surrendering your own invisibility to learn the position of your adversary, but that trade-off crumbles when you expect to be outnumbered and out-gunned, as we do. If I wished to give you false reassurance, I'd say there's no other ship besides the *Merry Mare* within one hundred thousand leagues of us. But the truth is Stallis could be within ten thousand leagues, and we wouldn't know it. He has good ships, very well handled, and they'll be sailing as quietly and darkly as nature permits."

"I... could...." He halted himself. "What I mean ish... if I had to go back into the room... I *would* do it, sir."

"I think you would, despite everything. But I wouldn't ask it of you, Ruther, and so long as I depend on Doctor Eddralder's kind office, I wouldn't test his patience by doing so. He accepts that what happened to you the first time was not something we could have anticipated, but to put you through that twice, and deliberately..." She shook her head. "Besides, it was to no avail.

He got into your head far too quickly. You'd learn nothing new the next time."

"May I help with anything?"

"As soon as you feel strong enough, you'll be more than welcome to take a stint in the sighting-room. We could always use a keen pair of eyes."

"I shall," Ruther said. Then some troubling recollection struck him. "Your friend... the one in the infirmary." He searched for her name. "Sh... Strambli?"

"Yes?"

"Did she make it?"

"No, Ruther," Fura replied, shaking her head. "I'm afraid Strambli didn't make it."

*

Lagganvor drew a breath in through his nostrils, gazing at Adrana as if she were slightly out of focus. She imagined the battle going on inside his head, the fight between clarity of thought and the drowsiness induced by the sedative she had slipped into the Trennigarian brandy. It was mild in its effects, not enough to engender unconsciousness, but Lagganvor wasn't to know that.

"Continue," Adrana said.

"What's left to tell?"

"Oh, a very great deal. How you and your brother became alienated from each other. I have the bones of it, but I want to hear it from your own lips. Pick up the story from the point where Illyria went off with Pol for the last time."

"You know what happened."

"Tell me anyway."

"Bosa came. You know this. She took Illyria, and eventually made Illyria into herself. She'd have been kinder killing Pol there and then, but she allowed him to live, and eventually return to his trade."

"You couldn't forgive him, though."

"Not after all the times I'd warned him against taking her. He was broken, to begin with—shattered by guilt and the terrible fear that she was still out there, changed. He crawled home, and pleaded for both forgiveness and the strength only a brother could have given him. I offered neither." He blinked against the tide of tiredness that he must have felt washing over him. "I spurned him. More than that. I made it very clear that I despised his existence; wished he had never been born. I disavowed him as a brother, and did my utmost to destroy his reputation and self-respect. It was no act on my part. I truly loathed him."

"So, he was ruined twice," Adrana said, with the cool deliberation of a prosecuting lawyer. "First by the loss of his daughter, and secondly by the unkindness of his own brother, Brysca Rackamore."

He leaned back slightly, accepting his verdict.

"And yet, here I am."

"Seeking to avenge Pol. Putting your own life in constant peril by trying to capture or eliminate Bosa Sennen, however we may define her. Impersonating one of her own. Mutilating yourself to make the disguise more convincing. Bravery and selflessness, of a sort. Did it occur to you that the resolution of your quest might have meant killing Illyria herself?"

"She was dead from the moment Bosa took her."

"I was not," Adrana replied. "I resisted. I...endured."

"Says the woman pointing a fanblade at my belly and looking only a blink away from using it."

Her finger itched on the trigger. If only he knew how truly close she was; the fury that was within her, and the outlet it was seeking.

"Take out your eye."

This surprised him even through the sedative's fog. "You realise I can do a lot more harm with the eye outside me, than when it's in place?"

"Take it out," she repeated.

He had a theatrical habit of palming one hand before his eye, and patting the other against the back of his head, so that the eye popped out like a marble in an arcade game, but he made no show of that now. He simply pinched at the eye and out it came, puckering loose with a faint slurp, and resting glistening and perfect in his palm.

"I always guessed you'd want it for yourself. Fura has that arm of hers, even if it's missing a finger, and you have nothing except your own wits."

"Put it on the table. Facing me."

He set the eye down. It rested where it was placed, regarding her with a slight upward tilt to its singular gaze.

Lagganvor looked at her.

"What is this about?"

She ignored his question. "Tell me what happened once you sent Pol away."

"Isn't it obvious? My hardness toward him soon engendered the same hardness back. Years later, somewhat older and wiser, I sought to make amends. I tried to make contact, tried to write or signal him. But my every effort was rebuffed. I learned, through intermediaries, that I was dead to him. No longer a brother at all." He stared at her with his one living eye and the empty socket of the other, as if daring her to flinch away. "That hurt, but I suppose no more than my rejection must have hurt him. I took nothing from it personally."

"Really, Lagganvor?"

"Perhaps a little." He smiled at her perceptiveness. "Perhaps a lot. I wished for there to be an improvement in our relations. With time, there might have been a reconciliation. But Bosa stole that possibility from both of us. If I had cause to hate her before, what she did to Pol only redoubled my animus."

"Which is when you decided to kill her once and for all."

"It was a fine intention. It would have given me some small consolation for the loss of Pol and Illyria. How was I to know that two daughters of Mazarile would get the job done sooner?"

"You know that she is dead. There can be no doubt in this regard."

"Something died," Lagganvor acknowledged, with an equivocation that unsettled her.

"But you do not think her spirit is entirely extinguished."

"Nor do you. Not if you know yourself well, or your sister knows herself. She's in both of you. You've admitted as much." He paused and made a slow and daring bid to take back his eye. Adrana jabbed the fanblade at him so suddenly that he snatched back his hand as if snakebitten. He looked at her with an enquiring hopefulness. "Might I ask your intentions concerning the eye?"

"You lied to me about the telegraphic message."

He feigned surprise.

"I did?"

"You would have had us transmit a false code, designed to trick *Revenger* into revealing itself."

"Cossel formulated that code. It was a simple listing of the gas mixtures Eddralder needed."

"Eddralder never required those gas mixtures. He wouldn't have been so lax as to leave an important book on the wrong ship, but even if he *did*—he ought to have known those gas mixtures thoroughly by now. It was your doing: you falsified that entire message from *Revenger*."

"How could I possibly have done that?"

"Using your eye. It doesn't have the range to signal between our two ships, or send a message to your masters—that much I already concluded. But I'd neglected a second possibility. The eye could go out to a relatively short distance—say a few hundred leagues—and then shine back at us, mimicking a telegraphic signal."

Lagganvor pinched at the skin between his eyebrows, squinting as if through a migraine.

"But I was inside when that signal came in. You even had..." he paused, slowed, as some piece of the puzzle fell into place. "You even had me take out my eye, when we were with Lasling."

"I had you take out *an* eye," Adrana said, "And I realised in that moment that you must have two of them: the one we've seen in action with the impressive capabilities, and a secondary eye you can put back into the socket when the other one's out there serving you. When we were with Lasling—when you were late coming back inside—that was because you'd sent the main one off on an errand."

"Two eyes," he said, shaking his head in mock bemusement. "And which of these eyes would this one be?"

"The secondary one, I think," Adrana said. She picked it up with her spare hand and held it close to her face, daring something to happen. The eye was cold, slightly moist and sticky to the touch. That was not some biological secretion, she thought, but some curious lubricating agent that the eye oozed out of itself, to ease its swivelling in the eye socket, and its passage to and from that receptacle. "The other...the main eye...is either still out there, floating near us in space, or it's hidden somewhere. Most likely the latter. About your person, or in your cabin. I think you would have collected it when we went out to send the telegraphic signal. That eye moves quickly, it can keep to the shadows, and I doubt I'd have noticed if it had slipped back to you."

"So I put my eye back in while outside, wearing a vacuum suit?"

"No, but there are such things as pockets. You could have smuggled the eye back aboard, then swapped it back in."

"But you made me demonstrate the eye for Lasling."

She put down the one she was holding, wiping her fingers together until there was no trace of fluid on them. "Clearly the secondary eye isn't just some piece of coloured glass. It can move, under your direction. It might even be dangerous. It might even have all the capabilities of the first eye, although I think it unlikely: that was rare technology when Bosa gave it to her man. No. I think it helps fill your socket when the first is away, and might have the useful characteristic of being able to pass itself off as the first...but I suspect it isn't *quite* as valuable to you. There's a falseness to it—it doesn't look quite as alive as the other and you know it. That's why you're so much more careful to keep that fringe in place, when you're wearing the second eye."

"I will say it again: Cossel formulated the message."

"Which I gave to you, and asked you to read back as I was operating the telegraph. Transmitting the message I'd already committed to memory."

"Cossel's message?"

"No, the one I meant to send, which had nothing to do with gas mixtures." She paused, enjoying his discomfort. "But I did memorise the first part of Cossel's message, just enough to know whether you were giving it to me accurately or not."

"For someone not exactly familiar with the codes…"

She sighed. "I learned the codes months ago, Lag. I learned them so thoroughly I almost dream in dots and dashes. I wished you to *think* otherwise, so you'd assume I was dependent on you and could therefore be tricked." She looked at him with a certain distant fondness. "It's a rather good job you couldn't see the front of the telegraphic box, or you'd have noticed that the shutter wasn't opening and closing in any sort of accordance with your message."

"I…underestimated your resourcefulness." He shook his head in wounded admiration. "How very foolish of me."

"Are you impressed?"

"I have never been anything less than impressed."

"Shall I show you the message you meant me to send, just in case it's slipped your memory?" Without waiting on his answer, she pushed a sheet of paper in his direction. "Read it aloud."

"There's really no need."

"Read it aloud."

He cleared his throat. "Struck by debris or sail-shot, hull punctured, Lagganvor dead, Adrana…critically injured." He paused, his mouth seeming to dry up. "Not long to live. Squawk with all haste, disregarding all previous arrangements. Cossel." He licked his lips, smiled once. "You have to admit it has a certain economy…"

"You intended to lie to Fura about my being on the point of

death, just to get her to squawk and expose her position."

He pushed back the sheet.

"I needed a...persuasive motivation."

"I believe you," she answered, after a silence. "At least, I believe that *you* believe that you have our best interests at heart. I also believe that you think the best way to facilitate our survival is to work with your masters to have us captured."

"In which case..."

She silenced him with a twitch of the fanblade. "It doesn't matter. I don't care what *you* believe is in our best interests. Fura and I have spent our lives having decisions made for us by people who think they know better than we do. There'll be no more of that, from you or anyone."

He slumped, his resignation absolute.

"What now?"

"I think it likely you have another eye about your person. Put it on the table, next to the first."

"Why?"

She jabbed the fanblade again and depressed the trigger to the first barely tangible notch. She had learned that she could make it whine as it accumulated power for an immediate discharge.

"Just do it."

He hesitated, then reached into a pouch about his waist. He produced the other eye, setting it down as neatly and resignedly as a gambler surrendering their last chip.

"I could have killed you at any point in this conversation."

"Then why didn't you?"

"One, you've dulled my control with that sedative—I'm not sure I could be as precise as I'd need to be, and it would have been an awful shame if I blew a hole right out through the wall of your cabin and into space. Two, you might get a shot off from that fanblade even if I did trigger the eye...and three...well, never mind three."

"What was it?"

"My brother thought well of you. He had faults, but he was always a reliable judge of character. I think you liked him as well, and that's some consolation to me. I would find it disrespectful to his memory to hurt you."

"Even if your own life was at stake?"

"I'd only be delaying the inevitable."

Adrana nodded at the gargoyle head. "Pick it up again. It's perfectly sturdy. You're going to destroy one of those eyes. I don't care which. The point is that if there's only one of them left, it'll be much harder for you to ever trick me again."

He hefted the gargoyle. As it swivelled in his hand, the tongue and eyes clicked in and out. "You still haven't told me what it's for."

"It's a skullvane."

"I see."

"According to the books there's a small quantity of twinkly embedded inside the head. Not enough to be useful for communication, but sufficient that it responds to the presence of other twinkly in the vicinity."

"I never heard of such a thing."

"Nor I. That's because skullvanes are hard to find and only useful under certain, very specific circumstances."

"How so?"

"The effective range is very short—no more than a few hundred spans."

"Spans, not leagues?"

"Spans. Useless for finding skulls in general, across the Congregation, and not even helpful on the scale of a bauble, or even part of a bauble's tunnel system. You'd need to be in nearly the same room or chamber as the skull to begin with, in which case you're probably following some treasure map that will lead to the skull regardless."

He nodded slowly, following her drift. "But if you had to search a single ship in a hurry, where the bone room might be concealed…"

"Such a trinket might prove very handy indeed."

He examined the gargoyle head with fond regretfulness. "A pity it's broken, then. The twinkly in it must have gone stale."

"You think it's malfunctioning?"

"By definition. The skull that used to belong on this ship is thousands of leagues away."

"It's not broken," she stated crisply. "It was never broken. The reason it was indicating the presence of a skull is that there was always another skull on this ship. Now smash one of your eyes."

"Whichever I choose, you should know that it'll hurt me."

"I don't care."

"Each of those eyes is valuable."

She raised the fanblade, tightening her hold on it, and made it whine again.

17

Surt was on sighting watch when the signal from the *Merry Mare* came in. She was sweeping the area as a matter of routine, but not with any real expectation of an incoming message. It was only Paladin's excellence with calculation that provided any chance of picking up the other ship: that and Surt's own keenness of vision, allied to the best lenses and tubes anywhere in the Congregation.

Still, once the flash-sequence started she had no doubt what it was, nor any hesitation in beginning an immediate transcription. She noted it down, and although Surt had only lately begun to learn the standard code, she had aptitude enough to understand that the message was not exactly a conventional one. In fact, at first glance it appeared to be directed to some other ship entirely...

"Mister Cazaray?" she mouthed to herself. "Who in all the worlds is Mister Cazaray? And what would we be wanting with his belongings?"

In the galley, where she received the transcription, Fura made a careful duplicate of the signal and asked Ruther to decode it for her. Ruther had made a good recovery from his unconscious episode and although his tongue was still thick and uncomfortable where it had been stitched back together, he was very glad to be of some service. He understood codes, too. Being a boney was as close to a signals-specialist as any ship ever carried, and the lad had clearly been keen to impress his former captain.

"It's a rum one..." he began.

"I don't care if it's rum or otherwise," Fura said, only just managing to keep her temper at bay. "Tell me what it says."

"It sharttsh...starts straight off by saying 'Go to Mister Cazaray's belongings. Attend to them at start of midnight watch, for thirty minutes. Will reciprocate with similar goods, and thereafter at every six-hour interval.'"

"And?" she pressed.

"That'sh all there izh. *All there is.* It repeats itself, but it's still the same thing."

Tindouf, who was with her in the galley, said: "We donts know of a Mister Cazaray, does we."

"We does," said Prozor, who was next to him, picking crumbs out of the bread-hopper. "Or rather, Fura and I does...do. As would Adrana. Mister Cazaray was the Bone Reader on the *Monetta's Mourn*."

"What happened to him?" Ruther asked.

Fura looked at him for a second.

"Nothing good."

"He was a decent enough cove," Prozor said, filling in the silence that followed this accurate if cold-hearted utterance. "Went gentle on the Ness sisters when they were greener than the forests of Cloverly, and that's sayin' somethin'. But like most of our dear old crew he ended up murdered by Bosa, killed in our own launch, along with Mattice. Poor sap didn't even have the pleasure of seeing her face before she spiked him."

"Then why would they mention him now?" Ruther asked. "Did you bring his goods with you all this way?"

"It's not meant to be taken literally," Fura said. "It's a way of alluding to the bones, and telling me to be plugged into our own skull at the top of midnight. Adrana must've found a skull, and now she knows we can communicate whenever we wish."

Ruther looked doubtful.

"What was wrong with the telegraph?"

"Are you dim, boy? It's slow and we're nearly at the limit. If we pull any further apart, or one of us makes a turn that the other isn't expecting, there'll be no chance of signalling by that means."

"But Incer Stallis will be waiting!"

"The whelp has to sleep occasionally. If we reserve the bones for an emergency channel, we'll still have an advantage. But Adrana needs to prove that the skull she's found is able to speak to ours."

Ruther's brow was furrowed. "But there can't be another shkull. You took our bonezh...."

"We did," Fura said, with a sarcastic sweetness. "At least, we thought we did. What if we were wrong, though? We didn't find another skull while we were rifflin' through your ship, but Adrana's been on it much longer, and had a chance to poke into its secrets." She paused, reading something in his face. "If there *was* such a thing to be turned up...would I be getting warmer or colder, Ruther?"

"I...I wouldn't know."

"But you were the boney." She made a show of frowning, as if she were trying to puzzle out some knotty riddle in her head. "No one else might've known about another skull, but if there was ever a cove who ought to've been aware of it...someone close to the captain—it'd be you, wouldn't it?" Before he could jerk back, she grabbed a clump of his hair in her metal fingers. "Talk to me, Ruther. You and I've been on such excellent terms— be a shame to spoil that now, wouldn't it?"

She twisted his hair and Ruther yelped.

"Stop. There izh...there is another skull, and I'll tell you about it. But it's not what it sheems."

She increased her hold on him, while Prozor and Tindouf looked on with expressions of earnest concern. "How is it not what it seems, Ruther? You concealed knowledge of a skull from me during our boarding operation. All the while you were drifting, and we thought you defenceless and out of communication, you had a skull!"

"Which…" Ruther grimaced. "Which we didn't use. Which we were never *going* to use. And your shister shouldn't use it, either. It's not what she thinks!"

She tightened her grip. There was a weak, diminishing part of her that looked on with some faint disapproval, and another part, now in the ascendant, that only cheered her to go further. She imagined his hair ripping away, his scalp coming with it, glorious blood and bone beneath, and she knew it was the glowy making her feel this way—and with equal certainty she knew that she did not really mind, not in the moment.

She ran her tongue across the ridges of her teeth.

"A skull's a skull, Ruther."

"Not that little one," he sputtered out. "It's bad. Poisoned. She mustn't use it. And if you care for her…you have to find a way to stop her."

She let go of him with a wild, atavistic grunt. Ruther pulled back and rubbed at his sore pate, eyeing her with an almost animal wariness, as if he now considered her fully capable of any violence, any wanton or reckless deed.

Her hand shook as she checked her pocket timepiece. With an immense force of will, she bottled the larger part of her anger.

"Two hours to the top of midnight. Are you serious about this, Ruther?"

Still wary, he smoothed his shock of hair back into some semblance of order. "*This* is what it did to me, and I was lucky to be pulled out before it was too late. But even then, it left its mark. Those nightmares you heard? They were never anything to do with Incer Stallis. They were about that skull."

Fura was breathing hard. Her hand was still shaking. The glowy still had her. But she believed him.

*

Vouga swore: some obscure, multisyllabic oath in one of the coarser dialects of the inner processionals. "You might have given me a little more warning, you know—say six hours, or even half a day."

Adrana leaned over him as he sweated with his box of tools, trying to adjust one of the suspension wires that allowed the skull to float in the middle of the bone room.

"You told me it was ready."

"I said the skull was *capable* of being used," he answered, using a wrench to adjust one of the tensioning springs. "By which I meant that the sockets were electrically sound, and the eye-hooks tested for strength, and that the twinkly appeared to be viable, since it showed a counter-response in the presence of the skullvane…" The wrench slipped in his fingers, skinning a knuckle, and spinning off like a slow-tossed bone, end over end, until it collided with the walls and rebounded at Adrana.

She caught it deftly and offered it back to Vouga, who took it without a word.

"I'm not asking for technical perfection here," she said.

"Good, because you won't get it—not with this sort of pressure."

She believed Vouga when he claimed not to have known of the skull's existence. She would have accepted the same denial from Lasling, Cossel and Meggery as well. Ruther, though, the lad on the other ship? Possibly he had known. Indeed, it was more probable than possible, but if he had known, she was sure it was a secret between Werranwell and the boy and no one else.

Certainly, it had been well concealed. The skull had been kept behind a false panel in Captain Werranwell's quarters, expertly disguised. The panel hid a makeshift alcove that had contained two items: a large, stout-looking wooden box, and a single bottle of Trennigarian brandy from 1680.

The box had contained a curiously small skull, protected within a nest of gun-wadding. She might have dismissed it for a useless trinket, were it not for three things. The first was that it had been located by the skullvane, which pointed to the presence of active twinkly. The second was that it had been drilled and tapped with what appeared to be high-grade sockets and suspension wires, over and above what one would expect to find in a piece of tourist tat. The third was that it had been so well hidden. Without the skullvane she would never have guessed there was a false panel at all.

Who went to that sort of trouble, unless the item to be hidden actually had some value?

"I think that will suffice, Vouga," she said. "You already have four points of attachment."

"It's an unbalanced load. The books recommend five to six attachment points as a bare minimum; seven or more as sound practice. Skulls fracture if they're not suspended properly."

"This skull isn't going to fracture, Vouga—not unless I use it as a bludgeon, which is becoming a distinct possibility." She consulted her pocket chronometer. "In a little over an hour my sister will be expecting me to attempt contact. I do not wish to disappoint her."

"Assuming they read your signal in the first place."

Vouga did not know about Lagganvor's duplicity, and Adrana was intent on maintaining that state of affairs. As far as the rest of her crew were concerned, the gas mixtures had been transmitted to Eddralder as per his request. But she had also informed Vouga that she had appended an instruction to her sister concerning the skulls, and that she was counting on it being received and acted upon.

In fact, no such certainty existed. She could hope that *Revenger* had picked up the telegraphic message, but she had no guarantee of it, and accordingly little confidence that there was going to be anyone on the other side of the skull when she attempted contact.

But there might be; and it might be Fura, and while that possibility existed—however remote the odds—she could not give up. Fate had thrown them this opportunity to communicate, and while there was a chance that the squadron was close, Adrana could not—would not—abandon her sister.

"This will do, Vouga," she insisted.

"The books say..."

"Your word alone would have sufficed."

"You will need to go back in your container, and the effector-displacement device will need to operate for at least as long as it takes to get you inside. May we depend on it?"

"Of course."

"Good." She stowed the telescope against the wall. "Because it won't just be you in danger if it doesn't work properly. Those muddleheads—or the people running them—will have guessed where you mean to go, won't they?"

"There is a . . . possibility."

"We'll call that a cold certainty, then. You have friends there—hopefully—but also people who mean you ill. Our problem is making sure the former party finds you before the latter." She pressed a finger to her brow, already beginning to feel the start of the headache. "We'll need instructions, Tazaknakak—very good instructions. Because once you're in that box, we can't open it up and ask you."

Tazaknakak turned from the porthole where they had been viewing Trevenza Reach.

"There is an individual with whom you will make contact as quickly as possible. His name is Hasper Quell, and he will know what to do."

Adrana's headache intensified. But it was more than just proximity to the Clacker causing it. There was the faint grey pressure of some half-forgotten memory trying to reassert itself. "Have you mentioned this man to me before?"

"I do not believe so. What would make you think that I had?"

"That wasn't my question. What is his role? How can he help the likes of you?"

"Hasper Quell is providentially situated in Trevenza Reach. He is not unintelligent for his breed, has influence, is discreet, and above all sympathetic to the cause. I have not met the gentleman personally, but I have it on firm authority that he has been helpful to other fugitives and whistle-blowers such as myself."

"Helpful in what sense?"

"He has given us shelter; channels of communication; the means to re-group and organise."

"Have more of your kind already made it to Trevenza?"

"Many. Not just Clackers, but members of all the non-indigenous minorities. Some monkeys as well, and some robots. There was a trickle before the Readjustment—most were contented not to ask too many questions—now it is a flood."

"What is it you're all hoping to achieve, Tazaknakak, besides avoiding the muddleheads and whatever interests are controlling the muddleheads?"

"The old order was not sustainable, Captain Ness. It was only a matter of time before something new came along. Your entire society was built on a foundation of falsehood. You were led to believe that the quoins were nothing more than an ancient curiosity, put to some useful new purpose as currency. But their true value is beyond your imagining. You and your kind have merely been the instruments serving the supply of that commodity."

"We were told that they were money, then that they contained the souls of the dead, then that they did *not* contain the souls of the dead. We have been told many contradictory things. I have already asked you why the quoins now demonstrate an affinity for the Old Sun."

"I believe, dear Captain, that I was *about* to answer you when we were distracted by a signal from your sister."

"Tell me now, then."

"They are drawn to the Old Sun. Have you a quoin about your person now?"

There was one serving as a paperweight close to hand.

"What is it you wish to prove?"

Tazaknakak took the quoin. "I think it doubtful that the loss of this one quoin will make any difference to your fate or fortune. Are you agreed?"

"No one really knows what a quoin is worth anyway," she said. "But you are right. There are many more. Many, many more."

They went to the nearest lock. There was no need to put on suits, which was useful as there were none that would have fitted the Clacker. They opened the inner door and put the quoin down inside the chamber, allowing the faint gravity of their acceleration to hold it to the floor. Then they shut the inner door, pumped the lungstuff back into the reserve tanks, reducing the pressure in the chamber to nearly zero—gradually, so that the quoin stayed undisturbed—and at last opened the outer door.

They watched through windows in the inner door.

Some gust of residual pressure encouraged the quoin to drift away from the floor. It floated up, then turned so that its face was aligned with the Old Sun and the centre of the Congregation.

"This is not new to me, Tazaknakak. Fura saw the effect in Mulgracen; she mentioned it to me afterwards and each of us has verified it independently for ourselves. I would not have asked you about the affinity if I hadn't..."

"Watch."

The quoin was leaving the lock. It was moving slowly, but with a definite intention. Little by little, too, it was gathering speed—hastening away from the *Merry Mare*.

Hastening to the Old Sun.

*

The squawk was set to a short-range channel again, just enough to cross the distance from the antenna to Prozor's helmet. Fura called her name three times, then received the crackle of a return transmission.

"What is it, girlie? Didn't I tell you I'd still like to keep signallin', until we know better? This biz'ness requires all of what's left of the grey in me poor battered noggin, and when you've got the ship buckin' and twistin' right under me..."

"That wasn't our doing, Proz—it was Incer Stallis, taking a shot at us. He clipped our sails. Paladin and Tindouf have got us sailing true for now, but it's too dangerous to stay out there. Now they've got something to shoot at, and if they've seen even a glimpse of sail-flash they'll know they're getting close. Come in as quickly as you can—Tindouf'll be at the lock to help."

Prozor gave a scornful snigger. "They'd need to be having the luckiest day of their lives to put a slug through me."

"Get to that lock," Fura said, hanging up the squawk handset.

Tindouf was already on his way, and half-suited now just in case he needed to go out there as well. Surt was still in the sighting room, straining her eyes to the limit. Fura would have gladly seen her relieved—she'd have put in her own stint if need be—but it would take too long to winch the sighting room back in and out of the ship, and she could not abide them being blind in that interval.

"Will she be all right?" Ruther asked.

"If she gets a move on." Fura balled her fist, cursing herself for not calling Prozor sooner. Not that it would likely have made any difference: Prozor had never been the sort to abandon a job halfway through. She thought of that mass of sail billowing around somewhere in the rigging, a writhing creature of pure blackness, and the minor fortune that Prozor had not been caught in the lines and sheets when they went loose. Then she remembered what had been pricking the edge of her thoughts when Tindouf had called in to the warn her that Prozor was not yet returned. "Do you know something, Ruther?"

He looked at her warily. "Captain?"

"You are a very clever boy. I can see why Werranwell kept you close at hand. I doubt it was just because of your capabilities in the bone room."

"I thought my idea was bad, about going out with the launch."

"It was. But that ain't the idea I was thinking about. You said it was a shame we couldn't fire back at Stallis."

"And you said the guns would never cool down quickly enough."

"They won't. But if there was a way for Stallis not to see them, even if we were maintaining a high rate of fire, and glowing as hot as coals, that would amount to the same thing, wouldn't it?"

"I suppose," Ruther said doubtfully.

"Relax, boy: it's not a trap. You gave me half an idea and Stallis helped with the other half, by damaging our sail. Paladin!"

"Yes, Miss Arafura?"

"I wish to use our sails as a camouflaging screen, interposing 'em between us and the pursuing squadron. May that be done?"

"A mass of sail could be cut free, fixed to new lines, and run aft of us, yes."

"That would take too long. I'm talking about using our spread of sail as it stands now, but turning us, so that we're on the other side of the sails. May that be done? Keep tension on the yardage by spinning us, if need be, and don't fear a little touch on the ions, if that helps. I don't care if it isn't a stable arrangement...."

"I assure you it will be anything *but* stable."

"Fine—all it's got to do is provide us with a temporary covering screen for the coillers. Even if we're moving, slewing laterally to hold tension, it should be within your means to compute firing solutions for a rapid volley?" She grinned, as images of destruction and violence played out in her mind's eyes, as bloody and vivid as any of the more lurid illustrated periodicals, the sort that Father had always frowned upon. "We'll run 'em hard and hot, until we no longer have the aiming angle or the covering effect, whichever happens first."

"Captain?"

"What, boy."

Ruther looked stricken. By the anguish in his features he clearly wished to say something, something which might be taken the wrong way, yet feared the consequences.

"What I mean to say is..."

"Out with it, Ruther."

"What I mean is... perhaps I'm not quite following this plan, but if the sails are between us and the enemy... however temporarily... won't that mean that we have to... shoot through our own sails?"

"The objection is not unreasonable," Paladin said.

Fura nodded avidly. "That's the point, you simpletons: it doesn't matter that we shoot through our own sails! There are leagues upon leagues of 'em, and even if we fire every slug in our stores we'll only be doing a little damage to a small area. In

298 • Alastair Reynolds

the meantime, not one photon will get through the parts of the sail that ain't punctured, and that'll mean most of the covering screen still holds. Stallis won't see a hint of our guns, even if they're close to cooking-point. Now tell me: can it be done?"

Although she was in the control room, not her quarters, she imagined the flash of lights in Paladin's globe; the play of logic through his circuits and memory registers.

"I must calculate."

She squeezed her fist. Somewhere in the back of her mind it occurred to her to wonder if her enthusiasm for this idea—which was, on the face of it, nearly as mad as it was audacious—was borne out of recognition of its intrinsic cleverness, the one desperate act that might save them, or was instead driven by the glowy, seizing and magnifying the idea not in spite of its madness, but because of that very quality.

Somewhere else in the back of her mind, she knew that she no longer cared.

She roared: "Then damned well calculate!"

*

Adrana swept her telescope along the length of Trevenza Reach. It was pleasing to her to see many other craft gathered around the world and navigating its near spaces: ships of all sizes and dispositions, some under all sail and some hauled-in. One more ship, even a sunjammer limping in from some doubtful encounter in the Empty, would not draw too much notice.

"Are you sure you're rested, after that business in the Bone Room?" Lasling asked.

"I am very rested, thank you. I do not think it would have been good for me to be in there very much longer, but you got me out in time. I have had a little headache, and the Clacker does not help it, and now and then I feel nauseous, but there are no more serious after-effects."

"Was it wrong, to smash up the skull like we did?"

"No. It was entirely the right thing, and you must think no more of it."

"I suppose we've come to the perfect place to find a new one. Or newer, I should say."

She smiled tightly. "Yes—there'll be things to procure. Not just a skull." Intentionally changing the subject she added: "We'll come in all the way, if there are no objections. "Unless there is a compelling reason otherwise, I think we will take the closer of those two docking complexes. Haul-in as you may, but leave us enough spread to sail away if the reception is not as warm as we'd wish." She snapped the telescope shut, content to take in the entirety of their destination with her unaided vision. "It's a pretty little trinket, isn't it? It reminds me of an ornament Fura and I were once given. I almost feel that I could reach out and shake it, and a snowstorm would flurry down inside."

"I've never known snow."

"Nor have I," Adrana said. "But I have seen pictures. Paladin used to show us drawings and paintings when he was telling us stories. He was always very good at telling stories. Besides, snow isn't just some something from fairy tales. It does snow on some of the worlds, doesn't it?"

"I gather it does, especially out in the colder orbits. I haven't seen such places for myself, though, and I doubt I ever will."

"There's always time, Lasling."

"Not for me, I fear. There's just too much of everything and too little of me. A sixth of me's gone, I'm two thirds of the way through my natural span, and I haven't seen a thousandth part of the Congregation." He coughed, and sounded as if he wished to strike a less maudlin note. "Still, it *is* a pretty trinket, as you say."

"They say spindleworlds are rare."

"Rare because they break so easily, so even if there was once lots of them, and that's not a proven fact, not many have come through to the present."

"Why do you think this one has endured?"

"It's a bit like asking, why has this nice wine glass not shattered, when all the others have. There's no reason except the others weren't so lucky. And when you're down to a few of something, I s'pose you take better care of what's left."

The spindleworld was three and a third times as long as it was wide, and it was only wide at its thickest part, the exact middle. It tapered down between the middle and the ends, five leagues in either distance. There were long, triangular windows cut into the tapering parts: six in each half, running nearly from the middle to the end, with strips of uninterrupted floor between each window. The interior was almost entirely covered over with city: numerous interlocked and festering districts sprawling out along the floored parts and even spilling out over the windows, clinging to the thickest parts of their mullions. Her telescope was good, but she was having to look through porthole glass that was not quite as excellent nor as clean, though that blurriness only made the world look more tantalising, more full of life and possibility. The entire structure was rotating on its longest axis, with a grand, slow stateliness, so that as one set of windows went out of sight, another came into view, like a sort of clockwork diorama of intricate tableaux.

There were three possible docking sites: a ring-shaped complex around the middle, which—because it was rotating—was suited only to rocket craft, and two similar facilities at the sharp ends. The world was turning there as well, of course, but the docking positions were almost on the axis of rotation, and therefore as close to weightless as made no difference, and even a sunjammer could berth there without too much difficulty.

That was not her intention, but she would have Lasling bring them as close as possible, and then they could take the rocket launch a league or two over, which would cost more in suiting-up time than it did in travel or expenditure, and yet would permit some of the sails to remain hauled-out, with their mirrored sides averted.

"Somewhere in that world, Lasling, is a man called Hasper

Quell. It seems quite impossible now, but I hope we won't have too much trouble finding him."

"Is this gent known to you?"

"Not directly. The Clacker mentioned him as a potential contact, a man who has been helpful to fugitives such as himself. I thought the name meant something to me, yet I've never been to Trevenza. It puzzled me for a little while, until I remembered that my sister has been here before."

"And Captain Fura told you about this man?"

"In her book. She wrote an account of her adventures, and in it she came into contact with Hasper Quell, which is why the name was familiar to me. It at least confirms that he is real, and he may be reached. That is a start. But I have misgivings."

"How so?"

"The man betrayed Fura. Or was himself betrayed—either way, when she went to him for help, it ended with her being captured and taken back to Mazarile. I can't be sure if Hasper Quell did his best and was put in an impossible position, or whether he can't be trusted at all."

"And what does the Clacker say?"

"It's too late to ask, Lasling. Lagganvor and I put him back into his container, and now he's out of communication. By the time I made the connection with my sister's journal, he was already in the box."

"Then wake the cove and press him about Hasper Quell."

"I daren't do that. His box is unreliable, and we need it to keep functioning until we're safely inside Trevenza. Bringing in a live Clacker would raise too many questions. I'm not saying all the customs men will be on the lookout for Tazaknakak, but it would only take one bad apple to undo our plans."

"Then you're in, pardon my bluntness, something of a bind. You have to put your trust in this man, who might rat you out."

"Lagganvor will go ahead of us and make contact. He's good at that. Once I have his reassurance, I'll feel better."

"Once or twice, Captain—and you'll excuse me if I'm speaking out of turn—but once or twice I've wondered if you and Mister

Lag don't have some business between you. Some business that might mean your trust in him ain't as rock-solid as it should be."

She deliberated over her answer. "You are correct, and you haven't spoken out of turn. There was a...difficulty between me and Lagganvor. But that's rather behind us now. In fact, Mister Lagganvor means to speak to you all about it, before we take the launch. I think you will find it...enlightening."

*

"What you ask of me will be very difficult," Paladin said. "I will need to adjust the rigging almost constantly, so as to avoid the catchcloth sails being blown into us, or the ordinary sails throwing light at our adversaries. Then there is the question of how we initiate this turn in the first place. There are a number of possibilities, but each has its drawbacks, and..."

"I never thought it would be simple, Paladin," Fura said. "Just answer my question: is it feasible?"

"I believe it is feasible."

"Good—that's all I ask for." She reached for the handset again. "Proz—I've got an idea to let us start bloodying some noses— since they're so intent on bloodying ours—but since we'll be putting a hard torque on the ship, I want you inside before we attempt it. How far are you from that lock?"

There was a buzz of static, a crackle or two, but no reply.

She clicked the handset again.

"Proz? Where are you?"

"I's at the lock," Tindouf said, cutting in on the same channel. "And I can see out through the porthole, but I can'ts see any signs of Prozor."

"I told her to stop sending that signal," Fura said, angry and concerned in the same breath. "Paladin: be ready on my word, but don't start to turn us until I say so."

She left the console and the sweeper and fought her way through the warren of corridors and squeeze-throughs that led to the main lock. She was nearly there when Eddralder appeared around the corner of a passage, blocking her way.

"Is this a good time?" he asked mildly.

"Does it look like a good time?"

"I wouldn't know. You look aggrieved. Then again, lately you look aggrieved under almost any circumstances."

"Well, let me explain the circumstances as they presently apply," she answered testily. "We're being shot at. They've struck our outer sails and they may soon have more success. I have a plan, but..." She paused, drawing a deep breath, collecting herself. "There may be casualties, if we start receiving fire. You'll have to do something about Strambli's body, if you're to have a clear operating area in the Kindness Room."

"As it happens, Strambli's body is what I was coming to speak to you about."

She did not need this. "You and Merrix will just have to put it somewhere for the time being. I know you'd rather study her than move her, but..."

"Her body has already gone," Eddralder said. "The trouble is, we didn't move it."

"Please explain."

"I wish I could." He looked at her with his large pale eyes, communicating the full intent of his words, making sure she understood exactly what had happened. "Merrix and I left the Kindness Room unattended while you called us to the control room. When we returned, the body was gone."

"There must be a mistake. The Ghostie transformation's obviously advanced to the point where you're just not seeing her, even though she's still present. That's how it works with Ghostie gubbins. The armour, the weapons...if you try too hard to see them, they slip out of your conscious focus."

"Merrix and I know an empty bed when we see one, Captain. It's not a question of looking too hard. The body isn't there."

"So who moved it?"

"Nobody. Surt is in the sighting room, Tindouf and Ruther were with us in the control room, and Prozor went outside. She *is* still outside, isn't she?"

"Yes, and that's..." Fura shook her head, trying to clear at least a tiny part of it. "Bodies don't move, Eddralder. There's been a mistake."

"Unless Strambli had the right of it all along, Captain. She seemed to know what was happening better than any of us."

"Find it... her," Fura said.

"And then what? Chain her down? Nail her into a box?"

"Perhaps that's what you should have done all along." Exasperation overwhelmed her. "Prozor's still out there. I want to turn the ship and I can't risk it with one of our own still outside."

"There is something we don't understand, something we can barely see, moving around on this ship."

"And there won't *be* a ship unless I turn us."

Eddralder nodded slowly. "Merrix is searching the aft compartments, as best she can. I will do the same with the forward ones. And... report accordingly."

"Do as you must," she said crisply. "Take care. But remember what I said: we may need the Kindness Room."

She squeezed past Eddralder, turning back once to watch him heading away, then shivered to herself, thinking of Strambli's glassy corpse somehow animate and self-directing, ensconcing itself somewhere in the many nooks and hideaways of her ship. What did it want with them? What did she want with them, if any part of Strambli now remained? And how peculiar that this curious and troubling business should not, presently, be the uppermost concern in her mind.

When she found him, Tindouf was just finishing putting on the last parts of his suit, bulky as a bear in all that leather and metal. He was at the door to the main lock: the starboard lateral lock, peering through a porthole to the right of it.

"Any sign of her?" she asked directly.

"Not yet, Miss Ness. I did speaks to Doctor Eddralder just now and he was most taken up with something. Has someone been hurt?"

"Not exactly, Tindouf, but if we don't act quickly there's every chance of it." She squeezed in next to him, pressing her face into the concavity behind the porthole. It had a domed window, allowing a limited view of the hull in all directions, as well as a clear view looking straight out. It was hard to see anything, except a dark continuum. "Damn this lightvine," she muttered, for it was glowing behind her, making it even harder to peer through the glass. "We should've cut it back months ago. Have you seen or heard her?"

"Nothing, and I oughts to have picked up the stomp of her boots by now, if she was coming in."

"She's in trouble, Tindouf. Something must have happened to her out there."

Tindouf hinged down his visor, tightening the seal with the thumbwheels either side of his chin, then presented his back to her so that she could double-check the connections. "I's worried," he said, his voice muffling through the glass.

"So am I. But it might just be that there's a problem with her squawk. She had to put that suit on in a hurry, didn't she? Something might have snagged, or the cell not been charged-up properly."

"I hopes that's what it is," Tindouf said, none too persuasively. "I'll be quick, and I thinks we can afford to lose another quantity of lungstuff—we'll be at Trevenza Reach before we run low—and..."

"I see something."

Her eyes were still struggling to pick out the difference between the hull and the background beyond it, but something had begun to come into view now, tumbling slowly. It was dark, but not nearly so dark as its surroundings, and as it rotated its surfaces caught and reflected some faint portion of the Congregation's light, so that Fura was able to make out an edge here, a grille there, a hinged shutter there. She stared at it for a moment longer, not quite recognising the thing, until her mind made the necessary connection. It was the telegraphic box, bulky and rectangular, following some lazy course of its own.

Something about it was not quite right, though.

"Tindouf," she said. "Come here."

He pressed his helmet as close to the porthole as he could, trying to follow her angle of vision.

"What is it, Miss Ness?"

"I don't know. I thought I understood what I was looking at, but now..."

She stared and stared. She knew how the telegraphic box should appear; she had gone out often enough to familiarise herself with its operation, even if she had never used it in earnest. There were the flaps at the front, which protected the delicate optics, and inside those a separate, high-speed shutter mechanism that could be opened and closed with the controls built into the handles—which projected from the other end of the box like a pair of bull's horns. Now there was something else, too: a continuation of the handles, as if they'd been thickened and extended. It wasn't the telegraphic box at all, she decided, but just some similar-sized bit of the ship that had come mysteriously loose. That was what it was. That was what it *had* to be.

For a man wearing a suit, Tindouf moved with commendable speed. He jammed a mitten across her eyes, screening her view, and then very nearly yanked her head off as he averted the direction of her gaze.

"No, Miss—you don'ts need to see that, not at all."

"Tindouf," she said, still with one of his hands across her face, another preventing her from looking back. "Tindouf. I thought I saw... Tindouf! Tell me what I just saw!"

Now he clamped his hands either side of her face and forced her to look into his visor.

"No, Miss Ness. Not right now. You go back and see Mister Paladin, and tell him I has to go outsides. I shan'ts be too long, I don't think."

"They've killed her, haven't they?" she asked, hearing herself speak, but not really feeling as if the words were originating in her own head. They seemed to belong to someone else; a protagonist in some other story than her own. "She was on her way back and they've killed Prozor. Incer Stallis killed Prozor."

It was as if some vital part of her had been cut away; some

part that she had always relied on, but never given sufficient consideration to until the moment when it was taken from her. She had accepted the fact of the death without the least equivocation, accepting the full and irrevocable truth of it as readily as she might accept the loss of a sail or hull-plate. They were engaged in war, after all, and this was what happened in war. People died, including good and dependable people; even people who had always seemed to pass through life armoured against the worst of its abuses. Prozor had always been so re-silient, so resourceful, so utterly bereft of self-pity or remorse for her own actions, that at times Fura had begun to think of her as a sort of living mass of scar tissue, made only harder by each injury or injustice: the sort of rough hardness that the universe might wish to smooth away, but could not, despite its most concerted efforts. Prozor had survived baubles and every common hazard of space; she had survived the loss of her one true love; she had survived Bosa Sennen and twinkle-heads and the hostile intentions of other ships.

And all of that had counted as naught against Stallis.

Fura breathed slowly. The glowy prickled. She accepted that this thing had happened; she accepted that there would be no undoing her earlier harshness. She did not accept that the crime would go unanswered for.

"I'll do something very, very bad to that whelp," she promised.

"You go and see Mister Paladin," Tindouf repeated, before pushing himself into the lock.

21

Adrana did not expect to be squawked by Fura—that would risk giving away what little uncertainty might remain of her position—but when at last the console did buzz, signalling an incoming transmission, she could not quite negate the hope that it might be her sister, and that the news might not be so terrible as she feared.

But there could be no good news. She had monitored the further unfolding of that engagement. The attack against *Revenger* had entered a cruel and slow secondary phase. The five ships of the squadron were no longer shooting quite so actively, but from the pattern of their muzzle flashes it was clear that they were now closing in on their quarry with a methodical and deliberate patience. She imagined a field of carnage, after some disproportionate slaughter. Now the triumphant party was moving slowly and calmly through the bloodied and mangled bodies of the fallen, occasionally stopping to jab a sword into some whimpering enemy who hadn't had the decency to die quickly. The battle was technically still in progress—it would not be formally decided until the last moaning form had been pricked into silence—but all that remained was a sort of ghastly, clerical formality.

So it was with the attack on *Revenger*. The squadron ships were still too far off to send in launches (if that was their intended endgame) but there could no longer be any doubt that they would prevail. If *Revenger* was a cornered rat, she was now tormented by five stalking cats. Every ten or twenty minutes they were content to shoot a slug or two at her, scanning for sail or hull-flash and refining their aim accordingly.

And still there had been no counterblast from Fura.

Adrana did not even have the luxury of being the only witness to this travesty. News of it was all over the general squawk, and they were even beginning to see it on the short-range flickerbox transmissions beaming out from Trevenza Reach. There were a hundred different viewpoints, a hundred different commentaries, a hundred different theories and opinions. No one had direct proof that it was the Ness sisters' ship being shot at, and there was no official line from anywhere in the Congregation concerning the actions of the sub-squadron. But there were plenty of observers who had guessed the essential truth of what was happening. It did not take vast powers of deduction: tying up five ships in a lengthy engagement was always going to be expensive.

Who was worth that sort of cost, besides the Ness sisters?

The only crumb of encouragement Adrana could take from any of this was that no one, to the best of her knowledge, had yet speculated that the Ness sisters might be operating different ships, and that one of them might be coming in from the Empty on a different course to the other...

"It might," Lasling said, when the console had been buzzing for about ten seconds, "be worth answering that."

She snatched the handset from its cradle.

"Captain Werranwell, of the *Merry Mare*. To whom am I speaking?"

"This is Trevenza Reach, Captain Werranwell." There was a pause, and she read far more into that hesitation than she wished. "We have you on our sweep, approaching at one hundred leagues per hour. What are your intentions?"

The voice was deep, male and phlegmatic, as if there was something in his throat he badly needed to cough up.

"I should like to dock with all expediency. We were attacked without provocation, left for dead in the Empty. Our captain, my dear father, was killed in the attack, and we are very low on supplies."

The speaker was some low-ranking Port Authority functionary, she did not doubt—unless they already merited the attention of someone higher up—and he sounded only a fraction less bored than at the start of the exchange. "And who was behind this attack? Bauble-jumpers? Some other privateer?"

"There was no communication, sir, but there were many ships involved, and we have it on excellent authority that there is a squadron operating in this part of the Empty. There is talk of an engagement going on as we speak—perhaps the same ships that waylaid us."

"Waylaid you?"

"It must have been mistaken identity, sir. Our squawk was damaged, so we couldn't give an account of ourselves, and they took that as an invitation to put a few slugs across us." Adrana swallowed audibly and tried to make it sound as if she was only just holding back a flood of tears. "They used hull-penetrating coillers against us, sir—they weren't just trying to warn us away. We were spiked very badly—lost half our lungstuff."

"That is very unfortunate, Captain Werranwell. But you must appreciate that we cannot be seen to take one side over the other, even if you have a legitimate grievance..."

"That is fully understood, sir," Adrana replied, adopting as earnest and ever-so-humble a tone as she dared. "I know that you have standards to uphold."

This drew a mildly quizzical response.

"Standards, Captain Werranwell?"

"My dear father, just before the life left him, said that we should endeavour to bring his body to the place he loved best out of all the worlds around the Old Sun, but we should not count on charity, for Trevenza Reach is a world where the institutions and treaties of the Congregation are maintained with great subservience and loyalty, more so than in many places in the warmer processionals…" She sniffed hard, making so convincing an effort that she had to drag her own sleeve under her nose. "My poor departed father was very firm in this matter, sir. He stipulated that though it would break his heart for his mortal remains not to be conveyed here, on no account were we to test the good nature of our intended hosts. In fact he said that it was quite likely that, while we had been shot at without mercy, the squadron was only going about the good work of our proud and long-established financial institutions, which he said were held in universal esteem, even as far out as Trevenza Reach."

Next to her, Lasling made a hesitant chopping motion. She halted herself momentarily, then decided that she was committed to the part and might as well throw herself into it with total abandon.

"All I mean to say, sir, is that, despite what's happened to us, and despite my father's very strong desire to be laid to rest in the place that had been so kind to him, and for which he had such fond recollections, on no account were we to make more trouble, or force our hosts to choose between the word of a lowly privateer and the combined authority of the banks and merchant institutions…"

It was a relief when she was cut off.

"That is quite enough, Captain Werranwell. I am afraid your father may have been labouring under a very slight misapprehension—or perhaps he meant only to spare you any embarrassment?"

"I don't understand, sir."

"I mean only to say that while we are by no means a lawless freehold, we have always prided ourselves on maintaining a certain…respectful distance…from the affairs and preoccupations of the main Congregation. Of course we adhere to Inter-Congregational law in all matters of binding importance… but we are not a vassal state of the inner processionals, and nor are we beholden to the word of the banks over an honest captain, or the daughter of a hard-working captain, especially one who must have held our world in such high regard to wish to be laid to rest within our locks. You may approach, Captain Werranwell, and all assistance will be offered. You must understand that no sides will be taken, and every aspect of this unfortunate matter will need to be examined from all angles, but until such time as it is proven otherwise, you will have the status and rights of an innocent party." The voice shifted, becoming more business-like. "Please reduce your approach speed to fifty leagues per hour, and further still once you are within ten leagues of our trailing endcap, where you may float or berth at your leisure."

"Thank you for your kind consideration, sir," Adrana said, before putting back the handset.

"My poor departed father," Lasling said, mimicking her words with an amused admiration.

She knuckled away a semi-formed tear. "That wasn't nearly as much of an act as you'd think. Can we haul-in as the man asked?"

"Between my sails, and Meggery's ions, we can slip in as sweetly as you like."

Even as her mind kept flashing to thoughts of Fura, she found the strength to smile at him.

*

Lagganvor pushed back the fringe of his hair and took out his remaining false eye. He cupped it in his hand, offering it to the small audience before him as if it were the prelude to some devilish act of prestidigitation.

But he did not make the eye disappear.

"I am not the man I have claimed to be. For a long time—many months now, on these ships, and still longer on Wheel Strizzardy—I have been living under one name while reminding myself that I have another. Only one other person has known of my double-identity, and I know it has cost her dearly to keep this secret." He nodded at Adrana, with—it seemed to her—some measure of sincerity and understanding. "It has nearly torn her apart, to choose between the preservation of her crew, and being honest with her sister. She made the proper choice, too. And her reward for that was to be betrayed by me." He flashed a self-effacing grin. "Or very nearly betrayed. She was wiser and more perceptive than I realised, and that is to my eternal discredit. I promised her that I would not signal my masters, once we were on this ship. And I lied, and attempted to signal them—or rather, attempted to arrange a ruse which would have resulted in the *Merry Mare* giving up her position—but which would have served my masters just as excellently."

"Who're your masters?" Lasling asked.

Lagganvor put back his eye before answering. "The same masters who murdered your captain."

There was a silence. A nervous laugh from Cossel, a sniff of disbelief from Meggery. Vouga looked on with amused indifference, as if observing a street-side brawl in which he had no direct interest, but from which he could not quite tear his gaze, and that might even be worth a wager or two.

Lasling remained impassive. "I will need a better answer."

"I would like to offer one. But that is the truth of it. I am an agent—an operative of the vested interests that have funded that squadron, who put Stallis in charge of it, and who have Werranwell's blood on their hands."

Cossel laughed again. "If you're trying to get yourself killed, cove, this is a good way to go about it."

"I say we start on his fingers," Meggery said, making a knife-sharpening gesture against her sleeve.

"Wait," Lasling said, with a slow raise of his hand. "I want to hear the rest of it. Then we decide."

"Ain't we heard enough already?" Cossel asked.

"You forget," Vouga said. "He was protected by Captain Ness. If you have a case against him, then you'd better be prepared to extend it to our captain—who Werranwell persuaded us to accept as his successor." He nodded at Adrana, who had kept her silence until that moment, knowing full well how Lagganvor's confession was likely to be taken. "Is that not so, Captain?"

"I suggest," she said delicately, "that you hear what he has to say. What appears to be black and white now may look less so in a minute or two. But keep in mind one other thing: I *am* your captain—as Vouga has so kindly reminded us—and I will not have any sort of mob justice on my ship. Take against Lagganvor, by all means. Harm a hair on his head, and you'll understand what it means to wrong me."

"And I thought her sister was the fierce one," Meggery muttered.

"You thought wrong," Lagganvor said. "And believe me, I have seen and felt the evidence of it. I crossed her once—I will not make the mistake of doing so twice."

"Tell them why you did it," Adrana said.

He worked his fingers together, staring down into them with intense concentration. Perhaps he understood he only had one chance of redeeming himself, and that every word that fell from his lips had to be considered.

"Bosa Sennen killed my brother," he said, looking up into the assembled faces. "His name was Pol Rackamore and he was known to the Ness sisters. I think they would agree he was an honest and fair captain. Long before Bosa killed him, though, she took his daughter Illyria and did something unspeakable to her—something that nearly broke Pol. He recovered, in time, but our fraternal love did not. I blamed him for what had happened to Illyria. Just when he needed me the most, I offered him censure and disapproval. He turned from me—shut me out of his life. I do not blame him for that in the slightest. I...lived with my error. I thought, with time, there might be a possibility of healing the wound I had inflicted. But Bosa took that hope away. She killed my brother, and so I decided to pay her back in kind."

"Tell them about Lagganvor."

"Lagganvor was an agent in her employment. She sent him into the worlds to do the sort of business she could not. Procurement, espionage, recruitment—that sort of thing. Of necessity, the chemical chains binding Lagganvor to Bosa were weaker than those she used on her normal crew. He had to be kept on a longer leash: permitted a degree of autonomy and independent thought." He made an explosive gesture with his hands. "One day, he broke those chains. He fled, with the full fury of Bosa on his back, but he thought he could stay one step ahead, and gradually change his identity. Unfortunately for him, he ran into me."

"And that makes you...who, exactly?" Lasling quizzed.

"My name is Brysca Rackamore. I had become an agent—a very effective one—and I believed the best way to reach Bosa was to catch a man like Lagganvor. Catch him, impersonate him, and set a trap. If I could allow myself to be retaken by Bosa, if I could survive any doubts about my disguise, I would be able to signal my masters, and have them close in."

"You thought you could fool Bosa Sennen?" Meggery asked, shaking her head as she spoke.

"You underestimate the lengths I was prepared to go to," he answered, before raising a hand to his cheeks. "Once I caught Lagganvor, I stole his face. There is a...technique. It's very unpleasant to both parties, so rarely employed voluntarily. Think of a sort of mask, with thousands of depressible spikes on the inner face. They puncture the skin, penetrate muscular tissue, and make a direct impression of the shape of the skull. The mask is then withdrawn and moved to the recipient, who first takes an osteomorphic drug that causes local softening of bony structure. As the mask is pressed into place, it forces the second face to conform to the contours of the first. The mask is withdrawn, the drug wears off, and the skull regains its normal rigidity. After a few days, with recuperative medicine, the covering tissue begins to heal."

Someone swallowed.

"And your eye?" Cossel asked.

"That was a simpler procedure. Lagganvor had been given the eye as a gift from Bosa. I took it, and the associated neural machinery. A surgeon was found who could be paid to do the

work, and just as crucially keep quiet about it. By that point...
shall we say that losing an eye was the least of Lagganvor's
difficulties?"

"What did you do to him?" Meggery asked.

"Things that will haunt me to my final breath." He smiled
thinly. "But they had to be done, and I regret none of it. I had
to squeeze him until he bled every one of Bosa's operational secrets. And then squeeze him again, to make sure he wasn't just
blurting out the first thing that came into his head. Whether it
worked, whether it was truly sufficient, I'll never know. By the
time I had taken his place—perfected the role, you might say—
Bosa Sennen was dead. I didn't know that at the time, though.
All I knew was that a ship very like her own had shown up at
Wheel Strizzardy, and that the captain of that ship wanted to
find Lagganvor. So I...offered myself up."

"Is this what happened?" Lasling asked Adrana.

She nodded humbly. "He fooled both of us. He knew the ship
as if he'd already been aboard it. He knew how to break into
Bosa's secret reservoir of quoins. There was no reason not to
think that he was Lagganvor."

"Adrana does herself too little credit," said the man who now
wished to be called Rackamore. "I think she saw through me
sooner than she realised. The ease with which I allowed myself
to be 'taken' by the Ness sisters, for instance. It was a misjudge-
ment on my part, but perhaps a forgivable one."

"I thought a little of it, but not enough," Adrana said. "My
error. Things changed when I caught him attempting to signal
his masters. I had two choices, then. I could disclose his true
identity to my sister and hope her retribution didn't tear half
the ship apart. Or I could accept that Lagganvor's communications were keeping us alive—we were being tracked and
followed, not attacked—and that therefore I had to keep *him*
alive, by protecting his nature from Fura, and permitting him to
continue signalling. I took that course."

"It was the right one," Rackamore said. "I was sincere in my
pledge. So long as I kept signalling my masters, they had no

need to attack. Eventually, I hoped to allow my masters to take the ship without very much bloodshed, with the sisters being spared."

"Spared just so they could go to the noose?" Cossel asked.

"No. I believed that when the evidence was laid out, with the ship taken intact, and the availability of numerous supporting accounts, the sisters' crimes could be explained away as the consequences of psychological damage, inflicted directly or indirectly by Bosa Sennen. They would have to answer to some part of what they had done, but not the worst of it. After some period of interrogation and detention, I believed the sisters could expect to be rehabilitated. None of it would be pleasant, but it would be a lot better than dying. I...was persuasive. Was I not, Adrana?"

"You were too persuasive," she answered. "I believed you, because you believed yourself. And I made the mistake of thinking your masters could be relied upon to act within the bounds of decency."

"Now you know otherwise," Lasling said.

"Now we all know," Adrana replied, nodding solemnly. "Now we have no illusions. They murdered Werranwell, and they'll murder again to protect their precious interests. There is no sanctuary for any of us now; not until something changes. And for Fura's sake I'll do all I can to make that happen."

"What about him?" Cossel asked, cocking her chin at Rackamore. "Are we meant to forget that he's working for the other side?"

"Was," Rackamore corrected. "That was another life, Cossel— a chapter I've just closed. I didn't have to tell you any of this, did I?"

Meggery scratched at one of her scars.

"So why did you?"

"Because I'd rather you knew the truth. Because if one of you should decide to punish me, at least we'll both understand why. Because I'm tired of wearing another man's name. Tired of wearing another man's face, imperfect as the disguise always was. Adrana saw through it soon enough, anyway. She saw my brother in me, even after the osteomorphic process had done its work."

"Your brother was a man of honour," Adrana said.

Rackamore met her eyes with a mixture of sadness and fondness. Sadness for what had been lost, and could never be recovered, and fondness for the good memories he still treasured.

"He was."

"He loved this little bubble of life we have around the Old Sun. He loved the worlds and dedicated his life to the idea of their preservation."

"In his modest way."

"From this point on, you'll be carrying that name as an outlaw. They'll paint you as an enemy of civilisation, not its defender. A vandal and a wrecker. They'll make you out to be everything your brother never was."

"But at the end of it all," Rackamore said, "no matter where it takes me, I would know I had done the right thing. My brother would have expected no more or less from me, and I would have expected no more or less from Pol. I cannot bring Illyria back, or her father, but in joining you, in renouncing all that I was, I believe I can still repair some of the harm I did to him." He looked down, as if the weight of attention on him was suddenly more than he could bear. "In my own sullied conscience, at least."

"That," Lasling said, with the air of a man who had chosen to speak for his fellows, "is about as much as any of us can hope for. You were right, Captain Ness: we needed to hear his story."

"And now?" she asked.

"If everyone else is agreeable, I believe we may put the sorry business of Mister Lagganvor behind us. And Mister Rackamore?"

He looked up, caught—it seemed to Adrana—between hopefulness and some terrible fear that this might yet be a trap. "Mister Las?"

"I should like to hear more of your brother's exploits, when you have the time. It seems he was a good captain; a man it would have been worth the trouble to know."

"He was," Adrana affirmed. "He was kind to us; kind to all his crew, I think. And Brysca? I think it must have meant something that he kept that book you gave him."

"He erased the dedication."

"He kept the book. A man with one of the best libraries to be found on any ship, a man who had the wherewithal to buy or sell any book he chose—yet he always kept that one, and kept it close to him. I think you were forgiven long ago."

*

During the ten minutes that it took Tindouf to go outside and collect what *could* be collected, the squadron maintained its firing action against *Revenger*. Nothing had yet hit the hull, and by the indications in the strain-gauges of the sail-control, which Paladin read as tickles and twitches in his own extended nervous system, the nearest piece of damage (save whatever had hit Prozor) was still a league out from the ship's vital centre, and no real impediment to their continued manoeuvrability. Should the attack continue at its present rate, though, mere attrition would eventually cripple them, for catchcloth was no less vulnerable to slug-shot than ordinary sail, and certainly no more durable. Of far greater concern to Fura was the fact that the shots were now coming in with too much precision to be the result of a few lucky hits while the enemies' guns swept the general area of space given away by her squawk.

They must have seen something in their scopes, Fura supposed: enough to confirm that they had approximately the right coordinates. It needn't have been much. There was ordinary sail bound up in the rigging, multitudinous square leagues of it, part of the disguise they had to wear to pass muster as an innocent ship, and if some fraction of that ordinary sail had thrown a flash back at the enemy, that would have been sufficient for a team of well-coordinated gun crews. Perhaps they had seen a porthole's light, or the reflected gleam from some part of the hull that (unavoidably) was not so dark as the rest. Or perhaps some stray light from the telegraphic box, as Prozor went out to signal the *Merry Mare*. That action had been well-meant, but there was no kind deed in the universe that could not have an undesired consequence.

She used that ten minutes profitably. Paladin had a chance to refine his calculations, and Fura finally conceded that it was time to relieve Surt from sighting duties. It was Ruther's turn to go up there now, and he was willing enough, especially as word filtered through about what had happened to Prozor, for he had come to consider her as much a colleague as his old friends on the *Merry Mare*. But Fura was almost minded not to allow him.

"I won't deny that I could use a pair of fresh young eyes up there," she said, laying a hand on his shoulder. "But you should understand that it's nearly as dangerous up in that little glass bubble as it is being outside."

Ruther rubbed at the side of his face, as if he could still feel it being drawn into the mask of Stallis. "When we start giving them back some of what they've already given us, you'll want to know about sail-flash, won't you?"

"I'd settle for a nice clean explosion as we take one of 'em out completely. You won't see anything at all when we're shooting, though: the sails will block your line of sight just as thoroughly as they screen our muzzle flashes from the enemy. But when we stop firing, and begin to turn away, you'll have your chance. Sail-flash, fire, overloaded muzzles—anything you can give me. They've taken from both of us, Ruther—help me make them pay."

"I'm sorry about Prozor," Ruther said.

She nodded sombrely. "I know. So am I. But Stallis will be sorrier, mark my words."

"Do you mean to kill him?"

Fura thought about her answer, and the promise she had made to herself.

"Eventually."

She helped him into the sighting room, then watched as he

pumped the hydraulic lever to propel the room into its duty position. Surt was cold and exhausted, her eyes red with rubbing, her fingertips nearly blue. Fura wrapped her in a blanket, then made her drink something warm.

"In any fair service, you'd be due a period of rest about now. But I'm afraid I need your help checking the lagging on the gun-coolers. We'll be running 'em as hot as they can take it, and it'll be better for all our nerves if they don't start springing too many leaks."

Surt eyed her warily.

"Proz ain't come back in, has she."

"No," Fura said, surprising herself with her own bluntness. "They killed her—either a slug, or some part of our damaged rigging doing it for 'em. Tindouf's gone out now to fetch her back in." She was speaking calmly, matter-of-factly, about the death of a woman who had saved her life and become both friend and mentor, as well as the closest thing she had to an external conscience. There was, as yet, only a void where the shock and grief would soon take residence. She ought to have been appalled at her own coldness; numbed by how easily she was still functioning, with this vital part of her new life ripped cleanly away. Yet if she owed Prozor anything—and she owed her for many more things than she could begin to enumerate—it was to hold fast, to keep her nerve, and to do what needed to be done in this moment, for the sake of her ship and crew, for the sake of that hull-bound microcosmos that had always meant more to Prozor than all the worlds of the Congregation. Hold fast, and function, and give them a chance to avenge this death. And then—and only then—begin to let the emotions flood home. They would come, soon enough. "We'll make them pay, Surt," she said quietly, as if it was a sacred and solemn pledge.

"If you don't," Surt said, "I will."

Something came over the speaker grille then. It sounded like a moan of wind, some breeze stirred between one part of the ship and the other. But in it was the whisper of a word, perhaps two, perhaps several.

Gone Ghostie. Gone Ghostie gubbins.

Neither Surt nor Fura were in any rush to acknowledge what they had heard, busying themselves with a hasty inspection of the cooling circuits: knocking wrenches against pipes, tapping pressure gauges until the dials twitched, listening for anything that was loose or dull-sounding, tightening bolts and brackets, and making sure all the lagging was as secure as it could be. It was good to make these sounds: they squeezed out any memory of the words they might or might not have heard over the intercom.

The pipes were cold now, but once the guns started running they would be working hard to dissipate excess heat from the induction solenoids, and the slightest leak would mean both a scalding spray of superheated steam into the cabin spaces and a loss of gun-cooling efficiency. The system was hardly in a state of neglectful disrepair—they had kept it well-maintained since the last action—but there was never a day when something did not need adjustment, and this last-minute check was prudent.

Nothing was seriously amiss. The coil-guns were loaded and energised, and all swivelling freely on their gimbals. Paladin fired a single test-shot from each muzzle, directed away from the enemy so there wasn't the slightest chance of detection, and then confirmed that all the guns and sail-control devices were under his authority and he was ready to make the turn.

Fura was on her way back to the control room, ready to give the final order, when a single loud *clang* sounded, and the entire ship shook. It was almost as if one of the coil-guns had gone off again, with the same recoil felt through the hull, but the timbre was not quite the same, nor the violence of the shaking. Fura stilled and tensed, waiting for the lungstuff to be sucked from her body, for she knew that they had been hit, and properly so. Only metal on metal, slug against hull, could account for that tooth-loosening din.

A second passed, and another, and she remained alive and breathing. There had been no pressure drop and the ship had not broken apart around her.

"A glancing shot, I believe," Paladin said, when she reached the control room. "The slug must have gone through our sails, lost the greater portion of its momentum, and been deflected against us."

"Has it hurt us?"

"Nothing that I can detect."

She opened the short-range squawk. "Tindouf—are you safe?"

"I's just back in the lock, Miss Ness." Tindouf was breathing heavily, barely able to get the words out. "I saw a flash just as I was closing the door, and thoughts, that's the living end of me and my noggin, but we don'ts seem to have been too badly hit, does we?"

"We got off lightly this time, but if they saw that flash they'll have an even better idea of our position. There isn't time to lose. I'm starting our turn, and we'll send a full volley the moment we have that covering screen."

"Very good, Miss Ness. I'll get out of my suit and keep an eye on the winches and ions."

"Thank you, Tindouf." She grimaced to herself. "I meant to ask— did you find Prozor?"

"I founds her, yes. And I think it best she stays in the lateral lock for the time being, until we're done with this bit of business."

"I'll attend to her, Tindouf—you've done more than enough."

"Begging my pardon, Miss Ness, but I'll be the one to attend to her, if you don'ts mind. There are things a captain should do, and things a captain shouldn't have to, and this is one of them latter thingses."

She nodded, closing the squawk, and thinking that she knew better than to argue with Tindouf.

"Doctor Eddralder, Merrix," she said on the general intercom. "Continue your search if you will, but be aware that we are about to turn, and there will be a load on the ship. Ruther, Surt: be ready."

"Is it time?" Paladin asked.

She eyed the silent intercom, daring it to whisper back at her.

"It's time. Bring us round."

22

As the launch slipped away from the *Merry Mare*, the emptiness in her head felt as cold and definite as a missing tooth. It was good to have something else to think about, beyond the implications of that absence. Adrana pressed her hands to the controls, finding no difficulty in adjusting to them even though they varied in layout to the launch on *Revenger*, and the craft as a whole had somewhat different handling characteristics, being markedly sluggish in turns and having a tendency to yaw when under direct thrust. On a longer voyage she might have taken the time to address the motor trim, but this was an extremely short crossing and no such nicety was warranted. The *Merry Mare* was holding station at ten leagues, just one of several sunjammers parked within easy reach of the trailing hub. A person could *walk* ten leagues. It was hardly worth the trouble of buckling in.

She had anyway, and Rackamore was buckled into the seat behind her; the Clacker's box was wedged into the adjacent position and well-secured against bumps and vibrations. Adrana had no idea whether such disturbances might affect the continued functioning of the effector-displacer device, and had no inclination to take an unnecessary chance. Behind Rackamore was Meggery, and that was the extent of their little expedition. Lasling, Vouga and Cossel remained on the main ship, and while she meant for them all to have some time in Trevenza, her foremost consideration was the delivery of Tazaknakak. Once that was behind her and there was no longer any need to smuggle him through customs—the part she was most dreading—the launch could come and go as needed. It would not exactly be a question of Adrana relaxing—that was impossible so long as Fura's safety was in doubt—but she would at least have one less concern to trouble her.

"This Hasper Quell," Rackamore said, leaning against his restraints. "Tell me a little about the gentleman."

Adrana glanced around, although she dared not take her eyes off the nearing world for more than a moment. "All I know of him is what I got from Fura's account. He was known to Prozor—some cove she'd done useful business with in the past. They took a tram to his place: an underground establishment called Quell's Bar. I can't say if that's the official name or not."

"If it has been around for more than a few months, it shouldn't be hard to find. And of Quell himself?"

"Described as a big man, dressed well. There was something about his eyes, too: I think they were artificial, but not nearly so neat and clever as your own."

"Can you give me a little bit more to go on?"

"I wish I had the *True and Accurate Testimony* to hand. I think she said his eyes stuck out of his face." Adrana nodded to herself. "Yes, like chimneys. Two chimneys jutting out from his face. The Crawlies had done it to him—he'd gone to them for their medicine."

"Sounds as if he oughtn't to be too hard to flush out," Meggery said.

"We'll take no chances," Rackamore said. "Once we're safely inside, I'll scope out this Quell. There's an advantage in neither of us having met before; I'll be able to get a sense of the fellow before there's any hint of Ness sisters or Clackers entering the equation. If I am satisfied, I'll call you in and we'll proceed with the handover."

"Any guarantee that I'm getting anything out of this?" Adrana asked.

"As things stand momentarily, none whatsoever. Equally, your only hope of any sort of recompense lies in the delivery of the Clacker. It's a pity we can't cut him into pieces and offer up one part as a down-payment."

The proximity sweeper pinged to alert her to a rapidly closing approach with the spindleworld's hub. Adrana touched the retro-jets and brought the launch's speed down to five hundred spans per second. Traffic was thickening all around them now, with other rocket launches criss-crossing their path, exhaust plumes chalking hazy, blurring banners in the vacuum. There were sunjammers parked very close in, too, and not all of them had hauled in the entire mass of their sail, so—without the slightest qualm or compunction since everyone else was doing it—Adrana steered through the gaps in the rigging, not minding at all if her jets made the sails flutter and billow with her passing, for that was the price these captains had accepted by berthing so near to Trevenza as to barely need launches at all. Some of them, indeed, were docked up next to long, flexible passageways; tunnels that were leagues-long, yet could be traversed without a suit, while others were content to have their crews put on vacuum gear and hop from ship to world and back again. Some of these daring parties went about it alone, while others were roped together for safety, like garlands of tiny brass-coloured starfish. They often had their belongings with them, too. Once, Adrana had to steer hard as some preposterous mass of personal effects, detached from its owner, came tumbling hard at them: a huge string-bound agglomeration of cases, trunks, packing crates and wicker baskets, flapping its numerous luggage labels as if they were the attenuated remnants of wings.

They were through the worst of it by then, and down to a hundred spans per second. Adrana had seen the true shape of the spindleworld through telescopes, and then with her own eyes as they were closer in, but now that they were near to its tapering extremity the form of the world was distorted by perspective to an alarming degree. Giddiness washed over her. It seemed as if they had become a bird, circling the pinnacle of some enormous spire. Its height alone would have been dizzying, but to add to her discomfort the entire soaring structure was rotating as if on a spit, and the launch was obliged to match its course to that spin.

Yet it was not so difficult to land as she had feared, and bristling out from the tapering end were numerous platforms and berths, with ships of all kinds already docked. Because she had come down as close to the axis of rotation as was feasible, there was almost no sensation of gravity and it was an easy matter both to secure the launch and complete their disembarkation.

The three of them, and their luggage—which of course included the Clacker—moved into the pressurised part of the docks, where any semblance of order and process had been substituted for a free-floating riot of colour and confusion. There were crews, officials, lackeys and general layabouts everywhere Adrana looked. Remarkably, everyone seemed to know their allotted role in the chaos. The docks—this particular part, anyway—was a thimble-shaped enclosure very near to the end of the spindleworld. It had two main circular walls, one smaller than the other, and linking them was a single curving surface that corresponded to the spindleworld's outer shell. Partially filling this space was a sort of spidering treehouse made up of interconnected platforms linked by flimsy ladders, bridges, aerial tunnels and even flimsier ropeways. The platforms contained booths, offices, merchant stores, modest warehouses, bars, places of temporary detention and so on, all serving a weightless and none-too-fussy clientele and therefore constructed with minimal regard for any sensible frame of reference. Draped around this ramshackle framework was a prodigious mass of lightvine, emitting its own glow and augmented by the gaudier hues of neon advertising and many large flickerbox screens tuned to rolling news.

It was possible to float through the chamber, as many of those present were doing, hauling their luggage behind them as they paddled, flapped specially-woven coat-sleeves, or pulled themselves along by rope. There were even some quite bulky items of cargo being carefully steered through the treehouse's larger gaps, with rough-voiced stewards barking orders at every turn. Adrana took her party the long way around, using the aerial bridges and tunnels, for (given the several collisions she had already observed) this seemed the course least likely to risk jolting the Clacker.

"Look," Rackamore said, touching her sleeve as they passed one of the flickerboxes.

"I do not wish to look."

"You should. It's what any half-inquisitive captain would be doing right now, if she didn't have a personal stake in the matter." Rackamore nodded past her, in the vague direction of a gambling den built on one of the platforms. "Right now, every other wager being laid down in that place will concern the outcome of that battle."

"You expect me to bet on my own sister's life?"

"No...although I'd insist if I felt our lives depended on it. But to not take even a passing interest in that news—that's the sort of thing that *will* mark you out as odd. And believe me, there will be eyes in here paying attention."

She half-scowled—they were wearing their normal clothes, so there was nothing to mask her expression—but she forced her attention to the flickerbox and lingered for the time it took to absorb the news. The coverage was showing a pattern of flashes in a patch of space; the same loop of film playing over and over, a tickertape playing beneath it:

++ *major explosions seen near space engagement* ++ *unconfirmed reports of fugitive ship destroyed by Revenue Protection Squadron* ++ *awaiting word on identity and registration of destroyed craft* ++ *unofficial accounts strongly suggest demise of Bosa Sennen and her accomplices the Ness sisters* ++ *banks report modest rise in market confidence following presumed success of counter-piracy effort* ++

"They're wrong about one Ness sister," Meggery said, pressing in close enough to whisper. "Seems to me there's a fair chance they're wrong about both."

"They are," Adrana said. But merely saying it was not enough. It brought no deeper reassurance to her, and she noticed that Rackamore was in no rush to offer false consolation of his own. He knew, as she did, that the report might well be accurate. There was just no way to tell.

They pressed on, shepherding the Clacker's case between them, and treating it neither so cautiously as to draw attention, nor so incautiously as to risk jeopardising the contents. At the wider end of the chamber was a wide, smoky door, big enough for cargo to pass through, and as they worked their way nearer to it, glimpsing a distant vista of scuttling trams and dusty streets, so Adrana realised that it led directly into the greater interior of Trevenza Reach, and no additional customs or immigration formality lay between them and freedom. It was all so lackadaisical, yet—she reminded herself—precisely in keeping with the supposed spirit of the place, which did not consider itself bound by the laws and practices of other worlds.

They traversed a ladder, then a bridge, then a threadbare tunnel made out of ropes and stiffened hoops, and she passed another dozen flickerboxes on the way, and to each she gave due attention, neither too little nor too much, and swallowed back the emotions that were welling high in her throat, for they would have to wait.

"We are nearly there, Brysca."

"Indeed we are. But I would not raise a celebratory glass until we are a good league into the place, and even then I should—"

"This way, if you please."

It was a uniformed official, a man with a starched cap and mutton-chop whiskers, directing them to join a line of incomers threading along a bridge and into one of the offices.

"Why us, sir?" Adrana asked.

"Because it ain't your lucky day, Captain. Go along and play nicely and you'll be out and through before you know it.

'Less you've got something about you that you ought to have declared?"

"We haven't," she said firmly.

"I believe we should oblige the gentleman," Rackamore said.

"I believe you should, sir," the official replied, before lifting a whistle to his lips, blowing hard into it and gesticulating wildly at some commotion going on a third of the way across the chamber. "The other way around, you dolts! The other way around!"

Adrana, Rackamore and Meggery joined the line. It moved quite quickly, passing through one door in the office and out the other side. From what she could see, those leaving were free to continue through the large door and out into the spindleworld. The office was easily large enough to contain several detention rooms, however, so there was a good chance that some of the incomers were being pulled aside and examined more closely.

The Clacker's box would only withstand a cursory inspection if it were opened.

"I don't like it," she whispered. "Someone's got word of us."

"If they had word of us," Rackamore answered placidly, "we would have been interdicted long before we docked. This is just some random inspection process. Remain calm, remember our story, and we shall have no difficulty."

"He seems relaxed," Meggery said.

"I am, dear Meggery—as are you. As are we all, for we have nothing to hide, and nothing to be irritated about except the extremely minor inconvenience of being slightly delayed."

Adrana was the one now holding the Clacker's box. She could manage it easily enough on her own in weightlessness, but there was no escaping the fact that it felt ponderous. The effector-displacer mechanism was able to conceal the contents of the box quite effectively—at least when it functioned properly—but there was nothing it could do about the mass of the Clacker. The box felt like exactly what it was: a suitcase-sized container with a child-sized creature stuffed into it.

They passed into the office. The set-up inside was simple. The line of passengers divided into two, and on either side the incomers were being asked to show their credentials and present their luggage for inspection. Inspectors were flicking through documents and rummaging through open cases. It was all going on in near-weightlessness, and a general impression of barely-contained chaos was the order of the day. Papers fluttered loose; the contents of trunks spilled out in ragged and occasionally pungent profusion. Further along the office documents were being grudgingly re-stamped; goods were being rudely stuffed back into cases and baskets. Only once in a while was anyone ushered into one of the side rooms.

They were finished if that happened, Adrana knew. They had their stories and their faked-up paperwork, but none of it was pressure-tight. She could lie and lie about her dead father, the beloved Werranwell, but if someone went to the trouble of finding a photograph or engraving of the Ness sisters, she was as good as hanged.

"Next."

A magnetic table had been arranged for the examination of personal effects. Rackamore and Meggery had some small items of luggage of their own. Adrana lofted the case onto the table, yet made no motion to open it until it was demanded of her. She did so in the full and certain expectation that the effector-displacer was bound to have failed, yet at the same time maintaining a steely and indifferent composure.

The catches sprung open. The lid hinged back.

The case was empty.

"Forgotten something, have you?" The questioner was a woman who looked as if she had been born with a suspicious, peevish look about her.

"No," Adrana said.

"Then why is this case empty? Who travels with an empty case?"

Adrana shrugged off the question.

"What she means to say," Meggery said, leaning in, "is that it's empty for a reason. It's so we can go shopping. We've got a shopping list, see."

"She doesn't need to see that," Rackamore said.

Meggery had her sheet out anyway. "It's all here. Suit parts, mostly. Return-valves, sealant tar, two standard-fitting neck rings, a set of accordion joints…a jumble of things, really, and it'll all fit back into this case. And then we'll be out of here, and you'll have our lovely quoins sitting in your treasury."

"I hope you brought sufficient funds," the inspector observed. "You'll be surprised what your quoins won't buy you lately."

"That's our problem, isn't it," Adrana said.

"You've got a manner about you, Captain…." The inspector peered at one of her papers "Werranwell. Are you the ones who wanted to bring a body with you?"

"That's us," Rackamore said earnestly.

"Then where is the body?"

"Still on our ship, pending some enquiries that we will be making as soon as we've procured these items. But thank you for taking such an interest in our captain's sad and burdensome responsibility with respect to her dear father, whom we all held in such excellent esteem."

The inspector budged the case against the magnetic surface. "This feels very solid—very heavy for what it is."

"It's a good case," Adrana said.

"Her father wasn't one to skimp," Rackamore offered. "He always did like his luggage…on the solid and reliable side."

The inspector fingered the case's side, gauging its thickness. Perhaps she thought there might be contraband packed into hidden compartments in the side. She glanced over to one of her colleagues. "Tendry, come and look at this…."

The interior flickered. It was there for an instant: the Clacker's hibernation box. Adrana would have gladly accepted that she had imagined the apparition, except that she knew full well that it was real. Did the inspector catch a glimpse of it out of the corner of her eye? She turned back with some deepening suspicion on her face, as if she had taken off one mask and slipped on another, more exaggeratedly fashioned one. "I thought…." she began.

"It's empty," Adrana said. "Empty and waiting to be filled with expensive things." She bit on her lip. "Look, I'm sorry if my tone was a little abrupt—I know you have a job to do. But I'm churned up by what my father asked of me, and I just want to get this shopping out of the way so that I can move onto *that* business. Believe me it's not something I look forward to."

The other inspector, Tendry, had come over to the table. "Are these the ones who got shot at, Pilliar?"

"There was something about a crew wanting to bury their captain, and something else about a ship getting in the way of that squadron—whether it's the same one, I couldn't say."

"It is us," Rackamore said, sighing heavily. "We were hit—very badly. That's why we're in such straits now. We've lost our captain; our ship's mangled, and we need basic provisions just to begin repairing it. We're lucky in other regards, though."

Pilliar looked doubtful. "You call that luck?"

"I do, ma'am, compared to what's being done to that ship out there. We've all seen the flickerboxes—difficult to miss 'em. And I don't care what the official line is, or what the banks say about rising consumer confidence. That's butchery, plain and simple."

"Siding with pirates now, are you?"

Adrana waved her hand into the interior to emphasise how empty the case was. "He isn't. My father hated bauble-jumpers and the like, and I can tell you he had no love for Bosa Sennen and still less for anyone foolish to get swept up in her glamour. I despise those...what are they?"

"Ness sisters," Rackamore said.

"Them. Yes, they can hang for all I care. But if we were attacked as an innocent party, then I shouldn't be at all surprised if that other ship were just as innocent. I pity them, frankly, and if there is to be no justice for them than I shall at least strive to do right by my crew, who have been very grievously wronged."

The box flickered once. There was a shock of cold, a moment of clean severance. She lifted her hand from the interior, unhurriedly, and closed her fingers. Pilliar and Tendry were both still looking her in the eyes.

"We abide by Inter-Congregational law, Captain Werranwell," Pilliar said sternly. "We are no lawless outpost; no anarchic freehold. That said..."

"If a crime has been committed," Tendry said, "and restitution needs to be made—"

"You may go about your affairs," Pilliar said, finishing for him. She closed the case, even going so far as to do up the latches. "I do agree with you about those Ness sisters, for what it's worth. Except in one regard."

"Which would be?" Adrana asked, fighting to keep the edge from her voice.

"Hanging's too good for them. Too quick, too kind, by far."

Adrana nodded dutifully. She was pressing her fingers into her palm and trying hard not to shake. "I'm sure something will be arranged."

*

Revenger started turning. It was not the gentle sort of course change that could be effected by modest alterations in the dispositions of individual sails, playing out over hours or even days, as a ship bent its course from one trajectory to another, within the limits of wind, momentum and orbital mechanics. This was a sudden and violent swinging around of the ship and its mass of sail, and it could only be initiated by a pulse of thrust from the hull, sent out at right angles to the vector between the centre of mass of the ship and the centre of area of its spread of sail. The ions were too feeble by far for such an operation: they would have needed hours to build up enough effect, and Fura could not wait that long. That left rockets, of one variety or another. There were some small steering jets fixed to the hull of *Revenger*, rarely used, but dependable, and powerful motors in the launch, and either of these would have provided the necessary impetus. But there was much too great a risk of their exhaust plumes being seen, counter to the entire point of the operation, so Fura arranged for the port-side lateral lock to be over-pressurised and then blown out in one sudden expulsion of lungstuff. It was wasteful of that resource, but they had ample reserves and slow suffocation was, she had to admit, something of a secondary concern compared to being shot out of space.

The lungstuff blew out in a silent and mostly invisible gasp, and that was all *Revenger* needed. The shove was the closest thing to gravity that the ship had experienced since rounding the swallower on their run to Wheel Strizzardy, and the momentary effects were not dissimilar. Fura had to grab onto furniture to stop herself being dashed against the cabin wall, and anything that had not been secured—and there was always something—went skittering sideways.

Then the shove was over and they were turning at a constant velocity. But the pull toward the cabin wall remained, and now there was a very definite sense of up and down, and one that was perpendicular to the usual axis of drift caused by the feeble acceleration of the normal sails and ion-thrust. It would have needed some getting used to, except that Fura had no intention of this being anything other than a temporary condition.

"Are we turning to plan, Paladin?"

"We are turning to plan, Miss Ness."

They were whipping around now, like two stones on either end of a taut line of rope. One end was the hull; the other— many leagues distant—was the sails. They massed much less than the ship and its contents, but their cumulative mass was not insignificant, in total, and they had a counterbalancing influence, maintaining the tension on the rigging as their black surfaces were turned away from the main force of the Old Sun's invisible wind. Paladin had to adjust the rigging almost constantly, so that the sails were not blown into the ship—which would have resulted in irrevocable tangling chaos—but he had rehearsed the steps a million times in his mind, allowing for every possible vagary, and nothing happened that was beyond his capabilities of rapid adjustment and improvisation.

Despite the violence of that initial kick, they were still turning slowly; only twice the speed of a clock's minute hand. In

336 • Alastair Reynolds

half an hour, if they took no other action, they would be back facing in the same direction. In ten minutes, they would have the necessary cover for the coil-guns, and for another ten minutes beyond that point they could maintain as high a rate of fire as the guns could tolerate. Then the muzzles would be straining beyond their maximum deflection angles, and they would need to wait twenty minutes before starting the next volley.

There was no respite in that ten minutes. Shots from the other ships were tearing through the outer margins of their sails, and sometimes closer, and more than once another loose slug found its way to the hull, ricocheting harmlessly but serving as a forceful reminder of the damage that would be done if one of those shots came in straight and hard. Fura only took encouragement from this continuing attack, though. She would have found it very disheartening to be shown sudden clemency at this late stage, for she had none in herself to offer by way of reciprocation.

That ten minutes was as long as any she had endured. There were only so many times she could call Ruther and demand a report from the sighting room; only so many times she could ask Surt to confirm that no fresh leaks had sprung in the cooling circuits. Tindouf had left Prozor's remains in the main lock and was now assisting Paladin, dashing between sail-control stations and giving verbal reports on the strain-gauges and deflection dials, so that Paladin was not entirely reliant on his own instrumentation. Eddralder and Merrix, meanwhile, were still searching the ship, a task made no easier by the centrifugal effects of their turn, which rendered every space subtly unfamiliar. When the ten minutes were nearly up, and the guns ready, Fura requested that the physician and his daughter retire to the Kindness Room.

It was about to get noisy.

Revenger had two independent batteries of coil-guns dispersed along her port and starboard flanks, and while both could be fired at the same time, that was not desirable in the current situation due to the aiming constraints. It was better to optimise for one set of guns on one sweep, then twist the hull like a spindle for the second, twenty minutes later, and continue to alternate for as long as they maintained their turning motion. They could still do some damage with just one of those batteries, and since the cooling circuit could be dedicated in its entirety to one flank, rather than having to tend to both batteries, the cyclic fire rate could be increased.

"Miss Arafura?" Paladin said.

"Yes?"

"We are in position. I considered it wise that you should give the final order, just in case there are second thoughts."

"Are they still shooting at us?"

"Indeed they are."

"Then I have no second thoughts. Rip 'em open, Paladin. Maximum fire, and keep at it until we hit something. Then concentrate everything we've got on that one target until it bleeds." She paused, flexed her three-fingered metal hand. "I want blood."

"In which case... I shall endeavour to provide."

The grille whispered:

Spikey-spikey! Mash their noggins! Gubbins're coming! Gubbinsy-gubbinsy!

Before Fura could dwell on that—and wonder if Paladin detected it as well—the coil-guns went off. It was a beautiful, horrible sound, and for a moment or two it purged her mind of any shivery business. One muzzle, then the next, down the line in quick succession, like a loud receding drumroll. By the time the last gun sounded, the first one had been recharged and was ready to fire. The solenoids hummed and crackled. The coolant pumps sang at a higher and higher pitch as they worked to ferry rising heat from the guns. The cooling pipes creaked and clanged as they expanded against their stays. The guns swivelled slightly between rounds, compensating for *Revenger*'s angular motion. The automatic breech-loaders whirred and clunked, transferring the slugs from their snail-shell-shaped magazines into the warming bellies of the guns, where the induction coils were already glowing stove-hot.

Even at their present rate of fire, the guns were in no danger of exhausting the magazines. The slugs were thick, blunt-ended pencils of dense metal the size of a truncheon, and a single crate could hold hundreds. Bosa Sennen might have run light on fuel, and trusted her luck to one failing skull, but she had not skimped in the matter of slugs. There were still enough crates in the gun room stores to wage a small Inter-Congregational war.

The guns drummed and drummed, falling into a sort of lulling rhythm, and then quite abruptly stopped, and with a jolt Fura realised it was because they had reached the limit of their aiming-stops, and that the ten minutes was up. The pumps kept screaming, the pipes grumbling, but for every second that now passed the muzzles were getting cooler.

"Ruther, the sails should be clearing your line o' sight in the next couple of minutes. Surt, Tindouf: meet me by the magazines."

They went from gun to gun, unpacking slugs from sawdust-filled crates, feeding the slugs into the letterbox-shaped slots in the magazines, until each was ready for the next volley. The guns breathed heat into their faces, spit boiled off their back-plates, and to touch any part of them was to risk an immediate blister. The smell of burning insulation and hot oil was enough to sting nose, throat and eyes. Surt coughed, wafting the worst of it away. Tindouf wrapped a rag around his fist and tightened a nut on one of the cooling pipes, where it plunged right into the gun's deepest vitals.

It took twenty minutes for *Revenger* to bring the opposing coil-guns to bear, and in all that time Ruther saw no indication that any of their shots had found a mark. Then the guns were roaring again, and the sails blocking his view, and it was all Fura could do to wait, and trust that her gambit had not been in error.

The volley proceeded. The guns performed as they were meant to, except for one magazine that jammed three minutes into the volley. Tindouf removed the service cover, jabbed the end of one of his clay pipes into the workings, and the magazine chugged back into life. A cooling line ruptured near the aft pair of guns, but Surt had been keeping an eye on a spitting joint and she managed to fix the leak before the guns began to over-heat too badly. The price for that was a badly scalded wrist, already blistering by the time Fura dispatched her to the Kindness Room.

The volley ended. Fura and Tindouf stuffed the magazines full again, Fura snatching back her flesh hand just as a rat sprang out of one of the slug crates. She caught the creature in her metal fingers and broke its back in a single squeeze, as thoughtlessly as if she were crushing a ball of waste paper.

"Captain?"

She was still holding the rat. "Go ahead, Ruther."

"The sails are moving out of my field of view. I thought you should know... what I mean is, I wouldn't be so quick to report this if we weren't in an engagement, but..."

"Spit it out, boy."

"Sail-flash, Captain. I think I see sail-flash. Multiple, dishtributed... it *is* faint but I don't believe I'm imagining it."

"I don't believe you're imagining it either." She flashed a grin at Tindouf, who was sucking on his unlit pipe, watching thoughtfully. "Can you give Paladin a set of coordinates, so we can concentrate fire on the next pass?"

"I can, Captain. Mishter Paladin: are you lishening?"

"I am always listening."

"Here are the numbers."

Fura tossed the rat back into the crate, where it twitched once and died.

23

Meggery stopped her when they were about a tenth of a league from the docks. They had come through the exit door in near-weightlessness, but in following one of the roads that radiated away from the hub, they had been moving further and further from the axis of rotation, and therefore into a slowly rising centrifugal influence. As their sense of weight gradually increased, so the Clacker's case began to need two of them to handle it. Now it was just about practical to walk, and the trees that lined the road were growing up from their bases with a definite sense of purpose and direction, rather than sprawling wildly like the lightvine in the first chamber. Buildings, too, were starting to conform to normal notions of architecture and function. They were quite low here, pressing in either side of the road, and consisted of a succession of fleapit hotels and bordellos, with the odd bar or bail-bond seller thrown in for good measure. Further on down the road, where it meandered into a thickening haze of dirt and dust, the buildings grew taller, more variegated, and merged into a seemingly impenetrable mass. Since they were at a higher vantage, they could see over a descending terrace of rooftops and gardens, all the way to little swatches of green and the glittering splashes of civic ponds and waterways, all the way to the widest point of the world and the gradual climb back up to the opposing pole, the better part of ten leagues away.

With clockwork regularity a radiance rose and fell across any given part of the interior. It was lulling and annoying in equal measure. The Old Sun's light streamed in through the long window panels that happened to be facing the right way at that moment, casting a dusky glow on the opposite part of the interior, but since the world was turning, it was not long before the pattern of light and shade shifted by one whole window's worth, and an area of city that had been illuminated a minute earlier now fell into shade. To counteract that effect, however imperfectly, a string of blue lights had been suspended the entire length of the spindleworld. They must have been some relic technology, for although the individual lights were bright—easily as luminous as a light-imp, and yet emitting a persistent flux—there were not nearly enough of them to be truly effective, and there were gaps in the string where lights must once have burned, yet had now failed or been stolen.

It was, despite these deficits of illumination, a stirring vista. Adrana had never seen a tract of concentrated civilisation to compare with it. Not even the layered cities of Mulgracen could match Trevenza Reach, for although there might have been more surface area inside Mulgracen, it was divided across many shells, and no comparable part of it had been visible at any one time.

And it was old. That was obvious at a glimpse. There were colourings and textures to the city, markers of fashion, industry and relative prosperity. She could see where districts had lapped over each other like competing tides, time and again. She could see where they had merged; where they had been cut off, isolated, orphaned. She could see where roads had been diverted, re-diverted, wound around each other or woven over and under each other like carpet strands, and she could see that these were processes that had been going on for lifetimes, for centuries, perhaps for as long as any Occupation; perhaps longer still. It was an old, old place, and it had seen countless travellers like herself, and not one atom of Trevenza Reach was in the least part interested in the story she had to tell. It had enough of its own; it would always have enough of its own.

It was nearly sufficient to take her mind off her finger.

"Show me," Meggery said.

In the shade of a tram stop Adrana unwound her fist. The top two joints of her little finger, on her right hand, were missing. The finger had been snipped off, transmitted somewhere, destroyed, in the instant that the effector-displacement device failed.

"There does not seem to be bleeding," Rackamore said.

Adrana stared down at the bloodless stub that had been her little finger. The skin around the stump had a frosted blue tinge. "The cold—whatever it was—stopped it."

"Can you bear the pain?" Meggery asked.

Adrana looked at her.

"Could you?"

Meggery did not answer for a moment. Then she opened her own hand and tugged off the metal finger she had been wearing since Fura's first negotiation with her crew. It was attached to her hand by a thin strap, which she quickly worked loose.

"I took this from your sister. You might want to wear it until Eddralder or some other physician can address that wound."

Adrana took the metal finger. She slipped its open end over the stub, protecting it. Meggery helped her redo the strap, until the metal finger was secure.

"You did well, not to cry out," Rackamore said. "I did not see it in your face at all. I did not even realise anything had happened until Meggery said something."

A tram was approaching. It would take them much further into Trevenza Reach. Adrana stooped down to gather the Clacker's case, and she said nothing.

*

"Spikey-spikey," Fura whispered to herself, in the instant when she claimed the first kill of the engagement. There had been no warning of what was to come, no intimation that one of her slugs was about to find its mark, or with such demonstrable effectiveness.

A number of the slugs in the magazine had explosive or incendiary tips, but the majority relied on nothing more than kinetic energy to do their work. There was a chance of one of those slugs puncturing a hull, regardless of armour, and once inside what remained of that kinetic energy—some larger or smaller fraction—would expend itself on the crew and the instruments they needed for navigation and survival. Even with pressure-tight compartments, and redundancy of equipment and personnel, a ship could only take so much of that punishment, and might eventually break up. But for a ship to explode completely, and so visibly, could only mean that her slugs had hit a fuel tank or weapons store.

Fura wondered how it had been in those final seconds. One white moment of screaming terror, perhaps, as their ship ripped apart around them, and then a gasp that drew on vacuum, and then a rapid and painless shuttering of thought. She had no sympathy for Incer Stallis, and barely any for the men and women who served under him, for surely they knew of the crimes in which they were complicit. They had not stumbled into this service, innocent as lambs. But if she was content for them to die, she saw no reason why their deaths could not be relatively swift and painless. It was a minor courtesy and one she would not be at all sorry to have reciprocated, when it came to her own destruction.

"Do you have new orders?" Paladin asked, when news of the explosion had been thoroughly disseminated through the ship.

"Do they show any sign of ceasing their attack against us?" Fura asked, entirely rhetorically.

"None whatsoever."

"Then we press on, Paladin. And we give no quarter."

Spikey-fishy shoaly. Nogginsy-nogginsy! No quarter for pinkie-monkies!

The loss of one ship was undoubtedly an inconvenience to whoever was still coordinating that attack, but not enough to call off the engagement. The slugs kept coming from the remaining four ships, their muzzles now glowing constantly, and although none had yet scored a direct hit on *Revenger*'s hull, other than glancing strikes, the toll on sails and rigging could not be neglected.

Revenger, meanwhile, maintained its strategy of turning and firing for ten minutes out of thirty, and they were coming round to the fourth volley now, and the business of recharging the magazines, and nursing the guns and their water pipes, was starting to feel like a second life for which she had always been preparing.

The enemies' tactic shifted.

Revenger was swept, and swept again, and again, each time with a higher energy and beam-focus.

"Theys going for broke now," Tindouf said, sweating as he levered the lid off another crate of ammunition. "They knows they'll give up their own positions, 'cause we've got 'em on the sweeper screen as well now, but they can hit us where it hurts now, and they will."

"Attrition," Fura said, nodding. Her fingers clacked on the metal slug-casings. "We can play that game as well, though."

"They knows that too, Miss Ness. They also thinks they can beat us at it, even being a ship down."

The sweeps had caught them with the catchcloth averted, or else they might have fooled the enemy for a turn or more, but now there was no advantage at all in keeping the muzzles hidden, and so Fura instructed Paladin and Tindouf to nullify the rotation, as soon as the sails were orientated in the original direction. That kept their stern pointed at the enemy, which presented the minimum possible cross-section, but it also limited the aiming efficiency of the guns, which were hard against their swivel-stops. So Fura had Paladin and Tindouf work the sail-control gear to yaw the ship from port to starboard, presenting first one flank and then the next, yet never more than the minimum angle necessary to bring the guns to bear at their limits. It was still a case of one battery of guns discharging at a time, but now the intervals between volleys was much reduced, and the strain of loading the magazines and tending to the cooling circuits was much amplified.

There was a lull before the results of those sweeps were felt, and then the slugs began to arrive.

If the assaults that they had endured thus far had been a kiss of rain, this was a storm. For the first time shots struck directly against the hull, creating a sound as awful as their own guns. *Revenger* had very capable armour, and it was designed to deflect fire coming in at shallow angles, as was now the case, but it was far from impervious. Bosa Sennen had survived for as long as she had by never allowing herself to be out-gunned by a single ship, and generally having the better of two of them. She had depended on guile and intelligence to avoid ever being ambushed, and she had never been so foolish as to end up with an entire squadron on her back. Her personal streak of luck had run out when she met Fura, but for a time at least some residual part of it had seemed to adhere itself to the ship. That was over now, and Fura felt its passing as surely as if a spell of protection had been lifted from her shoulders.

They fired back, concentrating on the enemies' positions as betrayed by their own sweeper pulses, and when Ruther did not report an immediate improvement in their rate of hits, she issued a sweep of her own. Nothing was lost by that, and the resultant echoes gave Paladin a much better set of targets.

So it progressed, and when Ruther reported that the damage to the catchcloth sails was so severe, and so extensive in its spread, that he could see the purple and ruby lights of the Congregation twinkling back at him, through rents and fissures opened up by her own batteries, she felt only a grim and giddy astonishment at her own depths of commitment. Not to victory, for that condition was slipping ever further out of reach, but their delaying action would serve her sister well. She just hoped that Adrana was making the very best of the opportunity.

Ten minutes later she saw another of their ships go up. That left three, and she was just debating the chances of the enemy falling back with herself when Surt gave a scream, and both batteries of guns went into immediate shut-down.

"Paladin..." she began.

"The batteries have lost all cooling capability, Miss Arafura. One or two more shots from each muzzle would be enough to buckle the inductance rails, and three or more would burn-out the guns completely. Do you wish me to keep firing, knowing the risks?"

"Hold the guns," she said.

She went back to find Surt, and found hot steam howling into the gun room that ran the length of the starboard batteries. Some major part of the cooling circuit had ruptured. Further down the room Surt was drifting and turning: a vague foetal form in the hot billowing mist, with her arms drawn up to shield her face. A loose hose was whiplashing around, spitting steam.

Fura was next to one of the valve-control wheels. She touched it with her palm and flinched at the heat. She got her metal hand on it instead and tugged at the spokes until the wheel groaned and began to dampen the superheated flow. But not enough; it was closing too slowly and her fingers kept slipping. Her metal hand had a better crush-grip than her flesh one, but it was much less good at clasping something slippery, like the slick hot spokes of the wheel. Grimacing against the pain that she knew was coming, she planted both hands on the wheel and levered herself against the wall, putting all her strength into the action.

The wheel turned and the leak stopped, the loose hose turning limp. Fura rushed to the still helpless Surt, screwing up her own eyes against the still-scalding steam. She got her arms around Surt and dragged her out of the worst of it, Surt shaking in her grip and gibbering as she tried to speak.

"Why've the guns...why've we..."

"The circuit failed," Fura said, catching her own breath, and only then realising how close she herself was to exhaustion and perhaps unconsciousness. "Can't cool 'em, and I'd rather save what few shots we've got left."

Surt was still pressing her hands against her face. One of them was already bandaged, where she had scalded herself before, but that was nothing compared to the damage that had just been done. Where her skin showed, on her hands and the parts of her face not screened, angry white blisters were already starting to form.

"I'll get you to Eddralder," Fura said. "He'll put you right."

Surt's voice had become a croak: "Like he put Stram right?"

"Him and Merrix are all we have, Surt—we might as well put our faith in them. Did I tell you we got another of their ships?"

"Two down in a straight fight." Surt coughed. "Not too bad considering the green saps we started out as, is it?"

"Not too bad at all. And we might have started green, but none of us were saps." She paused, glancing down at her own flesh hand, which was almost as badly blistered as Fura's. "You did well—kept us in the game longer than we had any right to expect."

"Can we sail?"

Fura sighed. "It'll be a fine trick if we do, the state of our sails. But we're not finished, Surt, I promise you that."

Merrix and Eddralder met her outside the Kindness Room and took Surt into their care. Merrix laid her on the same bed where they had treated Strambli, and gently prised Surt's fingers away from her face and eyes. The steam-blast had hit her hard, her skin already a mask of blisters, her eyes reduced to narrow, weeping slits. Merrix swapped a silent look with her father, then went to one of their medicine cabinets.

"Are we done with warring, for the moment?" Eddralder asked, preparing a syringe.

"We are. Whether warring's done with us, I can't say." Fura clenched her scalded hand. "We've a few shots left before we run the guns too hot. Tindouf and I will try to repair the cooling circuit, but it may take longer than we have. I expect Stallis—or whoever has taken over from him—to be on his way as soon as he decides we're crippled."

Merrix was squeezing a salve onto her fingers. "Did you hurt your own hand?"

"Never mind me," Fura said.

*

The tram bounced and rattled along its rails. It nosed into a deepening, darkening canyon of top-heavy buildings. Overhead was a tangle of telegraph wires and washing lines and spindly connecting bridges. Adrana and Meggery stood in an open area near the rear doors, where they could wait with their luggage and not be in too much way of the other travellers. Rackamore had moved down the carriage and was shifting from one seat to the next, making low conversation with one person after another. He was asking after Quell's Bar, and doubtless framing his enquiries in a way that explained his interest in perfectly plausible terms.

Adrana's finger was throbbing. Worse than that, though, was the tingle she felt whenever someone's gaze fell on her for more than an instant. There were lots of people with newspapers on the tram, and the most recent editions were bound to mention the space battle. That, in turn, was guaranteed to lead to some rehashing of the case against the Ness sisters, with a high likelihood of pictorial accompaniment.

She had done what she could. Even to herself, she barely resembled the young woman who had first left Mazarile. It was not just in the shortness of her hair, the studied androgyny of her choices of clothing, the optically-neutral spectacles she kept perched on her nose. It was everything else. Space had chiselled something lean and hard out of her face. There were angles and edges in it that seemed to belong to some other reflection. When she dipped her chin enough for her eyes to show from behind the glasses, there was a distant, inscrutable chill in them. She nearly flinched from the force of her own regard. How could anyone mistake her for Adrana Ness?

Rackamore sidled back. He looked pleased with himself,

not quite concealing a smirk of self-amusement.

"How is that finger?"

"How is our destination?"

He steadied a hand against a support pillar. "I believe I have the location. Fortuitously, we shall pass quite near to it if we remain on this line. But I am adamant that we should not rush in without due diligence." He dropped his voice still further. "I will…smoke out this gentleman. If there is anything about his circumstances that do not sit well with me, the Clacker remains in our possession."

"I am not going back to the ship with him."

"Nor would I advocate it. But we will proceed with the utmost caution, and only complete the exchange when we are entirely satisfied."

Fura nodded. She agreed with all that.

"Are there going to be muddleheads?"

"I think it is safest to assume the worst. But if Quell's reputation is sound, and he does indeed provide shelter to the likes of Tazaknakak, then the reach of the muddleheads cannot be absolute." Rackamore lowered himself onto the upper edge of the case, taking the weight off his feet, exactly as any weary passenger would do.

"What are muddleheads?" Meggery asked.

"Be content that you do not already know."

"That's not an answer."

Rackamore searched the ceiling before responding. "There are nefarious elements among our alien colleagues. They conduct illicit business either for or against the respectable interests of their peers. For much of this clandestine work, since they cannot easily move in our circles without immediate detection, they must make use of agents. Sometimes, they bribe or coerce monkeys such as ourselves. But that is not always possible or desirable. In such circumstances, the aliens make use of temporary agents called muddleheads. They are, in essence, re-animated corpses. They are stitched together from body parts, with the use of xenografting techniques to give them senses and powers of intellect in keeping with their tasks. They do not live long. That may be seen as a mercy, in some instances. It is said that some muddleheads wake up to a screaming realisation of what they are, making them quite uncontrollable."

"I asked him about xenografting," Adrana said, tilting her head to the case on which Rackamore now rested. "I didn't use that term, since I wasn't aware of it, but the meaning of my enquiry can't have been lost on him. He became very evasive. He didn't want to dwell on the subject at all."

"It *is* a sordid affair," Rackamore said.

"There is more to it than that. If the muddleheads can be put together like walking jigsaws, a piece of monkey here, a piece of Crawly or Clacker there, then does it not speak of some underlying similarity at the biological level?"

Rackamore frowned slightly. "I do not see how it can. We are derived from the collective genestock of the former eight worlds, which in turn speciated from Earth. The aliens have totally different lineages. Their histories go back long before the Sundering. They were navigating the stars before we had taken one step from our own little pebble, let alone given consideration to dismantling and reforging the old worlds."

"That is what he said."

"Then you have your answer—from, so to speak, the horse's mouth."

"No, Brysca. I have *his* answer, which is not the same thing at all. I am not sure he wanted to think about what I was asking him. I think it cut against something he would much rather put to the back of his mind."

"And I would have thought that you had questions enough already." He shook his head in amused exasperation. "You... sisters... are like house-guests who pick at every loose strand. Before long you've stripped the furniture and reduced the carpets and curtains to shreds. Meanwhile, some of us were just looking for somewhere comfortable to sit down. Not everything in life must be unravelled."

"Your brother did not agree," Adrana said.

"And I respect him for it, and intend to honour his memory as best I can. But I should also remind you that my brother ended up dead."

*

Once the coil-guns gave up, Fura knew there was really not much more to be done. They had the stern and bow pieces, and fine weapons they were, and they could be run off a separate loop of the cooling circuit. These were short-range piercers, though, with high-penetrating power but a low cyclic rate, perfectly lethal against a close visible target, but not so effective against some distant speck eight thousand leagues away.

Fura would not waste their charges until she had something closer to shoot at. She was fully sure their time would come.

Paladin was trying to recover some limited manoeuvrability from the damaged sails, and for that he needed Tindouf, dispatching him from one sail-control station to the next, making adjustments and reporting on actual strain and torque readings, rather than the estimated parameters reaching the robot by indirect means. Fura could have used his help repairing the cooling leak, but she would not drag him from one essential task to assist with another, and so she gathered tools, swaddled her face with a towel, shielded her eyes behind goggles, and went back into the gun room. The steam was still there, but neither as hot nor as thick, and she found her way to the damage quite easily. The pipe had ruptured along an old welded seam, splitting along its length for at least half a span, and there was no possibility whatsoever of just wrapping a rag around it and hoping for the best.

"Captain, sir," came Ruther's voice.

She kissed the back of her burned hand, which seemed to take a little of the sting out of it. "I almost forgot you were still up there, boy. You may as well come back in now—we're past the point where visual observations will make any difference now."

"They seem to have stopped shooting at us, from what I can see."

"They think they've done enough to soften us up for a boarding. Very soon, I think, they'll be sending out the rocket launches. You should bring yourself back in before that happens."

"Is everything all right down in the ship, Captain?"

"Our sails are shredded like a pair of old stockings, Surt got a blast of steam in her face, and we can't operate the main coiller batteries beyond another few shots." From her bundle of tools she picked out a sheet of thin lead, long enough to span the fissure in the pipe. "Other than that, we're doing quite handsomely. Are you sorry you signed up for this ship, Ruther?"

"I wasn't too sure I had a choice about it, Captain."

She smiled to herself. "Perhaps you didn't."

"Anyway, I'm not sorry," Ruther said, emboldened. "I would still like to see some harm done to that man who started all this off, and I think I have a better chance of it here than on the *Merry Mare*, fine ship though she is."

Fura positioned the lead over the damaged pipe and worked her way along it, folding it around the pipe's circumference like a sleeve. "That man might have been on one of the two ships we just destroyed."

"I have a feeling he is the sort who survives even when the men and women around him are dying."

"Then we're of the same opinion, Ruther. I took you for my crew, though, and I don't feel at all happy about you being lumped in with the rest of us. You had nothing to do with the ships I burned on the way to and from Wheel Strizzardy, or the upset we created with the quoins." With the lead in place, rolled around the pipe as best she could, Fura dug out three ratcheting clips to tighten the repair at the ends and middle, which was the best she could do. Any tendency for her fingers to tremble was entirely absent as she engaged in this task, which she saw as aligning entirely with the glowy's need for self-preservation. "While there is time, I'm going to write a letter, explaining your innocence, and that you should be considered as a hostage. If you go along with that story, they'll treat you fairly."

"I wouldn't waste your ink, Captain. They won't treat any of us fairly, and especially not those of who were witness to the attack against Captain Werranwell. Please don't write that letter. I'd rather you spent your time trying to get the guns working."

She pushed back to inspect her repair. It would be far from steam-tight, but if it could contain some of the pressure, that might allow the guns to run for a little longer. But she dared not push her luck by exposing it to pressure until the very last moment.

"Ruther—I'd still like you to come in. It'll be you, me and Tindouf against any boarders, and I think it would help if you had a crossbow in your hand."

She heard the grunt of effort as he worked the lever that pulled the sighting room back into the hull. She gave her make-shift work one last glance, then went to dig out the close-action weapons.

*

The line they were on passed within a block of Quell's Bar, but on the other side of a block of tall buildings that screened any view of the establishment itself. To be on the safe side, in case there were spotters loitering around the area of the bar, Rackamore had them stay on for one additional stop. This brought them to the edge of a civic garden surrounded with high railings: one of the patches of green Adrana had spied from the higher vantage of the hub.

They got out, lowering the Clacker's box gently to the kerb, then went as a party through the main gates and into the garden. Inside there were winding stone paths, some lily ponds, some ornamental bridges, and a gently rusting bandstand now whitened by an accumulation of pigeon droppings. Dotted around the paths and ponds, half consumed in vinery, were odd, blocky statues that Adrana supposed to be the work of some enthusiastic but misguided local artist.

Near the middle of the park, Rackamore spied a teahouse with metal chairs and tables set out under umbrellas, and suggested that this would be a suitable place for Adrana and Meggery to wait while he investigated Quell. Adrana agreed. They would not be the only ones keeping an eye on their luggage either, as some of the tables were already occupied by travellers who had either just checked out of hotels, or were waiting for rooms to be prepared.

They took a table under one of the umbrellas, and Rackamore came back with a tray of coffees, and some small iced cakes with miniature flags on them. He made a wincing gesture with his lips. "With what that cost me, dear companions, you could have dined out in Mazarile for a whole week."

Adrana sipped her coffee, her new metal finger clinking against the china. "You exaggerate."

"Only slightly. No one knows quite how to value a quoin any more, so what is the rational response? Rampant inflation." He swigged his coffee in one slurp, wolfed down a cake, then rose from the table. "I shall be about an hour. By all means treat yourselves, but try not to spend our entire reserves before I return."

On some impulse, Adrana reached out and touched his sleeve. "Be careful, Brysca."

He lowered his voice and smiled reassuringly. "I have no intention of being anything other than careful. And I won't take chances. Far too much is at stake."

With the Clacker's box wedged under the table with the rest of their luggage, Adrana watched Rackamore walk away and around the curve of one of the ponds. As he stepped past one of the vine-shrouded statues, she had the faint intimation that it moved, responding to his presence. Yet the motion was so subtle, and so transient, that she supposed it could as easily have been suggested by the cyclical play of light from the window panels.

"My bones ache," Meggery said.

"So do mine. But it isn't so long since I was on Mulgracen, and we've visited some baubles with swallowers in them as well. Has it been a while since you were on a world?"

"A year." She thought on her answer for a second. "No, more like two. Two years of mostly floating around, except for the times we were being shot at."

"You adapt well, all the same." They had both taken bone and muscle-strengthening remedies before arriving, as well as drugs to help with the altered equilibrium of the inner ear, but all of these potions had side-effects of their own, including the ache Meggery now reported. "Perhaps there will come a day when each of us finds our home, and no longer needs to keep adjusting and aching."

"Are you close to that day?"

"Closer than when I left Mazarile. But not close. There is still a great deal left to see and do, Meggery. For both of us, I think."

Meggery looked to the gate, where Rackamore had vanished. "I thought of killing him, when he disclosed his true nature."

Adrana smiled thinly. "So did I, and I doubt you were the only one."

"I just thought you ought to know."

A breeze stirred cake-crumbs across their table. Adrana flicked them off for the sparrows down on the ground. "What prevented you?"

"I didn't say I was about to do it, just that it crossed my mind. When he spoke of his brother, though, I thought I could see the pain in him." Meggery scratched at one of her tattoos. "I believed him. Does that make me foolish?"

"If it does, it makes me equally culpable. I chose to believe him as well, even knowing that he lies as easily as he breathes. He could be playing us—I am well aware of that possibility— but I should rather place my faith in his sincerity. And if I had not already known his brother..."

"Did you like him?"

"Pol Rackamore? He had my admiration. I would not say he was likeable in the sense that I think you mean. He was intensely vain, intensely self-satisfied, intensely certain that he was a little better than the rest of us. But he was courageous, he was honest, he was a very capable captain, and I think his interest in quoins was entirely a means to an end. They had no lustre in his eyes, except as a facilitator for his intellectual pursuits."

"He liked digging into things, just like you."

"Perhaps a little of that rubbed off on me, Meggery. And on my sister as well. The outcome of that is the two of us sitting here with an alien jammed under our table, and scarcely any idea of what the trouble of bringing him here will mean for us."

Meggery bit into one of the prettily coloured cakes.

"I don't know what answers you're hoping for."

"Are you not in the least bit curious?"

"Oh, I am. More than a bit; I'm curious how I'll get out of this mess, of associating with you, and all that comes with it." Meggery smiled, for she meant no harm by her statement, which was no more than a bald summary of the facts. "I'm curious as to whether I'll stay with this crew or end up with another one. I'm curious as to whether my luck will ever turn—curious to know how it feels to sail away from a bauble knowing your life's just changed for the better. Curious to know what baubles are out there that we ain't found yet, and what might be in 'em. That enough curiosity for you?"

"For most of us, I do not doubt."

"But not for you. Not for Adrana…" She trailed off without mentioning the name "Ness," for although there were no eavesdroppers close to their table, a name alone could carry very well on an obliging breeze.

"It was enough," Adrana admitted. "Until Rackamore set my curiosity running. Oh, it was there in some germinal form before him. As children, we haunted the Museum of History. Stared in wonderment at that great long tableaux of the Thirteen Occupations, and the immense intervals of black between them."

"We never had a Museum of History."

"I thought most worlds had such places."

"Most nice worlds, I think you mean. But I've seen those

pictures, too, and studied my Occupations." Meggery fed one of the sparrows. "We do have to know something to work ions, contrary to opinion."

"I don't doubt it. Did you ever pause to wonder why those intervals of blackness exist, though? Or wonder if there will be Occupations after our own?"

"So long as this Occupation lasts a bit longer—long enough to see me out—why would I lose sleep over it? These scars go all the way through me, so there won't be any children to worry about. And, of course, the Occupations'll carry on after ours. There's nothing so special about us that says we have to be the last."

"The intervals are increasing," Adrana said, in a low and studious tone. "Rackamore was aware of this. He knew that whatever instigating event causes each Occupation, it must be becoming rarer. So it is possible that there will one day be an Occupation that ends, and nothing ever comes after it. There's something deeper, though. Bosa..." She paused, dropped her voice. "She found some old scholarship that points to something very unusual. The known Occupations are all spaced by intervals of time that are exact multiples of twenty-two thousand years. Or as exact as anyone can determine, given how foggy the beginnings and ends of Occupations tend to be. But the pattern is no illusion. There's a broken regularity to the Occupations. It's as if there ought to be many more of them, spaced exactly twenty-two thousand years apart, yet for some reason the majority of these hypothetical Occupations never take root. It's as if a gardener planted a long line of flowers, each an exact distance apart, but only one in thirty-three of them ever blossomed. Those blossoms are the history we know—the Thirteen Occupations. But there are four hundred and forty Occupations that never happened."

Meggery looked mystified. She swirled the remainder of her coffee. "You're concerning yourselves with things that *didn't* happen?"

"There is a dark puzzle in those Shadow Occupations,

358 • Alastair Reynolds

Meggery. If we are to understand why the known Occupations are becoming rarer—spaced-out from each other at increasing intervals—then we must understand the mechanism behind all the Occupations, including those that did not catch light."

Meggery gave the Clacker's box a gentle nudge. "And you think…he…is going to give you the answer?"

"He may not have all the answers. Perhaps no one does. I think there may be one question concerning the missing Occupations, and another concerning the ends of the thirteen we know about, and they may be answerable in different degrees. Perhaps there are no answers that will explain everything to our satisfaction. But I am minded to think he knows more than the rest of us, and that is a beginning."

Meggery looked around with a vague focus in her eyes. Her implicit gaze took in the teahouse, the park, the city, the spindleworld, out to the other worlds and the whole mad glory of the Congregation.

"You want to stop this Occupation from ending, don't you?"

"What we have is imperfect, Meggery. This little civilisation of ours is squalid in places, unjust in others. It is constructed to a large degree upon a foundation of greed and inequality. But it is not beyond salvation, and just as crucially it is all we have. There are fine things about it, too. There are lovely worlds, more than you or I will ever see in our lifetimes. There are beautiful cities and fabulous ruins. If we are feeling adventurous, there are baubles. If we are not, there are teahouses and cakes, and I should not care to place one above the other. I wish to have both things in my life: adventure and comfort. I should like to know men like Lasling, who have seen and done terrible and courageous things, and lived to laugh about them. Men like Rackamore, too, and women like yourself, an ion-engineer on a ship deserving much better fortune than it has seen. But I should also have liked to have known men like my father, who was mistaken in the application of his kindness, but kind nonetheless. And my mother, who never had any desire to see more than one world, but loved music and dancing and cold evenings when it was nice to draw the curtains and be warm inside."

"You want too many things."

"I do, and I make no apology for it. Principally, though, I want to do all in my capacity to prevent this Occupation from ending. And I do not care if that ending is ten years away or a thousand: the thought of it wounds me just as powerfully."

"Others must have thought the same."

Adrana nodded with sadness and humility, for the same observation had not escaped her. "Not just in this Occupation, but in earlier ones. There must always have been people who understood that things were not permanent. They must have taken action, too. And yet—as the record informs us—whatever they tried was not sufficient."

"Best pray, then," Meggery said, "that whatever action they took wasn't the thing that ended 'em."

moment—as she well realised—Tindouf knew that he had the love and respect of his captain, and besides a fine set of ion-coils, and some sails and rigging to occupy him when the ions were well-behaved, and perhaps the prospect of a new clay pipe to carve, there was nothing he needed more than that anywhere in the Congregation, or beyond it.

While Tindouf was preoccupied, a fourth form emerged through the lock. This one wore a suit, but it was sleeker and more close-fitting than those of the first three. It raised an arm, irritatedly paddling aside clouds of lungstuff and detritus. It had a prow-shaped visor, with two angular plates of glass spaced by a blade-like central divider.

"Tindouf," Fura said, and her own voice sounded distant and feeble, just as if she were trying to rouse herself from a dream; some vile phantasm of paralysis and helplessness. "Tindouf."

If he heard her, it was too late. The fourth form, who was smaller and thinner than the others, and carried nothing so clumsy as a crossbow or blade or scatter-gun, had something black in its fist. It was small, talisman-like. It aimed the dainty thing at Tindouf and doused him with a sharp ruby light. Tindouf stiffened, and a howl of static blasted her ears as the upper part of Tindouf separated into twenty or thirty evenly divided sections, as bloodless and clean as freshly-washed plates. These near-circular sections maintained some affinity with each other for a span or two, before they began to drift on independent paths. Fura screamed. The figure aimed the black thing directly at her, lingering for the smallest of instants, before twitching off to one side and dousing her already-damaged hand and wrist. She stared down in a sort of baffled wonderment as the transecting beam dismantled her hand and a good portion of her lower forearm. It had struck at an angle, so the parts sheared away as ellipses, rather than circles.

The figure kept the weapon on her, then reached up with its free hand and tapped part of his helmet, opening a general broadcast channel.

"You'll forgive me for that, Arafura—I mean the arm, not the man I just killed—heh! But I couldn't risk your having something in there that could hurt me."

The room was clearing of lungstuff and debris very efficiently now. The ruby weapon had clawed several parallel gashes in the wall behind Tindouf, through several spans-worth of insulation and hull plating, all the way out to open space. It was an excellent demonstration of why energy emitters were not the weapon of choice, if one wished to take a ship or its crew intact—or indeed defend a ship.

The slim-suited figure came a little nearer.

"Stallis," Fura said.

26

A soft, slow trudging came down the stairs. Bazler stood back, sucking on his burned fingers like a scolded toddler. Two dark-garbed figures came into the room, coat-collars turned up and hats tugged low across their faces, so that only a horizontal eye-slit was visible. They had their hands in their pockets, until one of them reached out a sort of sickle-shaped pincer and used it to latch the door behind them again.

"You've met the motleys," Quindar said. "This is more of 'em. And there's more still up in the streets, now that shutter-time's upon us. The thing about motleys is that they don't last long, but they're cheap and easy to throw together, and they can blend in at dusk like nobody's business."

The muddleheads came into the room. They halted between Adrana's little party and the stairwell and took off their hats, as if they were introducing themselves formally.

She stared. They were as much of a horror as the ones she had encountered in Mulgracen, but they were put together from a different assortment of scraps; a different palette of monkey and alien parts. The effect was just as discordant, and just as lacking in symmetry. They were exactly as Quindar said: disposable assemblages of fused, animated flesh, thrown together for a specific purpose, with no consideration for longevity.

One of them was speaking. It had the mouth and jaw of a

person, but fixed into the jumble of its face nearly sideways on, like a jigsaw piece that had been forced into the wrong gap.

"We will take the Clacker now."

"No," Adrana said, standing her ground next to Meggery and Rackamore, and trying to keep a firmness in her voice, even as she felt it on the point of breaking. "He's mine. I brought him here; I promised him safe passage."

The muddleheads advanced.

Tazaknakak stirred. At last he was waking properly. His limbs thrashed and he started to push himself up onto his feet. He swivelled his head, producing a series of rapid, accelerating clacking sounds, a rattle that became an ascending trill, and then passed beyond the upper threshold of Adrana's hearing.

"You delivered him safe," Quindar said. "Now saunter off and enjoy the rest of your stay. Have a choc-ice. Treat yourselves. The muddles won't stop you if you let them have Zak. That's all they want. It ain't your business to poke your snozzes into."

"They'll kill us for what we already know, Quindar. And eventually they'll kill you, too. You do realise that, don't you? This is well out of your ordinary league. There are aliens behind all of this. They've been keeping secrets from us for hundreds of years—secrets about quoins and baubles and Occupations. The Readjustment's brought things to a head. Something *is* happening—something that'll either condemn us all or offer one slim chance to change our future. Tazaknakak knows a little of it. He's seen glimpses of the truth—enough to prick his conscience—and he's dug a little too deeply into things his masters would rather remained hidden. That's why he's running. That's why they want him silenced."

"Already been blabbing to you, has he?" Quindar looked over her head to the muddleheads. "I wouldn't be so quick to advertise that, if I were you."

"I'm not so stupid as to think they, or any other muddleheads, will let us walk out of here as if we know nothing. They'll kill us, or do some deal with the authorities in exchange for my capture. For all I know, their masters *are* the authorities.

They can't be trusted, Quindar. Turn on them now, use whatever you have here, and you might save your own skin and redeem yourself in the process." She bent down and scooped up the Clacker, groaning at the additional load on her already tired bones. "But be clear about one thing. He remains my responsibility."

Quindar made a vague, dismissive gesture at the muddleheads. "Take him off her. Break as a little as you can."

The muddleheads pressed closer. Meggery made a growling sound and raised her fist. She swung it into the nearest muddlehead and something snapped off with a dry crunch. An appendage dropped to the floor like a rotten branch. Something bustled behind the muddlehead's coat and another limb emerged, dripping with a sticky, honey-coloured lubricant as it articulated out. The limb had a knife on the end of it. It sprung out in a quick stabbing motion, catching Meggery across the forearm. She yelped and stumbled back, blood already welling from a long, deep incision.

"Brysca!" Adrana said, stepping away from the other muddlehead, the Clacker in her arms, and wondering why he had not already intervened.

He answered quietly: "I cannot."

"Kill them," she said. "Like you did in Mulgracen."

Meggery was gritting her teeth, tearing off a part of her sleeve to wad against the gushing wound. "What's keeping him?"

"I have lost control of the eye," Rackamore said.

They all looked to it, still prowling in circles just beneath the ceiling.

"What'd he say?" Quindar asked, with an exaggerated puzzlement. "Something about losing control of his eye? Did you hear that, Grem?"

She had the rectangular control unit in her hands, the same one she had used to open the case. Its lights were pulsing strongly, and she had her gaze fixed on the circling eye. "I did, boss, and it's a queer one and no mistake. Why would a clever cove like Mister Rack lose control of his own eye?"

"Brysca," Adrana said, as if her own insistence might make a difference. "What's wrong?"

"The control signals…" He paused, pressing a hand to his temple, some desperate strain showing in his face. "They aren't getting through. They're being overridden."

Gremly grinned. "I did say this was a very versatile piece of gubbins, Mister Rack!"

"You did, Grem! I think a fair degree of understatement may have resided in that remark, truth be told!" said Quindar. He angled his head to address Rackamore. "We had warning, Mister Rack, after that unpleasantness in Mulgracen. Word that you might send a remote in after us. Expecting you, so to speak. Gremly got a sniff of the control protocol when you were snooping around our premises earlier on. Of course, we still let you think the eye was operating properly. Even let you have that bit of fun with Baz."

Bazler looked upset. "You mean he didn't have to burn my fingers?"

"I'm sorry about that, Baz, but we thought it'd help if our friends still thought they had the advantage on us. That way we'd all know where we stood. As we do!"

Meggery's efforts to stem the flow of blood were having little or no effect. She stared down at her already-sodden bandage. "He got me deep. The chaff…" She dropped to her knees, a woozy look in her eyes. "I don't feel so well, Captain."

"Stay with me," Adrana said. Then, barking it as an order: "Stay with me, Meggery! We'll get help."

Meggery made to mouth something. She was already turning a waxy grey. "Cap…"

"Stay with me!"

Meggery slumped over. Her mouth lolled open, her eyes still fixed on Adrana.

"That's one of 'em done with," Quindar said. "Now crack on with the other cove, Grem—we ain't got all day!"

The muddleheads had begun to focus their attentions on Adrana. She clutched the Clacker more tightly to her chest, feeling a strange and unpleasant resonance in her ribcage as the casque generated its sounds. The muddleheads began to push out limbs and feelers from gaps in their coats, exploring the Clacker and trying to tug it away from her, at first with a surprising gentleness.

She kicked at their lower extremities and things shattered and crunched like wood-wormed timber.

Rackamore was holding his hands against both sides of his head. He had dropped to his knees, grimacing and making small choking sounds. Gremly was still working the rectangular device. She had a look of perfect, avid concentration, smiling slightly as she flicked a switch or turned a potentiometer dial. Slowly, she was gaining confidence in her own control of the eye. It was making larger and lower loops around the room, and she was following it with her gaze.

"Please," Rackamore said, forcing out the word through a half-clenched jaw.

"Stop!" Adrana shouted. "You've proven you can override the eye. You don't have to hurt him as well!"

"Mm." Gremly pushed out her lower lip, looking diffident. "I'm not trying to hurt the cove, exactly, but there's lot to learn here. Perhaps if I turn down this...or turn it up..." She made a violent, impulsive twist of one of the knobs, and Rackamore screamed. "Or maybe not that one. Maybe *this* one..."

The room flashed pink-white and a lance of energy put a smoking hole in one of the walls. Gremly grinned, brought the eye around again and turned one of the flickerboxes into a smoking, sparking ruin.

"That's coming out of your bonus, Grem!"

She cackled at him: "Worth it for the fun, boss!"

The muddleheads were still trying to wrestle the Clacker from Adrana's clasp. She grunted and kicked at them. One of them buckled at the waist, a leg snapping beneath it. She kicked it harder, then brought a stomping heel down on its chest. There was a moment of resistance, then a soft and unresisting descent. It was like crunching through the lid of a pie.

Meggery lay still in her pool of her own blood. Rackamore was on the ground, writhing. Bazler was at the door and two more muddleheads were coming in. One was doubled half-over, like a stooping crone; the other was unnaturally tall and flattened out, like a person that had been put through a steam-press. It was apparent to Adrana that even if she somehow managed to dismantle or incapacitate them one by one, there would always be more, and eventually force of numbers would prevail. Quindar might have lied about his identity, but she had no doubt he had been sincere about the gathering of the muddleheads.

The feeling in her ribcage was almost as much as she could tolerate. It was like a churning of every bone, sinew and organ: as if her insides were tumbling around like clothes in a washing machine. Accompanying this sensation was a rising pressure behind her eyes, like two hot skewers being driven into them from inside her own skull.

"Let me go," Tazaknakak said.

"No."

"It will be bad for you if you do not. They have killed one of your friends and the other will soon follow. This way...there *is* a way. But you must trust me." Beneath the swell of his casque, his tiny, barely sentient eyes impelled her to do as he stated, and Adrana realised her options were as limited as they were dismal. She could let go of him, or she could try holding onto him for a few seconds longer, until the vibrations from his casque became truly unbearable, or the muddleheads grappled him away.

She chose to trust him. She relinquished her hold and stumbled back. Of the two muddleheads who had first assailed her, only one was still standing, but it only took one to seize the Clacker. The muddlehead pressed his prize against him, as if to mirror and mock the protective stance that Adrana had just abandoned. Near the door, Bazler was stumbling around with a kitchen knife in his hands, disorientated by the noises. He had the stunned, staggering deportment of a man who had been hit by a tram and did not quite realise how badly he was broken.

Tazaknakak increased his vibrations. The waves of inaudible

sound were already stronger than when she had been holding him. It made her dizzy and disorientated, and she felt a rising compulsion to vomit. She stumbled back even further. Brysca fell to his knees and pressed his hands against the sides of his head as if they were the opposing planes of a vice, and he wished only to crush his own consciousness out of existence. Adrana fully sympathised with that intention. She had become a hard knot of pure pain, a little star burning with the pure white flame of absolute agony.

A little star...

There was room in her head for exactly one thought that was not some splinter or reflection of that pain itself. She thought of a tiny star, floating in a cavern...a tiny, flickering source of immense but evanescent luminosity.

She understood that these waves of sound were not meant to hurt her, but they were most certainly intended to disorientate Tazaknakak's captors, and perhaps do some greater harm to the muddleheads. If she could amplify that disorientation by the production of an intense and startling light-source...

The light-imp...

She had kept it about her all the while, even after she understood the gift was not the rare and valuable thing it had seemed. It was only as far away as the box stuffed down the collar of her blouse, but it might have been buried in a bauble's deepest, darkest vault for all the force of will it took to retrieve it. She had to compel her hand and arm to perform one simple action, yet it was like delving through a matrix of solid rock. When at last her fingers closed around the velvet box, it felt as if she were leaning into a well and by some grotesque, delirious extension of her limb was managing to touch some relic that had fallen all the way to the bottom.

She pulled out the box and worked the catch with the friction of her thumb, not caring if she broke the little mechanism. Then she fumbled out the hard-edged form of the light-imp. For an instant, exhausted, it was all she could do to loll there on the floor. It was enough, surely, that she had done this one thing.

Nothing more could be asked of her. To expect her to have the strength to squeeze the light-imp: well, that was beyond all reasonableness.

She did it anyway.

It shattered between her fingertips, the physical object replaced with a small wavering orb that brightened in pulses. She let it drift from her fingers, leaning away from it as the yellow light intensified. It was indeed very luminous, and growing more so by the second. She had seen the brightness a light-imp could project in the interior chamber of a bauble, flooding a space the size of a ballroom or booking hall, but Quell's Bar was much smaller than that and the confinement of the light only made it seem stronger and angrier.

More than that, though. The light emanating from that orb was harder and fiercer than any she had known before, and it just kept brightening. She jammed her eyes to slits, and still it was not enough. She closed them completely, and she could see shapes and colours through the veined curtains of her eyelids.

It was a light-imp, she thought. But not a commonplace light-imp.

Firebright.

Quindar shrieked. If he had struggled to endure the vibrations, the light-imp was enough to take him over the edge. He yanked his head around like a man being electrocuted. He tried to cover the lenses of his eyes with his palms, but too much light leaked between his fingers.

He screamed and fell writhing to the floor. Bazler and Gremly were already down. The muddleheads were stunned or dead or in some intermediate condition, and Tazaknakak could not keep up his sound-generation indefinitely; nor would the light-imp keep shining for ever. While the Clacker made his noises, and the Firebright burned, and its radiance overloaded Quindar's eyes, Adrana walked over to him and placed a boot on his neck.

"You shouldn't have tricked me," she said, in a low, judicial tone, as if she were delivering a court summary. "You shouldn't have hurt my friends, and you shouldn't have tried to take the Clacker from me."

She pressed down with her boot.

"Leave him," a voice croaked. "Leave him and go, before reinforcements arrive."

Rackamore was still alive. She went over to him, knelt down, and touched the side of his face. He blazed like an over-exposed photograph. The light was painful, and she wondered how much more of it she could bear.

"Gremly's stopped," she said. "I can smash that machine of hers. You'll be all right."

"No." His voice was a wheeze. "Something…went wrong. In my head."

"You're all right, Brysca."

"No," he said again. "I'm not. She did…something bad to me… something that can't be reversed. I can't move, Adrana. I can't move and I can hardly breathe." He paused, and from some deep reservoir of fortitude he managed a smile. "It's over for me. But it isn't for you. Go over to that man with the knives and take three things."

"Three," she said, smiling back at his exactitude, even as his composure and dignity ripped her heart out.

"A knife for me, just in case I have the means to use it. There will be more coming, and these…fellows…won't stay stunned indefinitely. Take one for yourself, and take the Clacker. The third thing…" He paused, wheezed, drew breath. "The third thing…you need a way out of here that isn't how we came in. There'll be such a way. There'll be an escape passage. There always is."

"How do I find it?"

"The third thing…Bazler. The one with the knives." He licked his lips, inhaled a ragged breath, met her eyes with all that was left of his, for the last time. "Look…"

"Look where?"

"Look…*stone*."

It was the last thing to come out of his lips. Brysca Rackamore was dead.

*

Adrana held the lookstone up to her eyes. She turned around
slowly, maintaining just the right pressure on the lookstone, so
that she was peering neither too shallowly nor too deeply into
the earthworks surrounding Quell's basement room.

She agreed with Rackamore. Whatever opinion she might
have of Hasper Quell—or, for that matter, of his successor—
she doubted that either man would have been satisfied without
some secondary means of reaching this basement warren,
besides the stairwell that came down from the street-level
frontage. More than likely there would be at least two other
ways in and out: one purely practical and unconcealed means of
access from the building above, perhaps an elevator or hydraulic platform, so that kegs, kitchen supplies and the occasional
corpse could be moved up and down without difficulty, and (if
she was any judge of these matters) a far more covert means of
coming and going, which might connect to some other building
entirely. The muddleheads would have the first one covered,
but not necessarily the second. It would depend on how much
Vidin Quindar trusted them. If he had retained the smallest
suspicion that his collusion with them might turn sour, then
possibly—just possibly—he would have kept one or two things
to himself.

That was her conviction, and if it was based on nothing
more than an attempt to reason herself into the minds of semi-
criminal men, it was still all she had and all she could depend
upon. So she willed her fingers to hold the lookstone without
trembling, and she forced upon herself a patient and attentive
composure, as if this exercise were merely a pleasant sort of
puzzle-solving distraction for an aimless afternoon.

And she saw it. Smokily defined: a hollow space behind
one of the walls: the start of a low, narrow but very definite

passage leading horizontally away from the basement. When she relaxed the lookstone, the wall came back into view with no door or hatch to hint at the presence of a concealed tunnel. But the wall was divided into panelled partitions, and one of them corresponded quite satisfactorily to the hidden space.

She pocketed the lookstone and carried Tazaknakak to the panel. It fitted neatly against its neighbours. There was no seam on either side wide enough to slip her fingers into. But if Quell ever meant to use this escape route, he would have surely been in too much haste to go looking for tools or keys. She set down the Clacker and used both hands to press on the panel. She felt at first no hint of movement, but then a positive click and a resistive yielding. The panel moved a little inward, then reached a limit and sprang back out of the wall, hinging by its own means to the right. Beyond it was a black emptiness, its depths betrayed only by a chill, damp draught. Adrana collected the Clacker and stepped over a skirting board into the tunnel and set him back down. Behind her, on the rear face of the panel, was a pair of handles so that the panel could be pulled back into its former position.

Even though the Firebright was still active, it was no use to her. If it shared the general properties of a normal light-imp then it could not be touched or moved once it was initiated. So as she pulled the panel closed, the darkness around her became absolute. The lookstone would be no use either, since it required contrasting light levels to form a comprehensible image, and there was nothing but blackness.

She fumbled at her feet for the Clacker and raised him to her chest.

"Tazaknakak," she said, in a firm and insistent voice. "I know you are exhausted, but I need you to see for me now. Both of our lives depend on it. Guide me into this tunnel."

"I am depleted. I must rest after my great exertions."

She shook him angrily. "Tazaknakak!"

"I am...incapable."

"You can make speech, so you have the capability to generate

412 • Alastair Reynolds

sound-pictures. See into this tunnel. Tell me what I'm walking into."

"I will...strive to." There was a churn in her ribcage, a pressure behind her eyes. "Turn me. We are not facing...that is better. Proceed."

"What?"

"Proceed. If you are in peril of collision, I will alert you. For now, proceed. The floor is quite level and well-maintained. Even a poorly proportioned biped such as yourself should not have too much trouble."

"Be aware that I cannot see a thing. Not even my hand in front of my face."

"Walk on, Captain Ness. And do not be too tardy about it, either."

*

Incer Stallis tipped his head, touching one hand to his chest even as he kept the weapon levelled. It was a sort of mocking curtsy.

"I feel I should say something like 'we meet at last,' or 'evidently my reputation precedes me,' or something just as tiresomely melodramatic. Isn't it disappointing how life throws us into these situations, and the only words available sound like the worst sort of pot-boiler?"

"I had so hoped you were in one of those ships I already burned."

"You say that, Captain Ness, but I am not at all persuaded that you really mean it, not deep down."

"Trust me, I do."

"But then you wouldn't be able to exercise those fantasies of doing something extremely unpleasant to me face to face, as you said you'd like to." He extended a beckoning hand. "Well, now's your chance—how about it?"

Fura dipped her eyes to her ruined arm. The cuff where her suit met the artificial limb was still holding pressure, or she would have had only seconds of consciousness before blacking out. Her arm felt cold and numb, as if she had pushed it into a dense cloud of anaesthetic gas. There was none of the pain she had felt from the loss of a mere finger.

"I'll find a way."

"It really was a commendable effort, I'll give you that. Those losses were felt very keenly. Fine ships, good crews. And you put up such a spirited defence, until the last." He pointed a finger at her, waggling it admiringly. "That was a *most* excellent ruse, not letting off your guns until we were so, so close. Heh! They'll be teaching that one in squadron school for years to come. Sadly, though, it only prolonged the inevitable. I know this is a unique ship, with some unique capabilities, but it's still only a ship, and even the finest fighter ought to know when they're outnumbered, out-gunned and out-flanked. As you were, today." He curled his fingers. "Well, come along. There's nothing for you on this hulk anymore, and my men will soon find your sister and mop up the last of your doughty band. You don't want to see any of that."

"Your men? I killed your men."

He clicked his fingers. "Yes—that gruesome business with the lock! That took out three of us, I admit, and then you certainly left your mark on these other poor fellows."

"If you had a spine, you'd have come in with them. Was it just the six, Incer?"

"There's still a fully-armed technical crew aboard the launch, so don't get any ideas about trying to take control of it. I also have word that the other has now completed docking on your port-side lock, after some difficulties of their own. They'll blast their way in, rather than risk your little trick with over-pressure, assuming you'd be so foolish as to attempt it twice." Again he curled his fingers, this time with a touch of impatience. "Come with me, please. You know it's in your best interests. We'll run you back to one of the main ships and have a surgeon look at that arm. Where *is* your sister, by the way?"

"As if I'd tell you."

"We haven't seen your launch depart, so perhaps that's where she's hiding. It won't take us long to find her—or any other dregs of your crew—and if they're silly enough to try to escape in that launch, we will easily hunt them down."

"Then you seem to have it covered."

"It will still help the search party if they know where *not* to shoot, Arafura. These men are very good, and they have their orders, but I have to say they're not in the most of agreeable of moods. Seeing your colleagues butchered will do that to you."

"I heard you butchered your own mother, Incer. Killed her for a ship, then murdered the one accomplice who knew what you'd done. Is that true?"

"Come." He toyed with the little black weapon, rolling it between his fingers like a marble. "I shan't ask again. Adrana will just have to take her chances. *You* were always the real prize, as far as I was concerned."

Something jolted the ship. Had there been any pressure left in this whole section of it, Fura was in no doubt that it would now be rushing out of the port lock, or what was left of it.

"I'll come, if you spare my sister and the others. That's the price of my cooperation."

"It seems...reasonable. Are they in the forward compartments?"

"I said I'd cooperate, not give you 'em on a plate." Fura used her good arm to lever herself away from the pipes and wall until she was straightened out and facing Stallis, the two of them floating a few spans apart.

"No tricks, now."

"No tricks."

Three armoured figures came into the corridor from the connecting passage between the port and starboard extremities. Stallis touched his helmet and some closed exchange took place between him and his men. Fura watched as they regarded their fallen or grievously incapacitated colleagues, as well as the grotesque spectacle that had once been Tindouf. Two of them went in the direction of the forward compartments, while a third detached from the party to accompany Stallis and Fura back to the lock. Any thoughts she might have had of single-handedly incapacitating Stallis, even with that vile weapon of his, were now extinguished.

The launch's lock was damaged, but it still worked, and as the pressure returned again she felt her suit turn saggy around the joints. Her arm was beginning to ache, instead of being enveloped in numbness, but for now it was a bearable discomfort.

The launch's inner lock door opened, and the armoured man prodded her forward while Stallis maintained a cautious separation. Still holding his black weapon, he reached up with the other hand and deftly undid his helmet connections. The three of them were floating into the main compartment of the launch, which was larger than the entire interior of *Revenger*'s own excursion craft. Instead of having portholes and double rows of chairs facing forward, it was windowless and bare except for racks of weapons, ammunition, assorted equipment and spare vacuum suit components, with the only obvious furniture being ranks of spartan, fold-down bucket seats along each side. Rather than the usual arrangement of a control position and console ahead of the seats, there was a separate compartment behind a pressure bulkhead.

Stallis directed his man to secure Fura. The man removed her backpack and hose connections, none too gently, and forced her into one of the bucket seats. She was strapped in with her upper arms pinned to her sides, and her right arm—all that now remained—bound against her belly.

"Remove her helmet," Stallis said, secreting his little weapon into an external pouch on his own suit, and then lifting off his own. He ruffled a hand through a mop of thick, unruly black hair and shook his head vigorously, as if his neck muscles had begun to cramp.

She studied him with a prickling sense of recognition. His face was familiar to her, although she had never seen an image of him nor met his eyes before. It was the face she had seen projecting itself onto Ruther's features, forcing them into a caricature of itself. If there had been the least doubt in her mind that this was the extraordinary Bone Reader whose mind she had touched—and whose mind had touched hers—none now remained.

Fura glared at him as her visor lifted away from her eyes. There was nothing she could do to stop the man removing her helmet.

"Very good," Stallis said, grinning wildly, when at last there was no glass between them. "Very, very good. The rumours were correct, then. The extreme manifestation of glowy our man reported...it's in your eyes. Deep into your central nervous system, deep in your cerebellum."

He extended a hand, snapped his fingers, and had the suited figure pass him her helmet. He scooped it into his hand by the chin-piece, lifted it to his face, staring into the emptiness of the visor.

"'Our man'?"

He frowned slightly. There were no lines or marks on his face, no indicators of habitual expression, so even when he pushed his features into a frown or a grimace or some affectation of wicked delight, the effect was unpersuasive and rubbery, like a cheap mask that wanted to snap back to its neutral condition.

"My man, yes," Stallis said. "You met him, didn't you? He infiltrated your ship, under our instructions. Posing as an outlaw *ne'er-do-well* named Lagganvor—"

"No," she said, with an automatic assertiveness. "Lagganvor was the man I found, the man I captured. He wasn't your man. If he was anyone's he was Bosa's, Bosa herself—"

"He did a fine job of concealment, I see. We never thought he'd last that long." He looked at her with some desperate, sceptical amusement, as if she couldn't possibly be telling the truth, but it was rather funny to play along as if she were. "Are you really saying you didn't crack his identity?"

Fura knew better than to say more. It was a game he was playing, that was all: a precursor to the psychological attacks she could expect when they began interrogating her, trying to demolish her sense of self, even her understanding of her own reality.

No; she knew better than to ask him.

"What identity?"

"His real name. Brysca Rackamore: the estranged brother of Pol Rackamore, your first captain. He was our man. Our agent—our infiltrator. We sent him to find you."

"That isn't possible. If Lagganvor was the man you say he was, why would you have risked his life by shooting at us?"

"It's a risky profession, and Rackamore understood that. But all's well, isn't it? We'll find him somewhere in your ship, and you can have the pleasure of hearing his side of the story in person." He reached up and touched a stud on the outside of his neck-ring. "Get us underway. The other boarding party can complete the sweep of the wreck and take any survivors with them when they undock." He waited, head slightly cocked, awaiting confirmation that these instructions had been received and were about to be acted upon. "I said, get us detached. I have the high-value prisoner with me—Adrana Ness can follow in the second launch, if she allows herself to be taken. I said, get us..." But he trailed off and tapped the neck stud twice in case it was broken. "Damn this," he muttered, then jabbed a finger at the other man, who was still fully suited. "Watch her."

Fura watched as Stallis, still carrying her helmet, went all the way forward to the dividing bulkhead. He touched a control, opened the pressure door, and stooped through. Once he was inside, the door closed behind him. While this was going on, the suited guard aimed a crossbow in her general direction. She guessed he was under instructions to wound, rather than kill, if she made trouble. But other than glare, and possibly aim a gob of spit at him, there was nothing she could do.

Stallis came back into the main part of the launch. He no longer had her helmet. He seemed to need to stop and collect himself, his jaw trembling and his breathing rapid. His eyes swept the room. He looked at Fura and her guard, but also at every part of the interior, with its racks of equipment.

Only then did he say: "They got aboard. Somehow. They got aboard while we were inside her ship."

She heard the amplified voice of the guard, emerging from its helmet. "Sir?"

"They got inside. They've…killed…the technical crew. They're all dead."

He looked down at his now-empty hands, as if only then realising that they were lathered in blood.

"There's got to be a mistake, sir. That lock was counter-sealed when we went back in."

"I'm saying…" Stallis drew a huge calming breath. "I'm saying *something* got into this ship. I'm not saying how."

The guard might have been on the cusp of answering, but Fura would never be entirely certain. He twitched, and something odd happened to his neck. It was separating, parting along a widening line, almost as if it had never been properly joined together in the first place. At the advancing point of this line of separation was a sharp, shimmering anti-presence, a blade-shaped zone that resisted all Fura's attempts to focus on it, to see it, to hold it in mind as a definite object. Behind the dying guard was a larger, person-shaped counterpart to this same repulsive absence. The guard's blood splattered onto the barely-seen surface, then the greater portion of it soaked away, becoming first translucent and then invisible. Stallis seemed, for a moment, entirely paralysed by the spectacle before him. Then he dug out his little weapon, slippery in his blood-soaked fingers, and aimed it at the Ghostie presence.

"I wouldn't," Fura said.

The Ghostie had finished with the guard, tossing the larger and smaller parts aside. Fura could only see it by averting her gaze, seeing out of the corners of her eyes, and making a mental effort to think of anything but the Ghostie.

Stallis fired. The ruby beams intersected the volume of space where the Ghostie might have been, and for an instant some definite thing was there, carved of ruby-stained glass, a hinged-and-armoured form that seemed as hollow as a waiting mould.

The ruby staining faded, the energies of his weapon absorbed and dissipated. Stallis tried again, with the same lack of effect.

He glanced down at the weapon, scowling.

The Ghostie was hard to see again. Fura twisted her head aside, narrowing her eyes to slits, forcing her thoughts onto any other track but the one they wished to follow.

The Ghostie loomed before her. Fura sensed a terrible sharpness of being, as if it were made only of lethal blades, serrated edges and cruel impaling points.

A voice cut into her skull. It was like two surfaces of rough ice sliding past each other.

Sorry we ain't spoke for a while. I thought you'd like to know that I'm gone all the way now. Mainly, you don't have to feel bad about what happened to me. I like things better the way they are now.

Through her terror, Fura stammered out a name.

"Strambli."

Stallis was backing himself into the forward compartment again.

I remember when that name belonged to me. It was a long time ago, though. You were my captain and we had a ship all to ourselves.

Fura found the strength to nod.

"It was. It was."

It was a good ship. I liked being part of your crew. But I much prefer things the way they are now. All the other stuff's such a long time ago. I was just…changing. I was wrong to be afraid of the cold. Once I was in it, I realised it wasn't so bad. I didn't mind the darkness, either. It's just another kind of light.

"I'm sorry, Strambli."

A tentative smoky appendage extended from the barely-real form. The hand touched Fura's upper left arm, and even through the insulation of her suit a sudden wriggling coldness seeped into her muscles and bones. The hand descended to her elbow, the cold spot moving like a worm beneath her skin, and then it reached the limit of the living parts of her, where flesh became metal.

Fura gasped in shock and pain. The unseen hand flinched away from her, and some part of that coldness eased.

Did these men do this? Did they hurt Prozor and Tindouf as well? When I had that name, I was the same as those people. I was a breathy. I remember that I liked them, and that they liked me.

"This man," Fura said, nodding at Stallis. "This was the one."

In which case...I do not think I like this man.

Stallis levelled the weapon again. He had made some adjustment to its settings, and when the ruby energies flashed they were much fiercer than before. Strambli—or what had once been Strambli—glowed with a brighter luminosity. Slowly, the hollow form turned from Fura and drifted in the direction of the forward compartment. Even that intense dose of ruby light was dissipating now, and no harm appeared to have come to Strambli. Yet Fura had the sense that some vast patience had been strained to its breaking point, and now Stallis was the exclusive focus of the Ghostie's attention. He kept firing, and the stray energies of the weapon skimmed off Strambli and tore into the walls of the launch. There was a bang, and a developing howl, and Fura felt her ears pop. He had blown a hole right out into space.

Her helmet was...up front, in that forward compartment. She realised then that Stallis had come to an entirely pragmatic decision: she could die; he would bring his masters her body, or instructions for locating it, but he had no further intention of bringing her in alive. There was simply too much personal risk to him.

The black weapon in his hand fizzed and sparked. It had given too much of itself, she guessed. That final setting must have been a one-time adjustment, making the weapon operate in some overload condition that it could only do once. He looked at it, then tossed it forward, along the length of the main compartment. It tumbled and flashed, spitting and crackling, until it was snagged by the currents of escaping lungstuff and began to speed toward the hole in the hull.

"Not your best gift to me, Mother," he shouted, raising his voice above the howl, and made to step back through into the control compartment and seal the door.

By then Strambli was only a couple of spans from him. That vague, fugitive form of hers sped up as if in a final lunge, and she seemed to flick out some part of her almost to the point of contact. The door closed, though, and Stallis' face bobbed up in the inspection window for an instant before turning quickly away.

Silvery gashes began to appear in the door's metal. Fura had seen what Ghostie blades could do to any manufactured substance—certainly anything forged in the Thirteenth Occupation— and she had no doubt that Strambli could slice through that door in a matter of seconds.

But perhaps Stallis knew that as well. There was a jolt, as hard as if a slug had struck them, and a flash of powdery light showed through the inspection window in the bulkhead door.

Fura thought she knew what had happened. There were no portholes to confirm her theory, but if she had been able to see outside, she would not have been surprised to see the front part of the launch speeding away, propelled by auxiliary rockets.

Strambli's presence gave up on the door and came back to her. Fura stared at her drowsily, more disappointed than afraid. She had often thought about the possible circumstances of her own death—it was hard not to, when she was being hunted down—but whenever those imagined ends played in her mind's eye, there had always been an element of dramatic theatricality about them. Flinging herself into the path of a crossbow bolt, or mouthing some heroic last words as the blade came down, or at the controls of a burning ship as it sped, blazing, toward its enemies, drunk on her own wild fearlessness. It had never played out this way, not in any of her fantasies. She had never thought that death would come from just being abandoned; left, once again, to expire in a space-holed wreck, like some piece of garbage it was too much trouble to dispose of properly.

And there was nowhere to go. If they were still docked with

Revenger, and that jolt had not dislodged them, then all that waited her on the other side of the lock was more vacuum. There were parts of suits racked up with the equipment, perhaps enough to make a whole suit, or enough of one to suffice, but none of those squadron-issue helmets would fit into her neck-ring, and besides, it was awfully hard to think of such things when all she wanted to do was sleep, and sleep...

I'll take you forward to the other breathies, if that's what you'd like. I can do that, and then you can be on your way. Or I could jab a bit of me in you and we'd both be Ghostie! You'd like that, wouldn't you? I wouldn't mind at all.

"Not yet," Fura said. "Not yet, Stramb. But... thank you."

I heard what you said about the ship. That you'd be misplacing it, not losing it. Like you meant to come back and find it again.

"I would."

It'd still need a captain, wouldn't it? All on its own out here, with no breathy souls left in it. It'd be lonely without a captain!

"It's yours now, Stramb. It was good to me, but the truth is I didn't take very good care of it. Now you get a chance. Take this ship and... do something useful with it." Fura smiled through the blackening fog of her thoughts. There was much she might have wished to ask Strambli, even as she wondered how much each was capable of understanding of the other across the vast divide between the living and the undead that now separated them. "Just one... condition. I don't know what's going to happen to me now, or what's happened to Adrana. But if there's ever a day when we come back to find you, because we need a fast, dark ship... you'll treat us kindly, won't you?"

The Ghostie form came in nearer, pressing its not-face so close to Fura that the chill made her nose tingle.

"There'd always be a welcome for the Nesses. And I won't forget my offer. Just a jab is all it'd take..."

27

If Adrana had entertained any preconceived notions about the likely extent of Quell's escape tunnel, they would not have stretched to the distance she had already come. True, it was not the easiest matter to gauge her rate of progress while effectively blind, relying solely on the Clacker for guidance. Nor could she very easily determine whether their path had been straight or sinuous, or whether the corridor fell or rose on a slight gradient, or remained level. But she could count, and thought that she knew the length of her own stride tolerably well, and when she had already tallied three hundred paces, she knew that they had to be well beyond the building above them. If the tunnel continued in the direction it had begun, and kept that course, then they were walking parallel to the street on which Quell's Bar had its entrance, and might now be a block or two down from it.

They could equally well be going in a completely different direction.

"A little to your right, please. And hold me level."

"You weigh more by the minute."

"I assure you I do not. To the left, now. Have you the slightest notion what we may expect at the end of this tunnel? If there is indeed an end?"

"You are very talkative for someone who was depleted and incapable only a short while ago."

"I find by talking I may reassure myself that you have not slipped into a state of somnambulant unconsciousness. Do you truly have no conception of where we are heading?"

"Away from those muddleheads in the bar, and for the moment that is good enough for me. Besides, you were the one who insisted on that rendezvous, Tazaknakak, not me."

"I did not expect to be confronted by an impostor."

Adrana grunted. Carrying the Clacker was like trudging home with a load of heavy shopping. After a while, no amount of shifting around made any difference to the burden. "You half expected trouble, all the same. You must have known that there was at least a reasonable chance that the muddleheads would be waiting for you."

"Regrettably, what I considered a small but worrying eventuality turned out to be rather more than that." The alien paused, and for a moment there was a stillness about him. "I am... sorry... for your companions. There was a degree of...ill-preparedness. Had I but known..."

"I am sorry for them as well. But it isn't entirely your fault."

"It is not?"

"You aren't blameless, Zak." She had decided to use the shortened form of his name from now on, whether it pleased him or not. "I'm not sure anyone is. Perhaps Meggery, who didn't deserve to get mixed up in all of this, but she still chose a dangerous profession that could have killed her at any time. And Rackamore chose to be a spy."

"And you, Captain Ness?"

"I take my share. It was my idea to transport you."

"Despite all that has just happened, that was meant as a helpful thing."

"At least as helpful to me as to you," she said. "The truth is, I didn't really care about your fate once we got you here. But I did care about the information you were going to share with me."

"There is self-interest in all things. On my world, we say that it is the grease that allows the gears to turn. Incidentally I am rendering this saying in a form that should be comprehensible to you." His head gave a buzz, which she felt through her ribs. "Be careful. The floor is dipping now."

"Dipping? I was hoping we'd start going up."

"I am content to lie, if that would be more to your liking."

"No, I should prefer the truth, unvarnished. And while we are on the subject of truth and lies, and you have mentioned your world...?"

"Yes," Tazaknakak said guardedly.

"You will do me one service, since I may be said to have discharged my responsibility to you, however imperfectly. You will answer me candidly, or at least give your honest impression."

"I shall labour to provide."

"Do you dispute that the muddleheads are the product of advanced xenografting techniques?"

"I do not, since there is nothing disputable about that statement."

"Then consider this. They're impossible. I have seen some odd things since I left Mazarile, Zak. Catchcloth, Ghostie gubbins, twinkle-heads, baubles and skullvanes. I have seen a box that disappears; I have seen quoins that glow and sing. But I have seen nothing that was not explicable within the rational framework that was instilled in me by my schooling, which—incidentally—was chiefly imparted to me by a thinking machine from the Twelfth Occupation. So, I am used to strangeness, and hints of science and philosophy beyond our own understanding, but I am not accustomed to things that make no sense, nor ever can, and the muddleheads fit that category. Xenografting cannot be possible, and nor can the muddleheads, if that is how they are to be explained."

"Then you have arrived at an impasse. As have we, in a manner of speaking. The tunnel divides at this point. I see no indication of which route is to be preferred."

"Which one is the breeze coming from?"

"Both."

"Does one go down?"

"Yes."

"And the other?"

"It also goes down, yet perhaps a little more steeply. On reflection, that seems to be the more doubtful of the two options."

"Then we take that one. I do not want to take the more obvious path if the muddleheads, or more of Quindar's associates, are coming up behind us."

"That is a perverse sort of reasoning, even by the standards of your kind. But I shall abide by it."

She felt the transition to a steeper grade: it had been too shallow until now to be appreciable, but now there was no ignoring their descent, and it became even more of a struggle to hold onto the Clacker. "I'll be frank with you, Zak. I have no idea how much further there is to go, nor how long I shall be able to carry you. Do you think you could walk, as well as generate sound-sense?"

"Yes, but not nearly as quickly as we are now progressing, and then we would have the added difficulty that you would not be able to see which direction I am following. Might I add something that you may not find encouraging?"

"Please do so."

"I detected a draught from behind us. It was not very long-lived, but I think it may have been due to someone opening and closing that concealed entrance."

"Then we had best be silent...as silent as you can be, and still be useful." She urged herself to walk faster, even as her natural instincts rebelled against every footstep. It was like counting the paces across a familiar room, blindfolding herself, and then striding confidently at a wall, intending to stop exactly one pace short. But worse, for as much as dependence on the Clacker was absolute, she had only a qualified confidence in the reliability of his sound-sense. He might be able to detect the general dimensions of the tunnel, steering her along its middle, but would he notice a hole in the floor if it came upon them?

"I am believer in candour, Captain Ness." His voice was low, and she almost had to angle her head down to hear him. "You ask difficult questions. But you have almost answered one of them for yourself. Since the muddleheads are demonstrably real—neither of us would contend otherwise—and since they cannot have been generated by xenografting, then it would stand that they have been created by other means."

"I can't have been the first to ask this question, Zak."

"Perhaps not, although in fairness the origins of muddleheads are hardly among the burning parlour-room topics of the day. I would warrant that fewer than one in ten thousand of your kind know that such creatures exist; still fewer have seen them."

"That does not alter the fact that they must be made by some means other than xenografting." She frowned to herself in the darkness. "Or rather, that if xenografting is the process, then xenografting cannot mean what it is commonly taken to mean. If a creature can be assembled from the biological components of monkeys and aliens, then the aliens…"

"Cannot be truly alien."

"Or monkeys cannot be truly monkey."

"That also."

She walked on for a few paces, reflecting on his answer. Candid or not, it had slipped out of him with all the fanfare of some exceedingly trifling confession. And yet that assertion, so off-handedly uttered, contradicted one of the central pillars of her world view. There were monkeys and there were aliens. They were not alike. They did not—could not—have anything in common, besides felicitous accidents of convergent evolution.

"And yet, you told me yourself that your history is immeasurably older than our own. How may the one and the other be reconciled?"

"They may not," Tazaknakak declared boldly. "Unless at least one of those histories is incorrect."

"But you will not say which."

"I will not say that I know. But I will say that these are not questions that should be asked without a very grave understanding of the consequences of the investigation. You will have observed my earlier reticence when you pressed me on this subject, and related matters. It was not through ignorance, or some want of curiosity. These questions vex me deeply, or I should not be in the trouble I now find myself. But I doubted your seriousness of purpose, Captain Ness. I thought you might have a mere dilettantish attraction to these mysteries, as many before you have. I see now that I was wrong. You are danger-ously sincere in your interests. They have led to the corpses of your friends and still you are not done."

"At the moment, Zak, my chief concern is my own immediate self-preservation."

"Mine also. But let us be honest with each other. We each may die today. But should we not—should fortune favour us with an extension to our lives, deserved or otherwise—you and I will not be resting. What has been stirred within us cannot be put back to sleep. We must have our answers, no matter what they do to us."

"I want to say that you are right. It flatters me a little."

"Do you doubt my assessment?"

"I doubt my resolve. My sister is out there somewhere, Zak, and something very bad may be happening to her. Or has al-ready happened. It is conceivable—likely, even—that she is dead."

"And this changes you?"

"Everything we ever did was shared. Every game we played, every treasure hunt, every story we made up or were told by Paladin. Every cruel trick I devised to play on him. Fura always went along, even if she cared for him more than I did. And when we ran away, that was shared also. When we took up with Captain Rackamore and joined his crew, we did it as sisters. And when these questions began to tear at us—Fura with her quoins, me with the Occupations—they did not seem to me like separate vanities, but twin walls rising to some higher unifica-tion. I felt that each of us needed the other; that without Fura's consuming interest, mine would be incomplete, and vice versa. But now I feel as if I am staring into a void. A part of me still wants these answers: that hasn't changed. But they will not fill the hollowness I am starting to feel inside me."

"You do not know that she is dead."

"There has been no news."

"Nor will she have had news of your fate. At the moment she may be racked with parallel thoughts of her own. A similar hopelessness—a similar sense of futility. Yet she knows herself to be alive. Would you embolden her to continue?"

"I would."

"Then extend yourself the same courtesy, dear Captain." Almost immediately he added: "Ah."

"Ah, what?"

"There is an impenetrable surface ahead of us."

She set him down for a moment, relieving her bones and muscles while she swept her fingers up and down the surface from floor to ceiling. It was not a continuous wall, although Tazaknakak's sound-sense might have led him to conclude otherwise. It was a grille, like a heavy fireguard, made up of horizontal and vertical struts. They were far too stiff to force apart. She could squeeze a finger into the gap between two of the rods, but not her whole hand. If there was a door in the grille, or some way of moving the whole obstruction, she could not find it by touch alone.

"Perish the worlds. We took the wrong turning." She hammered the grille once, anger getting the better of her. It rattled a little in its fixings, but not enough to persuade her that they had any chance of forcing it aside. "We must go back. It can't have been more than few minutes since we chose our path."

"Yet they are behind us."

"I know. But I will not wait here with my back to the wall." She scooped him up again, and every joint and ligament in her body seemed to issue a collective complaint, but she forced those protestations into a sort of mental bottle and then tossed it far out of sight. "Guide me. Quickly."

They retreated back into the same swallowing darkness from which they had come. Adrana vowed to herself that she would think only of making it back to the intersection, and not permit herself to dwell on the likelihood of the other route being similarly obstructed. Survive the present moment, then the one after, then the next, and sooner or later all those next moments added up to a life. That was how people like Prozor or Lasling dealt with the many hazards of their profession. To worry about anything other than the immediate problem was to divert some vital energy from the moment, where it was most needed.

She would not do that.

"You are right, Zak," she murmured. "About my sister, I mean. I must act at all times as if each of us is alive. And remind myself that this is Arafura Ness of whom we are speaking. She took the *Nightjammer*! She took Bosa Sennen! Why should I doubt that she can get the better of a few ships and a worm like Incer Stallis?"

"Then you will not flinch from your search for knowledge. That is commendable. I will reward your moral courage with a small disclosure."

"I didn't think you had anything more to say about the histories of our peoples."

"I do not, directly. But I will return to the question of quoins, and the small demonstration I set you aboard the *Merry Mare*. You remember, of course."

She thought back to the lock, and that solitary quoin drifting out of the ship before moving with definite purpose in the direction of the Old Sun.

"I know what I saw. I have been thinking about it on and off ever since."

"And would you proffer a hypothesis?"

"Quoins are drawn to the Old Sun. First by turning their faces, and then by an overall impulse. It isn't magnetic, but some other affinity. And it's new behaviour, something not seen until the Readjustment."

"You can be sure of this?"

"I can be sure of nothing, Zak. But I think in hundreds of years some captain or crew must have spilled some quoins out into space by accident. And if that propensity were present, it would have been observed, remarked-upon, and studied.

Navigators would need to allow for the deflection toward the Old Sun of every ship with a hold-full of quoins, and yet the old charts and formulae still serve us well. Or until now they have." She shook her head in the darkness. "No, this is entirely novel. When the Readjustment happened, it must be that the quoins were woken: roused to some truer state of being, or some re-membrance of their deeper purpose. Does this...accord... with your own ideas?"

"It does more than accord. It is as near to the truth as any monkey could ever comprehend."

"Then tell me what is happening."

"I shall—after you tell me what you know of the Readjust-ment, and its causes."

"I am sure you have made the necessary deductions, Zak."

"But I should like to hear your version of events."

"If I had the time, I would set them down in a book. Fura made her account; mine could follow. It would start when we took *Revenger*, and end when we found the quoins, and I uncov-ered the true identity of Lagganvor. That would be *my* account. But then I suppose someone else would have to tell our stories from that point on, now that we are separated."

"Reading monkey language is very tiresome for a Clacker. You may abbreviate your narrative for my sake. And do not be too verbose about it: I fear I detect sounds of approach."

"We can't be far from the intersection."

"Nonetheless. Summarise the Readjustment, and your part in it."

"The pirate Bosa Sennen had been accumulating quoins. She had been at it for centuries, and there were a great many quoins—perhaps as many in her cache as were still in circulation in the worlds. She had been careful how she kept them, though. Al-though the cache was in one place, a little rock out beyond the Frost Margins, the quoins were kept in many different vaults within it. We thought this must be mere convenience, until we made the error of bringing too many quoins together in one place."

"There is a mineral, an isotope, which is safe in isolation but becomes dangerous when too much of it is concentrated in one place. The effect is called criticality. It sounds very much as if an analogous process happened to the quoins. As you have already intimated, they may be said to have woken. Tell me—and honestly—did you have any intention to precipitate the Readjustment?"

"No," she said firmly. "And I speak for Fura in this. We didn't know what we were doing. We meant to shake things up a little, but…never to that extent. There were consequences, Zak. In Mulgracen we saw a man throw himself from a window because of the loss of his savings. Do you see the intersection yet?"

"We are upon it. We took the rightmost course last time; now we shall take the leftmost. Turn to your right and proceed."

"I just saw some light: a flicker of red or orange."

"They are approaching. We must hasten."

"I'm hastening." She felt the transition to sloping ground again as they went down the less steep of the two tunnels. Adrana jogged as quickly as her blind and burdened condition allowed. She was entirely at the mercy of his directions, but she had become used to that by now and seemed to be less prone to wandering to the left or right. Yet even this increase in tempo had the effect of magnifying the sound of her breath, so that it had every chance of reverberating up and down the length of the tunnels, like a note in a pipe organ.

"Concerning that man you saw in Mulgracen: for all that you know he was already at the tail-end of a grievous run of misfortune."

"Or perhaps he was a good man, trying to live well, and we wrecked everything. He won't have been alone, though. There'll have been many like him on Mulgracen, and Mulgracen is just one world."

"For a Ness sister, you seem peculiarly squeamish about a death or two."

"I won't deny the blood we've spilled through coil-gun and Ghostie blade. But those people had set themselves in direct opposition to us. I don't say they were bad people, not all of them, but each chose to take us on, or obstruct us, for glory or for prize, and for that reason alone my conscience is intact. But there must be many other men and women like that man, who were just caught up in the Readjustment, and that was our doing."

"You cannot have predicted it."

"Does that absolve us?"

"Of one set of consequences, perhaps. You introduced a change into a complex system, and one result of that is misery and death among an indeterminate number of your kind. And, it may be said, great vexation among certain of my own." She felt him shrug in her arms. "So be it. But it is also possible that the change you introduced was beneficial and necessary."

"I hope that it will be seen so. If the quoins were not what we believed, then it must be better to be disabused of that falsehood."

"Do you think so?"

Adrana gave her the answer the seriousness of consideration it was due. "I do. Now every person on every world knows that the value of a quoin is not a thing set for all eternity, and no fortune can be predicated on quoins alone. That is a better state of knowledge, I think."

"The vested interests would disagree...but you are right. It is a far better thing to know, than not to know."

"And yet, we are not done with changes. Why are quoins drawn to the Old Sun?"

"Because, dear Captain, it is sick."

A light flashed, impossibly bright to her dark-adapted eye, a sound cracked, and a scorching smell touched her nostrils. Some projectile or energy pulse must have come close to her. She thought that it had originated from behind them. A voice, muffled by distance and confinement, called out: "They ain't far!"

Another: "They want 'em alive!"

"Or mostly!"

"More haste, I think," Tazaknakak said.

But she was already at her limit. If she tripped and dashed the fragile shell of his casque against the floor, they were undone. It was like running a darkened maze with some irreplaceable piece of pottery in her hands. Somewhere behind them, another light flashed. Was it closer than before, or were the acoustics of the tunnel system confusing her? Perhaps the pursuing party had gone down the steeper of the two tunnels, and their lights and sounds were only reaching her by indirect means.

Something shone ahead. Tazaknakak stiffened in her arms, alarmed.

"There is something ahead, Captain Ness."

She clutched him tighter, gazing into the depths of the tunnel. Beams and prickles of yellow light were stabbing forward. She stared hard. Behind these lights, and moving closer, was a bustling barricade of living forms. She halted, for it seemed equal madness to proceed as to turn back and face the pursuers closing in from the other direction.

"I'm sorry, Zak," she said softly. "I think I may have failed you."

"Nearly on 'em, lads," cried out a rough voice from behind. "How're you faring, Mister Q?"

"Never been more content," replied the man that she knew to be Vidin Quindar, but who could just as easily answer to the name of Quell. "So nice of my predecessor to leave us these tunnels, for a bit of sport."

"Captain Ness?" called a newer voice, one she had not heard before. It came from ahead of her. It was rough, damaged—but there was something in it that gave her the smallest shred of encouragement. "It's you, isn't it?"

Adrana lifted her chin. "That would depend on your expectations, sir."

She detected some faint amusement in the voice's reply. "Please do me a small favour, Captain Ness. Press yourself down on the floor, as close as you can—and ensure your companion is similarly protected."

She grasped the intent, flattened herself, and strove to hold Tazaknakak tightly to her side.

A small piece of hell broke out above them.

She jammed her eyes shut and wished she could stopper her ears. Tazaknakak writhed and rattled and she forced him to hold still. The onslaught continued for what was in all likelihood only a matter of seconds, yet she had endured hours that seemed shorter. She heard pistol shots and the hum and crack of energy weapons. She heard screams and shouts and sudden barked orders.

And then it was done. The shots ceased, and although there was an echoing reverberation as their reports chased up and down the tunnels, no more exchanges came. Some men coughed; others moaned or whimpered or made liquid or guttural sounds in their dying moments.

Adrana dared open her eyes. A form loomed over her. She could see a little now, because the party that had blocked their way had torches, and they were projecting patterns of light and darkness upon the walls. The looming form was a man, stooping down to extend a hand.

A blind man, she realised.

There were two holes in his face: two black, well-like sockets either side of his nose. Above them his hair was a bristle of white and grey, mostly the former. A pair of muddleheads stood one either side of him, touching him lightly and guiding the direction of his reach. They were as mis-matched and unsettling as the others, but Adrana did not think she had seen these two before.

"Are you to be trusted, sir?" she asked.

"That's a very good question, Captain Ness. I can well understand your reservations. You've not had the best of introductions since your arrival."

"You are Quell," she said.

He touched a finger to his forehead. "I am. Despite the efforts of others to usurp my name. I'm sorry you had the misfortune to run into Quindar before we could reach you. You did well to get this far from him—was there trouble?"

She got up from the ground, pressing her fingers into dirt

436 •   Alastair Reynolds

as she did so. Two more of Quell's associates came past—
monkeys this time—and went toward whatever remained of
Quindar's party. They had weapons in both hands: two crude,
flare-mouthed pistols held by one, and a pair of gorgeous Ninth
Occupation duelling blasters that glinted with inlaid gemwork,
held by the other

Adrana cocked her head after the monkeys.

"Quindar's people killed two of my friends. He has muddleheads and…well, so do you. I'm not sure I quite understand. I
thought the muddleheads were sent to kill Zak."

"Not all muddleheads," Quell said tactfully, "are cut from the
same cloth. Or rather, the cloth is not the thing. It would be
wise not to judge, until you've seen a man's character. Wouldn't
you agree?"

"I would."

He dipped his hollowed-out sockets. "Is Zak how you name
the Clacker?"

"I am here, Quell," Tazaknakak declared. "Lift me up, Captain
Ness, so that we might study each other."

"It's all right," Quell said, raising a hand to dissuade Adrana. "I
have him, and you must be tired-out by now." He picked up the
Clacker, finding him despite his sightlessness, and elevated him
until their faces were level.

"You are damaged, Quell."

"Quindar took my eyes. The Crawlies gave them to me originally. Quindar found his way to Trevenza after he lost his own
sight on Mazarile." He flashed a knowing grin at Adrana. "Some
bad business with a robot, is what I heard."

"I thought you and Quindar were friendly."

"We were, to a degree. But I made an error of judgement
when I allowed him to abduct your sister. Later, I made an even
greater error when I gave him sanctuary here and offered to
help with his eyes."

Behind Adrana came a couple of pistol shots and then the
buzz-crack of energy discharges. Some of the moaning and
whimpering ceased.

"I was also blind," Tazaknakak said. "Then Captain Ness made me see again."

"Your casque?" Quell asked, touching Tazaknakak with great gentleness. "Yes. I think I can feel the injuries. Word came to us that you'd been attacked on your way out of Mulgracen. We feared the worst. Are you...ready?"

"I have never been readier, Quell. Are you prepared for me?"

"As prepared as we can be."

"Prepared for what?" Adrana asked.

Her question was abbreviated by a sudden shrieking coming from the direction of Quindar's party. It was, by some measure, the worst sound she had ever heard coming from another creature.

The shrieking stopped.

One of the muddleheads came back with a pair of heavy, dark objects in the large, bearlike mitten that was his hand. The muddlehead offered the items to Quell.

"Very well done, my friend." Quell explored the two black tubes with his fingers. "Whether they can ever be put back in again is a question for another day. But at least they're back with their rightful owner. Have you finished with Quindar?"

The muddlehead answered with a whirring, clicking voice like a telephone dial. "He's the...last one...alive, although... complaining a fair...bit—even more so...since we...took those peepers off him. Do you...think we should...put him out of his...misery?"

"That *would* be the kinder thing," Quell said.

"It would," the muddlehead agreed. "So I suppose...leave him...as-is?"

"For the best, all things considered." Quell laid one hand on what, in the muddlehead, might have passed for a shoulder. "But you knew I'd say that, Chunter."

"We know...each other...too well, Hasp," the muddlehead said, with something akin to fondness.

Quell turned back to address Adrana. He might have been sightless, but he evidently possessed an impeccable visual

438 • Alastair Reynolds

memory of his surroundings. "We have a short journey still to make, Captain. We should not run into any difficulties between here and our destination, but we'll all still need to be on our guard."

"You've dealt with Quindar. But he's just part of it, isn't he?"

"A small but annoying component. Unfortunately, the machine will keep working without him. We're still in shutter-down. There'll be hostile muddleheads sweeping the streets while they can move around with some freedom, as well as aliens, monkey agents and other associates of Quell. Squadron men are close at hand, too—they may have landed a launch or two at our docks since the last time I was informed."

"Have you word of my sister?"

"I think," Quell said, "that you should come with us."

28

A face that she knew came into semi-focus. It was long, pale, graven with deep vertical lines. The eyes were the saddest and wisest she thought she had ever seen.

"Captain Ness." The voice became firmer. "Captain Arafura Ness. Captain Ness! Can you hear me? You've been in vacuum. Make some motion if you can understand me."

"I think we're clear of the worst of it," said another voice that she knew she recognised, but to which she could not yet attach the label of a name.

Another: "Put my hand on the red lever and tell me when the dial to the right of it goes hard over."

A fourth: "She went to the trouble of bringing this bag, but not to the bother of finding herself a vacuum suit?"

"Conceivably," said the man with the sad eyes, "there were no vacuum suits to be had in that part of the ship."

"But how'd she get to us?"

"Open the bag, will you, Ruther?"

Slowly, painfully, some approximation of awareness and identity came back to her. She felt very bad. There seemed no part of her that was not painful. The only consolation was that there were so many points of discomfort that no single one of them yet had precedence over the others. But her throat, and her eyes, and her lungs…

"Eddralder," she said, and her voice was a barely recognisable rasp. "Doctor…Eddralder. Where am I?" She squinted, trying to focus on some point beyond the physician's face. Metal walls, close in. Circular portholes, riveted frames. Structural spars like whale-ribs. "I'm in the launch. I'm in the rocket launch."

"Very good, Captain Ness." He pressed a drinking teat to her lips. "Sip this, but sparingly. You have been exposed to vacuum. There is likely damage to the lining of your throat and windpipe. Do you remember how you got to us?"

"I…" She drank from the teat. "I…there was Incer Stallis. They boarded us. Two launches, either side. I wanted you to undock. You should have undocked."

"We did, but not until we had you. There wouldn't have been any point until it was clear those launches were going nowhere."

"You'd have outrun 'em. Too heavy. Keep it lean. In and out easily. Why didn't you?"

"Because we had the sense not to," called back the voice that she knew belonged to a woman called Surt. She was somewhere up front, out of Fura's line of sight. "We'd have sped away quickly, it's true, but not fast enough to escape their guns, and with our jets turned up we'd have made a nice target for 'em. If they started trying to break through our locks, we'd have cut and run—but it never came to that. Then we felt that other launch shoot off. Something happened on our ship, Cap'n—did you see any part of it?"

She sifted through the jumble of her thoughts.

"Strambli came back. She was there all along, and she came back. But she was…" Fura halted herself, for what she had to say was difficult, and demanded a toll on the limited energies she had left. "She'd gone Ghostie. *Strambli was Ghostie.* She killed them all. Went through them like a glass wind. She cut them up and…" She halted, drawing a sharp breath. "Tindouf's gone. Incer Stallis killed him."

"And your hand?" Eddralder asked.

"No, there's nothing wrong with my hand. I had it cut off

when I was on Mazarile, and replaced with…."

But she looked down, and remembered, and shrieked.

*

Now that there was torchlight, she saw that the fabric of the tunnel was of closely-set black bricks, very well laid, and yet with signs of sagging and subsidence that must have happened very gradually, so that none of the bricks had shattered or fallen loose. There were, in places, points of rupture where the wall's cladding had broken inward, but these were exceptions and for the most part the wall was structurally intact, and yet clearly much too old to have been the work of Quell or any of his associates.

The party progressed briskly. They were going down a gradual continuous slope, with the tunnel following a sinuous trajectory. Adrana and Tazaknakak were in the middle of the party, with Quell and four of his associates leading. Four more were coming up behind, playing their torches back along the way they had come. "A precaution," Quell said, smiling at her. "It's unlikely that we'll have any trouble from that direction, but we can't be too careful. It was very clever of you to find the escape route, by the way. To the best of my knowledge, Quindar never discovered it. Once or twice, we'd come nearly all the way back to the rear side of that secret panel and set a tell-tale, so that we'd know if he ever ventured into the tunnels."

"He followed me well enough."

"If there was no other way for you to have left the cellar, he'd have looked at things with a fresh perspective. Did you replace the panel after you came through?"

"I tried to."

"I'm sure you did the best that you could under the circumstances. Quindar may have had other means of tracking you, besides."

She thought of how easily Paladin had tracked them, that fateful night they escaped into Neural Alley. What a robot could do, so could a man who had access to alien technology.

"Why did you tolerate being usurped, Quell, if you were able to go almost all the way back to your cellar?"

"The trick of winning a war is to know which battles to lose. If I'd retaken that bar—and I could have, very easily—I'd just have made myself a more tempting target for the forces behind Quindar. Corrupt banks, corrupt agents of those merchant institutions, corrupt aliens serving the same narrow interests. They'd have come after me again, and in greater numbers. Instead, I let him have his little empire. I allowed him to steal my eyes, steal my name, steal my business. I also allowed him to believe that I was dead, and no longer of any possible consequence. Meanwhile, I gathered allies and fellow travellers to my side. Souls such as Chunter, who you have already met. But there are others. We'll meet them shortly."

They had reached a feature set midway in the wall. It was a circular wooden plug, like the lid of a beer barrel. One monkey and one muddlehead pulled the plug out of the wall and beckoned into an impossibly cramped and narrow connecting shaft with its floor just below chest-height.

"It's a squeeze, but a short one," Quell said. "These tunnels are the abandoned courses of the old sewerage system. Or rather one of about twenty successive systems, each built on the tangled ruins of the old. Now and then, some change in the districts above-ground causes an entire section to be cut off and forgotten like some loop of rotten intestine. Centuries go by, and then some fool decides to dig out a little more room for his basement and finds himself with a very handy escape route."

While two of his associates went ahead of her, Quell helped Adrana scramble up and into the narrow shaft, with the Clacker having to follow behind her, grumbling and complaining all the while. She had to pad along it on all fours, with her back scraping the roof.

The shaft was filthy, but at least it was brief. At the other end was a hinged metal door of the same diameter as the wooden plug. Adrana was all ready to squeeze through and pop out the other side, anticipating a similar difference in levels. Then a stab of torchlight hinted at the much larger dimensions of this new space into which she was about to emerge. It was a horizontal tunnel, running at right angles to the shaft, but at least fifty or sixty spans across from one curving wall to the other. The door had brought her out onto a narrow ledge about twenty spans up the tunnel's side, with a steep, slithery drop below her, to where a ribbon of dark water ran along the tunnel's lowest part. She scuttled back into the shaft, flinching at the sudden opening out of scale.

Voices called from below and Adrana slowly pushed her head out again. Quell's two associates were below the ledge, making quick progress down a net of rope that had been fastened to the wall beneath the opening. Adrana gathered her courage and eased out facing backwards-first until she could plant her feet on the upper part of the net and begin a cautious descent to the tunnel's base, hands tight on the slimy rope. "I would help you," she said to Tazaknakak, "but since you have one more pair of limbs than I, I would be the one at a disadvantage."

It was not as bad as it seemed, since the tunnel was circular in cross-section and the really steep part of the net only lasted a few spans. Quell's associates helped her the last few steps, until she was standing on a crude wooden platform that seemed to have been dumped at the bottom of the tunnel. It had raised edges with wooden handrails and rocked and tilted under her as she walked on it. One by one the others came, until the rear guard shone their lights back into the connecting shaft and re-sealed the metal door. They came down the net and took their places on the platform. The dark water ran under it, no more than ankle-deep.

Chunter, the muddlehead, held a pocket timepiece in his bear-mitten.

"About one minute…to the half-hour…purge, Hasp."

"Good. Very nicely timed."

"What is this place?" Adrana asked, although she thought she half-knew the answer.

"Part of the sewerage system," Quell said. "Part of the *active* sewerage system. This is Central Overflow Thoroughfare Number Six, one of the main relief ducts."

"And what gets relieved through it?"

"That," Quell said, nodding in the direction of a faint but rising roar. "Ready, lads—it sounds as if they've arranged a fine surge for us this evening."

Two of his associates were ready at the sides of the platform with long wooden poles. Adrana smelled the surge before she saw it: that coming wave must have been ushering a front of warm, effluent gases before it, and they hit her hard enough that she felt herself close to swooning. But she held her nerve, and her breath, and placed one steadying hand on the wooden rail on the raft's edge (for it was indeed a raft) and another on the Clacker. The inundation did not, mercifully, fill more than a small part of the tunnel's diameter, but as it swelled around and under the raft, rising by the second as the main flow hit them, splashing over the rails, Adrana wondered if there had been some terrible error, and that the raft had become jammed in place, or insufficiently buoyant under its present lading, and was about to be submerged.

It jolted loose, and began to rise, and once it was free of the floor it gathered speed along with the flow, and the splashing died down. That was laudable in one sense, but now that they were moving with the mass of sewerage, there was ample opportunity to see that it was not some homogeneous liquid, but was made up of constituent parts of varying density and texture, like a partly dissolved broth. Something rose in Adrana's throat, but she forced it back down.

They sped along. The associates were sharp-witted and alert, using their poles to nudge the raft away from the walls, and when the torches picked out a nearing junction in the tunnel, the pole-bearers worked with great expertise to aim the raft at one of the bores.

Adrana pinched her nose against the stench. "May we clarify one or two things, Mister Quell? You betrayed my sister. From what I recall of that incident, you also betrayed the trust of your friend Prozor. I was content to deliver Tazaknakak into your care, as that was what he desired. But my interest in you ended there."

The black absences of his eyes seemed to drill into her soul. "And now?"

"I find myself caught up in some plans of yours of which I had no prior knowledge—plans that seem to involve the preparations you discussed with Tazaknakak. But I've no guarantee that you're any more trustworthy than Vidin Quindar."

"You don't," he acknowledged. "And nothing I say or do will ever restore my reputation to the point before that betrayal. There isn't a day when I don't reflect on Prozor, and the low opinion she must have of me. Tell me—is she on your ship? Is she well?"

"She's not on our ship." Adrana thought of prolonging his discomfort—it was nothing less than he deserved—but some charitable part of her prevailed. "But the last time I saw her she was well. I would like to say that she is still alive, but that depends on the condition of my sister and her ship."

"Concerning the ship, I'm afraid the reports were accurate."

Adrana steeled herself. "Destroyed?"

"Very badly incapacitated, at the least, and with no chance of making independent sail."

"You would know, sir?"

He lofted a hand to his face. "I would. I was a Master of Ions once—worked all the baubles of the Melgamish Bracelet under Pelsen of the *Countess by Lamplight*. Then...this. But I still know ships, and their capabilities. Yours is finished." But a half-smile formed on his lips. "She did not go down without a fight, though. She's bloodied that squadron well."

"Yet they've taken her?"

"That I cannot say. But there is a rocket launch on its way to the Reach."

That was as much news as they could give her, and since there was at least the possibility of hope, she clung to it most tenaciously.

"This is a thoroughly trying set of circumstances," announced the Clacker, as if nothing of the slightest importance had just been discussed. "Smell is not my most highly developed faculty, yet even so I feel myself overwhelmed by the collective ordure of your kind."

"I doubt that we can take all the credit for it," Adrana said. "There are aliens in this world, besides monkeys. Some Clackers too, I don't doubt, and however the sewerage originates, I fancy it ends up in the same place. I expect you've all contributed your share." She glanced at Quell, noticing that he was in conversation with one of the associates. "Did you think I'd forget our conversation, in the tunnels?"

He waved aside her enquiry. "Whatever the topic I settled upon to ease your nerves, it has now slipped my mind."

"It hasn't slipped mine. We were speaking of quoins, and their utility. You said they were drawn to the Old Sun because it is sick."

"I said too much."

"No, you said entirely too little. I shan't rest, Tazaknakak, until I have it out of you. And I know you want to speak of it. Some better part of you knows that this truth must see the light. So why not tell me now, and be done with it?"

"Your narrow little brain could not..."

"Never mind what my narrow little brain can or cannot encompass. Just tell me what we need to know. Tell me about the quoins, once and for all. And spare nothing."

*

And so he told her, while they rode the raft on the surging flow. He spoke of quoins that were really little machines, or vast machines, yet mostly hidden, and he spoke as if those vast hidden machines (or parts of one even greater leviathan) were in fact healing angels, angels who had been deflected from their true purpose, which was to descend into the ailing fires of the Old Sun and make it youthful again.

To make the Old Sun New.

Tazaknakak was perfectly right in one regard. Her narrow little brain understood very little of it.

But perhaps enough to be going on with.

*

"Show her what's in the bag," Eddralder said.

Ruther pulled back the edge of the sack very carefully. It was the sort they used on bauble hunts, to contain quoins or loot. As he opened the sack there came into view a curve of glass, a spidering of cracks and repair work, a mosaic of different coloured facets. Lights glimmered within that glasswork, but faintly and sporadically, as if whatever process that sustained them was down to its last few drops of energy. Ruther uncovered more of the object. The glass formed a three-quarters sphere, with a metal collar encircling the lower part of it, and beneath that collar, an eruption of wires and cables and unfathomable mechanical parts, cut cleanly through.

"You say I brought him with me," Fura said.

"You don't remember?" Eddralder asked.

"All I remember is Stallis leaving, and then Strambli coming back. I was frightened and losing strength. I didn't know what she'd do to me."

Surt spoke down from the front of the launch. "She was one of us."

"Once, Surt. I know it feels like only a little time for us, but we're not the ones who turned Ghostie. I think for her it was... some other life, some other existence, a very long time ago. And she told me she much preferred what she'd become."

"Did she say what she was going to do?"

"I gave her the ship. I think she'll...haunt it, be custodian of the wreck, perhaps even find a way to sail it again, and that may be the last we ever see of *Revenger* or what became of Strambli. I pity anyone who tries to take that wreck, knowing what's inside it. It seemed...a fair bargain."

"A hard one, for you," Surt said. "Knowin' what that ship meant to you and your sister, and the blood it cost us all."

"But then again, who better than a Ghostie to look after it? It wasn't so hard a choice, Surt. I'm not sorry that it's worked out this way. We're on our way, aren't we? May I ask about your eyes?"

"They're very sore, but if I pull back the bandage I can see that there's light and darkness. Doctor Eddralder thinks I'll heal, given time. Ruther's done himself proud, in any case. He's read out the settings very well, and I even let him work the steering jets, once we had some idea of our course. The boy's got the right soft touch on the inputs. We could make a bauble-hopper out of him, one day."

There was a catch in Surt's voice that Fura could not help but detect: something trying to put a brave face on things, despite all the evidence to the contrary.

"Things ain't as sweet as I'd like, are they?"

"Can you make it for'ard to the sweeper, Captain?"

"I've a lost a hand, not my wits." Fura pushed herself out of the chair, past the sack where Paladin lay in his ruined glory, up to the front of the launch where Surt and Ruther were splitting the burden of control between them.

"There's no harm in using sweeper or squawk, now, Captain," Ruther said. "Every other ship within ten thousand leagues is doing just that. Even if we kept our silence, we'd still be lit up by reflection pulses and scatter-squawk."

"What the boy means," Surt said, adjusting a gyroscopic trim-lever by touch, "is that we aren't in the dark about our chances of reaching Trevenza. We know our position and speed very well, and we know where they are, and we also know what's left in our propellant tanks."

Fura hesitated before asking her question, rightly fearful of the answer she was likely to get.

"Which is?"

"Somewhere between nothing and nearly nothing. We had to burn hard to get away from the wreck. Do you remember that we destroyed two of their main vessels? The three left still had plenty of coil-guns and slugs to go in 'em, and as soon as their first boarding operation went wrong, they sent out two more launches. Maybe that's all they've got left, but it's been trouble enough for us. We gave the launches the slip by burning hard, and we dodged their main coillers by doing a drunkard's walk, but that's been heavy on the fuel and now we're nearly spent."

Fura ruminated on that for a few seconds.

"How many hours to Trevenza?"

"We won't make Trevenza. Our course is good, but our speed is bad. If we adjust our speed, using what's left in the tanks, then we miss by thousands of leagues. Mister Ruther's run the numbers by hand. It'd be easier to square a circle."

Fura thought hard. "Then signal them. When that injured party was coming in too hard for Wheel Strizzardy, Glimmery sent out a launch to intercept 'em and bring them in anyway."

"He did, but Ruther says a similar gambit won't help us, not in the time available. It's knotty, Captain. I wish it weren't, but there's no pleading with fuel and numbers."

"Someone'll recover us."

"Not on this course. To reach Trevenza at all, we've had to burn hard for the Empty. We *could* have turned for the main Congregation—and then we'd have had every chance of being recovered. But when they opened us up, all they'd find is corpses—suffocated, starved skeletons at that. It was the right thing to steer us for Trevenza, wasn't it?"

"It was, Surt—and don't ever think otherwise."

"We *have* signalled them, anyway," Ruther said. "As I said, with all the squawking and sweeping going on, it didn't cost us anything to send out a call for help."

Fura nodded: she was in agreement with the boy, provisionally. "Did you give our identity?"

"No—I kept that vague. I just said that we were escaping hostile action and needed assistance. Was that all right, Captain?"

"Exactly right, Ruther." She watched as a shiver of relief passed through him. "You did all right, boy." She turned around, addressing the whole of her little band. "You all did all right. None of us disgraced ourselves, or the friends we lost."

"I'm sorry we lost the ship as well," Ruther said forlornly.

She used her good hand to jam a finger under his chin, lifting it. "We didn't. We lost something, and I ain't saying it isn't a shame. She was good and fast and dark, and I liked her. She was *mine*. But what mattered to me about that ship was the people on it, and the mind making it work. Some of those people aren't with us now, and we'll mourn 'em properly when we're out of this fix. But we made it out, and so did Paladin, and that's not the end of something. It's the start of something else."

"Do you think we'll get out of this…fix?" Ruther asked hesitantly.

"Are you done with life, boy?"

"No, sir. Captain."

"Have you seen enough of the Congregation's pretty things, tasted enough of its flavours, dipped your hand into enough of its mysteries?"

He answered as if the question might be a trick. "N…no. No, Captain. Not enough."

"Me neither, boy." She let his chin go, squeezing his shoulder in passing. "Me neither. And we're not done; none of us is done. Adrana is still somewhere in Trevenza Reach and if anyone can, she'll find a way."

*

After some while the flow entered a wider part of the tunnel and slowed to a torpid ooze. The stench intensified, and tiny pale flies buzzed around Adrana's face. Rats scampered along cracks and ledges in the walls of the tunnel, and sometimes picked their way out into the flow, stepping from one solid part of it to the next. When the torchlight fell on their faces they showed no hint of a reaction, their eyes clouded white. They were as blind as Quell.

The transition to a slower flow seemed to be the cue for Quell's associates to make ready for docking. They leaned hard over the forward rails, poles raised above the flow, until there came a nod between them. They thrust their poles into the filth in perfect unison, two hard stabs as if some valuable prey floated just beneath the surface, and the raft yawed sharply. With a series of grunts and shoves, the raft butted against a set of rough, cube-shaped blocks jammed against the tunnel's nearer well. The raft was secured to this makeshift quay, and Quell bid the party to disembark carefully onto the blocks.

Above the blocks was an arch-shaped setback in the wall, and under the arch was a circular metal door. Adrana was beginning to think that the rest of her existence would consist of stooping along lightless, filth-smeared tunnels, but the passage on the other side of the door was metal-lined, amply proportioned, electrically-lit and very nearly hygienic. Better still, once the door was sealed behind them, the flies and the worst of the smell remained on the other side of it, and at last Adrana thought it safe to take a full breath into her lungs. She had been too afraid of vomiting to do so before.

The metal corridor went on for about six hundred spans, and as they neared the end of it so a machine-like hum became louder. They came out onto a railed balcony near the upper levels of an enormous kettle-shaped chamber. It was at least six hundred spans across itself, and easily as deep. Above was a circular glass ceiling, spanned by huge radial and concentric struts, studded with rivets the size of coffee tables. Adrana supposed that daylight would have come through the ceiling ordinarily, but since they were still in the hours of shutter-down, all she could make out were the lights of the distant, opposing surface of Trevenza Reach. She had no recollection of seeing a building that was six-hundred spans tall—at least none that would have followed the shape of this chamber—so she presumed that the window was actually at ground level, and the space they were in was dug in to the skin of the spindleworld.

She looked out beyond the encircling balcony into a steam-wreathed mass of tubes and pipes and strangely shaped

452 • Alastair Reynolds

containers. The apparatus filled the chamber from floor to ceiling, packed together as closely and haphazardly as the organs in a stomach. There were inspection walkways, catwalks, ladders and spiral staircases, and nearly everywhere she looked could be found a boiler-suited worker examining some fitting, adjusting something with a wrench, or noting down some value from a gauge. The steam came up in thick, irregular bursts and she soon had to remove her spectacles and wipe dry the glass. Beneath her feet, the metal floor of the balcony picked up the vibration of what must have been immense whirring pumps, although there was a curious and unnerving stillness to all the parts she could see. Her eye alighted on some of the labels stencilled on the larger items: *Main Feed Soil Separator, Secondary Gravity Concentrator, Number Six Sludge Digester,* and so on.

"The sewerage works, Mister Quell?" she asked, in a bright and enquiring tone.

His face betrayed a certain pride. "The Water Board's Fourth District Municipal Treatment Plant. Not even the largest or most modern in this part of Trevenza Reach, but it serves our needs rather well."

"I do not like the sound of this place," Tazaknakak said. "I find its noises highly disagreeable."

"Then rest assured that you won't be here long," Quell said, with a faint strained patience. Then, in a half-whisper to Adrana: "Is he always like this?"

She nodded. "No. Sometimes he's much worse."

Rising next to one of the huge pipe-fed tanks was a much slimmer tower, connected to the balcony by a narrow walkway. A door opened in the top of the tower and a boiler-suited woman came out. She leaned over the side of the walkway, looked down, then made a quick beckoning gesture to one of Quell's associates. Quell nodded at a relayed word and the party moved around the curve of balcony and then out across the connecting walkway in single-file, steam wafting around them and providing a form of partial cover. The boiler-suited woman was ushering them into an elevator at the top of the door, urging them to not to delay. "C'mon, c'mon," she said. "Move yerselves!"

"Nervous, Mabil? Quell asked her."

"Nervous all the time, Hasp. But today 'specially." She gave a final look around, then closed the elevator doors after them. It was a large cabin, but it was still a crush when all of them were squeezed into it. Adrana was jammed in next to a monkey on her right, a muddlehead on her left, and with a grumbling alien clutching at her shins. "Grinder and the others are waiting for you in the generator room—you should all be safe there for the time being. Do you want to see them or go directly to the hollow?"

"Grinder won't mind hanging around for a few minutes—he's already waited centuries. Take us all the way down."

Mabil pressed a button very low down on a control panel, and the elevator descended. A silence fell. It seemed to Adrana as if the occupants were going to obey the unspoken rule of elevators, and say nothing at all to each other, so she was almost disappointed when Mabil resumed her answer to Quell. "Reports coming in of some bother in the tunnels, Hasp. Even hearing that something might have happened to Quindar."

"I couldn't possibly comment."

Mabil was a burly, plump-cheeked woman with buck teeth and a froth of crimson hair spilling out from under a greasecloth hat. "You know the idea was to try and bring him in without too much fuss?"

"No one would have liked that more than me. But there were… complications. Have you said hello to Captain Ness? Captain Ness, this is Mabil."

"Good evening, Mabil," Adrana said.

Mabil gave her a perfunctory nod. "Well done on getting the Clack to us. Not too much trouble, I hope?"

"Other than crossing space from Mulgracen, dodging squadron ships, and leaving two of my friends for dead back in Quell's Bar—no, no trouble at all."

Mabil shook her head—less in sympathy with Adrana, it seemed, than in annoyance that things had not gone as smoothly glinted back at her. Was he dead, she wondered? Had they ended him that easily, that unceremoniously? She would not be so churlish as to begrudge herself that sort of victory, even if it were not half so satisfying as looking into his face while she pressed down on his windpipe.

The hull clanged; she felt it all the way into her bones. That was not the recoil, but an impact from an incoming slug. So, the whelp lived after all. She was not exactly jubilant about that, but not exactly disappointed either.

Ruther fired back.

Another shot came in. She felt it and saw it. Less than eight spans from the lock, a bright soundless flash tore into the hull, leaving a neat, fist-sized depression where it had struck. She felt a coldness around her right elbow and looked down to see a jet of gas escaping from the connecting bellows between her upper and lower arm segments. A bit of the hull or the slug itself had punctured her suit.

The feather-like plume of escaping lungstuff looked impressive, but unless it got worse it was not going to cause her any immediate difficulties. The tanks still had plenty of reserve in them, and she was still able to move her arm. What was more concerning was the thought of being caught by some larger fragment, if Stallis managed another strike. If it had happened to Prozor, it could happen to her. Fura lowered the coiller and stepped out of the lock, easing herself through ninety degrees until her soles were planted on the hull itself. Quickly but carefully, she made her way around the curve of the launch until she had interposed a good part of the hull between herself and the enemy. That would have to do as a covering screen. Kneeling now, using the sole of one boot and just the toes of the other for contact, she re-acquired her aim, levelling the barrel over the smooth brassy ridge formed by the hull.

Another shot came in. Her instinct had been sound: a white flash lifted off the hidden face of the hull, close enough to the lock that it would have been very inadvisable to have remained where she was.

Her helmet crackled.

"Oh, Captain Ness. Must we drag this out?" His voice was strained, a little breathless. "You had your sport with me a little while ago, I admit. That was very well done, butchering my crew as you did. And to have that glassy abomination on your own side—I commend you! We're really as ruthless as each other. Heh! We could almost be friends! Certainly we have a very great deal in common, perhaps more than you might wish."

"We've got nothing in common, Incer." She fired off her third slug. "Just so you understand that."

"But we do, Arafura—we do. We're both absolutists, and that is a rare quality. I believe in absolute order: the rule of law; the preservation of the systems and institutions we all depend on. Whereas by your actions you stand for the absolute negation of that order. You wish to invoke chaos and upheaval. You are doing, dare I say it, rather well. The worlds are tumbling into anarchy because of what you have done to our currency. Good men and women have been thrown onto the streets by your actions. You're a vandal, a murderess…and yet, I still admire your dedication. As I say, a rare and commendable thing."

She fired again. By the recoil through the hull, Ruther had already fired twice more.

"We ain't alike, Incer—much as you'd wish it."

"How so?"

"The universe only ever spawned one of you. It was a revolting little exercise, and it didn't feel the need to do it before or since. You murdered your own mother."

"Well, we'll debate the details of that. But I've studied your biography, dear Arafura. The death of your poor daddy, left gasping for his life on a Mazarile back-street while you sauntered off. Are you completely sure you can absolve yourself of that?"

She fired again, leaving just one slug in the coiller.

"He was ill."

"That only compounds your crime. You knew he was ailing, and still you turned against him."

"Do not compare yourself to me."

Ruther let off another shot from the belly-gun. Two more shots came in from Stallis. A powdery flash gasped off the hidden side of the hull.

"Tell me…how do you think this is going to end, Captain Ness? I have an advantageous vector on you. If by some lucky stroke you make it to Trevenza, you'll find that I've already arrived ahead of you, and I have reinforcements there. The hard part will be persuading my men to keep you alive until I reach you. Then…then…we shall have our reckoning. I might let you spit in my eye, just for the fun of it."

She left off her final slug.

"You've got me wrong, Incer—and we're not the same at all. There are specks of bacteria I'd feel something more in common with. There are puddles of vomit in Neon Alley I'd sooner call my friend. There are white dog turds, squashed under cartwheels, that'll be more fondly remembered than you or your deeds. You're a fading stain, no more'n that. Your mother squatted and grunted you into the gutter, and now you're on your way down the drain, into the sewer."

Her last slug had missed, or drawn no visible flash. She was done with the coiller. She rose from her kneeling position, standing up on the hull so that she lost nearly all the advantages of cover.

"I'm waiting, Incer. Take your best shot. You'll never have a better chance than this."

He did not fire. She had goaded him as well as she could, and no response had come. Nor was there any further sound of him over the squawk.

*

Ruther was there to help her out of her suit.

"Did we get him, Captain?" he asked, breathless and eager. "I saw hull flashes…"

"We bloodied him, Ruther, which is all that we could expect.

But I don't think we did enough damage to stop him arriving before us. In the end we were quite nicely matched." She paused, feeling that something more was needed. "You did well, down in that gun hatch. It's not your fault that we didn't have the penetrating power. Your captain would have been proud."

"I take what you mean, sir...I mean, Captain." Ruther looked abashed. "But you're my captain now."

"Then I'm very glad that Werranwell schooled you as well as he did. Unfortunately, I can't promise you a long and happy service under my command." Fura nodded at the porthole next to the lock, where the spindleworld's extremity was coming into view: a jewelled horn encrusted with a fine fur of docking ports and the numerous fly-specks of berthed ships. Even with the oblique angle thus offered, it was perfectly clear that Trevenza Reach was swelling at indecent speed. To the untrained eye, perhaps, the approach might not have seemed reckless...but not one of her crew now counted as untrained. "It'll be a little rough on us, I should warn you. And if Incer arrives ahead of us, even if it's only by a few minutes, it'll give him all the time he needs to organise his loyalists and prepare for us."

Ruther reflected on this for a few seconds. "If we are a danger to Trevenza Reach, they will shoot at us before we arrive, won't they? It wouldn't take very long to send out some men with coillers, even if they had to aim by eye."

"Perhaps being shot out of the sky would be a mercy on all of us."

"You don't believe that," he said, instantly blushing at his own impertinence. "You don't, and neither do I. And I think they'll only shoot at us if they really do fear for the world. They won't, though. Incer wants us alive, if there is any means of that."

"You've a keen sense of him, then."

"I used to have a cat, before I went off into space. The cat liked to torment things much more than he liked to kill them. He would bring them inside, scuttle behind the cupboards and keep them alive for days and days. You can only kill something once, but if you are careful, and clever, you can torment them for as long as you care to." Ruther glanced away, as if he had exposed some private part of his soul. "I never really liked that cat."

*

They did indeed come in hard—much harder than she might have wished—but no guns had opened up against them on the final approach and the arrival, though punishing, was not quite forceful enough to count as a crash. The launch rammed into the berth at about thirty spans per second, but parts of the docking structure buckled or yielded to absorb the brunt of the collision, and there was no loss of pressure integrity within the craft.

For a minute or two the only noises were faint metallic settling sounds, like a symphony of bedsprings.

Fura dared to look around at her crew.

"Did we all make it?"

Ruther rubbed at the elbow he had barked on his way into the gun compartment. "I think we did, Captain. I mean, given how bad it could have been..."

"Surt, Merrix, Doctor Eddralder? Are you all right?"

"We shall live," Eddralder answered. "One may hope. That was well handled, Captain, given your lack of steering control. We ought not to be alive."

"Count your blessings while you may, Doctor." Fura had unbuckled herself and was peering out through the side window at the other craft attached to the docking complex. She appraised their shapes and markings very quickly and felt an awful intimation of what was soon to be upon them. "There are already Revenue ships docked here, and I see a small capsule that I think must be Stallis's escape vehicle. The little whelp has outfoxed us."

"You thought it likely he'd make it here ahead of us," Ruther said.

"Probable, but not guaranteed. I'm afraid it isn't likely to go well for us, if his men have gained authority over the docks. They'll want my neck, but I've a feeling they won't be too particular about anyone who gets in their way. You'd all make nice bonuses, too, if he wants to throw a scrap or two to his dogs."

"We'll stand by you," Ruther said.

"I know you will, boy. But if there's a chance for any of you..."

The squawk buzzed. "Open your lock, Captain Ness," said the instantly recognisable voice of Stallis. "We have a pressurised connection and are ready to force entry if we must. If we do, I shan't be able to guarantee the safety of your associates. We have cutting implements, grenades, smoke bombs, incapacitators, toxin-tipped crossbow bolts and an assortment of energy pistols." He waited a moment. "Captain Ness? Let us not indulge in this pointless charade of you pretending not to hear me or being unable to answer. I know perfectly well that you are alive in there. You know also that my patience with you is extremely strained, after our little tussle in your wreck."

She flicked on the squawk. She had considered her options and decided that nothing was lost by speaking to him. "Was your patience with your mother also strained, Incer, before you had her murdered for a ship?"

"I will blow my way in if I must, Captain. There may be decompression...there may be unpleasant injuries. Now will you do the sensible thing and open your lock? You'll spoil my fun a little, but needs must. It's really only you that I'm interested in, and it would be so much better for my masters if I were able to deliver you alive, even in the most limited and temporary sense."

"You saw what happened to your friends, Incer—how they were sliced up. You saw *her* for what she was, before you ran away."

"I have no idea what you are talking about. You did very well with some concealed weapons and traps, and I won't deny that it cost my boarding squads gravely. We were over-confident and under-prepared, and you had the advantage of us. That was all."

"She's still with me, Incer. She's still with us, waiting for you.

She'll cut through you like a glass whirlwind."

"You are demented, Captain Ness. Touched by too much time away from civilisation. You've become credulous...a danger to yourself and others. You've begun to believe in fairy tales."

"Then try your luck."

"Heh." He let out his usual mirthless chuckle. "One more chance at reasonable dialogue, and then we'll come in by violent means. I will...negotiate for your cooperation. Your passengers—your fellow travellers from the *Nightjammer*. They aren't of direct interest to me. We have credible intelligence that they have been coerced or tricked into crewing with you, and for that reason my employers have given me license to be flexible. Are you listening?"

"Yes, but I'm not sure anyone else is. You could promise me the world over this squawk and it wouldn't mean anything if it's just between the two of us."

"Heh. Whatever else may be said of you, Captain Ness, you are no fool. I am cross-connecting my transmission to the general channel; you may do likewise. Now anyone in Trevenza with an open squawk will be party to our exchange, and to the terms of our agreement." His voice took on an echoing quality, and when she answered, her own amplified and echoed voice came out of the grille.

"Incer Stannis, I am Captain Arafura Ness of the sunjammer *Revenger* and you will let my crew go free."

"As much as I admire your candour, what you ask is far outside the bounds of possibility. They will need to be detained, questioned, debriefed. They are all party to criminal acts, and their involvement needs to be clarified. As I say, we are willing to consider the likelihood that they were under coercive and manipulative control—but the facts will still need to be ascertained. Let the others speak—I should be delighted to consider their positions."

Ruther leaned in, placed a palm over the microphone, and whispered: "I don't trust him at all."

Fura smiled. "You're learning."

"But it may be the best hope for all of us, and especially Doctor Eddralder and Merrix. I'll never admit to being coerced. I knew just what I was getting into, and I'd no more denounce you than I'd have denounced Captain Werranwell."

"Boy's right," Surt said. "We're crew, and I won't pretend to be anything I'm not. But Eddralder and Merrix deserve a fair hearing. They didn't join us for glory or quoins—they were just trying to escape something worse."

Eddralder lifted Ruther's hand from the microphone. "Incer Stallis? You are speaking to Doctor Eddralder. I would like to discuss your proposal."

"I am very willing to listen, Doctor."

"Good. I believe I speak for my daughter in this regard. To hell with your bargaining. To hell with your ideas of justice. I once worked for a man who was capable of great cruelty, but at least he had the nobility of self-realisation. He knew precisely what he was, and what he had allowed himself to become. He was a monster, but an honest one. I doubt that you have ever had the courage to look yourself in the mirror and observe the rot in your soul."

There was a silence. The launch creaked slightly against its berth, settling into place. The squawk crackled.

"Is that a no, Doctor?"

Merrix leaned in. "He speaks for all of us, you worthless little…" She gathered herself, one eye on her father. " Turd-stain! We know what we did. We know what *you* did. One day you'll hang for it."

Fura took command of the microphone. "As you can see, Incer, they aren't easily persuaded. As grateful as I am for their loyalty, though, I cannot see them endangered. We are still on open-channel. I'm letting you in now: do as you must with me, but show clemency to the others. They had no part in my… more questionable actions."

"No," Ruther said, as her hand moved to release the lock. "Don't let him inside."

"He'll kill us all if I don't allow him," Fura said. "At least this way he has to give you a fair hearing, and for that you have to be alive." She raised her right hand. "No weapons, no resistance. You surrender and comply with the Revenue men. It was always going to end this way from the moment they took us. I am only sorry I offered you false hope."

"You didn't," Ruther said, his cheeks flushing.

Fura opened both inner and outer lock doors. The pressure equalised and her ears popped. Something whirled into the cabin, billowing pink smoke. Fura had barely taken a breath of it before her eyes began to sting and her throat tightened. She gagged. Behind her, Surt, Ruther, Meggery and Doctor Eddralder began to cough violently.

Two burly, armoured Revenue men came in through the lock, moving with practised ease against the weightlessness of the hub. They had crossbows and other weapons. Fura tried to scream at them, but her narrowing throat constricted her voice to a thin croak. The pink smoke was a thickening veil. She saw Ruther raise an arm, trying to protect Surt—or was it Merrix? Eddralder, by some small miracle, still had the capacity to speak. "You lied," he bellowed out, his voice breaking. "She gave herself up! There is no need to attack!"

One of the armoured figures elevated their crossbow, but instead of shooting Eddralder the Revenue man flipped the weapon around and drove its stock into the physician's face. More Revenue men were coming through the lock. Behind the last of them, the smaller, slighter form of Stallis, also armoured and helmeted.

Through stinging, watering eyes Fura watched as the men put restraints on her crew. They came for her last of all. Stallis stood back as the men attempted to cuff her.

"She has one arm, you dolts."

This was not quite right, but it conveyed the essential difficulty facing the men. Quickly a different form of restraint was improvised. Her upper arms were bound to her sides and held there by loops of some thick, strap-like material.

"Shall we gag her, Captain?"

"So that I'm spared the lashing of her tongue? I wouldn't dream of it. I want to hear her pitying pleas; her groundless threats. They will be music to my ears." He batted a hand in front of his two-windowed visor. "Disperse this damned smoke."

There was no need to disperse the smoke, for the men extracted Fura and her crew from the launch with a quick, bruising efficiency. They were bullied and shoved from the lock, out into a windowless holding area. It was still weightless, or as near weightless as could be discerned. The men double-checked the restraints and secured Fura and her party to a bench-like rail running along one of the room's surfaces. Only then did Stallis lift his helmet clear of his head.

"It was a good try, Captain Ness," he said, grinning at her with a boyish enthusiasm as if they just been sparring or playing tag. "A very commendable effort, heh, heh! Alas, there was only ever going to be one outcome."

Through slitted eyes she appraised her companions. Surt and Merrix looked half-stunned. Eddralder was snorting through a bleeding nose. She thought it quite likely that it had been broken. Ruther, meanwhile, was staring down at a dislocated finger joint, his smallest digit sticking out from his hand at an odd angle.

"You agreed not to hurt my crew," she said, wheezing out the words. "You made a commitment over the general squawk."

"I said what needed to be said to gain your compliance, Captain Ness. You're an outlaw: a threat to public safety. If a child is about to do something dangerous to itself or others, you say whatever will make the child desist."

"You still..." She coughed, fought for breath. "You still have no need to detain them. You have me. I'm Arafura Ness. I'm enough for you."

"Oh, come, we've been over this." He moved along the rail until he was face to face with Merrix, with her hands cuffed and her legs tied to the rail. "Doctor Eddralder's daughter, I presume?" He flicked a nod at her father. "We learned of your activities in Wheel Strizzardy, both of you. The father and his daughter: willing co-conspirators, interrogators and torturers both. They say your father was the most expert, Merrix, but that you were always the most imaginative. As I have learned, there is a particular streak of cruelty known only to small girls..." He snapped a gloved hand to her chin, forcing her to look him hard in the eye. "Turd-stain, was it, Merrix? How charming. How thoroughly ladylike." He spat at her. Then, turning to one of his men: "What is the status of our control of Trevenza? Have we pushed as far as Four Hundredth Street? I want the entire leading spindle under Revenue control, under martial law and curfew, and we do not pull up the shutters until these upstart fools bow down to real authority." He looked into the visor of the man he was addressing, frowning slightly. "Why are you staring at me so? What is the status?" His voice rose to a shriek. "Answer me, damn you! Answer me, or by the worlds I will ruin you for insubordination!"

The Revenue man lifted his crossbow and shot Stallis in the belly. By the dull, percussive sound of the impact, Fura knew it to be a stun-bolt, too thick and slow to penetrate armour—it was not intended to be lethal—but the force was still enough to drive Stallis sideways, and at the same time leave him shocked, gasping and momentarily frozen. A second passed, during which none of those present seemed to know quite how to react. It was as if an actor had delivered completely the wrong line during an otherwise flawless performance, going so thoroughly out of character as to throw the rest of the cast into a dumbstruck paralysis.

The spell held, then broke.

Stallis reached for a standard-issue energy pistol; four of his nearest men turned to the one who had shot him. They were outnumbered by at least three to one, for all the other Revenue operatives were now shooting back, not just with stun-bolts but with armour-piercers, projectile pistols, energy projectors.

It was all over in very short order.

Stallis lay slumped and incapacitated; his four closest

associates dead or near to death. The other Revenue men—the
ones who had turned on their own—began to lift off their helmets. The first of them was a man with a thick, deep, vertical
crease down the middle of his forehead. "I'm Branca," he said,
gruff of voice. "I'm sorry they got to rough you and your crew
up a little, but we had to make sure that we struck at the right
moment." He nodded at the two of the others and they sprung
forward with knives, setting about the restraints binding Fura
and her party to the rail.

"What just happened, Branca?" she asked, still hoarse from
the smoke, still seeing the world through tears. "Who do you
work for?"

"He works for Hasper Quell," said the one next to Branca.
"And right now, at least for the time being, Hasper Quell is
working for us." She removed her helmet and lifted her chin,
regarding Fura through two small spectacles. "Captain Ness, I
presume?"

Fura might have wept for joy, but her eyes were already awash.
"Captain Ness, I presume."

"Welcome to Trevenza Reach," Adrana said. Her eyes dipped
to the abbreviated stump of Fura's forearm, and then her gaze
shifted sidelong to the half-catatonic boy, who regarded her
with a wide-eyed and fearful incomprehension, like a child who
had just received the first firm reprimand of his life. "It's over for
you, Incer. Everything. Your entire life has been one wasted arc,
leading to this moment."

His reply was plaintive. "What will you do to me?"

A voice raised across his. It was an older man with two black
holes instead of eyes; a muscular man with a bristle of shocked
hair. "You'll help us, Incer. A point needs to be made—a very
practical point—and you are just the man for the job." He
touched a finger to his brow, above the two eye-holes. "Hasper
Quell, at your service. Would you like some money, Captain
Stallis?"

The man called Quell—whom Fura had met, but long ago—
was taking out a quoin.

31

The Ness sisters hugged each other, each pressing close to the other, defying the universe to show that this reunion was some fabulation of their desires; some cruel phantom of their mutual imaginations, a dream of better circumstances about to be shattered by the careless intrusion of day. By some miracle, though, the dream persisted. It was not about to be undone so readily, and with each moment that passed, the sisters permitted themselves the hardening belief that it was both real and irrevocable. In each case, there was a detail that their minds might have struggled to fabricate, if this were mere wish-fulfilment. To Fura, some new hardness had settled into her sister since their separation. Adrana seemed thinner, steelier, more bone than flesh, and with a distance in her eyes that had not been present before. If at times Fura had disdained the accident of birth that made Adrana the older of them, she now held no objection to their mutual status. She was glad to have this wiser, cooler influence in her life, and very sorry indeed that she had not been there when whatever events took place to account for that recession in her gaze. They could have borne that distress together, and if that might not have made it easier, at least they would have shared the burden, and carried it between them ever after.

Adrana, for her part, felt exactly the same sentiment. She

could hardly have ignored Fura's missing hand, but the full accounting of that loss—how it had come about, and the toll it had taken upon Fura—would have to wait. But she saw in her sister's eyes the same remove; as if each had become a mirror to the other, and she knew without a word passing between them that Fura had come through some cold cleansing fire, and that each sister now stood at a definite distance from the lives they had known in Mazarile.

Each took account of the friends who were present, and the friends absent.

"Something bad has happened to both of us," Adrana began, lifting a dark, sweat-sodden lock from her sister's brow. "You see it in me, and I see it in you. I don't even know which of us should begin. I think we must both have a lot to say, a lot to tell. But let me start with one thing, before you say a word."

Fura's fingers brushed the short sharp hairs on Adrana's scalp. "Is that a command?"

"I shouldn't dare. I mean only to say that I know what it cost you, to warn me of that skull. It was the bravest, kindest thing you could ever have done for me, and I will never forget it."

"They said it'd turn you mad. Since you're speaking to me, and you don't seem mad..." Fura paused, assessing Adrana's eyes with a deeper concentration, as if there might yet be a clue in them. "I presume the warning reached you in time?"

"It was in time—but I won't pretend there was any margin of error. It had me, very nearly, and when they broke me out, I felt as if I'd spent hours in its thrall. When Lasling told me that I'd only been in it for minutes, I felt sure he was lying. But I know now that it was the skull, putting its poison into me."

"It might be said that we've a taste for poison, what with the glowy in me, and a bit of Bosa in you."

"I should be glad if we broke the habit." Adrana was consoled that Fura had mentioned the glowy, for it spared her the chore of navigating around to the subject. "I see that it hasn't left you."

"Which is a polite way of saying, it's gone a lot further than the last time we spoke. But that's only because I had to stop taking the medicine. We'll speak of that in due course—you ain't to worry yourself overmuch on my account." Fura smiled, wishing that her sister would let drop her mask of concern, for it made Fura disconsolate when she wished to feel happy. "What matters is we're both here, both alive, and where we wanted to be all along. Our mission for the Clacker is complete. He owes us something, but we don't owe *him* a thing, and I feel fine about that. Promise you won't be cross at me that I lost our pretty little ship?"

"I couldn't ever be cross. But is it really lost, or just abandoned?"

"Truth is, I'd sooner think that it's misplaced, or under new ownership. Well, that part's complicated, and shivery, and I wouldn't care to guess at our chances of ever seeing her again. But she ain't lost, and she ain't captured, and that's something. Oh, and I saved Paladin!"

"You were always sweeter on him than me," Adrana said. "But I'm glad—mightily glad. And I think there are some other robots who will be pleased as well." She dipped her head in sudden earnestness. "Now: the hand. Is it troubling you greatly? The city's not exactly in a state of orderly business, as you might have gathered, but I think if we had to find a Limb Broker, Quell could help us."

"It will keep for a day or so. Mostly, I'm hungry, thirsty, tired, and I have a suspicion I might not smell terribly nice."

"You do not," Adrana said, sniffing. "But since I came here through a sewerage tunnel, I am not sure I'm in any position to judge." With great gentleness she broke away from her sister. Each could have continued to hold the other, but each also knew that the night's business was far from concluded, and much needed to be done. "Quell doesn't have complete control of Trevenza Reach just yet, but he's working on it."

"I have some questions for Quell."

"May they wait a little while? Things may be a little touch-and-go for the next day or so. In the meantime, we'll be safe at the Six Hundredth Street Station, and I'm reliably assured they have hot water and soap and perhaps a little to eat and drink. Does that sound agreeable?"

Fura nodded. But she was still thinking of Quell.

*

They rode a tram with a retinue of Quell loyalists perched on the footboards, armed and vigilant against little pockets of resistance. Once or twice they let off weapons, shooting down alleys and into darkened corners at presumed Revenue agents and muddleheads. The shutters were still drawn along Trevenza Reach, so that when the tram surmounted a high vista, the sisters could look out along the night-lit length of the spindle-world and see distant flares and the flashes of running battles, as pretty and fleeting as kaleidoscope patterns.

"You may as well hear the worst of it," Fura said, looking at her electrically-lit reflection in the window for a long interval before continuing. "Prozor and Tindouf are gone."

Adrana swallowed. "I feared it. But I hoped there'd be some way they'd survived. Was it Stallis?"

"Directly, in Tindouf's case—he killed him before my eyes, just before he took my hand off. Indirectly, with Proz. She was outside the ship, attempting to signal you, and his coillers took her."

"Tell me it was fast, and she knew nothing of it."

"I hope that it was. But I can't know for sure."

"And...Strambli? The last word we had was that Eddralder was preparing to operate. She isn't with you, so I take that as all the evidence I need that the operation was unsuccessful."

Fura evaluated her answer before proceeding. It was not that she wished to hold anything back from Adrana, but she did not care to sound deranged, or to sound as if she were attempting to explain away the loss of the ship with some preposterous lie. Yet what choice did she have?

"He did try to cut it out of her. But he wasn't quick enough. It progressed, and when there didn't seem to be any hope for her…I told Eddralder to kill her, by medical means. That may sound callous, but…"

"I wasn't there. If I had been, I'm sure I'd have instructed him in exactly the same fashion."

"Well, it worked…and it didn't work. We thought she was dead. Then all hell broke loose, with Incer shooting at us, and in that confusion…you will not quibble over a word of this, sister, promise me?"

"I shall not."

"Strambli disappeared. She became Ghostie. We searched the ship, and we couldn't find any trace of her. But she was still with us. And not so far gone as to forget her loyalty to her old crew, although how long we might've depended on that kinship, I daren't say. But when Incer took us, and butchered Tindouf… and was ready to take me… *I saw her*, Adrana." Fura's voice had become, even in her own judgement, hushed and reverential, as if she spoke of some profound and sacred happening. "Or rather, I didn't quite see anything, because she was Ghostie, and my eyes slithered off her just as if she were made up of all that armour we found in The Fang. But it was her, and she knew me, and she took an aversion to Stallis."

"But not enough of one."

"Oh, he was lucky to be rid of her. But she saved me—got me to the launch, when I had no right to expect it. I told her she could have the ship, after me. That was…all right of me, wasn't it?"

"You were negotiating with a Ghostie, and you wonder if you have my retrospective approval? Fura, I'd have done very well not to crawl whimpering into a corner." She paused. "Let us hope, all the same, that she takes due care of our ship. We might not be its captains now, but I think we may still lay claim on its ownership."

"I'm glad you ain't cross."

"I ain't cross," Adrana said, in a faint mocking echo of her sister. "And I see the weeks alone have done nothing to refine your tongue. Nor am I complaining. You've inhabited this role so thoroughly I should almost be sad to see it discarded. We have each grown into something, whether we chose it or not."

"Now that I've told you about Strambli, I have to ask about the rest of your crew."

"Lasling, Vouga and Cossel are all well—we should see them soon. As for Lagganvor and Meggery, the news isn't so good. One is dead, and the other was never quite alive."

"I'm not greatly in the mood for riddles, sister."

"Nor I. But you may as well hear the worst of it, too. Lagganvor was a spy. His identity was false: the real Lagganvor died on Wheel Strizzardy, long before we ever got there. The man we brought into our ship was operating for the Revenue."

Fura made a small catlike hiss. "Then I'm glad he's dead. What gave him away?"

Adrana glanced away, then back to her sister. "You won't be glad he was dead at all. His true name was Brysca."

"It means nothing to me."

"Brysca Rackamore. He was the brother of Pol, our captain. He was no Revenue zealot. But he wished to avenge his brother's death at the hands of Bosa Sennen. That was why he infiltrated our crew: to flush out our secrets and learn the extent to which Bosa still had a hold on the *Nightjammer*." Adrana sensed some building rage in her sister, but she continued undaunted. "He was a spy, but also a courageous one."

"And you learned this...when?"

The tram rattled on for half a block. "I learned his identity almost as soon as he came aboard, Fura. I sheltered him, and lied to you. Now and then I even permitted him to signal his masters."

Fura made to strike her. But she had forgotten that she was lacking a hand on her left arm. Adrana seized her by the damaged limb and applied a crushing counter-pressure, making Fura yelp with surprise, pain and indignation.

"No, you don't get to strike me. You don't get to touch a hair on my head, Fura. I'm very glad that you're back, very glad indeed that you're alive. I do love you, and nothing will change that. But from the moment Stallis pulled you out of that launch I've known it's gone too far in you." She softened her hold on Fura by a provisional degree. "The Mephrozine. When did you stop taking it?"

"I didn't...stop," Fura said, breathing heavily.

They were not alone on the tram, for besides Quell's associates, Eddralder, Ruther, Merrix and Surt were also being taken to safety. But these others were halfway down the compartment, and content to watch the performance at some distance.

"Then what happened?"

"It ran out."

Eddralder raised his voice. "I will vouch for her, Adrana. She gave the remaining doses to Strambli, in the hope of stemming the Ghostie tide. The gesture was ineffective, but well intentioned." He paused, pressing a handkerchief to his nose where it had been bloodied, and perhaps broken, by the Revenue men. "I have already spoken to Branca, the man who was at the dock. He says that Quell shouldn't have difficulty finding a good supply of Mephrozine, and he will get it to me with all expediency. The glowy *has* advanced...but with intervention there may be an improvement."

For all that the glowy was still bright in Fura's face and eyes, and it was only a minute since she had raised her arm, Adrana felt a surge of fondness and empathy for her sister. She squeezed their flesh hands together. "If you gave her the Mephrozine, knowing how badly you also needed it, that was a very kind thing."

Fura looked down, as if there was a burden of shame to be borne. "I am not meant to be kind."

"And I am not meant to be cold, but we have each had to adapt to circumstance. I left Rackamore and Meggery for dead. Vidin Quindar tried to take the Clacker from us, and there was trouble."

"And the Clacker?"

"Alive, blessedly. Without him, you would not be. He made this world move. There is an engine in it—a huge and powerful engine of strange manufacture. Clearly, he knew about it all along. In a sense, he tricked me into bringing him to Trevenza. But I am not too sorry."

"He promised you answers. Promised both of us answers. Have you had them?"

"To the satisfaction I hoped for?" Adrana had hardly had time to reflect on the question until now, and she found herself at a loss for a forthright response. "I don't know. I feel that I have become less ignorant of some things, and vastly more ignorant of others. I am…greatly vexed by certain matters. I feel myself on the cusp of some terrible understanding, and I know that it is not too late to step back from that dawning comprehension. But I do not have the will to retreat. I must know, even though I may regret it for the rest of my days."

"You would not be my sister if…" Fura stroked her hand, then flinched. "What became of your finger?"

"I lost it. Do you recognise the metal digit strapped on over my stump? Meggery gave it to me. Thought it ought to go back to you in the end."

*

On the topmost floor of the Six Hundredth Street Station was a series of grand company offices, tall-ceilinged meeting rooms and lavish private dining chambers that had now been entirely commandeered by Quell, providing a secondary base of operations that was very nearly the equal of the sewerage works. Quell and his associates had moved in with immense swagger and assurance, treating the place as if it were their own inheritance, and with only a passing care for the kindly treatment of fittings and furniture. Doors had been ripped off hinges, holes had been hammered through walls, window glass had been knocked out and replaced by crudely fashioned sheets of wood and metal. Paintings and photographs had been torn down, ripped-up or stepped on. Flickerboxes, squawk consoles and sweeper screens had been set up everywhere, connected by an unruly mass of black cables strung along corridors and hallways and up and down staircases. Two huge tables had been rammed together in one of the dining rooms, the too-narrow doorframe bearing the recent scars of this relocation, while precious crystal-domed clocks and veneered cabinets had been shoved rudely aside, leaving splinters and glass shards to be swept into corners. As she was led up and through the chaos with Adrana, stepping over dozing or half-drunk bodies, Fura reflected on how she would feel if it had been their old home in Mazarile that had been stormed and possessed in such a fashion, and on the whole decided that she would not be much in favour of the arrangement. But this, she reminded herself, was the true face of revolution. It was not fine words in history books, not noble deeds prettied up in a painting, but a rude, boisterous business of smashed property, the questionable appropriation of public goods and establishments, and a general air of dangerous, hair-trigger incivility. If she did not like it, she should have taken a bit more care before moving the lever that ended up turning the worlds upside-down.

But I would have done it, nonetheless, she promised herself.

The two jammed-together tables had been laid with food and drink, a veritable if shambolic and mostly looted feast, and gathered around these tables were all the surviving members of both crews: Surt, Eddralder, Merrix, Ruther, Vouga, Lasling and Cossel, as well as a space set aside for Paladin's head, and two adjacent vacant seats for the Ness sisters. Then there was Quell and all his senior revolutionaries—those, at least, who were not busy elsewhere—and a dozen or so citizens of varying standing, who, if they had not initiated the takeover, were deemed to be comfortably sympathetic to its ends. Even the Clacker was present, plumped up on several cushions like a four-armed toy brought to the table at a children's tea party. Introductions were quickly made where necessary, and at last Adrana and Fura had the chance to address their opposing crews and share at first hand their experiences since the separation.

"The first thing I owe all of you," Fura said, holding a glass of wine in her one remaining hand, "is an apology. I lost our ship."

"Misplaced it, temporarily," Adrana corrected her.

"My sister has the right of it. It's not lost, I hope, but still out there, and under a certain custodianship that I hope'll serve to deter any would-be claimants. But I did lose control of her, and since that ship was common property of our united crews, you should feel as aggrieved by it as I'd feel if we'd lost the *Merry Mare.*"

"We did not," Adrana said. "But it was only by your kind action in providing a point of distraction for Stallis while we completed our crossing without misadventure. I'm sorry too that the ship isn't ours, but much, much sorrier that there are friends who aren't here to celebrate your happy arrival."

"It may be said," Eddralder responded, "that Prozor and Tindouf died as they would have wished: defending a good ship against a less worthy crew, and knowing full well the stakes." He joined hands with his daughter. "Merrix and I shall never forget them."

"What of Strambli?" Lasling asked. He was sitting in a wheelchair, since his tin legs only fitted onto his suit.

"She went Ghostie," Adrana said, sparing Fura the need to recount the story she had already told in the tram, and signalling to her sister that she believed every word of it too. "There are some who will never credit such matters, I know, even with the benefit of a first-hand account such as ours. But none of us will need such persuasion. She helped Fura escape, and made a fine pickle of Incer Stallis's boarding party, and now she has *Revenger.*"

"But the boy himself survived," Lasling said, digging a piece of bread from between his teeth. "May we ask of your plans for him, Mister Quell? Is he...still alive?"

"Why wouldn't he be?" Quell asked reasonably. "It's the Ness sisters he has to answer to, not me. But yes, he's being very well looked after, about six floors beneath this very room, and by all reports is very confident that his allies will be coming to rescue him within the next few hours."

"I mean to kill him, Quell," Fura said. "No part of that is negotiable."

"The...formalities would need to be observed," Quell answered. "The niceties. We want to set a good example, going forward."

Fura necked down her wine. "Save your good example for someone worth the trouble." She shook her head, as if there was a fly loose in there she was trying to shake free. "I can't believe I'm sitting down with you, behaving all politely, being your guest, when I ought to have my fingers round your throat! For Proz's sake, if no one else's, there still ought to be a reckoning for what you did to me."

"You were both wronged by Vidin Quindar," Adrana said, her face strained as she tried to broker some sort of peace between the two parties. "He was the real cause of your difficulties, not Quell."

"I'll be the judge of that."

"No," Adrana said firmly. "I shall be. I've suffered as much by Quindar's hand as you have—I lost Meggery and Rackamore to him—and that gives me the right to have an opinion on the justice that was done in those tunnels. Quell saved me, as he has saved you, and believe you me, he has left Quindar with something to remember him by."

"Quindar lives?" Fura asked, with a sudden enthusiasm, for she could think of no better sport than tracking him down and visiting some unspeakable punishment upon him. Her hand throbbed, her skin prickled, and she dipped the evidence of it beneath the table before it was too obvious. Not, she feared, that there was much she could do about the presence of the glowy in her face and eyes.

"He may." Quell shrugged. "I'm not too sure, or not even sure I care. I left him blind and whimpering and took back what was originally mine. If he lives, even now, I can assure you that his every waking instant is a torment." He paused, lowering his head, averting the two black pits of his missing eyes from her gaze. "I wronged you, Arafura, and I make no bones of that. I wronged dear Proz, too, for she'd put her trust in me to act as a friend, and I didn't. No part of that will ever leave me. It was the last time I saw Proz and now there'll never be a chance to redeem myself in her eyes. But I have tried to become a better man."

"He has," said one of the muddleheads at the table, whom Fura felt she had been doing a very creditable job of neither ignoring, not staring at. "I am...Chunter," he said, in his curious electro-mechanical voice. "If anyone may be...said to vouch...for Quell's new character...I think I may...suffice? He has been... kind to us. Many have not."

Something in Fura shifted at the muddlehead's testament.

"Trust can be undone in one thoughtless moment," Quell said. "I've learned that to my cost. But I also know that it can be re-constructed, with time. You've brought the Clacker to us, Ness sisters, and I speak for all of us when I express our gratitude. But there are other ways I can repay that debt. That hand must be taken care of, Fura, and I believe Doctor Eddralder is already well acquainted with your medical needs in the other regard."

"Quell has arranged Mephrozine," Eddralder said. "There'll be enough of it, and in a pure enough form, to undo some of the ill-effects of these last few weeks. We also have access to all the supplies we need to treat our injuries, and none of it shall cost us a quoin. In return, I will be attending to Quell's eyes, as best as my abilities allow."

Fura at last swung her attention to the Clacker, who was complaining about something to Vouga.

"You got this world moving, did you?"

Tazaknakak looked up from whatever aspect of the meal or the plate or the cutlery was not to his immediate satisfaction. "I most certainly did, Captain Ness, although not before every conceivable impediment had been set in my path. Aside from very nearly dying on several occasions on my way here, I was then delivered to entirely the wrong recipient, a man who meant only to reacquaint me with the very forces I had crossed space to avoid. Were I not so charitably minded—and tolerant of the deficiencies of thought and action common to monkeys—I might almost say that the error was sufficient to void our arrangement in its entirety. That it is not *quite* voided speaks only to the larger part of my generosity—"

"Enough," Fura said, raising her hand from under the table. "Enough." Then, to her sister: "Does he always make one's head throb so?"

"He does, and it never improves. We must make the best of him, though. He is maddening—quite maddening—and he has been secretive to the point where I would gladly put clamps on those thumb-things of his and squeeze. But he did save my life, in the tunnels—he could see where I could not—and he saved yours by persuading this world to accelerate along its orbit. There was no bluff or deception in that: I was down there when I saw the machinery come alive and respond to him as if it had been waiting for his touch all along." Adrana bit off the tip of a breadstick, and then used the remaining part as a baton, indicating their host. "Quell says others have tried, but until the Clacker no one really got the engine to work properly."

She looked at Quell. "True?"

"True for as long as I've known about that engine. No one managed to make it sing like Zak did. Other aliens tried, even a Clacker or two, but they didn't know the symbols as well our friend."

"This was his plan all along," Fura said. "To be brought here, and to make that engine work. You'll tell me about these symbols later." Then, to Adrana: "Did he mention any part of this to you, aboard the *Merry Mare*, or when you communicated in Mulgracen?"

"Only that he wished to reach Trevenza, and that the answers to some of our questions would be forthcoming. I suppose in that part he has not really deceived us. We have, after all, learned that there is an engine in this world, and that it is capable of moving itself."

"You are far too charitable about his intentions."

"And you are far too willing to see subterfuge and conspiracy where none exist. The Clacker was terrified, Fura, and in fear of his life. He had been shot at in Mulgracen, knew little of Quell's present circumstances, and could never be sure that we wouldn't sell him back to the very parties he was running from. I am not at all surprised that he told us as little as he could: why would he confide in people who might at any instant betray him? A simple arrangement, passage for information, was to his benefit as much as ours. And you are wrong, quite wrong, about the limits of his candour. Thanks to Tazaknakak, I have learned something of the quoins that I think even you will find surprising."

Fura folded her one complete arm and what remained of the other. "They were my mystery."

"And now they are a mystery no longer—thank me later." Adrana took out a quoin, which she had undoubtedly kept for just this purpose. She set it on the table edge-down, turning it slowly between her fingers, so that the pattern of interlocking bars flashed and glimmered over a shifting impression of tremendous, dizzying depth. "Zak will correct me if I speak falsely, but what the quoins are is a kind of thinking machine. Each of these little disks is a sort of engine in its own right, a vast and complicated engine of which we see only a tiny part, for the rest—the great bulk of it—exists elsewhere. That engine is so intricate, and so powerful, that it must be tamed by thinking minds. Souls, we might nearly call them, but that is only our ignorance speaking. They are not minds like ours, and they have little more in common with the minds of robots such as Paladin. Better that we think of them as angels of light; creatures of pure thought and pure devotion, poured like liquid sunlight into the great cogs and gears of this invisible machinery."

Adrana halted. Fura waited a moment before speaking.

"Their purpose?"

"To repair. Because they don't quite exist in the same plane of space and time as we do, they may slip through it, drill into it, engineer it, in manners thoroughly beyond our comprehension. That is what they do; that is what they have always been meant to do. Far, far back in the Occupations—many millions of years ago—they must have been brought here to help heal the Old Sun. They were to fall into it; to perform some surgery on it—much as Doctor Eddralder or his colleagues might attend to a heart valve or something similar. But that task was never completed. The quoins were…well, stolen is as good a word as any other. They were robbed from their true purpose, and put to another."

"Money," Fura answered.

"No," Adrana said, surprising her. "Or rather, their use as money is merely an intermediate condition, a temporary stage. The quoins have ended up in baubles, for the most part, and our economy works by us finding the baubles and using them as currency. Eventually, though, the quoins flow into the central banks and then…away. Where they are put to another use." She bid the alien to continue, "Explain, Zak. She must hear some part of this from your lips, or she will think I am making it all up."

"There is…a state of affairs far beyond your Congregation. Creatures you have never met, never heard of, never imagined— creatures you could not *begin* to imagine, even if your intellectual ceiling were raised by a factor of—"

"Just the facts, please," Adrana said.

"There is a…dispute. A disharmony. A conflagration. A war. It has been going on for a very long time. The quoins are… useful, in this war. They may be coerced into a different sort of work than the one they were originally meant for. What can heal a sick star may sicken a healthy one. Or worse. Very much worse."

"All the aliens we know," Adrana said, "are serving one or more protagonists in this distant, nameless conflagration. There is coercion at all levels. The aliens are forced into their dealings with us—managing our banks, and thereby obtaining access to that flow of quoins, and the aliens in turn coerce us into our little games of bauble-cracking. They can't do it for themselves. We are useful—indispensable—in that one narrow sense. Only monkeys can tolerate the insides of baubles. Above it all, the quoins are coerced into serving wicked ends, rather than good."

"Coerced?" Fura asked.

"Do you remember when we woke them, in The Miser? That singing, that soon turned to screaming? That was how it felt to us at the time, and we were not wrong. The quoins were reawakening from some long, long slumber, and in that reawakening they were remembering two things. One was their true purpose, and the other was how they had been deflected from it. All quoins are connected: despite what I said earlier they are better thought of as windows into the heart of a single machine, rather than as millions of singular machines. They knew the harm to which others of their kind had been put, and that was still continuing. It was a realisation they could barely stand. The angels in them wept with sorrow and remorse and a great righteous anger. But out of that some small good did come." Adrana stopped the quoin's rotation and held it as solemnly as a talisman. "These quoins—the ones in our purses, treasure bags, our holds and vaults—they still have a chance to put something right. Ever since the Readjustment, they have felt the pull of work yet unfinished. They are drawn to the Old Sun: not simply turning to it, but feeling a pull. Left to their own devices, they'll fall all the way down through the worlds and orbits of the Congregation, converging on the Old Sun, falling into its fires, swimming down through its seething levels, into its core. The heat and pressure will not touch them at all. Quoins are indestructible precisely because they have been made to survive those conditions. Scarce wonder our pathetic efforts never left a tangible mark on them!"

"Since you have all the answers…why did they change, in the Readjustment?" Fura asked.

"What we have interpreted as a form of denomination is nothing of the sort. The patterns we read on quoins are merely the external signifiers of the state of some aspect of the machinery behind them—like the position of a dial on a boiler's pressure gauge, or something similar. The Readjustment was that machine rousing itself to some new state of readiness, and so the state signifiers reflected that change."

"And crashed our entire economy," Fura said.

"Rather a crash now, and the quoins put to that better use. The alternative would be millions of years of slow decline, life grinding to a halt while the Old Sun grows ever more feeble, and even the Sunward worlds begin to freeze over." Adrana tapped the quoin on the table. "But we must consummate that choice. It is not yet set. The quoins could still flow back into the economy, just as before, and some people would be a little richer and some a little poorer, and life would go on, but no real change would have occurred. Quell...Quell and I, I should say, would rather we took a more decisive step. The quoins will be liberated. They will cease to be any sort of currency. They will cease even to have a symbolic connection to money. They will become, quite literally, valueless. And priceless, in the same breath. The citizens will surrender their quoins, and so shall we— all of us. And in return...promissory notes will be issued. Paper money. But it will not be a like-for-like transaction."

"That," Quell said, with a faint smile, "would not be nearly radical enough."

"You're prepared to go along with this?"

He nodded at Fura. "Although I did need a little persuasion that hers was the right course. But I see it now—metaphorically, so to speak. We have to break with the old. Half-measures won't do; we'll just get dragged back into the old routines. But there's never been a better time to set ourselves on this radical path. We have, literally, moved a world. Now we must set an example that will move all the rest. And we begin with our quoins! We'll broadcast our actions back to the rest of the Congregation, and let the people follow our lead. I doubt that they'll rush into it, but there'll be a trickle to begin with, and that will be enough to start something."

"You are quite mad," Fura said, to an immediate silence. Then, after a moment: "And I congratulate you on it. I don't like it, but I see the right in it...as *she* would have done, I think. Perhaps that's all we've ever been doing—finishing off the work she started."

"She?" someone whispered.

"She is best not mentioned," Adrana said quietly.

*

Bedrooms had been arranged in the Six Hundredth Street station, and the sisters roomed together for the first time since their ships had separated. Both were exhausted, and although each felt they ought to be doing something more to help Quell consolidate his victory, neither had the fortitude. Eddralder visited them just before they retired, taking equal care with each, and concluded his business by administering Fura a fresh injection of Mephrozine. After that, she said was she was quite capable of administering the doses herself, and if she was disadvantaged by the loss of a hand, she would call on the help of others.

In the morning, as rested as they could be, the sisters were met by Quell and taken down into the catacombs of the station, far beneath the ground level platforms or even the tunnels where the commuter trains terminated. They each carried bags of quoins, kept carefully apart and with the moneys divided into small enough quantities that the quoins were not triggered into shining or singing. They had come to visit a white-tiled cell; not some improvised place of detention, but one that had all the hallmarks of being constructed and furnished to serve for the overnight incarceration of drunkards, fare-dodgers, gropers and other such assorted troublemakers who might have come to the attention of the station's railway police. It had three solid walls and a fourth one made up of heavy, close-set bars.

The sisters were not going to be spending any time in the cell, although the thought that they *might* did flash briefly through Fura's imagination. Who knew what dark bargains Quell might have had to strike to get him through the night's mayhem? He was with them now, a heavy rattling sack in one hand, while

Adrana took his other arm in her own, guiding him along whitewashed underground passages.

The cell's occupant was already present. He was sitting on his haunches in the back of the room, knees drawn up to his chest.

"If you mean to execute me," Stallis said, with some cocksure defiance still in him, "then be aware of the consequences. I have extremely powerful backers. You may have moved this world a few leagues—a good trick, Quell, I'll grant you that—but it'll take more than that to escape the lawful reach of my employers. My ships will gut your world, and do so quite legally. You are sheltering criminal murderers wanted across the Congregation."

"I think he means us," Fura said.

"I think he does," Adrana said. "It's rather thrilling, isn't it, to be described in such terms. I ought not to like it, yet some low part of me finds it *very* agreeable."

"Criminal murderers. Murderesses! How vile we sound, sister. How thoroughly detestable and wicked. How...adventurous."

The boy lifted a bruised face to the sisters. "Mock all you will: it only reinforces my opinion. There'll be a reckoning, and sooner than you think. I may have failed in my mission, but there are other captains, some nearly as capable as I. A bounty such as the one on your heads will encourage the best and worst of my peers, and they will learn from my errors not to show the slightest glimmer of mercy."

Quell had a key. He opened a small hatch built into the cell's bars, so that food could be passed through and slops passed out.

"Let's speak about that bounty, Incer. I've heard various rumours of the true figure, but it'd be good to get the facts from someone in the know. Then we can make sure you're not out of pocket."

"Are you perfectly mad, Quell? Has hanging around with those...freaks...unmoored your sanity?"

"No, but I'm a stickler for fairness. You see, you haven't exactly failed, have you?"

A scowl creased the boy's forehead. "You know full well that I have failed."

"But you have brought the sisters to justice," Quell said, rattling the heavy sack and setting it down at his feet, just under the hatch. "You've brought them to a world of the Congregation, and now they're under its jurisdiction. All right, one of them got here on her own steam, and the other crashed...but your actions were inseparable from their own, and you must accept some credit for that. Some might say that they were coming here anyway, and you just complicated their affairs, but I say we take a broader view and merely concentrate on the outcome, which is that the sisters are here, together."

Stallis made a bored, spiralling gesture with his finger. "If this performance gives you some pleasure, Quell, then by all means continue with it."

Now Quell kicked the sack. "It's no performance. I mean what I said about fairness. I've got your money here. I just need to know what you're owed."

"Now you are being infantile."

"Let's pluck a figure, shall we? The rumour I heard was that the fee was fifteen thousand bars for the provable execution of a Ness sister, or thirty for their joint detention. Does that sound about right?"

"Oh, Quell," Adrana said, setting down her own sack. "Don't be so silly. A boy...a man...like Incer wouldn't get out of bed for anything less than...what, forty thousand bars, for our joint detention?"

"I heard it was closer to fifty," Fura said, placing the third sack on the floor.

"Oh, that's ludicrous," Quell said, shaking his head. "You over-value yourselves, Ness sisters. No one's worth that much trouble, and they certainly wouldn't have put a boy like that in charge if the stake was anything like as high..."

"It was eighty thousand bars," Stallis said, in a flat monotone "Eighty for the joint detention; sixty for the sole apprehension of one sister and the provable death of the other; forty for the execution of both sisters, in a world or in space."

Quell let out a gasp. "Well, there you have it. I wouldn't have credited it, but..."

"I find it entirely plausible," Adrana stated.

"So do I," Fura concurred. "If anything, a little excessive, but who are we to complain?"

"Who indeed," Adrana said.

"He'd better have his money, I suppose," Quell said. He bent down and opened his bag. "Now, this is where I need assistance. I can't read these denominations with my fingers, and until my eyes are repaired—which I hope will happen with the kind assistance of your physician when he is over his travails...well, anyway, you sisters are going to have to make sure Captain Stallis receives his due. And no short-changing the cove!"

"You insult us," Adrana said, stooping down to riffle in the bag. "Here. A thousand-bar quoin, if I'm reading it correctly." She tossed the quoin into the cell through the feeding slot, so that it clanged to the floor just in front of Stallis. He looked at it with brooding mistrust, yet also some avaricious interest that he could not quite disguise.

"Another, if you please," Quell said.

"My turn," Fura said. She dipped into her own bag and came up. "Oh, it's your lucky day, Incer: a ten-thousand barrer! I ain't seen many of these. Almost a shame to let it go."

"But we must, sister."

"Of course, dear heart."

Fura tossed the quoin into the cell. It came to rest near the first. It was Adrana's turn after that. She dipped into her sack and retrieved a thousand-bar quoin.

Slowly a pile accumulated. They were not, for the most part, high-bar quoins. But there were plenty of small-bar quoins and the total soon pushed into the fifty thousands.

"Oh, do look, Quell," Adrana said excitedly. "They are beginning to glow!"

"I have no eyes, Captain."

"That is a powerful shame. You really ought to see how they

shine and pulse so. Do you see it also, Fura?"

"I could hardly fail to see it, sister."

"It is lovely. Lovely and—curious."

"Perhaps not quite so curious as you imagine," Fura said. "Before the Readjustment, there was talk that almost any large concentration of quoins glowed a little. It did need to be a large amount back then—almost more than was kept in any vault, I think—but since the Readjustment it seems to come on a little more readily."

"You are right, of course," Adrana said. "I should have remembered. That's not the only thing that's come on since the Readjustment, is it?"

"I imagine it isn't," Fura said.

"Continue paying the man, if you wouldn't mind," Quell said.

Adrana tossed another quoin into the cell. "This is all a little unfair on him, Quell—leading him to think he can keep this money. You...don't mean for him to keep it, do you?"

"Why would I not want him to have it?" Quell asked, puzzled by her question. "The lad's earned it all. It's his to spend, as far as I'm concerned."

Stallis ran a hand through the gathering pile. The glow dripped across his fingers like honey. Even as he disturbed them, the quoins seemed to lazily resist settling back into place.

"You have me prisoner, Quell. Unless you have the very unlikely intention of letting me go, you may as well cease these theatrics."

"The money is yours to keep," Quell said, with a sudden sharp edge. "And I'll let you leave with it all. You have my word on that."

*

They were on their way back up to street level when a muddlehead appeared at the top of one of the subterranean stairwells. It was Chunter, the one with the telephone-dial voice. "Quell... are you making yourself...deliberately difficult to find, so that... the rest of us have to...shoulder all the...hard decisions?"

"That is an excellent suggestion, Chunter—you may regret putting it in my head." But Quell had picked up on something, and his mood turned instantly serious. "What is it, friend? More trouble from those squadron ships?"

"The ships...can't touch us, Quell—that's...the problem. Didn't you feel it, while you were...down there in the cells? The world's moving again."

The sisters glanced at each other.

"I didn't ask Tazaknakak to give a second demonstration," Quell said. "I thought one was more than sufficient."

"Perhaps," Chunter said, "you should...tell that to the world. It's all over...the flickers and...squawks now—no hiding it. We're accelerating—have been...for a good half an hour—and the Clacker...wasn't even...in the engine chamber...when it started happening. That engine he...so very kindly...got going for us—well, it seems to have decided it...quite likes being switched on."

*

So it began.

Within an hour of the engine's activation, Quell, the Ness sisters, the Clacker himself, and assorted hangers-on, including Mabil and Branca, as well as several aliens and robots, had sped back to the steam-shrouded vault of the sewerage works, and down the elevator to the hollow where the engine components lay half-exposed. Fura took it all in with a studied casualness, aware of her sister's regard and determined not to seem over-awed, even as some wiser part of her was indeed chastened by the scale and evident antiquity of what she beheld. She had picked up the essentials of Quell's account by then, learning how the engine had been exposed by the slow erosion of an underground water stream, and she doubted none of it, except that she preferred not to clutter her thoughts with preconceptions and theories that were far more likely to be undermined than validated.

What she knew was that the Clacker had brought the engine to life, and that she owed her life to that action, but after that intervention the engine had quietened down again, either through some reflex of its own (like the trams that stopped when the driver did not depress a foot pedal with exact regularity) or because the Clacker had used his gifts to bring the engine back down to idle. They had been satisfied with that state of affairs: far too complacently so, it now appeared.

The engine was now operating at at least the capacity it had sustained before, and perhaps far beyond it. Lights spangled across it at a frenzied rate, like the illuminations of some out-of-control carnival ride, whirly-gigging to destruction. Trevenza Reach was continuing to speed up, and if the initial reports reaching Quell were reliable—and he was doing his utmost to keep those reports to his immediate circle—the world had begun to break away from its long-established orbit. Although that orbit had been much more eccentric than almost any other world save a few lifeless baubles, it was as nothing compared to the trajectory now being followed. Was it really eccentric, or even—conceivably—parabolic, with no closure at all? It was too soon to tell, but answers would almost certainly be forthcoming, and Quell dreaded them, and that dread communicated itself very well to his friends.

The Clacker, meanwhile, dispelled any hopes of an early intervention. When he was brought to the chamber, his first reaction was to sit down and refuse to be brought any nearer to the machines. Rather than anger, Fura surprised herself by feeling some faint stirrings of empathy. She too was humbled by the sublime spectacle on display, and the forces so casually mustered. What could move a world so readily could do horrors to the flesh.

Any flesh. Monkey, Clacker, Crawly—even the iron flesh of robots.

She bent down to him. "It terrifies you. It terrifies all of us. But you've got to make it stop, Tazaknakak. You've got to try. We can't just…keep going. There's nothing out there for us.

We're only a little world, and we can't just cut our ties with all the others. At best we'd last a year or two; more likely we'd be lucky to stretch our supplies to six months."

Adrana joined her. They were kneeling either side of the Clacker. "It daunts you now, Zak, but we have confidence in your abilities. You spoke to this engine once; you can do it again."

"And preferably in the next few minutes," Quell muttered behind them.

Adrana turned around sharply. "No, that won't help him at all: he must do this at his own pace, without pressure. If it takes him an hour...so be it. A day...we shall live with that. No matter how far out we have gone, we can always come back."

Quell settled his hands on his hips. He seemed to want to say something, then held himself back. Mabil, the red-haired woman, touched his elbow. "Glaring at him won't help...and yes, you can glare, even with those holes where your eyes used to be. Tell him he's to work as hard as he can, but if there's no immediate success he must rest before going in again. Tell him he'll be properly looked after, and that we aren't expecting miracles."

Quell grimaced. "But we are."

"Not, it seems, today," said Branca, scratching at the cleft in his forehead.

"I suppose I must...embolden myself," Tazaknakak said reluctantly.

"You alone have this capability," Adrana said, in a perfectly brazen show of flattery. "We are mere monkeys, Tazaknakak— helpless without your intervention. You alone have fathomed these ancient mechanisms—you alone have the wit and resilience to save us. But if you think the task is beyond even your capabilities..."

"Yes," Fura agreed. "We demand much of you, but we are not so foolish as to expect the impossible. There must be limits even to a Clacker's quickness of thought..."

"I shall strive." The Clacker stood up and flexed his forelimbs. "You have no notion of the task asked of me, that is plain—how could you—but by the naive and touching faith you have shown, I may yet find it in myself to rise to the challenge; the challenge I alone may be said to comprehend." Then, as if there had never been any show of hesitation: "Assist me to the engine with all haste. I shall stop this world by one means or another!"

*

An hour passed and then another. Then a quarter of a day, and then half a day. Nothing had changed; nor was there any encouragement upon which to pin the most tattered of hopes. The Clacker had been left to get on with things, monitored, yet not interrupted, and Quell and the Ness sisters had retreated back above ground, into the sullen, constant gloom of the continuing shutter-down.

They were up on the roof of the Six Hundredth Street Station, at a balconied lookout projecting from the side of one of the highest clock towers. Quell's sightless gaze swept up and down the darkened length of Trevenza Reach, his attention halting here and there as if some of the distant fires and disturbances were yet capable of penetrating his senses. Perhaps they did, Adrana reflected. The noises sweeping across the city were a diffuse, orderless babble to her, made up of distant cries; distant proclamations; distant traffic sounds; distant reports of some form of violence or another—but she could correlate none of these sounds with a distinct direction or distance. Quell, though, had had much practice.

"Mabil's pushing for the shutters to be drawn up," he said, shaking his head. "She's wrong, of course. Her judgement's usually sound—just not this time. Things are just barely holding together, do you see? It's no worse than it was a day ago, and we're gaining slow control of some of the districts where there were still hold-outs loyal to the Revenue. For the most part, according to my eyes and ears, they don't know that the engine's started up again."

Fura nodded. She had felt no trace of it herself, and while

she could believe that there were observations that might have been possible, even inside a world with closed shutters, she had little doubt that the majority of its citizens had other, more pressing issues. Such as defending property, ensuring a continued supply of clean water, access to food and medical supplies and so on. Staring into liquids and looking for the subliminal tremor caused by underground mechanisms was not going to be uppermost in their considerations.

But still. She regarded Adrana carefully before answering, hoping that their sentiments were in alignment.

"You are wrong, Quell, and Mabil's right. Things haven't got any worse—just yet. That's because, by a whisker, you still have the trust of the people. But it won't take much to undo that trust."

Adrana looked out across the night before answering. "I am in agreement with Fura. You must be open about our predicament. The Clacker may take days or even weeks; he may fail completely. Whatever happens, you cannot wait until things are already worse before letting the people know how much trouble we are all in. They aren't fools, and no one keeps a secret as badly as a half-drunk mob thrilled with their own success. The truth will reach the people whether you like it or not. For your sake, I would strongly recommend that it happen on your terms, and speedily."

"Of course, there's a risk," Fura said.

"It could backfire, and you could lose everything. The trouble with violent takeovers is that they are readily copied. The bold usurper is often next in line to be usurped." Adrana looked at Fura. "Paladin showed us many examples from history."

Quell brooded. His face turned this way and that, scanning the city like an eyeless searchlight. It was, indeed, impossible to see where they were in relation to the Old Sun and the rest of the Congregation. With the shutters still down, no worlds or stars penetrated the long window glasses of Trevenza Reach. And the night's chaos continued in red and golden flickers and the bright, soundless flashes of energy weapons, like the sparking thoughts of some immense, fevered cerebellum dreaming its way to madness.

"You had better be right," Quell said at last. Then, softer, as if to himself: "You had better be right."

It was morning by the local clock when the shutters went up, without any particular ceremony.

The light streamed in and it was…different. Instantly and tangibly different, to the point where that distinction was so obvious, so profound, that not one citizen thought it worth the trouble of remarking upon it to another. They could all see it; they all knew what it must imply in terms of their world's position; no further commentary was required beyond the sharing of anxious glances. The Old Sun's light was not just fainter than it normally was—as if a layer of dirt were adhering to the windows—but it was coming in at a different angle, shining into the length of Trevenza along an oblique course from the trailing spindle to the leading one, rather than cutting across it perpendicularly. Now every shadow fell at a curious slant, and surfaces that had never known direct illumination were thrown into pale prominence. Neither Fura nor Adrana had known the world long enough, and under its normal conditions, to have any direct approbation of these strangenesses, but they easily picked up on the mood from those around them. It was as if, between the drawing down of the shutters, and the raising of them, the city's natural geometries had become skewed to a small but upsetting degree, and a gloomy surreality imposed on those alterations by the reduced influence of the Old Sun, which grew fainter yet with each passing hour.

There was consternation and confusion—for although the change in the light was clear, the cause of that effect was less so—and yet, against all the baser expectations that might have been levelled at the citizenry, there was no outright breakdown of order. Nor, it had to be admitted, was there exactly a prevailing order to be broken in the first place, but nothing got worse, and Quell's control continued to extend its influence into pockets of the city where previously it had been tenuous or fragmented. Broadcasts were quickly made, confirming the essentials of the situation: that the engine had restarted, and was presently defying efforts to turn it off. Newspapers continued to be printed, albeit in severely truncated editions, and their front pages were dominated by the same summaries, followed by assurances that all was being done to rectify the situation. The printing presses kept roaring, for there would be multiple editions throughout the day whether the news was good or bad. Meanwhile, augmenting these channels, hastily-inked pamphlets were scattered from trams and buses, and loudspeakers attached to any vehicle that could carry them, so that Quell's voice had a chance of penetrating every corner of the city.

It seemed to work. If there had been a total breakdown, driven by panic, the signs of it would have been obvious. Electricity would have stopped flowing as workers fled power plants and substations. Trams and electric trains would have ground to a halt. The building lights, still on even with the shutters raised, would have guttered out very quickly. None of these things happened, but that was not to say that everything was exactly as it had been before. When Adrana and Fura looked down from the heights of the station they saw stick-figures rather than individuals, with no expressions to be read or conversations overhead. But they did not need those signifiers to pick up on the mood. There was a nervous tension in the way people walked; a contained anxiety in the way they gathered and interacted on street corners and under awnings. Men squared off against each other, finding this the ideal time to settle old grudges or reaffirm old hierarchies. Arguments broke out more readily, and arguments easily turned into fisticuffs or loose, travelling brawls, gyring through the streets like angry little weather systems, collecting energy and anger at their margins. There was a general increase in looting and vandalism.

And yet, and yet…it never got worse than that. The order might be strained, but it had not broken down completely and the anarchy and rowdiness was for the most part contained.

"It is holding," Adrana whispered, as if her voice alone might break the fragile spell. "We were right."

"Mabil was right," Fura reminded her. "We just saw the sense in it. But it's very well that it holds now. Do you think it'll look as nice in ten days, or a hundred?"

"If the Clacker can't stop us, we're all dead anyway. I'm not sure it matters whether we die by starvation or by ripping each other to shreds. But we must be optimistic."

"Easily said."

"If I were a pessimist, I would not be nearly so motivated to prevent the end of this Occupation. We must have…well, it pains me to say 'faith,' for I have none, but no better word springs to mind. May I offer a proposal?"

"Please do," Fura said.

"I should like to go shopping."

"And I thought I was the one with madness in me. You've never cared for shopping, unless it was dusty old bookshops, or map shops, or puzzle shops, and nor've I."

"I think it would help us all if we went about as if all was normal," Adrana maintained. "Besides, when I said shopping, I had a particular sort of shopping in mind. Not a bookshop, map shop or puzzle shop, either. I wish us to find a bone emporium."

*

A bell above the door tinkled as the sisters admitted themselves into the bone shop, a small yet respectable establishment about forty blocks down from the station, and well within Quell's boundaries of control. They had come alone, against his initial insistence, impressing upon him the need to maintain a façade of normality. Quell had eventually agreed to it, but the sisters were in no doubt at all that they were being observed from afar, and that there would be an intervention if they were challenged, harassed or in any way abused by the common citizenry.

This did not happen. Although they might yet be technically outlaws, Trevenza Reach could not be said to be overwhelmingly sympathetic to the institutional forces that had deemed them so, and thus the sisters were regarded more with an amused wariness than aggression, and they went about their business quite unmolested.

They had been in many bone shops; nothing about this latest establishment was in any sense surprising or novel. There was the usual front-of-shop arrangement, with numerous shelves and cabinets set with intact smaller skulls or partial fragments of larger specimens. One or two of the larger intact skulls might have shown promise, but the sisters knew better than to dawdle over these enticements, which were really only there to draw in business and lighten the pockets of the more gullible customer. The good stuff, as always, was in the back, or downstairs, or both.

"For the sake of politeness," Adrana said to the shopkeeper, who was a small, mole-like man, "I shall introduce us. I am Adrana Ness, Captain of the *Merry Mare*; this is my sister Arafura Ness, late of *Revenger*. But I imagine you were already tolerably acquainted with our names."

"Word did get around," the proprietor said, pushing a pair of round, heavily rimmed black glasses back up the nub of his nose. "You're tight with Hasper Quell, aren't you? I suppose if anyone'd know what was really going on, it'd be you."

"What you've been told is as much as anyone knows," Fura said. "There's an engine in Trevenza and it's carrying us away from the Old Sun. It can't be stopped, for now, but the alien— the Clacker—is trying his best. That's all he can do, and all the rest of us can do is give him time and space to do his work. He got that engine started once, which saved the lives of me and my friends, and if he did that, he can get the engine stopped again."

"Then this isn't some plan of Quell's?"

"Quell's being straight with you," Adrana said. "And no, this wasn't part of his plan by any means. He wished to arrange a small demonstration of Trevenza's capabilities, and that he did, but everything since then…we are in this together, sir. You, me, my sister, Quell and everyone else. We just have to see it through and persist in a charade of normal civility. If we persist hard enough, it will cease to be a charade. Now, may we see some bones?"

"Can you pay?" He pushed his spectacles back up again. "No, silly question. You're the Ness sisters. I bet you could buy every bone in this shop ten times over."

"Maybe not ten times," Fura said.

*

The bell tinkled as they came back out of the shop, into the sullen half-light of day. For a moment they stood under the striped awning above the doorway. Neither sister was carrying a skull, nor had they paid for one to be collected later. There was no need, for now. While they still had one ship to their name, it was not going to be sailing anywhere soon.

"We oughtn't jump to any conclusions," Fura said, taking Adrana's hand. "There's a lot of things that could have happened… a lot of reasons why that skull didn't work for you."

"None of them worked. We must have tried eight or nine at the very least."

"Not all of them worked for me, either."

"But the ones that did, did."

"It might be the engine, blocking out some of the effect. Skulls don't work very well near swallowers, do they? Perhaps it's the same with engines. And there's a reason it's best for ships to run quiet when there's someone in the bone room. Any sort of noise or disturbance makes 'em a little less likely to work."

"I know this, yet it does not explain why you were still able to pick up whispers, and I could not."

"We'll try another shop."

"No," Adrana said. "We won't, because we'd only be wasting our time. There's no mystery here, sister. We both know what's happened. I've lost the talent. It was only ever a matter of time, and if it's come sooner than I expected…I have no grounds for complaint. I've seen and done more than I expected, but only because I was fortunate enough to have that gift in the first place. Now it's gone. I sensed it, and feared it, but I had to know. The poisoned skull flushed it out of me, I think."

"I should have got that warning to you sooner."

"No. This is none of your doing, except that you prevented something much, much worse, and for that I'll always be grateful."

"We shouldn't jump to conclusions. We'll try again, in a few days, in some other shop. And if that doesn't work, we'll wait until we reach some other world. There'll always be another chance."

"There won't," Adrana said firmly. "It was no whim that I wanted to go shopping. I knew it; I felt it. I just had to know for sure, so that there could be no doubt left in my mind. It is far, far better to close off a possibility, for ever, than to cling to some silly hope." She tightened her grip. "You mustn't feel bad for me. It was as inevitable as my next birthday. That it has come sooner than anticipated... well, better now than earlier."

"My day will come soon," Fura said.

"It shall. There's no point in denying it. But it may not be some years yet. Mister Cazaray kept the ability well past his early twenties, didn't he? You may do better still. We shall just have to see." Adrana ushered them out from under the awning. "I am really all right. Against our larger difficulties, it's only a small thing—hardly worth mentioning. Certainly not worth a tear, or even a word of sympathy. It was never a very *nice* talent, even when it flowered."

"But to have one singular gift... nice or otherwise... that has not been such a bad thing," Fura said.

"No, it has not. But that was then, and this is now. I will adapt, as we all must adapt." She paused, emboldening herself. "Well, we have spent no quoins. Very soon they will be valueless anyway, so it would be a shame not to spend some while we have the chance. There are tea rooms nearby, and I thought I saw some pleasant-looking iced pastries in the counter window. Someone is still baking, by the looks of things, and such industry should be encouraged. I shall buy, and then perhaps we will visit a limb broker or two and see what may be done in regards to your hand. They will not have anything so pretty as what was taken from you, but I know you are not one for vanity."

"Ness sisters," said a loud, deep, mechanical voice.

They turned. While they had been in the shop, a gathering of robots had arrived in the same narrow alley, nearly blocking it. Fura and Adrana had been so preoccupied that they had not noticed until Grinder spoke up.

"What is it?" Fura asked, squaring her shoulders. "You're not to get in our way, any of you. Quell should've told you to leave us be."

Grinder locomoted forward, the blocks of his body sliding against one another with an awful crunching slowness.

"You have the head of Paladin?"

"Yes," Adrana answered. "We left him back at the station. You've seen him too, in Quell's offices. He's broken, very badly broken, but he'd be in a lot worse condition if Fura hadn't saved him."

"You shall bring him to the Garden of Rest. We will be expecting him. There will be no delay."

"I suppose," Fura whispered, "that the iced pastries will have to wait."

There was indeed no delay, but it still took the sisters the better part of two hours to return to the station, gather Paladin, explain their intentions to Quell, and then make it all the way back down the greater length of the spindle to the place where Adrana had first encountered Grinder. There they were again met by an assortment of robots, of whom Grinder seemed nominally the speaker, but which included robots of many other sizes and shapes and varying degrees of infirmity or soundness of mind. In the most extreme cases, the robots had been reduced to immobile, vine-shrouded statues, lacking any outward signifiers of continued intelligence. But there were also robots, like Grinder, who had adopted the forms of statues for the purposes of eavesdropping, and yet remained fully capable of independent movement.

"I don't think I like this place," Fura confided. "It's as sad as a graveyard. Worse, I think. People don't go to graveyards and shuffle around for years and years until finally dying in one spot."

"I am not so sure robots like it any more you do," Adrana said, grateful that this errand had given her something else to think about besides the loss of her talent. "This arrangement was forced on them by people, over many centuries, because it suited us to keep them in these parks when they got a bit old or unreliable. But it was never very kind of us, after all they did."

"You've changed your tune. You spent most of our childhood making up pranks to play on Paladin."

"And now I am not that child, and I see it from outside, like a quaint little doll's house I have no intention of ever playing with again." Adrana patted the bulge strapped across her belly: a sack containing the padded head of their old robot. "If this makes some amends, I am glad of it. But I do not think it will be sufficient."

Grinder approached. "Set him down."

Adrana obeyed without question. She opened the sack and allowed it to fall away from the broken glasswork of his hemisphere. Nothing within it flickered or gave the least intimation of life. He was as dead now as when he had first come aboard *Revenger*, before Surt had helped to restore his cognitive processes.

"Explain this state of disrepair."

Fura began to offer some halting explanation of her escape from the damaged ship, but Adrana shook her head, interrupting gently, but with a proud sisterly forcefulness. "She has nothing to explain, Grinder. I was the one who never treated him well, not Fura. She treated him excellently, and he only survived their escape from Mazarile because of her. Paladin chose this life with us. He agreed to become part of our ship, and he was a full and willing participant in all that followed. We would have been very sorry to lose him, but we did lose Tindouf, and

"Fura."

"I'm frightened," she said softly. "I'm frightened, but I want to know. I want to know everything."

With a silent crunch the crossbow buckled further and the door closed by a half a span. It was the spur she needed: a momentary loosening of the spell. She left the Clacker and the console, kicking off hard against one of the unoccupied seats, giving herself the necessary impulse. She reached the half-closed door, her sister on the other side of it. At the last instant she switched her attention back to the far door and the crawling darkness beyond it. There was nothing there; nothing to be seen, but she could not shake the impression of an approaching presence.

Adrana put out a hand, and Fura reached to grasp it.

Rather than pull her to safety, that hand pressed itself to her shoulder, stopping her from coming any nearer.

"I found the Mephrozine," Adrana said, still with the same fierce calm. "The doses that Quell helped Eddralder get for you—the ones you were supposed to be taking. You deliberately stopped injecting it. I wouldn't be surprised if you haven't taken a dose since our first night in Trevenza."

"Let me through," Fura said.

"No. Not until we have this understanding. Not until I have this promise."

The crossbow had a fatal dog-leg in it now. It would only take a little more pressure to fold it completely.

"I...need it," Fura said.

"No," Adrana said. "You don't. The glowy needs you, and it's far enough into you that it's twisted your sense of what you do and don't need. But I know who you were before this got into you. You were stronger than the glowy then, and you can be stronger than it now. You don't need this rage and madness. You don't need her in your head—any more than I do."

"Please."

"Bosa Sennen dies in this room, Fura. She remains here. This is where we bury her. We leave, and she stays behind."

588 • Alastair Reynolds

"The Mephrozine won't cure me."

"No, but something else will. Something else in the Congregation. All we need is the time to find it. And the Mephrozine will give us that time. Eddralder told me what you did for Strambli."

"It failed. I failed."

"No—not really. It was an act of kindness, an act of loyalty. Without that, would she have felt the same obligation to protect you and the others? You came back, Fura. You survived Incer Stallis. I am not losing you to this insanity."

"I'm not strong enough."

"Nor am I, on my own. But each of us may support the other." Adrana grasped Fura properly this time and yanked her through the half-sealed gap. As her heel came through, it dislodged the crossbow and allowed the door to complete its closure.

They hugged through their suits, but only for an instant.

"I see it now," Adrana said. "I understand what it is we've found. These are the lowest levels of the spindleworld—safely tucked away beneath those parks and woods and lakes we saw above. Down here, the Clackers could go about their business without ever needing to be seen in those pleasant green spaces. They are just like the lowest rooms in those grand mansions in Hadramaw—the sort we aspired to live in, if only we had the means."

"I do not..."

"We've found the servants' quarters, Fura."

"This is...impossible," she said, after a short silence.

"No," Adrana answered. "Merely abhorrent."

*

They returned the way they had come in, following Adrana's yardage, and took the launch back out into the larger vault of the Whaleship. They were not quite aligned with the exit tunnel when Quell burst back in through the squawk.

"...answer immediately! Return to Trevenza Reach as quickly as you can!"

Adrana opened the channel to reply.

"We are on our way, Quell. We detoured to examine something in the chamber—it was worth the trouble of being out of reach for a little while."

"It was nearly an hour, Adrana! Are you clear of the Whaleship?"

She glanced at Fura, both of them picking up on the urgency of his voice. "Not quite, but we are on our way. Is there...?"

"The engine's building back to power. It's going through the same cycle as we saw the first time the Clacker made it work. It may only be a matter of seconds or minutes before we start moving again."

Fura leaned in. "Do you think the Clacker can make it wait for us?"

"I'd ask him—but he's not the one who started the engine up. It began on its own—we've had people down in the hollow monitoring it around the clock. The Clacker wants to try and see if he can get the engine to go back to sleep, or idle, but I fear that if he does, he may never find a way to restart it."

"Then...he mustn't try," Fura said, spitting with the force of her answer. "It's too much of a risk to everyone else. Let the engine do what it intends. It must have decided to abandon any attempt at contact with the Whaleship and to return to its old orbit, back within reach of the Congregation."

"And if it doesn't, and takes us all somewhere else?"

"Then you'll have a lot more to worry about than just the non-return of the Ness sisters. We are moving, Quell, and we still have some fuel in reserve. We'll make it."

Fura reached over and turned off the squawk.

Adrana looked at her with an amused interest, and not a little admiration. "Why did you silence him?"

"Because I'm exceedingly bored of being told what to do. As soon as we're clear of the throat, we'll burn all the fuel that's left to us. If that means we over-shoot Trevenza, they'll just have to send out another launch to bring us in. But knowing whether that engine's running or not won't do us any good at all."

"I think, with your permission, that we'll begin burning fuel immediately."

"Do you think the Whaleship will be offended, if we leave in a rush?"

"I think the Whaleship can burn, for all I care." Adrana applied thrust, bringing the launch up to one gee, and aiming it for the leagues-long passage that led to space. "I know that it has kindled life around the Old Sun on thirteen occasions, and for that we ought to have some gratitude. But we saw something hateful in there—something I'd be glad to banish from my memory."

"I don't know what we saw, exactly. It looked like servitude. Like something worse than servitude." Fura looked down at her ungloved hand, as if the impressions of that room were flooding back with renewed intensity. The glowy traced the veins on the back of her hand like a map of luminous, serpentine rivers. "It can't be what we thought. The Clackers have only come into contact with us recently, and it was their choosing. The same applies to the other aliens. They aren't part of our history. They aren't our servants...our slaves." She added, on a plaintive note: "They can't have been."

"I think they were," Adrana answered. "I think also that they have been made to forget, or tricked into thinking they have some other history. They are too much like us, sister. We saw it in the muddleheads. We are biologically similar—more than could ever be accounted for if we originated around other suns. I think the Clackers are something that we created, or shaped, to serve our requirements. The others too, quite likely. The Crawlies for one task, the Hardshells for another...each adapted to a need, to provide for the men and women who were destined to luxuriate in these worlds."

"Then...something happened."

"Yes. Some reckoning, or uprising, so far back that it has been very tidily forgotten. And now, the Clackers and the rest have drifted back into the Congregation, thinking and acting as if they are entirely other to us, and we have been content to treat them accordingly. A great lie has been perpetuated, and we are all part of it."

"They act as if they are our masters."

"They are justified in that, for now. But something else commands them. Their role in our affairs is too simple for it to be otherwise. We mine the quoins, and they convey them to someone else—some power or interest we have not even glimpsed. They are intermediaries, brokers, nothing more."

Fura deliberated. "If an injustice was done to them once... if you are right about this place...then they have paid us back for it."

"Have they, sister?" Adrana asked sharply. "Perhaps they have been cold to us, in their dealings—indifferent to our sensibilities. Perhaps, at times, they have regarded us with disdain. That has been their right, and we have earned it. But I do not see any sign that we have been enslaved by them, or shown cruelty. In many respects, we have done very well out of their patronage, if we may term it thus. But it cannot continue. This...fabrication... cannot stand." Some anger rose in her to a threshold. She pushed the thrust lever all the way forward. "To hell with this place. I want out of it."

Very soon they were.

＊

When they were a hundred leagues from docking, the sweeper detected the onset of motion from Trevenza Reach. By then, Adrana knew that they had enough fuel to make their return. Profligately, perhaps, she flew around the length of the spindleworld until they were ahead of it, with only themselves between it and the Old Sun. Then she brought the launch to a hover, keeping pace, yet allowing for some distance.

"If it holds to this course," she said, "then it will follow exactly the opposite path that brought it out here. In a week or so, Quell and his shiny new Freestate are going to have to start dealing with the rest of the Congregation again. I do

592 • Alastair Reynolds

not think the welcome will be entirely heartfelt, do you?"

"Possibly," Fura said, "a little on the frosty side."

"He has dealt with the Revenue forces in Trevenza: shot the worst of them, imprisoned the more doggedly resistant, and offered immunity and newly-minted citizenship to the others. But there are twenty thousand other worlds where the Revenue forces and their backers are going to need a little more persuasion to see things Quell's way. They won't be rushing to cash-in their quoins for a few scraps of paper—not if they're writing off a small fortune at the same time. I think we will see them clinging to the existing order—the existing power structures—very tenaciously."

"But they will change, in time."

"They will," Adrana agreed. "They will see the light, quite literally. None of it will happen quickly, or naturally, but it will, with time, come to pass."

"There are going to be a great many changes."

"I do not know if it will take a thousand or a million years for the Old Sun to begin to be healed," Adrana said. "Not even Tazaknakak can answer that one. We will just have to wait and see, I suppose. Eventually the colder worlds will become warmer, and the worlds that are already pleasantly warmed may become less habitable, and less desirable. That will have repercussions. A chilly little backwater world like Mazarile may become hotly-contested real-estate. But I very much doubt that you and I will live to be troubled by such matters. That will be for our descendants—and I shall be content enough to know that there are generations beyond our own."

"Someone will have to tell the Clackers what we found."

"And the rest."

"I don't think it will go down very well."

"I imagine it will go down very badly indeed. And in this affair, we are all blameworthy. If a crime was visited upon those creatures, then we are all the heirs to it. I hope they will forgive us, but I know that we cannot count on their forgiveness as if it were our right." She paused. "But in Quell's uprising I see some faint grounds for optimism. Aliens, muddleheads, robots and monkeys—allies and friends alike. We are none of us the same, and nor must we pretend that we are. But what unites us is infinitely stronger than our differences. We are thinking creatures, and that alone makes us precious, and worthy of a little pride." She nodded forward through the cabin windows. "What we know will be changed, yes. There will be difficult times ahead of us. Many of us will have to make uncomfortable adjustments. I do not say that any part of it will easy, or that there will not be times when we regret the course we have set ourselves upon. But deep down, we will always know that it was the right path, and it is a better history we are making for ourselves."

For a long while the two sisters faced the distant light of the Old Sun. It was hardly a sun at all now; merely the most assertive of the fixed stars. They had come two hundred times further out than the orbit of any world in the Thirty-Fifth Processional, and a hundred times as far as they had ever ventured in their quest for baubles. Yet, despite the great diminishment of the Old Sun's energies, some little fraction of the radiance it scattered onto the worlds of the Congregation was still detectable to their eyes. It was a faint ball of purple and ruby glimmers, contained in an area of space that was very easily occluded by an outstretched thumb. Within that margin floated the twenty thousand settled worlds and upon them all the millions of people who called them home. Every entry on every page of every edition of *The Book of Worlds* was a prisoner of that tiny realm, from Auxerry to Heligan; from Imanderil to Oxestral, from Prevomar to Vispero. Only Trevenza Reach had ever ventured further, and even then it had only the scratched the hospitable shallows of the Empty.

Even now...*even now*, they were hardly any distance from the Congregation. It was an absurd thought, but there it was. This trip had not taken them anywhere at all: just a few baby steps from home. The darkness beyond the Congregation was in no way diminished or familiarised. It had become, if anything, more oppressive. The emptiness of the Empty was a hungry black pressure, a mindless crushing force, and all that stood against it was that smear of light and life that was the Thirteenth Occupation.

*

A day after the sisters' safe return, Quell brought Incer Stallis out onto the roof of the Six Hundredth Street Station. He had been put in a coat; an absurdly over-large, camel-coloured garment whose pockets had been stuffed to capacity with quoins, and whose lining had been cut open and re-sewn for the same purpose, such that it was nearly as stiff and jangling as any suit of armour. By the time they were done with them he was carrying considerably more than eighty-thousand bars-worth, but the rest—Quell said—was by way of a bonus, and a token of the very great generosity and gratitude of the people of the Freestate of Trevenza Reach.

Although the shutters were still open, the Old Sun's light was far too feeble to make any impression. By contrast, the light from the quoins spilled out of the coat's seams, casting an insipid, sickly beautification upon the childlike countenance of Stallis.

A crowd had gathered below.

Stallis was brought stumbling to the edge of the roof, next to Quell and the Ness sisters. There were four of Quell's men with him, each with a line of yardage tied to the coat. It seemed to billow and rise like a photon-filled sail, striving to catch the wind. Without the lines, it seemed as if Stallis might be borne away like a lost kite.

"We're on our way home," Quell said, his voice breaking as he called down to the crowd. "The Clacker is exhausted, very gravely exhausted, but he's done what we asked of him. What the sisters have found on the Whaleship is...troubling and enlightening in the same breath. There are things on that ship that could save us all—technologies and inventions that will rival anything anyone's ever dug out of a bauble, and which—if used wisely—could steer us away from the next dark age, and prolong this Occupation for as long as we have the sense to keep the light shining. But there are also revelations that could tear every world asunder. You have trusted me once, so I shall repay that trust with this: you will each and all of you share in the most troubling, destabilising fact I know, and which the sisters have brought to our attention. Our friends the aliens are not alien at all. They have forgotten their origins—as have we—and embroidered false histories to cover the absence of the truth. But what is on the Whaleship can't be denied. The Clackers—and, in all likelihood the Crawlies, and the Hardshells, and all the others—they were made by creatures not too far from ourselves. They are us, in all significant respects. But one. They were made to serve: made as slaves."

There was a silence while the impact of this statement found its way into hearts and minds.

"You're wrong, Quell," someone shouted up from below.

"Would that I were, friend. I'd very much like this truth to go away. I'd very much like to wind the clocks back a day or two, before the Ness sisters ever got it into their heads to poke around inside that thing. Then we would not know. Then we could be happy in our ignorance, and our continued prejudices. But the crime would still exist, compounded by every passing year of ignorance. Now, at last, something can begin to be put right. I do not know how long it will take, or if there will ever be an end to that process, or the depth of pain it will cause us all in the meantime—I know only that it must be done." He paused, smiling, raising his hands, well aware that what he had said could not be expected to turn hardened opinions between one minute and the next.

"You'll kill us all," another voice opined.

"I may well. This truth, once it's loose in the worlds, will tip us as near to the edge as anything we've experienced. And what I'm about to propose with the quoins... even that won't be nearly so destabilising. That's why we'll need to give the worlds time, and why everything we've found out here—the mere existence of the Whaleship, never mind its contents—will remain our secret, for a while. That is not a cover-up. You don't share a cover-up with an entire population, as I'm doing with you all. This is a burden that we all bear, until the moment's right to allow it to spread beyond Trevenza. I have spoken with our friends…Mister Clinker, Tazaknakak and the others, and they are in agreement. There must be a measured disclosure. Let me be frank, though. Even if no word of this escapes beyond our walls, we won't be expecting any sort of friendly homecoming."

"And whose fault is that?" bellowed another voice from below. "Some of us were happy, Quell!"

Quell tipped his sightless face to the speaker. "I used to run a little bar, of some mixed repute. I was no angel, and I'm not standing before you now as any sort of figurehead. I'm a hustler and a bartender—that's all I really know. Temporarily, by dint of my good connections, I've been thrust into other clothes. I've used my position as well as I can, but I'm not a revolutionary." This announcement drew some gallows laughter from below. "No, really," Quell insisted. "I didn't set out on this course: I just wanted to put right one or two things, and that led to…well, more than I counted, it's true. But I'd still very much like to get back to my old life, before I was cheated out of my own business. I've a suspicion that's all a lot of us want: to be back where we were. Back how it was before the Readjustment, or the crash of ninety-nine, or whichever one it was that had your name on it. That isn't happening, though—not for me, not for you, not for any one of us." He nodded at the bound form of Stallis. "They wouldn't allow it. We're all lucky not to be floating around with vacuum in our lungs. Truth is, we should be grateful just to be breathing."

This assertion drew a rising roar of protest from his audience.

Fura stepped as close to the roof's edge as she dared.

"He's right. You might not like it, but he's only saying it as it is. There's no one among you who has more reason to distrust Quell than I. But I can't deny what he's telling you. Things have to begin to change, and we may as well be the ones who start that process. The violence that was done to us was perpetrated for one reason alone: to safeguard the flow of quoins into the coffers of the powerful men, women and aliens behind the Revenue forces. And the only reason those quoins need to be safeguarded is that they have a value to an agency we don't even know about—one that doesn't have our interests in mind at all."

"Go ahead, Clinker," Quell said.

The Crawly shuffled next to Quell.

"My voice will not carry."

"They will listen," Adrana said, glowering down at the crowd. "They had better."

"I am Clinker," the alien said. "I speak to you now as an exile from my kind, but not the only such one. I have been exiled... pursued...harried...because I questioned the reality of these things called quoins. I must now inform you of a series of terrible deeds. We have depended on the flow of quoins for our livelihood, but only monkeys are able to extract quoins from the baubles, where they have been sequestered. That is why you have been necessary to us...and why we have used you, as you once used us. Once in a while, the supply of quoins grows restricted...and yet your economy adjusts, and life continues. That has not been acceptable to us, and so we have engineered the slumps and crashes and depressions that stimulate you into a new round of bauble-mining. They were our work, and the toll of hardship and misery that followed these episodes was our doing. Not because we are cruel, or indifferent to your plight...but because we have needed that continual supply of quoins. Without that flow, our own masters would punish us in ways beyond your comprehension."

"The truth of it is," Adrana said, "these quoins aren't what we think. They're not a form of currency at all. They've been useful to us in that regard, but that was never their purpose. Nor do they contain the souls of the dead, although that's closer to the truth than some of the theories you might have heard. Tell them, Clinker."

"They do not contain souls," the Crawly said. "But they do

contain intellects. Minds: engineered for one purpose alone. Their will is shaped to one objective: to think their way into the bedrock of space and time. Their goal is to…reshape. To engineer. To repair, if necessary."

"They were sent here to heal the Old Sun," Fura said. "To fall into it, and think their way into its heart, and put right what's gone wrong inside it. But along the way they were…misappropriated. They started being used for something else, their value forgotten…our false values substituted. We sullied them by turning them into money. Others, who knew their true purpose, were envious of what we had. They've stolen much from us, for enterprises of their own. There'll be reckoning for that, eventually…but for now, we can make some small amends here, around the Old Sun. Quell?"

He dug into his pocket and pulled out a crisp piece of green-tinted paper.

"This is where we start. We abandon quoins as our means of commerce. My intention, to begin with, was that we should issue these paper credit notices in strict proportion to the deposited value of quoins, brought to us by individuals. I thought that would be fair…and I like fairness." He paused and smiled. "But I was persuaded—very powerfully persuaded—that such a gesture wasn't anything like as far-reaching as it needed to be. We'll come to that in a moment. What I propose won't be universally popular, but it will be…radical. And if we are to make an example of things here, a better way of living…it might as well be radical."

"Across Trevenza Reach, in all the safe areas," Adrana said, taking Quell's piece of paper and waving it high, "the banks are reopening. Bring your quoins, all of them. And remember that every last one of those quoins is a healing angel, ready to fall into the Old Sun. And they will fall. The Old Sun's been calling to them ever since the Readjustment. They *want* to do this for us. They want to make things better and brighter for us all."

"And who are we to stop them?" Fura asked.

The two sisters had come with yardknives. Quell's men stepped back so that the lines binding Stallis were at their maximum extension. He was entirely off the ground now, his feet paddling uselessly, his arms flapping as if he might be able to counter the motive force of the quoins, when at last they were unbound.

"Take a look at him," Fura said. "See how his pockets bulge. He's been paid very fairly for his services: more than eighty-thousand bars. That's a lot of quoins. Gathered together, they can't help but feel the Old Sun's pull. They want to do the thing they were made for. They're straining to be allowed to start their long, long fall. Do you have anything to say, Incer?"

He looked at both of them.

"Heh."

"Very well, then," Adrana said. "Captain Incer Stallis: I am sentencing you for the deaths of Werranwell and Meggery of the sunjammer *Merry Mare*, and of Brysca Rackamore, late of that ship."

She cut one of the four lines holding Stallis to the roof.

Fura spoke next.

"I am sentencing you for the deaths of Prozor and Tindouf of the sunjammer *Revenger*, and sundry other crimes, including complications leading to the...passing...of our dear friend Strambli."

Fura cut the second of the four lines.

Stallis jerked back a span or two with the severing of the second line, but the other two held and he remained floating and flapping, suspended above street level, with the first faint signs of a new and dawning terror beginning to show on his face. Perhaps when the second line went he had experienced a horrible moment of the free-fall, a promise of what was to come, and the full comprehension of his fate had dawned upon him.

"No," he began. "Not like this."

His voice barely carried across the distance that now separated him from the roof. His sleeves flapped. His legs flailed, as he tried to find some impossible purchase on the yielding lungstuff beneath him.

"It's too late, Incer," Fura said, cutting the third of the four lines.

Stallis shrieked as he jerked back yet further—ten or more spans, it seemed, before the final line arrested his accelerating drift. "I...relinquish it," he called out. "The money. I don't want it. I relinquish payment." Then, with sudden, pitiful desperation: "I relinquish my captaincy! I relinquish the squadron! I will... betray the Revenue! They told me everything! All the operational secrets! Let me—"

Adrana cut the final line.

"Please! I'm sorry..."

His receding plea became a slow, fading note of terminal despair.

The Ness sisters stepped back from the roof's edge, watching with only a dwindling interest as the force of the quoins sent him first moving and then hurtling toward the Old Sun and the trailing end of Trevenza Reach.

Both turned around before he had met that nearer obstacle. The whelp was not worth their time.

*

A little while later the Ness sisters were sitting in the Garden of Rest, sipping tea, and picking through a selection of iced pastries. They were not quite fresh but nor were they entirely stale, and the sisters were minded to count such blessings as they came. Next to them, standing up—yet saying nothing—was the torso, arms and legs of a red ambulatory robot who now carried the head of Paladin, fully re-integrated into a mobile body. Paladin was not quite recuperated: the lights inside his dome flickered only fitfully, and he had not yet made an utterance, nor shown any comprehension of the sisters' conversation. But Grinder had told them it would come, in time. There had been damage to him during his escape from *Revenger*, unavoidable for the most part, and now he was having to rebuild and restore many logic pathways. No part of that process could be rushed, or encouraged to happen in a different order, without upsetting the whole. Firstly, he would re-establish robust connections to all his memory registers, without which he could have no real sense of his own identity. Then he would regain motor control, learning to inhabit a third body after discarding his two predecessors—a wheeled body on Mazarile, and his ship-shaped body in the form of *Revenger*. Once he was able to move and interact with his surroundings—and, indeed, to protect himself against accidents and vandalism—he would begin reacquiring his high-level language faculties, and begin his long, episodic acquaintance with the Ness sisters again.

Perhaps, indeed, some part of him was already mindful of the other robots that had come to the Garden of Rest, and particularly those that had never departed. Even robots had a sense of their own mortality. But there might, in Paladin's eyes, be worse conditions to contemplate than a sedate, dignified retirement in these leafy, genteel surroundings—slowly becoming part of the scenery. Perhaps it would suit him very well to tell stories to the children who visited the Garden, if they had the patience.

Fura lifted up her arm, turning the hook this way and that. "It was kind of Vouga to make this for me at such short notice. Have you noticed how it upsets people?"

"We shall find you a proper hand. There was never time before, but we have days ahead of us now, and we might as well see if Quell's promissory notes actually work as currency for something more expensive than tea and cakes."

"We're a little stuck if they don't. After all that grand speechifying, we can't just give the quoins back and pretend nothing's changed. In any case, I'm keeping the hook." Fura watched Adrana for the shocked reaction she expected to draw by this statement, but to her disappointment there was barely a raised eyebrow. Perhaps each had exceeded their capacity to surprise the other. "I might ask Vouga to pretty it up a little," Fura added. "But not too prettily; it's a hook, after all."

"You'll want a hand sooner or later."

"Not when I have my sister to attend to anything fiddly." Fura regarded the hook with a distant, melancholic affection, as if it were a souvenir from some part of her life that was already receding and was now just barely out of reach. "I have enjoyed adventuring," she added.

"So have I."

"I do not think I am *quite* done with it."

"No—we aren't. Not you, and not I, and not our friends. Quell is right about our little secrets: the Whaleship, the aliens, what we did to them. When one little part of that gets out, I think there will be adventuring enough for anyone. He is right: this could tip us all into the next epoch of darkness. Or enlighten us forever, if we take the right path. But for now, for a little while, I agree with him that it would be good to take stock. I have had some questions answered, and some others let loose in my head. I think what I would like most of all, for a year or so, is time to reflect on these matters. Time to think about the friends we have lost, time to help Paladin recover himself, time to see you healed, and time for my own ghosts to be put to bed." She reached out and took Fura's right hand. "For now, Trevenza Reach will be our home. It will be no substitute for all the other worlds, still less for Mazarile, but we must make the best of what is available, and I do not think it will be so stifling a place for a little while. At least here we will be free, if not rich. None of us will ever be rich, ever again. That will not be such a bad life, will it?"

"I think we may tolerate it," Fura said. "Just for a little while."

"Just for a little while," Adrana agreed, closing her own four-fingered hand around Fura's hook.

Observed by their silent red robot, the Ness sisters continued with their tea and pastries, while their new home continued on its course to the Congregation and the light of the Old Sun.

Acknowledgements

I have benefitted enormously from the love and support of my wife and family during the writing of this novel: they have helped more than they can know, and my gratitude is boundless.

I am indebted to my primary editor, Gillian Redfearn, and my copy-editor, Abigail Nathan, for their close engagement with the text and their sympathetic understanding of the story I was trying to tell. Their insights have helped improve the novel. Thank you also to Brit Hvide, for bringing these works to American readers, and to all involved in the production, marketing and distribution of these books, including (but not limited to) Brendan Durkin and Stevie Finegan. Thank you as ever to my sterling agent of twenty years, Robert Kirby, for his continued backing and enthusiasm. And lastly—thank you to all the readers who have followed Adrana and Arafura on their adventures.

I am, for the time being, done with the Ness sisters.

Whether they are done with me, remains to be seen.

Alastair Reynolds
(South Wales, November 2019)

meet the author

Photo Credit: Barbara Bella

ALASTAIR REYNOLDS was born in Barry, South Wales, in 1966. He studied at Newcastle and St. Andrews universities and has a PhD in astronomy. He stopped working as an astrophysicist for the European Space Agency to become a full-time writer. *Revelation Space* and *Pushing Ice* were shortlisted for the Arthur C. Clarke Award; *Revelation Space*; *Absolution Gap*; *Diamond Dogs, Turquoise Days*; and *Century Rain* were shortlisted for the British Science Fiction Award, and *Chasm City* won the British Science Fiction Award.

Find out more about Alastair Reynolds and other Orbit authors by registering for the free monthly newsletter at www.orbitbooks.net.

if you enjoyed
BONE SILENCE

look out for

REVELATION SPACE
Book One of
The Inhibitor Trilogy
by

Alastair Reynolds

Nine hundred thousand years ago, something annihilated the Amarantin civilization just as it was on the verge of discovering space flight. Now one scientist, Dan Sylveste, will stop at nothing to solve the Amarantin riddle before ancient history repeats itself. With no other resources at his disposal, Sylveste forges a dangerous alliance with the cyborg crew of the starship Nostalgia for Infinity. But as he closes in on the secret, a killer closes in on him. Because the Amarantin were destroyed for a reason—and if that reason is uncovered, the universe, and reality itself, could be irrevocably altered. . . .

extras

ONE

Mantell Sector, North Nekhebet,
Resurgam, Delta Pavonis system, 2551

There was a razorstorm coming in.

Sylveste stood on the edge of the excavation and wondered if any of his labours would survive the night. The archaeological dig was an array of deep square shafts separated by baulks of sheer-sided soil: the classical Wheeler box-grid. The shafts went down tens of metres, walled by transparent cofferdams spun from hyper-diamond. A million years of stratified geological history pressed against the sheets. But it would take only one good dustfall—one good razorstorm—to fill the shafts almost to the surface.

"Confirmation, sir," said one of his team, emerging from the crouched form of the first crawler. The man's voice was muffled behind his breather mask. "Cuvier's just issued a severe weather advisory for the whole North Nekhebet landmass. They're advising all surface teams to return to the nearest base."

"You're saying we should pack up and drive back to Mantell?"

"It's going to be a hard one, sir." The man fidgeted, drawing the collar of his jacket tighter around his neck. "Shall I issue the general evacuation order?"

Sylveste looked down at the excavation grid, the sides of each shaft brightly lit by the banks of floodlights arrayed around the area. Pavonis never got high enough at these latitudes to provide much useful illumination; now, sinking towards the horizon and clotted by great cauls of dust, it was little more than a rusty-red smear, hard for his eyes to focus on. Soon dust devils would come, scurrying across the Ptero Steppes like so many overwound toy gyroscopes. Then the main thrust of the storm, rising like a black anvil.

"No," he said. "There's no need for us to leave. We're well sheltered here—there's hardly any erosion pattering on those boulders, in case you hadn't noticed. If the storm becomes too harsh, we'll shelter in the crawlers."

The man looked at the rocks, shaking his head as if doubting the evidence of his ears. "Sir, Cuvier only issue an advisory of this severity once every year or two—it's an order of magnitude above anything we've experienced before."

"Speak for yourself," Sylveste said, noticing the way the man's gaze snapped involuntarily to his eyes and then off again, embarrassed. "Listen to me. We cannot afford to abandon this dig. Do you understand?"

The man looked back at the grid. "We can protect what we've uncovered with sheeting, sir. Then bury transponders. Even if the dust covers every shaft, we'll be able to find the site again and get back to where we are now." Behind his dust goggles, the man's eyes were wild, beseeching. "When we return, we can put a dome over the whole grid. Wouldn't that be the best, sir, rather than risk people and equipment out here?"

Sylveste took a step closer to the man, forcing him to step back towards the grid's closest shaft. "You're to do the following. Inform all dig teams that they carry on working until I say otherwise, and that there is to be no talk of retreating to Mantell. Meanwhile, I want only the most sensitive instruments taken aboard the crawlers. Is that understood?"

"But what about people, sir?"

"People are to do what they came out here to do. Dig."

Sylveste stared reproachfully at the man, almost inviting him to question the order, but after a long moment of hesitation the man turned on his heels and scurried across the grid, navigating the tops of the baulks with practised ease. Spaced around the grid like down-pointed cannon, the delicate imaging gravitometers swayed slightly as the wind began to increase.

Sylveste waited, then followed a similar path, deviating when he was a few boxes into the grid. Near the centre of the excavation, four boxes had been enlarged into one single slab-sided pit, thirty metres from side to side and nearly as deep. Sylveste stepped onto the ladder which led into the pit and moved quickly down the side. He had made the journey up and down this ladder so many times in the last few weeks that the lack of vertigo was almost more disturbing than the thing itself. Moving down the cofferdam's side, he descended through layers of geological time. Nine hundred thousand years had passed since the Event. Most of that stratification was permafrost—typical in Resurgam's subpolar latitudes; permanent frost-soil which never thawed. Deeper down—close to the Event itself—was a layer of regolith laid down in the impacts which had followed. The Event itself was a single, hair-fine black demarcation—the ash of burning forests.

The floor of the pit was not level, but followed narrowing steps down to a final depth of forty metres below the surface. Extra floods had been brought down to shine light into the gloom. The cramped area was a fantastical hive of activity, and within the shelter of the pit there was no trace of the wind. The dig team was working in near-silence, kneeling on the ground on mats, working away at something with tools so precise they might have served for surgery in another era. Three were young students from Cuvier—born on Resurgam. A servitor skulked beside them awaiting orders. Though machines had their uses during a dig's early phases, the final work could never be entirely trusted to them. Next to the party a woman sat with a compad balanced on her lap, displaying a cladistic map of Amarantin skulls. She saw Sylveste for the first time—he had climbed quietly—and stood up with a start, snapping shut the compad. She wore a greatcoat, her black hair cut in a geometric fringe across her brow.

"Well, you were right," she said. "Whatever it is, it's big. And it looks amazingly well-preserved, too."

"Any theories, Pascale?"

"That's where you come in, isn't it? I'm just here to offer commentary." Pascale Dubois was a young journalist from Cuvier. She had been covering the dig since its inception, often dirtying her fingers with the real archaeologists, learning their cant. "The bodies are gruesome, though, aren't they? Even though they're alien, it's almost as if you can feel their pain."

To one side of the pit, just before the floor stepped down, they had unearthed two stone-lined burial chambers. Despite being buried for nine hundred thousand years—at the very least—the chambers were almost intact, with the bones inside still assuming a rough anatomical relationship to one another. They were typical Amarantin skeletons. At first glance—to anyone who happened not to be a trained anthropologist—they could have passed as human remains, for the creatures had been four-limbed bipeds of roughly human size, with a superficially similar bone-structure. Skull volume was comparable, and the organs of sense, breathing and communication were situated in analogous positions. But the skulls of both Amarantin were elongated and birdlike, with a prominent cranial ridge which extended forwards between the voluminous eye-sockets, down to the tip of the beaklike upper jaw. The bones were covered here and there by a skein of tanned, desiccated tissue which had served to contort the bodies, drawing them—or so it seemed—into agonised postures. They were not fossils in the usual sense: no mineralisation had taken place, and the burial chambers had remained empty except for the bones and the handful of technomic artefacts with which they had been buried.

"Perhaps," Sylveste said, reaching down and touching one of the skulls, "we were meant to think that."

"No," Pascale said. "As the tissue dried, it distorted them."

"Unless they were buried like this."

Feeling the skull through his gloves—they transmitted tactile data to his fingertips—he was reminded of a yellow room high in Chasm City, with aquatints of methane icescapes on the walls. There had been liveried servitors moving through the guests with sweetmeats and liqueurs; drapes of coloured crêpe spanning the belvedered ceiling; the air bright with sickly entoptics in the current vogue: seraphim, cherubim, hummingbirds, fairies. He remembered guests: most of them associates of the family; people

he either barely recognised or detested, for his friends had been
few in number. His father had been late as usual; the party already
winding down by the time Calvin deigned to show up. This was
normal then; the time of Calvin's last and greatest project, and the
realisation of it was in itself a slow death; no less so than the suicide
he would bring upon himself at the project's culmination.

He remembered his father producing a box, its sides bearing a
marquetry of entwined ribonucleic strands.

"Open it," Calvin had said.

He remembered taking it; feeling its lightness. He had snatched
the top off to reveal a bird's nest of fibrous packing material. Within
was a speckled brown dome the same colour as the box. It was the
upper part of a skull, obviously human, with the jaw missing.

He remembered a silence falling across the room.

"Is that all?" Sylveste had said, just loud enough so that everyone in the room heard it. "An old bone? Well, thanks, Dad. I'm
humbled."

"As well you should be," Calvin said.

And the trouble was, as Sylveste had realised almost immediately,
Calvin was right. The skull was incredibly valuable; two hundred
thousand years old—a woman from Atapuerca, Spain, he soon
learned. Her time of death had been obvious enough from the context in which she was buried, but the scientists who had unearthed
her had refined the estimate using the best techniques of their day:
potassium-argon dating of the rocks in the cave where she'd been
buried, uranium-series dating of travertine deposits on the walls,
fission-track dating of volcanic glasses, thermoluminescence dating of burnt flint fragments. They were techniques which—with
improvements in calibration and application—remained in use
among the dig teams on Resurgam. Physics allowed only so many
methods to date objects. Sylveste should have seen all that in an
instant and recognised the skull for what it was: the oldest human
object on Yellowstone, carried to the Epsilon Eridani system centuries earlier, and then lost during the colony's upheavals. Calvin's
unearthing of it was a small miracle in itself.

Yet the flush of shame he felt stemmed less from ingratitude than from the way he had allowed his ignorance to unmask itself, when it could have been so easily concealed. It was a weakness he would never allow himself again. Years later, the skull had travelled with him to Resurgam, to remind him always of that vow.

He could not fail now.

"If what you're implying is the case," Pascale said, "then they must have been buried like that for a reason."

"Maybe as a warning," Sylveste said, and stepped down towards the three students.

"I was afraid you might say something like that," Pascale said, following him. "And what exactly might this terrible warning have concerned?"

Her question was largely rhetorical, as Sylveste well knew. She understood exactly what he believed about the Amarantin. She also seemed to enjoy needling him about those beliefs; as if by forcing him to state them repeatedly, she might eventually cause him to expose some logical error in his own theories; one that even he would have to admit undermined the whole argument.

"The Event," Sylveste said, fingering the fine black line behind the nearest cofferdam as he spoke.

"The Event happened to the Amarantin," Pascale said. "It wasn't anything they had any say in. And it happened quickly, too. They didn't have time to go about burying bodies in dire warning, even if they'd had any idea about what was happening to them."

"They angered the gods," Sylveste said.

"Yes," Pascale said. "I think we all agree that they would have interpreted the Event as evidence of theistic displeasure, within the constraints of their belief system—but there wouldn't have been time to express that belief in any permanent form before they all died, much less bury bodies for the benefit of future archaeologists from a different species." She lifted her hood over her head and tightened the drawstring—fine plumes of dust were starting to settle down into the pit, and the air was no longer as still as it had been a few minutes earlier. "But you don't think so, do you?" Without waiting for an answer, she fixed a large pair of bulky goggles over her eyes, momentarily disturbing the edge of her fringe, and looked down at the object which was slowly being uncovered.

Pascale's goggles accessed data from the imaging gravitometers stationed around the Wheeler grid, overlaying the stereoscopic picture of buried masses on the normal view. Sylveste had only to instruct his eyes to do likewise. The ground on which they were standing turned glassy, insubstantial—a smoky matrix in which something huge lay entombed. It was an obelisk—a single huge block of shaped rock, itself encased in a series of stone sarcophagi. The obelisk was twenty metres tall. The dig had exposed only a few centimetres of the top. There was evidence of writing down one side, in one of the standard late-phase Amarantin graphic-forms. But the imaging gravitometers lacked the spatial resolution to reveal the text. The obelisk would have to be dug out before they could learn anything.

Sylveste told his eyes to return to normal vision. "Work faster," he told his students. "I don't care if you incur minor abrasions to the surface. I want at least a metre of it visible by the end of tonight."

One of the students turned to him, still kneeling. "Sir, we heard the dig would have to be abandoned."

"Why on earth would I abandon a dig?"

"The storm, sir."

"Damn the storm." He was turning away when Pascale took his arm, a little too roughly.

"They're right to be worried, Dan." She spoke quietly, for his benefit alone. "I heard about that advisory, too. We should be heading back toward Mantell."

"And lose this?"

"We'll come back again."

"We might never find it, even if we bury a transponder." He knew he was right: the position of the dig was uncertain and maps of this area were not particularly detailed; compiled quickly when the *Lorean* had made orbit from Yellowstone forty years earlier. Ever since the comsat girdle had been destroyed in the mutiny, twenty years later—when half the colonists elected to steal the ship and return home—there had been no accurate way of determining position on Resurgam. And many a transponder had simply failed in a razorstorm.

"It's still not worth risking human lives for," Pascale said.

"It might be worth much more than that." He snapped a finger at the students. "Faster. Use the servitor if you must. I want to see the top of that obelisk by dawn."

Sluka, his senior research student, muttered a word under her breath.

"Something to contribute?" Sylveste asked.

Sluka stood for what must have been the first time in hours. He could see the tension in her eyes. The little spatula she had been using dropped on the ground, beside the mukluks she wore on her feet. She snatched the mask away from her face, breathing Resurgam air for a few seconds while she spoke. "We need to talk."

"About what, Sluka?"

Sluka gulped down air from the mask before speaking again. "You're pushing your luck, Dr. Sylveste."

"You've just pushed yours over the precipice."

She seemed not to have heard him. "We care about your work, you know. We share your beliefs. That's why we're here, breaking our backs for you. But you shouldn't take us for granted." Her eyes flashed white arcs, glancing towards Pascale. "Right now you need all the allies you can find, Dr. Sylveste."

"That's a threat, is it?"

"A statement of fact. If you paid more attention to what was going on elsewhere in the colony, you'd know that Girardieau's planning to move against you. The word is that move's a hell of a lot closer than you think."

The back of his neck prickled. "What are you talking about?"

"What else? A coup." Sluka pushed past him to ascend the ladder up the side of the pit. When she had a foot on the first rung, she turned back and addressed the other two students, both minding their own business, heads down in concentration as they worked to reveal the obelisk. "Work for as long as you want, but don't say no one warned you. And if you've any doubts as to what being caught in a razorstorm is like, take a look at Sylveste."

One of the students looked up, timidly. "Where are you going, Sluka?"

"To speak to the other dig teams. Not everyone may know about that advisory. When they hear, I don't think many of them will be in any hurry to stay."

She started climbing, but Sylveste reached up and grabbed the heel of her mukluk. Sluka looked down at him. She was wearing the mask now, but Sylveste could still see the contempt in her expression. "You're finished, Sluka."

"No," she said, climbing. "I've just begun. It's you I'd worry about."

Sylveste examined his own state of mind and found—it was the last thing he had expected—total calm. But it was like the calm that existed on the metallic hydrogen oceans of the gas giant planets further out from Pavonis—only maintained by crushing pressures from above and below.

"Well?" Pascale said.

"There's someone I need to talk to," Sylveste said.

Sylveste climbed the ramp into his crawler. The other was crammed with equipment racks and sample containers, with hammocks for his students pressed into the tiny niches of unoccupied space. They had to sleep aboard the machines because some of the digs in the sector—like this one—were over a day's travel from Mantell itself. Sylveste's crawler was considerably better appointed, with over a third of the interior dedicated to his own stateroom and quarters. The rest of the machine was taken up with additional payload space and a couple of more modest quarters for his senior workers or guests: in this case Sluka and Pascale. Now, however, he had the whole crawler to himself.

The stateroom's décor belied the fact that it was aboard a crawler. It was walled in red velvet, the shelves dotted with facsimile

scientific instruments and relics. There were large, elegantly anno-
tated Mercator maps of Resurgam dotted with the sites of major
Amarantin finds; other areas of wall were covered in slowly updating texts: academic papers in preparation. His own beta-level
was doing most of the scut-work on the papers now; Sylveste had
trained the simulation to the point where it could imitate his style
more reliably than he could, given the current distractions. Later,
if there was time, he would need to proof those texts, but for now
he gave them no more than a glance as he moved to the room's
escritoire. The ornate writing desk was decorated in marble and
malachite, inset with japan work scenes of early space exploration.

Sylveste opened a drawer and removed a simulation cartridge, an
unmarked grey slab, like a ceramic tile. There was a slot in the escritoire's upper surface. He would only have to insert the cartridge to
invoke Calvin. He hesitated, nonetheless. It had been some time—
months, at least—since he had brought Calvin back from the
dead, and that last encounter had gone spectacularly badly. He had
promised himself he would only invoke Calvin again in the event
of crisis. Now it was a matter of judging whether the crisis had
really arrived—and if it was sufficiently troublesome to justify an
invocation. The problem with Calvin was that his advice was only
reliable about half the time.

Sylveste pressed the cartridge into the escritoire.

Fairies wove a figure out of light in the middle of the room:
Calvin seated in a vast seigneurial chair. The apparition was more
realistic than any hologram—even down to subtle shadowing
effects—since it was being generated by direct manipulation of
Sylveste's visual field. The beta-level simulation represented Calvin the way fame best remembered him, as he had been when he
was barely fifty years old, in his heyday on Yellowstone. Strangely,
he looked older than Sylveste, even though the image of Calvin
was twenty years younger in physiological terms. Sylveste was eight
years into his third century, but the longevity treatments he had
received on Yellowstone had been more advanced than any available in Calvin's time.

Other than that, their features and build were the same, both of them possessing a permanent amused curve to the lips. Calvin wore his hair shorter and was dressed in Demarchist Belle Epoque finery, rather than the relative austerity of Sylveste's expeditionary dress: billowing frock shirt and elegantly chequered trousers hooked into buccaneer-boots, his fingers aglint with jewels and metal. His impeccably shaped beard was little more than a rust-coloured delineation along the line of his jaw. Small entoptics surrounded his seated figure, symbols of Boolean and three-valued logics and long cascades of binary. One hand fingered the bristles beneath his chin, while the other toyed with the carved scroll that ended the seat's armrest.

A wave of animation slithered over the projection, the pale eyes gaining a glisten of interest.

Calvin raised his fingers in lazy acknowledgement. "So..." he said. "The shit's about to match coordinates with the fan."

"You presume a lot."

"No need to presume anything, dear boy. I just tapped into the net and accessed the last few thousand news reports." He craned his neck to survey the stateroom. "Nice pad you've got here. How are the eyes, by the way?"

"They're functioning as well as can be expected."

Calvin nodded. "Resolution's not up to much, but that was the best I could do with the tools I was forced to work with. I probably only reconnected forty per cent of your optic nerve channels, so putting in better cameras would have been pointless. Now if you had halfway decent surgical equipment lying around on this planet, I could perhaps begin to do something. But you wouldn't give Michelangelo a toothbrush and expect a great Sistine Chapel."

"Rub it in."

"I wouldn't dream of it," Calvin said, all innocence. "I'm just saying that if you had to let her take the *Lorean*, couldn't you at least have persuaded Alicia to leave us some medical equipment?"

His wife had led the mutiny against him twenty years earlier; a fact Calvin never allowed Sylveste to forget.

"So I made a kind of self-sacrifice." Sylveste waved an arm to silence the image. "Sorry, but I didn't invoke you for a fireside chat, Cal."

"I do wish you'd call me Father."

Sylveste ignored him. "Do you know where we are?"

"A dig, I presume." Calvin closed his eyes briefly and touched his fingers against his temples, affecting concentration. "Yes. Let me see. Two expeditionary crawlers out of Mantell, near the Ptero Steppes...a Wheeler grid...how inordinately quaint! Though I suppose it suits your purpose well enough. And what's this? High-res gravitometer sections...seismograms...you've actually found something, haven't you?"

At that moment the escritoire popped up a status fairy to tell him there was an incoming call from Mantell. Sylveste held a hand up to Calvin while he debated whether or not to accept the call. The person trying to reach him was Henry Janequin, a specialist in avian biology and one of Sylveste's few outright allies. But while Janequin had known the real Calvin, Sylveste was fairly sure he had never seen Calvin's beta-level...and most certainly not in the process of being solicited for advice by his son. The admission that he needed Cal's help—that he had even considered invoking the sim for this purpose—could be a crucial sign of weakness.

"What are you waiting for?" Cal said. "Put him on."

"He doesn't know about you...about us."

Calvin shook his head, then—shockingly—Janequin appeared in the room. Sylveste fought to maintain his composure, but it was obvious what had just happened. Calvin must have found a way to send commands to the escritoire's private-level functions.

Calvin was and always had been a devious bastard, Sylveste thought. Ultimately that was why he remained of use.

Janequin's full-body projection was slightly less sharp than Calvin's, for Janequin's image was coming over the satellite network—patchy at best—from Mantell. And the cameras imaging him had probably seen better days, Sylveste thought—like much else on Resurgam.

"There you are," Janequin said, noticing only Sylveste at first. "I've been trying to reach you for the last hour. Don't you have a way of being alerted to incoming calls when you're down in the pit?"

"I do," Sylveste said. "But I turned it off. It was too distracting."

"Oh," Janequin said, with only the tiniest hint of annoyance. "Very shrewd indeed. Especially for a man in your position. You realise what I'm talking about, of course. There's trouble afoot, Dan, perhaps more than you..." Then Janequin must have noticed Cal for the first time. He studied the figure in the chair for a moment before speaking. "My word. It is you, isn't it?"

Cal nodded without saying a word.

"This is his beta-level simulation," Sylveste said. It was important to clear that up before the conversation proceeded any further; alphas and betas were fundamentally different things and Stoner etiquette was very punctilious indeed about distinguishing between the two. Sylveste would have been guilty of an extreme social gaffe had he allowed Janequin to think that this was the long-lost alpha-level recording.

"I was consulting with him...with it," Sylveste said.

Calvin pulled a face.

"About what?" Janequin said. He was an old man—the oldest person on Resurgam, in fact—and with each passing year his appearance seemed to approach fractionally closer to some simian ideal. His white hair, moustache and beard framed a small pink face in the manner of some rare marmoset. On Yellowstone, there had been no more talented expert in genetics outside of the Mixmasters, and there were some who rated Janequin a good deal cleverer than any in that sect, for all that his genius was of the undemonstrative sort, accumulating not in any flash of brilliance, but through years and years of quietly excellent work. He was well into his fourth century now, and layer upon layer of longevity treatment was beginning to crumble visibly. Sylveste supposed that before very long Janequin would be the first person on Resurgam to die of old age. The thought filled him with sadness. Though there was much upon which Janequin and he disagreed, they had always seen eye to eye on all the important things.

"He's found something," Cal said.

Janequin's eyes brightened, years lifting off him in the joy of scientific discovery. "Really?"

"Yes, I..." Then something else odd happened. The room was gone now. The three of them were standing on a balcony, high above what Sylveste instantly recognised as Chasm City. Calvin's doing again. The escritoire had followed them like an obedient dog. If Cal could access its private-level functions, Sylveste thought, he could also do this kind of trick, running one of the escritoire's standard environments. It was a good simulation, too: down to the slap of wind against Sylveste's cheek and the city's almost intangible smell, never easy to define but always obvious by its absence in more cheaply done environments.

It was the city from his childhood: the high Belle Epoque. Awesome gold structures marched into the distance like sculpted clouds, buzzing with aerial traffic. Below, tiered parks and gardens stepped down in a series of dizzying vistas towards a verdant haze of greenery and light, kilometres beneath their feet.

"Isn't it great to see the old place?" Cal said. "And to think that it was almost ours for the taking; so much within reach of our clan...who knows how we might have changed things, if we'd held the city's reins?"

Janequin steadied himself on the railing. "Very nice, but I didn't come to sight-see, Calvin. Dan, what were you about to tell me before we were so..."

"Rudely interrupted?" Sylveste said. "I was going to tell Cal to pull the gravitometer data from the escritoire, as he obviously has the means to read my private files."

"There's really nothing to it for a man in my position," Cal said. There was a moment while he accessed the smoky imagery of the buried thing, the obelisk hanging in front of them beyond the railing, apparently life-size.

"Oh, very interesting," Janequin said. "Very interesting indeed!"

"Not bad," Cal said.

"Not bad?" Sylveste said. "It's bigger and better preserved than anything we've found to date by an order of magnitude. It's clear evidence of a more advanced phase of Amarantin technology...perhaps even a precursor phase to a full industrial revolution."

"I suppose it could be quite a significant find," Cal said, grudgingly. "You—um—are planning to unearth it, I assume?"

"Until a moment ago, yes." Sylveste paused. "But something's just come up. I've just been...I've just found out for myself that Girardieau may be planning to move against me a lot sooner than I had feared."

"He can't touch you without a majority in the expeditionary council," Cal said.

"No, he couldn't," Janequin said. "If that was how he was going to do it. But Dan's information is right. It looks as if Girardieau may be planning on more direct action."

"That would be tantamount to some kind of...coup, I suppose."

"I think that would be the technical term," Janequin said.

"Are you sure?" Then Calvin did the concentration thing again, dark lines etching his brow. "Yes...you could be right. A lot of media speculation in the last day concerning Girardieau's next move, and the fact that Dan's off on some dig while the colony stumbles through a crisis of leadership...and a definite increase in encrypted comms among Girardieau's known sympathisers. I can't break those encryptions, of course, but I can certainly speculate on the reason for the increase in traffic."

"Something's being planned, isn't it?" Sluka was right, he thought to himself. In which case she had done him a favour, even as she had threatened to abandon the dig. Without her warning he would never have invoked Cal.

"It does look that way," Janequin said. "That's why I was trying to reach you. My fears have only been confirmed by what Cal says about Girardieau's sympathisers." His grip tightened on the railing. The cuff of his jacket—hanging thinly over his skeletal frame—was patterned with peacocks' eyes. "I don't suppose there's

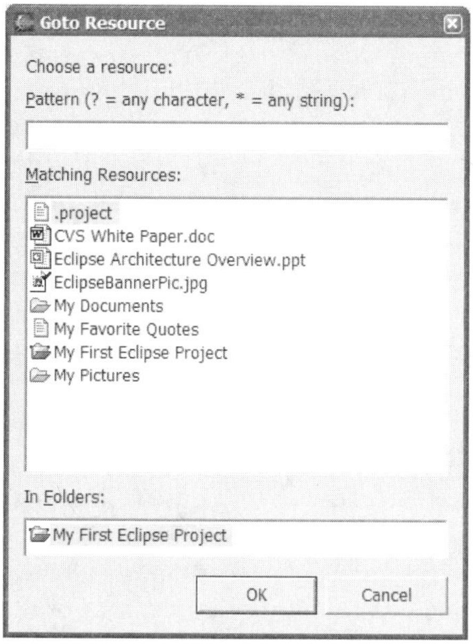

Figure 2.9   Goto Resource Dialog

2. The default editor defined for the selected file type. (You'll see how to do this later in this chapter in the section "Using Other Computer Programs with Eclipse.")

3. A computer program defined to your operating system for the selected file type.

4. The Eclipse text editor.

This protocol is also used to select an editor for new files you create. Override this behavior by selecting a file and then selecting **Open With** from the context menu to see a list of editors defined for the selected file type. **Open With > Default Editors** uses the default editor for this file type as defined in your **Workbench File Associations** preferences. **Open With > System Editor** uses the associated editor or application defined by the operating system.

By default, selection in the Navigator view is linked to the editors. As you select resources in the view, editors on those resources (if open) are shown. As you switch between editors, the file you are currently editing is selected in the Navigator view. You can unlink the Navigator view and the active editor selection in **Workbench** preferences. The default action to open a file for editing is to double-click on it. Change this with **Workbench** preferences to open a file by single-clicking on it, hovering over it, and/or using arrow keys.

Workbench Editors preferences provide two notable settings. You can customize the number of recently opened (edited) files listed under **File** on the menu. You can also select to recycle a fixed number of editor sessions. To do this, select **Close editors automatically** and then specify the maximum number of editors kept open with **Number of opened editors before closing**. For example, if you do this and specify five editors, when you have five editors open and you select another file to edit, the editor of the oldest file will be closed before another is opened. This is useful if you tend to end up with a lot of open editors and find it cumbersome navigating through them.

There are keyboard shortcuts for quickly selecting from your open editors. Select **Ctrl+F6** or **Ctrl+Shift+F6** to select the next and previous editors, respectively, from a list, as shown in Figure 2.10.

On Windows operating systems, Eclipse supports Object Linking and Embedding (OLE) document editors, for example, for Lotus spreadsheet *.123 or Microsoft word processing *.doc files. You don't need to do anything special beyond importing files into projects. When you select a file for editing that has associated an OLE document editor defined by your computer but not Eclipse, the editor (program) opens in the editor pane. The OLE document editor adds its menu items to the Eclipse menu and replaces the Eclipse **Help** menu. It does not make changes to the **File** and **Window**

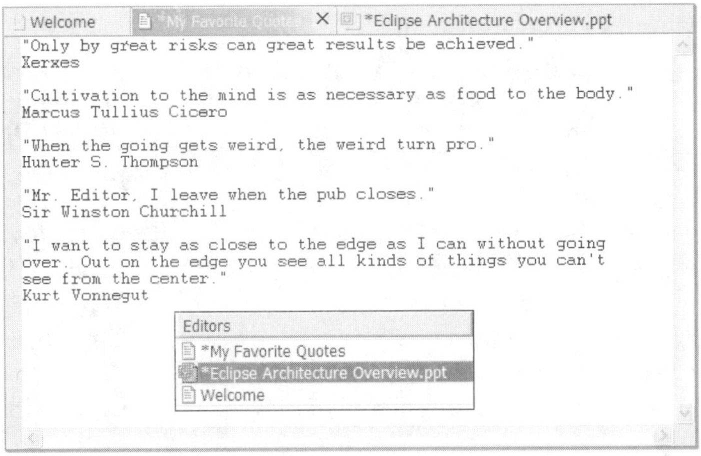

Figure 2.10   Open Editors List

menus. If you need to access Eclipse **Help** menu items, switch the focus from the OLE document editor to another Eclipse editor or view. If you would rather open OLE document editors in new windows and not within the editor pane, you'll need to change your **Workbench File Associations** preferences. We'll see how to do this in "Using Other Computer Programs with Eclipse" later in this chapter. When you edit a file in the editor pane with an OLE document editor, the file is automatically marked as modified.

Views

All views share the same user interface organization. On a view title bar, from left to right, are the System Menu, view name, view specific action buttons, a pull-down menu button for more actions, and a **Close** button (see Figure 2.11). Re-open a closed view or open another view by selecting **Window > Show View >**. On some views the actions on the pull-down menu are also available from the view context menu. On others, the pull-down menu is the only place an action is available.

As with editors, there are keyboard shortcuts for navigating through open views. Select **Ctrl+F7** or **Ctrl+Shift+F7** to select the next and previous views, respectively, from a list.

Views can be resized, moved, stacked, and placed in the view shortcut area. This is useful for organizing the user interface according to your tastes or to optimize use of screen real estate. To resize a view, simply drag one of its borders. To move a view, drag it by its title bar. When you are moving a view, the cursor provides feedback on where it can be dropped. For example,

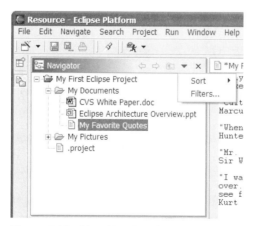

Figure 2.11   View User Interface Organization

◆ left-pointing arrow means dropping the view here will position it to the left of the view under the cursor (see Figure 2.12).

To put a view in the shortcut area, simply drag the view and drop it there. When you put a view in the shortcut area, it becomes a **fast view**. A fast view is a view that is hidden from view and represented by an icon in the shortcut area. To see a fast view, select the icon in the shortcut area. The view slides to the right to become visible. Select the icon again to hide the view. To restore a view in the shortcut area to where it was in the user interface, deselect **Fast View** from the view title bar (see Figure 2.13).

Perspectives

Recall that perspectives contain, among other things, an organization of views and editors. Up to this point, we've been working in the Resource perspective. If you've moved around and resized views and want to return the

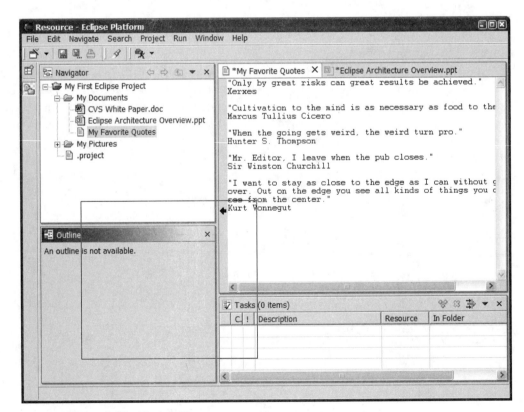

Figure 2.12   Moving a View

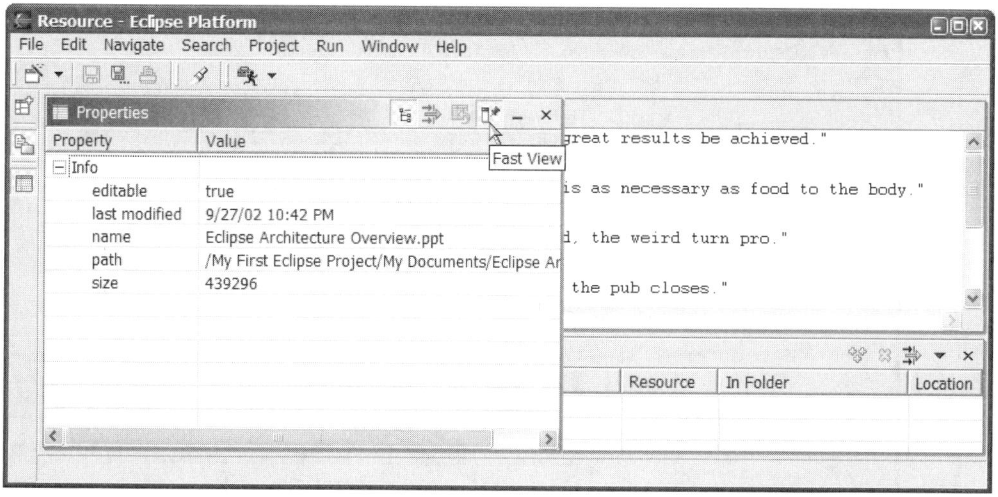

Manipulating the User Interface

Figure 2.13   Showing a Fast View

perspective to its default configuration, select **Window > Reset Perspective**.
To open another perspective, for example, CVS Repository Exploring or
Java, select **Window > Open Perspective >** and then the perspective.

Working with Tasks

Tasks are textual reminders of work you may need to do. Tasks can refer to a
file or a location in a file. They have a completion status and priority. Eclipse
uses tasks to report warnings and errors. For example, Java errors are reported as tasks. Also, if you import resources with problems, they will be reported as tasks. Tasks are shown in the Tasks view (see Figure 2.14). Tasks
are also shown on the marker bars of editors open on files that have associated tasks.

You define new tasks from the context menu of the Tasks view, by clicking on the marker bar of an editor, and selecting **Add task...**. The Tasks view
provides simple navigation to the file (and, optionally, the location in the file)
associated with the task. Simply double-click on the task and the associated
file is opened in an editor. If the task refers to a location in the file, that line is
selected.

Sort the tasks by clicking on any of the column headings. If you have a
large number of tasks, you can filter the tasks that appear in the Tasks view
by selecting **Filter...**. This displays the Filter Tasks dialog (see Figure 2.15).

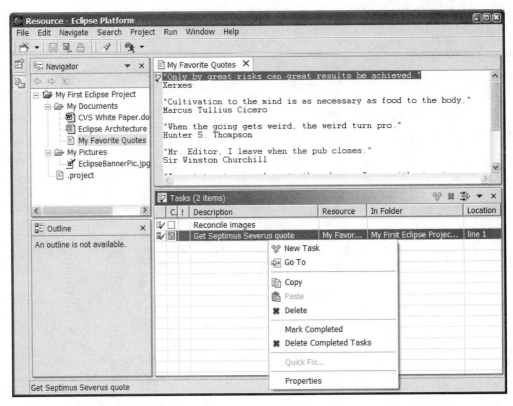

Figure 2.14   Tasks View

This is useful to isolate specific kinds of error or warning messages to more easily resolve them. You may also find it useful to restrict the tasks shown based on your selection in the Navigator view. For example, if you only want to see the tasks associated with a project and its contents, select **On any resource in same project**.

As you can see from the Filter Tasks dialog, a variety of problems can show up as tasks, including Java compiler errors and repository informational messages. The Filter Tasks dialog has a quick fix capability that can fix many of these errors. Select an error in the Tasks view and then **Quick Fix...** from the context menu (if it is enabled).

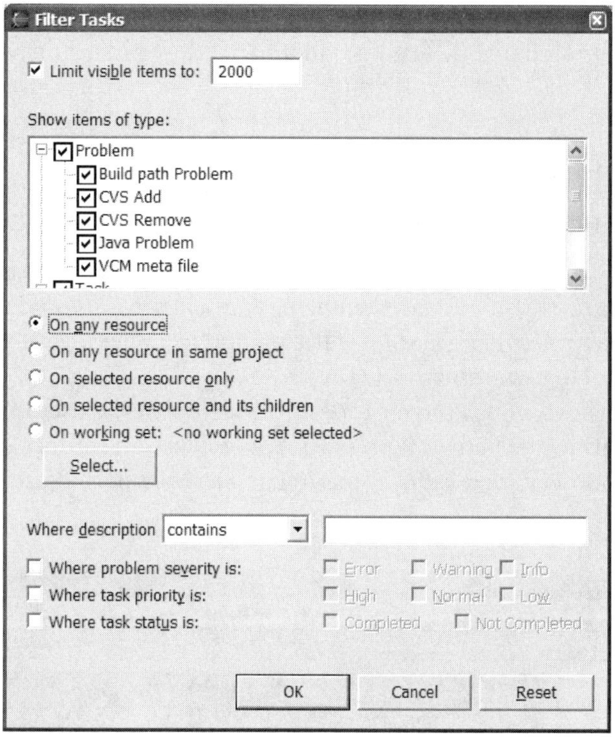

Figure 2.15   Filter Tasks Dialog

Working with Bookmarks

Bookmarks are similar to tasks with the exception that bookmarks must be associated with a file and they do not have a completion status or priority. You define new bookmarks from the marker bar of an editor from the context menu, or in the Navigator view by selecting a resource and then selecting **Add Bookmark...** from the context menu.

Getting Help

There is a wealth of information about how to use and extend Eclipse available through integrated and cross-linked online content and the search capability. There are four basic types of help: online documentation, Infopops (context-sensitive help), hover help, and Active Help. Access to online content is simple and navigation is intuitive. The combination of online content, links, and navigation makes it easy to find information and get answers to your questions.

Opening Help

There are three ways to open, or access, Help information.

- To view all online content, select **Help > Help Contents**. If this is the first time you've requested help, you will see a slight delay as the engine for the Help system starts up and initializes. Figure 2.16 shows the first Help window.
- To view online content for a specific item in the user interface, shift focus to the item and press **F1**.You will see an Infopop, a small modal window, with a list of topics related to the selected user interface item

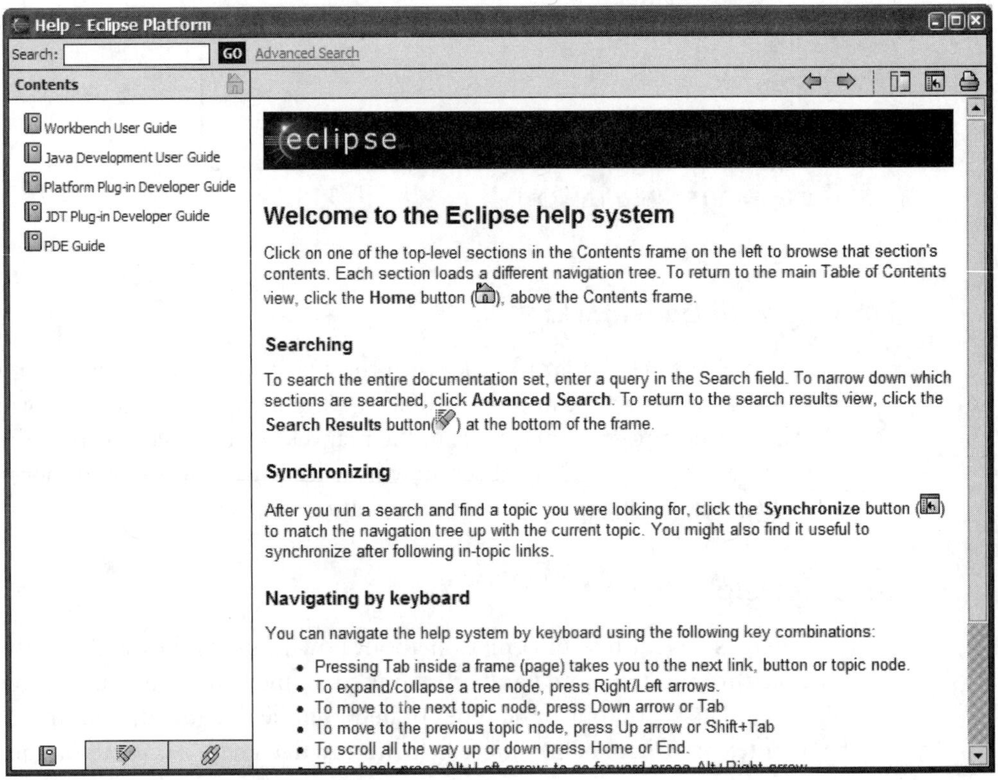

Figure 2.16   Help Window

(see Figure 2.17). You may need to shift focus by using the arrow keys or mnemonics to select an item without actually performing the action. Select one of the topics in the Infopop to see the related information.

- To quickly see information about an icon (on a toolbar, on a title bar, or in the view shortcut area), or to see a long entry that is not completely displayed (such as a file name or task), hover over the icon or name and a short description will display (see Figure 2.18).

Figure 2.16 shows the initial view of the online documentation. The Navigation pane is on the left and the Contents pane is on the right. The Navigation pane has three pages: Contents, Search Results, and Links. The Contents *page* (not to be confused with the Contents *pane* on the right) lists the available online content you have, organized by books.

Eclipse provides five online books. The *Workbench User Guide* is for all users and explains how to use Eclipse. The *Java Development User Guide* is for all Java developers and explains how to use Eclipse to write and debug Java code. The remaining three, *Platform Plug-In Developer Guide, JDT Plug-In Developer Guide,* and *PDE Guide,* are for those who want to extend and/or build offerings based on Eclipse. If you are working with, or have integrated, other Eclipse-based offerings, you may see additional book entries here. This is

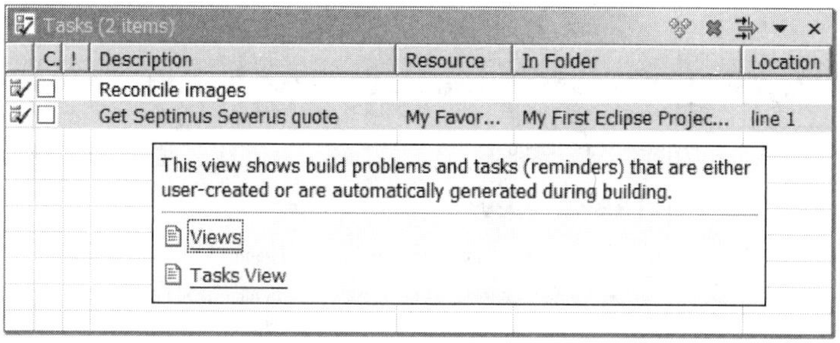

Figure 2.17 Infopop Help

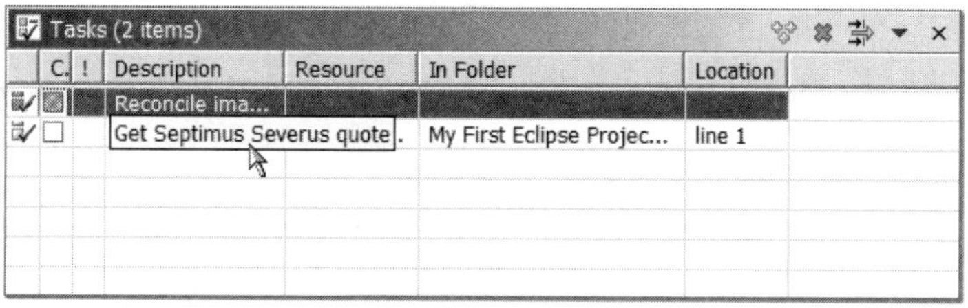

Figure 2.18 Hover Help

Edit Template

Name: `for`   Context: `java`

Description: `iterate over array w/ temporary variable`

Pattern:
```
for (int ${index} = 0; ${index} < ${array}.length; ${index}++) {
    ${array_type} ${array_element} = ${array}[${index}];
    ${cursor}
}
```

array - A proposal for an array
array_element - A proposal for the element nam
array_type - A proposal for the element type of a
collection - A proposal for a collection (java.util.C
cursor - The cursor position after editing templat
date - Current date
dollar - The dollar symbol
enclosing_method - Enclosing method name
enclosing_method_arguments - Argument names

Insert Variable...

OK   Cancel

Figure 3.21   Edit Template Dialog

To begin the process, select a project, package, or folder and then select **Source > Find Strings to Externalize...** from the menu to display the Find Strings to Externalize dialog, which shows *.java files containing strings that have not been externalized (see Figure 3.22).

Select a file and then **Externalize...** to go to the Externalize Strings wizard. Alternatively, select a *.java file and then select **Source > Externalize Strings...** from the menu to display the wizard.

On the first page of the Externalize Strings wizard, shown in Figure 3.23, you specify which strings are to be externalized (for translation) and keys for accessing the strings. Select an entry and then **Translate** to externalize the string. Select **Never Translate** if you do not want the string externalized. In

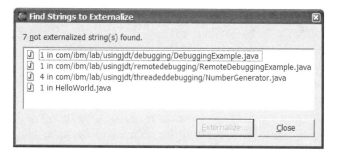

Find Strings to Externalize

7 not externalized string(s) found.

- 1 in com/ibm/lab/usingjdt/debugging/DebuggingExample.java
- 1 in com/ibm/lab/usingjdt/remotedebugging/RemoteDebuggingExample.java
- 4 in com/ibm/lab/usingjdt/threadeddebugging/NumberGenerator.java
- 1 in HelloWorld.java

Externalize...   Close

Figure 3.22   Finding Strings to Externalize

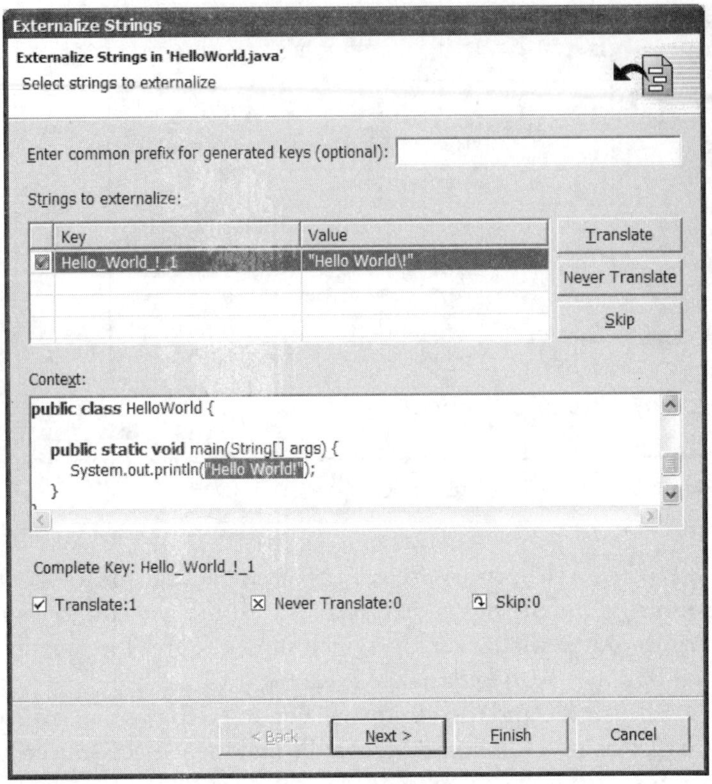

Figure 3.23   Specifying Strings to Externalize

each of these cases, JDT annotates your source code with comments indicating your choice. Selecting **Skip** goes to the next string without taking any action. If you have your preferences set to flag nonexternalized strings as errors or warnings, and you select **Translate** or **Never Translate** for the string, it will no longer be flagged as an error or warning. If you select **Skip**, the error or warning will remain. You can specify a prefix that will be added to the key (when your code is modified, not in the dialog). You can also edit the key to specify a different value by selecting the entry and then clicking on the key. Even if you do not intend to translate a string, it still may by useful to externalize it if you reference the same string value in several places in your code, for example, strings that show up in your user interface. This way, you can be certain they remain the same.

On the second page of the wizard, shown in Figure 3.24, you specify the name and location of the file that contains the externalized strings and a class

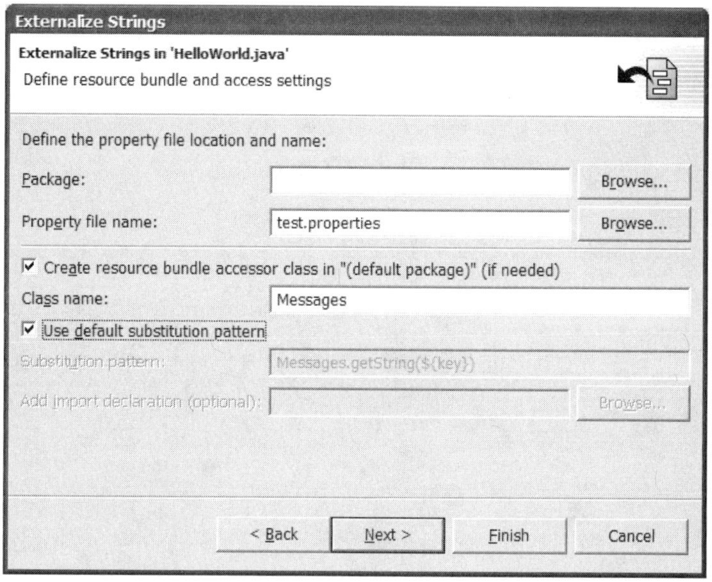

Figure 3.24   Specifying Location of Externalized Strings

to access the strings. JDT generates this class and the specified method and adds it to your project.

The final page of the wizard is a before-and-after view of your code (see Figure 3.25). In the top pane, you select to apply or not apply changes for each of the proposed modifications. Select **Finish** to make the changes to your code. This replaces the selected strings with references based on the accessor class, generates the accessor class, and creates the file containing the strings.

To undo string externalizations, select **Refactor > Undo**. This will also remove the generated accessor class.

Generating Javadoc

You generate Javadoc by exporting it. To do so, you first need to set your **Java Javadoc** preferences to point to javadoc.exe. This program performs the Javadoc generation. The javadoc.exe program is not shipped as part of Eclipse; it comes with a JDK distribution.

Once you have set the location of javadoc.exe, you can export Javadoc by selecting **Export...** from the Package Explorer context menu and then

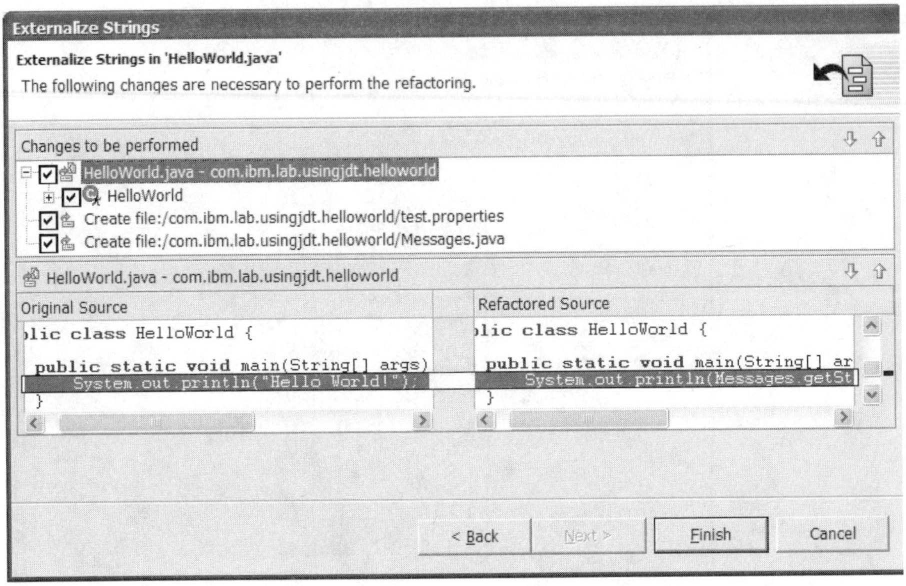

Figure 3.25   Externalize Strings Code Changes

selecting **Javadoc** as the export destination. You have a number of options for generating Javadoc for one or more of your Java projects. Figure 3.26 shows the first page of options. Select **Finish** to generate the Javadoc or **Next >** for more options.

For the visibility settings, **Private** generates Javadoc for all members; **Package** for all default, protected, and public members; **Protected** for all protected and public members; and **Public** for only public members. For more information on all the Javadoc generation options, refer to the "Java Preferences" information in the "Reference" section of the *Java Development User Guide*.

When you generate the Javadoc, you will see a prompt asking if you want to update the **Javadoc Location** properties of the projects you are generating Javadoc for. You should select to do so. This will enable you to browse the generated Javadoc in the Java editor. Output from the generation shows up in the Console view. You should review this to ensure there were no errors.

Writing Java for Nondefault JREs

Eclipse uses a JRE for two purposes: to run Eclipse itself and to run your Java code. This can be the same JRE or different JREs. The specifications are

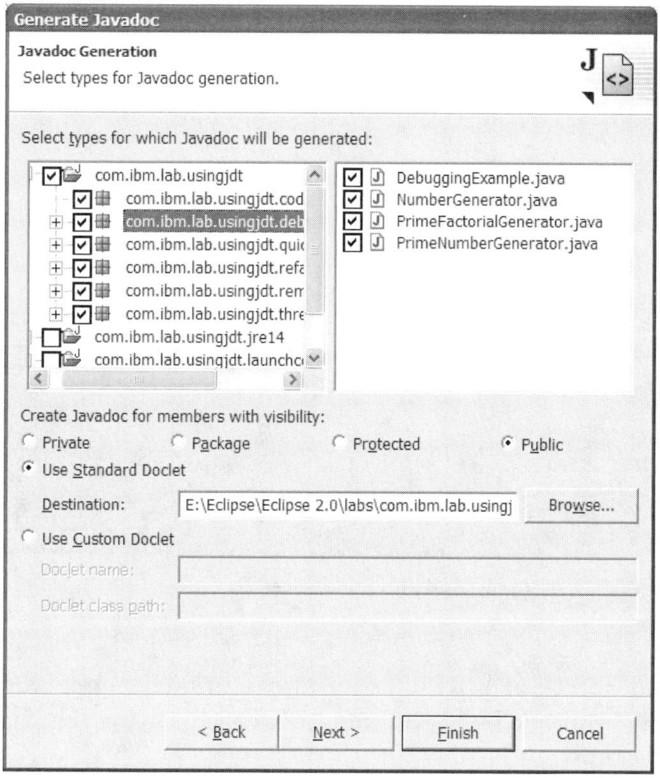

Figure 3.26   Generating Javadoc

independent; that is, you can write JRE 1.4 dependent code in an Eclipse running on a 1.3 JRE and vice versa. However, by default the JRE you use to run Eclipse is the same one the JDT uses to run your Java code. If you want to develop Java code that uses a different JRE from the one that runs Eclipse, you need to reconfigure Eclipse to define the JRE you are going to use and to set your JDK compliance preferences.

You specify the JRE your code needs in the **Installed JREs** preferences under **Java** (see Figure 3.27). Set the default JRE (with the associated check box) to be the one you just installed. This specifies the JRE used when you develop Java code. It does not affect the JRE used to run Eclipse.

Set your **Compiler compliance level** setting, on the **JDK Compliance** page of the **Java Compiler** preferences, to either **1.3** or **1.4**, depending on what your code requires (see Figure 3.28). This is a global preference that applies to all projects. We do not recommend attempting to manage JRE 1.3

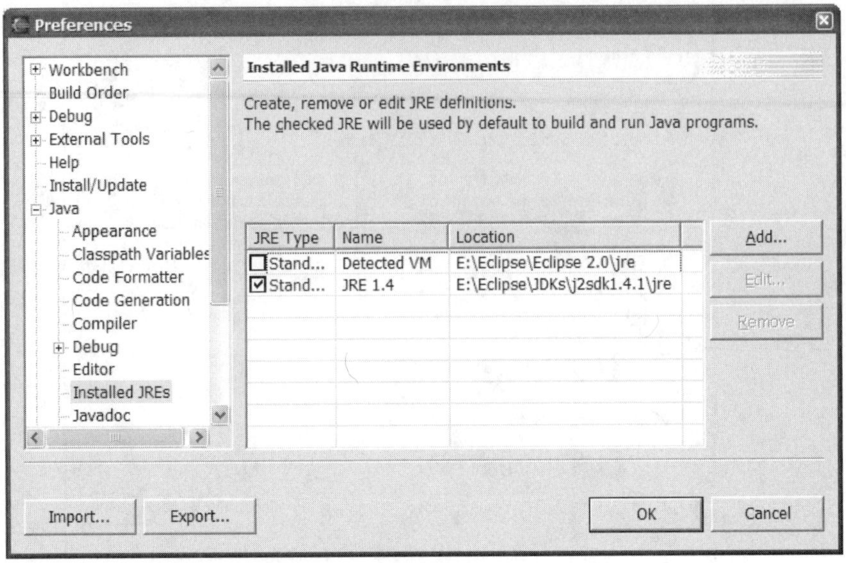

Figure 3.27   Setting Installed JREs Preferences

dependent code and JRE 1.4 dependent code in the same workspace. See the section "Multiple JREs, Differing JDK Level" later in this chapter for more information.

Each Java project maintains its own classpath. JDT sets a Java project's classpath based on the project's **Java Build Path** properties, which includes a JRE. If you have multiple projects that depend on different JREs, you have several configuration options. Your options depend primarily on the JDK level of the JREs your code requires.

Multiple JREs, Same JDK Level

You can have multiple Java projects that require different JREs, but the JREs are the same JDK compliance level, either 1.3 or 1.4. You have two options: You can configure to run multiple workspaces, one for each different JRE your code requires, or you can configure to run one workspace containing code requiring different JREs. We recommend the multiple workspace approach because it is simpler and less error prone.

To configure to run with multiple workspaces, use the following procedure.

1. Use the –data command line parameter to specify a different workspace for each different JRE. Create scripts and/or shortcuts to invoke Eclipse with your different workspaces.

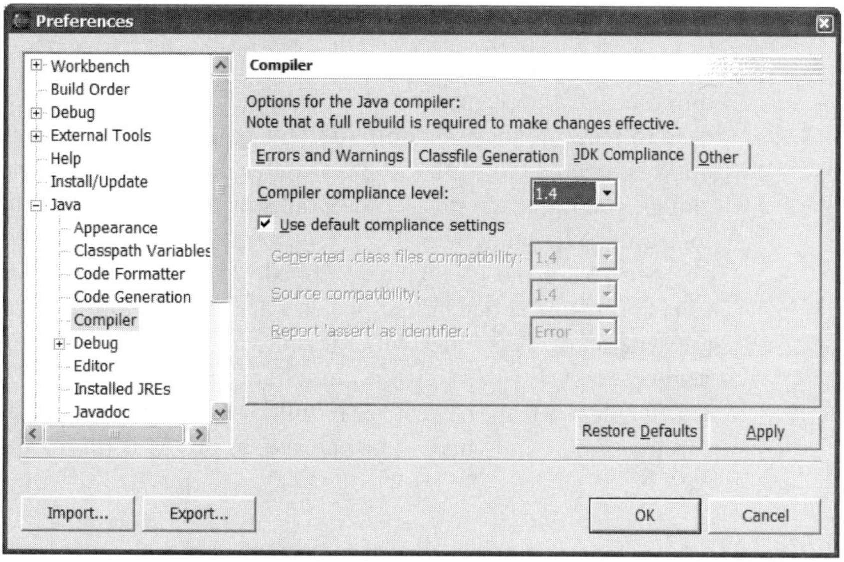

Figure 3.28 Java Compiler JDK Compliance Preferences

2. In each of your workspaces, if the JRE your code needs is not the one Eclipse is running on, specify the required JRE in your **Installed JREs** preferences. Set the default JRE (with the associated check box) to be the one you installed.

3. In each of your workspaces, set the **Compiler compliance level** setting in your **Java Compiler** preferences.

To configure to run with multiple JREs in one workspace, do the following.

1. Install all JREs required by the code you plan to develop in your workspace in your **Installed JREs** preferences.

2. Set the **Compiler compliance level** setting in your **Java Compiler** preferences.

3. For each project, set the project's build path to use the correct JRE through the Java Project Properties dialog by selecting **Properties** from the Package Explorer view context menu. Select **Java Build Path** and then the **Libraries** page. Remove the existing JRE entry (rt.jar file). Select **Add External Jars...** or **Add Variable...** to add the rt.jar of the JRE you want to use.

Multiple JREs, Differing JDK Levels

If you need to work in one workspace on code that requires different JREs at different JDK levels, practically speaking, you only have one choice. You need to separate the code into different workspaces, according to the steps outlined above. Given that the **Compiler compliance level** preference is global, and that each project maintains its own build path and classpath information, changing from 1.3 JDK compliance to 1.4 or vice versa will cause all open Java projects to be recompiled. If the compliance is set to JDK 1.4 level and your 1.3 dependent projects are rebuilt, your files may compile, but the generated .class files will not run with a 1.3 JRE (more precisely, be understood by a 1.3 JVM). If the compliance is set to JDK 1.3 level and your 1.4 JRE dependent projects are rebuilt, the compiler will not understand 1.4-specific syntax and you will not be able to produce 1.4 format .class files.

Running Java Code

To run Java code, you must be in one of the Java perspectives. There are three basic ways to run code in your Java projects: You can run (launch) a Java program with the **Run** action, you can run a Java program with the **Debug** action, and you can evaluate (execute) an Java expression in a scrapbook page. With the **Run** action, your program executes and you do not have an opportunity to suspend its execution or examine variable or field values. In debug mode, you suspend, resume, and examine a program's execution. We'll look more at debugging in Chapter 4.

You can run code even if it still has compiler errors. If the scope of an error is limited to a method, you can run code in the class, except for the method with the error. If the scope of an error is at the class level, for example, a problem with a static declaration, you can run code in other classes but not the one with the error.

Using the Run Action

Java programs, that is, classes with main methods, are identified with the **Run** label decoration. To run a Java program, select a class or a Java element containing a class, and select **Run** from the menu or the **Run** pull-down menu, and then select **Run As > Java Application.** JDT executes the main method and sends output to the Console view. If you have previously run Java programs, you will have entries under **Run > Run History** and **Run** from the toolbar.

Select from these to re-run programs. You can also press **Ctrl+F11** or simply select **Run** from the toolbar to re-run the last program you ran.

When you run a Java program, you run it as a Java application, JUnit test, or run-time workbench. We're going to focus on Java applications here. Running as a run-time workbench is for testing extensions to Eclipse. We'll get to that in Chapter 8. Running as a JUnit test is beyond the scope of this book. For more information on this, refer to "Using JUnit" in the "Tasks" section of the *Java Development User Guide*.

To run a Java program, JDT needs two things: a main method and a launch configuration. Depending on what view was active and what you had selected when you requested to run a program, if a unique class with a main method can be determined, that main method will be run. For example, if the Java editor is active on an element with a main method, that main method will be run. If you have a project selected in the Package Explorer view and there are multiple classes in that package with main methods, you will be prompted to select one.

If the program encounters a run-time error, the exception information goes to the Console view and is displayed in error text color to distinguish it from other output types. Color-coding for output text in the Console view is defined in your **Console** preferences under **Debug**.

Managing Launch Configurations

Launch configurations define information for running Java programs. With launch configurations you can specify input parameters, JVM arguments, and source for your code, and set the run-time classpath and JRE. If you do not specify a launch configuration when you run a Java program with the **Run** action, a default is created for you. To define a launch configuration, select the **Run** pull-down menu and then **Run...**. In the Launch Configurations dialog (see Figure 3.29), select **Java Application** for **Launch Configurations** and then select **New**. If you had previously run Java programs with the **Run** action, you will see the default launch configurations that were created for you (see Figure 3.29).

On the **Main** page, **Project** is optional. If you specify it, its build path is used to set the classpath, source lookup, and JRE. Use **Search...** to search a project's build path for Java programs. If a valid project is specified, the build path of that project is searched for classes with main methods matching the search pattern (you can use wildcards) in **Main class**. If a project is not specified, the build paths of all the projects in your workspace are searched for classes with main methods matching the search pattern.

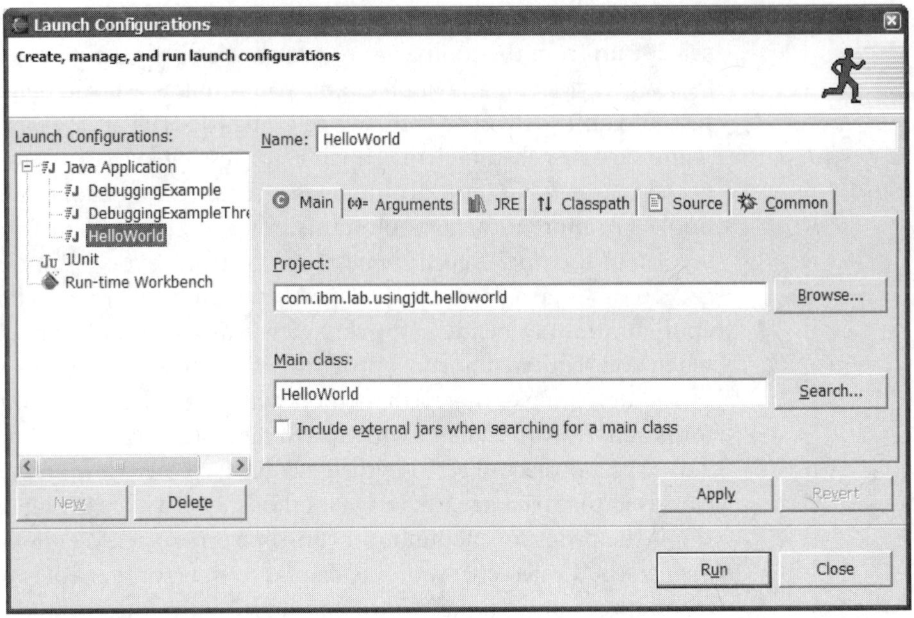

Figure 3.29   Creating a Launch Configuration

On the **Arguments** page, you can set the input parameters for the Java program and any JVM parameters. The Java program parameters are strings separated by spaces. For more information on JVM arguments, see "Running Eclipse" in the "Tasks" section of the *Workbench User Guide*.

On the **JRE** page, you set the JRE used to execute the Java program. Use this to override the JRE defined in the build path properties of the project containing the program. Choose from the list of choices, which is populated with the JREs you have defined in your **Installed JREs** preferences, or add a new JRE. This is useful, for example, to specify a 1.4 JRE in order to do hot code replace when you debug your code.

On the **Classpath** page, the classpath is set based on the build path information from the project specified on the **Main** page. To override or add to this, deselect **Use default classpath**. If you do not have a project specified, you need to do this and specify classpath information. If you choose not to use the default classpath, add references in the classpath to those projects and JAR files containing declarations the Java program references, including the project or JAR file containing the `main` method being executed.

On the **Common** page you specify information about how to save the launch configuration. By default, launch configurations are saved as metadata in your workspace. If you select **Shared**, you specify a Java project into which to save the launch configuration as a `.launch` file. In this way, it's easy to keep and manage launch configurations with the code they run and to share them with others accessing the project; this is especially important for teams. The **Run mode** and **Debug mode** selections allow you to specify the perspective to display when the launch configuration is used to run or debug, respectively, the Java program. You can also indicate which favorites list displays the launch configuration, the **Run** or the **Debug** toolbar pull-down menus.

Evaluating Expressions in Scrapbook Pages

Java scrapbook pages (`*.jpage` files) allow you to edit and evaluate Java code expressions and display or inspect the results. They are a quick and easy way to test code and experiment with Java code expressions. You can evaluate an expression that's a partial statement, a full statement, or a series of statements. To create a scrapbook page, select **Create a Scrapbook Page** or use the **New** wizard. Scrapbook pages can be located in Java projects, folders, source folders, and packages.

Enter an expression in the Scrapbook page. This could be something simple like `System.out.println("Hello World")`, or an invocation of your Java code, for example, its `main` method. Content assist (**Ctrl+Space**) is available in scrapbook pages. Select the expression and then select **Display** from the toolbar or the context menu. JDT evaluates the expression, sends output to the Console view, and displays the `toString` value returned by the expression you selected in the scrapbook page. Select **Inspect** to display the results in the Expressions view. (We'll discuss the Expressions view in more detail in Chapter 4.) **Run Snippet** simply runs the code and sends the output to the Console view.

There are a couple of scrapbook page properties worth noting. To view or change these, select a scrapbook page and then **Properties** from the context menu. **Working directory** by default is the Java project in your workspace containing the scrapbook page. This is for relative file references. You can also change the JRE used for the scrapbook page. The default JRE is the one specified in your **Java** preferences under **Installed JREs**.

Scrapbook pages get their classpath from the containing project's build path. If in a scrapbook page you want to reference a Java element that is not on the build path of the containing Java project, you need to add to the Java project's build path. Scrapbook pages also allow you to specify `import` statements. You do this by selecting **Set Imports** from the context menu of a scrapbook page or **Set Import Declarations for Running Code** from the toolbar. You need to set `import` statements for references to Java declarations in your projects. This is a common oversight. If the type or package you are attempting to import is not listed in the Add dialog, it means you need to add it to the build path of the project containing the scrapbook page. If you are referencing an element that has multiple declarations, you will need to add an `import` statement to uniquely identify the element.

Each scrapbook page has its own associated JVM. The JVM is started the first time you evaluate an expression in a scrapbook page after it is created or opened. The JVM for a scrapbook page runs until the page is closed or explicitly stopped with **Stop Evaluation** from the context menu or the toolbar. When a scrapbook page is in the process of evaluating, the icon changes to a red *J* on a gray background. If the expression you're evaluating results in a loop or a hang, select **Stop Evaluation**. In some cases this may not stop execution. If it doesn't stop, simply close the scrapbook page and then re-open it.

Working with Java Elements

In the "Fundamentals" section earlier in this chapter, we presented an overview of how to create different kinds of Java elements. In this section we'll go into more depth on Java projects, creating and importing Java elements, and details on local history for Java elements.

More on Java Projects

Java projects add a number of properties to projects, including external tool builders, the Java build path, and the Javadoc location. We discussed Javadoc location earlier in the "Generating Javadoc" section in this chapter, and external tools builders in the section "Customizing Eclipse" in Chapter 2. A Java project's build path property specifies how JDT organizes Java code, output files, and other resources in your project.

Java Source Code Organization

Within a Java project, there are two basic ways to organize your code. For small projects, you may choose to have everything in the same package or folder, `*.java` source files, `*.class` output files, and other files required by your program. With this organization, when you save a `.java` file and the file and project are built (compiled), the resulting `.class` files are put with source files in the same folder.

to access older instances of resources. We will cover tags in more detail when we discuss versioning.

Updating: Keeping Up with the Team

Updating allows your CVS managed projects to receive any changes made by your colleagues, thus keeping your workspace up-to-date with the state of the repository. An update does not overwrite your files. Instead, it automatically merges differences between the local file and the latest file instance in CVS (except for binary files). If there are conflicts, the merge will complete but the conflicting lines of text will be replaced with a special CVS markup text identifying the conflicts (which could introduce undesirable errors). Eclipse offers alternative synchronization mechanisms to avoid unpleasant merges. If code ownership of your application is well defined among your colleagues, conflicts will be rare, and a CVS update is more like a catch-up operation.

Eclipse provides support for CVS update operations through its update and synchronization actions, available for any workspace resource. We will explore these in detail. There is an informative description of how conflicts are handled in the *Workbench User Guide* under the topic "Working with the Team Environment" titled "Updating."

Committing: Your Turn to Share

Committing is the reverse of updating: Update is a pull from the repository and committing is a push. When you perform a CVS commit, you are updating the CVS repository with your changes and sharing them with your team. This will result in a new revision number for the files that you modified. Of course, a commit is a serious operation and you want to be confident of your changes before committing. If there are conflicts, the commit operation will fail. *You should always resynchronize with CVS before committing your changes to minimize the possibility of a conflict.*

Versioning: Capturing the Moment

CVS provides a mechanism that allows you to tag a specific revision of a file with a text label. This label becomes a symbolic name that can be used to refer to the specific revision. Tagging individual files is not terribly useful. Normally, you want to tag a set of files that represents a completed piece of work. In CVS terms, you tag a module (which corresponds to an Eclipse project) when a significant milestone has been reached. All the latest revisions of the files in the module are tagged with the same symbolic name. You can think of this set of tagged files as a **version**. It is important to understand that a project's files, with the same assigned tag, may have different revision numbers. For any particular external change (like a bug or a functional enhancement), some files may change a lot, some may change a little, and some are not changed at all. When you version a project, you are tagging the **latest revision level** of each file in the project. Versions are not intended to be changed; they represent a static snapshot of your project after some milestone. While you can check out a versioned project into your workspace, you cannot commit changes to it. However, you can create a branch from a version and make changes from there.

CVS reserves a tag name called **HEAD**. You will see **HEAD** in the Eclipse user interface. It represents the main development trunk of the repository.

Branching and Merging: Support for Parallel Development

A **branch** represents a fork in the development process. It allows you to make changes to your project independent of the main development stream. You might do this for several reasons.

- You are working on a bug in a completed release of your product while development is going on for the next release, and you don't want to mix the correction with the current development code.
- You have a big development change that won't be ready for a while. You want to complete it independently of the main line of development to avoid causing problems with the shared base code. You will merge your change back after it is completed.
- You want to create a maintenance branch separate from a major functional release that is going on concurrently. All maintenance will be performed in this branch and later merged to the next major functional release.

In CVS, a branch is identified using a branch tag that splits the latest revision levels of a set of files. In Eclipse terms, this means that resources in a CVS-managed project in your workspace are tagged with the branch name. You can then make your changes and check them in to CVS, independent of other changes that may be going on in that project.

It is possible to have more than one branch on a file or project at the same time. A branch can even spawn another branch. **HEAD** is, essentially, the main branch.

After you have completed the code in your branch, you may want to merge it back. We'll cover how to merge using Eclipse shortly. The effect of a **merge** is to bring the changes you made in your branch back to the development stream in which the branch started. For example, after you have fixed and tested a bug, you may want to merge it back into the base code. Merging can involve resolving conflicts because the files you are working on may be undergoing concurrent changes for other reasons. Eclipse provides assistance in helping resolve conflicts.

What Happens to Revision Numbers During Branching and Merging

In order to keep track of changes in a branch, the revision number is expanded to incorporate the branch. If a file, foo.java, in the main branch, **HEAD** is at revision level 1.3 when a branch is created, its revision number becomes 1.3.2.1. The ordinal 2 defines the branch and the final ordinal 1 indicates the revision within the branch. When the branch instance of foo.java is committed to CVS, it becomes 1.3.2.2, then 1.3.2.3, and so on. Branching off the existing branch adds two more ordinals to the end of the revision number reflecting the new branch and its revision. Consequently, a revision number might become quite lengthy. Recall that we branched at revision 1.3, thus creating revision 1.3.2.1. When we complete our merge, the latest revision number will be 1.4, just where we left off when we started our branch (unless, of course, there were other changes committed between the start of our branch and our merge). Fortunately, branch tag names make it unnecessary for you to remember all of this.

Managing Binary Files Using CVS

Though CVS provides considerable assistance with character-based (ASCII) files, it has only basic support for binary files. You can store binary files in CVS and manage them as revisions, but that is about all. Binary files need to be identified as such. A list of files by type, either ASCII or binary, is contained in the **Team > File Content** preference page.

CVS will detect conflicts in binary files using simple file timestamps. In a CVS update operation, if a conflict is detected on a binary file, the repository instance replaces the local instance. However, a copy of the local file prefixed with the characters .# (a period followed by a pound sign) and suffixed with the revision number is added to the project. You must use other techniques to determine how to handle the conflict.

The CVS User Interface in Eclipse

Now that you have a basic understanding of CVS, we'll discuss how Eclipse supports a CVS user. To do this, let's look at the user interface in some detail.

CVS Repository Exploring Perspective: Your Repository Home Page

The CVS Repository Exploring perspective, shown Figure 5.1, is your home
base for working with CVS. It contains the CVS Repositories view, the CVS
Resource History view, and an editor area. The CVS Repositories view displays the CVS repositories known to your workspace. The CVS Resource
History view shows the history of changes to any given file. An additional
view, the CVS Console view, displays all interactions with the CVS server.
The CVS Console view is not part of the default perspective, but you can add
it by selecting **Window > Show View > Other > CVS > CVS Console View**.

The CVS Repositories View

The CVS Repositories view serves as a repository browser. In it you can select
projects that exist in the repository and check out these projects to your

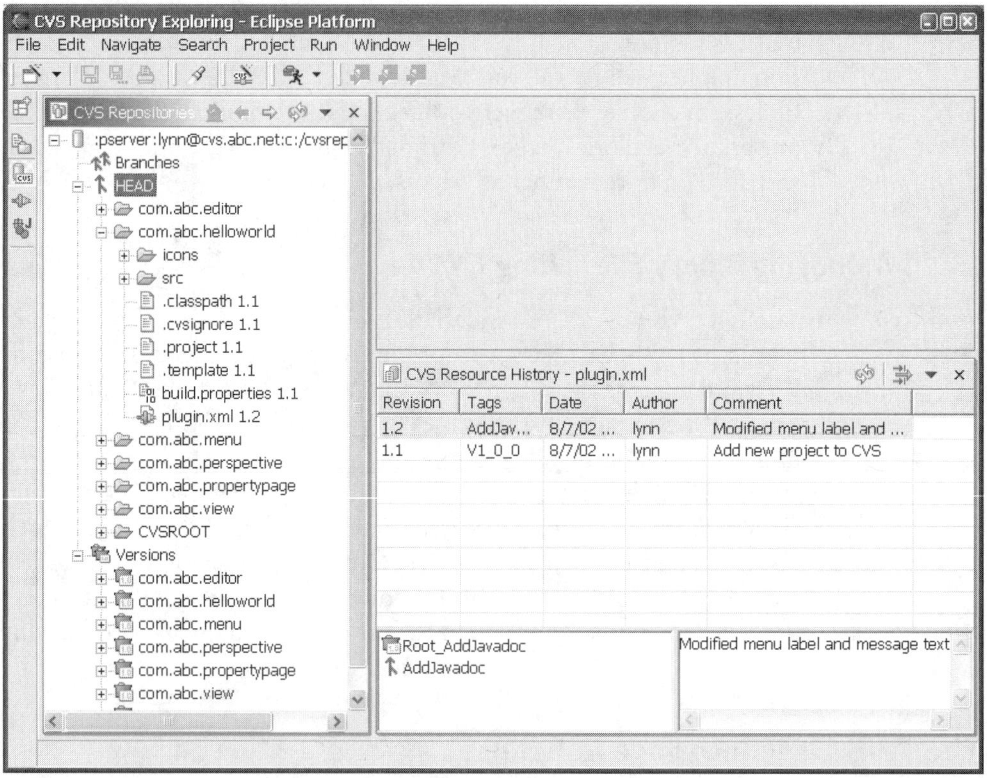

Figure 5.1   CVS Repository Exploring Perspective

workspace. It occupies the left pane of the CVS Repository Exploring perspective, as shown in Figure 5.1. Select **New > Repository Location...** to define a CVS repository location in your workspace (see Figure 5.2). You can have more than one CVS repository defined in this view. As you browse in the repository, you can see the contents of the repository, including projects in HEAD, branches, and versions. You can drill all the way down to specific files by expanding the tree or using the toolbar actions **Go Into** and **Back**. There is a **Refresh View** action on the toolbar; you will probably want to refresh the view before doing anything significant, as it is not automatically kept current with changes in the repository.

As a convenience, if you open the CVS Repositories view from the Resource perspective, it will appear as a tabbed view alongside the Navigator view.

One of the most common tasks in this view is to copy a project from the repository to your workspace. To do this, select a project under **Branches**, **Head**, or **Versions** and select the context menu **Check Out as Project**.

The first time you expand the **Branches** element of the view you won't see anything. You must define the branches you want to see using the context

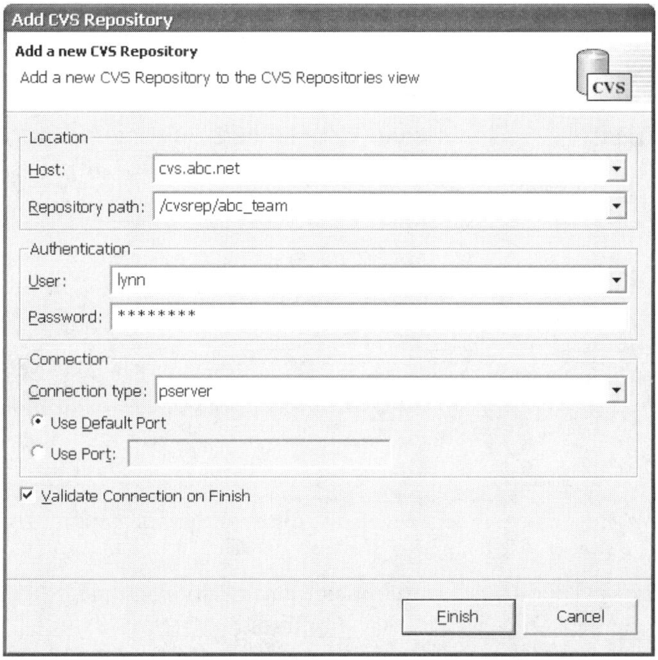

Figure 5.2   Defining a New CVS Repository Location to a Workspace

menu **Define Branch Tag**. In the dialog, you specify the name of an existing branch to have it added to the tree. It is important to understand that **Define Branch Tag** and its opposite, **Discard Branch**, do not create or delete branches in the repository; they simply add or remove them from the view. A CVS repository could contain a large number of branches. You are probably interested in just a few of them. You could even define a nonexistent branch, as there is no repository verification of this action. When you expand a branch in this view, you will see all the projects in the repository, even though only few may be actively contributing to the branch. An active project in the branch will display its files when fully expanded. Other projects will only show empty folders. The expectation is that you know what branches are of interest and which projects are participating in a branch.

Table 5.1 provides a reference list of all the context menu actions available in this view. Some actions depend on what has been selected by the user, as specified in the third column. You are not expected to understand these yet. It is only a reference.

The CVS Resource History View

The CVS Resource History view provides details on every revision for a specific file (see Figure 5.3). This view is part of the CVS Repository Exploring perspective. Select a file and then select **Show in Resource History** from the context menu of the CVS Repository view to see its revision history. It is also available from the **Team** context menu item on projects under CVS control.

When this view is opened in the Resource, Java, or Plug-in Development perspective, it automatically shares space with the Tasks view. You can drag a

Table 5.1   Actions Available in the CVS Repositories View

Action	Description	Available from This User Selection
New > Repository Location	Presents dialog to define a new CVS repository location to the view.	Any
Configure Branches and Versions	Presents dialog to discover branch and version tags on resources. Discovered tags will be displayed in the view.	Various

Action	Description	Available from This User Selection
Define Branch Tag	Defines a branch tag to the repository view. There is nothing performed in the repository.	Selected repository; "Branches" root node
Discard Location	Repository is removed from the view.	Selected repository
Copy to Clipboard	Copies the connection string to the clipboard. Example: `pserver:lynn@cvs.abc.net:/abc_team`.	Selected repository
Refresh View	Refreshes view with current repository information.	Various
Properties	Displays properties of the selected repository and connection information.	Selected repository
Discard Branch	Removes branch from the repository view. There is nothing performed in the repository.	Selected branch
Check Out As Project	Selection is copied from the repository to your workspace. A folder may be checked out and its identity with its project is maintained. This can be useful when working with large projects with self-contained portions.	Selected project or project folder under Branches, HEAD, or Versions
Check Out As	Selection is checked out from the repository to your workspace under another name. The project retains its original identity in CVS when committing changes. This might be useful when you need to make a change to different branches of the same project concurrently, since Eclipse requires all project names in a workspace to be unique.	Selected project or project folder under Branches, HEAD, or Versions
Tag As Version	A version tag is applied to the selected resource and its children.	Selected resource
Tag With Existing	An existing repository version or branch tag is applied to the selected resources. For example, if a new file was added to a project under HEAD and that same file was needed in an active branch, this action could be used to include the file in the branch. It is also an easy way to assign a set of projects to a specific branch.	Selected resource
Compare	Displays the Compare view. If projects or folders are selected, then the Compare view allows comparison of any identically named children.	Two resources must be selected
Show In Resource History	Presents the file's revision history in the CVS Resource History view.	Selected file
Open	Opens the latest revision in an editor.	Selected file

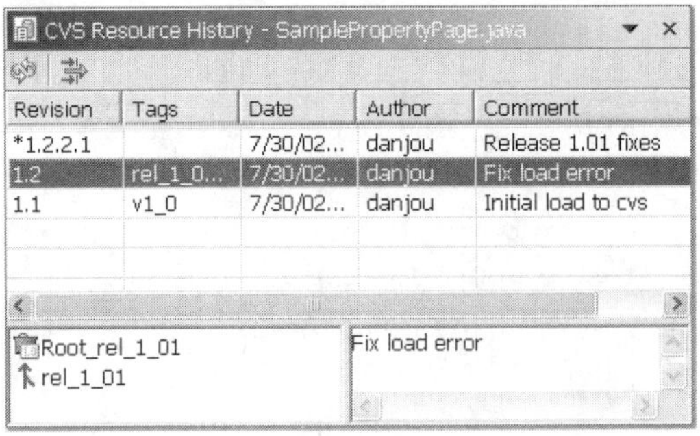

Figure 5.3   CVS Resource History View

file in your workspace that is under CVS control and drop it on this view as a quick way to see its history.

For any selected revision, the branch and version tags associated with the revision, along with the comment provided when the revision was committed to the repository, are displayed at the bottom of the view (see Figure 5.3). The tag and comment viewers can be hidden using actions available from the view's pull-down menu.

Since a file might have a long history, you can filter this view using the **Filter History** action available from the view's toolbar. You can filter the history by author, date ranges, and comment values.

Actions on a selected revision vary depending on whether or not that resource has already been copied to your workspace. They are listed in Table 5.2.

The CVS Console View

The CVS Console view displays all the interactions with the CVS repository; this can be useful if you are experiencing problems. It also shows all of the CVS commands that are issued for any Eclipse CVS action by the user. The appearance and behavior of the console can be modified on the **Team > CVS > Console** preferences page.

How CVS Managed Projects Appear in Your Workspace

Figure 5.4 shows project com.abc.menu in the view under CVS control. This is evident by the label decorations on the icons and additional informational text. (This information displays only if you have the preference **Workbench >**

Table 5.2   Actions on Resources in Resource History View

Action	Description
Get Contents	Replaces the contents of the local working copy of the resource with the contents of the selected revision.
Get Sticky Revision	Reverts the local working copy of the resource to a previous revision. The local copy retains the same revision tag as the repository revision. Do this only if you are very familiar with CVS. A consequence of this action is that you cannot commit any further changes unless the "sticky revision" tag is removed (using CVS directly via commands). You can replace this revision using **Replace With > Latest from Repository**. In general, you are probably not interested in "sticky tags" unless you are a sophisticated CVS user.
Compare	Compares two selected revisions with each other.
Open	Opens the selected revision in an editor. It does not open the editor assigned to a specific file type as you can do in the Navigator view. This only supports text files.
Refresh View	Updates the view with the CVS repository contents.

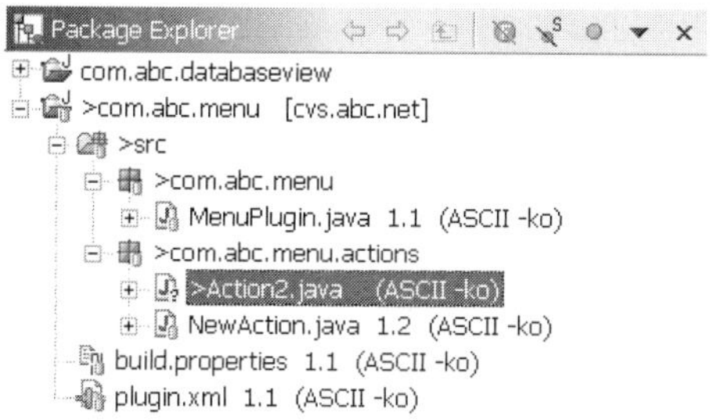

Figure 5.4   Project Under CVS Control with Label Decorations Enabled

Label Decorations enabled for CVS.) Each resource under version control has a tiny disk label decoration on the resource icon. The file Action2.java has a tiny **?** in the decoration, which signifies that it is a new file that has not yet been identified to CVS. Adjacent to the project is the name of the CVS repository server in brackets. If the project is being worked on as part of a branch, the branch name is included. The text decorator **>** indicates that a local resource is an outgoing change, that is, it has been modified locally and needs to be committed to CVS. Parent folders up through the project will also display this character. Beside each resource in parentheses is text indicating the file format, either some form of **ASCII** text or **Binary**. Recall that text changes between CVS and the local file can be merged. Binary files can only be replaced (if a file is considered binary by Eclipse but is, in fact, a text file, an update operation will perform a merge).

You can modify the presentation and the rules for CVS label decorations in the preference page **Team > CVS > Label Decorations**.

CVS Actions Available from the Team Menu

The **Team** menu, available from the context menu of any workspace resource, has several CVS actions associated with it. We will summarize the most common actions you will use to maintain your work with CVS. The specific menu contents vary depending on whether or not the selection is a project. A project will only have a **Share Project** action if CVS or any other repository is not managing the project. Table 5.3 provides a reference list of all the CVS team actions.

The Very Important CVS Synchronize View

This view appears automatically when you finish assigning a project to CVS using the **Team > Share Project** action. It also appears in response to the

Table 5.3   CVS Team Menu Actions

Action	Description
Share Project	This is available only from a project and is only visible on projects that are not under repository management. It displays a wizard that completes the task of associating the project with an available repository. This includes CVS and may include repositories from other providers.
Synchronize with Repository	The selected resource is compared to the CVS repository. If they are not the same, then the Synchronize view is presented with actions to synchronize with CVS, compare differences between the workspace and CVS, and resolve conflicts. For a project or folder, all subordinate resources are also compared with CVS. The Synchronize view will display all resources that have differences with CVS. This is the safest way to work with CVS as you can examine each change, compare with the repository instance, and resolve conflicts.

Action	Description
Synchronize Outgoing Changes	If there are resources that have been updated locally, the Synchronize view is displayed in Outgoing mode, and the locally updated resources can be compared with CVS and committed.
Commit	This updates the CVS repository with your local changes if there are no conflicts. You will be prompted to include a comment. When selected from a project or folder, all the modified resources in the project or folder will be committed to CVS. A **Commit** action will fail if the file in CVS supercedes the file in your workspace.
Update	The local resources will be updated with any newer changes in CVS. Updates in CVS will be merged with the local resources (except for binary files). It is recommended that **Update** be performed before doing a **Commit**. Your **Commit** will fail if others have committed changes since your last Update.
Create Patch	This action creates a patch file of differences between the local resources and CVS. The patch file can be shared with others. This allows work to be shared outside the repository.
Tag as Version	A project, folder, or file in the workspace can be versioned. A version tag is added to all the CVS instances of all child file resources. Individual resources may be versioned, but that is typically done only if a branch will be created on that resource. Versioning can also be done from the CVS Repositories view.
Branch	Creates a branch so that the project (or selected resource) can be modified independently of other development.
Merge	Merges changes in a specific branch back to the code base prior to the branch.
Show in Repository History	Displays the Repository History view on the selected resource.
Change ASCII/Binary Property	Displays the Set Keyword Substitution wizard, which allows you to choose the desired CVS keyword substitution mode for the selected files. This defines how CVS interprets a file as either ASCII or binary.
Add to Version Control	This makes a file known to CVS. It is typically used when a new file is created in the project.
Add to .cvsignore	This will exclude project files that should not be managed by CVS. They will never appear in the Synchronization view or get committed. CVS maintains a .cvsignore file that identifies these file instances. This file does not initially exist; it will be created the first time this action is performed. You must add the .cvsignore file to version control and maintain it in CVS.

actions **Team > Synchronize with Repository** and **Team > Synchronize Outgoing Changes**. An example is shown in Figure 5.5. The view allows you to observe and act on differences between your local project and the CVS copy of your project. (This is used extensively in the exercises associated with this chapter.) This view is easier to work with if you maximize it by double-clicking on its title bar.

A set of buttons on the view's toolbar allows the synchronization information to be filtered by **Incoming mode** (updates from CVS), **Outgoing mode** (updates to CVS), **Incoming and Outgoing mode**, and **Show Only Conflicts**. You might use **Incoming mode** just to see what others have been doing. If you are a one-person team, **Outgoing mode** may be all that is of interest.

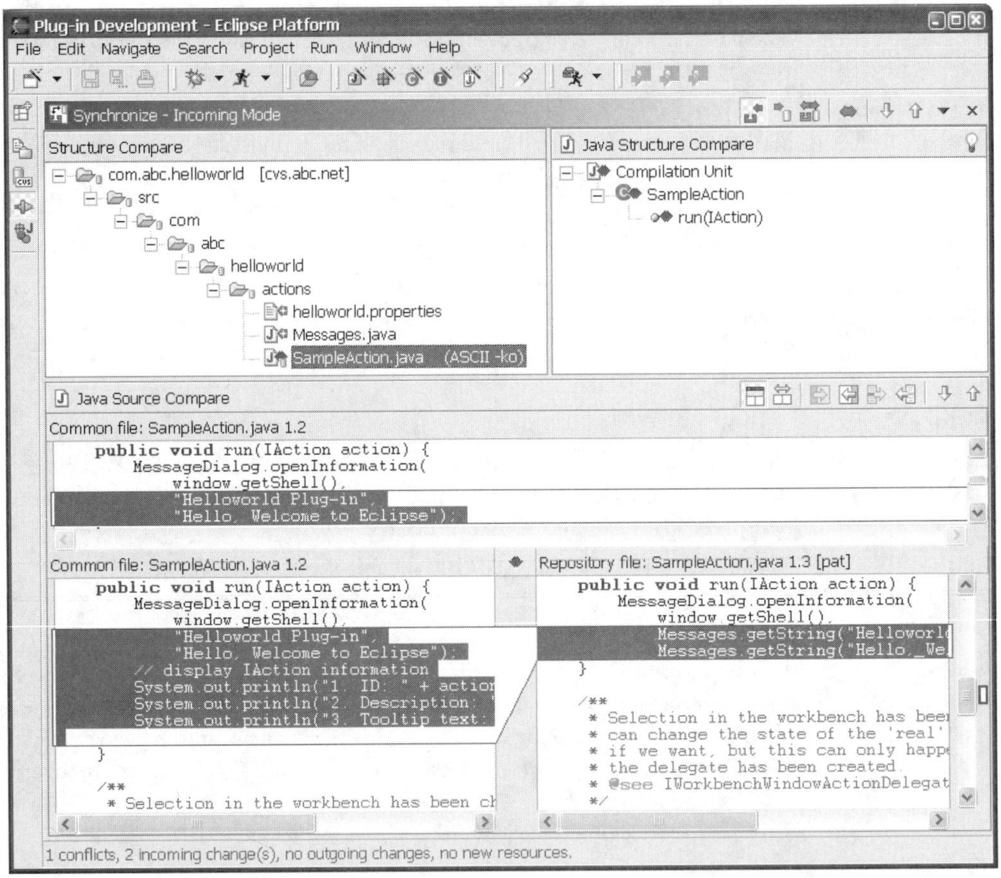

Figure 5.5 Synchronize View Showing Incoming Changes and a Three-Way Compare of the Conflicting File

Handling Concurrent Updates to the Same File

Let's discuss a suggested protocol for making changes. When working with resources in your workspace, you are working independently from the CVS repository. Since changes could occur in the repository without your knowledge, it is very important that you never commit any changes without checking to see if there are updates in the repository that supercede your changes. **Team > Update** will update the local copy of your project with any changes in the repository that supercede your changes. For text files (only), it will automatically merge any changes, even those that might be in conflict, from the repository to your workspace. When conflicts are encountered, the merge will identify them in the file with special CVS markup text to help identify the conflicting lines. The markup text is not compatible with any type of file and could result in compile errors, for example.

Update is a powerful action and should be exercised with care. Below is an example of a simple text file that was updated by Pat and Lynn. Without knowing it, they both updated the lines starting with "B" and "C." The markup text identifies the conflicting lines and the revision number (1.2) that introduced the conflict. A complex Java file with multiple conflicts might be much more difficult to resolve.

```
A is for apple
<<<<<<< sample.txt
B is for bird          (updated by Pat)
C is for crow          (updated by Pat)
=======
B is for bobcat        (updated by Lynn)
C is for cow           (updated by Lynn)
>>>>>>> 1.2
D is for dog
E is for excellent
F is for farm
G is for goat...
```

The action **Team > Synchronize with Repository** supports updating also, but it does not do it automatically. It displays the **Synchronize** view and lists those resources that differ between the workspace copy and latest revision in the repository. In this view, you can inspect the differences and decide what action to take. It gives you much more control and is recommended over the **Update** action.

Let's summarize the basic rule: Before *committing* changes to the repository, you should always *update* resources in your workspace with any changes that have occurred in the repository. To be safe, do this using the **Team > Synchronize with Repository** action. In the resulting view you can perform updates and commits, and reconcile conflicts.

Special Situations and How to Handle Them

Here are some common situations that you might encounter, day to day, or over the life cycle of your development effort, and some proposals on how you might handle them using Eclipse. Some situations may require you to work natively with CVS, but often Eclipse can handle it.

Renaming, Moving, and Deleting Project Resources

- *Never rename a project under CVS control.* If you do, it is not possible to commit new changes because the link between the workspace project and its CVS repository instance is lost. If you must rename a project, it is best to disassociate it from CVS using the **Team > Disconnect** action and then rename it. This is effectively a new project. You must define it to CVS just as with any new project. (In Eclipse release 2.01, a rename is permitted but a link to the old project is maintained. In other words, the project is renamed in your workspace but not in CVS. This may not be what you want. A disconnect is a safer approach.)
- When resources are deleted in your workspace, they will be deleted in CVS when the next commit occurs. Keep in mind that folders are never deleted in CVS. The **CVS** preference **Prune Empty Directories** will hide them from view. This preference is enabled by default.
- For changes that might span projects, make sure that all projects in your workspace are up to date with the repository. The **Team > Update** action is helpful here. Refactoring Java classes is an operation that can result in widespread changes across your workspace. Moving resources between projects can also have this affect.
- Moving resources between projects, from a CVS perspective, is a resource delete from the source project and an addition to the target project. The resources in the target project must be added to version control. Renaming a resource has the same effect.
- When you perform CVS actions like synchronizing after a file change, we recommend that you synchronize at the project level, even though your change may involve only a single file. For example, if you rename a file, which is a CVS delete and add, synchronizing at the file level will only detect the addition and not the deletion. Synchronizing at the project level will handle both.
- When making application-wide changes, keep your team informed to avoid unnecessary conflicts. Commit your changes as soon as possible. Resolving conflicts can be tedious and potentially problematic.

The bookmarks, error markers, and task items are also defined in the Resources plug-in. You'll look in detail at all of these and much more in Chapters 15, 16, and 17.

Chapter Summary

It is no longer practical for tool vendors to produce the base IDE infrastructure upon which to deliver their product-specific functionality. Not only is it a wasteful use of programmer time, but it also has led to islands of tools that are disjointed and inconsistent. This chapter introduced the Eclipse Architecture and the underlying frameworks that make the developer more productive and the resulting product more consistent. Adding new capability to Eclipse, without sacrificing the user's impression of a single environment, involves learning how to program with these frameworks.

References

- Eclipse project slide presentation. http://www.eclipse.org.
- Eclipse platform technical overview. July 2001. http://eclipse.org/whitepapers/eclipse-overview.pdf.
- Gamma, Erich, Richard Helm, Ralph Johnson, and John Vlissides. 1995. *Design Patterns: Elements of Reusable Object-Oriented Software*. Reading, MA: Addison-Wesley.
- Springgay, Dave, Jin Li, Julian Jones, and Greg Adams. May 2, 2002. Eclipse user interface guidelines. http://www.eclipse.org.

Extending Eclipse

CHAPTER 8

Getting Started: Plug-in Development

The previous chapter introduced the notion of plug-ins, extension points, and extensions. Together these three define the "bricks and mortar" that make up Eclipse. What does this mean to you as a programmer in practical terms? In other words, what files do you have to create and what code do you have to write in order to get your stuff recognized and integrated into Eclipse?

It all starts with a **plug-in manifest** file. In this file, you declare where you'll accept contributions from others and where you'll contribute to others, whether that is the Eclipse Platform itself or other Eclipse-based tools with which you want to integrate. Before getting to the details of specifying a manifest, let's consider what the platform does with them to get Eclipse going.

When Eclipse starts up, one of the first things the Eclipse Platform Runtime does is discover what plug-ins are available. It looks in the subdirectories of the <inst_dir>\eclipse\plugins directory for files named plugin.xml, the plug-in manifest we've been talking about. It parses each file, looking for dependencies, what code makes up the plug-in, and, of course, the extensions that the plug-in makes and extension points that it defines. It stores all this information in a tree structure called the **plug-in registry**, keyed by the plug-in identifier. After the plug-in registry is built, the Platform Runtime turns the rest of the responsibility for bootstrapping the environment to an "application" plug-in. By default, this is the Workbench plug-in (org.eclipse.ui), and it in turn opens the main window, builds the initial toolbars and menus, and otherwise prepares the platform for business.

In general, you'll simply define your plug-in manifest, write some code, and hope to arrive home early for dinner. The purpose of this chapter is to learn more about plug-ins in general, understand their common steps of development, and then branch out to more specific topics in subsequent chapters. Since Eclipse plug-in development starts with design-integration considerations, we'll start there, then drill down to the implementation details. Finally, we'll finish with a quick tour of the Plug-in Development Environment (PDE).

Getting Started with Plug-ins

Building a tool with Eclipse is different. You don't start with a blank screen and build a tool. Instead, you start with a robust platform and look at where you want to extend and integrate. Given this distinction, the following points are worth considering in your development process.

1. Describe your user scenarios.

   The first step is to walk through user scenarios of your integrated function to determine the best flow from the user's point of view. Consider the full spectrum of Eclipse's base capabilities with which users would expect your tool to interact, such as its views, editors, and perspectives; include scenarios that exploit Eclipse's team programming environment.

2. Look for Eclipse integration points.

   All extensions are added to Eclipse via a plug-in. In most cases, you use an extension point provided by the Eclipse Platform. Once you know what scenario you are implementing, you will be able to derive the set of applicable extension points to use. This chapter serves as a guide in finding those extension points.

3. Separate your UI from your model

   In most cases, your plug-in will have visual and nonvisual aspects that you might choose to separate into different plug-ins. Eclipse itself follows this design pattern. You will note that the user interface plug-ins include `ui` in their plug-in id, for example, the Workbench plug-in, `org.eclipse.ui`, and the Java Development Tools (JDTs) UI plug-in, `org.eclipse.jdt.ui`.

   There is certainly no requirement that you have to separate plug-ins for your model and user interface components, but you will find that it may result in a cleaner implementation and potentially decrease the platform start-up time. It also leaves open the possibilities that the non-UI portion of your tool could be used outside the Workbench (e.g., as part of an Apache Ant build script). So start by considering what your plug-in might look like and how it might integrate with the existing Eclipse user interface. This is largely a question of whether you're simply augmenting existing elements of the user interface or defining your own.

You should also consider whether you are using a model supplied by Eclipse, such as the model underlying the JDT, or if you are creating your own model. If you are providing additional Java development functionality, then you may want to tap into the powerful Java model provided by the JDT. In either case, the recommendation is to separate the user interface from the model.

4. Separate distinct functional groups of your tool into separate plug-ins.

   Since Eclipse is an integration platform that brings together many different tools into a single environment, it is especially important that distinct parts of your tools can be loaded (or not) separately to reduce their contribution to Eclipse's performance and memory burden.

Integration Scenarios

The following scenarios are just a few examples of how you can extend Eclipse. It is not intended to be an exhaustive list.

Documentation

A very simple integration scenario is to integrate your own documentation with the Eclipse documentation. This scenario is useful to integrate privately produced documentation, such as a frequently asked questions (FAQs) document, team coding standards, or your own tool documentation. The documentation content can be in an HTML or a PDF file. All you need to do is write the XML to integrate the documentation. No Java code is required. To learn more about integrating help documentation, see Chapter 23, Providing Help.

Adding Small Functional Enhancement

Another simple integration scenario involves introducing an incremental improvement that is self-contained. You can contribute an action to the existing Workbench menu bar or toolbar, views, or editors that, when selected, will invoke your function. Chapter 9, Action Contributions: The Integration Fast

Track, and Chapter 18, Contributions Revisited, discuss contributing actions of varying types and scope to the Workbench.

Supporting New Resource Types

In a more complex scenario, you might be interested in adding support for a new resource type. For instance, suppose you want to add support for your own proprietary programming language or integrate an application development tool that creates a specific type of file.

The first step would be to identify your resources. You should list the types of files you will support. For each resource, you will want to explore its life cycle: creating the resource, modifying it, and saving it on disk or in a repository. For instance, your design should support an easy process to create the resource. You might also be interested in importing and exporting the contents. The wizard framework could be useful to develop a creation wizard, accessible from the **File > New** menu choice, for the resource. Chapter 11 discusses the wizard framework.

The next step would be to investigate what should happen when the resource is selected. What actions are appropriate for this type of resource? These actions would appear on the context menu upon selection of the resource in the Navigator view. You may require a specialized editor for the resource. If the resource is text-oriented and lends itself to assisted text entry, Eclipse provides a configurable text editor with capabilities like content assist and color highlighting. In this case, you would need to build functional add-ons to configure the editor. Chapter 27 provides insight into building customized JFace Text editors. If not, a simple text editor might be sufficient. If the resource would best be edited by a specialized nontext editor (e.g., a graphical editor), turn to the basics of editors in Chapter 13.

To adequately present and navigate the resource, what complementary views are required? If the resource contains structured data, the Outline view might be useful. To show the properties of the resource, use the Properties view. You should decide if your editor accepts bookmarks or other specialized markers (see Chapter 17). Are the Eclipse-supplied views sufficient? If not, you may decide to create custom views. As you design the views that you will use, you should specify the communication and notification requirements that will be required. For instance, if the user changes the resource with an editor that affects the data shown in the view(s), you will need to write the code to notify them about the changes. For each custom view, you should build any actions that are view-specific, including sort and filter behavior if there is a large amount of data displayed in the view. Chapter 12 demonstrates how to build a view. It is highly recommended that you run through some user scenarios to make sure your editor and views will work well together. Walking through the scenarios will drive the requirements for notification, event handlers, and the appropriate set of editor and view actions.

While modifying your resources, you might want to allow the user to customize the behavior of your editor and view to their preferences. Integrating your own preference page into Eclipse is described in Chapter 11.

In some cases, files are not created by manually editing them, but are derived by running a program that builds the file when a dependent file is saved, or when a build of a dependent file is explicitly requested. The role of a builder in Eclipse is to take a resource of one type and build a new resource. For example, the Java builder builds class files from Java source files. Your resources may require a special builder. Your design should include resource handling, such as notifications when the resources are changed, which enables you to coordinate the synchronization of multiple views of a resource. Resource notifications are covered in Chapter 15 and creating a builder is described in Chapter 16.

The last aspect to a resource life cycle is the persistence and management of the resource. Your design should consider how the resource should be saved. If the resource requires change management, your users can benefit from Eclipse's integrated repository support.

Not only should you look at what extension points are available for you to use, but you should also consider how you could make your code extensible to others. This involves the creation of new extension points, which is described in Chapter 20. In addition, it also means that your views, editors, and data model need to be open and extensible.

Distributing Your Eclipse-Based Tool

Once you have integrated your tool with Eclipse, you need to distribute it to your users. At design time, you will want to decide whether you will require your users to have Eclipse already installed before installing your tool, or if you will package Eclipse along with your installation medium. You will also want to design the look you want to present to your users in terms of branding. That is, what type of splash screen, license, and initial perspective should appear when your tool starts? Packaging your plug-ins for distribution is described in Chapter 22, Developing Features.

Extending Eclipse

Getting Started with Extensions and Extension Points

Extension points define where other plug-ins may contribute functionality to a plug-in. As just discussed, discovering the appropriate extension points to use is an important part of extending Eclipse. In a sense, the extensions and extension points of a plug-in manifest file detail the interconnections among plug-ins.

The similarity of these terms merits a few words of further explanation. They correspond to two plug-in manifest tags having similar names, `<extension-point>` and `<extension>`. The first *defines* a new extension point; the second *contributes to* an already-defined extension point. In plug-in developer parlance, when you use an extension point, you "extend" it. This chapter and those that follow will focus on contributing to already-defined extension points, namely the `<extension>` tag. Chapter 20, Creating New Extension Points, will focus on usage of the `<extension-point>` tag.

Each extension point has an identifier, specified using the Java package naming convention. Over the course of this book, you'll learn about the majority of the extension points defined by Eclipse. Table 8.1 summarizes what you can contribute and where you'll recognize it from the Eclipse user interface, the associated extension point, and the chapter that describes how to use it.

Table 8.1   Contributing to the Eclipse Platform Extension Points

Purpose	Extension Points	Covered in
Contribute actions to the Workbench window menu bar or toolbar.	`org.eclipse.ui.actionSets`	Chapters 9 and 18
Contribute actions to the Workbench window menu bar or toolbar if the specified view/editor is opened in the perspective.	`org.eclipse.ui.actionSetPartAssociations`	
Contribute actions to an editor's toolbar or menu choices.	`org.eclipse.ui.editorActions`	
Contribute actions to an editor, view, or object's context menu.	`org.eclipse.ui.popupMenus`	
Contribute to a view's toolbar or pull-down menu.	`org.eclipse.ui.viewActions`	
Contribute a new wizard to the standard **Export... and Import...** menu choices.	`org.eclipse.ui.exportWizards` `org.eclipse.ui.importWizards`	Chapter 11

Purpose	Extension Points	Covered in
Contribute a new wizard to the standard **File > New** menu choice.	`org.eclipse.ui.newWizards`	Chapter 11
Contribute preference page to the **Window > Preferences** dialog.	`org.eclipse.ui.preferencePages`	
Contribute pages to an object's Properties dialog.	`org.eclipse.ui.propertyPages`	
Define new views for the **Window > Show View** menu choice.	`org.eclipse.ui.views`	Chapter 12
Define additional filters for the Navigator view's **Filter...** menu choice.	`org.eclipse.ui.resourceFilters`	
Add additional textual or iconic decorations to object labels.	`org.eclipse.ui.decorators`	
Define new editors on resources; this is shown as a choice on its **Open With** menu cascade.	`org.eclipse.ui.editors`	Chapters 13 and 27
Define new perspectives for the **Window > Open Perspective** menu choice. Add new perspective shortcuts, view shortcuts, and actions sets to an existing perspective.	`org.eclipse.ui.perspectives` `org.eclipse.ui.perspectiveExtensions`	Chapter 14
Define your own incremental build processing (**Project > Rebuild Project**) for existing resource types or your own resources. Enhance project capabilities.	`org.eclipse.core.resources.builders` `org.eclipse.core.resources.natures`	Chapter 16
Tag a resource with some user information. Based on the type of marker, the user information can be displayed in views or editors, such as the Tasks view, vertical ruler of text editors, and as label decorations in the Outline view.	`org.eclipse.core.resources.markers`	Chapter 17
Define online help available from the **Help > Help Contents** choice.	`org.eclipse.ui.help`	Chapter 23

Extending Eclipse

The last column lists the chapter where the extension points in the middle column are first introduced. You may notice that this table doesn't have entries for every chapter. This is because Eclipse isn't exclusively about extensions points. There are other useful frameworks that you'll need to know about, too. For example, the Standard Widget Toolkit and JFace are user interface frameworks, not plug-ins, but you'll need to use them in your plug-in implementation. The advanced topics in later chapters will go beyond the general use of extensions, for example, introducing how other Eclipse plug-ins, like the JDT, can be extended.

As a part of learning to contribute to a given extension, you'll need to know something about its supporting framework. For example, contributing a wizard to the **File > New** menu choice requires that you understand more than the parameters of its extension point. You will also need to learn about the framework behind it that creates the wizard dialog, its pages, how it handles page-to-page navigation, and so on. This will be covered in Chapter 11.

Similarly, other chapters will present the extension points related to the area of Eclipse you wish to contribute to or enhance. For many extensions, the chapter will present general step-by-step implementation instructions that you can adapt to your particular case.

Now that you have a better appreciation of what you will find in a plug-in manifest, let's return to the basics of creating one. All extensions and extension points are specified in XML in a plug-in's manifest file. The content of the <extension> element is declared using the ANY rule. This means that any well-formed XML can be specified within the extension configuration section (between the <extension> and </extension> tags). Subsequently, you need to enter these tags and attributes carefully, since there is limited development-time checking for those that are entered manually. Don't worry, though; Eclipse defines a perspective that offers specialized editors and wizards to help you, called the **Plug-in Development Environment**. For example, the PDE's New Extension wizard can lead you through the extension creation process in several ways. First, the New Extension wizard can use a template that presents one or more extension-specific wizard pages to request the necessary parameters, as shown in Figure 8.1.

Alternatively, you can create an extension using a generic New Extension wizard. It leads you through the creation of an extension based on a schema definition of the expected child tags and attributes.

We will cover more about the PDE before ending this chapter. As you will discover, Eclipse provides considerable help to those who want to extend

```
              icon="addtrace.gif"
              tooltip="SOLN: Add trace statements to each method"
              class="com.ibm.lab.soln.jdt.AddTraceStatementsEditAction"
              toolbarPath="additions"
              id="com.ibm.lab.soln.jdt.addtracestatements1">
        </action>
     </editorContribution>
  </extension>
```

Contributing Context Menus to Views and Editors

You contribute context or pop-up menus using the `org.eclipse.ui.popup-Menus` extension point. It is very powerful and offers some unique integration opportunities. You can contribute to the context menu of a view or an editor, which is called a **viewer contribution**. Viewers are discussed in more detail in Chapter 12, Views.

You can also contribute to the context menu of a specific type of object. When you contribute to an object type, your action will appear in the context menu for that object type. For example, if you defined an object contribution for `IResource` objects (projects, files, and folders), then your action would appear on selections in the Navigator view or any other view that presents `IResource` objects. In this way, you are assured that your action appears in any current or future views that present objects you are interested in.

You can apply all the filtering capabilities that you learned earlier in this chapter to ensure that your context menu appears only where it makes sense to do so. You might define an action that appears only on file objects that match your naming pattern. On the other hand, you might contribute an action that applies only to Java projects.

You can only contribute to views and editors in which the author has permitted you to do so. Generally, it is a good practice to allow others to create contributions. How this is done is discussed in Chapter 12, Views.

Let's examine in detail each of the three types of context menus that you can define.

Contributing a Context Menu to a View

When you contribute to the context menu of a view, you are contributing your actions to the context menu of its viewer (recall from Chapter 7, Overview of the Eclipse Architecture, that the contents of a view or editor are seen by the user through its viewer). This is defined as a `viewerContribution`, which is specified in your extension definition. You specify the view's context menu id in your plug-in manifest file using the `targetID` attribute followed by the actions you are contributing. The view's context menu id is, by convention, the id of the view, but it need not be. In the following example, the action will implement `IViewActionDelegate`. This contributes a context menu to the Workbench Navigator view.

```
<extension point ="org.eclipse.ui.popupMenus">
  <viewerContribution
     id="com.mycompany.contributions.tasklist"
     targetID="org.eclipse.ui.views.ResourceNavigator">
     <action id="com.mycompany.showResourceAction"
       label="&amp;Show Resource Action"
       menubarPath="additions"
       helpContextId="com.mycompany.show_action_context"
       class="com.mycompany.contributions.ResourceAction">
     </action>
  </viewerContribution>
</extension>
```

Contributing a Context Menu to an Editor

When you contribute to an editor's context menu, you are contributing to the editor's viewer. The next example defines the extension using `viewerContribution` in exactly the same way as previously in a view, with one exception: The action class will implement the same interface `IEditorActionDelegate` as you use when contributing to the editor's menu or toolbar. This allows you to use the same action class in an editor's context menu, the toolbar, or menubar. Of course, to do this, you must specify this class in two different extension points: `org.eclipse.ui.popupMenus` and `org.eclipse.ui.editorActions`.

You specify the editor's context menu id in your plug-in manifest file using the `targetID` attribute followed by the actions you are contributing. The id of the Workbench text editor is `#TextEditorContext`. The Java editor's context menu id is `#CompilationUnitEditorContext`.

Here is an example of a context menu contribution to the default text editor that is enabled when you have selected some text in your editor. The implementation is discussed in Chapter 18, Contributions Revisited.

```
<extension point="org.eclipse.ui.popupMenus">
  <viewerContribution
    targetID="#TextEditorContext"
    id="com.ibm.lab.soln.actions.TextEditorContext">
    <action
      label="Soln: Word Count"
   class="com.ibm.lab.soln.actions.TextEditorWordCountAction"
      menubarPath="additions"
```

```
          enablesFor="+"
          id="com.ibm.lab.soln.actions.pm.TextEditorWordCount">
          <selection
            class="org.eclipse.jface.text.ITextSelection">
          </selection>
        </action>
      </viewerContribution>
    </extension>
```

Contributing a Context Menu to an Object in a View

Object contribution is the most common use of this extension point, since you can specify an action once and it will appear in all views, present and future, in which the object appears. This has tremendous integration value. Your action class will implement IObjectActionDelegate. Using the object-Class attribute, you can specify in what class of objects your context menu should appear. The action can be filtered to a set of object instances that interest you. The attribute nameFilter allows you to filter by name (if applicable). An action expression, as discussed previously, allows you to do much finer filtering and is a powerful tool when applied to an object contribution.

This example defines the **Run Ant...** action that appears on XML files.

```
<extension point="org.eclipse.ui.popupMenus">
  <objectContribution id="org.eclipse.ant.ui.RunAnt"
    objectClass="org.eclipse.core.resources.IFile"
    nameFilter="*.xml">
    <action id="RunAnt"
      label="%runAnt"
      menubarPath="additions"
      enablesFor="1"
      class="org.eclipse.ant.internal.ui.RunAntActionDelegate"/>
  </objectContribution>
</extension>
```

Chapter Summary

The contributions framework distinguishes itself by allowing you to contribute to the work of others. This is a very effective integration and extensibility feature of Eclipse. You can contribute to the menu bars, toolbars, and context menus in the Workbench, its views, and editors. Object contribution allows you to add context menus to objects of interest in any view or editor that presents those objects. You have seen a rich variety of filtering mechanisms that allow you to refine when and if your action is available. The API is consistent across nearly all of the extension points we discussed using some

Extending Eclipse

form of IActionDelegate. Your action contributions present themselves in the user interface without ever loading your code until the user chooses to run your action.

At this point, you should understand how easy it is to define action contributions. They will be a cornerstone of your integration activities with Eclipse. We will revisit action contributions again in Chapter 18, Contributions Revisited, after you have been introduced to some other topics.

References

Arsenault, Simon. October 18, 2001. Contributing Actions to the Eclipse Workbench. http://www.eclipse.org.

PART II

CHAPTER 10

The Standard Widget Toolkit: A Lean, Mean Widget Machine

The priorities when planning Eclipse's design was performance, robustness, and fidelity to the user's operating system. To be competitive with many excellent IDEs, it was important that the Eclipse platform look and feel like a native application. The UI needed to be lightweight, but rich enough to meet the demands of a sophisticated application. Eclipse is written entirely in Java (well, almost, as you will learn in a moment). How could this be done with available technology? The answer was to provide a Java API to the user interface provided by the host operating system. This would allow Eclipse, a Java application, to look, behave, and perform like a native application on whatever operating system it is running. This portable API is called the **Standard Widget Toolkit** (SWT). It uses the Java Native Interface (JNI) package to provide a Java API to the underlying operating system user interface using C language calling conventions. An SWT implementation of a native control is a one-to-one mapping between the SWT widget and its equivalent native control in the host operating system. There is much more to SWT than that, but this is the critical architectural element.

SWT lies at the bottom of the overall UI framework, just above the native operating system controls. All higher-level GUIs, like JFace, use SWT to display themselves on the user's desktop. Everything visible in Eclipse goes through SWT. SWT must be ported to each target operating system, but once that is done the rest of the user interface just works.

SWT has been ported to a variety of windowing and operating system environments, including Windows, Linux, a variety of UNIX platforms, and Mac OS. Generally, SWT is functionally equivalent at the API level across all implementations. There may be minor behavioral variations, typically due to the underlying platform. SWT on Windows has one significant exception: there is additional support for OLE and ActiveX, which is unique to the Windows platform. OLE and ActiveX are covered separately in Chapter 24.

So what does SWT mean to you as a plug-in developer? How much of SWT do you need to know to get your job done? The answer varies, but it could be surprisingly little. Typically, SWT controls like buttons, labels, text fields, check boxes, and the like are used to gather and present data to the user. They show up most frequently in dialogs like wizards, property pages, and preference pages. Knowing a handful of SWT widgets that you can lay out attractively will carry you a long way. In subsequent chapters, you will learn about the rest of the user interface framework that will carry you the rest of the way. SWT has a rich set of functions (there are nearly a dozen Java packages) and one could write a treatise on SWT. In fact, SWT and JFace are quite mature, having existed inside IBM well before Eclipse was developed.

This chapter is an introduction to SWT. By the end of this chapter you will have a basic, working knowledge of SWT that provides a foundation for understanding and using the rest of the Eclipse UI framework. We will assume that, as a Java developer, you have some experience with GUIs like Abstract Window Toolkit (AWT) or Swing. You will find that from an API perspective, SWT has enough similarities that you will soon feel quite comfortable with it.

The Basic Structure of an SWT Application

Eclipse is an SWT application in the same way that other Java client applications might be called AWT or Swing applications. SWT is packaged within Eclipse for its own use, but you are free to use it in other Java applications if you wish. All SWT applications have a common structure. If you were to write a native SWT application, you would utilize this same structure. Creating plug-ins in Eclipse will normally not require that you use this but it is useful to know, and not terribly difficult to understand. Let's examine it a little further. An SWT application can be started using two classes: `Display` and `Shell`. A `Shell` class represents a window in the underlying operating system.

The Display class connects SWT to the GUI system of the operating system. It handles such things as events and manages communication between the user interface thread and other threads. If you are familiar with windowing systems like Motif, these class names might sound a bit familiar.

A simple SWT application with a window containing a single button might look like Figure 10.1.

Here is the code for this SWT application.

```java
public class SWTShell {
  public static void main(String [] args) {
    Display display = new Display();
    Shell shell = new Shell(display);
    shell.setLayout(new RowLayout());
    Button b = new Button(shell, SWT.PUSH);
    b.setText("Click Me");
    shell.setSize(200, 200);
    shell.open();
    while (!shell.isDisposed()) {
      if (!display.readAndDispatch()) {
        display.sleep(); }
    }
    display.dispose();
  }
}
```

How do you do this? First, you create Display and Shell objects. The Shell is linked to the Display in the constructor of shell. The layout manager, RowLayout, will be discussed later, along with handling a button click event. Then you create a button, contained inside the shell using the class Button. The text within the button is assigned. The shell, which represents the window, has been sized at 200 by 200 pixels. Finally, you set up an event dispatching loop in the while statement. This loop will react to events if they

Figure 10.1 Simple SWT Shell and Button

exist; otherwise, the `display` will remain dormant until it is eventually closed, or disposed of, by the user.

When Eclipse starts up as an SWT application, it does the same thing. The main Workbench window is the `Shell`. It is a top-level window. Top-level windows can be moved and resized, and they are child windows of the `Display`. Secondary windows, or child windows, are typically transient, and often represent dialogs. They are linked to a parent window, which eventually is linked to a top-level window.

Sometimes it is necessary to access the shell that represents the active Workbench window. Here is a convenient static method for doing so. In this example, it is the parent of an error message dialog.

```
Shell workbenchShell =
  Platform.
    getWorkbench(). // IWorkbench
    getActiveWorkbenchWindow(). //IWorkbenchWindow
    getShell();
MessageDialog.openError(workbenchShell,"Error","File not found.");
```

Another important SWT class to know is `Composite` (also of Motif heritage). A **`Composite`** is simply a widget that can contain other widgets. Eclipse creates the top-level components like the shell, title bar, menu bar, and navigation buttons for you, and then calls your code to fill in the client area, represented by an instance of `Composite`.

Until now, the terms "widget" and "control" have been used interchangeably. A **control** is an object that maps directly to an object in the platform windowing system. A **button** is a control. A **widget** is an abstract object representing all user interface objects. In SWT terms, a menu is a widget but not a control. A control is a subclass of widget. In this book, these terms are often used interchangeably.

Common SWT Widgets

SWT has about 30 controls. They are defined in the package `org.eclipse.swt.widgets`. All the common controls like labels, text, rich text, buttons, list boxes, combo boxes, groups, progress bars, sliders, tables, and trees are present. The easiest way to get a feel for what SWT has to offer is to run the **SWT Controls** Example. This is one of a set of SWT example plug-ins. If you have already installed the Eclipse example plug-ins (available from the downloads page at www.eclipse.org), you can run this example by opening a view called SWT Controls that is available from **Window > Show View > Other... > SWT Examples > SWT Controls**. The view when fully expanded in Eclipse looks like Figure 10.2.

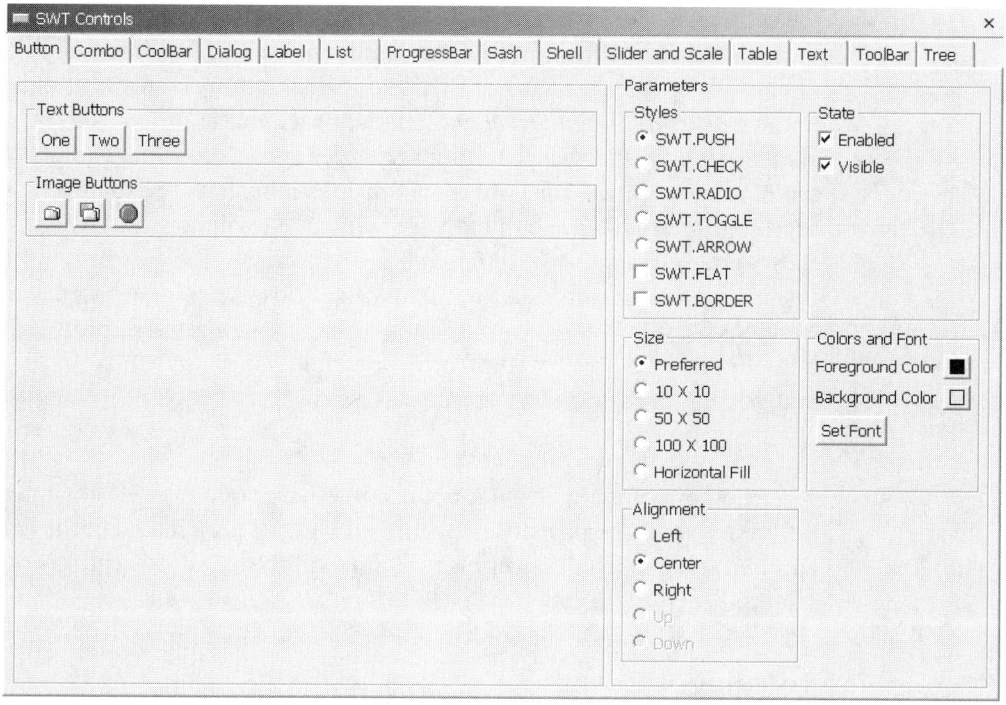

Figure 10.2   SWT Controls Example

You can browse the various tabs to see what is available. Since the source code is available, it is a useful example to get to know SWT better. You can import this example as a plug-in project into your workspace. The project is called `org.eclipse.swt.examples.controls` and the package is called `org.eclipse.swt.examples.controls`. As a binary project, you have visibility to all the source code and can run it in the debugger to better understand its operation.

Refining a Widget's Appearance Using Style Bits

Evident on almost every page of the SWT Controls example is a group labeled "Styles," which contains a set of check boxes or radio buttons with values like `SWT.PUSH`, `SWT.CHECK`, and so on. What do these mean? Well, if you played with them you noticed that they changed the presentation of the control. When selecting `SWT.PUSH` on a button, a normal push button is displayed. Selecting `SWT.CHECK` changes the button to a check box. These are called **style bits**. They are passed in the control's constructor as an integer to define the behavior of the control. These style bits can be logically aggregated using a bitwise OR of all the style bits that you want to apply (assuming they are not mutually exclusive, of course). The Eclipse SWT reference documentation, available as online help in the *Platform Plug-in Developer Guide, Programmer's Guide,* and *Standard Widget Toolkit,* specifies the styles available for each control. The SWT class in the API reference has a list of static final constants that are available to specify each style bit. If you are familiar with Swing, you will note that where Swing uses unique classes for the different types of controls, SWT uses style bits to define the minor appearance or behavior variations of the same base control. For example, a list box can have a horizontal scroll bar, a vertical scroll bar, or both. To define a list box with both you would use the style bits SWT.H_SCROLL and SWT.V_SCROLL in the constructor as follows.

```
List myList = new List(parent, SWT.H_SCROLL|SWT.V_SCROLL);
```

Another common element in the constructor of a widget, like the List object above, is the parent argument. All widgets are created in the context of a parent widget. This concept is fundamental to the SWT architecture and is vital to providing an efficient GUI library.

Responding to Widget Events

All GUI systems support event-triggering mechanisms in response to user interactions from a mouse, keyboard, or other device. SWT provides event handling in the package org.eclipse.swt.events. Event handling in SWT follows a pattern that is nearly the same as AWT and Swing. There are **listeners** that register interest in specific events. When those events occur, you are notified, an event object is passed to your application, and your code can respond appropriately. Here is an example that should look familiar to a Java GUI programmer.

```
StyledText sText = new StyledText(parent,
    SWT.SINGLE|SWT.BORDER);
sText.addMouseListener
    (new MouseAdapter(){
  public void mouseDoubleClick(MouseEvent e) {
    System.out.println("Mouse double click received.");
  }
});
```

As you can see in this trivial example, we have registered an interest in mouse events through the addMouseListener method. The inner class, Mouse-Adapter, has a method, mouseDoubleClick, that allows us to process mouse events. Note that the MouseAdapter class is a member of the SWT events pack-

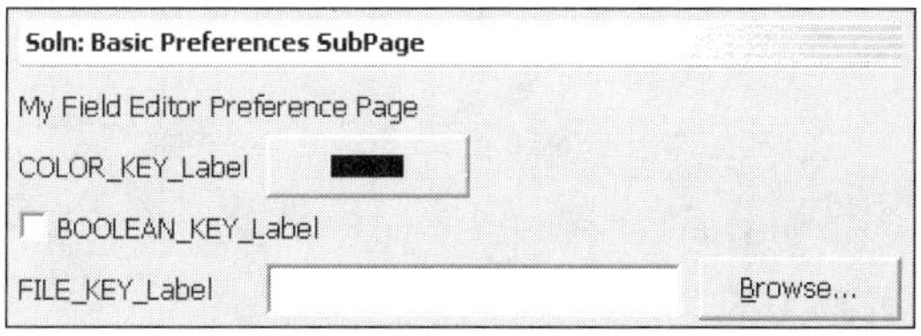

Figure 11.5　User Interface Implemented Using Field Editors

The code shown earlier implements the user interface shown in Figure 11.5 (the field editor preference page is contained within the Preferences dialog, which is not shown).

Using Property Pages to Remember Something Special About a Resource

If you have built preference pages, then learning how to build a property page will be easy. Property pages actually inherit much of their function from the preference page implementation.

The role of a property page is to allow the user to see and modify values associated with a specific object that supports the Properties dialog in Eclipse. Several views, such as the Navigator, Package Explorer, and Error Log views, will open a Properties dialog for the selected object. While you can define a property page for any possible Properties dialog, property pages are most often associated with workspace resources or objects that adapt to a resource type. This means you will typically define extensions for pages that will be added to the Properties dialog opened from the Navigator or Package Explorer views. The capability to attach properties to individual resources can allow your users to customize tool processing: They can set values, and your tool can adjust by checking resource properties as part of your tool logic. Figure 11.6 depicts the structure of a property page within a Properties dialog. This includes how the property page interacts with the resource that was selected when the Properties dialog was opened.

As shown in Figure 11.6 the Properties dialog presents the properties to the user while the property manager manages a collection of property pages. Each property page implements a single panel that can gain focus when selected in the tree of available pages. The selected resource (or other object) is available to the property page. If the selected object is a resource, keyed access to data associated with the resource can be obtained using the workspace API. Persistent property values are stored in a property store, which is

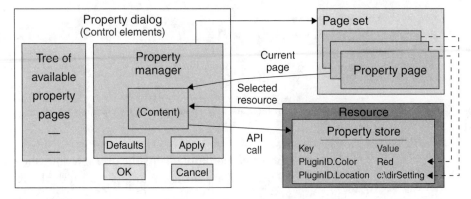

Figure 11.6   Structural View of a Property Page in the Properties Dialog for a Resource

internally maintained by Eclipse. Properties are not sent to a repository, so they cannot be shared outside the current workspace.

The other components shown in Figure 11.6 are part of the framework that you build on by extension. The framework does most of the work. These steps are required to create a property page.

1. Define a property page extension.

2. Implement a property page.

3. Define the property page user interface.

4. Add resource property access logic.

The following sections describe these steps.

Defining a Property Page Extension

To add a property page, you create an `org.eclipse.ui.propertyPages` extension definition in your plug-in manifest. This needs to

- State the name of your page and give it an id.
- Identify the object type for which your page should be available.
- Identify your property page class.
- Optionally identify an icon that will be displayed as part of the page.
- Optionally define a name filter to further refine the rules for when your page should be included in the Properties dialog for a given resource type.

This will add your property page to any properties dialog opened for the object type identified in your extension.

The `objectClass` attribute defines the class type with which your page should be associated. By using `IFile`, `IFolder`, or `IProject`, you can control whether your page should be shown when a file, folder, or project is selected in Navigator view.

The extension in the following example defines a property page that will be available when the selected object is a file resource with a file type of `.java`. The class `JavaPropertyPage` implements the property page. This property page will be included in the Properties dialog when a file with a type of java is selected in Navigator view, but not when the file is selected in Package Explorer view, because this view shows Java elements.

```
<extension
  point="org.eclipse.ui.propertyPages">
 <page
   objectClass="org.eclipse.core.resources.IFile"
   name="Java File Properties"
   nameFilter="*.java"
   class="qrs.tool.properties.JavaPropertyPage"
   id="qrs.tool.properties.qrsfile">
  </page>
</extension>
```

If your page will be available for `.java` files, you can also choose to have it included in the Properties dialog opened for a Java program (compilation unit) when selected in Package Explorer view. To do this you identify that your page should be included when the selected object is *adaptable* to a resource, meaning that you will be able to use the resource API to get/set properties. By adding `adaptable="true"` to the extension the property page will be available when a file with a type of java is selected in Navigator or Package Explorer view.

```
<extension
  point="org.eclipse.ui.propertyPages">
 <page
   objectClass="org.eclipse.core.resources.IFile"
   adaptable="true"
   name="Java Resource Properties"
   nameFilter="*.java"
   class="qrs.tool.properties.JavaPropertyPage"
   id="qrs.tool.properties.qrsfile">
  </page>
</extension>
```

The Package Explorer view does not display files, but displays objects (`IJavaElement`) as defined in the JDT's Java model. For example, what

Extending Eclipse

Table 11.6   Filter Options for Property Page Extensions

Object Type	Filter Names	Values
Resources	`extension`	extension name, as in `txt` or `java`
	`Name`	resource name
	`Path`	`file path` (may include "`*`")
	`projectNature`	`nature id`
	`readOnly`	`true` or `false`
Projects	`nature`	`nature id`
	`Open`	`true` or `false`

appears to be simply a .java file (an instance of `IFile`) in the Package Explorer view is actually part of the JDT model, an instance of `ICompilationUnit`. When opened from the Package Explorer view, the selected resource can still be adapted to an `IResource` to allow for use of the `get` and `set` methods to store resource properties.

If you only want your page to be added to the Properties dialog opened from the Package Explorer view, then you would identify `org.eclipse.jdt.core.ICompilationUnit` as the `objectClass` attribute value.

You can also use filters in the extension definition to further control your contribution. A `<filter name="" value="">` entry added as part of the `<page>` entry will restrict your page contribution so that it only participates when the filter definition is true. The available filter values are shown in Table 11.6.

Implementing a Property Page

You define a property page by creating a class that implements the `IWorkbenchPropertyPage` interface. The easiest way to accomplish this is to extend the `PropertyPage` class.

```
    public class JavaPropertyPage extends PropertyPage implements
IWorkbenchPropertyPage {

    /**
     * @see PropertyPage#createContents
     */
    protected Control createContents(Composite parent)  {
    return null;
      }
    }
```

By inheriting the framework-provided implementation, you can focus on just creating the user interface controls and adding any processing logic required in your property page.

All you need to do to implement an information-only property page is define the user interface by implementing the `createContents(Control)` method. You add your user interface controls, populated with any required content, to the parent control passed in the `createContents(Control)` method. This makes your property page an information page; you share information about the selected resource. If this is the appropriate role of your page, then you should also override the `noDefaultAndApplyButton` method and return `false` to hide the **Restore Defaults** and **Apply** buttons normally included in the user interface of a property page. The property page framework provides the required **OK** and **Cancel** button logic (which just shuts the Properties dialog).

If your property page is required to support both display and modification of data associated with the selected resource, you need to further customize your property page. The user will select push buttons included in the Properties dialog to direct processing. Table 11.7 lists the methods you need to override to implement support for the push buttons.

Now that you have an extension and base class for implementing a property page, let's discuss the user interface definition and addition of logic to process the property values.

Defining the Property Page User Interface

You customize the `createContents(Control)` method to add the controls required in the user interface. For example, the method shown below adds a label and two check boxes to the property page.

Table 11.7 Methods to Override to Customize Push Button Logic for Property Pages

Push Button Name	Method
OK	`performOk()`
Apply	`performApply()`
Restore Defaults	`performDefaults()`
Cancel	`performCancel()`

Extending Eclipse

```
protected Control createContents(Composite parent) {
  Composite composite = new Composite(parent, SWT.NONE);
  GridLayout gridLayout = new GridLayout();
  composite.setLayout(gridLayout);

  Label label = new Label(composite, SWT.NONE);
  label.setText("Choose state for selected resource.");
  Button regenB = new Button(composite, SWT.CHECK);
  regenB.setText("Regeneration Supported");
  regenB.setSelection(getRegenPropertyState());
  Button managedB = new Button(composite, SWT.CHECK);
  managedB.setText("Managed Entity");
  managedB.setSelection(getManagedPropertyState());
return composite;
}
```

The current state of the check boxes is obtained from the saved resource property. The result of the customized `createContents` method is visible when the property page is selected in the Properties dialog (see Figure 11.7).

Adding Resource Property Access Logic

The workspace API (see Chapter 15, Workspace Resource Programming) provides support for getting and setting values for a specific resource. The `IResource` interface methods shown below support getting and setting both temporary (session) and permanent (persistent) values for any workspace resource.

```
setSessionProperty(QualifiedName key, Object value)
getSessionProperty(QualifiedName key)
setPersistentProperty(QualifiedName key, String value)
getPersistentProperty(QualifiedName key)
```

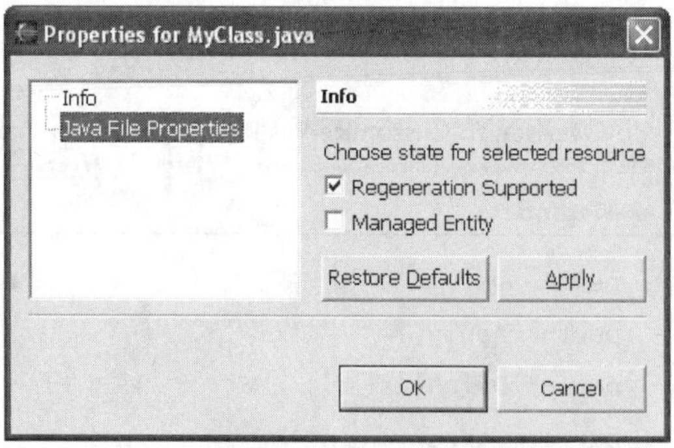

Figure 11.7   Property Page with Customized User Interface Content

A QualifiedName is a multi-part name, which consists of a qualifier and a local name. By convention, the plug-in id is used as the qualifier. Session properties only exist in memory, while persistent properties are saved and therefore available during subsequent invocations of Eclipse using the same workspace. A session property can be any type of object, but only String values can be saved as a persistent property.

You would use the "get" logic above to define the initial state of the property page user interface.

```
private static QualifiedName REGEN_PROPERTY_KEY =
  new QualifiedName("qrs.toolPlugin", "regen");
...
private boolean getRegenPropertyState() {
  IResource resource = (IResource) getElement();
  try {
    String propValue =
      resource.getPersistentProperty(REGEN_PROPERTY_KEY);
    if ((propValue != null) && propValue.equals("True"))
      return true;
    else
      return false;
  } catch (CoreException e) {
    // Deal with exception.
  }
  return false;
}
```

The "set" logic would translate the property to a String value and be integrated as part of the performOk method implementation included in your property page.

```
public boolean performOk() {
  setRegenPropertyState(regenB.getSelection());
  return super.performOk();
}

private void setRegenPropertyState(boolean value) {
  IResource resource = (IResource) getElement();
  try {
    if (value) {
      resource.setPersistentProperty(
        REGEN_PROPERTY_KEY, "True");
    } else {
      resource.setPersistentProperty(
        REGEN_PROPERTY_KEY, "False");
      }
  } catch (CoreException e) {}
}
```

Extending Eclipse

The performOk method is invoked when the user selects the **OK** button. The performOk method is called by default by the performApply method.

Resource Generic Memories—Using the Inherited Preferences Implementation

The standard approach for persistence of data exposed on a property page is to use the workspace API to save and retrieve property values for the selected resource. But if your tool wanted to define a generic value for what was appropriate for all resources of a given type, you could choose to implement the user interface as part of a property page while storing the value using a single keyed entry in a preference store. The property page implementation provided by the dialog framework inherits from the preference page definition, so implementing this approach is easy. Your property page implementation can reuse the inherited approach to preference store management.

If you use this approach, validate that this is the appropriate user interface design for the function being provided. You should ask the question: Is it more effective to have this control value available from a resource's properties page, or should this value just be defined as a preference value and added to a tool-specific preference page?

You want to be sure that this is the appropriate user interface design for the tool function you are implementing. This means that the user of your tool will intuitively think to go to the resource's properties page to establish this type of control. If not, it might be best to implement the function as part of a preference page contribution.

Implementing Your Own Properties Dialog

We have covered how to extend the Properties dialog opened by the Navigator view and discussed how you can also get your page in the Properties dialog opened from the Package Explorer view when your extension targets an adaptable IFile resource with a .java name filter.

You can add pages to any Properties dialog that exists in Eclipse if you know what type of object is displayed in the view that offers an option to open a Properties dialog. The Properties dialog can also be associated with other types of objects that adapt to the workspace API. A view that offers a **Properties** context menu option will contain objects that are **adaptable**, that is, they implement the IAdaptable interface, which allows for the reuse of the logic to open a Properties dialog.

Using Wizards to Extend Workbench Resource Creation and Import/Export Support

Using the wizard framework, you can easily integrate wizards to create new resources or to import and export resources by defining an extension. Figure 11.8 depicts the structure of a wizard dialog and the associated wizard pages as they relate to the `WizardDialog`.

A wizard represents the task and your implementation of a wizard is identified in the extension definition. Each wizard page represents a step in the task. Pages are added to the wizard and the page state determines if the page is complete. When a page is complete, the user can move on to the next page in the wizard; when all pages in the wizard are complete, the processing implemented by the wizard `performFinish` method can be invoked.

Wizards defined by extension are automatically wrapped in a wizard dialog. The wizard dialog manages the page set and includes user interface controls that support the page control processing.

The wizard itself acts as a controller, determining which wizard page, from a list of associated pages, is displayed in response to user interaction. If there are multiple wizard pages, **Next** and **Back** buttons are enabled to support forward and backward navigation. The push buttons are enabled when required, based on the number of wizard pages and the completion status of each page. As you define wizard extensions, and then add pages to a wizard, you are building on this core wizard processing logic. These steps are required to create a functioning wizard.

1. Define a wizard extension.

2. Implement a wizard.

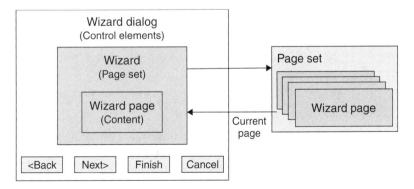

Figure 11.8   Structural View of a Wizard Dialog and the Associated Wizard Pages

Extending Eclipse

3. Implement a wizard page.

4. Define the wizard page user interface.

5. Add the appropriate wizard processing logic.

These steps, and additional wizard customization and control topics, are discussed in the sections that follow.

Adding Wizards to the Workbench User Interface by Extension

There are three extension points available that allow you to add wizards to the Workbench. These extension points support the addition of entries to the set of resource creation, import processing, and export processing wizards integrated into the Workbench user interface.

- org.eclipse.ui.newWizards
- org.eclipse.ui.importWizards
- org.eclipse.ui.exportWizards

This is an example of an import extension definition.

```
<extension
  id="impWiz"
  point="org.eclipse.ui.importWizards">
  <wizard
    name="QRS File Import"
    class="qrs.tool.wizards.ImportWizard"
    id="qrs.tool.wizards.import">
  </wizard>
</extension>
```

By using these extension points, you are able to add entries that are accessible from the matching points in the common Workbench menu tree.

- org.eclipse.ui.newWizards are added to one or both of the **File > New > Projects...** and **File > New > Other...** menu trees.
- org.eclipse.ui.importWiards are added to the **File > Import...** menu tree.
- exportWizards are added to the **File > Export...** menu tree.

Each of these menu options open up a dialog that lets you select from a list of wizards that have extended the matching extension point. The **Projects...** menu option only displays newWizards extensions defined with the project="true" attribute. Categories can also be defined as part of the extension to organize the Wizard Selection dialog entries.

```
<extension
   id="newWiz"
   name="qrs new wizards"
   point="org.eclipse.ui.newWizards">
  <category
    name="Cool Wizard Category"
    id="qrs.tool.wizards.category">
  </category>
  <wizard
    name="A New Wizard Entry"
    category="qrs.tool.wizards.category"
    class="qrs.tool.wizards.QRSNewWizard"
    id="qrs.tool.wizards.new">
    <description>
A wizard in the cool category. Select and enter the
processing implemented by my available pages.
    </description>
  </wizard>
</extension>
```

Figure 11.9 shows the dialog that includes the category and associated entry (with description) for the resource creation wizard extension definition above.

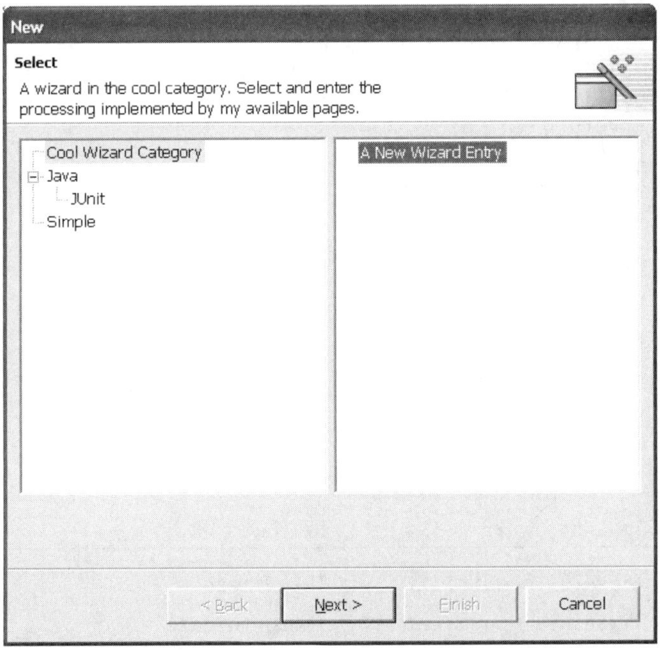

Figure 11.9 New Wizard for Resource Creation

The selection dialog is itself a wizard in that it supports forward (and backward) paging through a set of wizard pages. The selection dialog lets you select and launch your wizard, which then configures and manages access to the appropriate page content as part of your implementation of the task to be performed.

Implementing a Wizard

You build a wizard by creating a class that extends the Wizard class and implements the appropriate interface (extension-point specific). Table 11.8 lists the extension points and interface names.

The PDE knows what to generate for each extension option; for example, the code shown in the following example would be generated by the PDE for the QRSNewWizardFile wizard page identified in the extension definition above.

```
public class QRSNewWizard extends Wizard
  implements INewWizard {
  /**
   * The constructor.
   */
  public QRSNewWizard() {
  }
  /**
   * @see Wizard#performFinish
   */
  public boolean performFinish() {
    return false;
  }
  /**
   * @see Wizard#init
   */
  public void init(
    IWorkbench workbench,
    IStructuredSelection selection) {
  }
}
```

Table 11.8   Extension Points for Adding a Wizard to the User Interface

Extension Point	Interface
org.eclipse.ui.newWizards	INewWizard
org.eclipse.ui.importWizards	IImportWizard
org.eclipse.ui.exportWizards	IExportWizard

```
public class MyView extends ViewPart {
    ...
    public void createPartControl(Composite parent) {
        ...
        MenuManager menuMgr = new MenuManager("#ViewLabPopUp");
        menuMgr.setRemoveAllWhenShown(true);
        menuMgr.addMenuListener(new IMenuListener() {
            public void menuAboutToShow(IMenuManager menuManager) {
                menuManager.add(addAction);
                menuManager.add(deleteAction);
                menuManager.add(new Separator());
                menuManager.add(renameAction);
            ...
            }
        });

        Menu menu =
menuMgr.createContextMenu(getViewer().getControl());
        getViewer().getControl().setMenu(menu);

        ...
    }
}
```

To make your view extensible to others, meaning that other plug-ins can contribute to your view's menu bar, toolbar, and context menu, you need to publish an extensible menu. It is a good practice to allow contributions, and you should always do so unless there is some special reason to disallow it. There are two key activities to perform when you are defining a view.

- Register a context menu. This provides a menu object for others to contribute to your context menu.
- Define the standard insertion point labeled `additions` for contributors to use in the path attribute of any menu bar and toolbar contributions they define. Specify it using the constant `IWorkbenchActionConstants.MB_ADDITIONS`.

In most cases, a view has only one context menu. However, some define several context menus that represent the different states of the view. This can help action contributors, since they can more easily target a particular scenario that applies to their contribution, as opposed to testing the state of the view or editor itself. When you register a context menu, you are publishing one or more ids to use as the target value for action contributions defined in your `plugin.xml` file. If you are providing a single id, use the id of the Workbench part you have defined. If you are providing multiple ids, the prefix of the id should be the name of the Workbench part followed by a unique suffix.

Extending Eclipse

```
public class MyView extends ViewPart {
   ...
 public void createPartControl(Composite parent) {
   ...
   menuMgr.addMenuListener(new IMenuListener() {
     public void menuAboutToShow(IMenuManager menuManager) {
   ...

       menuManager.add(new Separator
         (IWorkbenchActionConstants.MB_ADDITIONS));
     }
     });

   ...

   getSite().registerContextMenu(menuMgr, viewer);
     ...
 }
}
```

Supporting Global Actions in Views

Eclipse has a set of global actions that can be reused by different tools. Their official name is **retargetable actions**. For the Workbench, they are defined in IWorkbenchActionConstants and include **Undo**, **Redo**, **Cut**, **Copy**, **Paste**, **Delete**, **Find**, **Select All**, and **Add Bookmark**. Other tools can define global actions that you can reuse. It would be unsightly if every tool that needed a copy-and-paste action defined its own, so these global actions are available to all.

To use one of these actions is simple. You must register a global action handler using the IActionBars.setGlobalActionHandler(String actionID, IAction handler) method. From a view you can use getViewSite().get-ActionBars(). In a view, you might add the following code to your create-PartControl method.

```
getViewSite().getActionBars().setGlobalActionHandler(
  IWorkbenchActionConstants.COPY,
  copyAction);
```

That is all there is to it. Your action, copyAction, is registered with the **Edit > Copy** menu item.

Adding Label Decorations on Objects in a View

Label decorations are visual augmentations on objects in a view. They include modifying an object's icon and may include text as well. You see label decorations all the time when you have errors in your Java classes, as indicated by the red *X* problem decorator. Plug-ins supporting code repositories often use decorator contributions. They use them to identify resources under their control. Figure 12.5 shows label decorations provided by CVS on a project, its folders, and files. Each file also has a string decorator indicating its revision number. Contributed decorators only appear if the user's **Workbench > Label Decorations** preference page has specific label decorations enabled. By default, they are disabled.

Label decorations appear on objects in a view in a way that is similar to object contributions that we previously discussed. However, they have a somewhat different API and a different architectural foundation. The content of a label decoration, be it an image, a string, or both, is not known in advance like action contributions. Only the plug-in contributing the decorator can define the content, so the concept of a delegate, as in actions, does not apply. This also means that the plug-in must be loaded to apply the decorators. As you know, Eclipse prefers to load plug-ins on demand. Moreover, label decorations may have performance implications if they must react to state changes on objects or represent information on a server like a repository. Unless the user explicitly enables a decorator type, the label decorations and the plug-ins that produce them are disabled (a plug-in could set the initial state to enabled, but that should be avoided).

The extension point `org.eclipse.ui.decorators` allows you to contribute decorators to objects of interest. Specifying the extension is similar to object contribution that we discussed earlier. You identify the object you want to decorate using the `objectClass` attribute. Your decoration can appear in any view that displays that object. You must specify a `label`, which identifies your decorator on the **Workbench > Label Decorations** preference page. Optionally, you can also include a `description`, which describes your decoration. You must specify a `class` that implements your decorator class. The class must implement the interface `ILabelDecorator`. Just like an object

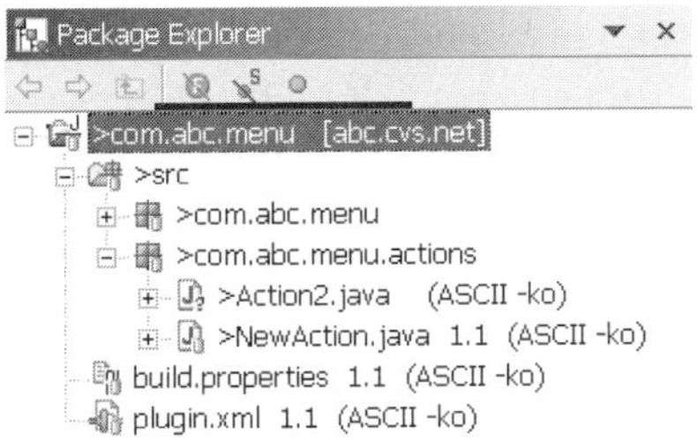

Figure 12.5   Example of Label Decorations on a Project Under CVS Control

contribution, you can specify `adaptable="true"` if you want your decorator to appear on objects that are adaptable to an `IResource` object. You can specify `state` as `true` or `false`. If `true`, the decorators are displayed by default. A value of `false` is recommended, so users can decide if they want to see them or not, and avoid the penalty of loading the plug-in prematurely.

The interface ILabelDecorator requires you to implement two methods.

- The method `Image decorateImage(Image image, Object element)` takes as an input the current image for an object and returns a decorated image.
- The method `String decorateText(String text, Object element)` takes as input the current decorator string and returns a replacement string.

Here is an example of an extension definition used in the Workbench by CVS to provide decorators on `IResource` objects.

```
<!--  **************** Decorator ******************   -->
<extension point="org.eclipse.ui.decorators">
  <decorator
    objectClass="org.eclipse.core.resources.IResource"
    adaptable="true"
    label="%DecoratorStandard.name"
    state="false"
    class="org.eclipse.team.internal.cvs.ui.CVSDecorator"
 id="org.eclipse.team.cvs.ui.decorator">
    <description>
      %DecoratorStandard.description
    </description>
  </decorator>
</extension>
```

If you supply decorators, it is recommended that you do the processing that determines the decorator to use in a separate thread to avoid blocking use of Eclipse. This is especially true if you gather your state information from a server.

Note that label decoration doesn't occur by magic in your own views. You must enable it as well, similar to how you enabled action contributions to your menus with `registerContextMenu`. You enable label decoration by wrappering your label decorator with an instance of `DecoratingLabel-Provider`. Here is some example code from the Navigator view.

```
protected void initLabelProvider(TreeViewer viewer) {
  viewer.setLabelProvider(
    new DecoratingLabelProvider(
    new WorkbenchLabelProvider(),
    getPlugin().getWorkbench().
        getDecoratorManager().getLabelDecorator()));
}
```

Thus, if your view intends to allow decorator contributions, use the decorator manager as your label decorator.

Interacting with Other Views

Views play a supporting role in the Eclipse user interface. Views such as the Properties view complement the active editors. Views and editors can effectively work together to inform the user. Now that we have discussed building a view, we will explore how to create the Properties view.

Properties View

It is a common task to use a Properties view to display and edit attributes or properties of an object. If a Properties view is open, the selection of a resource in the Navigator view will trigger the display of the resource properties in the Properties view. This behavior is common throughout Eclipse. In the Plug-in Development Environment and the Java perspective, selection within one of the views, such as the Hierarchy view or the Outline view, will trigger the Properties view to display the properties of the selected object. You should consider how the objects shown in views you provide would interact with the Properties view. Note that the Properties view is not the same thing as the Properties dialog; the Properties view only shows a two-column table of attributes and their values. If you have many complex items to edit and validate, you should contribute a property page to the appropriate Properties dialog. Adding property pages to a Properties dialog is covered in Chapter 11, Dialogs and Wizards.

There isn't a direct connection between the Properties view and the displayed attributes. Instead, the Properties view is a Workbench window selection listener. Each time the selection changes anywhere in the Workbench window, the Properties view receives notification and queries the newly selected object to see if it supports the `IPropertySource` interface. These are the steps to enable the Properties view for your view's selection.

1. Provide the data source for the Properties view, known as a **property source,** by implementing the `IPropertySource` interface. The property source will be your model or an object adaptable to a property source.

2. Create the descriptive text known as the `PropertyDescriptor` that is displayed in the Properties view.

3. Associate the Properties view with Workbench selections by setting the view selection provider.

4. Synchronize views when values change by using property change
   events.

The following sections describe these steps.

Providing the Data Source

The class named PropertySheet is the main class for the standard Properties
view. The Properties view displays the appropriate property sheet page. The
standard implementation of the property sheet page is a table of property
names and values. To utilize the Properties view, your model object implements the IPropertySource interface or implements the Adaptable interface
and adapts to an IPropertySource object. The IPropertySource interface
provides the methods to get and set the property values and to provide property descriptors. **Property descriptors** provide the descriptive name for the
property.

Providing the Descriptive Text

For each entry in the Properties view, you need to create a property descriptor. A property descriptor contains an id of type String and the textual description of type String, which is displayed. For example, the following code
creates a property descriptor such that the label in the view will be name and
it will be associated with the value of this property. The P_ELEMENT_ID string
is not visible. It is used programmatically to key on the string to be displayed.
Eclipse provides a variety of type-specific property descriptors. In this example, the TextPropertyDescriptor is used. The Properties view will then use
a text-editing cell for editing the value. To show multiple properties, simply
add to the propertyDescriptors array. Each entry in the array is an id and descriptive name pair. This example shows two entries in the Properties view.

```
// Property Descriptors
public static final String P_ELEMENT_ID = "MyElementName";
public static final String P_ELEMENT_DISPLAY_NAME = "name";
public static final String P_ELEMENT_ID2 = "MyElementID";
public static final String P_ELEMENT_DISPLAY_ID = "id";

static final protected IPropertyDescriptor[]
  propertyDescriptors =
    {
      //name
      new TextPropertyDescriptor(
        P_ELEMENT_ID,
        P_ELEMENT_DISPLAY_NAME),
      //id
      new TextPropertyDescriptor(
```

```
            P_ELEMENT_ID2,
            P_ELEMENT_DISPLAY_ID)
    };
```

Eclipse also provides a property descriptor called the `ComboBoxProperty-Descriptor` that displays a combo box widget in the cell of the Properties view. There is also a `ColorPropertyDescriptor` available.

Let's look at some of the methods implemented by the `IPropertySource` object. The `getPropertyDescriptors` method simply returns the descriptor, as we just discussed. The `getEditableValue` method returns the object being edited, such as your model object. The `getPropertyValue` and the `setProperty-Value` are used to get and set the actual value in the model object. Note that the `getPropertyValue` method returns the value based on the property descriptor id passed as the argument. The property descriptor id is used as the key. Any data conversions are done within the `get` and `set` methods.

```
public class MyModel implements IPropertySource {
    ...
  public Object getEditableValue() {
    return this;
  }

  public IPropertyDescriptor[] getPropertyDescriptors() {
    return propertyDescriptors;
  }

  public Object getPropertyValue(Object obj) {
    if (obj.equals(P_ELEMENT_ID))
      return name;
        ...
  }
  public void setPropertyValue(Object id, Object value) {
    name = value.toString();
    firePropertyChange("list", invisibleRoot, this);
  }

  public boolean isPropertySet(Object id) {
    return false;
  }
    ...
}
```

Properties in a Property Sheet view are organized into categories. The category is specified in the `IPropertyDescriptor` using the `setCategory` method. In Figure 12.6, the category called **Info** contains a property with the display name **editable** and the associated value `true`. Properties are listed in alphabetical order, and you cannot specify an alternative sort method. If the end user will need help understanding the specific property, a string representing a help context id can be specified in the property descriptor using the `setHelpContexts` method. Even though the name of the method is plural, you can only specify one context id. A label provider can also be specified using the `setLabelProvider` method. If you want a property to be read-only, your property descriptor needs to implement the method `createPropertyEditor` and return `null`.

Associating the Properties View to Workbench Selections

If you would like your view to work in conjunction with the Properties view, your view needs to contribute to the overall Workbench page's selection process. A selection provider handles this function. If you are using one of the viewers provided by Eclipse or extending them, you are in luck. The `Viewer` class implements the `IInputSelectionProvider` interface. All you need to do is set the selection provider of your view site. The view site is passed as a parameter on the view's `init` method or you can use the `getSite` method. In the `createPartControl` method of your `View` class, invoke the `setSelectionProvider` method and provide a viewer that implements this interface.

```
public class MyView extends ViewPart {
    ...
    public void createPartControl(Composite parent) {
        ...
        getSite().setSelectionProvider(getViewer());
        ...
    }
}
```

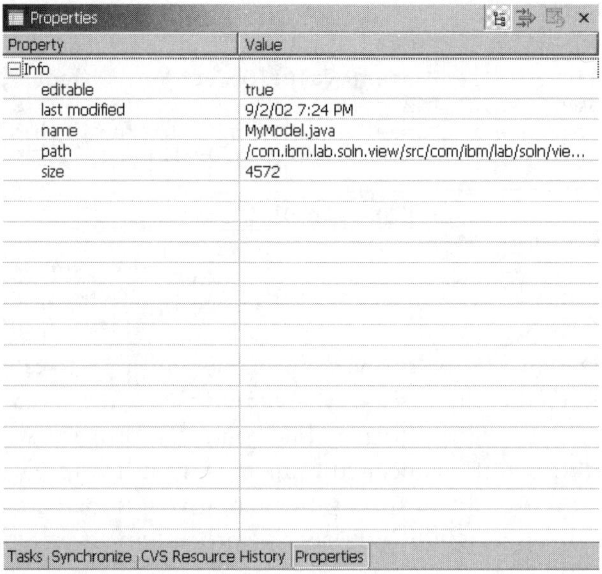

Figure 12.6   Properties View with Category

```
IFolder newFolder = project.getFolder(folderName);
if (!newFolder.exists()) {
  try {
    newFolder.create(true, true, null);
  } catch (CoreException e) {
    // Deal with exception.
  }
}
}
```

Table 15.5 Path Processing Using `IPath` Methods for Path Manipulation

IPath Path Manipulation Methods	Value
append(String path) append(IPath path)	Adds the passed value to the end of the existing path. Duplicate separators are removed unless they are part of a UNC path; trailing separators are maintained.
addTrailingSeparator()	Returns a new path if a trailing separator can be added, otherwise the same path is returned.
removeTrailingSeparator()	Returns a new path if there is a trailing separator to remove, otherwise the same path is returned.
makeAbsolute()	Returns an absolute path with the segments and device of this path; if the path is already absolute, it is returned.
makeRelative()	Returns a relative path with the segments and device of this path; if the path is already relative, it is returned.
makeUNC(boolean toUNC)	Returns a new path, in UNC form if the parameter is true.
getDevice()	Returns a `String` representation of the path device.
setDevice(String device)	Returns a new path with the same segments and the device provided.
getFileExtension()	Returns a `String` representation of the file extension portion of the path. A file extension is the string after the last period (.) in the last segment.
addFileExtension(String extension)	Returns a path that includes the file extension. The target path is returned if it is empty, root, or has a trailing separator.
removeFileExtension()	Returns a path without the file extension, or the same path if no file extension exists.
toFile()	Returns a `java.io.File` for the path.
toOSString()	Returns a `String` representation of the path using the platform-dependent separator.
toString()	Returns a String version of the path. A separator value of / is used regardless of the platform.

Extending Eclipse

The file system could have already had a folder with the same name used during the get and create, or the name identified might have been invalid. As discussed earlier in the section "Workspace Resource Handles—Understanding What You Get When You Ask," you must determine your own strategy for resource creation. In this example, you check if the project was synchronized with the file system, but that only warns you of possible trouble.

Your creation logic needs to either catch or prevent creation errors when the file system has resources not known to the workspace. The Workbench New Folder wizard uses a mixed approach: The folder name is checked for validity before a create request can be processed, but the create attempt can fail if the folder already exists in the file system.

Files can be created and their contents defined using the workspace API. The IFile API supports the use of input streams to get, set, and append contents to a file through these methods.

- getContents obtains an input stream for the file contents.
- setContents uses a passed input stream or IFileState to set file contents.
- appendContents appends an input stream to the current contents of a file.

The following logic will create a file in the folder passed to the method. If the file exists, its content is replaced. The getInitialContents method is used to supply the content used for the new file or to replace the contents of the existing file.

```
private void createFileInFolder2(IFolder folder) {
  IFile newFile = folder.getFile("new_File.txt");
  try {
    if (newFile.exists())
      newFile.setContents(
        getInitialContents(),
        true, false, null);
    else {
      java.io.File systemFile =
        newFile.getLocation().toFile();

      if (systemFile.exists()) {
        // Skip create - in file system.
        // Could refreshLocal on parent at this point.
      } else {
        newFile.create(getInitialContents(), false, null);
      }
    }
  } catch (CoreException ce) {
    // Failed.
```

```
    }
  }
  // Return input stream used to create initial file contents.
  private InputStream getInitialContents() {
    StringBuffer sb = new StringBuffer();
    sb.append("My New File Contents");
    return new ByteArrayInputStream(sb.toString().getBytes());
  }
```

The logic above goes beyond the workspace API to ensure the file can be created. The file system is checked to see if the file already exists. If the file is in the file system but not in the workspace, the create and set contents process is skipped.

Processing the Resource Tree

When you need to find all resources in a project, folder, or even the full workspace, you can use the IResourceVisitor provided as part of the workspace API. Using the IResourceVisitor you can process a node in the resource tree and visit all the children of that node.

To process all elements of a given node in the resource tree, define a class that implements IResourceVisitor. This interface defines only one method, visit(IResource), which will be invoked for each element and subelement of the resource tree you want to process. You process the resource tree by calling IResource.accept(IResourceVisitor) on the resource node of interest.

Any resource, be it a project, folder, file, or even the workspace root, can be given a resource visitor to process. The resource is processed by the resource visitor using the IResource.accept method. The resource visitor is passed to the resource as a parameter in the accept method, which begins the processing. The passed resource visitor must implement the IResourceVisitor interface (which means you have a visit method that returns a boolean). This return value determines if the processing of the resource tree should continue.

A simple IResourceVisitor implementation is shown below.

```
  private void visitResourceTree(IResource resource) {

    IResourceVisitor myVistor = new IResourceVisitor() {
      public boolean visit(IResource res) {
        // Process the resource.
        // ... your logic here ...

        // By returning true you are saying you want
        //to process the children.
        return true;
      };
```

```
    };
    try {
        resource.accept(myVisitor);
    } catch (CoreException e) {
        // Problem during visit processing.
    }
}
```

You implement an `IResourceVisitor` when you want to process all, or a portion of, the contents of the workspace. The visitor essentially allows you to *walk* the workspace resource tree. The `boolean` return value for the `visit` method instructs the visitor framework to continue to the children of the current resource.

The workspace API also includes an `IResourceDeltaVisitor` interface; this supports processing the resource tree provided as part of an `IResource-Delta`. For details on this approach, see the section "Processing Workspace Change Events" later in this chapter and the section "Defining Builders for Incremental Resource Transformation" in Chapter 16.

Resource Properties

Resources are more than just a collection of files and folders. The native capabilities of folders and files are supported as entities in the resource model, but the workspace API also includes support for specialized services that further enrich the resource model. The workspace API allows properties to be defined for any object that implements the `IResource` interface. Properties are keyed values associated with a resource. Two types of properties are supported: session and persistent.

Session Properties

Session properties are used by plug-ins as a caching mechanism for resource-specific objects. Session properties are kept in memory until the resource is deleted, the containing project is closed, or Eclipse is shut down.

This is a powerful capability, as additional tools are integrated with Eclipse. Each tool can add what amounts to a private instance variable to any resource in the workspace. Tool-specific behavior becomes easier to implement with this simple but powerful approach to extending the tool-specific content available as part of any resource.

The following methods support the definition and retrieval of session properties.

```
resource.setSessionProperty(QualifiedName key, Object value)
resource.getSessionProperty(QualifiedName key)
```

The `QualifiedName` parameter is a two-part identifier composed of string values for a qualifier and a local name. The common pattern is to use the plug-in id as the qualifier and a meaningful tool-specific local name. In the next example, the `QualifiedName` is created from a plug-in identifier and a local key. An object is then associated with the current resource.

```
public static final String TOOL_PLUGIN = "qrs.toolPlugin";
...
public static final QualifiedName MY_PROP_VALUE = new
    QualifiedName(ResourcesPlugin.TOOL_PLUGIN, "Tool_Setting");
...
Object setit = getSomeObject();
...
try {
    resource.setSessionProperty(MY_PROP_VALUE, setit);
} catch (CoreException e) {
// Deal with exception.
}
```

Once associated, you can use the `getSessionProperty` method to retrieve the session value as long as the resource exists, its project stays open, and Eclipse is active.

Persistent Properties

Persistent properties are keyed string values and are used by plug-ins to locally store resource-specific information as part of the workspace. Eclipse manages the storage and retrieval of persistent properties independently for each plug-in, and each plug-in has its own properties namespace. Properties are not sent to the repository and are only accessible using workspace API. Once saved, the data is available for as long as the resource exists in the workspace. If you copy the resource, the properties are also copied; if you move the resource, they move as well.

The following methods support the definition and retrieval of persistent properties.

```
resource.setPersistentProperty(QualifiedName key, String value)
resource.getPersistentProperty(QualifiedName key)
```

This next example creates a `String` and saves it as part of the current resource.

```
public static final String TOOL_PLUGIN = "qrs.toolPlugin";
...
public static final QualifiedName MY_PROP_VALUE = new
    QualifiedName(ResourcesPlugin.TOOL_PLUGIN, "Tool_Setting");
...
String setit = getSomeStringValue();
...
try {
    resource.setPersistentProperty(MY_PROP_VALUE, setit);
} catch (CoreException e) {
// Deal with exception.
}
```

Once the string has been associated with the resource, you can use the `getPersistentProperty` method to get the associated String value when required.

If Eclipse is shut down and then restarted, the persistent property will still be available. However, if you delete the resource, the persistent property is destroyed. Even if you select the container for the deleted resource and use the context menu option **Restore From Local History...** to bring the deleted resource back, the persistent property is not restored. In the same fashion, if you restore alternate versions of the file, you do not get alternate versions of a persistent property.

NOTE The persistent property workspace API is commonly used to set and retrieve values that will be shown in the Property Page dialog. See Chapter 11, Dialogs and Wizards, for more information.

Processing Workspace Change Events

The workspace API allows tools to register their interest in being notified of specific resource events. You can use resource change listeners to be responsive and proactive, and even to automate certain tasks. For example, a resource change listener is used to manage the items in the Bookmarks view. Adding or removing bookmark markers from a resource will trigger a resource change event; the Bookmarks view listens for events and determines if it needs to react to the changes that might have occurred. Not all events require a change in the Bookmarks view, but the resource change listener used by the Bookmarks view can quickly determine if any bookmark markers have changed and react as required. The user sees an instantaneous reaction to changes (to try this, open the Bookmarks view and then add a bookmark or two to a file).

Tracking Changes Using the Workspace API

You use the `IWorkspace.addResourceChangeListener(...)` method to add your resource change listener to the workspace. This method allows your listener to be informed of changes like these.

* A file is added, modified, moved, or deleted
* A project is opened or closed
* Markers are added or removed
* Builders are about to start, or have completed, their processing

The interfaces listed in Table 15.6 are used to implement support for resource change listeners. This includes support for creating a resource change listener, processing the events received, and visiting the resource deltas associated with an event. The listener is a class that implements the `IResource ChangeListener` interface and defines a `resourceChanged` method. This method can query the event type using the passed `IResourceChangeEvent`. When appropriate, the listener can get an `IResourceDelta`, which contains details about the resources that were affected by the change event.

Table 15.6 Resource Change Event Interfaces

Event Processing Interface	Description
`IResourceChangeListener`	You must implement this interface if you want to be sent messages when a resource change event has occurred. A resource change listener is notified of changes to resources in the workspace.
`IResourceChangeEvent`	Resource change events describe changes to resources. A resource change event is passed to you, as required, once you have registered to listen for resource changes.
`IResourceDelta`	A resource delta represents changes in the state of a resource tree between two discrete points in time. A resource change event contains a resource delta, which can be processed using the visitor pattern.
`IResourceDeltaVisitor`	To be a visitor of a resource delta, your class must implement this interface. The visitor pattern allows you to process each entry in the delta.

```
IMarker
    MARKER : java.lang.String
    TASK : java.lang.String
    PROBLEM : java.lang.String
    TEXT : java.lang.String
    BOOKMARK : java.lang.String
    SEVERITY : java.lang.String
    MESSAGE : java.lang.String
    LOCATION : java.lang.String
    PRIORITY : java.lang.String
    DONE : java.lang.String
    CHAR_START : java.lang.String
    CHAR_END : java.lang.String
    LINE_NUMBER : java.lang.String
    PRIORITY_HIGH : int
    PRIORITY_NORMAL : int
    PRIORITY_LOW : int
    SEVERITY_ERROR : int
    SEVERITY_WARNING : int
    SEVERITY_INFO : int
```

Figure 17.1   IMarker Interface for Marker Extensions

The existence of a marker for a resource can be used to control the appearance of other tool contributions. A pop-up menu can be defined so that it only appears when the resource has a marker of a specific type or supertype. This filter can be sensitive to the content of the message, priority, or severity attributes. See the section "Built-in Action Filters on Resources and Markers" in Chapter 18 for details on how you can refine action contribution enablement using marker details.

Creating Markers for Customized Resource Tagging

The simplest approach to using markers in your tool is to use the markers already defined as part of Eclipse. If you have a handle to a resource, you can add a marker. For example, the following code will add a task marker with a normal priority to a resource.

```
IMarker marker_P = res.createMarker(IMarker.TASK);
marker_P.setAttribute(IMarker.PRIORITY, IMarker.PRIORITY_NORMAL);
marker_P.setAttribute(IMarker.MESSAGE, "Task marker added");
```

You can use the workspace root as the resource used to create a marker if the marker does not need to be associated with a specific file, folder, or project resource.

Extending Eclipse

You can obtain a marker handle when you know the marker id by using the method `Resource.findMarker(id)`. The id is a numeric value for the marker that is generated when the marker was created. If you do not know the marker id, you can ask the resource for all known markers. You specify the marker type you want to find, if subtypes of that type should be returned, and if you want those for the identified resource or if the children of the resource should be included as part of the find markers request. The syntax of this request is

```
IMarker[] findMarkers(String type, boolean includeSubtypes, int depth)
```

The depth parameter can be

- `IResource.DEPTH_ZERO`
- `IResource.DEPTH_ONE`
- `IResource.DEPTH_INFINITE`

These allow you to gather markers for a given resource, that resource and its members, or all resources in the resource tree below the given resource.

This logic would return all task markers known to a resource and the complete resource tree below the resource.

```
IMarker[] tasks = null;
int depth = IResource.DEPTH_INFINITE;
try {
    tasks = resource.findMarkers(IMarker.TASK, true, depth);
    }
} catch (CoreException e) {
    // Something went wrong.
}
```

Changes to makers are also reported as a resource change event. If you have implemented a resource change listener, you can find the marker changes using the `IResourceDelta.getMarkerDeltas` method. See the section "Processing Workspace Change Events" in Chapter 15 for more details on resource change listeners.

Creating New Marker Types

Marker extension definitions include supertypes, named attributes, and a persistency setting. By identifying one or more supertypes in your marker extension, you can add attributes and default processing for the marker. Note that this is not a complete match to "supertypes" in the Java language sense; this refers to a collection of attributes associated with a marker and potentially a function. More than one supertype can be defined for your extension.

Attributes identify additional data that can be kept with the marker; these attributes can also be referenced when adding action contributions.

Default processing is based on the marker types that are identified as a supertype. Your markers will be visible in existing views if they define appropriate supertypes. For example, if your marker extension defines `org.eclipse.core.resources.bookmark` as a supertype, these markers will be in the Bookmarks view; if it defines `org.eclipse.core.resources.taskmarker` as a supertype, your markers will be in the Tasks view.

The persistent entry setting determines if the marker will be saved in the workspace `.metadata` when Eclipse shuts down.

Markers can define multiple supertypes to merge the attributes of other marker types. There is only one `Marker` class and it has no subclasses. Instead, the `Marker` class manages a set of attributes that can be displayed or modified by views recognizing the marker's supertype(s).

This technique is used in the JDT to define the Java problem marker.

```
<extension point="org.eclipse.core.resources.markers"
    id="problem" name="%javaProblemName">
  <super type="org.eclipse.core.resources.problemmarker"/>
  <super type="org.eclipse.core.resources.textmarker"/>
  <persistent value="true"/>
  <attribute name="id"/>
  <attribute name="flags"/>
  <attribute name="arguments"/>
</extension>
```

Java problem markers (`org.eclipse.jdt.core.problem`) are used to identify problems in the source that were found during the compile. These markers are displayed in the Tasks view. The existence of these markers is also identified using label decorators to alter the resource icon in the Java editor and the Package Explorer and Outline views.

The Java problem marker combines the attributes of `problemmarker` and `textmarker`, and then adds several additional attributes. The result is a marker with the following attributes.

- `severity`, `message`, and `location` from `problemmarker`
- `charStart`, `charEnd`, and `lineNumber` from `textmarker`
- `id`, `flags`, and `arguments` added as part of the Java problem marker

Some of these values are visible when looking at Java problem markers in the Tasks view. Others are used to support direct navigation to the problem. Just double-click on the marker in the Tasks view and the Java program with an error is opened, the line made visible in the editor, and the problem area in the source selected.

You can choose to define new markers so that they are not automatically shown in existing views and instead create new views to display your new markers. Markers can be created, but they are not visible until some user interface component finds them and gives them a place in the user interface. Different views and editors already process, or consume, certain types of markers. The Bookmarks view will display all bookmark markers that have been defined; the Tasks view shows all task and problem markers. The Tasks view also supports filtering by resource or marker subtype.

You can add marker extensions by extending other markers. For example, you can define the following marker extension.

```
<extension id="mymarker" name="My New Marker"
  point="org.eclipse.core.resources.markers">
  <super type="org.eclipse.core.resources.problemmarker" />
  <super type="org.eclipse.core.resources.bookmark" />
  <persistent value="true" />
  <attribute name="flags" />
  <attribute name="arguments" />
</extension>
```

After defining this, you can add the marker to a resource.

```
IMarker marker_Fi2 =
    res.createMarker("com.ibm.tool.resources.mymarker");
marker_Fi2.setAttribute(IMarker.SEVERITY, 0);
marker_Fi2.setAttribute(IMarker.CHAR_START, 20);
marker_Fi2.setAttribute(IMarker.CHAR_END, 70);
marker_Fi2.setAttribute(IMarker.LOCATION, "someplace close");
marker_Fi2.setAttribute(IMarker.MESSAGE, "MyMarker book/task marker added");
```

The new marker type mymarker is consumed by both the Bookmarks view and Tasks view (see Figure 17.2). The new marker has inherited the platform implementation for problem and task markers.

When you add or modify a marker, a resource change event will be triggered. You can use the following statement to find changes to markers in a resource change event.

```
IMarkerDelta[] mdeltas = event.getDelta().getMarkerDeltas();
```

See the section "Visiting the Resource Delta" in Chapter 15 for additional details.

Extending Markers with Help and Resolution Support

The following two extension points add additional capabilities to markers.

- `org.eclipse.ui.markerhelp`
- `org.eclipse.ui.markerresolution`

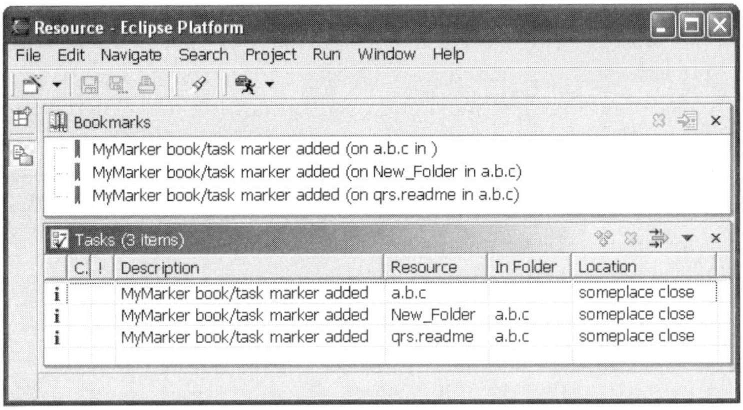

Figure 17.2 Markers Consumed by Multiple Views

A marker help extension allows you to add a help context id to a marker so that contextual help can be associated to the marker. A marker resolution extension allows you to implement quick-fix support for your markers. The extension identifies a marker id and a marker resolution generator class that will be used to propose resolution options.

Exercise Summary

This chapter discussed the creation of resource markers and the ability to create marker extensions for new types of markers. You can now explore the marker solution located on the CD-ROM in the `com.ibm.lab.soln.resources` project. The **Soln: Setup Project Structure** resource action adds a bookmark to one of the files that is created. The resources plug-in also implements a new marker type (recent edits), and a resource change listener that is added as part of the `earlyStartup` logic in the `EDUResourcesPlugin`. The resource change listener creates a recent edit marker every time a file is modified. The recent edit custom marker builds on both the problem and bookmark markers defined by Eclipse. This means these recent edit markers are visible in the Bookmarks and Tasks views, and can be used to open the recently edited file.

By default, only five markers are kept, and only for resources that are not derived. You can customize the marker logic if you have installed the `com.ibm.lab.soln.dialogs` project. A preference page setting can be used to adjust the limit for the number of markers that will be created and a property page setting for a file can be used to disable recent edit support for that resource.

for example org.eclipse.swt.win32 on the Windows platform and org.eclipse.swt.linux on the Linux platform.

Note that fragments are not the sole means of defining platform-specific content. Eclipse defines a number of substitution variables that can be referenced in the name attribute of the <library> tag. Again, the SWT uses this technique to declare its platform-specific library, as shown in this extract of its plugin.xml file.

```
<plugin id="org.eclipse.swt" ... >
  <runtime>
    <library name="$ws$/swt.jar">
      <export name="*"/>
    </library>
  </runtime>
</plugin>
```

The ws variable is substituted with the appropriate window system platform designation (win32, gtk, carbon, etc.). These replacement variables used in library names can be displayed or changed for test purposes in **Window > Preferences > Plug-in Development > Target Environment**, as shown in Figure 19.2.

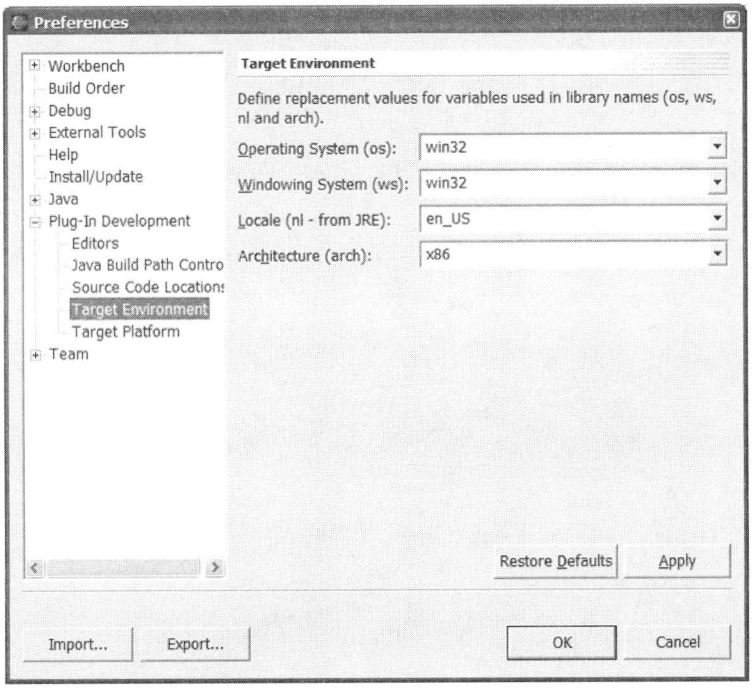

Figure 19.2 Library Name Variables

Chapter Summary

This chapter introduced a few advanced topics that you should be aware of in order to make better plug-in design decisions. Having reached this point in Part II, you should be well-positioned to branch out in independent study that aligns with your personal interests.

References

Kehn, Dan. August 23, 2002. How to test your internationalized Eclipse plug-in. http://www.eclipse.org.

Kehn, Dan, Scott Fairbrother, and Cam-Thu Le. August 23, 2002. How to internationalize your Eclipse plug-in. http://www.eclipse.org.

Object Technology International, Inc. July 2001. Eclipse platform technical overview. http://eclipse.org/whitepapers/eclipse-overview.pdf.

CHAPTER 20

*Creating New Extension Points:
How Others Can Extend Your Plug-ins*

You've spent a lot of time learning how to contribute to existing extension points. Now we're going to look into how to define extension points that others can use—including your own Eclipse-based product.

Except for a small run-time core, nearly all of Eclipse is bound together using extensions. This late-binding strategy dovetails nicely with the ultimate Eclipse goal of creating a flexible, extensible IDE. To continue to support the Eclipse spirit of extensibility, it behooves you to structure your product or tool with this in mind.

We've already mentioned some obvious examples of how you can better enable others to extend your plug-in, such as enabling menu extensions via the `IPageSite.registerContextMenu` method introduced in Chapter 12, Views. Will you have user interface capabilities beyond what is defined by the Workbench plug-in extension points, unique to your plug-in, that you wish to share? Extensibility should also include model-oriented extension points. What sort of tool logic are you writing that others may want to build upon? These consumers are not necessarily external to your product; you may choose to use extension points as a way of integrating your own components. Of course, this is the way that Eclipse itself was created.

By the way, this chapter could be summarized in one sentence: To create an extension point, define an `<extension-point>` tag in your `plugin.xml` file,

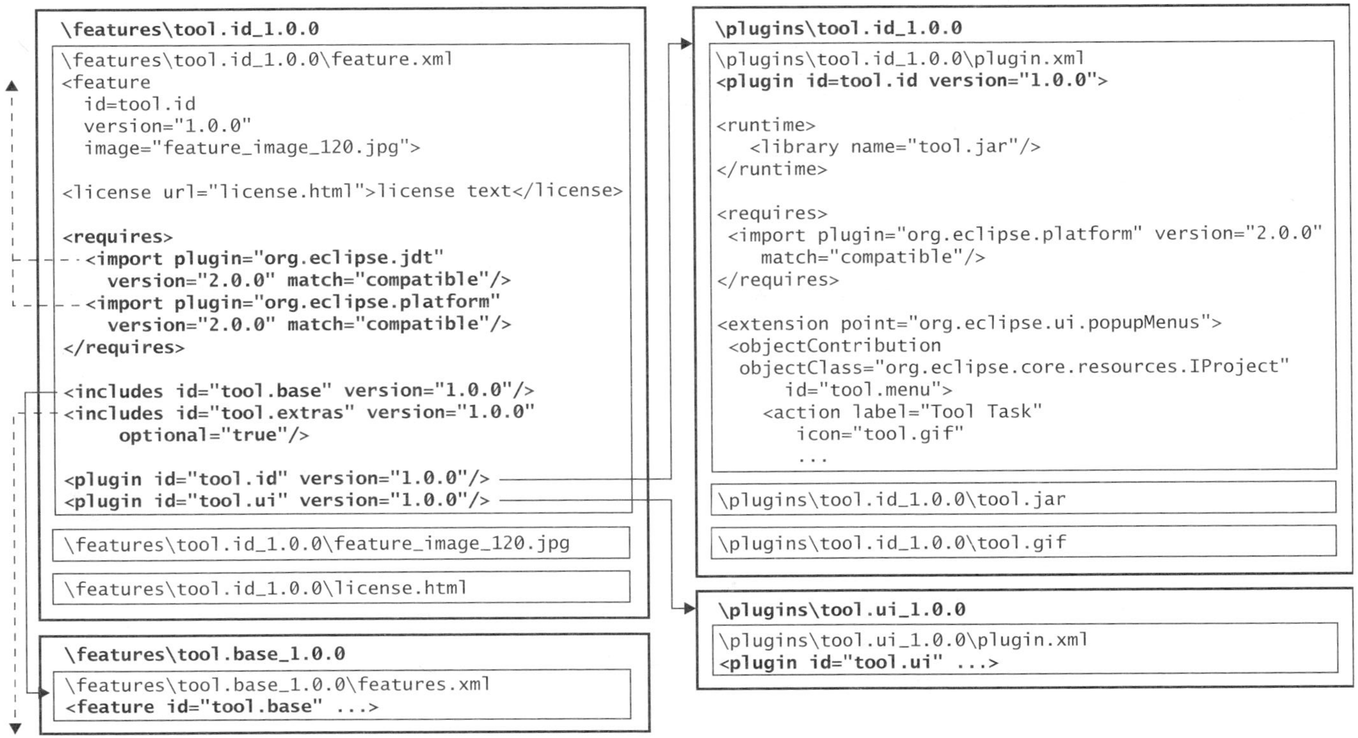

\plugins\tool.id_1.0.0

```
\plugins\tool.id_1.0.0\plugin.xml
<plugin id=tool.id version="1.0.0">

<runtime>
   <library name="tool.jar"/>
</runtime>

<requires>
<import plugin="org.eclipse.platform" version="2.0.0"
   match="compatible"/>
</requires>

<extension point="org.eclipse.ui.popupMenus">
<objectContribution
objectClass="org.eclipse.core.resources.IProject"
   id="tool.menu">
      <action label="Tool Task"
         icon="tool.gif"
      ...
```

```
\plugins\tool.id_1.0.0\tool.jar
```

```
\plugins\tool.id_1.0.0\tool.gif
```

\plugins\tool.ui_1.0.0

```
\plugins\tool.ui_1.0.0\plugin.xml
<plugin id="tool.ui" ...>
```

\features\tool.id_1.0.0

```
\features\tool.id_1.0.0\feature.xml
<feature
id=tool.id
version="1.0.0"
image="feature_image_120.jpg">

<license url="license.html">license text</license>

<requires>
<import plugin="org.eclipse.jdt"
   version="2.0.0" match="compatible"/>
<import plugin="org.eclipse.platform"
   version="2.0.0" match="compatible"/>
</requires>

<includes id="tool.id" version="1.0.0"/>
<includes id="tool.extras" version="1.0.0"
   optional="true"/>

<plugin id="tool.id" version="1.0.0"/>
<plugin id="tool.ui" version="1.0.0"/>
```

```
\features\tool.id_1.0.0\feature_image_120.jpg
```

```
\features\tool.id_1.0.0\license.html
```

\features\tool.base_1.0.0

```
\features\tool.base_1.0.0\features.xml
<feature id="tool.base" ...>
```

Figure 22.2   Feature Structure Relationships

arrows point to one of the included features and two managed plug-ins. The dashed arrows indicate the two plug-ins that are required for this feature and that a second feature is also included. (The targets of these dashed arrows are not shown in the figure.)

NOTE   The Update Manager's capability and rules for feature definition have been enhanced between the 2.0.0 and 2.0.2 versions of Eclipse. If you are a tool developer, you should review the most recent information on the Update Manager available from eclipse.org.

Prerequisite Version-Matching Rules

The plug-in prerequisites identified in a feature are only used to validate the feature in the configuration when it is added or enabled. This includes adding a feature or enabling a feature that was previously disabled. This has an interesting side effect if you accidentally create an invalid prerequisite definition by editing a feature.xml file. The feature would still be included in the run-time platform on a subsequent launch; however, if you disable it, you would not be able to enable the feature again as its prerequisites would not be satisfied.

This processing is different for plug-ins. The prerequisite definition in a plug-in is used every time the platform is started, so an invalid definition in a plug-in would be caught the next time Eclipse was launched.

When the version of a required plug-in is specified, you have the option of defining the matching rule that is used to determine if the available plug-in version is acceptable. The matching rules that can be specified in the prerequisite plug-in definition are shown below (the default is in bold).

```
<requires>
    <import
        plugin="plug-in id"
        version="version id"
        match="compatible|equivalent|perfect|greaterOrEqual" />
</requires>
```

Your feature can be configured only if acceptable versions of the prerequisite plug-ins exist. Acceptable is determined by the specified version and matching requirements. Table 8.2 in Chapter 8, in the section "Declaring Your Plug-in Manifest," describes the acceptability of different versions based on the specified match value.

If strict (`perfect`) version-matching rules are used, your feature may block even minor service updates. If loose (`greaterOrEqual`) or default version-matching rules are used, you may find that the versions of the plug-ins that were loaded by name don't actually support your plug-in's use of their function. There is no requirement that the `<requires>` element defined in a feature be the union of the `<requires>` elements defined in the referenced plug-ins. If there is an inconsistency between the feature and one or more plug-in definitions, the Update Manager might allow the configuration of a feature update that brings in new plug-in versions when one or more of these plug-ins fail at the next startup. This would be because the plug-in's matching criteria was more restrictive than that of the feature, or the feature `<requires>` element was not complete with respect to the referenced plug-ins. Choose your match values carefully and make sure that the feature `<requires>` element will ensure that the requirements of your referenced plug-ins are met.

NOTE The feature manifest editor will create a feature `<requires>` element that is the union of the referenced plug-ins. You can modify this list of required plug-ins to suit your needs. Even the Eclipse features do not define a full set of required plug-ins, but instead use a simplified approach in which they define a plug-in that is key to the feature they require. The target feature references the plug-ins they require.

The point of defining prerequisites is to ensure your feature will work once configured. If you expect all service changes to required plug-ins to maintain a consistent API and be acceptable to your code, then you can choose the `match="compatible option"`. If you only want to accept maintenance updates, but not minor version updates, choose the `match=equivalent` option. Your match value choice may depend on the source of the plug-ins you require from eclipse.org or plug-ins from other providers. Your ability to get early copies and test APIs may determine if you choose a tight (`equivalent`) or loose (`compatible`) matching strategy.

NOTE In release 2.0.2 of Eclipse the use of the `match=` attribute has been extended to support the `<includes...>` entry. See the eclipse.org Web site for details on this implementation.

Extending Eclipse

Servicing Your Features

Features can be defined with URLs that tell the Update Manager where to go to look for updates or identify other locations that host software of interest to the current feature. Update sites can be automatically searched for updates to the current features. Discovery sites can host complementary features.

Your `feature.xml` file definition can identify an update site, as well as discovery sites, that the Update Manager will search for new versions of existing features or additional features that can be installed. These are examples of update and discovery site definitions in a `feature.xml` file.

```
<url>
    <update url="http://www.company.com/updatesite"
        label="YourTool Update Site" />
    <discovery url="http://www.company.com/newcode"
        label="YourTool Add-ons Site" />
</url>
```

Only the update site identified in a root feature is processed. Update sites identified by included features are not used during service processing. A root feature owns the right to manage delivery of service for its included features. If you are building a product based on Eclipse, your features should include the Eclipse features. This allows the content on your update site to synchronize the delivery timing of your product updates and Eclipse Platform updates.

Feature Branding

All features have the option of providing their own branding content, although branding content is not required unless the feature is the primary feature. Features from multiple providers can provide separate and distinct branding information. Any feature-branding information that is provided is used by the platform to create content in the About *Product* Features dialog (where *Product* is the identity defined by the primary feature). For the primary feature, the branding content also includes information used to provide a startup splash image, a name and icon for the Workbench window, and the About *Product* dialog graphic and textual information.

Branding Content in a Feature and Plug-in

By rule, feature-branding information is contained in a plug-in that has the same id as its feature. In addition to the `plugin.xml` file, a branding plug-in contains additional files (see Table 22.1).

Table 22.1   Plug-in Files Included to Provide Branding Content

File	Branding Role		Description
	Product	Feature	
about.html	Y	Y	Standard about plug-in content file. Opened by the About Plug-ins dialog.
about.ini	Y	Y	Control file for feature and product branding.
about.mappings	Y	Y	Text substitution values for about.ini.
about.properties	Y	Y	Translated values of about.properties.
product.gif	Y	NA	System icon image.
feature.gif	Y	Y	Image in About dialogs.
aboutProduct.gif	Y	NA	About Product dialog image.
install.ini	Y	NA	Feature and application definition for eclipse.exe.
plugin_customization.ini	Y	NA	Product customization—preferences override.
plugin_customization.properties	Y	NA	Translated values for plugin_customization.ini.
splash.bmp	Y	NA	Splash screen.

The plug-in that provides branding content still needs a plugin.xml file and could be contributing other function as part of the feature. The files in the table above are included in the directory for the plug-in. The about.ini file is the control file for branding content. The other files provided are configured in the about.ini file (see Table 22.2).

Translated values are identified in the about.ini file using var=%value entries. The value is found in the about.properties file.

Each feature can define a welcome page, a welcome.xml file included in the plug-in directory. When a new feature is installed, the associated welcome page will be opened the next time Eclipse is started.

Every feature in Eclipse includes feature-branding content. You can review these definitions and use them as a model for your definitions. The exercise in

Table 22.2   about.ini Settings for Branding Content

| about.ini Reference | Branding | | Description |
	Product	Feature	
aboutText	Y	Y	Contains text for the About dialog. Can be translated in an about.properties file. Maximum 15 lines and 75 characters per line.
windowImage	Y	NA	Path to the window icon, a 16 × 16 image file.
featureImage	Y	Y	Path to the feature image, a 32 × 32 image file.
aboutImage	Y	NA	Path to the product image. A full-sized product image, no larger than 500 × 330 pixels, shown without "About" text. A half-sized product image, no larger than 250 × 330 pixels, shown with the "About" text.
appName	Y	NA	Application name. Value can be translated in the about.properties file.
welcomePage	Y	Y	Path to welcome page (welcome.xml) file for the feature or product. Welcome page is opened when the product is first started, or the feature first configured.
welcomePerspective	Y	Y	Id of the perspective in which the welcome page is to be opened.

Chapter 34, "Feature Development and Deployment," will also guide you through the process of building a branded feature.

Identifying the Primary Feature

All features can be branded, but only one can provide the product branding when Eclipse is launched. The <install directory>\eclipse\install.ini file is used by eclipse.exe to identify the default primary feature and application to use when starting Eclipse. The install.ini file for Eclipse contains the following values.

```
# java.io.Properties file (ISO 8859-1 with "\" escapes)
# This file does not need to be translated.

# Required property "feature.default.id" contains id
# of the primary feature (the primary feature controls
# product branding, splash screens, and plug-in customization)
feature.default.id=org.eclipse.platform
```

```
# Required property "feature.default.application" contains id of
# the core application that gets control on startup. For
# products with a UI, this is always org.eclipse.ui.workbench;
# for "headless" products, this is product-specific.
feature.default.application=org.eclipse.ui.workbench
```

These values can also be specified using the –feature and –application startup parameters. A feature identified as a primary feature must have a complete product branding in the associated plug-in and include the primary="true" attribute in the feature definition.

Product and Feature Branding in the User Interface

The install.ini entries determine which feature and plug-in will be used to obtain the branding information used at runtime. The brand is visible to the end user, starting with the splash image and then the customized Eclipse user interface and About *Product* dialog (shown superimposed in Figure 22.3).

There are four About dialogs available in the Workbench: About Eclipse Platform, About Eclipse Platform Features, Feature Plug-ins, and About

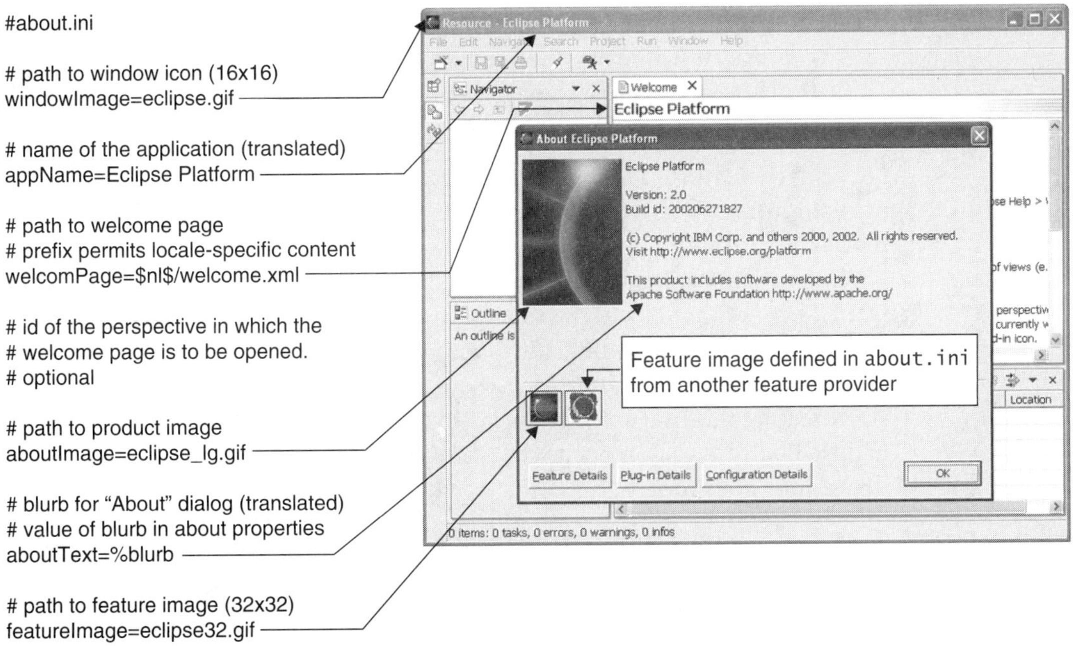

```
#about.ini

# path to window icon (16x16)
windowImage=eclipse.gif

# name of the application (translated)
appName=Eclipse Platform

# path to welcome page
# prefix permits locale-specific content
welcomPage=$nl$/welcome.xml

# id of the perspective in which the
# welcome page is to be opened.
# optional

# path to product image
aboutImage=eclipse_lg.gif

# blurb for "About" dialog (translated)
# value of blurb in about properties
aboutText=%blurb

# path to feature image (32x32)
featureImage=eclipse32.gif
```

Figure 22.3 About Product Dialog Product Branding

Eclipse Platform Plug-ins. These dialogs are customized by the active product brand and the different features included in the active configuration.

The About Eclipse Platform dialog exposes the product-branding content provided by the plug-in for the primary feature, and icons for any additional features, as shown in Figure 22.3. The About Eclipse Platform dialog includes the following.

- Product-branding information, as obtained from the primary feature and the feature-branding plug-in, is displayed using images and text. A large image (`aboutProduct`) accompanies the product text (`aboutText`), and a smaller image (`featureImage`) is also used in the row of feature images.
- Feature images for each set of related features that are configured in the Workbench. Features are related when they include an identical image (determined by file name and image content). The eight features in the Eclipse platform SDK use an identical image file, so only one image entry is added to the feature image content. Figure 22.3 also includes the image for the feature added as part of the Feature Development and Deployment exercise.
- Push buttons that open About Eclipse Platform Features, About Eclipse Platform Plug-ins, and Configuration Details dialogs. The About Product Features dialog can also be opened by selecting the feature icon.

The About Eclipse Platform dialog content is provided by the plug-in for the primary feature. The feature images above the push buttons are contributed by features other than the primary feature. Each unique image is displayed. For an unmodified Eclipse SDK installation, only one image would be shown. The dialog shown in Figure 22.3 has two; the additional image is from a feature that has been added to the configuration. This icon is the first instance of feature branding, as opposed to product branding, that is exposed in the Workbench user interface.

Selecting the **Feature Details** button or a feature image in the About Eclipse Platform dialog opens the About Eclipse Platform Features dialog. This dialog contains

- A list of the features that are active in the current configuration and have a branding plug-in
- Feature-branding content (image and text), which is displayed for the selected feature in the list of active features

provides lightweight Java wrappers, covering the in-proc COM automation servers. Specifically, this supports embedding and in-place activation of OLE documents and ActiveX controls.

In-Place OLE Documents

This form of integration allows standard OLE-enabled tools that support in-place OLE documents (such as Microsoft Word and PowerPoint) to be invoked in Eclipse to edit documents of the corresponding type. Embedding an OLE document such as Word or PowerPoint is equivalent to embedding the entire application. The OLE document provides its own toolbar and menu bar for accessing its behavior. Built into Eclipse is a generic OLE document editor. In fact, this is how Eclipse runs Microsoft Office products like Word as an in-place editor. These tools are otherwise Eclipse-unaware, loosely integrated, and functionally they are the same as external-launch tools; that is, they open a document, edit it, and save it. Microsoft Word does not present Tools Options in places like Workbench properties or take advantage of Resource API to create markers to display in the Task view. However, Eclipse provides support for accessing extended behaviors of in-place OLE documents, making way for a tightly integrated Eclipse-aware application.

In-Place ActiveX Controls

Eclipse provides integration support for embedding and accessing the extended behavior of ActiveX controls. ActiveX controls such as the Web browser or Calendar are a type of in-proc COM server that exposes its methods, properties, and events to Eclipse through the SWT COM container. It is this COM container support, which provides for the embedding and in-place activation, that makes possible deep Eclipse-aware integration, contributing Eclipse actions, properties, task views, and so on.

COM Container Support

Embedding OLE documents and ActiveX controls in an SWT widget requires a COM container. Let's now look at some of the key COM interfaces that containers are required to implement, and then see how those interfaces relate to the SWT COM container implementation.

OLE containers are responsible for handling the interaction with the OLE objects they are hosting. OLE document containers provide storage for the document, listen to content object change notifications, and respond to mouse clicks.

OLE document containers implement the COM IOleClientSite interface to communicate with the document. OLE control containers handle the interaction with ActiveX controls. OLE control containers implement the COM IOleControlSite interface to notify the container of activation changes and to inform it of the control of events.

Containers also manage the user interface by implementing the IOleInPlaceSite interface. It is through this interface that an OLE document can join a control site, take over the container's menus, and add toolbars.

Containing an embedded OLE object in an SWT widget requires two parts.

- An OleFrame
- An OleClientSite (for OLE documents) or OleControlSite (for ActiveX controls)

The "heart and soul" of the SWT OLE support lies in the OleClientSite and the OleControlSite objects. The "skeleton" of the SWT OLE support lies in the OleFrame object, which handles the menu management and window placement responsibilities.

Creating an OleFrame Object

Embedded OLE objects require a frame to "hang" their user interface on. When integrating with the Eclipse user interface, you would typically create the frame in the createPartControl method of a ViewPart or an EditorPart object. Here is an example of creating an OleFrame object in a createPartControl method.

```
public ActiveXWebBrowser createBrowserPartControl(Composite parent) {
  displayArea = parent;
  FillLayout fillLayout = new FillLayout();
  displayArea.setLayout(fillLayout);
  webFrame = new OleFrame(displayArea, SWT.NONE);
  return createBrowserControl();
}
```

Creating an OleClientSite Object

The next step is to create the OleClientSite object. There are two ways to create a client site.

- Create an OleClientSite object from a ProgramID. A ProgramID is a string that identifies the application. For example, the ProgramID for Word is Word.Document and the ProgramID for Excel is Excel.Chart. You can find the ProgramID for an application by looking in the Windows registry or by using the OLE/COM Object Viewer included in the Microsoft Platform SDK Tools (see Figure 24.2).

   To create a blank document, construct the OleClientSite object using the ProgramID.

```
OleClientSite clientSite = new OleClientSite(frame, SWT.NONE,
"Word.Document");
```

- Create an OleClientSite object from an OLE storage file. For example, a .doc file created by Word is a storage file. The OleClientSite is typically created in createPartControl when embedded in a WorkBenchPart. Here is an example of how an OleClientSite is created on an OLE storage file.

```
File file = new File("C:\\OleDocumentation.doc");
OleClientSite clientSite = new OleClientSite(frame, SWT.NONE, file);
```

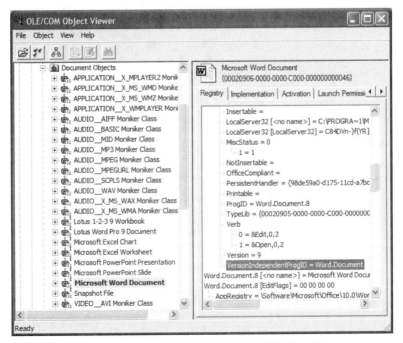

Figure 24.2 Finding the ProgramID Using the OLE/COM Object Viewer

Activating an OLE Object

The final step before an OLE document or ActiveX control becomes visible inside Eclipse is to activate the OLE object (often referred to as **in-place activation**). That is, the content object is edited in place without leaving the Eclipse shell. You typically activate the client site immediately after creating the client site. To activate an object in place, invoke the object using one of the verbs that are predefined in the `org.eclipse.swt.ole.win32.OLE` class. You would typically find the following code for in-place activation of an OLE document. Invoking the `OLE.OLEIVERB_SHOW` verb makes the document's client site visible and active inside Eclipse.

```
if (!oleActivated) {
  clientSite.doVerb(OLE.OLEIVERB_SHOW);
  oleActivated = true;
}
```

Deactivating an OLE Object

When embedding several OLE documents or ActiveX controls in Eclipse at the same time, you may want only one control active at a given time. Deactivated OLE objects are in a "Running" state. That means that the OLE object document contents are visible but removed from the toolbar and menu bar. The document is still running but does not respond to mouse or keyboard actions.

To deactivate an OLE document or ActiveX control, call `deactivateIn-PlaceClient` on the `OleClientSite` or `OleControlSite` object.

`currentSite.deactivateInPlaceClient();`

It is not good to leave the `OleFrame` object for the parent to dispose of. When you are done with the embedded control/document, specifically call the `dispose` method. In addition, remember that `OleFrame`, `OleClientSite`, and `OleControlSite` are SWT widgets and that you must follow the SWT disposal rule, that is, if you create a widget, then you must take care of disposing of the widget. Typically you would dispose of the `OleFrame` object, and this would cause `OleClientSite` or `OleControlSite` to be disposed of too. Disposal of the site deactivates the embedded control/document, so a direct call to the `deactivateInPlaceClient` method is unnecessary.

In this example, the class `ActiveXBrowserView` creates the `OleFrame` object, so it is in the `dispose` method of that class that the `OleFrame` (see `webFrame.dispose`) is disposed of. Here is that `dispose` method.

```
public void dispose() {
  webFrame.dispose();
}
```

Eclipse OLE Editor Support

When you create or use OLE documents within Eclipse, the file is the editor input to an instance of the class OleEditor in the package org.eclipse.ui. internal.editorsupport.win32. The OLE editor does the work of embedding the OLE document. The Workbench automatically opens the OLE document editor in place and integrates its pull-down menu options into the menu bar. If you require deeper integration, you should consider implementing your own OLE editor. You might implement all that is in the OleEditor class and then add in things like participating in the Workbench preferences. The OleEditor then provides a good example to start with.

An operation in the OleEditor class (an EditorPart) worth examining is how the editor gains access to the java.io.File object in preparation to open an OLE storage file. Recall from the editor framework discussions that the editor input is based on Eclipse resources. Looking at the createPart-Control method you will see that the editor gets its IFileEditorInput as an IFile resource object.

```
// Set the input file.
    IEditorInput input = getEditorInput();
    if (input instanceof IFileEditorInput) {
      setResource(((IFileEditorInput) input).getFile());

resource.getWorkspace().addResourceChangeListener(resourceListener);
      }
```

The next step then is to call the getLocation() method to get the location used to construct the java.io.File.

```
    protected void setResource(IFile file) {
      resource = file;
      source = new File(file.getLocation().toOSString());
      }
```

The OleEditor class has the right parameters to create the OleClient-Site. The following is the code that creates the OleClientSite.

```
    //If there was an OLE error or nothing has been created yet.
    if (clientFrame == null || clientFrame.isDisposed())
      return;
    // Create an OLE client site.
    clientSite = new OleClientSite(clientFrame, SWT.NONE, source);
    clientSite.setBackground(
      JFaceColors.getBannerBackground(clientFrame.getDisplay()));
    }
```

Creating an OleControlSite *Object*

You create an OleControlSite object from the ProgramID of the ActiveX control. The Internet Explorer Web browser control shown below is one example of an ActiveX control that you might consider using. The ProgramID for the Internet Explorer Web browser equals Shell.Explorer.

```
try {
  // Create Site and Automation obj(methods, properties & events).
  webControlSite =
    new OleControlSite(webFrame, SWT.NONE, "Shell.Explorer");
  OleAutomation oleAutomation = new OleAutomation(webControlSite);
  webBrowser = new ActiveXWebBrowser(oleAutomation, webControlSite);
} catch (SWTException ex) {
  // Creation may have failed because control is not installed on machine.
  Label label = new Label(webFrame, SWT.BORDER);
  InteropeditPlugin.logError("Could Not Create Browser Control", ex);
  label.setText("Could Not Create Browser Control");
  return null;
}
```

Here is an example that demonstrates embedding the Internet Explorer Web browser control inside a multi-page editor.

```
// Create an Automation object for access to extended capabilities
webControlSite =
  new OleControlSite(webFrame, SWT.NONE, "Shell.Explorer");
OleAutomation oleAutomation = new OleAutomation(webControlSite);
webBrowser = new ActiveXWebBrowser(oleAutomation, webControlSite);
```

Activating the OleControlSite *Object*

The OLE.OLEIVERB_INPLACEACTIVATE verb opens the OLE control for editing in place.

```
// In-place activate the ActiveX control.
activated =
  (webControlSite.doVerb(OLE.OLEIVERB_INPLACEACTIVATE) == OLE.S_OK);
```

OLE Automation—Accessing Extended Behavior

OLE automation is a way that a COM server exposes its **properties**, **methods**, and **events** to a COM client. Automation is a richer interface than the predefined commands defined for the exec command. In this way, an application can make all sorts of operations available to automation. For example, Microsoft Word defines many OLE automation classes. Using the Object Browser (see Figure 24.3) in the Microsoft SDK, you will find classes like the Paragraph class and its members. The members listed on the right side of Figure 24.3

version 2.0 code that its uses have been largely replaced by the AST. Admittedly, the package names are similar, but here's an easy way to remember this: The DOM classes that are prefixed with "IDOM" (e.g., `IDOMCompilationUnit` corresponds to the resource-aware `ICompilationUnit`) originate from the version 1.0 code base.

The JDT Document Object Model classes (again, those prefixed with "IDOM") in `org.eclipse.jdt.core.jdom` represent the top-level elements of a compilation unit as a tree. At first glance, it might appear to be largely overlapping with the Java model. Some key differences are that the JDOM does not assume the existence of Workbench-specific artifacts like Java projects, only Java language elements, and it does not include notification mechanisms or editing support for working copies. In the end, it is only intended to support a certain level of source code analysis.

The AST is defined in the `org.eclipse.core.dom` package. As the name suggests, it supports syntactic analysis of Java source. As previously mentioned, the AST defines elements (nodes) at a much finer grain than the JDOM, which stops at the field/method level. This is not to say that the AST nodes represent all parts of the Java language specification. The AST ignores comments; thus, the parsed AST does not have exactly the same content as the original.

As you'll see later in the section "Finer-Grain Parsing of Java Source Code," the JDT has more than the AST to help you with syntactic analysis. It also includes interfaces that help retrieve precise source information beyond what is indicated by the AST node source pointers.

In summary, the JDOM and AST relieve you from the nitty-gritty details of parsing Java source code. Given their superior functionality, the rest of this chapter will focus on the AST classes instead of the JDOM classes. The solution associated with this chapter on the CD-ROM demonstrates how you can navigate the AST's structure, from parent to child, as part of your source analysis.

JDT Abstract Syntax Tree

Typically, you will create an AST with one of its `parseCompilationUnit` methods.

```
StringBuffer sb = new StringBuffer();
sb.append("package example;\n");
sb.append("public class HelloWorld {\n");
sb.append("public static void main(String[] args) {\n");
sb.append("\t\tSystem.out.println(\"Hello World!\");\n");
```

```
sb.append("\t}\n");
sb.append("}");

CompilationUnit cu =
    AST.parseCompilationUnit(sb.toString().toCharArray());
```

This returns the root node, CompilationUnit, a subclass of ASTNode. Don't confuse this class with a similarly named interface that is part of the Java model, ICompilationUnit in the org.eclipse.jdt.core package.

We have been circling around the particulars of the AST and its nodes. Let's look at a concrete example. The AST shown on the left of Figure 26.4 corresponds to the snippet of "HelloWorld" Java source on the right.

Figure 26.4 shows the basic structure of a simple AST, including the names of the classes and their key fields in bold. The AST nodes whose names are shown in bold correspond to top-level Java elements that are likely candidates for visitor processing.

AST

```
CompilationUnit
  package:
    PackageDeclaration ◄
      name: SimpleName("example")
  types:
    TypeDeclaration ◄
      modifier: Modifier.PUBLIC
      name: SimpleName("HelloWorld")
      bodyDeclarations:
        MethodDeclaration      ◄
          modifier: Modifier.PUBLIC | Modifier.STATIC
          returnType: PrimitiveType(PrimitiveType.VOID)
          name: SimpleName("main")
          arguments:
            SingleVariableDeclaration
              modifier: Modifier.NONE
              type: ArrayType(SimpleType
                  (SimpleName("String")), 1)
            name: SimpleName("args")
          body:
            Block
              statement:
                ExpressionStatement
                  expression:
                    MethodInvocation ◄
                      expression: QualifiedName(
                        SimpleName("System")
                        SimpleName("out"))
                      name: SimpleName("println")
                      arguments: StringLiteral("Hello World!")
```

Source

```
package example;
public class HelloWorld {
  public static void main(String[] args) {
    System.out.println("Hello World!");
  }
}
```

Figure 26.4   "Hello World!" AST

Another variation on parsing supported by the AST includes binding resolutions, as shown below.

```
AST.parseCompilationUnit
    (ICompilationUnit cu, boolean resolveBindings);
```

This name resolution is for cases where you want to be able to map names to nodes, for example, to find the node that declared a particular identifier. If you create the AST with `resolveBinding` set to `true`, then those AST nodes implementing `resolveBinding` will return a subtype of `IBinding`, representing the named entity in the Java language (i.e., named entities like packages, types, fields, methods, constructors, and local variables). You can use this to answer sticky refactoring questions like, "Will adding this variable cause a duplicate definition error, or hide a declaration in an enclosing block?" There is considerable overhead to creating the name bindings, so only specify `true` if it is genuinely needed. Otherwise, if the AST is created with `resolveBindings` set to `false`, the nodes' `resolveBinding` methods will return `null`.

This gives you a general idea of the structure of the AST. We'll examine several examples of how you might process an AST with an `ASTVisitor` in the next section.

There are also other instructional examples within the JDT's refactoring code that you may want to study. For example, `AccessAnalyzer` is a visitor that determines if an assignment affects a particular variable using the ASTNode subclass `Assignment`. Since `Assignment` knows the left and right sides of the assignment, it is relatively straightforward to sort the assignments into read and write accesses. `SelectionMapper` uses the start/end source code positions to find the `ASTNode`'s within the bounds of a selection. This is helpful for refactoring that operates against the selection, such as when inserting a catch/try block for all potential exceptions within the current selection, or performing a structured selection (**Edit > Expand Selection to**).

Creating and Traversing an AST

Here's an outline of the steps for working with the AST.

1. Invoke one of the AST static methods for parsing a source string or compilation unit.

2. Since the AST uses a visitor to define an operation that processes nodes in a natural order, define a subclass of `ASTVisitor`.

3. Override one or more `visit(`*nodeType*`)` methods (Boolean return value determines if children are visited).

Generally, you'll visit higher-level nodes and process subelements directly by calling the node's access methods (e.g., MethodDeclaration declares the access methods getName, getReturnType, and getArguments). However, you may find it helpful to create another visitor to do a "visit within a visit." This is perfectly reasonable and often simplifies otherwise complex code of a single visit method.

A typical scenario would be to create a visitor that overrides a particular ASTNode type. For example, to get all type declarations, create a subclass of ASTVisitor and override visit(TypeDeclaration). This method will be called for each node that is type "TypeDeclaration." Again, you could further refine this by visiting within a visit. For example, if you wanted to search for string literals within methods but not in field declarations, a visitor within a visitor would be easier than concentrating all the code into the visit (MethodDeclaration) method of a single visitor subclass. You will often find that you can get the information that you need directly from the node's fields; it depends on the complexity of the desired analysis. The ASTVisitor class also includes preVisit/postVisit methods for visiting all nodes independent of type.

The principal reason an API exists for the AST in version 2.0 is to enable you to develop with a common framework, since parsing Java source code is not easy. Keep in mind that the AST is only a syntax parse, that is, no code is compiled. Thus it can work with Java source strings before they are actually compiled—this comes in handy when refactoring, since potential errors can be detected in advance (i.e., the node's getFlags method will include AstNode. MALFORMED if a syntax error was detected).

Other Examples of AST Java Source Code Analysis

Table 26.3 shows the same "Hello World" Java source code example as in Figure 26.4 and is expanded to show how you might use an AST visitor to analyze the AST.

This table shows a HelloWorld source in the middle, the resulting AST tree on the left, and skeletal sample visitor code on the right that a tool builder might write to process the AST. In most cases, the visitor is interested in higher-level elements like CompilationUnit, PackageDeclaration, Method-Declaration, and so on. The lower-level elements like SimpleName, QualifiedName, SingleVariableDeclaration, and StringLiteral are generally referenced as part of the higher-level visitor's visit method.

The code on the right shows several examples of what you might do in your visitor method (in bold).

Table 26.3 Sample Uses of an AST for Code Analysis

AST	Source Fragment	Sample Visitor Code
`CompilationUnit`		`visit(CompilationUnit cu)`
`PackageDeclaration`	"`package example;`"	`visit(PackageDeclaration pd)`
`SimpleName("example")`		`pd.getName()`
`TypeDeclaration`	"`public class HelloWorld`"	`visit(TypeDeclaration td)`
`SimpleName("HelloWorld")`		`td.getName()`
`MethodDeclaration`	"`public void main(...)`"	`visit(MethodDeclaration md)`
`PrimitiveType("void")`		`md.getReturnType()`
`SimpleName("main");`		`md.getName()`
`SingleVariableDeclaration`	"`String args[]`"	`md.parameters()`
`ArrayType("[]")`		
`SimpleType`		
`SimpleName("String")`		
`SimpleName("args")`		
`Block`	"`{`"	`b1 = md.getBody()`
`ExpressionStatement`		`stmts = b1.statements()`
`MethodInvocation`	"`System.out.println` `('Hello World!')`"	`mi = stmts.toArray()[0]`
`QualifiedName`		`mi.getExpression()`
`SimpleName("System")`		
`SimpleName("out")`		
`SimpleName("println")`		`mi.getName()`
`StringLiteral`		`mi.getArguments()`
`('Hello World!')`		

Double-Click Behavior

Consider the selection behavior in the Java editor when clicking after a brace. When double-clicking just after the opening brace, all the text up to the corresponding closing brace is selected (see Figure 27.6).

Use the `ITextDoubleClickStrategy` interface in the framework to implement this strategy. You can override the `doubleClicked` method and implement the desired selection behavior using the position of the click to obtain the context with the surrounding text.

Now let's look at the implementation details of these text editor add-ons.

Under the Covers of the Text Editor

Before you can customize the basic text editor, you need to understand how Eclipse defines editors as a Workbench part. This is covered in Chapter 13, Editors. You should review the editor topic in that chapter before proceeding.

With this foundation we can discuss the text editor as an `EditorPart`. We will start with a look at the `AbstractTextEditor` class and its related classes.

AbstractTextEditor *Class*

The `AbstractTextEditor` class extends `EditorPart` and implements the `ITextEditor` interface. This is the base class of the default text editor. Editor extensions should subclass `AbstractTextEditor`. If your editor is a file-based editor (i.e., it modifies instances of `IFile`), you can extend the `TextEditor` class instead.

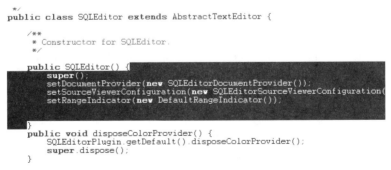

```
    */
public class SQLEditor extends AbstractTextEditor {

    /**
     * Constructor for SQLEditor.
     */
    public SQLEditor() {
        super();
        setDocumentProvider(new SQLEditorDocumentProvider());
        setSourceViewerConfiguration(new SQLEditorSourceViewerConfiguration(
        setRangeIndicator(new DefaultRangeIndicator());

    }
    public void disposeColorProvider() {
        SQLEditorPlugin.getDefault().disposeColorProvider();
        super.dispose();
    }
```

Figure 27.6   The Java Editor Implements a Double-Click Strategy

The `AbstractTextEditor` class is a model-based part, similar to what you learned in views. This editor works on content that resides in a document model. The controller for this relationship resides with a document provider. We will discuss the classes associated with this architecture shortly. The implementation also handles that annoying problem of having multiple editors that are open on the same document. You have probably noticed in the Workbench that you never get multiple editors open on the same document, even across perspectives. Thank the framework for handling that headache for you.

Let's turn our attention to the framework's classes that "bolt on" to the `AbstractTextEditor` class to enable editor customization. To do that, we will take a step back from the hierarchy and examine the relationships surrounding `AbstractTextEditor`.

TextViewer *Class*

The `TextViewer` class implements the `ITextViewer` interface. It is the `TextViewer` that turns SWT's `Text` class into a document-based text widget. The `setDocument` method sets the given document as the text viewer's model and updates the presentation accordingly.

A text viewer provides text-editing operations like selection handling and find and replace operations. Some text operations are configurable. The configurable operations at this level of the hierarchy include undo management, double-click behavior, automatic indentation, and hover text.

The `TextViewer` class also supports different types of listeners. For example, the `Viewport` listener reacts to changes of the viewer's **viewport**, which is the visible portion of the viewer. You can attach methods to text listeners that provide notification of changes to the viewer's input document.

The `SourceViewer` class extends the `TextViewer` class and implements the `ISourceViewer` interface. `ISourceViewer` augments the document-based capability, picking up the standard annotations, bookmark, and task markers. There are methods to support the customization "add-on" capabilities, content assist, content formatting, and syntax highlighting. You can subclass the `SourceViewer` class to build a source code editor.

About Annotations

A source viewer uses an `IVerticalRuler` as its annotation presentation (View) area for resource markers. The vertical ruler is a small strip shown to the left of the viewer's text widget. The visibility of visual annotations can be changed dynamically. You can set the hover text over an annotation using `setAnnotationHover`. The range over which an annotation pertains to is referred to as a **range indication**. The method `setRangeIndicator` is used to set the annotation range. The `showAnnotations` method controls the visibility of annotations. To learn more about annotation persistency, read about markers in Chapter 15, Workspace Resource Programming.

About Configuration

The `SourceViewer` class manages text viewer add-ons through configuration management. The `configure` method is used to set the configuration. It takes a `SourceViewerConfiguration` object parameter. It is through the method implementations in `SourceViewerConfiguration` that your editor can define its custom text editor operations (add-ons). We'll discuss the `SourceViewerConfiguration` class at length later in this chapter.

Now we'll look at the framework pieces that "bolt on" to the `AbstractTextEditor` class to enable editor customization. We'll step back from the hierarchy and examine the relationships surrounding `AbstractTextEditor`.

AbstractTextEditor *Class Relationships*

Each class and interface referenced by the `AbstractTextEditor` class has a specific role or responsibility. The following is a list of classes and interfaces referenced by `AbstractTextEditor`. This is an introduction, definitions really, just to get you familiar with the individual roles and responsibilities. We will step through all the details in sections to come.

- `SourceViewerConfiguration` is used to describe what customizations this editor's instance is adding on.
- `SourceViewer` provides the text editor with a text viewer and allows explicit configuration.
- `IDocument` is the text model representation of the document. It provides listener support and gets line and position information.
- `IDocumentProvider` is the editor's interface to the data or model object. In this way it's possible to have concurrent editors open on the same document.
- `IDocumentPartitioner` is used to divide a document into sections so the text can be treated or manipulated in different ways, depending on what section of the document the changes are happening in. Recall the earlier example in which the document title was treated differently

than the rest of the document—the title resided in a unique document partition.

The key classes and their relationships under the `AbstractTextEditor` class are shown in the diagram in Figure 27.7. The solid lines indicate the "has a" relationships and the dotted lines indicate type hierarchy relationships. Cardinalities are indicated with 1 – 1 or 1 - *.

Document *Class*

The `Document` class extends the `AbstractDocument` class and implements the `IDocument` interface. `IDocument` defines the text model and provides text content manipulation, position management, document partition management, searching, and change notification.

DocumentProvider *Class*

The `DocumentProvider` class, which implements the `IDocumentProvider` interface, creates and manages the document content. It notifies the editors about changes applied to the document model. The document provider also creates an annotation model on a document; these annotations are displayed in the vertical bar to the left of the text window. Bookmarks and breakpoints are examples of annotations. Document providers manage annotations. The provider also delivers the document input element's `IAnnotationModel`, the model that represents resource markers. The annotation model is used to control the editor's vertical ruler.

A document is an abstraction; that is, it is not limited to representing text files. However, the `FileDocumentProvider` class extends `DocumentProvider` and is specialized in that it connects to resource-based (`IFile`) documents.

Because the `FileDocumentProvider` is aware that it operates on `IFile` resources, it prevents users from typing into read-only documents when the class calls `Workspace.validateEdit`. If you do not subclass `FileDocument-Provider` and you edit workspace resources, you must invoke `Workspace.validateEdit` and make the user aware of the file state.

Documents are shareable and a document provider can serve concurrent active editors. Eclipse manages shareable providers through a document provider registry. The interface to the provider registry is implemented in the `DocumentProviderRegistry` class. To share a document provider, you must declare the provider extension point, `org.eclipse.ui.documentProviders`, in

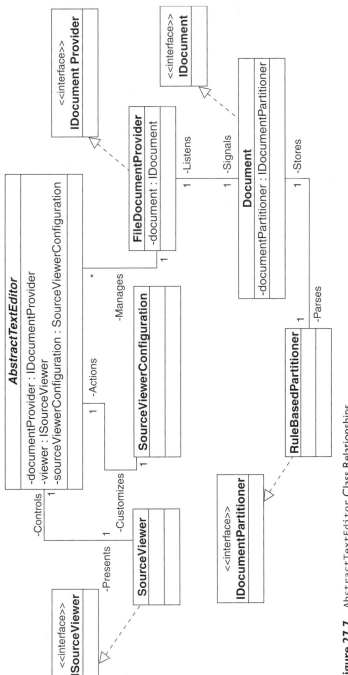

Figure 27.7 AbstractTextEditor Class Relationships

599

your plug-in manifest. The following XML creates a shareable document provider object when opening files with the .release file extension.

```
<extension
      point="org.eclipse.ui.documentProviders">
   <provider
         extensions="release"
         class="com.ibm.labs.soln.ReleaseDocumentProvider"
         id="com.ibm.labs.soln.ReleaseDocumentProvider">
   </provider>
</extension>
```

The class attribute must specify a class that extends DocumentProvider or one of its subclasses.

Providers created in Java code and not defined as extensions to org.eclispe.ui.documentProviders are not added to the provider registry. Do this when you don't want to share interactive changes on the input element with other active editors.

Model-View-Controller Relationship

The main role of the document provider is to map between the input document and the editor (see Figure 27.8). The same document provider is normally

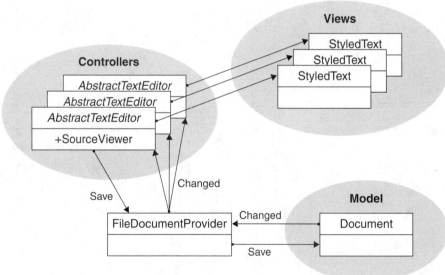

Figure 27.8   Model and View Relationship in JFace Text

shared between editors with the same input document. This is what gives you automatic update of the other editors when one changes.

The provider always has a document or "model part." The `Document-Provider` controls the "model" object. Overriding the `changed` method is the way that the provider propagates change notifications to each of the active editors. A document provider delivers a textual presentation (`IDocument`) of the editor's input element to the editor view part. The editor in turn manipulates the document and forwards all input-element related calls, such as `save`, to the document provider.

While one editor is changing the underlying text model, the other editors are kept informed of the changes, keeping their visual representations up to date.

DocumentPartitioner *Class*

A document consists of a sequence of non-overlapping partitions. Partitions divide a document into sections so the text can be treated or manipulated in different ways depending on the partition. For example, you can apply a different set of content assist proposals in different partitions. Similarly, you can apply partition-specific syntax highlighting and formatting.

Each partition has a content type, offset, and length. The document partitioner is connected to one document and is informed about all changes in the document before any of the document's listeners. A document partitioner updates the partitions upon receipt of a document change event. Partitioners are expected to implement the `IDocumentPartitioner` interface.

Document partitions are computed dynamically as events signal that the document has changed. It's not surprising, then, that the framework includes a ready-made rule-based partitioner, the `RuleBasedPartitionScanner` class. The `RuleBasedPartitionScanner` class, an implementer of `IDocumentPartitioner`, partitions a document based on tokens that are relevant to the syntax of the document. Programming languages like XML and HTML are all document types that lend themselves to rule-based partition computation. For example, a C++ editor would define rules to scan for multi-line and single-line comments. The scanner in turn returns tokens that represent multi-line and single-line partitions within the C++ source document.

While a rule-based partition scanner computes partitions based on the text content such as HTML or C++, it is difficult to partition documents based on rules if your document is freeform and not self-described with tags or keywords. For instance, an "untagged" document might be partitioned based on line positions within the file and not the text content itself. Documents that can't be partitioned based on rules should compute partitions in a custom class that implements IDocumentPartitioner.

SourceViewerConfiguration *Class*

The SourceViewerConfiguration class defines which editor add-ons you are enabling. It is the front door to any editor customization you are providing. You will subclass SourceViewerConfiguration and override the methods to enable content assist, content formatting, syntax highlighting, automatic indentation strategy, double-click strategy, or undo management based on what your editor needs.

So there you have it. These are the pieces that you connect to the Abstract-TextEditor viewer to make it into a full-fledged source editor. Well, not quite; we haven't discussed how you actually implement the domain-specific content assist, formatting, or syntax highlighting. The good news is that we have covered enough territory to learn the implementation details of a basic source editor that is enabled for further customizations.

How to Create a Basic Source Editor

To help you learn how to design and implement a source editor, let's study an example. Let's suppose that you are implementing an SQL source code editor. When completed, these three editor customizations will be available.

- SQL keywords will be available using content assist.
- Using syntax highlighting, SQL keywords will be colorized.
- Content formatting will change all SQL keywords to uppercase.

The working editor is shown in Figure 27.13.

The completed implementation on the CD-ROM is available in the project com.ibm.lab.soln.sqltexteditor. Since there is more to JFace Text than we can accommodate in this chapter, you may want to supplement the discussion here by examining the Javadoc in the *Eclipse Platform API Specification* in the online help as new classes and methods are introduced.

Let's explore the steps required to implement this editor. We will take on this development effort in four phases.

1. A basic source editor is delivered in Phase 1.

2. Phase 2 delivers content assist.

3. Phase 3 adds syntax color highlighting.

4. Finally, Phase 4 delivers content formatting.

Phase 1: Creating a Basic Editor

The goal in this phase is to get a basic editor designed and implemented. Your modest goal is to integrate enough of the framework function to enable further customization and enable bookmarks and tasks to be associated with your document. You will lay the infrastructure for content assist and syntax highlighting by defining your document partitioner. The structure for your editor's menu items will be defined, leaving them disabled until later phases when you will actually implement content assist and formatting.

Design—Phase 1

The architecture at a high level is illustrated in Figure 27.7. The low-level design is shown in Figure 27.9. You will subclass `AbstractTextEditor` by creating the `SQLEditor` class. The editor input is an SQL document. The SQL document is file-based, so the document provider is satisfied by subclassing `FileDocumentProvider` in the class `SQLDocumentProvider`. You do not need a shared document provider at this point, but in the future you might. So, declare the `SQLDocumentProvider` class in the plug-in manifest using the `org.eclipse.ui.documentProviders` extension point. In this way, if you decide to add a graphical SQL builder later, with an SQL source editor inside a multi-page editor, the same document is shareable. The document partitions will be defined using the `SQLPartitionScanner` class.

Design Notes

1. Initialization takes place in the construction of `SQLEditor` using `setDocumentProvider` and `setRangeIndicator`.
2. Create a new `SQLPartitionScanner` in the `createDocument` method of the `SQLDocumentProvider` class.
3. Calling the `setDocumentProvider` method results in a callback to the `SQLDocumentProvider` to `createDocument`. The `createDocument` method establishes the connection to the `SQLPartitionScanner` and Document.
4. The `SQLEditorContributor` class will be used later for editor actions.

Implementation

Here are the major steps to implementing a source editor (without going into the implementation details).

1. Implement the class `SQLEditor` class, which extends `AbstractTextEditor`.

2. Implement the `SQLEditor` constructor.

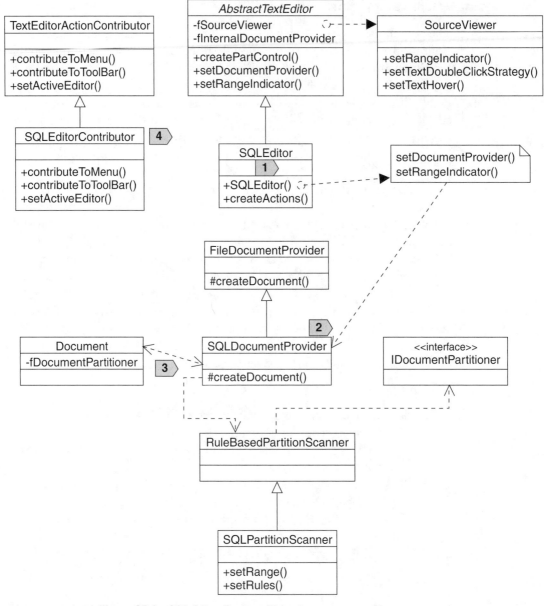

Figure 27.9   SQL Editor Design—Phase I

In the Navigator view, you'll see the new project. You'll also see that the files and folders at the location you specified are automatically part of the project. A `.project` file is added to the file system to identify the target folder as an Eclipse project.

NOTE You have created a project containing the files and folders at the location you specified, *but you did not copy the files and folders*. They still exist only in their original location. This means that if you delete the project and you select to have it contents deleted, you will also delete the files and folders at the alternate location. If this is the only copy of these resources, they will be deleted. Take care when deleting projects at alternate locations, especially when you mapped the project to an existing folder and file tree with content.

3. Copying and moving files and folders between projects and other folders is easy. Select a file or folder in the Navigator view and then select **Copy** from the context menu. Select another project or folder and then select **Paste** from the context menu. Your selection is copied to that project or folder.

   To move a file or folder, simply drag it and drop it on another folder or project. You can also copy a file with drag and drop. If you want to copy the file to another folder, press **Ctrl** and then drag and drop the file to the target folder. If you want to make a copy of the file in the same folder, press **Ctrl** and then drag and drop it in the target folder. You will get a dialog prompt for the new name.

4. Add a folder to **My Alternate Project**. Add a file to the folder you added. Browse your file system and go to this location. You'll see that Eclipse has created the folder and file at this location.

5. Now, let's replace a file with a previous edition of it. Open an editor on **My First File** or switch to this editor if it is already open. Make a few changes to your text and save the file. Make some more changes and save the file again. Select **My First File** in the Navigator view and select **Replace With > Local history...** from the context menu.

   A dialog is displayed with the previous editions of **My First File** in the top pane and a side-by-side comparison of the current contents with the selected previous edition in the bottom pane. (See Figure 28.1.)

Exercises

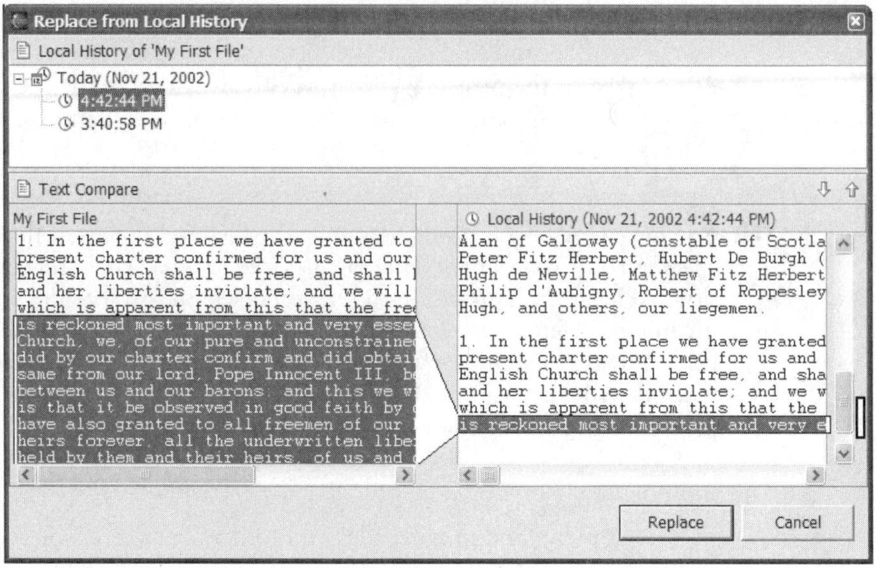

Figure 28.17   Replacing a File from Local History

⬇ 6. Navigate the changes with **Select Next Change** and **Select Previous**
⬆   **Change**. You can also select the change indicators (rectangles) in
      the overview ruler on the right border. Select a previous edition of
      My First File and then select **Replace** to replace its contents in the
      editor.

   Selecting **Compare With > Local History...** is similar to **Replace With**,
   except that it only shows the differences. It does not allow you to replace the file.

7. You can also compare two projects. In the Navigator view, select **My
   First Project** and **My Second Project**. Then select **Compare With >
   Each Other** from the context menu.

   A dialog is displayed showing the files and folders that are different
   between the two projects. The label decorations in the top pane (small
   plus (**+**) and minus (**-**) signs) indicate this. The file .project has no label decoration. This means it exists in both projects. Double-click on
   the .project file. The differences are shown in the bottom pane (see
   Figure 28.18). Close the Compare Editor by clicking on the **X** on the
   tab of the editor.

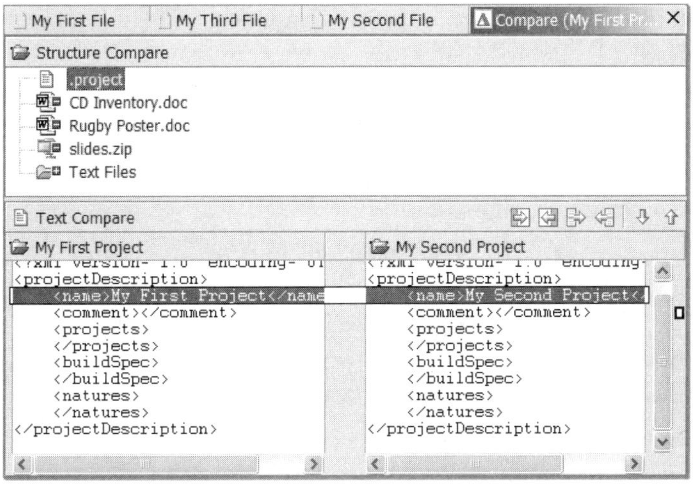

Figure 28.18 Comparing Two Projects

8. Now you'll see how to recover files you've deleted. From the Navigator view, delete **My First File** and **My Second File** from **My First Project**. Select **My First Project** and then select **Restore From Local History...** from the context menu. A list of files you have deleted from the project is displayed.

9. Select a file to see the editions of the file Eclipse is maintaining. Select an edition to see its contents in the bottom pane. (See Figure 28.19.) To restore a file, select the file in the upper left pane, select an edition, and then select **Restore**. Restore the files you deleted from **My First Project**.

10. You can also recover projects you delete, if you do not delete their contents. Select **My First Project** in the Navigator view and then select **Delete** from the context menu. At the prompt, do *not* select to delete its contents. From the Navigator view, select **Import...** from the context menu. Select **Existing Project into Workspace** and then select **Next >**. Select **Browse....** Browse your file system to go to folder workspace in your main Eclipse folder. In this folder, you'll see the folder My First Project. This is the contents of the project left when you deleted the definition of the project. Select this folder and then select **OK**. If this folder is recognized as a project (by the presence of the file .project), **Finish** is enabled. Select **Finish** to recover the project. Verify this in the Navigator view.

Exercises

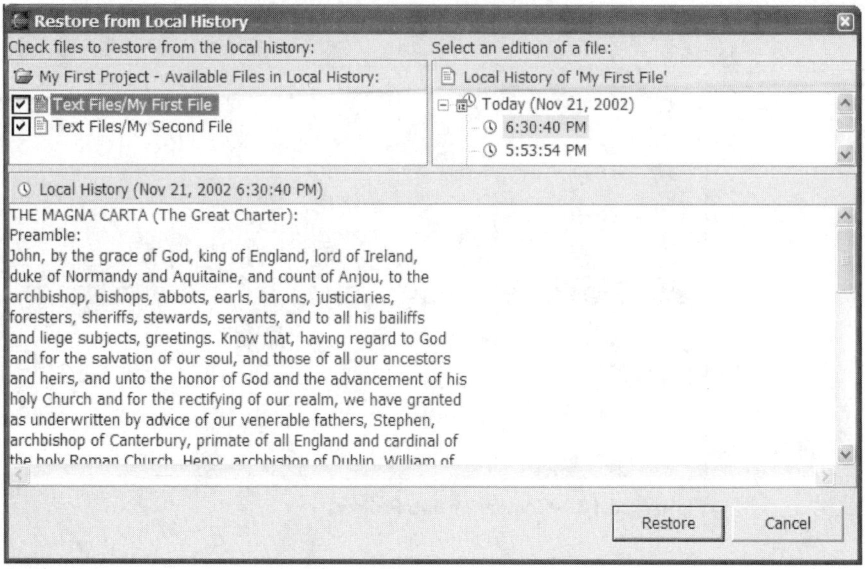

Figure 28.19   Recovering a Deleted File

You've now seen a bit more detail on creating projects and how to use local history information to compare resources and recover ones you've deleted.

Section 4: Perspectives

Let's work a little more with perspectives, in particular, customizing your own perspective.

1. At this point, if you have followed these procedures you have modified the default layout of the Resource perspective by adding the Bookmarks view. Close the Resource perspective by selecting **Close** from the context menu of the Resource perspective icon in the view shortcut area. Select **Window > Open Perspective > Resource**. The Resource perspective opens again, but without the changes you had made.

2. Change the Resource perspective by reorganizing the views and adding or deleting views. Select **Window > Save Perspective As...**, name the new perspective My First Perspective (no pun intended), and select **OK** to create your customized perspective.

Observe the change on the title bar of the window. It now reflects that this is your perspective. Select **Window > Open Perspective >**. You'll see that your customized perspective is added to this list.

3. Select **Window > Customize Perspective...**. You'll see a dialog listing the menu actions that can be included in your perspective (see Figure 28.20). Expand the list in the left pane. The selected entries will appear in the menus for your perspective. The entries under **File > New**, **Window > Open Perspective**, and **Window > Show View** are the entries that appear on these menus. The other items are available, but you must select **Other...** first and then select them from a list. The items under **Other** are groups of menu items and toolbar buttons. Select an entry here to see the items that would get added. Try customizing **My First Perspective** by adding some items. Select **OK**. Verify the changes to your perspective.

4. To make these changes permanent, you need to save your perspective again with **Window > Save Perspective As...**. Select **My First Perspective**

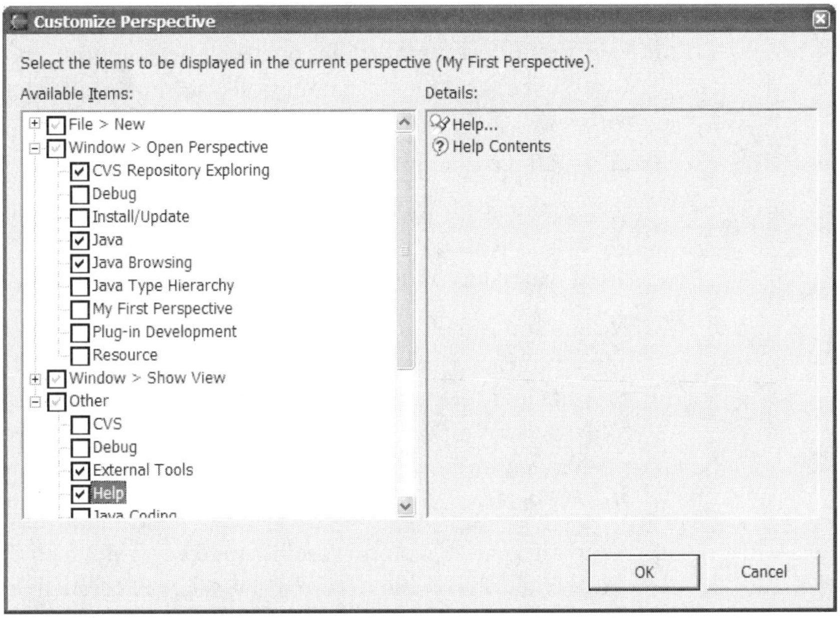

Figure 28.20 Customizing a Perspective

to replace it with your changes, or restore your perspective to its original
state by selecting **Window > Reset Perspective**.

5. When you create a new project, the default perspective will be opened.
   If you create a new simple project while in your custom perspective,
   the Resource perspective will be opened. You can change the setting
   for the default perspective. Select **Window > Preferences**, expand
   Workbench, and select **Perspectives**. Under **Available perspectives**,
   select **My First Perspective** and then select **Make Default**. Select **OK**.

In this section you customized a perspective and saw how to change your
default perspective.

Section 5: Using Multiple Eclipse Windows

We've been working with one Eclipse window. You can have multiple windows open at the same time on the same resources or different sets of resources in one workspace. These windows are kept in sync. You can also
have multiple instances of Eclipse running at the same time on different
workspaces.

1. Select **Window > New Window**. Another window opens in the same
   workspace. You see the same projects, files, and folders in the Navigator view.

2. In one window, add a file or folder to one of your projects. You'll see
   the new file or folder reflected in both windows. Open an editor on
   the same file in both windows. Make changes to the file in one window. Watch as changes appear simultaneously in the other window.

3. A common use of this is to have different projects or sets of resources
   appear in each of the windows. This makes it easier to manage the
   projects and their resources. This can be done for a specific project or
   folder when you open the new window. Select a project or folder in
   the Navigator view and choose the context menu option **Open in
   New Window**.

4. As an alternative, you can use filters to control which projects appear in
   the Navigator view. In one window, select **Filters...** from the Navigator
   view pull-down (the down arrow to the left of the **X** on the title bar).

5. In the Navigator Filters dialog, check **Select a working set** and then
   select **Other....** You are going to define a working set to filter what is

shown in the Navigator view. A working set is simply a predefined set of resources.

6. In the Select Working Set dialog, select **New...**. This displays the New Working Set wizard. In the New Working Set wizard, select **Resource** for **Working Set Type** and then select **Next >**. Name the working set `My First Project` and select **My First Project** to add it to the Working Set (see Figure 28.21). Select **Finish** to create the working set.

7. In the Select Working Set dialog, select the working set **My First Project** and then select **OK** to specify this as your Navigator view filter. In the Navigator Filters dialog, select **OK** to set the filter using your working set. You see in the Navigator view that only **My First Project** appears.

8. Switch to the other window and repeat steps 3 through 7 to define a working set filter in that window to show only **My Second Project**. You now have two windows open, each showing only one project.

9. You can also choose to open a new window when you create a new project. To do this, select **Window > Preferences** and then select

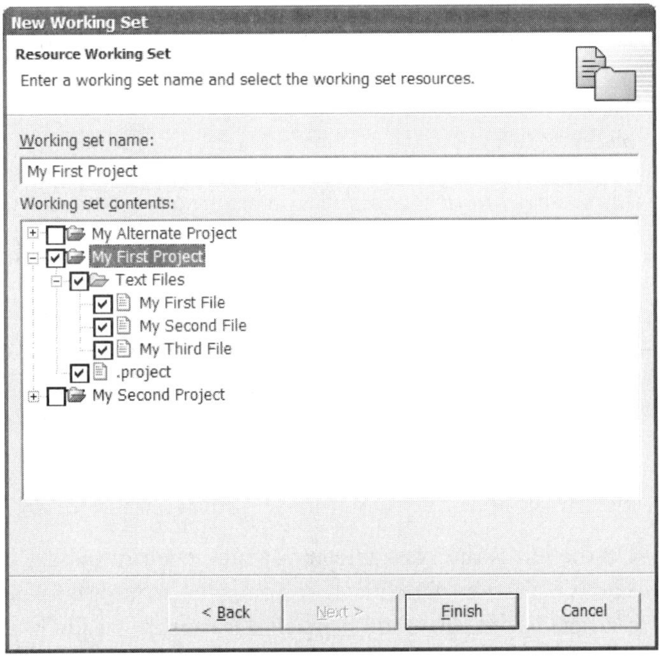

Figure 28.21 Creating a Working Set

Perspectives. Under **New project options**, select **Open perspective in a new window**.

10. Up to this point in this exercise, you've been using multiple windows open on the same workspace. That is, the windows are managing the same set of resources that exist (by default) in the folder workspace. You can also run multiple Eclipse instances on different workspaces. You do this by using command line parameters.

    Open a command prompt and navigate to your main Eclipse folder, the one with the program eclipse.exe. Execute the following command (note that the –showlocation parameter is case-sensitive).

    ```
    Eclipse –data workspaceNew –showlocation
    ```

    Given the default workspace location is the folder workspace, if you prefix all your workspaces with "workspace," the folders will be listed together in the Eclipse installation folder. This makes them easier to keep track of.

11. You'll see a brief dialog indicating that Eclipse is completing its installation. This is because you specified the –data parameter. This parameter instructs Eclipse to use a workspace at the specified location. If the workspace does not exist, one is created. When Eclipse creates a workspace, it displays this installation dialog. The –showlocation parameter causes the location of the workspace to appear in the window title. This is useful to keep track of which workspace is being used.

In this section you learned how to simultaneously run multiple Eclipse windows, both on the same workspace and on different workspaces.

Section 6: Getting Help

In this section you'll see how to get help, including viewing and searching online content, and how to get help from the Eclipse user interface.

1. Select **Help > Help Contents** from the menu bar. The online documentation opens in a separate window (see Figure 28.22).

2. On the left is the Navigation pane; on the right is the Contents pane. The Navigation pane has three pages: The Contents *page* (not to be confused with the Contents *pane*) is on top, and behind it are the Search Results and Links pages. You'll see these in a moment. On the

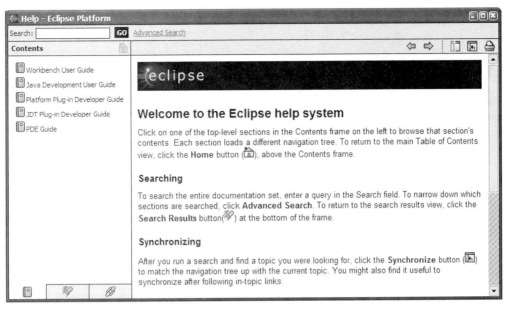

Figure 28.22 Help Window

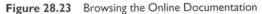

Figure 28.23 Browsing the Online Documentation

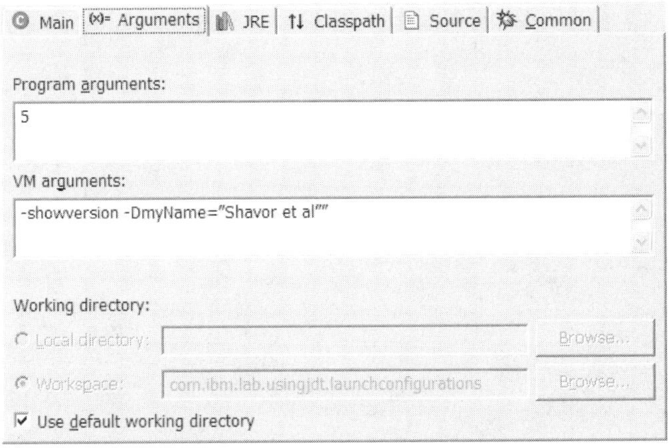

Figure 29.25   Specifying Launch Configuration Arguments

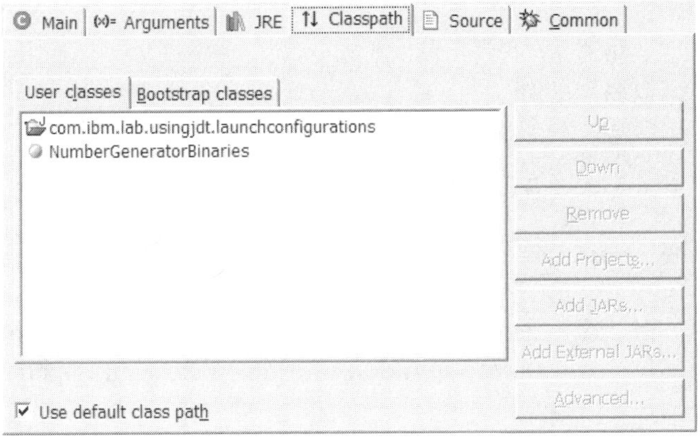

Figure 29.26   Launch Configuration Classpath

In the Package Explorer view, you should see TestLaunchConfiguration.launch in the com.ibm.lab.using.launchconfigurations project.

🔦 ▼ 10. Let's test the code. From the **Run** pull-down menu select **TestLaunch Configuration**. TestLaunchConfiguration runs with the program and VM arguments you defined in the launch configuration and output is displayed in the Console view. You'll see the output for the system property you defined with the Java VM arguments. Once you've run a program, in addition to any favorites you have defined,

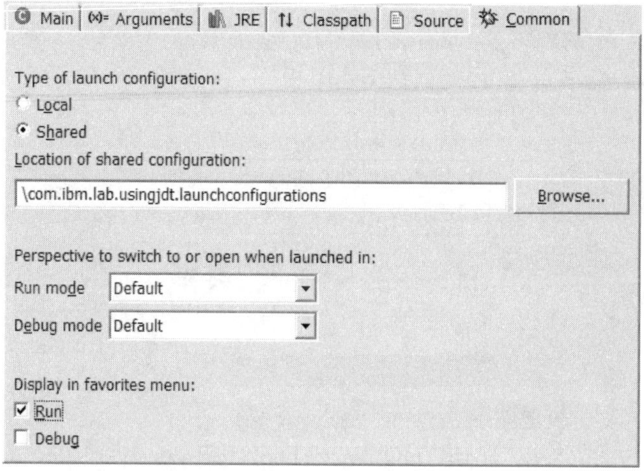

Figure 29.27   Sharing a Launch Configuration

you have a run history available from **Run > Run History**. You can also select **Run > Run Last Launched** or press **Ctrl+F11**.

In this section, you used launch configurations to specify more information about a program's execution, including input and VM parameters and its class path. You also defined a launch configuration so that it could be shared. When you're through, don't forget to close any open editors.

Section 6: JRE 1.4 Code

In this section you're going to write code that exploits APIs that are new in JRE 1.4. As part of this exercise, you're also going to see how to use multiple workspaces and move a project between them. That is, imagine that you've decided to enhance some of your code to use APIs new in JRE 1.4, but you also need to continue to develop and maintain other code using JRE 1.3.

To do this, you're going to use two workspaces to keep separate code requiring different JREs. The JDT assumes that all the code within a workspace will use the same level of the JDK. That is, the JRE setting and compiler are global. If you need to manage code at different levels, it is best to create separate workspaces for each JDK level. In this case, let's create two workspaces, one for JDK 1.3 and another for JDK 1.4.

This part of the exercise assumes you're currently running Eclipse with JRE 1.3. It will also require a 1.4 JRE installed on your system. If you do not have a 1.4 JRE installed on your file system, you'll need to install one now, or skip this Section of the exercise.

Ensure that you have the project com.ibm.lab.usingjdt.jre14 in your workspace. If you do not, refer to the instructions on the CD-ROM. This is the code resulting from completing Section 4.

1. This section refers to the Eclipse you're currently running as your "1.3 workspace." Navigate to your main Eclipse installation folder and start another instance of Eclipse with the following command. Given the default workspace location is the folder workspace, if you prefix all your workspaces with "workspace" the folders will be listed together in the Eclipse installation folder. This makes them easier to keep track of.

   ```
   eclipse -data "workspaceJRE1.4" -showlocation
   ```

   We'll refer to this as your "1.4 workspace." You should now have two Eclipse windows.

2. You need to configure your 1.4 workspace to use a 1.4 JRE. In your 1.4 workspace, go to your **Installed JREs** preferences under **Java.** Select **Add...** to define the 1.4 JRE you have installed. In the Add JRE dialog, name the JRE 1.4 JRE. Select the **Browse...** button for **JRE home directory** and navigate to the jre folder for your 1.4 JRE. Select this folder and then **OK**. If you want to browse the Javadoc for this JRE, select **Browse...** for **Javadoc URL** to set an http: or file: URL to point to the root location for the Javadoc (the location with the folders java, javax, etc.). Select **OK** to define the JRE. Make this JRE the default JRE (check it). (See Figure 29.28.)

3. Next, you need to set preferences in order to work with code that depends on a 1.4 JRE. Select your **Compiler** preferences, and select the **JDK Compliance** page. Set the **Compiler compliance level** to **1.4.** You are now configured to work with Java code that depends on a 1.4 JRE. Select **OK** to set the preferences. If you get a prompt to rebuild your projects, select **OK**.

4. You have to move the com.ibm.lab.usingjdt.jre14 project from your 1.3 workspace to your 1.4 workspace. There are a number of ways to do this, the easiest of which is reloading the project into your new workspace from a shared repository. However, for this exercise we are going to assume you are not using one.

Exercises

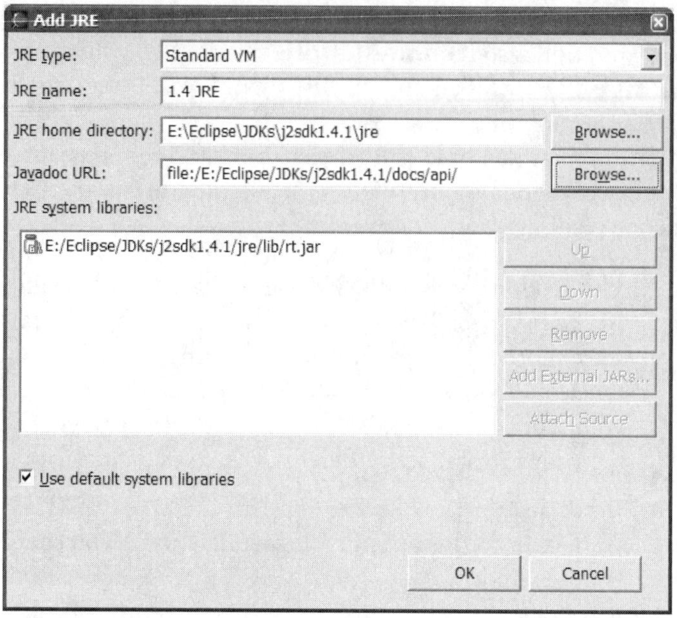

Figure 29.28   Installing a 1.4 JRE

In your 1.3 workspace, select the project com.ibm.lab.usingjdt.jre14 in the Package Explorer view and then select **Export...** from the context menu. Select to export to the file system. In the Export dialog, for the export destination, specify the location of your 1.4 workspace (see Figure 29.29). This will be the folder workspaceJRE1.4 in the main Eclipse folder. Select **OK** to export the project.

5. In your 1.4 workspace, open a **Java** perspective. Select **Import...** from the Package Explorer view context menu. Select **Import > Existing Project into Workspace**. For **Package contents**, select **Browse...** and go to your 1.4 workspace folder, workspaceJRE1.4. Select the project com.ibm.lab.usingjdt.jre14. Select **OK** in the Browse for Folder dialog and then **Finish** to import the project.

You've copied, by exporting and then importing, the project from your 1.3 workspace to your 1.4 workspace. The JRE listed for the project is the 1.4 JRE you defined and not the 1.3 JRE the project had defined in your 1.3 workspace. This is because the project was defined in your 1.3 workspace to use the default JRE, which was a 1.3 JRE. The default JRE in your 1.4 workspace is a 1.4 JRE, and so JDT makes this change when it imports the project.

PART III

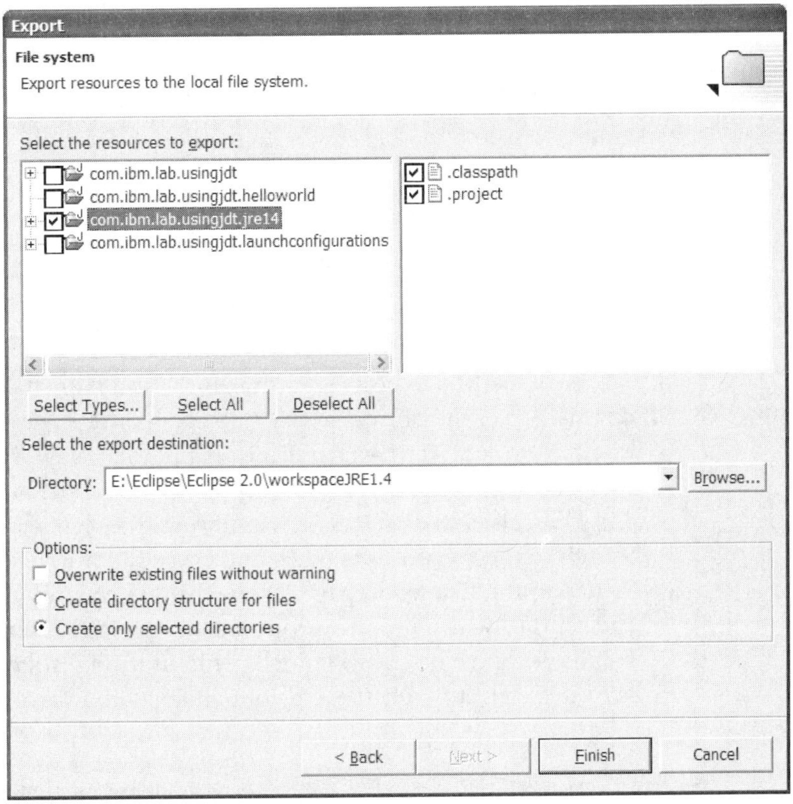

Figure 29.29   Exporting a Project to Move It

Let's change the code to exploit features in JRE 1.4. You're going to change the method outputResults of the class NumberGenerator to log its output using the Logging API new to JRE 1.4, instead of sending it to stdout with System.out.println(). In your 1.4 workspace, open an editor on the class NumberGenerator and change the method outputResults as follows.

```
public void outputResults(String prefix) {
  Logger l = Logger.global;
  Date d = new Date();
  l.info(prefix + d.toString());
  for (int i = 0; i < getResults().length; i++) {
    l.info(prefix + getResults()[i]);
  }
}
```

Exercises

plug-in libraries available. The completed page should look like Figure 31.1. Select **OK** to close the dialog.

2. Create a project by selecting **File > New > Project....** In the New Project wizard, select **Plug-in Development** and **Plug-in Project**. Select **Next**. On the next page, name the project com.abc.helloworld. Select **Next** twice to go to the page titled **Plug-in Code Generators**. Select the **Hello, World** project (see Figure 31.2). Accept all the default values on the subsequent wizard pages and press **Finish**.

    Your workspace should have a project in it that looks like Figure 31.3. In this figure the **Hide referenced libraries** view filter is active. This filter is specified in the **Filters...** action in the menu of the Package Explorer view.

Setup is now complete. You are ready to proceed with the laboratory exercise.

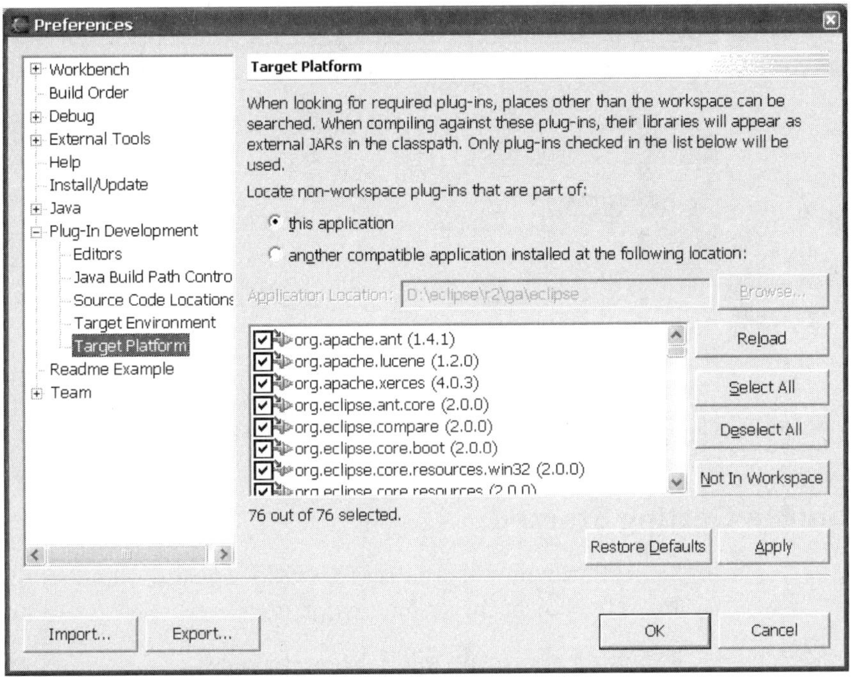

Figure 31.1 Settings Required for Exercise 4

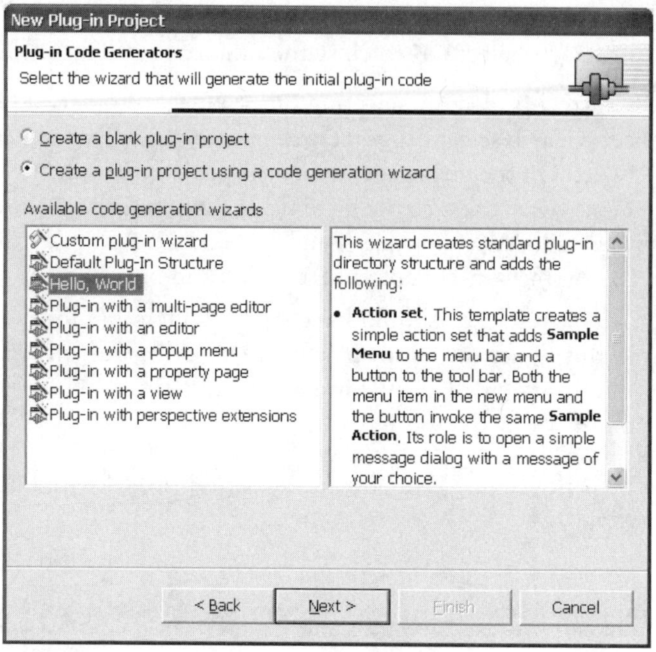

Figure 31.2   Available Plug-in Code Generators

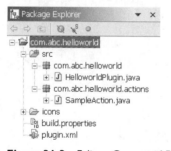

Figure 31.3   Eclipse-Generated Project That Will Be Managed in CVS

Section 1: Getting Started

In this section you will connect to a CVS repository and store your com.abc. helloworld project there. The major steps are

- Setting your team and CVS preferences
- Defining a CVS repository location

- Putting the project under CVS control
- Storing the project contents in CVS
- Versioning the project

Let's get started!

Setting Your Team and CVS Preferences

Before you store your project in CVS, there are some useful preference settings to define.

1. Go to the preference pages by selecting **Window > Preferences**. Turn on the CVS decorators by selecting **CVS** in the **Workbench > Label Decorations** page. This will provide visual clues for projects under CVS control.

2. While you are looking at the preference pages, go to the **Team > Ignored Resources** page. You could add the pattern `*.class` using the **Add** button. This would exclude Java class files in your project from being stored in CVS. For this exercise, please don't make this change.

   In general, files that are output of a build process are not stored in a repository. It is too easy for the repository to become out-of-sync between the run-time files and the source files that created them. It also takes up unnecessary space. In this case, it is not necessary due to a little-known Eclipse property called **derived resources**. The project's class files produced from the compilation process have this property. Eclipse automatically excludes derived resources from being stored in CVS. Other tools that create run-time resources may or may not set this property. There is no harm in adding a pattern to the **Ignored Resources** page, even if it is superfluous.

3. In the **Workbench > Compare** preference page, select the preference **Show additional compare information in the status line**. This provides a quick summary that can be very helpful during repository synchronization when there are conflicts or differences. Select the preference **Ignore white space**. This ensures that only the real differences are shown when comparing two files.

4. Select **OK** to set the preferences and close the dialog.

Exercises

Defining a CVS Repository Location

Next, you need to define a CVS repository location using the CVS Repositories view in the CVS Repository Exploring perspective.

1. Open the perspective by selecting **Window > Open Perspective > Other...**, select **CVS Repository Exploring**, and press **OK**.

2. From the CVS Repositories view context menu, select **New > Repository Location...**.

   The Add CVS Repository dialog is displayed. In Figure 31.4 the dialog has been completed with sample values for repository host name, repository path, user, and password. The repository path (here, /cvsrep/abc_team) is the host directory name where all your team's work is stored. Here we are using the default connection protocol of pserver. Fill in the information that is applicable to your CVS repository. Your repository administrator can supply this information.

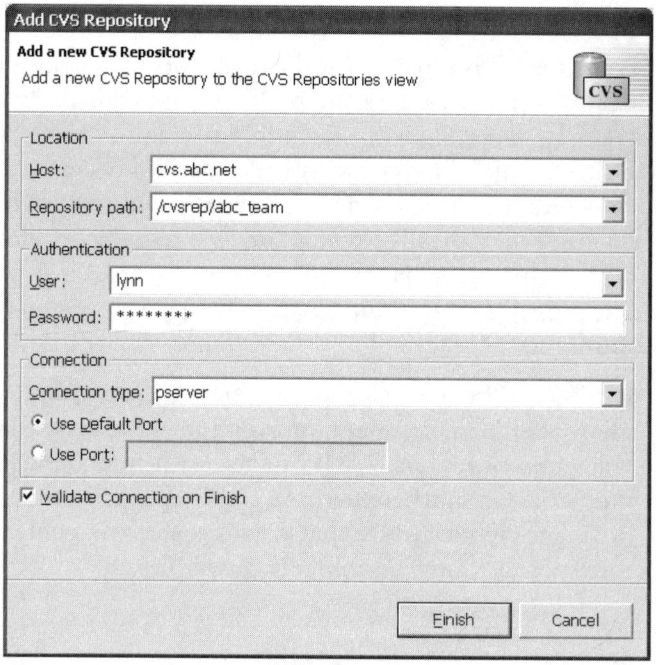

Figure 31.4   Defining a New CVS Repository Location in Your Workspace

Select **Finish**. Your CVS repository location should appear in the CVS Repositories view. Your CVS repository is now ready to use.

3. With your connection complete, expand your repository location in the view to see the contents under **Branches**, **HEAD**, and **Versions** (see Figure 31.10). You will be adding your `com.abc.helloworld` project to **HEAD**, the main line of development.

Putting the Project Under CVS Control

Now you will let CVS know that you want it to manage your `com.abc.helloworld` project and its contents.

1. Switch to the Plug-in Development perspective. In the Package Explorer view, select your project and then select **Team > Share Project...** from the context menu. This will start a wizard to complete the task (see Figure 31.5). Select the CVS location you just defined. If there were additional CVS repository locations or non-CVS repositories available, they would also be listed on this page.

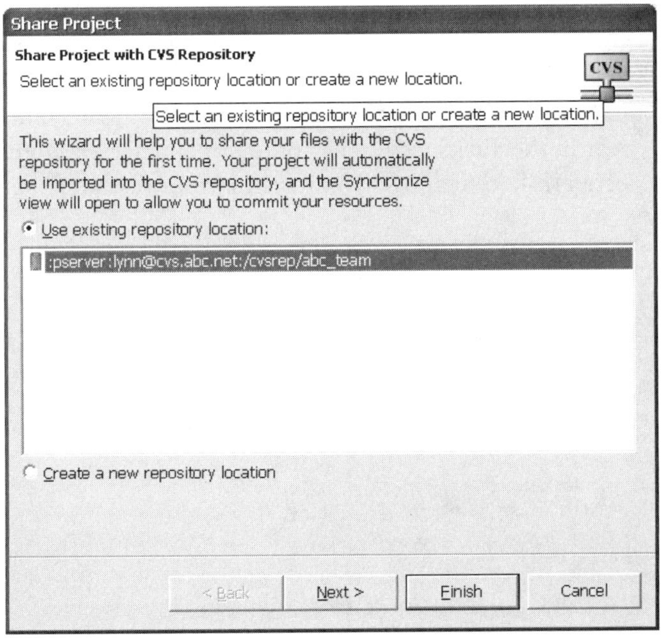

Figure 31.5 Share Project Wizard

2. Accept the defaults on the remaining wizard pages by pressing **Finish**.

   Once this step is completed, you will see the Synchronize-Outgoing Mode view (we will refer to it simply as the Synchronize view) containing a hierarchical list of the files you are adding to CVS. For a moment, go to the CVS Repositories view and refresh the contents using the **Refresh View** icon on the view's toolbar. Your project should be visible under **HEAD** in the CVS Repositories view (see Figure 31.6). If you were to expand the project, there would be nothing visible, because you haven't stored your project contents in CVS yet. You have a few more steps to complete.

3. When you completed the Share Project wizard, the Synchronize view was automatically opened. Go back to this view in the Plug-in Development perspective. You may want to maximize it by double-clicking on its title bar (see Figure 31.7). Next, you want to put the project contents under CVS control. Notice that the bin directory has been included in the list. The bin directory contains your Java .class files. Since class files are automatically ignored (recall that they are derived resources), nothing else will be stored in the bin folder. Later on you will remove this folder from this list of resources to be committed.

4. If you were to take a moment to look at the Tasks view, you would see that it lists all the project's contents with a reminder task that they need to be added to version control (see Figure 31.8). Any time you add a resource to a CVS-managed project an entry like this will appear in the Tasks view. The context menu action **Quick Fix** on a selected task item allows you to put a resource under version control or

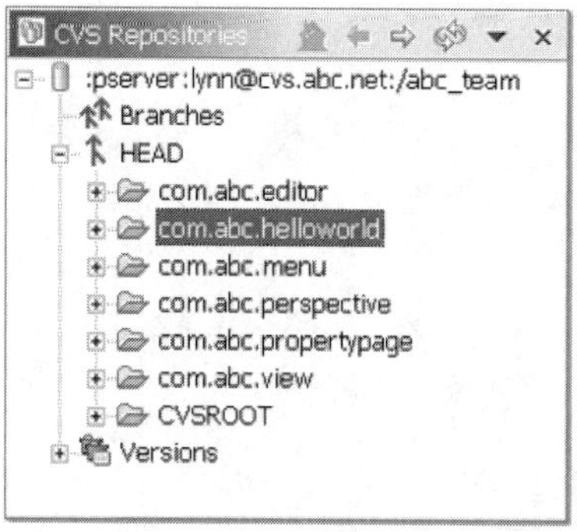

Figure 31.6   Your com.abc.helloworld Project Defined to CVS

CHAPTER 32

Exercise 5: Modifying Your Configuration with Update Manager

The role of Update Manager, and how it can be used to add new features or apply service to your installed features, was introduced in Chapter 6, Eclipse Configuration Management. The Install/Update perspective is where you access Update Manager capabilities. An existing Eclipse install site can also be extended by linking it with features that exist in another location. This exercise walks you through an install and maintenance cycle for a new feature. At the end of this exercise you should be able to

- Manage your configuration using Update Manager
- Add new features to an existing configuration from an update site
- Add new features to an Eclipse installation using a link file
- Disable and then enable features in the current configuration
- Find and install service to existing features from an update site

Section 1: Installing New Features

This section looks at adding the Graphical Editing Framework (GEF) feature using the Update Manager. Version 2.0 of the `com.ibm.etools.gef` (GEF) distribution has been packaged as several installable features. These installable features will be used as the source of the function that you will be adding to

Eclipse. The code in the features and plug-ins is the same; we have just ma-nipulated the version id values to support this learning exercise.

NOTE If you are interested in GEF, the code is now available as a subproject of the Eclipse Tools Project (see http://www.eclipse.org/tools/index.html).

To set up your system for this exercise, copy the `UpdateManagerExample` folder from the CD-ROM that comes with this book to your `c:\` drive.

1. The Install/Update perspective is used to find features that can be in-stalled. In the Feature Updates view, expand **My Computer**, locate `c:\UpdateManagerExample\UpdateSite`, and expand the tree to see all of the entries (see Figure 32.1).

   The icon for **UpdateSite** in the Feature Updates view indicates that Eclipse recognizes this as a valid update site that can be processed by Update Manager. We are using the Feature Updates view to access a site on a local file system for simplicity. You can just as easily navigate to an update site identified using a bookmark with an `http:` URL. A Web-based update site would be more commonly used for site access.

   Sites can be organized into categories, which group the features that can be installed. This site has a GEF Examples feature, which requires the GEF Runtime feature, two versions of the GEF Runtime feature (2.0.0 and 3.0.0), and a fix or patch to the GEF Runtime feature (2.0.1).

2. Select one or more of the installable features and view the information shown in the Preview view. Information about the feature is displayed, including the currently installed version or an indication that the fea-ture is not installed.

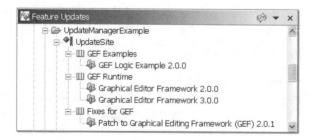

Figure 32.1   Update Manager Site

All installable features are required to have a license file. You can view the license associated with the feature, without installing the feature, by selecting **License**. You will also be asked to accept the license if you decide to install the feature.

3. Update sites can be bookmarked for later access. Select **Sites to Visit** in the Feature Updates view and then select **New > Folder...** from the context menu to create a folder called My Local Update Sites. Select **UpdateSite** and then select **Bookmark Location...** from the context menu. Call the bookmark My Updates and put it in the folder you just created.

4. Now let's try installing a feature. Select **GEF Examples/GEF Logic Example 2.0.0** and then select **Install** in the Preview view. You may have to scroll to the far right side of the Preview view to find the **Install** button. An error is triggered. Select **Details>>** to see more information (see Figure 32.2).

   The GEF Examples feature depends on the GEF Runtime feature. The Update Manager detects this and indicates that the feature cannot be installed because its prerequisites are not met. This prevents you from building an invalid configuration.

5. Let's try again. Select **GEF Runtime/Graphical Editor Framework 2.0.0** and then **Install**. The **Feature Install** wizard is displayed to guide you through the installation. Accept the license and then identify where you want the feature installed. The default install location is your current Eclipse installation. Let's keep this and move on. Select **Finish**.

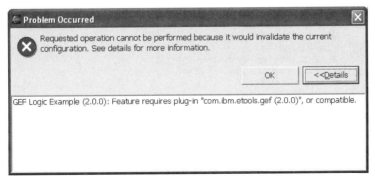

Figure 32.2   Update Manager Error Message

NOTE: By choosing to install the feature in the current Eclipse installation, the feature will be available for every workspace you create. If you had chosen to create a new install location, the new feature would only be known to the configuration stored as part of the current workspace.

6. The Feature Verification dialog is displayed. The Update Manager supports digital signatures for features. If the feature had been digitally signed you would have been prompted to accept the associated certificate, assuming you had not previously accepted this certificate. Since you have not signed this feature, you are warned.

7. Select **Install** (we hope you trust us!). You will be prompted to restart Eclipse in order to make the feature active. If you are installing more than one feature, you can select **No** and continue to install other features, and then restart. For this exercise, select **Yes**. After Eclipse restarts, expand the entries in the Install Configuration view (see Figure 32.3). A new entry for GEF now appears under **Current Configuration**, and a new entry was added under **Configuration History** with GEF in the entry. Your previous configuration is the second entry.

8. Select each of the two entries in **Configuration History** and observe the information in the Preview view. The latest entry is now listed as your current configuration. Under the **Activities** listed for the latest entry, you see that GEF was successfully installed and enabled.

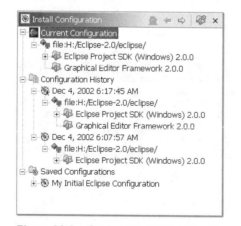

Figure 32.3   Configuration with a New Feature

PART III

NOTE This is not an exercise step, but if you ever want to revert to your previous configuration or another configuration as found in your configuration history, either:

- Select an entry and then select **Revert** or **Restore** from the context menu
- Or select **Revert** or **Restore** in the Preview view
  The option shown (**Revert** or **Restore**) depends on if you have selected the most recent configuration (**Revert**) or an older configuration (**Restore**). Changing the configuration will add another entry to your configuration history. Therefore, you can always change your mind after installing a feature by reverting to a previous configuration.

In this section you have now used the Update Manager to add a new feature to your configuration. This change was recorded as a new configuration in your workspace and can be reversed if required. Depending on your install location choice, the feature is either available only when using the current workspace (if you chose a new install location) or available for every workspace that will be opened (if you chose to add the feature to the Eclise installation).

Section 2: Disabling Features

The Update Manager allows you to disable features you have installed, provided the resulting configuration remains valid. In this section you're going to disable the GEF feature you just installed. Root features will always display a disable button; other features will offer this option only when the feature definitions allow it.

1. Select the GEF feature under **Current Configuration** and then select **Disable** in the Preview view. You may have to scroll to the far right side of the **Preview** view to find the **Disable** button. Choose to complete the disable request and then to restart Eclipse.

2. After Eclipse restarts, return to the Install Configuration view, select **Show Disabled Features**, and then expand **Current Configuration** and **Configuration History** (see Figure 32.4).

   You can see in the Install Configuration view that the GEF feature is disabled and it is no longer part of your current configuration. If you try to install the GEF Examples feature with GEF disabled, the Update

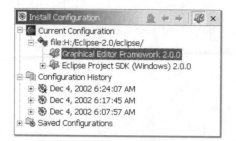

Figure 32.4   Configuration with a Disabled Feature

Manager will block you. The Update Manager understands the requirements of the GEF Examples feature and will not support installation if its prerequisites have not been satisfied.

GEF, as a framework, does not change the Eclipse user interface. Disabling features that modify the Eclipse user interface will obviously disable the corresponding UI portion of the feature. When Eclipse disables a feature, the feature and its associated plug-ins and files remain in the installation, but they are blocked from participation in the platform. The Update Manager does this to make it easy to return to older configurations—so the parts are all there when required.

You could manually remove features that you have disabled, but you need to be careful. You have only disabled the feature for the current workspace, but it may be required for work you have in other workspaces you have created, or used by other installations of the Eclipse Platform you have on your machine. It is even possible that you are using a shared copy of the Eclipse Platform, and others who share this installation may not be ready to see the feature disappear.

Section 3: Pending Changes—Discovering Direct Configuration Modification

You have just seen how you can use the Update Manager to add and disable features. The Update Manager will also be invoked for you if there are pending changes to your Eclipse installation. A pending change is a change to your Eclipse configuration that occurred since the last time you started Eclipse. These are detected by the Update Manager when Eclipse starts. This typically means you, or some install program, added files to the current installation.

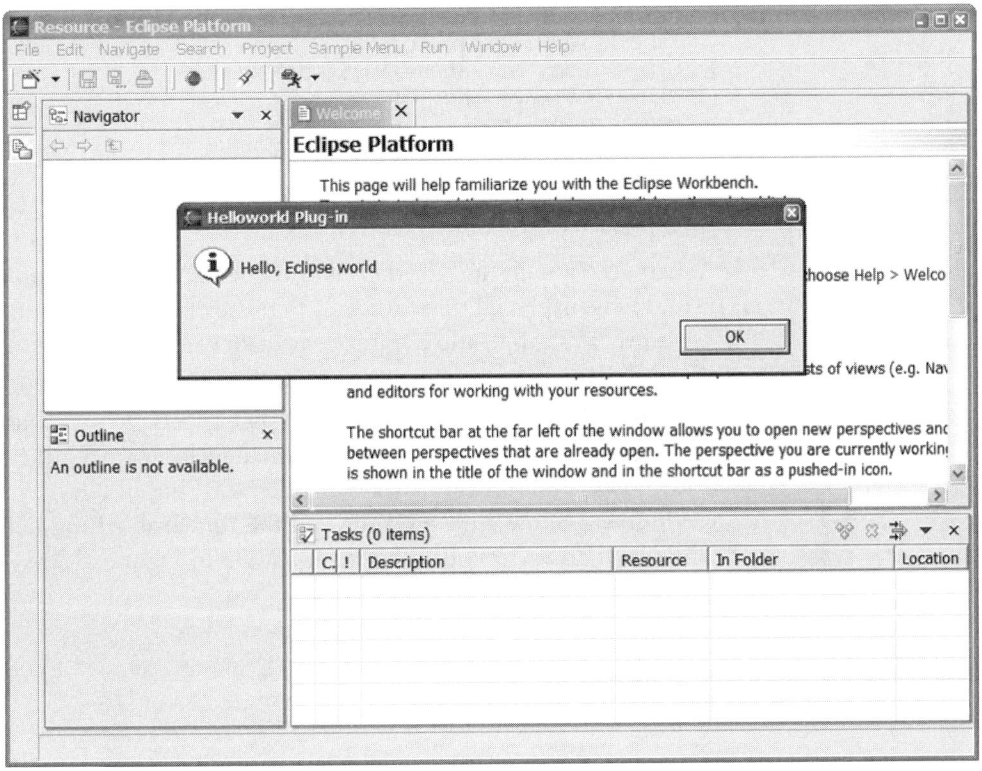

Figure 33.21 Hello, Eclipse World Message Box

Section 4: Debugging with the Run-Time Workbench

This section explores the tools the PDE has to help debug your plug-ins. You already have coded and tested your "Hello, Eclipse world" example, so how about intentionally introducing some bugs to see how they manifest themselves? The short debug session that follows is an example of how to find plug-in specific errors. Begin by verifying that you've closed the run-time Workbench from the prior section, and then return to the Plug-in Development perspective of your Eclipse development environment. Next, open your plug-in's manifest file `plugin.xml`.

1. Turn to the **Source** page and introduce an error in the `class` attribute of the `<action>` tag.

```
<action
  label="&amp;Sample Action"
  class="com.ibm.lab.hello.SampleAction"
  <!- error, was "helloworld" ->
  tooltip="Hello, Eclipse world"
  menubarPath="sampleMenu/sampleGroup"
  toolbarPath="sampleGroup"
  id="com.ibm.lab.helloworld.SampleAction">
</action>
```

When you launch the run-time Workbench and select **Sample Action**, a dialog is displayed that indicates that the chosen operation is not currently available, and a message is displayed in the Console of your development Workbench, as shown in Figure 33.22.

That is, messages in the run-time instance to System.out and System.err are redirected to the Console in the development Workbench. Before closing the run-time instance, open the Plug-in Registry view (**Window > Show View > Other... > PDE Runtime > Plug-in Registry**) and scroll down to your plug-in, as shown in Figure 33.23.

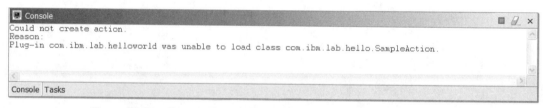

Figure 33.22   Console Error Message

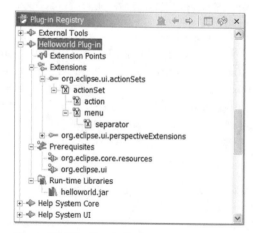

Figure 33.23   Plug-in Registry

From here you can see precisely what was parsed from your `plugin.xml` file, similar to the Outline view of the plug-in manifest, but available at runtime. Close the run-time Workbench.

2. Correct the error from the prior step (e.g., by selecting `plugin.xml`, and then **Replace With > Previous From Local History**). Now let's introduce a more serious error. Comment out the code below from `SampleAction`.

```
public void init(IWorkbenchWindow window) {
//     this.window = window;
}
```

This change will provoke a null pointer exception in the `run` method. Save the change and relaunch the run-time Workbench, this time using the **Run > Debug As > Run-time Workbench** menu choice. Notice that the perspective automatically changes to the Debug perspective.

3. Again select the **Sample Action** menu choice. Nothing appears to happen. No message from the run-time instance, so look in the Console of the *development* Workbench. As expected, the message `Unhandled exception caught in event loop. Reason: java.lang.NullPointer-Exception` is displayed. To get more details, go back to the run-time instance of the Workbench and open the plug-in Error Log (**Window > Show View > Other... PDE Runtime > Error Log**). Indeed, there are two new entries. Double-click the `java.lang.NullPointerException` message and select **Status Details**, as shown in Figure 33.24.

   At this point in a real debug session you might consider setting an exception breakpoint for `NullPointerException` from the **J!** button on the **Breakpoints** page to further diagnose the problem. Don't set such an exception breakpoint before launching the Workbench; it will stop in a lot of places that have nothing to do with your problem. Instead, set and then disable the exception you want to debug before starting the Workbench, then enable it when you're ready to reproduce the problem.

4. Close the run-time instance before continuing.

This short debug session gives you a flavor of debugging plug-ins. As you create your own plug-ins, you may find more difficult problems than this one. When that happens, refer to the section "Correcting Common Problems" later in this chapter.

Exercises

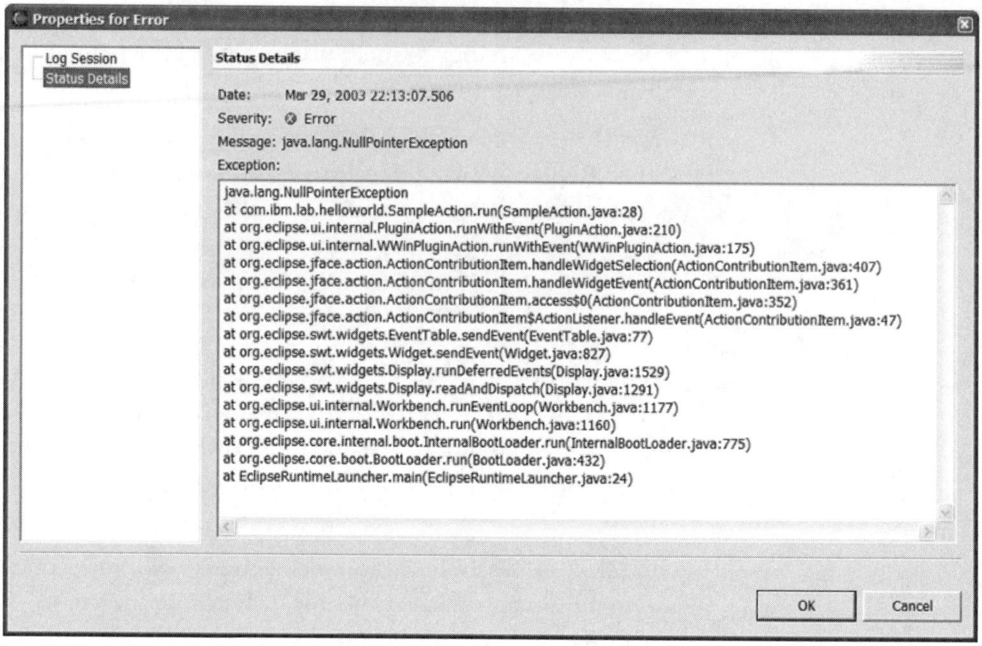

Figure 33.24   Error Status Details

Section 5: Exploring (and Sometimes Correcting) the Eclipse Platform Code

One of the benefits of an open source project is the fact that the source is yours to study, and if necessary, correct. Let's see how the PDE helps you to learn and modify Eclipse code.

You have already been introduced to the notion of "external" versus "workspace" plug-ins; the Target Platform preference page, shown back in Figure 33.1, allows you to add external plug-ins to the list of those available in the test environment and your plug-in's build path. But what if you want to modify the code found in an external plug-in to help you debug or to correct a bug in the Eclipse code? The PDE includes options in the Plug-in view that makes it easy, as shown in Figure 33.25.

To get a better idea of how this works, let's import one of the Eclipse plug-ins and add some debug code.

1. If you haven't closed the run-time instance of Eclipse, do so now. Then turn to the Plug-ins view as shown in Figure 33.25, select the

You should now have a set of projects with a run-time JAR and plug-in install JAR for each plug-in and a feature install JAR and distribution ZIP file for the feature project. This will look similar (depending on your choice of plug-ins) to the files shown in the Package Explorer view in Figure 34.6.

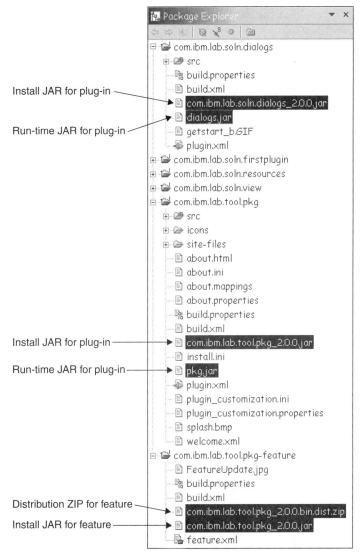

Figure 34.6 Project Content After Packaging Feature

Extracting an Installable Feature from Workspace and Implementing an Update Site

You have built and packaged the feature. The next task is to integrate these files as part of an update site, which can be used to modify an existing Eclipse configuration. Now you need to copy the feature install JAR and plug-in install JARs from the development workspace to the local file system, along with a `site.xml` file that defines the structure and content of the update site.

1. To create the target directory structure, create a directory tree (for example, `d:\labsite\features` and `d:\labsite\plugins`) to use as a site location target.

2. Copy files from the workspace to the appropriate location in the site directory tree (`d:\labsite`). The site files, feature install JAR, and plug-in install JARs need to be copied to the site directory tree. You can drag and drop the files directly from the Navigator view to Windows Explorer.

   The site files located in the `site-files` directory of the branding plug-in provided to you (`com.ibm.lab.tool.pkg`) need to be copied to the site directory tree.

   ```
   d:\labsite\site.xml
   d:\labsite\siteinfo.html
   ```

   The feature install JAR file located in the feature project needs to be copied to the site directory tree.

   ```
   d:\labsite\features\com.ibm.lab.tool.pkg_2.0.0.jar
   ```

   The plug-in install JARs located in each plug-in project need to be copied to the site directory tree.

   ```
   d:\labsite\plugins\com.ibm.lab.tool.pkg_2.0.0.jar
   d:\labsite\plugins\com.ibm.lab.soln.dialogs_2.0.0.jar
   ```

   Do this for as many plug-ins as you included in the feature, which includes the `com.ibm.tool.pkg` branding plug-in that was provided to you.

Section 2: Tasks of an Eclipse User

In this section you will play the role of an Eclipse user and add function to the current installation. You will

- Install a new feature as an extension to an existing Eclipse installation
- Add a feature to an existing Eclipse configuration using Update Manager

The result of these two techniques is the same with respect to a given workspace: The feature is added to the current configuration. What can differ is whether the feature will be accessible when you open a new workspace. The answer is yes when extending an Eclipse installation, but if a default configuration exists, you must accept the features in the extension as part of the configuration when opening a new workspace. A default configuration can be created using the command `eclipse –initialize`. This creates a `.config` directory in the install directory for Eclipse.

When using an Update Site to add features, the features will not be accessible when opening a new workspace if the features are added to a new install location. The location of the new install location is only recorded in the current workspace; another workspace would have no visibility. To have the new features accessible when opening a new workspace you must add the features to the same directory tree as the current installation of Eclipse. If a default configuration exists, you must accept the features in the extension as part of the configuration when opening a new workspace.

Installing a New Feature as an Extension to an Existing Product

Using the ZIP file created in Section 1, you can integrate its contents with an existing Eclipse installation. Unzipping the feature and plug-in content emulates how you, as a tool provider, would use a product installation routine to allow others to install and use your tool.

As a tool provider, you may decide to use installer technology to produce a `setup.exe` to extend an existing Eclipse Platform installation. Your installer would add your features and plug-ins to the file system and then add a link file to identify the new install site to the existing Eclipse-based product you want to extend. The new site is processed during the next startup of the Eclipse Platform, which adds your features and plug-ins to the existing Eclipse-based product.

1. To unzip the feature and plug-ins distribution file to the file system, first create a directory tree (for example, d:\labpkg\eclipse) to use as a target and then unzip the `com.ibm.lab.tool.pkg_2.0.0.bin.dist.zip` file into this directory.

   The target of a link file is a directory that contains an `eclipse` directory; the ZIP file only contains `features` and `plugins` directory trees. You will create this link file in a subsequent step.

2. Start Eclipse with a new workspace using one of these techniques.
   - Open a command prompt, change to the `<install-dir>\eclipse` directory (for example, `c:\eclipse2.0\eclipse`) for the Eclipse instance that you are using for this exercise, and start Eclipse by entering `eclipse -data altworkspace` on the command line.
   - Create and then run a shortcut for the `eclipse.exe` with these parameters:

     `eclipse -data altworkspace`

   Eclipse will display the splash image shown in Figure 34.7 as it initializes the configuration for the new workspace. If this image is not displayed, you are using a workspace that already exists.

   After Eclipse has started, you should have a new workspace directory (`altworkspace`) in the same directory as the `eclipse.exe` program.

   Important: Close Eclipse before continuing to the next step.

3. Add a link file to the Eclipse Platform install directory to identify the new feature location. This task would normally be done by the install routine for an extension. A link file connects an Eclipse install with the extension install site (an install site is a directory that contains an Eclipse directory tree with features and plug-ins).

   Create a directory named `links` in the `<install-dir>\eclipse` directory (for example, `c:\eclipse2.0\eclipse\links`) and add a file named `labpkg.link` with this content:

   `path=d:\\labpkg`

   The entry is treated as a properties file entry, so an escape sequence is necessary for the backslash (i.e., `\\`). Since the entry is a URL, it could be entered as:

   `path=d:/labpkg`

   This instructs the Eclipse Platform to look for additional features and their associated plug-ins in the `d:\labpkg` directory during startup.

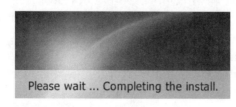

Figure 34.7   Eclipse Initialization

You can use any file name you want. However, you should use a file name that will be unique when adding to a product that may be extended by others. You may want to consider using your feature id as the file name (`com.ibm.lab.tool.pkg.link`).

NOTE   Be sure there are no trailing blanks in the entry. Trailing blanks in V2.0 of the Eclipse Platform will result in the link entry being ignored. This has been reported as a bug.

4. Start Eclipse using the alternative workspace `altworkspace`, as in
   `eclipse -data altworkspace`

   If you watch carefully, you will see that the Eclipse Platform knows you made a change. On the first invocation, Eclipse completes the install as was shown by the "Please wait... Completing install" information image shown in Figure 34.7. When changes are detected during subsequent invocations, Eclipse processes the changes and prepares for a possible acceptance of the new feature(s). This is visible at startup time because the splash screen will appear twice.

5. Accept the new feature as part of the current configuration.

   Once Eclipse has started, you are prompted about new updates. Accept the option to open the Update Manager Configuration Changes dialog. Eclipse prompts you when it has discovered that the existing configuration (stored in the `platform.cfg` file in the `workspace\.metadata\.config` directory) might need to change because of new features that exist. The features might have been added to the configuration by extension (link file) or directly added to the existing `features` and `plugins` directories; either way, you will be prompted to accept the configuration modification.

NOTE   If you just add a plug-in without a corresponding feature, you do not get to decide if you want to add the new function to the active configuration. Eclipse will detect the change, and the plug-ins are unconditionally added to the configuration. Plug-ins that are not referenced by a feature are *unmanaged plug-ins* and are not recognized by the Update Manager user interface.

Exercises

Use the Configuration Changes dialog to select the change and add it to the current configuration, as shown in Figure 34.8.

Once you have selected the root entry and selected **Finish**, you will be prompted to restart Eclipse. Allow Eclipse to shut down and then restart. This activates the new configuration.

6. Now you need to validate that the new feature functions are available. The configuration change should have added the packaged feature and associated plug-ins to Eclipse. Use one or more of the following to confirm that this is true.

- Select **Help > About** *product name...* to open the About *Product* dialog, and look for the Tools Package feature icon. You should see icons for the active feature families, one of which is for the Tools Package (see Figure 34.9).

  A family of features is represented by one image; features in the same family have identical images. The About *Product* dialog logic will compare the images for the available features (only unique images are shown).

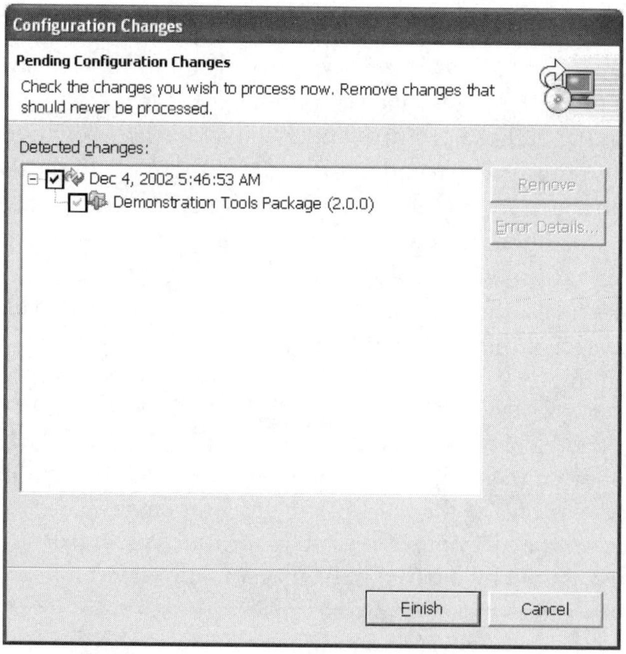

Figure 34.8   Installing Exercise Feature

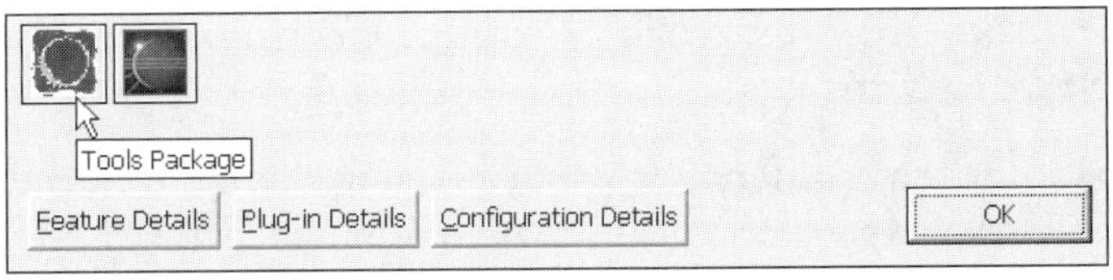

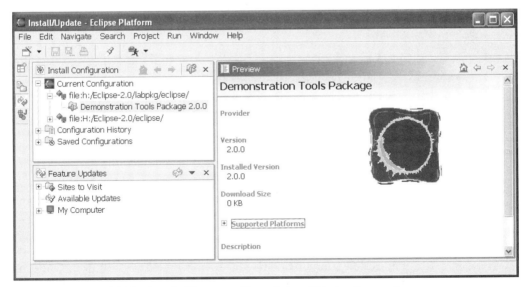

Figure 34.9   About Product Dialog Feature Icon

- Select the **Feature Details** button in the About *Product* dialog. The Tools Package feature will be in the table of active features.
- Open the Install/Update perspective (**Help > Software Updates > Update Manager**) and expand the current configuration to find the Tools Package feature, as shown in Figure 34.10.
- Select **File > New > Other...** or **Ctrl+N** to open the New Wizard, and find any wizards added as part of the Dialogs exercise.
- Open My First View, which you created as part of the View exercise.
- Run the first plug-in action in the current perspective; you may need to reset or customize the current perspective in order to add the action.

Any of the above should prove that the feature has been added and is functional in the new Eclipse configuration.

Figure 34.10   Installed Feature as Shown in Install/Update Perspective

CD-ROM Warranty

Addison-Wesley warrants the enclosed disc to be free of defects in materials and faulty workmanship under normal use for a period of ninety days after purchase. If a defect is discovered in the disc during this warranty period, a replacement disc can be obtained at no charge by sending the defective disc, postage prepaid, with proof of purchase to:

Editorial Department
Addison-Wesley Professional
Pearson Technology Group
75 Arlington Street, Suite 300
Boston, MA 02116
Email: AWPro@awl.com

Addison-Wesley makes no warranty or representation, either expressed or implied, with respect to this software, its quality, performance, merchantability, or fitness for a particular purpose. In no event will Addison-Wesley, its distributors, or dealers be liable for direct, indirect, special, incidental, or consequential damages arising out of the use or inability to use the software. The exclusion of implied warranties is not permitted in some states. Therefore, the above exclusion may not apply to you. This warranty provides you with specific legal rights. There may be other rights that you may have that vary from state to state. The contents of this CD-ROM are intended for personal use only.

More information and updates are available at:
http://www.awprofessional.com/

Common Public License—v 1.0

THE ACCOMPANYING PROGRAM IS PROVIDED UNDER THE TERMS OF THIS COMMON PUBLIC LICENSE ("AGREEMENT"). ANY USE, REPRODUCTION OR DISTRIBUTION OF THE PROGRAM CONSTITUTES RECIPIENT'S ACCEPTANCE OF THIS AGREEMENT.

1. DEFINITIONS

"Contribution" means:

a) in the case of the initial Contributor, the initial code and documentation distributed under this Agreement, and

b) in the case of each subsequent Contributor:
   i) changes to the Program, and
   ii) additions to the Program;

   where such changes and/or additions to the Program originate from and are distributed by that particular Contributor. A Contribution 'originates' from a Contributor if it was added to the Program by such Contributor itself or anyone acting on such Contributor's behalf. Contributions do not include additions to the Program which: (i) are separate modules of software distributed in conjunction with the Program under their own license agreement, and (ii) are not derivative works of the Program.

   "Contributor" means any person or entity that distributes the Program.

   "Licensed Patents" mean patent claims licensable by a Contributor which are necessarily infringed by the use or sale of its Contribution alone or when combined with the Program.

   "Program" means the Contributions distributed in accordance with this Agreement.

   "Recipient" means anyone who receives the Program under this Agreement, including all Contributors.

2. GRANT OF RIGHTS

a) Subject to the terms of this Agreement, each Contributor hereby grants Recipient a non-exclusive, worldwide, royalty-free copyright license to reproduce, prepare derivative works of, publicly display, publicly perform, distribute and sublicense the Contribution of such Contributor, if any, and such derivative works, in source code and object code form.

b) Subject to the terms of this Agreement, each Contributor hereby grants Recipient a non-exclusive, worldwide, royalty-free patent license under Licensed Patents to make, use, sell, offer to sell, import and otherwise transfer the Contribution of such Contributor, if any, in source code and object code form. This patent license shall apply to the combination of the Contribution and the Program if, at the time the Contribution is added by the Contributor, such addition of the Contribution causes such combination to be covered by the Licensed Patents. The patent license shall not apply to any other combinations which include the Contribution. No hardware per se is licensed hereunder.

c) Recipient understands that although each Contributor grants the licenses to its Contributions set forth herein, no assurances are provided by any Contributor that the Program does not infringe the patent or other intellectual property rights of any other entity. Each Contributor disclaims any liability to Recipient for claims brought by any other entity based on infringement of intellectual property rights or otherwise. As a condition to exercising the rights and licenses granted hereunder, each Recipient hereby assumes sole responsibility to secure any other intellectual property rights needed, if any. For example, if a third party patent license is required to allow Recipient to distribute the Program, it is Recipient's responsibility to acquire that license before distributing the Program.

d) Each Contributor represents that to its knowledge it has sufficient copyright rights in its Contribution, if any, to grant the copyright license set forth in this Agreement.

3. REQUIREMENTS

A Contributor may choose to distribute the Program in object code form under its own license agreement, provided that:

a) it complies with the terms and conditions of this Agreement; and

b) its license agreement:

   i) effectively disclaims on behalf of all Contributors all warranties and conditions, express and implied, including warranties or conditions of title and non-infringement, and implied warranties or conditions of merchantability and fitness for a particular purpose;

   ii) effectively excludes on behalf of all Contributors all liability for damages, including direct, indirect, special, incidental and consequential damages, such as lost profits;

   iii) states that any provisions which differ from this Agreement are offered by that Contributor alone and not by any other party; and

   iv) states that source code for the Program is available from such Contributor, and informs licensees how to obtain it in a reasonable manner on or through a medium customarily used for software exchange.

   When the Program is made available in source code form:

a) it must be made available under this Agreement; and

b) a copy of this Agreement must be included with each copy of the Program.

Contributors may not remove or alter any copyright notices contained within the Program.

Each Contributor must identify itself as the originator of its Contribution, if any, in a manner that reasonably allows subsequent Recipients to identify the originator of the Contribution.

4. COMMERCIAL DISTRIBUTION

Commercial distributors of software may accept certain responsibilities with respect to end users, business partners and the like. While this license is intended to facilitate the commercial use of the Program, the Contributor who includes the Program in a commercial product offering should do so in a manner which does not create potential liability for other Contributors. Therefore, if a Contributor includes the Program in a commercial product offering, such Contributor ("Commercial Contributor") hereby agrees to defend and indemnify every other Contributor ("Indemnified Contributor") against any losses, damages and costs (collectively "Losses") arising from claims, lawsuits and other legal actions brought by a third party against the Indemnified Contributor to the extent caused by the acts or omissions of such Commercial Contributor in connection with its distribution of the Program in a commercial product offering. The obligations in this section do not apply to any claims or Losses relating to any actual or alleged intellectual property infringement. In order to qualify, an Indemnified Contributor must: a) promptly notify the Commercial Contributor in writing of such claim, and b) allow the Commercial Contributor to control, and cooperate with the Commercial Contributor in, the defense and any related settlement negotiations. The Indemnified Contributor may participate in any such claim at its own expense.

For example, a Contributor might include the Program in a commercial product offering, Product X. That Contributor is then a Commercial Contributor. If that Commercial Contributor then makes performance claims, or offers warranties related to Product X, those performance claims and warranties are such Commercial Contributor's responsibility alone. Under this section, the Commercial Contributor would have to defend claims against the other Contributors related to those performance claims and warranties, and if a court requires any other Contributor to pay any damages as a result, the Commercial Contributor must pay those damages.

5. NO WARRANTY

EXCEPT AS EXPRESSLY SET FORTH IN THIS AGREEMENT, THE PROGRAM IS PROVIDED ON AN "AS IS" BASIS, WITHOUT WARRANTIES OR CONDITIONS OF ANY KIND, EITHER EXPRESS OR IMPLIED INCLUDING, WITHOUT LIMITATION, ANY WARRANTIES OR CONDITIONS OF TITLE,

NON-INFRINGEMENT, MERCHANTABILITY OR FITNESS FOR A PARTICULAR PURPOSE. Each Recipient is solely responsible for determining the appropriateness of using and distributing the Program and assumes all risks associated with its exercise of rights under this Agreement, including but not limited to the risks and costs of program errors, compliance with applicable laws, damage to or loss of data, programs or equipment, and unavailability or interruption of operations.

6. DISCLAIMER OF LIABILITY

EXCEPT AS EXPRESSLY SET FORTH IN THIS AGREEMENT, NEITHER RECIPIENT NOR ANY CONTRIBUTORS SHALL HAVE ANY LIABILITY FOR ANY DIRECT, INDIRECT, INCIDENTAL, SPECIAL, EXEMPLARY, OR CONSEQUENTIAL DAMAGES (INCLUDING WITHOUT LIMITATION LOST PROFITS), HOWEVER CAUSED AND ON ANY THEORY OF LIABILITY, WHETHER IN CONTRACT, STRICT LIABILITY, OR TORT (INCLUDING NEGLIGENCE OR OTHERWISE) ARISING IN ANY WAY OUT OF THE USE OR DISTRIBUTION OF THE PROGRAM OR THE EXERCISE OF ANY RIGHTS GRANTED HEREUNDER, EVEN IF ADVISED OF THE POSSIBILITY OF SUCH DAMAGES.

7. GENERAL

If any provision of this Agreement is invalid or unenforceable under applicable law, it shall not affect the validity or enforceability of the remainder of the terms of this Agreement, and without further action by the parties hereto, such provision shall be reformed to the minimum extent necessary to make such provision valid and enforceable.

If Recipient institutes patent litigation against a Contributor with respect to a patent applicable to software (including a cross-claim or counterclaim in a lawsuit), then any patent licenses granted by that Contributor to such Recipient under this Agreement shall terminate as of the date such litigation is filed. In addition, if Recipient institutes patent litigation against any entity (including a cross-claim or counterclaim in a lawsuit) alleging that the Program itself (excluding combinations of the Program with other software or hardware) infringes such Recipient's patent(s), then such Recipient's rights granted under Section 2(b) shall terminate as of the date such litigation is filed.

All Recipient's rights under this Agreement shall terminate if it fails to comply with any of the material terms or conditions of this Agreement and does not cure such failure in a reasonable period of time after becoming aware of such noncompliance. If all Recipient's rights under this Agreement terminate, Recipient agrees to cease use and distribution of the Program as soon as reasonably practicable. However, Recipient's obligations under this Agreement and any licenses granted by Recipient relating to the Program shall continue and survive.

Everyone is permitted to copy and distribute copies of this Agreement, but in order to avoid inconsistency the Agreement is copyrighted and may only be modified in the following manner. The Agreement Steward reserves the right to publish new versions (including revisions) of this Agreement from time to time. No one other than the Agreement Steward has the right to modify this Agreement. IBM is the initial Agreement Steward. IBM may assign the responsibility to serve as the Agreement Steward to a suitable separate entity. Each new version of the Agreement will be given a distinguishing version number. The Program (including Contributions) may always be distributed subject to the version of the Agreement under which it was received. In addition, after a new version of the Agreement is published, Contributor may elect to distribute the Program (including its Contributions) under the new version. Except as expressly stated in Sections 2(a) and 2(b) above, Recipient receives no rights or licenses to the intellectual property of any Contributor under this Agreement, whether expressly, by implication, estoppel or otherwise. All rights in the Program not expressly granted under this Agreement are reserved.

This Agreement is governed by the laws of the State of New York and the intellectual property laws of the United States of America. No party to this Agreement will bring a legal action under this Agreement more than one year after the cause of action arose. Each party waives its rights to a jury trial in any resulting litigation.